YOU BRI[...]

William T. Vollmann was [...]
Deep Springs College an[...]
summa cum laude in comparative literature. In 1982 he crossed into
Afghanistan with Islamic commandos, and afterwards lived for
several years in San Francisco. Vollmann's books include the novels
You Bright and Risen Angels, *The Ice-Shirt*, *Fathers and Crows*, and
Whores for Gloria (all available from Penguin); three story collections,
The Rainbow Stories, *Thirteen Stories and Thirteen Epitaphs*, and *The
Butterfly Stories*; and a work of nonfiction, *An Afghanistan Picture
Show*. Vollmann won a 1988 Whiting Award in recognition of his
writing achievements and the Shiva Naipaul Memorial Award in
1989. He is currently engaged in writing a series of seven novels
exploring the repeated collisions between North American native
populations and their colonizers and oppressors; the sixth volume,
The Rifles, has just been published by Viking. William Vollmann lives
in California.

WILLIAM T. VOLLMANN

YOU BRIGHT AND RISEN ANGELS
a cartoon

with drawings by the author

PENGUIN BOOKS

PENGUIN BOOKS
Published by the Penguin Group
Penguin Books USA Inc., 375 Hudson Street,
New York, New York 10014, U.S.A.
Penguin Books Ltd, 27 Wrights Lane,
London W8 5TZ, England
Penguin Books Australia Ltd, Ringwood,
Victoria, Australia
Penguin Books Canada Ltd, 10 Alcorn Avenue,
Toronto, Ontario, Canada M4V 3B2
Penguin Books (N.Z.) Ltd, 182–190 Wairau Road,
Auckland 10, New Zealand

Penguin Books Ltd, Registered Offices:
Harmondsworth, Middlesex, England

First published in Great Britain by Pan Books Ltd. 1987
First published in the United States of America by
Atheneum Publishers 1987
Published in Penguin Books 1988

10 9 8 7 6 5 4 3

PUBLISHER'S NOTE
This novel is a work of fiction. Names, characters, places, and incidents are either
the product of the author's imagination or are used fictitiously. Any resemblance
to actual events or persons, living or dead, is entirely coincidental.

Extract from Peter Green's translation of Juvenal's *The Sixteen Satires* reproduced by permission of Penguin Books Ltd. Extract from "Balade" in *The Poems of François Villon* translated by Galway Kinnell. Copyright © 1965, 1977 by Galway Kinnell. Reprinted by permission of Houghton Mifflin Company.

The author has based the opening pages of the chapter "The Battle of the Swimming Pool" in part upon certain passages from Alan Bullock's *Hitler: a Study in Tyranny*. He does this by kind permission of Curtis Brown Ltd., London and Harper and Row, New York.

LIBRARY OF CONGRESS CATALOGING IN PUBLICATION DATA
Vollmann, William T.
  You bright and risen angels: a cartoon/William T. Vollmann;
with drawings by the author.
    p. cm.
  ISBN 0 14 01.1087 9
  I. Title.
PS3572.O395Y6 1988
813'.54—dc 19   88–17451

Printed in the United States of America

For Paul Foster,
true friend

Only the expert will realize that your exaggerations are really true.

KIMON NICOLAIDES
The Natural Way to Draw

This book was written by a traitor to his class. It is dedicated to bigots everywhere. Ladies and gentlemen of the black shirts, I call upon you to unite, to strike with claws and kitchen pokers, to burn the grub-worms of equality's brood with sulfur and oil, to huddle together whispering about the silverfish in your basements, to make decrees in your great solemn rotten assemblies concerning what is proper, for you have nothing to lose but your last feeble principles.

William T. Vollmann

Karachi – Anatuvuk Pass – San Francisco
(1981–85)

A Social Gazette of the Personalities Interviewed for this Book

Our hero (Bug)
Atheist, spy, revolutionary, one-time insect ally; founder of the Kuzbuite movement; aged 44 in the Year 1 of the Revolution; university graduate.

Sammy Allen
Reactionary, electrician and inventor; tool of the blue globes; aged 97 in Y.R. 1. At Mr. White's disposal.

Clara Bee
She stung a Beetle to death.

Big George
Apolitical, tropical explorer; hard-coded and ubiquitous; immortal. Extremely dangerous. At everyone's disposal.

Phil Blaker
Reactionary, industrialist; owner of Mars; Mr. White's archrival; aged 188 in Y.R. 1.

Coldwell and Stringfellow
Reactionaries; insurance brokers. Long dead.

Fred Dalton
Reactionary; reinsurance man; died at age 55. A tough cookie. At Mr. White's disposal.

Milly Dalton (the Match-Girl)
Revolutionary; his daughter; escaped book character; mortal. At Bug's disposal.

Dr. Samuel William Dodger (a.k.a. Dr. William Samuel Dodger)
Reactionary, inventor, lecturer, psychiatrist, small businessman (mail order and retail), senator, member ex-officio of all city councils in our great Republic; aged 79 in Y.R. 1. Mr. White's righthand man. At Phil Blaker's disposal.

Electric Emily
Revolutionary, circuit-dweller; aged 78 in Y.R. 1. Paranormal but entirely natural powers.

Frank Fairless
Double agent; darkroom technician, documentary slide show producer; loser; tool of Dr. Dodger and the blue globes; aged 48 in Y.R. 1. The reincarnation of Roger Garvey. At Bug's disposal.

Parker Fellows
Reactionary, insurance executive; darkroom god; aged 46 in Y.R. 1. Many supernatural powers. Tool of the plants and the blue globes.

Roger Garvey
Reactionary, follower, petit-bourgeois; aged 18 when executed by Wayne. At Parker's disposal.

Wayne Hysaw
Reactionary, sailor, commando; aged 45 in Y.R. 1; holder of the Iron Cross, First Class. At Parker's disposal.

Susan Lingenfelter
Reactionary; revolutionary; school teacher; swim team fan; aged 46 in Y.R. 1. At the disposal of Bug and Wayne.

Katie White
Apolitical; talk show announcer; aged 42 in Y.R. 1. At Mr. White's disposal.

Stephen Mole
Revolutionary; darkroom technician; xerox boy in White's employ; bug subway observer; active Kuzbuite; aged 56 in Y.R. 1. At the disposal of Bug and Katie.

Catherine O'Day
Fellow traveler; law clerk; aged 52 in Y.R. 1. Worshipped by Roger Garvey until his death. At Susan's disposal.

Newton Payne
Reactionary; engineer; defense strategist; inventor; weapons designer; aged 98 in Y.R. 1. At Mr. White's disposal.

Earl Ward
Reactionary; inventor; aged 97 in Y.R. 1. At Mr. White's disposal until captured by the bugs.

Mr. Jack White
Reactionary; industrialist, Commander-in-Chief of the Merchant Marine Guard; aged 253 in Y.R. 1 (being immortal). A political leader of some ability. At the polar bears' disposal.

The affinity group
Extremist reformers – Bug, Ellen, Barb, Tina, Mary, Jerry, Simon, Sophie, Sandy and Barnaby. At Wayne's disposal.

The electric gang
Boy Cryption, Vern Puckett, Tippy Selenoid and Parker.

The programmers
Mr. White, Dr. Dodger, Big George, Parker, Sammy, Violet, Ron, Taylor, Eileen, Tracy and Chuck. At Mr. White's disposal.

(As I, the author, am myself a programmer, I have thought it fitting to award these fortunate souls a prominence of their own, the better to honor that glorious profession which we share.)

The prostitutes
Brandi (at Frank's disposal), Carla (at Wayne's disposal), Ginger (at Frank's disposal), Natalie (at Curtis's disposal), Georgette (at Natalie's disposal).

The reinsurance syndicate
Mr. White, Mr. Dalton, Dr. Dodger, Catherine, Big George, Parker, Coldwell, Stringfellow, and who knows who else. At the disposal of the Vegans.

The swim team
Parker, Wayne, Chip, Big George, Bug, Roger, Glenn, Doug and Bob. At the nation's disposal.

The Great Beetle
Leader of Bugdom.

The Boreal Bee
His queen.

Beetle-Guards
The name sums them up.

Mantis
   Revolutionary, spy; insect bartender in Oregon.

The Caterpillar Heart
   The instrument of Parker's damnation. At Bug's disposal.

Various mosquitoes, ants and spiders
   A rabble.

A cricket
   Mantis's envoy.

Vampire-bugs and assassin-bugs
   Hardly anything to worry about.

The Blue Globes
   Where the real power was.

Makers of the Macropedia
   Vegans.

Martians
   Also Vegans. At Phil Blaker's disposal.

The plants and plant-people of Omarville
   Reactionary reserves. At Parker's disposal.

Polar bears
   The terrestrial managers of the reinsurance syndicate.

TRANSCENDENTAL CONTENTS

SHAPE-SHIFTING 〰〰〰〰

Men should stop fighting among themselves and start fighting insects.

LUTHER BURBANK

If I can send the flower of the German nation into the hell of war without the smallest pity for the shedding of precious German blood, then surely I have the right to remove millions of an inferior race that breeds like vermin.

ADOLF HITLER

Just because they found Martin Bormann's skull doesn't mean he's dead, my best beloved; for everyone knows that competent observers from every neutral country have reported sighting an old man in Argentina whose head is wrapped in bandages, and only the hunted eyes show, winking and blinking beneath the thousands of cranial splints; – and Anastasia Romanoff, I know her: when Yurovsky and his Cheka men were murdering her family she fainted and they took her for dead; they piled her into a truck with the others, and while they were getting the hatchets and caustic acids ready she came to herself, ran into the deep dark taiga, and flung herself into the arms of the Whites just in time, where she was treated as befitted her nobility; and that's how the leopard got his spots. As for Mr. Ambrose Bierce, he really was shot as a spy by Pancho Villa, but I happened to pass by the grave before it was too late. Not all the brain cells had died, and with a minimal application of Dr. Dodger's Special Elixir I was able to save him, although it took months before he was up to the effort of breathing again, and even now he swears that he cannot remember the month of July 1899, *hanged* if he can. I can only conclude that God did not intend him to remember it. Such mental haziness is in order, given the delightful vagueness of the terrain – springy moss padding the continent, golden idols and lost gimcrack empires a dime a dozen, sentient insects and clean mountains without sharp peaks to puncture balloons and dreams; and a foggy sort of peace generally – for I am of course referring to South America, where many such persons hide; where everybody hides who is so base and eccentric as to show up death for a fumbler. So it is that when I myself take short-term refuge in that Shangri-La of displaced persons, which I do from time to time as a vacation from the grim and grinding world where one must stand one's ground like a salaried office worker, like the rest of the Romanoffs, I find ever so many beguiling faces: – here is exhibited some old American ambassador whose body was supposedly claimed by the State Department in a sealed casket after the ransom was not paid (funny things those sealed caskets; they invest their occupants with more vitality than they ever had previously; for look, this Ambassador fellow is rather more lively than a crayfish; he gets up when company arrives and then sits down again in his rattan chair, he consumes dark rum punches at a respectable clip, and after two or three in the afternoon he makes an effort at sincerity); and over here, just right of progress, we have the only Turkoman who is of a direct line of descent from Genghis Khan; he was once a good oil prospector* who had the misfortune one day to meet a dust demon whose riddle he could not answer; and that about sums it up for Turkomans and Mongols alike, or at least what electrified people in this part of the biosphere think about Turkomans and Mongols, fucking foreigners out to ruin our freedom to bear arms ("Turkmenians?" they speculate. "Mongolians? Mongoloids?"), which is a good thing since I like some of my acts to be easier than others; similarly, when dealing with your typical average everyday white man, it is child's play to impersonate a shameless Arab, snaggle-toothed darky, Grecian babbler, Macedonian spawn, without at all foreclosing the option of becoming, through the use of makeup, a necklace, and sheer plastic mobility, that woman whose face was doomed to give Octavian the scepter of the world, the eyes that launched a thousand rockets. We all work together, or rather, I work. – "Everyone who at that time did not stand on his own feet," says Hitler in another context, "joined in such working federations, no doubt proceeding from the belief that eight cripples joining arms are sure to produce one gladiator." – Standing on your own feet, naturally, is as tiresome and dangerous as standing your ground; and when the wild dogs begin to circle grinning round you with their dripping tongues hanging out and you know that with mock servility they like to go for your toes first, why, then, you should stand on someone else's feet, or head if necessary. It is a point of faith for me never to be Hitler; he stood his ground in his own two shoes in his own little hole almost to the end, the fool. But I may disguise myself as any other animate or inanimate object in what follows. I can be eight lame women with falsies, eight cracked chamberpots, or – let's get right to the point – a gladiator who is actually constructed of old clothes, brooms, and a paper plate with a face daubed on in finger-paints, not to mention two vagrants inside

---

*Before the revolution Turkmenia occupied only 488,100 square kilometers. It had nothing but a few barbaric handicrafts to offer us in the days of the tsars, such as wind-up gliders and popsicle sticks. In Soviet times these have been rooted out to make room for chemical, gas and engineering industries, as well as the most modern oil refineries, which are very susceptible to sabotage. Turkmenia now rules the world through its Secret Council of Elevated Grand Dragons and Dust Demons.

each shirt-sleeve and pant-leg, moving Goliath's limbs at my s̶
but as long as you believe in the gladiator, you are whipped, and the
Museum people will set out on your track, and then once they catch
you, don't think I won't come study your exhibit until I can convince
your own sweetheart that I am you come back from the dead. For I
am Big George, the eternal winner.

THE HISTORY OF ELECTRICITY

Only when the country is electrified, when industry, agriculture and transport are placed on a technical basis of modern large-scale production – only then will our victory be complete.

V. I. LENIN
address to party congress

To talk of atomic energy in terms of the atomic bomb is like talking of electricity in terms of the electric chair.

PETER L. KAPITZA

Synthetic Cognitions a Priori

~~~~~~

> . . . but if after death we are no longer able to exist, why do I see
> most nights each grave opening and its inhabitants gently lifting
> the leaden lids, to go out and breathe the fresh air?
>
> LAUTRÉAMONT
> *Maldoror*

Oh, you bright and risen angels, you are all in your graves! I, your author, am lonely; there is no one left in the world. Since I run things here half the time, I am going to call you up for another of my meaningless judgments — meaningless because you are all so eager and try so hard that I could never punish any of you, no matter how villainous you might be. I press the resurrection button; and here you come as large as life. Our hero, Bug, climbs diffidently out of his grave-pit, very polite and maybe a little embarrassed as he brushes the mold and ashes from his face (I know it's not his fault). Now here comes Wayne bursting from his tomb with a glower, looking around for Parker and ready to hurt somebody . . . I put out my hand to help Catherine up into the light, and she smiles nervously, as pretty as ever with just a hint of sulfur about her. Dr. Dodger pops forth from someone else's coffin, not looking at me (or is he?), and commences to build something out of a handful of rusty paper clips in his pocket. Milly, the Little Match-Girl, is not in evidence; she is trapped inside a rotting paperback in some garbage can, and even I will never be able to see her again, though if I close my eyes I can almost envision her white desperate face uplifted as she begs me to help her . . . Parker's gravestone tilts slowly with a sound of tearing grass and snapping roots and grinding gravel, and suddenly it sinks into the mud and almost topples as a stink gets stronger and stronger and a long yellow-green arm extends itself and flexes its fingers and the rest of Parker's body contracts and squeezes and just kinda oozes out of the crevice and Parker slouches against a family mausoleum and picks worms out of his teeth and Wayne comes running up to him almost crying for sheer happiness. – Aha, that mausoleum – so lordly it is! – must belong to the White family; for this looks like Mr. White himself marching up to us, in what seems a very bad humor, fifty years of decaying curses on his lips; and he spies Bug and shakes him by the shoulder and hauls off and punches him, but Bug is as polite as always and merely nods and turns away to wipe his bloody nose (though I can tell he is scheming inside). Now they are showing up faster and faster at this compulsory reunion: – Katie and Susan and Roger and Frank and Sammy and Newt and Earl; and even the Great Beetle burrows out, golden-green and shiny in the light; and Katie screams and Wayne and Mr. White come running up kicking at it, and Dr. Dodger has completed his little device; it is a catapult; he cranks it up and launches pebbles at the Great Beetle, which lumbers over to our hero to protect itself. Roger hesitates and finally bestirs himself to join Parker and Dr. Dodger; and now everyone is dividing up into reactionaries and revolutionaries just as predictably as choosing sides for grade school kickball, except for Frank, who stands in the middle and gets hurt by everybody. – Mr. White fires his pistol, and Wayne and Sammy and Newt and Earl come charging, and Bug awaits his doom along with Catherine and Susan and the Great Beetle; this will not be a great day for their revolution; no sirree, though at exactly this moment an elevator hums and Coldwell and Stringfellow arise from their graves, looking gaunt; and they approach Bug and pat him on the shoulder and give him and every other revolutionary a handful of sharpened pencils. Then Stringfellow takes Bug by the hand and Coldwell puts an arm around Catherine and Susan and begins leading them up to Mr. White, with the Great Beetle dragging itself resignedly after. – Phil Blaker is nowhere to be seen, perhaps because he is buried on Mars, but we have seen almost everybody, haven't we? – No, wait a minute, here comes Big George, juggling a handful of electric-blue globes; he grins and steps closer and closer and suddenly folds his arms piously so that the globes shatter on the ground and a hundred bolts of lightning strike everyone and when the smoke clears I see nothing but craters and bones and one of Susan's high heels. – Poor Susan! – Big George is still walking, almost out of sight now on the great graveyard of history, but he turns and waves, without any malice or triumph; that is just the way things are; and the sun sets and I didn't even have my judgment and I won't be able to sleep tonight because it is cold and foggy and anyhow here come all the

Great Beetle's little followers to eat the remains and make me itch, so I suppose I might as well get up and break into the caretaker's office and have a midnight snack and then sit down at the business typewriter amusing myself ... The typewriter hums, *uh*-uh-uh, *uh*-uh-uh, *uh*-uh-uh, and as I hold my hands above the keys I pretend that this will be as good as kissing Electric Emily ... (Maybe she was inside one of the blue globes.)

IN THE JUNGLE

~~~~~~

> Oh! did I not say you were clever, Macumazahn, you who know
> where madness ends and ghosts begin, and why they are just the
> same thing?
>
> H. RIDER HAGGARD
> *Child of Storm*

I will be especially faithful for these first few pages, since in
beginning the story I cannot but be reminded that every key-stroke
I make upon my typewriter may be transmitted through the wall
outlet just behind my head (for I do not pretend to understand
electricity) and left naked to the public, in radiant droplets on one of
the power grids or telephone lines of this world. As the saying goes,
you really have to see the *humor* of that situation. – Not that I
intend to demean the seriousness of purpose which I continue to
treasure in myself, for I do have my own goals, both long-range and
intermediate; and I am confident that my presence here makes some
difference. For example, in this room there are two spiders upon
the ceiling; it is my conviction that without me there would be
more. As I tread the shag carpet, observing it sternly, like one of
our surveillance planes high above the jungles of southeast Asia, I
wonder what new decisions the ants are making among the crumbs.
It must be dark down there, and endless with a horrible sort of rayon
vitality of fronds and threads and rotten yarn-boles. Billions of miles
above even me hangs the sun in its socket, warming the rubber trees
down to their wretched attachment points, and setting the working
day for the ants, their domestic animals the aphids, and many other
creatures, which sometimes appear in closer proximity than might
be wished, owing to the bald patches near the walls. This is in the
dry season. In the winter, or wet season, when I have gone out and
come in again, the water drips from my shoes and raincoat, the

insurgents retreat behind my bookcases, and their places underneath are occupied by river creatures, alligators, water-snakes, and repulsive fish, of which persons outside South America know nothing. As to the space behind my traveling trunk, had I been small enough to explore it I should never have proceeded without a loaded Winchester; for having gone undisturbed for a great while it is a sanctuary for all the vermin of the Amazon, these being dangerous and poisonous, not merely the chitin-faced guerrillas we know, not just the roaches and bottle-beetles hanging on the walls of the kitchen when you put on the light in the middle of the night when you are ill, and you bring your ear close to them to find out if it is really true, that you can hear them, and you discover that you can, that it sounds like frying bacon, and then you feel a tickling, and raising your hand you feel dozens of them crawling down your collar – no, rats were there, and deadly scolopendra and centipedes, and large bird-eating spiders with the expressions of Tartars were daily seen promenading up and down the walls. In such unexplored latitudes I always made a point of setting my watch to the local time. I prefer to title all such exercises: "The Celestial Sphere: Solved Problems." A correction must be made in each apparent hour to compensate for the refraction of the sun's rays by the earth's atmosphere and the glass of my fog-dulled instruments. This procedure was not only essential for chronological accuracy in my log-book entries, but also distracted me for at least the calculation period from worries about my home. I knew, for instance, that my bathtub faucet had a leaky washer. It was quite possible that the tub was now an inland estuary of the sort that I had been exploring for the past three days: – all crawling with brine shrimp from hidden eggs on the drain plug; and flamingoes, mangroves, cypresses, electric eels; and brackish, tea-colored water slopping gently against the weeds grown up around the bones of poor lost men.

As Sergio Bologna noted sarcastically in his famous analysis "The Tribe of Moles," "in its most shameful form, this egalitarianism assumes tones of workerist chauvinism. It appears that it is no longer capital that exploits the worker, but the postman, the milkman and the student." Because I expected to be myself considered by the authorities to be an exploiter – for I had made up my mind to kill those authorities – I decided to establish a base in parts unknown. Already Mr. White's power in our great Republic was impressive; it had become clear that his aim was absolute control over all matters. Of course, he was to underestimate us for several decades while he concerned himself with the more immediate problem of expanding his own influence and strategic capabilities; for which one can scarcely fault him, for he did have things on his mind like the menace of Phil Blaker, and his own little philanthropic projects, and then, too, he ran a family; and in those days electricity boondoggled on the horizon as the answer to all output concerns, so that he was flypapered like all the others in the distraction of its sticky blue radiance; and finally there was the indisputable fact that we could not dislodge him; there was no such possibility, never, *nein, nie*; we were no more effective than bugs in a rug. We set out to find our weapons in the wilderness, where strange plants grew seven hundred feet high, bearing drug-pods for every conceivable use. – In the month of June, the dry season having commenced in earnest, a trader published a notice to the effect that he would send a launch up-river. I do not recall the exact wording of his notice, but then, neither can I say precisely what the population of St. Louis was in 1962, though I do know that every day that year the afore-mentioned city discharged 200,000 gallons of urine and 400 tons of excrement into the accommodating river. That sounds like perhaps three North American families, wouldn't you say, since at that time we Big Georges had the highest standard of living on earth. Now it is all I can do to eat one steer a week.

STATION IDENTIFICATION

~~~~~~

It is now almost certain that as living beings we are alone in the solar system.

ZDENEŇĚK KOPAL
The Solar System

The keys of my typewriter depress themselves and clack madly, like those of a player piano, like (more appropriately still, since we are in the age of electricity) a teletype machine in some computer center at three in the morning, with the lights glaring steadily down, failed programs in the wastebasket and punchcards on the floor; and far off somewhere at the other end of the dedicated synchronous modem line, a sunken computer swims in its cold lubricants and runs things, and there is nothing to do but wait until it has had its say; the keys do not feel my touch; they do not recognize me; and all across the room the other programmers rest their heads in their arms as Big George dictates to them as well, garbage in and garbage out, screwing up everything with his little spots of fun, refusing to drowse in the spurious closure of a third-person narrative (think how lonely he must be if he has to play such stupid games with me); when what I really wanted to do was write about our hero and how he got his earplugs, or look into the heart of Catherine's pink face freckled like flowery darkness, as she sits in the office doing law briefs with the sunlight purple on her hair coming in through the window in striped shadows (due to half-sealed blinds) with the texture of cotton candy; I would rather be deceived by her perfection than by the boasting of Big George, but it doesn't matter; she may be the one I searched for and scratched for but she will never see or hear me; I remember the awful look in her eyes when she fell and hurt her knee and got up as I did nothing to help her because I could not; I could only see her vaguely and there was nothing I could do for her

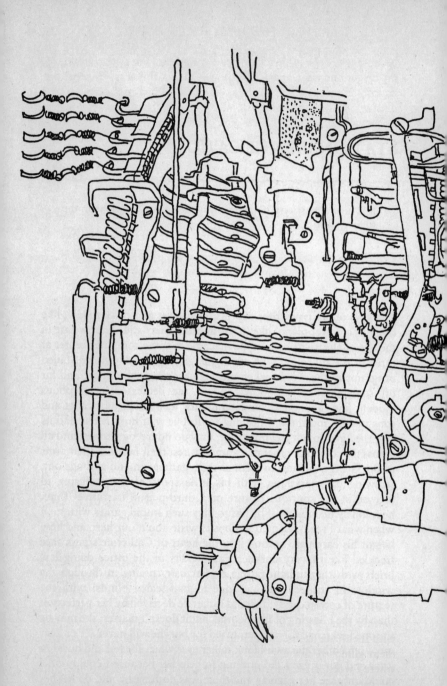

because while she is alive I am dead and when I am alive she is dead, my bright and risen angel, and though I want this story to come out happily it will not and Catherine will fall down and die; can you understand that, she will die, and our hero will die because though I pound at the keys, trying to type in

REFORMAT PROGRAM COMMAND 25 SAVE CATHERINE AFTER ALL
PLEASE I BEG YOU SAVE CATHERINE

it will do no good because such writing is a big fake that doesn't even show up on the roll of blue-lined computer paper; only what Big George vomits from his hard heart is what stains the story and even my skilled skull is full of it; and as I see her sublime mouth, and her head moving up and down, up and down with nervous theatricality right now I know she will be destroyed; and I want to send history to the bright fires. — Well, there is nothing for it but to endure; and she will never hear me anymore or come to see me; of course she is a very difficult girl. — It seems as if we have no choice but to go back almost to pre-settlement America and work through the history of electricity which Big George is determined to stick us with, lying through his teeth and confusing the astute reader with discrepancies in places and dates, for he just doesn't care; and all I can hope to do is to type in a little ameliorating detail here and there so that my angels will at least have the dignity of consistency as they are made to kill each other, and fall and die, and maybe Big George will draw a long breath at the end of this section and I can make adjustments, but I doubt it, I really doubt it; and all I can say is that I'm very sorry and that I'm dying, too.

And now it's back to Big George's war stories about what he did and didn't do in South America around the turn of the century, when he wasn't even there but actually ran the show, I believe, in the Philippines; and he tries to make himself out to be a revolutionary hero, maybe to mollify me so that he can get away with even more of this; my only consolation is that if he sees fit to mollify me he must not be omnipotent and perhaps I can find some way to assert control; but then maybe it has nothing to do with mollifying me at all and it's simply a new way for him to please himself so that he can while away another long chirring sleepless night of his immortality until with the dawn and the swollen orange sun the freeway will sparkle again with the colorful turtle-like cars of the programmers with their cute license plates and classical music, smog after smog of them glimpsed through the smoked-glass windows of the facility where I work, a freeway north of me and a freeway west of me, and the cars are crawling now thanks to some accident; the programmers are fuming and sweating and swearing and calling in late on their shoe-phones; now at ten in the morning it is as still as a Roman frieze, each bright metal-and-glass shell stalled and welded into place like a brick in the Great Wall of China; they say the Great Wall is about the only sign of humanity you can see from the moon; well, certainly you could see this yellow-and-blue-and-scarlet disturbance from a traffic helicopter, and it is really something to consider that by now every hood of every car is pretty and bright and burning to the touch. The cars are idling; this is all very hard on an engine; the drivers are going out of their minds with fear for their lovely machines and anxiety about being late for their latest screen polygon sizing project; but at length the tow-trucks come and clear a lane by the standard method of crushing all cars in the way into scrap for the good of the organization. This eases the bottleneck somewhat; and everyone roars off to work choking, and the helicopter reports all clear, so that the international public loses interest; at twelve comes the lunch hour panic; then at three the rush hour begins and the sky gets yellower and yellower and black dingy clouds grow around the sun's yellow skull; and it gets darker and harder to breathe and the night shift comes in; as Big George swivels round and round in his chair and perhaps looks over his big assignment cards and little personnel cards, matching them up, and decides to visit my cubicle unannounced tonight to see whether I am doing my work; he will tiptoe across the deep grey carpet and look over my shoulder for a long time before I realize he is there; or perhaps he will simply use his privileged user status to turn the inside of my terminal into a great lens so he can look from his screen directly into my face as I yawn, maybe, and close my eyes, and waste time, thinking I'm all alone . . . And the night solidifies; yes, no doubt he'll be identifying himself with the reactionaries next; and there's just no stopping him. At this point I'm too tired to care. My head is in my hands.

SNAKES AND LADDERS (1909)

~~~~~~

> It is better to play at marbles on a sepulcher than to lift the lid and
> peep inside.
>
> H. RIDER HAGGARD
> *Jess*

As the launch rounded bend after bend, the same scene repeated
itself: — here stood a tall matamata tree in a little accidental clearing,
tinseled with parasitic vines and creepers, and swinging with little
brown monkeys chattering as nervously as cabinet ministers; while
running the length of the entire shore on each side, as far as could be
discerned, jungly matter walled us in, a hundred feet high and
exuding death and chlorophyll. The river might have been one of the
forest bower-paths at Versailles, meandering from park bench to
fountain to trash can in a fashion that but accentuated the lacquered
monotony of the whole enterprise; for nothing displays such an
artificial nature as "life as we know it." Between the nasty lux-
uriance of the Amazon and the mediocrity of the New Hampshire
woods (where the narrative will presently take us) there may be
differences of scale and density, but the vegetable economies are the
same: more produce grows in the jungle but precisely so much more
is rotten. — However, while not dismissing these sage conclusions
from my mind's own shady paradise, I stood on deck straight as a
stick, with a half-smile on my face that expressed some enjoyment as
well as contempt. What pleased me was the thought of the *hidden
life* going on in the interior: — the unknown mineral-intelligences in
lava-caves, the snakes that watched us, the villages built entirely
upon the boughs of monstrous trees, where the cries of roosting
birds punctuated the howling prayers of these wretched children of
Tarzan to the gods that deprived and tortured them, the dangerous
local distempers, poxes, and putrescences (about which more later);

the little orphan boy who was warmed and raised within the waxy leaves of some capriciously carnivorous plant, the tribe of men with two heads each, and the tribe with their heads up their asses. I thought, also, without much straining my capacities, of the interesting conservatism of nature, that perpetrated the same sadisms everywhere in superficially diverse guises. How elegant, really, that along the mountainous fringes of this Amazon territory there undoubtedly ran a stream whose bed of sand and gravel was pure gold, that these nuggets, so rare in civilized lands and so difficult of access, would one day be the pocket-dandruff of rich men, who had dribbled out pittances to their compradore cavaliers, with much the same abandon with which they expelled their mouthwashes from their puffed cheeks, in the privacy of their echoing bathrooms, so that from a minimum investment, accompanied by a minimum obligation, the gold might be located for them, and dredged, and hauled; that then it would be no more or less difficult of access to your average loser than before! Certainly this promising new force of electricity (which I myself had discovered when, stooping to rub together two pieces of insect-amber in the late Jurassic, just to be doing something, I detected a static attraction now sticking the lumps each to each) would eliminate many spurious situational differences; – though I am a spy I have always, oddly enough, been a foe of hypocrisy – for electricity would crush things and make them over, and soon there would be no gold-stream to confuse the issue; they might call the place El Creeko Park or Riverita Road because they had to call it *something*, but it would be all flat and laid out with generating stations and Peruvian soccer fields and rubbish dumps. Then wealth would be unavailable only for the one reason that Mr. White or Mr. Morgan had it all sewed up; ah, it would be plain, you see, that unavailability is an ontological mudbank that no tin-pat gringo can cross. We ourselves had crossed the mudbanks only with the most elite and selective exertions, in the earlier stages of our voyage, when it was so hot and damp that we were thankful when our clothes only rotted off us once an hour; and all aboard, with the exception of Captain de Silva and myself, were kept occupied chopping and burning the bimbo-weeds and bonsai trees that continually took root upon the deck. – The first attack involved squadrons of spiky ferns. Within moments these organisms, which had sprouted as if at the behest of the triumphantly coiling vines in our rigging, had grown so high as to entangle us in the muju-wuju trees on either side. Indeed, our craft was lifted from the water and raised up into the tree-tops in the space of two revolutions of the second hand of my chronometer, such was the growth rate. — I ascended the crow's nest with de Silva for consultations, but there was nothing to see save white fog, which could be firmly squeezed in the hands until it turned into lukewarm water. We remained in our state of arboreal shipwreck for a week, foraging sadly for kapapoki fruits in the topmost branches, as Noah must have done with trawling lines as he sailed over the submerged forests of Ecuador; until at length, becoming annoyed with the affair, which could only delay my timetable if it persisted, I recommended that we act against our environment. We were by this time sealed into a catacomb of brownish vines. The senile fronds, which at first had wilted like limp old scallion-ends, gradually baked hard as pretzels in one of those humorous jungle droughts which surprise one every now and then due to meteorological upsets, so that our wicker-woven bower grew brittle and stiff, and the stems around us resembled nothing so much as dried kelp upon a beach, beaded with salt. Occasionally we heard some great leathery snake sliding overhead. We would have died of thirst were it not for the fact that it remained hot, so that the sweat ran from us at all times and filled our trouser-pockets; thus, we had but to sip this meaty, nutritious substance through long straws to instantly feel fit and fortified. — Meanwhile the foliage continued to thicken and compact itself over our heads. Thirty-seven-pound beri-beri berries ripened, fell, and burst into a noisome glue to which stuck broken twigs, broccoli-carcasses, coconut-fuzz, lizard skins, nut-pods, dead leaves made rigid by crystals of milky sap, thorns, burrs and prickle-shells, feathers, droppings, and similar matter, making the living stuff that it permeated more impenetrable than ever. — Next we had a drumming hour of rain, which restored a khaki hue to ferociously budding surfaces. Far off we could hear the cinnamon-trees (C. zeylanicum) growing so fast that the air whistled. The new growth beneath us began thrusting us upwards again the following afternoon, greedy as it was for the light; this gave me the idea of lowering a lantern on a line to the level of the river, which, as we could all see when we crowded like little boys round the hole we had chopped with our machetes to permit the execution of my plan, was as black as a mummy's cunt in a pyramid at midnight; for the foliage was now so thickly matted and stratified upon its branch-buttresses, like leaves clogging a gutter in a city and being stamped upon all day by millions of commuters and packed down and crushed, that we would soon be sealed in a layer of oil shale. We seemed to be peering down from the nave of a cathedral, or (equivalently) the manhole of a sewer. The river flowed viscously in the darkness. A fetid holiness of suffocating night-life arose to my nostrils like incense; and pushing the others aside I took three deep breaths of it. The lantern illuminated a whole desperate cicada-orchestra on the riverbank, their pointed musical knees slung over their shoulders like bayonets as they drilled their sad tunes in yellow-green formation, mourning this state of continuous blackout as they must have been required to do, not that they didn't love it since it gave them an unlicensed nightclub ambience down there, which was why they screeched their scaly bows with increasing abandon, oh, me, bruising the shin-barked tree-legs with raspers and timbrels until I wished that I had opera-glasses. – But back to business. At my direction, Captain de Silva rapped on the hard darkish matter which now enclosed our party; I had furnished him with a special rubber hammer, well suited to determining the hardness of minerals on the Lamarckian Scale. The noise was dull and heavy; fossilization was progressing rapidly; we were already encased in a seam of coal! But the lantern was too succulent a lure for the jungle not to grow towards, even if that meant rendering us less hermetically secured. It burned quite gently and steadily above the water, like a moon in a cave. – At once night-flowers budded from apical meristems; and groaning branches shifted downward toward the light. I glimpsed a shower of bugs pelting down against that distant lantern, so eager were they to die brightly. Then the unfolding leaves obscured everything down there in an olive-colored twilight, and the wood creaked anxiously up and down like a worried bed when a honeymoon couple is screwing away, excited beyond dreams but fearful that what they crave will elude them at the last minute. The walls of the coal-seam fissured slowly, and our boat rocked. – Being a member of the dominant race, I gave the signal to cut, and at once all the crew, not excepting Captain de Silva this time, began to lay about them with their imported blades. Bravo! Bravo! Lumps of coal clattered around us and splashed into the river; some few of these I secreted on my person for later sale, anticipating the continuing popularity of the steam engine. – Our faces were smeared with soot. The stratum shattered brilliantly, with a hard cold noise like breaking mirrors. – We fell; we caught; my fine men cut and cut; we fell again; we stuck; but the boughs on which we were snagged were already growing downward desperately to reach the lantern before their fellows; we rocked; we slipped; SPLURSH! back into the river; and we blew a leaf out of the engine and gunned it. – Now, I said to myself, for the punishment. Taking aim with my Browning pistol, I sternly shot out the lantern, which dangled above our heads like a chandelier in the clutches of the greedy trees. A great rustling hiss of disappointment arose from the foliage, at which my fellows and I smiled cruelly. Then we all dismissed the matter from our minds, for such happenings were commonplace in the days before electricity.

So we voyaged through this lonely country, the mosquitoes tracking us gamely over the water; and I swiveled my head from bank to bank not without an anticipatory nostalgia for this eco-system which already had its death-bloom on it. — Onward, onward! — The launch chugged sadly. One cylinder had slipped a bearing, or untoothed a cog (for I do not pretend to any mechanical knowledge). All along the bank was a stirring and chittering. Green serpents writhed gorgeously upon the overhanging branches. They flickered their cool tongues on the tree-boles, tasting the air; and they studied the tactical situation with their shiny yellow eyes. One spied us, and bellied its way through the foliage to poise itself above the cabin, at which I was alarmed (although I also wanted to collect it), because snakes can dangle from the trees like fruits, and multiply on jungle islands so that when you row your boat through the archipelagoes of the China Sea they'll come dropping ripely down from the trees above you and weight your boat more and more heavily, and squirm over you and ogle and fondle you, paying genuine attention to you, and struggle to be among the first to clog your oars with their bodies, and they'll unhinge their jaws in absentminded yawns so that the venom-drops roll off their fangs, which are inlaid with blue floral designs like Dutch tiles, as you see quite plainly just before they nip you, injecting the best of themselves into you, striking all together; and then they pile themselves on the starboard side, yellow and green like a hundredweight of ripe and unripe bananas, to capsize you once you are puffy and paralyzed from their bites, and you drown before the poison can kill you, and all the snakes swim back to their tree-roots, making long leisurely wakes in the water because they have a reptile truce with the guardian crocodiles; or else the snakes will sink to the bottom and coil into figure-eights and play games down there among all the interesting treasure-chests. But worldwide electrification is now putting a period to this nonsense. We will place them in lit cages. — Here came the curtain of hanging flowers that smelled of strawberries, and then there was the bend again, with the serpent up ahead waiting. By the fifth or sixth iteration we had perfected our maneuvers to such an extent that the monster never had a chance to get us. – Onward, onward! – This repetition was the jungle's defense against explorers. The wearisome monotony of it rendered civilized faculties insensible, confused the perception of time, and destroyed the will to slog on. Retreat, on the other hand, was easy; all one had to do was nose the launch around and head back downriver, cornering that same dark bend, but only once, and one would find oneself on the outskirts of Rio (which Mr. White had just bought, and which would in three decades have become another of his blaring electric fortresses). But we continued on, for thousands and thousands of miles. Had I, Big George, been a violent man, I could have gotten a great deal of target practice on that serpent, leaving it to thrash and finally dangle, loosen its coils just like Parker when I destroyed *him*, and plop into the muddy river a multiple number of times, always to be devoured by an identical crocodile (reptile-truces only go so far). But I just stared back up at it, unwinking and baleful behind my spectacles.

Would anyone think, O Best Beloved, that the trees, which looked so beautiful and harmless by day, have in fact a miasmatic breath which at night produces a severe fever in anyone exposed for too long to their influence? This was, alas, the case, and as dusk fell, and the river began to take on its humid phosphorescence, the night-ferns to uncoil their sensitive fingertips, the mosquitoes to swarm evilly, the vampire bats to ascend in winged file from some cave or hollow tree, then Captain de Silva lit the bow and stern lanterns, and we bound across our faces lengths of surgical gauze soaked in rum. Only this kept the vapor-disease at a distance. If one discarded the gauze, he would, I was told by my fellow reactionaries, feel a terrible thirst and dizziness, so that he'd rush to the side of the boat and greedily scoop up the river water with his hands. As he brought his cupped palms to his lips, the dreaded polukaru – a long, bee-striped polliwog with teeth – would leap down his throat and begin to devour his internal organs. Maddened by this new pain, the dumb shit would fall overboard in his convulsions (for no one could attempt to save him without risk of infection), and in due time be ripped apart by squat shapes unknown to current zoological nomenclature, whereas if, as described above, he had fallen into the China Sea, the underwater snakes would have been gentle with him, and played innocent tricks with his nodding skull, and hidden in his eye-holes with real gratitude when the junks of Chinese pirates passed overhead; this is the main difference between Asia and South America. I have fond memories of these days of old-style water-deaths, back before electricity had combined with the aqueous element (hydroxic acid) to create painful episodes, such as teenagers listening to the Dr. Dodger Show on the radio while they are in the bathtub and reaching out to tune in a little better, and their wet sleek arms bring the electrons rushing into their brains and hearts, or the way street people kill themselves in New York by pissing on the electric third rail. — Here in South America there were only natural sounds and sights if a man went over. For a moment his teeth might shine in the dark. If by some miracle he did not fall into the river, rolling instead, say, into the fo'c'sle so that we could all gather round to watch the spectacle as the ship's doctor shook his head sympathetically (all the rustic virtues still exist among these people), then the fever itself would kill him before morning — another grisly victory for the trees!

Oh, how hard it is to begin a truly worthwhile project, to break ground, to clear underbrush, and leave everything flat and smoldering to fertilize new growth!

The river was indeed a marvelous display of natural history. It reminded me of a long corridor lined with elementary school dioramas built out of shoeboxes stolen from home's black closets, and as you walked along the hall at the exhibition on parents' night you had to stop and get down on your knees to see anything because the budgets had been cut back in our great Republic, and there were no long light-tables or glass cases as you might expect to scratch and sniff, say, at the Aquarium; and the boxes on the floor disappointed you by their shabbiness, containing as they did clumsy dinosaurs squeezed from playdough, magic markered trees spreading their sad scribbly branches in the painted background like retarded children's hands, and the same old snake in each box, flicking its tongue (maybe it only *looked* poisonous), so trapped and miserable for Thailand or Sumatra or wherever it had come from; at least Clara Bee, my fiancée, always kept her snakes like candies or pills in a clean clear tank on the bureau, and she played her records at low volume so as not to disturb them by the vibration, and she fed them regularly and hung tiny pieces of No-Pest Strips in their cage when they had mites; and she watched the thermometer strip with conscientious alarm, so that when our coastal bedroom cooled off in the evenings or in rainy weather, and the temperature inside the snakes' cage, which was warmed by the light bulb of a study lamp pressed up against the glass, decreased by four or five degrees, then my sweet Clara Bee cried and worried that the snakes would die. They were called Fred and Harrison, and were almost always good.

These names Clara had decided on, the snakes being hers. She had bought them, as I, the author, never paid for anything, being a miser because already I understood that all my days I'd be working for Big George, and if I needed to ask him a question on a program or go to the bathroom he'd look up from his brochure on jungle studies and say, "I'm sorry, but I'm really not available right now" — well, it was those bright nickels and dimes I was humiliating myself for; so by rights I should save every one in my cookie jar, correct? and never ever spend them but always ask Clara dear to buy me treats. Thus it was she, as I said, who actually put the money down for the snakes, and now I do not live with my darling anymore and my heart is so sick that I will kill myself soon I shall hardly be able to see the snakes again (though I can still read about snakes in books, and dream about snakes in the graveyard where I am holed up; for from the layman's point of view there is not much difference between snakes in the trees and fat white corpse-worms snaking along underground). — My Clara Bee bought "Fred" to start with; Fred was in effect her first-born child. We picked Fred out together at the Vivarium in Emeryville; and how it hissed when the man took it away from the rest of its brood . . . All the vipers seemed very happy crowded together in the adults-only section at the Vivarium; and I liked the black, dangerous snakes, although Clara was afraid of black snakes, especially black racers, which I thought would be good fun to own and let zip around the living room and up the walls and across the ceiling to eat furry spiders that they thought were rodents. Still I was very proud of my Bee despite her phobias because she wanted to be brave and said that she would not even mind if Fred struck at her and bit her. — This was a possibility, especially in the beginning, for Fred was very frightened of Bee when she bought Fred and took Fred home with us, and I think that Fred had still not accustomed itself to living as a caged thing indoors, where wires ran through everything like veins, and there was no way to comprehend smooth surfaces. It hid in its straw. Once Clara looked for Fred and could not see it there in the straw and thought that it had escaped because it had secreted itself behind the water dish for reasons of prudence and safety; because it genuinely believed that it could hide itself away for good from its Bee. But Bee would not let it hide, and she played with Fred every day for forty minutes or so until it became agitated. (Jungles one may escape, maybe, but when electricity comes, it walls its prisoners off forever.) At that time, children, Fred was only as thick as a pencil. But already it could flicker its tongue and coil up and bask beneath the light bulb, and the household current pulsed like blood in the filament of Clara's study lamp, and made fun of the snake and tricked it with every amperic cycle, because the snake could not understand that this was not the sun, although it did sense something insidious and artificial about its surroundings. – Big pink meats came and grabbed it and watched it and handled it and fed it; they were too big to eat. The pink meats presented Fred with things, and were always there, even after Fred had forgotten about them. They kept Fred in a place where it was always light and the warmth never changed, and there were no waving leaves or wise tree-boughs to whisper to Fred or teach Fred stalking tricks, and there was nobody there but Fred. When Fred looked out, it could see the pink meats coming, and then it tried to hide in its sad boring desert, but the pink meats always found Fred. They never tried to eat Fred, though, so Fred became calm and sluggish. Sometimes it crawled slowly up inside Clara's sleeve, across her hot bare back, where it basked in the darkness like a schoolchild staying indoors at recess in the rain, until the scent of Clara's flesh reminded Fred that it wanted to go hunting and it fumbled and flickered inside Clara's sweatshirt (it cannot do any of this anymore because it is too big and will not fit inside her sleeve, just as it has had to stop sliding across the bridge of her glasses the way it did when it was a baby), and finally exited from the opposite sleeve. My Clara Bee laughed and stroked Fred's flat little head because she liked Fred to be close to her and she was proud of Fred for finding the way out, as if Fred were still a cunning jungle snake. But Fred just lay still, with only its head poked out of Clara's sleeve, and its long body wrapped back across her doughy shoulders inside her sweatshirt, and its tail still in the other sleeve, for Fred was daily growing in length. When she rubbed its head it became hypnotized or paralyzed, as frogs will when you caress their bellies slowly with a circular finger-motion, and if you then drop them back into the pond they just float helplessly for a moment, goggling at you in shock, until suddenly their functions are restored, and they can dive under the water. – Something terrible had happened to Fred. It could not understand exactly what that was, but it knew it could not do what it wanted to anymore.* The situation had something to do with the light bulb that shone down so watchfully and dazzled

---

*"At the least," says Haggard in Swallow, "allowances should always be made for the susceptibilities of a race that finds its individuality and national character sinking slowly, but without hope of resurrection, beneath an invading flood of Anglo-Saxons."

Fred's lidless eyes, but it warmed Fred and relaxed Fred's interlocking spine, so Fred lay coiled and basked and was patient, because one day Clara Bee might let it go or it might escape. Besides, it did not really mind because it liked to bask. But it was always hungry. Bee worried that it was lonely, so "Harrison," who was more sickly and beautiful and difficult, was purchased as a companion for Fred. It cost more than Fred had, being a reticulated python, not a mere Burmese like poor Fred. The financial aspect was not, however, a road-block for my Clara Bee because she very much wanted to have her dear snakes since they were all she could have; earlier that year, having turned eighteen, she had gotten herself sterilized. The snakes could be loved and would never cry. They grew and were good. In those days they each ate one mouse per week. Fred, who was the dark green one, became big, fat and olive-drab. After a month it had settled down and forgotten the notion of freedom, like a castrated tomcat. Then I loved Fred. I used to talk to it in the last few months before Bee became certain that she did not love me anymore and sent me away; I am convinced that Fred understood my every word. Sometimes it opened the lid of the cage with its nose and slithered into our bed in the middle of the night to keep warm. I'd wake up feeling a smooth cool entity, not unlike a wallet in texture, hugged around my thigh, and would lie very still so as not to hurt it. I wondered whether the snake's journey along the smooth glass cage-top, down the great precipice of the bureau, gliding cautiously from knob to knob, and across the rug to the hot mammal-smelling caves beneath the rumpled blanket mountains (it must have slithered in where my foot stuck out from the sheets, or where my sweet Clara had outflung her arm in sleep, with a corner of the blanket clutched in her plump fingers; the snake might have entered there gently, remorselessly, and glided across Clara's breast to come and see me) — I wondered whether this trip had seemed desperate and dangerous to it, or whether it was only looking for mice. — When Clara Bee woke up the next morning she was hysterical. We might have killed it. It might have crawled under the bookcase and gotten lost. Clara herself, who was plump, might have rolled over and suffocated it. It could have escaped through the open window and been killed by a cat. In pet magazines we had read accounts of snakes that hid in heating ducts and were fried, or worked their way earnestly under doors and along the carpeted hallways of apartment buildings; and came at last into the open air of Oakland, California, where if they avoided the broken glass on the sidewalk (which would have slit their poor narrow long bellies so badly I cannot even think about it) one would eventually come to the notice of one of the neighborhood kids who, in response to Big George's advertisements in the comic books, mailed it to a secret post office box in Mexico and received his nine dollars and fifty cents in cash and forgot all about the snake, but the snake didn't forget, because it was cramped and afraid in the dark box although at least it got warmer and warmer as it traveled farther south every day, third-class mail, in a great swaying stack of parcels all brown-paper-wrapped; and its packet was on top and had two air-holes punched in it with a fork, and the kid had written PERISHABLE – LIVING CULTURES on the address as per Big George's specifications so everyone would just assume it was some kind of mold virus or you know, nothing to worry about because it fell under the heading of science; so the snake traveled southward, southward, into Mexico where it smelled the big rats and was hungry and wanted to eat one, just one, but it couldn't; and kept traveling south and was scared by the pelting and pattering of Venezuelan gravel-storms; and then the air got very cold and sharp as the mule-train humped it over the Andes, descending in due time into mists and vapors, and the driver spat into the rain and wondered what could be so important about that bundle on the top that had faint slithering sounds coming out of it (or rather they had come out of it at first but now all was quiet because the snake was weak and afraid and dehydrated) and fog swirled into the air-holes of the poor snake's box, and from far below came the woobles and weebles of bloodthirsty Indian-calls; so that it was a mercy that the snake was deaf and could not be further frightened, though it could certainly sense the vibration and lurching and jouncing of the wooden wagon-wheels in the swamps, and the air became humid and the snake got encrusted with a fungal infection all over, which as Clara explained to me is usually the kiss of death for a snake; and so the prisoner arrived at last at the Enchanted Python Forest of the Amazon, and ranchero henchmen took the snake and massaged it with their big hands, which were as callused as baseball gloves, and force-fed it back into its prime; and raised it on rabbits and quarters of goats for about ten years; until finally it was ready for Big George's pleasure; who was now in the form of a small boy, wearing a sailor suit and a cowboy hat made of suede leather; and Big George had himself a popgun . . . They set the snake up in the crotch of a tree that looked much like the other trees; and now Big George could practice to his heart's content going around the bend and having a snake for target shooting; BING! the poor, poor snake . . . – Harrison, the lighter-green one with the yellow spots, which was by far the prettier of the two, and very vicious and nervous, gradually became a yellow-brown shade. It was always long and thin and irritable, and wriggled quickly. Clara loved it best. I remember the way it wrapped around my shoulders and arms and flicked its tongue in my ear, rolling its yellow eyes at me to see whether I would hurt it; and I felt sorry for it and wanted to explain to it that I would never hurt it, but I was also afraid of it because it moved so fast and struck at things and when I let it out of the cage it hugged itself around me or Clara's bookshelf or the table leg very very tightly like a lover, so that when I pulled it away — as I had to do when I put it back in its house where it never wanted to go, just as it never wanted to come out when dearest Clara reached inside to play with it or take it to its mouse — it would always realize that it was going back to its luminous prison, and would resist hopelessly, popping its head out again while Clara was still trying to introduce its middle third back into the cage, and flickering its tongue at the sweet bright bulb of Clara's study lamp by the cage (if Clara Bee was not vigilant it would burn itself) so then Clara would have to confuse it and trick it until finally it slipped and tumbled in, and its tail fell into the water bowl; then it scudded determinedly into a cardboard box which we had awarded it, where it could hide and think that it had escaped; and putting the snake back inside tested almost all my strength, like opening an oyster shell to eat the oyster alive when the oyster knew it and fought it; so perhaps then I did hurt it, and I always felt guilty about compressing the poor unwilling thing into its cage again, for it occurred to me that at such times it might strike. — But Clara loved it better precisely because it was so active; she was convinced that it was intelligent, compared to Fred. Once it bit Fred when it was hungry, and Clara screamed and sobbed and dropped them both in a sinkful of cold water to separate them. Fred harbored no grudge. It slid and basked in its box, and never minded when Harrison crawled on it or coiled around it. Perhaps it could not distinguish where it left off and Harrison began. Perhaps it just made allowances. I was never afraid of it the way I was of Harrison. But Clara, as I said, loved Harrison best and was always careful to see that it came to no harm. The cold water she had dropped it into was bad for it; it got a cold, which can be fatal for tropical snakes. But Clara Bee put it in a paper bag so that it would not be scared on the bus and took it to a veterinarian in Kensington and gave it medicine through a new eye-dropper, so it recovered its constitution, and grew; and the cage smelled more and more strongly of reptiles as Fred and Harrison basked and grew and ate and were good and fouled the pine shavings once a week with their long white cigar-shaped excrements. I hear that they each eat six mice per week now. Reptiles do get large, especially in the tropics. As I, Big George, traveled up the Amazon, secure and grinning, with hate-filled eyes spotlighting the noon to midnight mists we were at sea among, the trees drenched us with voluptuous dews; and as we passed a tall matamata tree in a little accidental clearing I caught a glimpse of Angkor Wat or maybe Tenoctitlan, and every ruined idol was black with shiny beetles in a trance of some kind; the mist was issuing from the spiracles of these bugs, intoxicating us, making us see double; I could have sworn I'd run across that serpent before. – Something pattered on the roof of the cabin ... Water gurgled at the bow, a crafty noise not unlike laughter or other classic enigmas, and the river wound back and forth like a dying snake, but by God we were overcoming it; and now and again a huge treetrunk slipped swiftly past us in the current like an advance signal of our victory.

On the sixteenth of June we arrived at our nameless port, a harbor with one hut. I followed Captain de Silva and his clerk ashore, where we were welcomed by a large bare-breasted Negress, her teeth filed to points, who bore a tray of tiny cups of jet-black coffee. I showed the varnished card identifying me as a white man, and was rewarded with two cups. After downing this delicacy in appropriately lordly style, I bade farewell to de Silva and paid him off. With whistles and rifle shots, the launch departed. It was going back downriver; it would be in Rio in an hour. They had washed their hands of me, no doubt; they assumed that I would hire bearers, who would desert me when we approached some sacred and terrible spot, whereupon I might well be ambushed by Indians who would revere me as a god. But, you see, comrades, it was entirely necessary for me to assume the disguise appropriate to my mission. I was no exploiter, no exterminator of indigenous aboriginal peoples – and if such feelings did come over me from time to time I had merely to call Dr. Dodger on my pocket wireless, and he would be happy to schedule an appointment. Cooperation, alliance, holy rolling – that was my keynote, you see; I intended to find the bugs and enter into partnership with this jungle.

We had our reasons, the author and I, for knowing that results must be achieved. Already Mr. White was blueprinting his subroutines so that it would be impossible to divert his program; what bug could escape the spiderwebs of power wires and interlocking directorates which would soon cover the country, especially once the juice was turned on? Of course in years to come I would much relish using the network against itself, recoding my identities as pleased me, like a snake, magnetizing the reactionaries' data banks in subtly different configurations, and making all slot machines pay me off; but in the meantime the bugs might prove useful; I enjoyed the blue-grey cap of a revolutionary, and I was restless . . .

PREMONITIONS OF THE IDEAL (1805–1878)

~~~~~~

In this movement the passive Subject itself perishes . . .

HEGEL
preface to the *Phenomenology* (1807)

The Society of Daniel, my dears, was founded in Colorado in 1911, a year when "the picturesque arrogance of the older academics was being replaced by a new generation of mercurial and spent individuals," as Bologna puts it (picturesquely) in another context altogether. In the universities of the country, hidalgos strutted round and round their endowed chairs to great effect, recalling to the uninitiated our victories in Mexico and Cuba. Mercurial and spent Full Professors meanwhile readied us for the trenches in Flanders a half-decade hence. We memorized statistics on pig-iron production and prepared to be engineers in the erection of that transnational superstructure known variously as the White Man's Burden, the Good Neighbor Policy, the Open Door, and Our Oriental Heritage (Vietnamization). Every one-room schoolhouse had its blackboard and its calisthenics area. And it was very common then, Virginia, to whistle hymns in front of the Stars and Stripes: "Und der *Hai*fisch, der hat *Zäh*ne; und die *trägt* er, im Ge*sicht*," dum-de-*dum*. By 1907, as Lenin points out in "Imperialism, the Highest Stage of Capitalism," the American General Electric Company (G.E.C.) had ceased competition with the German General Electric Company (A.E.C.). Cartels in railroads, merchant shipping, oil, steel and the slave populations of Asia and the tropics succeeded in establishing similarly beneficial zones of power, so that the great Vogelstein could write in his *Organisationsformen* (1910) that "the division of the world is complete, and the big consumers, primarily the state railways – since the world has been parceled out without consideration for their interests – might as well now dwell like the poet in the heavens of Jupiter." Good working-class theory rejoices at this. The forefathers of the movement, brooding in their villas on the shores of Lake Geneva (for at this time we had quite a European character) had determined that all we need do was wait until the multinational concentrations had become more and more acute, until it would simply be a matter of displacing a few dozen members of the reactionary elite and we would control the entire world. All this is no more saddening than a quick perusal of manifestoes a mere decade old, still speaking of "irresistible pressure" and a "qualitatively new element." Everybody makes mistakes. We were too optimistic, or too ruthless, or not ruthless enough.

Nowadays, as one lounges out on the porch of an evening, in a folding lawn chair of finished redwood, it is scarcely possible to recall the limitations of those days. It seems that our memory typewriters and compact disk players have been around forever, like wise infinitely reliable mentors and administrators of our sport. In front of me the automatic sprinkler crawls steadily along the garden hose which my father has cunningly laid across his lawn; and from the Carsons' house on Woodbine Court I can hear the metronome-like ticking of the children's robot playing house with Robbie in the garage. A jet plane shoots happily through the blue sky, bound, perhaps, for another covert bombing mission in Nicaragua, where the colorfully dressed, brown-skinned population still resists our directive to BUCKLE DOWN and WORK because for them every day is a fiesta day in their pink or yellow or green brick houses in the cool mountains when WE are drumming our fingers and impatiently waiting for our Buddy Brand or Dodger's Choice instant coffee to be harvested so that we can zip down to the office in our station wagons and set new goals and trends in productivity, because without us electrical consumption would sink to its nadir. – But if you will just stop dancing with the dishwasher for a moment I, Big George, will describe to you in loving detail how it all came about, and what life was like for our pioneers in the 1860s and 1870s. – No one had even heard of the blue globes then, if you can imagine such a thing! In the popular mind, the crawly hive consciousness, electrical philosophy had made no progress since that afternoon (some time ago now) when Ben Franklin flew a kite in a storm to determine the composition of lightning. These, and other foolish experiments, were satisfying to the credulous, who were thus lulled into the belief that electricity was nothing but a mindless natural force, existing for their use, like pyrites, alum, arsenic or cobalt. Even Dr. Dodger, ordinarily such a canny old man, was taken in by its transitory and contingent utility once Mr. White had made him aware of it; to him, as he sat at the window of his hotel room in Barker, Missouri, looking out at the yokels and the horse turds on Main Street one last time before setting out west for the Jenny Lode, even Dr. Dodger, who quaffed his whiskey as fast as he wiggled his toes (for Dr. Dodger's philsophy was: What better than drink to round off every extreme of emotion? to bring the flush of success to one's cheek? to dull a gnawing sorrow?) — even Dr. Dodger was anxious to hitch his wagon to that never-twinkling star; and the rare stories of accidental electrocutions which were to come to his ears in succeeding decades (several of which you and I, oh reader, will explore in detail) he dismissed as of no more account than some Indian tale about a yellow bluff inhabited by demons with sharp arrows that killed at a great distance. But then, as Lewis and Clark relate, the Indians were often amazed by no-account items, such as air guns and magnets and various other curiosities which were shown to them, so you couldn't have much faith in their absolute Being of Reason; by and large they were troublesome, was what it boiled down to, consistently begging for whiskey and fishhooks, then not being at all satisfied with what they got. But our own pre-electrical personalities were scarcely on a higher plane. The median man's ambition was to wend through the wind in the bottoms and the wolves in the willows, establish himself a crapulous little fort, and eke out the winters without losing more than two toes per blizzard. Our industrial procedures were administered in a similarly halfhearted fashion, involving as they did unspecialized apparati driven by unskilled persons of a generalist temperament, who imagined that anyone ought to be able to read a book as well as milk a cow. — But digging and placer activity continued gamely. There was no time to wait for DuPont. The newest immigrants drew stakes and ran for the mountains fast, because they had SPUNK. Folks generally hired Injuns to conduct them across the major fords, although they would rather have dickered with the bugs because the bugs knew good safe snug tunnels, but the bugs could not or would not communicate with us, so we were stuck with these Cayoose savages out to impede OUR progress; and sometimes when trusted Tonto led us to the river and said, "Cross here!" and we thanked him with a plug of tobacco, a handful of beads and a slap on the back, the brown water turned out to be higher than it looked, so that the wagon tore downstream and smashed into the rocks and the howitzer would get swept away a~ the mules would nearly be drowned; but then you could easily s' the offending Redskin, ker-BLOOWIE! to restore the moral ʰ of the universe, and roll onward, onward, ha ha! but perpetually on watch when we played cards in the wagons at night, particularly if we had ourselves some fine horseflesh or womanflesh to ride because as Grandad used to say back on the Santa Fe Trail, "Injuns can't forgo horses any more than a negro can leave a hen roost alone," and that is why we had to get our own back, the way our predecessors and preprocessors did; as, for instance, Jesse Applegate (1843) relates: — The wagons of the settlers had come within sight of Fort Boise, Idaho. The children found numerous small white beads in an anthill. Excitedly they ran around looking for more, for it was not every day that one discovered such playthings as these, which could be kept or sold or traded; and grubbing the ground they did find more, many more, which were polished like dice, thanks to the obliging ants, who despite what Mr. White may tell you are our best friends; and all went well in the gratification of the young collectors' passions until suddenly somebody looked up and spotted the source of the beads: — a broad platform strewn with decayed Indian corpses, many yet rolled up in their blankets and robes, some torn to fragments by the crows. We trust that those former persons had earlier been informed, as Captain Clark put it, "what they might depend on if they didn't open their ears." ("That's a good one," goes Wayne.) Applegate does not say whether or not the children threw away the beads, but I bet they didn't because we were a thrifty and frugal bunch. — So on we went. — The wagons wound around steep precipices, but the tough guys made it into gold country, awright; the second-best found silver; and all the rest had to be content grubbing rusted iron bars from Spanish auto-da-fé garages and cutlass shops. Clapboard settlements popped up like toast in your electric toaster. We went back over the trails we had made and widened them into log roads, erecting toll booths every fifty miles. The immigrants continued to arrive. (Narcissa Prentiss Whitman, one of the first white women to cross the Rockies, mentions in her diary how surprised the poor Indians were!) It was the work of only one or two generations of these traveling parties to make the land comfortable for the blue globes. Their mission in history was now accomplished. — Nowadays you can see their descendants in the casinos at Reno and Tahoe, putting quarter after quarter into the slot machines and hanging on tight when the painted apples go round *k-k-k-k-k-whoomp,* then the oranges go round *k-zzzzzzzzzzzz-thonk,* then the pears go round like an orbiting orchard *whoo-whoo-whoo-whoo-neeeeeee-donk!,* but they don't get three apples (not even one crab-apple), nor three orangey-

orangey oranges, nor three mathematically perfect green pears; nor (confound it!) do they land the triple sevens which would have given them everything, nor the triad of black bars which would have meant a new car; but at least the hostess comes by with cheap drinks because she knows how a guy can work up a thirst and be a-lickin' his lips a tad when he sees the mortgage money going the way of spilled water in the salt flats, so thankee, honey; and when they tip her for being God's little blonde she smiles and winks and says, "Thank you *so* much, gentlemen" and they say, "Thank *you*," and she says, "*My* pleasure," so all concerned feel reinforced; it's a real mutual admiration society here and what the hell, mebbe I lost them quarters on account of I didn't pull the lever just right or something but I betcha I could bang her for a couple of twenties because I'm on the Nevada side of the line IF you know what I mean, boys; well, now it's back to inputting the quarters, a-one, a-two; for there's the pay-off to prepare for, that delightful tinkling rain of quarters in the aluminum basin, which comes around in the place as regularly as Fasten's Eve, although (isn't it strange?) the big jackpots always grace yer elbow-neighbor; yer own return consists of two-bits, four-bits, six-bits, chicken grits plinking out to keep the rooster pecking the dung-heap in a frenzy, momentarily expecting new riches to cram in his gizzard; and in the process the manure gets nicely aerated for Mr. White. – Back in the founding days we refined silver according to those selfsame principles of classical mechanics; i.e., trial and error, instead of the special electronic relativity used now by America's brown slender Indochinese refugees down in Los Altos and Los Gatos and Santa Clara and Sunnyvale who respectfully raise and lower the eyepieces of their company microscopes in perfect drill order when so commanded by their pocket calculators at the sound of the tone, and the pace is pretty fast because we have to beat the Japanese who are themselves going *Itch! Knee! Son! Shee!* in industrial calisthenics on every level of their factories, but I am confident that our workers will beat their workers, because here in the computer center where I sit working for Big George I can hear nothing but the earnest clacking of keyboards and I feel as if we are going to do such a good job on the release this time that there will never ever have to be another one; and up past the chip manufacturing companies I know that electricity is being used wisely in perpetual darkness of top secret projects, where well-trained Chinese men and women are tapping and coaxing the sly electricity into the ingots in a different way every week to give our country intelligent silver to make satellite warfare monsters out of, spheres in space like great spiked diatoms inlaid with copper nerves and golden brains of the highest conductivity, spinning and spinning and spinning overhead; whereas back then, we had to make do with the alchemical procedures of the two-storey Nevada retort houses, where after being crushed by nine-hundred-pound weights, the virgin ore was sifted with water into a whitish paste, and then you should have seen those laborers bust their guts for us, for themselves, and for Mr. White, scrubbing down the screens and agitating the mixture with long wooden poles, *ah-one! ah-two!* until at long last, amalgamated with quicksilver, copper sulfate and salt, the slurry was strained, settled in great barrels and then baked into bullion. The gravel heaps of Dutch Flat, Telluride, Red Dog and Secret Town Ravine grew weekly in height, and the population increased, too. In those happy times a man loved his work and bore his fate uncomplainingly; and everything was oh so quiet, because revolution was like an undiscovered ore far down in a dark cavern. Barbed wire had only just been invented in Germany (1874), where dress rehearsals were being conducted for 1933–45; and we scarcely knew the lore of guns at that time; we were all separate but equal then, you see; even the greatest ideologues had not established the difference between echo and batch mode; it was only later, in the mysterious days when electricity had grown up all around us, that there were little folks and big folks towering like weeds; oh, yes, there was so much to be done! – But, alas, we Kuzbuites were in no way interested in electricity, which at that time was far inferior in beauty and dignity to the songs of Ireland.

Mr. White Makes His Million (1898)

~~~~~~

This 'homing' stroke is so simple it seems almost obvious afterwards; yet the effect never ceases to tell.

Liner notes for Beethoven's Piano Concerto No. 5
(Solti/Ashkenazy/Chicago Symphony Orchestra:
Decca Records, 1976)

In our red and yellow deserts the prophets of harsh new industries went wandering. Where in the 'seventies, 'eighties and 'nineties noisy tent cities of gold-struck fellows had unfurled themselves, to vanish within weeks or months of their erection, leaving behind only footprints, marker-stones and crushed tin cans which had once contained Dr. Dodger's Narcopathic Trail Food, now came the lone professionals. These men, upon whom the destiny of our young Republic so depended, were reactionaries in no devil-may-care sense. It was their sincere and unvarnished aim to make us over. With sacks of flour and lead shot lashed to their burros, they subdivided the land into zones of investigation, each zone being comprised of thirteen sectors, and each sector being administered and burnished with all zeal, as was the right of its owner, for property-polishing goes hand in hand with the natural affections of the superior mind. Every now and then, the private traveler, outlaw, or surveyor might meet one of these Imperators squatting in a river bend, say, looking underneath rocks for glints of color. The new arrival would nod, touch his hat for a Western how-d'ye-do, and begin to unhitch his knapsack to offer a chaw, for he did not yet know with whom he had to do; but at once a long-barreled "Empire" or "Terrier" shotgun appeared on the stream proprietor's knee, not pointing at him or nothin' like that because that would've been unnecessary in those subtle times when all firearms were loaded; but the intent was clear: Get the fuck off my land, Bo, and you'd better reckon to twinkle your moccasins pretty lively on the count of three and keep up a spanking pace for a godfearing distance, because this here stream, and these tamarisk trees, and that valley yonder where ya see the blue sparks comin' out of the rocks, and all the springs beyond the pass, and the mountain range over the horizon, are now under reactionary management and development! — So, my friends, the traveler bit his lip, bye-bye, and tightened his pack-straps and continued on his way with downcast face, while the great man remained in the middle of his stream like a spider in a web, monitoring the fading clinks of rock against rock that marked the intruder's departure, for the double-back and doublecross were not unknown then. — Not that bushwhackings were as common as one might suppose, either, thanks to the precautions generally taken. The reactionaries did not yet have their electronic "Sentry" alarms, but they built diverse snares and deadfalls around their camps. Had the traveler decided that he would rather ambush this greedy dingo than continue on with an empty canteen, he would have circled behind the ridge overlooking the stream. As he crept back up the slope, his own gun unslung now, he came upon a little arroyo, choked with bushes, which would take him up over the shoulder of the ridge to allow him to squeeze off a shot in concealment. Trampling unsuspecting over the skeletons of his predecessors (for the grey wiry grass had grown up over everything), he kept his head down, crawling closer and closer to the top of the ridge; and now all he had to do was part a screen of mesquite branches to get a bearing on the camp; and as he brushed a twig aside there was a creak of rope and a click of a pin disengaging; and then an arrow tipped with fish-hooks shot into his brain. So trespassers learned the error of their ways.

Nowadays, thanks to the enterprise of the great man, our deserts are covered with solar collectors, freeways and taco stands. Restful motels exist at thirty-mile intervals. One never has to worry that the gas stations will be pillaged anymore, that, coasting down through the salt flats on your last drop of gas, putt-putt-putt, you'll see black smoke rising from what was once the snack shop, and in the lurid red glow coming from the wreckage of the gas pumps you can make out the fuel jockey sprawled beside the rest room area with his scalp gone; no, my special one; these things never happen. And the technological picture is even brighter and yellower than the social one which I have just sketched for you.

This progress did not, as you can well imagine, occur in a day and a night. I, Big George, invite you to imagine the difficulties, distractions and divagations of these elder days, when exploitation came slow and hard, like a dying prospector stumbling out of H. Rider Haggard's Africa (for Sutter's Mill and the Klondike were hardly a flash in the pan), asking only for a little water, if you please, before expiring quietly, a treasure map on billion-year-old parchment to be found on his cold breast: "𝕱𝖗𝖔𝖒 𝕰𝖑𝖉𝖗𝖎𝖌𝖊 𝕸𝖙. take bearings on 𝕲𝖑𝖆𝖈𝖎𝖊𝖗 xxx 𝕯𝖊𝖌𝖗𝖊𝖊𝖘, proceed iv 𝕳𝖚𝖓𝖉𝖗𝖊𝖉 steps and kill 1st 𝕴𝖓𝖏𝖚𝖓 you meet. 𝕱𝖔𝖑𝖑𝖔𝖜 𝖁𝖚𝖑𝖙𝖚𝖗𝖊𝖘 to 𝕰𝖑 𝕯𝖔𝖗𝖆𝖉𝖔." — The arc lamp was invented in 1878. A steam plant was established by the Salt Lake Power, Heat and Light Company on the present site of the Capitol Theater, with a capacity of 46 arc lamps. The "Front Line Soldiers of Technology" program (Friday, November 19, 1943, radio station Alpha Gamma Bravo, 10:00 p.m.) quotes a resident's journal: "It's beautiful, that's what it is! It's something I'll always remember, an' it's a mighty big step in the way of modern Progress, those lights! Almost as bright as moonlight they are — or would be, if they gave just a bit — MORE — light!"

Mr. White, private citizen, packed a spring wagon and set out for Colorado. Rocks gnashed their teeth at him in the streams. There was snow on the bristlecones. Bluejays starved to death that winter; the ice was so thick they couldn't break through it to get to the nuts and seeds that they had buried. At Telescope Peak, where the wind was blowing so strongly that it folded half the mountain-tops in the state quite flat and stamped them down good (and that's where mesas come from) Mr. White shot the last aboriginal squirrel for his breakfast, *poom!* (In a slide-show talk which he gave to the Rotary Club in 1955, he reported that the squirrel's ribs had "stuck out like rails. Damned thing was probably mighty happy I finished him off.") Two days after this his supplies began to give out. Tightening his belt, he went on over the mountains, crossing his arms and frowning while his mare picked her path behind. He was a man in early middle age, was Mr. White, with grey hair, blue eyes, and an inexhaustible vigor. His underjaw, lined with a thick cartilaginous membrane, which added greatly to its length, protruded considerably beyond the upper. He wore boots of Mexican leather, and a web belt. His trousers were hitched up with stout galluses. In his wagon he carried a blanket roll, a haversack, a factory, and a Brown Bess musket rubbed bright with water and wood ashes. — It would never have contented him to be a mere onlooker. — Not infrequently he was forced to set the wagon on its side, climb on, set the mare in his lap like a baby, and toboggan down some sixty-degree ice-slide. In this fashion he encountered various lamaseries of lost civilizations hidden in pocket-shaped valleys; they were so removed from history that they still used Kerensky notes; but we have already done the lost civilization thing, so we will skip over the passes and the tribes that he left behind; in fact he was pretty brisk about it, down one cliff and up the next, march-march-march and out of MY way! – whereas Dr. Dodger dawdled in any Fertile Crescent he happened to find, making eyes at the high priestess in whose crescent he was while he lay refreshing himself with a lump of sugar soaked in adrenalin. And this, perhaps, was why Dr. Dodger was only Number Two, but Mr. White was Number One, hacking away at the glaciers to make steps for his horse until the chips flew up around his head and some hit the horse and made her jump and sneeze, while Dr. Dodger traveled freely and irresponsibly, warbling like a bird, carrying nothing but a roll of dogeared blueprints and a Hammer pocket pistol ("Hammer the Hammer!" went the ad); so when he came to the ice-falls he skated down them nimbly, glissading down the screes and bounding along the ledges and twanging the scrub pines, for he knew that no matter what might befall he would come to no harm. – But Mr. White was out of contact with him for some months during the journey (it was thought best that they travel separately, in order to avoid alerting any squatters who might perhaps be occupying some quadrant which Mr. White and Dr. Dodger had designs on), so he did not know of Dr. Dodger's lax and traitorous behavior. – Emerging from a little congregation of bare aspens, which somewhat sheltered him from the sleet, he looked round warily, and the mare stopped clopping behind him. The snow was relatively shallow here. Air bubbles and mouse footprints pockmarked its surface, so that from close up it resembled a frothing of crystallized spit. A few tall strands of grass stuck out, golden from the previous fall, but folded by wind into inverted Vs, like maimed cricket-legs. – The skinny mare snapped them up. – Everywhere grey twigs protruded from the snow like dead coral. The bark of the trees was a faint green color, as if tinted with moss-pigment; and each tree-trunk was tattooed with hundreds of oval shapes, the counterpart of the air bubbles in the snow. Every branch extended from the center of a web of concentric markings, like wrinkles around an armpit. In the cool blue shadows there was no sound but an occasional tree-creak or the abrupt snapping of a branch. At the edge of this grove, which was demarcated by a fallen log which was half black (its natural hue) and half white with snow, like a chocolate mousse, stretched a plateau upon which the snow had fallen with treacherous evenness, like democracy, concealing thin-crusted brooks and who knows what else. Beyond this was a zone of exquisitely bare dead bushes, their branches twisted into giant tassels. It was toward this vegetation, and the great mountains beyond, that Mr. White now proceeded after due consideration, seeing no ambushes, which was almost a pity because he was ready to beat anything or anybody bloody who tried ANYTHING; he'd give 'em the Star-Spangled What-For! To his right, as he cleared the aspens, he could see pine trees standing gloriously at the shore of a sullen little lake, like green plumber's brushes against the blue sky; and meanwhile the snow-clouds, white on the top and grey in the under-belly, came down lower and lower around the mountains, so that to Mr. White, striding across the snowy plain *crunch crunch crunch*, with the wagon squeaking along behind and the mare picking her way and farting and rolling her eyes, the range of peaks seemed to degenerate from pyramids into squat trapezoids as he scanned them through his British field glasses without pausing in his progress. These mountains had never been scaled by anyone of European stock (but there is always a first time). Long vertical blue-grey ridges ran up their walls, resembling streaks of muscle in a beef carcass, while between them meandered other vertical stripes of featureless white, not unlike marblings of fat. – Or, if you've already eaten, we can say with equal truth that Mr. White observed steep, narrow defiles bordered by grey-green trees, as in a Chinese painting. The rock was chiseled with striations and ledges, and extended north and south as far as the eye could see, extending great spurs from time to time to take in even more territory, such as the sullen lake, the blue-grey waters of which ground silently against the icy beach. – Onward, onward! The plain seemed to go on forever, and it was nearly as smooth as the snow made it look; it was a sage plain strewn with frozen broken cinders which were damned easy to stumble over or stub your toe on, 'ticularly fer a draggle-ass mare – and in case you didn't know, a horse with a broken leg has practically no resale value – and while we're complaining, even through the snow, which was as crunchy as styrofoam (Dr. Dodger would manufacture THAT commercially half a dozen decades hence) Mr. White could smell the detestable odor of greasewood, which always made him queasy, but what the bloody cunting hell, a man had to go on. – At the base of the mountains there were many short, steep ascents, exhausting the strength of his worn-out horse, but the summits ahead certainly had a grand appearance, huge masses of ice and snow piled peak upon peak, and almost every slope covered by timber of quality sufficient to make a fine lot of firewood. Meanwhile Mr. White had to clear a passage through the ravines for the wagon, leaping over rocks and hacking the tinkling-frozen bushes aside with his MacKenzie knife as he headed away from the redundant populations in the east. The horse struggled on behind, weakening by the hour. Sometimes the wagon got stuck all the same, and then there was nothing to do but get behind the back wheel and give it a tremendous kick so that it wrenched out of whatever rockbed rut it had caught in; and then he'd kick the wagon again so that it caroomed into the mare's backside, and he'd yell, "Move it, dog meat!", for Mr. White was not a boss to be trifled with. – Frequently he saw snow-covered beaver dams at the bend of some icebound creek, and he almost considered chopping through one of them and dispatching a few of the varmints for his larder, which was running thin indeed; what he wouldn't have given for plenty of potatoes, coffee and Safeway quality ground beef! but he figured if he kept going he might see something more worth the trouble, like a grizzly bear or a mountain sheep the horns of which were as thick as a man's leg, so on he went, forgetting that an old-timer had once warned the trekkers on the Oregon Trail, "Take my advice: anything you see as big as a blackbird, kill it and eat it." What was Mr. White's surprise and vexation to find as he proceeded higher and higher that the Sioux or the Sandinista or the Pueblo or whichever of 'em was poaching here must've run off with every last mountain bison because *he* sure as conscription didn't see any; plus he could've sworn the streams'd be black with trout, too; for you could tell when you were approaching an Indian encampment by the bright red strips hanging in the sun which you figured were barbaric menstrual wipes or mail-order L.L. Bean leisure flannel shirts stolen from travelers but which turned out to be salmon, so much salmon that everbody got lazy and insolent and wouldn't work for you; why, it was practically doin' 'em a favor to strip off the bracelets of brass that the Indian women wore, or the broad gold rings on their fingers, or the red ribbons in their hair (which did, Mr. White would have been the first to admit, make a fine contrast to their brown skins and glossy black hair; he was not made of wood) because at least then they'd have to exert themselves for once to get more of the same; and that was good for them, keep 'em from suffering from a case of the yaws; and it was good for you, too, because you could sell the gold, at least, and thereby afford your Christmas hams, flour and other comforts; but as it was, Mr. White

was getting pretty hungry; why, he could eat a spoiled ox paunch! —
At length he came to a steamy little dell in the mountains, where he
discovered a nice bubbling set of lime hot springs, which had a smart
taste like small beer. The vapor reminded him of inhaling hartshorn.
He made a note of that because he knew that once he and Dodger
had polluted all the water in these western states but *good*, the way
it is now in Silicon Valley from Mountain View down to San Jose,
then maybe you could sell mineral beverages at a dollar a glass,
without even making proclamations as to its supreme salubrity, and
they'd be mighty glad to pay all the same. That would sure be fine! —
The springs seemed to go back into a sort of cave that was all glaring
white with subterranean alkali lagoons, like a VT100 computer
terminal in reverse-contrast mode. (In fact a chalky water-bug was
receiving Mr. White loud and clear on its feelers back in there. A
message was sent to the Great Beetle.) But this bonus of water aside,
the area seemed almost wholly unfit for cultivation, unless he could
bring some Swiss engineers here to bolt pylons onto these four-
hundred-foot vertical rock walls, skirting the stream beds, which
were choked up by masses of boulders fallen from above, and then
get Dodger to make a giant band-saw or something to clear away a
big wide swatch of trees all the way back down to that lake, which
he could see excellently right now as he clambered up the rock face,
pulling himself up overhand, grabbing grass-blades and teeny-weeny
bits of gravel stuck in crevices even smaller and uglier than his wife's
crack; fortunately, Mr. White didn't have fits of acrophobia or other
doubt; if he did you think he'd be here? — so he went on up, hauling
the horse and wagon up after him because he'd trained that mare
pretty good to clamp on tight to his boot with her horsey-teeth, yes,
she could be pretty smart and obliging, so it was just a question of
strength and will, of which Mr. White had a good supply, so on he
went, continuing to plan out his dream of development for the
region: — after he had the pylons in he'd bring in the tramway and
the rope tow; and then it would all take shape; and he'd get himself
some Rocky Mountain blondes with nice bazoombas to be tour
guides in orange ski parkas with purple triangles sewn to the
shoulder: — "Please hold on as we cross the third tower," they'd say
to the passengers standing packed together with wet skis and poles
and everybody fogging up the windows with their breath so that
they wouldn't even be able to see the view they'd paid for, the
stupes; "Here we are, ladies and gentlemen, so enjoy your stay at the
Top of the World! There will now be a slight jolt as we come into the
dock!" — and there was indeed a jerk as poor Bessie the mare almost

let go of Mr. White's foot, and the wagon behind her creaked in the middle of the air, hanging from the end of her tail with its wooden wheels spinning . . . There'd be a big restaurant, packed full of fries and Crystal Brand real orange juice in cartons; and here we see the European tourists in their matching designer parkas, the wind blowing outside on the picnic tables that adorn the snowy deck beneath the light-globes; as meanwhile the skiers' silhouettes wind by on the chairlift in infernal silence against the sun-shadowed snow. A young couple in new goosedown jackets are sitting at one of the drift-piled picnic tables. The steam rises from their french fries, upon which sleet pelts. – Inside, it sounds like a robot factory with the constant thump of ski boots up and down the wet plank stairs, and all the skiin' men squint and look tough as they light up Camels with a flick of a pocket device which also has a built-in compass. Spilled salt glitters on the fake-wood tables, vainly reflecting every countenance in its grains, not that that is uncommon, for I, the author, can see a middle-aged lady's face imprisoned in a puddle of ketchup. Snow swirls outside until White Lake is just a blue-grey smudge a couple of thousand feet down, like a place these folks have never seen before; they sure couldn't get any more lost than they already are, could they? Over by the rest rooms a little blond boy sits mournfully at the High Altitude Table. He wears a yellow knit sweater and holds a purple-tasseled cap in his hands. Is he Big George? – Actually, Your Majesty, I was the woman in the black checked shirt at the adjoining table, my back turned to you, but I have eyes between my shoulder blades. Footprints swirled in the powdery snow out on the deck, where the multitude crowded to watch the ascending trams. I saw you get a hamburger and some fat, limp fries about the consistency of wax beans. You sat down and looked around joylessly, uncertainly, as you generally do in your struggles to locate me, but at best your unsuspecting gaze only fell on my back for a moment, soiling my shirt (which I have since discarded) before passing on to the fathers showing their sons the lore of unshelling the burgers from their styrofoam tombs, discarding the lettuce and other alien materials. – "I think it was . . . the fuse box," it was my pleasure to hear a superfluous oldster announce to his Coke; and I conceded that he might have scored a minor debating point there; – for I can assure you, ladies and gentlemen, that when something goes wrong it is always the fuse box. Fortunately one can replace a fuse at any hour of day or night, as I can replace you, my angels . . . – "I only got three fries!" a six-year-old cried indignantly, showing her almost empty carton.

Her father chewed stolidly. – "Well, go ahead and complain," he said at last. "You like to complain." – "No!" cried her four-year-old sister. "I do! I do!" – "Terri, YOU stay here and eat your french fries." – And now to enjoy the slopes. – "You see how Daddy keeps his knees together?" I, the author, was there with a bug. The bug was excited and asked me to take pictures of it. We went up and down a little white hill. At last it was time to descend back to White Lake. – All aboard! – "Now, isn't this MUCH better than freezing on that chair lift listening to YOU?" yelled some Texas wise guy. But his buddy, cut by this remark, pressed his nose against the window and did not reply. – "Okay," said the hostess, "watch your step, folks, because it'll be just a little slippery with the snow on the bottom of your boots." – "This parking lot is nothing," a man complained. "My cat has a bigger parking lot." – Some people are born complainers. But the bug did not complain. When we got back down, we sat in its car and it turned on the engine. For a long time the bug sat in the car, thinking hard. Finally it turned off the ignition. "Clean the window," it explained. "Little dirty."

Now there was a real nice view, so Mr. White stopped for a minute halfway up the cliff-wall, jamming the blade of his skinning knife into a crevice to keep himself and his horse and wagon from falling; and he looked out into space and saw all the rivers and willow islands he had passed – and by jingo! those places had been infested with Mosquetors all the way up the Peninsuler! – and there was the clearing where he'd felled some trees to take observation about a month ago, and then about a hundred acres of dead timber where he'd blazed the path for Dodger; and beyond that the lead ore flats full of quicksand that had sharpened pencils stuck point-upward on purpose to prick the soles of your feet; and then the lowland bluffs full of osage plums and grapes, plum apples, wild cherries &c, where he had killed two goslings and three hundred and eighteen pike in the space of fifteen minutes; and beyond that some more willows where he'd killed an elk in a heavy fog the month before last; and 'way down away from there, in the direction of Powder River or mebbe McCone County, the Great Plains started, the flat ground cracked into trillions of jigsaw polygons where Mr. White had pumped out the water to drive the price up later; then nothing but flat yellow sand for a good long stretch until finally in the middle of that nothing he could just make out the long furry carcass of a poisoned coyote, nailed head-downwards to the post of a barbed-wire fence – impossible that the creature could have been stretched so thin in life; somebody must've pulled him into the wanted shape, or else in his convulsions he'd burst his own bones like a sausage; Mr. White wasn't positive because he hadn't come from that direction; nope, that looked more like Dodger's tracks, and he was damned if he wasn't proud of that fella Dodger, following orders like a good subordinate; and just on the horizon was a black cloud of bearded bison; on the Kansas Pacific train you could sometimes run into a herd of buffalo a hundred and twenty miles across; the sportsmen had a real field day then, popping them off through the open windows; and let's see, over there to the west, that must be the Sierry Range, though with all this dust and grit flying around from erosion his field glasses were finally starting to get kinda crapped up, scratched like Capra's 1931 photo of Trotsky: — round-faced, pale, moustached, in his big black glasses, wearing black and a black hat (or so it seemed in the high-contrast print), with his arms up by his face as he orated; and long white scratches on the left, running through the black silent crowd; black like the mouth of a screaming Vietnamese wearing a conical hat whose relations Wayne had killed with one hand tied behind his back in his fucking SLEEP ("Haw!" goes Wayne), for as Edwin Tunis explains in his patriotic work on weapons, "Precision bombing at high altitudes is an American speciality." — As for Mr. White, *he* had missed the altitude at twelve o'clock with the quadrant, so he'd have to try for it later with the sextant, because he was measuring every square fucking inch to have all the details down for a future Intention of Government which Dodger would write out for him on parchment, and then they'd haul logs up with the wagon to build log cabin villages and then everybody would kill seven turkeys apiece. — Now over to the northeast, those must be the Grand Tetons — but here I, the author, had better explain that in those days the Tetons were volcanoes; when you went over the range you had to proceed with many instruments and green-tinted spectacles to circumspectly circumnavigate the various gas pockets, which were unpredictable in their properties and effects: — some would poison you invisibly right through your skin, and you'd sway and fall into a chasm the way that partridges come tumbling out of the air in Afghanistan nowadays when the Soviets launch their gas grenades, which kill my friends and aquaintances there without leaving external wounds; and others would make you lighter than the air, and you'd go shooting up into the falling stars, swing low, sweet chariot, dodging the twinkling comets that scorched your collar up there in the shadow of the moon and you'd be holding your breath so long your cheeks would be bulged out and your fingers and toes would go numb in the vacuum until all the mysterious gas would have chilled to rainbow crystals at absolute zero and you'd brush it out of your hair like snow and you'd dust off your jacket, still holding your breath, and flicking the stuff away in careful mincing motions to keep from spinning head over heels in the zero gravity; and as each fleck of it fell off into orbit your feet got heavier and heavier, then your legs, and then your calves, as was the case with Socrates after drinking the hemlock; or like, for that matter, the hysterical paralysis that often occurred among women during the open-air demonstrations of mesmerism at the True Electrical Revival meetings in the clearings of Ohio where Dr. Dodger felt your pulse and gave you a special syrup to drink and made you look at a ball of Turkish glass; so you started to sink back into the atmosphere again and enjoyed your first real breath in ages, keen the way that mountain air should be; and a nice breeze ruffled your hair and enveloped you in the pine incense of the Siberian taiga, for you were dropping through the global slipstream, faster and faster now; and the wind picked up as you fell faster and faster, down between the pointy mountain peaks ... watch out! – the mouth of a volcano licks out a big red puff of smoke that chars the soles of your boots! – you're falling right into it! – oh, *look* at it down there, all crawly with bright orange lava glaring through the smoke like a monster lurking behind window-curtains – but fortunately you're prepared for that, having prudently left a few smears of the condensed gas on your trouser kneecaps; and it sublimes and exerts greater and greater strength in the course of its expansion, lifting you up and bearing you safely to the other side of the range, whereupon you raise your bent knees as if you were doing the jellyfish float and cup your hands and blow firmly to dissipate the remainder of the gas-cloud; so that you settle into a bed of moss, which is not a bad resting place unless you are a most fastidious high-strung renegade.

Meanwhile Mr. White had to keep slogging, kicking the sinking horse harder and harder; and every night he had to pitch camp, get wood, feed the horse, make a fire, cook, eat, load more gunpowder into the buckskin carry-sack, grease the axles and mend the pack saddle, which were tedious chores almost guaranteed to bleed the enthusiasm of most wanderers and *voyageurs*, but fortunately Mr. White was unaffected by this syndrome, believing in himself, as he did, with great conviction. The hills were mighty steep and rough, and ya ran into strange things in them elevations. Every now and then, on some protected ledge, families of ruined idols or cigar store Indians would leer at Mr. White most ominously, bearded with ice like Yetis or Abominable Snowmen or something; their frozen frowns seemed to say, "You no belong here!" – but Mr. White just yelled, "*You* stay right where you are or I'll hack you for firewood!" and at this threat the zombie malice generally left their eyes, but if it didn't Mr. White'd run 'em right through their brisket! – and then he continued on his way in triumph. These successes could not, of course, blow away the pall of peril that hung over him; this was the Hunger Trail, no mistake; if Mr. White didn't watch his step it was gonna be goodbye, Old Paint. In the evenings he made a wretched camp in some snowy gulley, listening to the wind groan as he lay there in the wagon like a match in a matchbox, with nothing but the Aurora Borealis to warm his hands by. In the mornings he went on, tightening his belt notch by notch. He hadn't seen a nice juicy marmot in weeks, much less an antelope. At last he was forced to eat his horse and abandon his wagon, not that that was much of a loss because the wheels wobbled and squeaked like a mouse on a honeymoon; in fact the wagon hadn't been worth the horse, and horse hadn't been worth the motherhumping feed, Jesus Christ; every other minute she kept trying to lie down and die, hypocritical as a Catholic and parasitical as a Jew. Mr. White went on, so hopping mad he kind of forgot about thirst and hunger and cold. Icicles hung from his moustache, and all his fingers and toes were frostbitten. It was so cold he had to jump out of the way every time he exhaled because his breath froze solid into a big blue hailstone that must've weighed a ton since the ground shook when it hit. And scaling the ridges was no picnic; nope, not with the sun dazzling your snow-blind eyes, reflected from great faceted ice-boulders, black and shiny like obsidian; it was worse than staring at the aforementioned video display terminal for sixteen hours; and the wind practically knocked Mr. White off the mountain sometimes so he had to slam his axe into the ice at some of the more powerful gusts and cling to the handle for an anchor; it was about as easy getting the Statue of Liberty to spready cunny, which did take some dynamite persuasion. Every hill had to be stormed. As he ascended Beatty Pass an avalanche rolled over him. He had time for just one prayer to the Great Dynamo before he lost consciousness miles beneath the hardening snow. A mammoth dug him out with its tusks, evidently scenting the vegetable fiber in the fabric of his trousers, and began to browse on the cuffs. When he opened his eyes, it raised its head and trumpeted. – "You goddamn fucking thing," said Mr. White, "you've really had it now; don't even try to get away because that'll only make the agony longer," and he kicked it in the kneecap as hard as he could, so that it lowered its head to gore him, which was just what Mr. White had been waiting for; he shinnied up its left tusk quick as Jack-Be-Nimble and pulled himself up by clutching handfuls of the creature's fur, and, acting hardily and resourcefully, as ever, choked it to death with his belt. To keep warm during a blizzard which had sprung up in the meantime, he cut open the mammoth's stomach and crawled inside, where he found a lump of gold as big as his head. Why, the money had been lying idle for years! – It is impossible to say where it came from. But then it is impossible to say with certainty where mammoths came from, although they wind up nonetheless with monotonous regularity in tarpits. – Mr. White invested the gold in minerals. The following year he cashed in on the formica deposits in Tombstone, Arizona. There was a Tex-Mex insurrection in Durango at the time; with six percent of his newest profits Mr. White recruited a regiment of godfearing Kentucky and Tennessee sharpshooters to take care of the problem, and the town made him Mayor out of gratitude. Next came the Piute War, the shootout at Big Bonanza, and the formation of the Sierra Guard. Now things were rolling, that was as sure as bears shit in the woods; whenever anything went wrong, people looked to Mr. White to make it right; and all he had to do was levy improvement taxes until he had enough capital to go into the power industry . . .

THE RISE OF THE BLUE GLOBES (1663–1900)

~~~~~~

This is simply wonderful and good proof that the cause of the
spark is a new unknown force.

<div align="right">

EDISON
Notebooks (1875)

</div>

Here a quick résumé of electromechanical development may be
useful. I, Big George, discovered centuries ago that tourmaline
(sometimes called *lapis electrus*) is electrified when heated; this is
also true of Siberian topaz. So it is not surprising that initial research
involved minerals. The first machine for the generation of electrical
force was invented by Otto von Guernicke in 1663, consisting of a
globe of sulfur which was excited by the friction of human hands.
Tiny blue sparks were thrown off. Newton's innovation was to
make the globe out of glass, which Hawksbee (1709) set revolving.
From there it was a matter of course for Böse of Wittenberg to add
the metal chain and prime conductor supported, like a rich girl, on
silk strings. Winkler of Leipzig cleverly substituted a leather cushion
for the hands of the operator; then came Ramsden (1768) with his
plate electrical machine, which was insulated and had metal forks
embracing glass. Three-inch sparks were achieved. – We did not
take unduly long to recognize that the earth could remove our
negative electricity for us without charge; and that rubbers covered
with bisulphide of tin or Kienmayer's amalgam were an accessory
which we could not do without. Next Nairne added the glass
regulators, despite the problems in his personal life; and in no time
we could obtain either positive or negative electricity whenever we
wanted. Influence machines now entirely superseded the frictional
kind, though for a time we retained our habit of inducing static
induction between a pair of Leyden jars, calculating the doubler
charge R as P over the quantity $P + P'$, all times quantity $I + Q$

squared over *P* squared. Four-inch sparks were soon the industry standard. – The axis *PN* was now varnished by Nicholson in 1788 (Old Nick, we used to call him); and he made several other changes of equal significance upon the suggestion of his Döppelganger. We still had to compensate for 99 parts of opposite electricity, so we proposed the notion of a revolving plate for universal adoption. A field plate and a neutralizing conductor were added by majority decision. In 1860 Varley unveiled his classic influence machine, which was marked by the addition of ebonite, tinfoil and a winch. It was capable of emitting six-inch sparks from a Danell cell, according to a moldy old report which I still have in my scrapbook. Using Varley's principles, suave Toepler constructed a device comprised of two disks on the same shaft. Then, sometime between 1864 and 1880, Hotz used a multiplying gear with a pair of discharge balls at a distance which could be varied at will. Even the witless layman could now hear a most energetic hissing sound once the disk began to revolve (always assuming, naturally, that the paper armature had been properly electrified); and the seven-ought-five-inch sparks were like vile blue spheres. – We next invented comb points at opposite ends of the diameter. Voss of Berlin (1880) combined these like a good fellow, though Wimshult had already added belts, pulleys and a minimum of sixteen to twenty tinfoil carriers with brass buttons to his own apparatus back in 1878. Finally, after careful study of the inner coating of our Leyden jars, we commenced operations. Multiple plate influence machines were used instead of induction coils to excite Roentgen ray tubes. By 1900 Tudsbury was already getting eight-inch sparks at forty-five pounds above atmospheric pressure once the machine was suitably enclosed in a carbon dioxide chamber, and Kelvin, in one of his most astounding breakthroughs, used a mouse mill to electrify ink with a siphon recorder.

MOTIVES AND MISCONCEPTIONS
(1878–1911)

~~~~~~

The definition of reliability is quality over time.

National Semiconductor ad in
*Electronic Technology for Engineers and
Engineering Managers* (6 September 1984)

Even in those last days before the débâcle, my children, we did not trust electricity completely, though I grant you that we did not turn back, partly because the radical universality of the phenomenon had not yet become apparent. "The subdivision of the electric light is impossible of attainment," Hippolyte Fontaine had reassured us back in 1878. It was the contention of all authorities that if you took an electric current and ran it into ten houses, it would be only one-tenth as bright in each house as the source. This sounds like a logical and therefore absolute restriction, but the forces of electricity, as we shall see, could do almost anything. Voltage which may be harmless one day may be fatal the next, if atmospheric conditions are right. Current flows as small as 10 mA are potentially lethal.

All around the world, but particularly in our great Republic, inventors and professors set about applying the universal intrinsic principle. Some worked with formless Unchangeables in their seance lounges, others with religious Notions, and a rare few, such as our Mr. Edison, with bulldog Actualities. The way he looked at it, if your calculations showed you couldn't do something, then you went ahead and did it without the calculations.* – Here was one for whom the forces of electricity had been waiting! Once, in the laboratory, as he worked on a revised version of the carbon microphone, experimenting with charcoal buttons on springs and a

---

*"At the time I experimented on the incandescent lamp I did not understand Ohm's Law," he said later. "Moreover, I do not want to understand Ohm's Law. It would prevent me from experimenting."

diaphragm of moistened paper, he told his hired Harvard fella to work out the volume of a pear-shaped light bulb (this being no merely industrial calculation, for I remind you all that the world, too, is pear-shaped). Well, the geek calculated and calculated till a feller could trip over the square roots and he STILL wasn't done. Finally Mr. Edison just took the light bulb and poured water into it, then drained the water into a graduated cylinder and read off the number. He was practical. When a competitor developed an electric-powered lamp, Mr. Edison rushed off to take a look. He was fascinated, whereas Mr. White would have been puffed purple with rage. When he had studied the gadget to his satisfaction, he stood up and said, "I believe I can beat you at making electric lights." And he did, too. – In 1878 a reporter for the *New York Tribune* asked him what he did it all for. "I don't care so much for a fortune as I do for getting ahead of the other fellows," he said. But this might have been just modesty, for to a *Sun* reporter he made a statement which revealed him, in the light of the Insect Wars of the following century, to be a true-hearted ideologue: "My object is to keep the bugs out of it."

Already the bugs were in it. In the hot summer of 1885, while Mr. Edison rested at home in Woodside Villa, New York, taking perhaps the only self-prescribed vacation of his life, as he was still somewhat debilitated after the death of his first wife, they came buzzing all over the house – for bugs, like viruses, must be quick, and take advantage of any passing weakness to get their start. – On 16 July, he wrote in his diary, ". . . I learned the girls how to make shadow pictures by use of crumpled paper – We then tried some experiments on mind reading which were not very successful, think mind reading contrary to common sense . . ." – But the bugs buzzed in the parlor, trying to read his mind. The electric light had been a reality for almost ten years. As yet the blue globes had not shown *their* dreadful light, but the bugs sensed a threat of some kind. – Too bad for you, bugs! No, the bugs were not yet in full alarm, but uneasy, as when one's shadow falls upon a swarm of flies on a dunghill they rise up and their buzzing shrills, to show that they have been disturbed in their ritual practices, but they are not really frightened; if they were frightened they would scatter and the biggest fattest greenest bluebottle would drive bravely into your face to give the others a chance to escape. – It was very hot, as I said, and hazy, like the hot afternoon in upstate New York when Big George and I sat facing each other in the common room, trying to negotiate your fate, my bright and risen angels; he was tall, straight, blond, blue-eyed: — a wholesome Schweizerdeutsch sort of character, whereas Bee was soft and pink, like a Pink Pearl eraser. — "Read account of two murders in the *Morning Herald* to keep my interest in human affairs," he continued unaware. "Built an air castle or two — Took my new shoes out on a trial trip." The heat was conducive to lethargy for many creatures, but not bugs, who were cold-blooded. They buzzed and watched. At night when you sleep on the sofa in someone else's living room, and you wake up suddenly in the darkness and hear the whine of a single mosquito, then you know that it is only a matter of time before the bugs will get you. So it was in this case. But Mr. Edison did not know it because he dreamed heavy complicated dreams so that he could not even feel the mosquitoes piercing the skin of his face or his hand and injecting the anticoagulant preparatory to sucking his blood. They were dedicated bugs; they flew back to their superiors and regurgitated the blood so that it could be analysed and special tracing-bugs could be set to follow anyone with that kind of blood; and they would stick to him tighter than ticks then and never let him out of range of their pincers. So the sun came in and woke him up in the empty bed, and he rubbed absently at the itching welts. "I think freckles on the skin are due to some salt of Iron," he reflected (12 July); "sunlight brings them out by reducing them from high to low oxidation — perhaps with a powerful magnet applied for some time and then with proper chemicals these mudholes of beauty might be removed." He was curious about everything. He noticed that he had dandruff, and immediately he wanted to read about dandruff in the encyclopedia. He ordered loads of books from Brentano's and even read them. He remained at all times a man of science. In due time he was to propose to Miss Mina Miller in Morse code. Two children from his old marriage he nicknamed Dot and Dash. He observed a bumblebee ("this armed flower burglar"), but what he did not know was that the bumblebee was also observing him. She returned a condition code of 013 (missing or conflicting DCB information) to the hive. A yellow alert was instated at once. Swarms of expendable spy-flies began to drone through the house. On 14 July he "dreamed of a Demon with eyes four hundred feet apart." Later on he dreamed of finding Napoleon stuck by himself on a lonely planetoid. Napoleon was the past; the demon was the future. On 15 July, he "breakfasted clear up to my adams apple." Toward noon he patronized a "no-bread-with-one-fishball restaurant." — "The Governor whom I know and who is very deaf greeted me with a boiler yard voice. He has to raise his voice so he can hear himself to enable him to check the accuracy of his pronunciation." The flies buzzed in the living room. "Madden looks well in face but I am told its an Undertakers blush." Now for a tinker with the phonometer (he had already built the tasonometer, on which the odoroscope was based). He met a charming woman of his acquaintance; she "plays the piano like a long-haired professor." And now to bed. "That part of my memory which has charge of the night shirt department is evidently out of order," he reprimanded himself, but it was time to close his eyes and maybe dream about Big George off wandering farther and farther into the muggy jungles, playing dully with treasures and oddities that aroused no wonder. – The lights were now officially off. In the humid darkness, as the household tried to sleep, the flies droned very very steadily. The sheets felt heavy on the sleepers, and the pillows were hot and sticky. Over in his laboratory grasshoppers ran a riot of panicky investigation, springing all around the coils; yes, something awful was in the works; for the first time there was going to be real difficulty for the insect kingdom. – The next day it was still hot. "We are going out with the ladies on Yachts to sail perchance to fish, the lines will be bated at both ends." They took a course past Apple Island. Later everybody went to the theater: ". . . the curtain arose showing the usual number of servant girls in tights." But the actresses were perspiring, just like he was. The next day it was still hot. "Mem – Go to a print cloth mill and have yourself run through the Calico printing machine, this would be the Ultima Thule of thin clothing." Now for a game of Memory-Scheme. Then for a recital. "Boy is quite a prodegy on the piano, plays with great rapidity, his hands and fingers went like a buz saw, played a solemn piece which I imagined might be God Kill the Queen . . ." And the flies buzzed, buzzed, buzzed, trying to get to the bottom of this threat and cling to it and smear it around on their little bristle-feet and bear away bits of it to Headquarters for analysis. 20 July: "Mrs. [Scribble] has placed a fly paper all over the house. These cunning engines of insectivorous destruction are doing a big business . . . One of the first things I will do when I reach heaven is to ascertain what flies are made for . . ." The next day was hot, and he sat there dreaming. "I wonder if there are not microscopic orchids growing on the motes of the air."

"As for that despicable puppy Sawyer," he had cried back in the 1870s, "he never believed a word he ever said. He's nothing but a bag of miasma under pressure." But Sawyer was not his worst enemy.

He hated unions and leftism, of course, and he did fine work, so the reactionaries threw him bones. Of course they did not finance Mr. Edison alone; that would've been contrary to the laws of social development. So now this dude Westinghouse slimed his way into the market; he even had the nerve to talk about sending super-currents for super-distances, which Mr. Edison knew was impossible; Mr. Edison roasted stray cats in front of reporters, by means of the Westinghouse current, to show how dangerous it was, compared to the mild Edison current which only killed linemen once in awhile. And these objective demonstrations certainly helped the cause of justice in the end; for the state of New York agreed to use the Westinghouse current to electrocute condemned criminals in the most humane and up-to-date way! (The first time they tried, the current was too weak, so they had to do it again.) — The power industry was beginning to look pretty darn practical if you saw farther than the tip of your own long lying Pinocchio-nose, sir, believe you me; but most of you can't do precisely that; it takes an iron man to take the jump, because if you fall boy do you FALL, though if you make it to the fruit tree you can help yourself to the shining blue-globe fruits of electricity and stuff your pockets full of them or eat them and spit them out or sell them and shit on everybody down in the lower branches of the Iron Age.

THE SWITCH IS THROWN (1911)

~~~~~~

> The party will stand for the first kind of democracy and will carry
> it out with an iron hand.
>
> <div align="right">STALIN</div>
> "The Discussion, Rafail, The Articles by Preobrazhensky
> and Sapronov, and Trotsky's Letter"
> (*Pravda*, No. 285, 15 December 1923)

As the radio series tells it, Mr. White was standing with his associate
R. L. Stableford (the same Stableford who was later to be J. P.
Morgan's most tenacious antagonist during the Helium Wars) on a
high butte or alluvial fan near one of the lost cities of Idaho. It was a
windy day, or else mighty elevated and lonely, because the sound
effects man is whistling through his teeth into Stage Mike 3 in order
to help you understand what it was like for Mr. White and Mr.
Stableford to be up there by themselves on that spring afternoon,
with their neckties blowing horizontally below their chins, beckon-
ing them into the reddish-orange precipice below, with a waterfall
down the rock face; and Stableford chewed at his glasses and took a
new pencil from the pocket of his dress shirt and sharpened it with
his Butch knife and hurled it over the edge like a dart to impale a
passing antelope (here Lem the sound effects man increases the pitch
and intensity of his whistle to simulate the noise of the falling missile
– he has become expert at this in the series called "The Kamikaze
Kidz"). Mr. White, inhaling robustly, gave Stableford a wink of
appreciation at his shooting, and they both took more deep breaths
of the invigorating air (in order to stay alive) and Stableford told Mr.
White a couple of inside jokes about Dr. Dodger that Mr. White had
already heard, and they looked down at the brown hills, which
resembled dinosaur collarbones, and they walked to and fro in the
crisp sand that pillowed their overlook (to replicate their historic

footsteps Lem chews crushed ice with the microphone against his cheek); and as they walked they chatted about various things – death and taxes, most likely, for there is little else of interest to the great – when Mr. White stopped and kicked a shower of quartz crystals over the edge and squinted down at the waterfall.

WHITE: You know, R.L., that stream down there gives me an IDEA.

STABLEFORD: Layin' down there a thousand feet below, it's enough to give a feller any NUMBER of thoughts, like how we kin make the Stock Exchange do that. That Dr. Dodger we was jest talkin' about (you know he's got an in with McKinley), he's been sayin' that 'twenty-nine is gonna be a boom year.

WHITE: Well, I was hatchin' up a different scheme. Have you heard of those experiments in electrical power that young George Westinghouse has been conductin'?

STABLEFORD: Not THAT again. Now, you listen to me, White. Electric power is as dead as phlogiston. There ain't no way to make it, an' there never will be. How could you bottle it? What'd keep it from going bad in the summertime? And besides, what in the name of Behemoth do you NEED it for? You want a crank turned, you PAY somebody to do it for you. You want light at night, you stick yer plumber's candle up a squaw's ass.

WHITE: No, you're wrong there, R.L. All we need's venture capital, an' then we set up a couple dozen high-voltage stands in Salt Lake and Omaha. The sons o' bitches'll be gallopin' from miles around to get a little shock. You'll see. It'll start off in the circuses, but within twenty years the Chambers of Commerce'll be wantin' me in. You mark my words. It's the first thousand volts that'll be the hardest to sell. But after that, all the have-nots'll be whinin' that they jest got to have it. An' in THIRTY years we kin make 'em DIE for it, accordin' to the supreme protocols of war!

STABLEFORD: Well, I'm not gonna back you, White. You jest get yer tackle an' harness, an' go find yerself another pretty boy.

WHITE: All right then, you prick-nosed stingy yellowdog, I'll buy YOU out in the gubernatorial races, an' before you kin piss an' say porky you'll be wishin' you'd pork-barreled with ME; you'll be so far out in the cold you'll be wantin' to hump the polar bears to keep warm but my demolition experts will be wipin' your installations off the map because I've been a union buster from 'way back an' I travel in a limestone limousine so don't think you kin get through MY defenses.

STABLEFORD: Well, p'raps I'll reconsider.

WHITE: No one's askin' you, Dumbass Stonewall Jackson; I've gone to the Syndicate fer financial backin' and they're in on the ground floor because they kin see the day when everybody'll be buyin' electric do-dads and dildoes and humdingers, an' before you kin piss an' say porky I'll be the richest man in the entire solar system, 'ceptin' maybe Phil Blaker on Mars who has a conceptual JUMP on me.

STABLEFORD: White, you're a GENIUS. How do you plan to start?

WHITE: Well, I'm gonna need me some MEN, hard, tough, skilled MEN who will KNOW their BUSINESS. These men are gonna be the ELECTRICIANS of the FUTURE. An' fer that reason I'm gonna establish a school —

STABLEFORD: A SCHOOL? A SCHOOL fer grown men? So they kin twirl their peckers in their hands on MY capital?

WHITE: — Which I shall call the Society of Daniel, after our national hero, Daniel Boone, and which'll devote itself solely to the creation of an electric élite which'll reap untold benefits as long as every man jack does jest what I say.

STABLEFORD: Well, it all sounds mighty interestin', White. I'll have to get back to you on this.

NARRATOR: And that, folks, is how it all began. This is Big George concluding yet another segment of the "Front Line Soldiers of Technology" series.

Meanwhile, me boys, Mr. White prospered.

THE SOCIETY OF DANIEL (1913)

∿∿∿∿∿∿∿∿∿∿∿∿∿∿∿∿∿∿∿∿∿∿∿∿∿

In the middle of the square inch dwells the splendor.

T'AI I CHIN HUA TSUNG CHIH
The Secret of the Golden Flower

Standing upon the observation platform of the ball-lightning tower, and facing White Falls, one may observe at the foot of the right-hand wall of the gorge a long, brick building, its farther end obscured by spray from the cataract. This powerhouse, long since gutted and abandoned in favor of more modern technologies, was once the main generating station of the region. To the right, high above and behind it, stood the distributing station. To enter the training institute it was necessary to walk up the steep path to this latter, where once inside your firearms were checked with the day engineer, a young nervous lad named Newt, upon whom Mr. White relied absolutely. Passing through along the main floor, you would see the 12,000-volt automatic circuit-breakers in double column. Perhaps if the young man were not in too much hurry to get back to his work (for he lived in constant fear of Mr. White), he might let you peer into one of the transformer rooms, where between various pipes and cables stood (naturally) the transformers in pits six feet deep, along with other grand protective apparatus. Each transformer was fitted with a recording thermometer, and if that goddamned graph ever went five degrees out of true during that fellow's shift, you can guess what happened to him. Looking in and listening with half an ear to his awkward, stammering explanations (for they were not much used to visitors at the Society of Daniel), you would end up not having the slightest idea what any of this was for. Maybe he pointed timidly to one of the four doors spaced evenly along the main floor. These led upstairs to the gallery floors, where marble slabs bore integrating instruments, arranged in a twenty-two-point semicircle about a central spot. Higher up still was Mr. White's control room. The concentration here of all regulatory monitors, busbars and antljehosaphats — the brain of all electrical operation — provided Mr. White a quiet and secluded place for resynchronization and punishment, surrounded as he was by multiple classes of apparatus. He could detect trouble in any transformer room, and in fact he was probably watching you right now on your tour, rearing back and shaking his head in disgust, with a finger on his stopwatch so as to dock Newt's pay appropriately for having spent too much time with you. Sensing this, the boy led you on quickly through the dank building (the crashing of water always in your ears, like in some World War II movie about the submarine springing a leak) — the boy led you on, I say, showing with halfhearted waves of his hand that everything was in perfect order, and finally sent you out the back door. As you turned back to thank him you saw him already tiny in the distance, scampering along the braided cables to get back to his post. You turned forward again. Ahead was a small trestle bridge over a creek; and beyond lay a little triangular valley or dead-end canyon, sandy and devoid of trees, in which stood a three-storey stone building with a gabled roof — the student dormitory and laboratory; a garden plot adjoining the river; and a number of well-kept sheds and outbuildings. Mr. White might have been expected to live with his family in a manor set above and apart from the rest, but in fact he lived on the third floor of the dormitory, believing as he did that everything required constant supervision.

Around this establishment the cliff-walls rose sheer. These divides were bare ridges reaching an altitude of 16,000 feet, inaccessible in winter and swept by constant snow-slides. From the window of our student quarters we could see the valley floor slope up, up in a bowl-curve, then steeper still so that not even the parched sagebrush or rabbit-brush could dig in, then steeper and steeper until the scree of feldspar and granite gave way to a single brown wall of solid rock, dust-blasted and treacherous, with patches of snow glaring unbearably from their hollows year-round. From my window it seemed like a sick man's face, with the snow-patches forming sunken, clouded eyes sparkling with the iridescence of death, and the rock itself that ghastly brown of gangrenous skin stretched tight over the contours of the anguished rock. In winter the entire valley was covered with snow, and the face disappeared, but I always knew that it was there; and eventually it reappeared, sometimes (depending on precipitation for that year and the vagaries of the slides) twisted and screaming with long lines of snow extending from the eye-sockets as if the eyes were screwed so tight as to have almost pulled the cheeks inside themselves; and other times calm, dusty and resigned with tears melting and running on the hot summer days. But I, the author, hasten to admit that I can see a sad face in anything, the knobs of my dresser drawers pouting at me in the morning as I approach to pull out the hollowed wood-flesh where my trousers are stored. And bugs, lobsters and invertebrates generally have always excited my pity and championship when I look into their hard shiny eyes. At night the phosphenes dance behind my eyelids like a rainbow of fireflies bubbling out of the darkness; gradually they swirl purposefully and begin to form a face – but I know that they are really only another kind of electricity, malign and intelligent with its own face that no human being will ever truly see. This we frequently observed as students at the Society, for despite our imposing marble rheostats mounted at switchboards like grand organs, our synchrophones to call up the circuits and our magnetophones to repalatalize the B-vectors into some semblance of torque in duplicate aluminum strips, our electrophones to eavesdrop on the whispering cracklings of force, fszzzzz-fszzzzz, we were often tricked. Over a hundred distinct lightning charges were counted sometimes within a single hour, blowing out our armatures and rising blue and exultant into a great sphere upon some power pole until the wire was burned to a crisp . . . I used to think that I saw mocking faces in those spheres, evil round-faced Buddhas of static made visible, all serene and confident in the knowledge that certainly they would bankrupt Mr. White despite his new T-toothed armatures and replaceable coils, eight of which were burned out on one motor in a single week; but the worst grounds were prevented by using manufactured arrestors; and then we developed the radial commutator switch which turned from fuse-block to fuse-block as each fuse was blown, so that no gap in the line could ever again come into being to let the poor electricity escape; and then for the last few months of the blue discharges I thought I saw the faces terribly blue and unhappy, almost as if they were lobsters that knew they were about to be boiled; but once, out working on the line in the middle of a desert night, I looked deep into one of those doomed slave-faces (*our* slaves!), and discerned an unsettling swirling vagueness lurking, as it were, behind the texture of the swollen blue cheeks, the puffed-out blue tongue salivating dying blue sparks like the condemned on the gallows, the trapped but still malicious eyes; and I could not help but wonder if this were *really* the face, whether perhaps despite this show of resistance against our crushing counter-

ohms, the electricity was something quite other, and it was up to no good, so that as we constructed our grids and boosting stations and lines across the entire world, we increased its mobility and power; and someday perhaps a hundred years from now (actually, as it turned out, a quarter of that time), when everything was electrified, then we would see the true face . . . – But the face on the ridge was, I knew, the sad genuine article; for what can rock do when it is chipped away? We put up a long span right along the bridge of the nose, an 1175-foot line of No. 1 hand-drawn copper, supported by half-inch plow steel cable, both carried by the same insulators. The deflection was approximately 35 feet. There was a switching junction on the far side of the ridge; and then another long span to the tower on the summit of Catherine Divide, where the last knife-edge of rock stood beset by swirling snow (and who knows? perhaps also by chuckling volts of electricity dancing about our tower when we were not there). Beyond Catherine Divide we could perceive through our pocket-telescopes the thousand rocky vulvas of the Colorado Rockies, waiting to be impregnated or neglected by us in our postgraduate projects as Mr. White would see fit. (What we did not know was that in one of those valleys the ants kept a perpetual watch on our movements, long columns of their black-segmented soldiers marching up the lonely bypaths in formidable lines, with every detachment being reviewed by the most severe and poisonous gold-plumed ant-commanders. They never let us or a single wire out of their sight!) Meanwhile, we worked hard in our valley, investigating self-exciting motors in the privacy of the early student laboratory with its German-made benches and glass-fronted cabinets stacked with platoons of experimental battery acids. And each of us, in addition to being given his own room (the hardwood flooring alone of which I could not hope to afford today) was inculcated with electrical engineering principles according to the most modern methods (that is to say, the Dodger Process). – There were thirteen of us, and we were young and ductile. Our elbows were out and our feet were bare, as an old proverb has it. For months and months the drill went on in our shiny plating cells, with conducting fluid pumped in to the level of our knees; we had special copper waders, and I for one could fancy myself on some excursion in Rhode Island's marshes, slopping gingerly through the salt muck in high hopes of blue-crab; and it was not so bad at all after we got used to it. Mr. White expected a seriousness of purpose in us which provided discipline and willpower in those early years; and we learned the electrical and ideological trades from the ground plug up; for there's no substitute for brain conduction.

If I may be permitted to generate a personal transmission, we had few conveniences, and we had to make our own fun. There were no soda fountains in those days, so after the inductance sessions, which lasted from 7:00 a.m. to 12:00 midnight, with half-hour breaks for meals and an optional ten minutes to use the privy when we chose, we used to take a pinch of Mrs. White's bread dough and some sweetened shortening, roll it out in a thin sheet, sprinkle some ground-up bugs or iron filings on it for nourishment, and pop it into the stove. Then we crumbled it up in milk and added a heaping teaspoon of malt syrup. It was damned good.

We also had an intercom in each room. It was a favorite prank of ours to call a guy up on his intercom in the middle of the night and tell him that he was summoned to Mr. White's study for a beating. The younger ones sometimes wet their pants. So no one can say that we didn't have fun.

We were soon responsible for servicing and operating the power-house and the distributing station. When a motor dropped out of step we had to break the circuit with the rather crude interrupter switch of the period. This always drew a heavy, vicious arc, which clung to the full length of the cable like a poisonous blue caterpillar; and we had to take the precaution of coating the floor of the station with paraffin wax so as to avoid the hazard of fire. Coolness and competence were obviously required. Aside from one or two inferior persons, from whom Mr. White soon withdrew the scholarship, we all did very well, and we worked hard so that our hearts went thumpety-thump in our boyish chests, permitting us to come into the common room at the end of the day with a sense of real manliness which despite other things I must credit Mr. White for; and I know that he was genuinely fond of us, having made us. In the common room we sat reading the *Electrical Times* and other trade journals, all personnel washed and in the black suits which Mr. White had given us. There was also a bulletin board, on which Mr. White every day stuck the letters which had come for us from home, so that we could all read each one and learn about the other fellows' home lives. Mr. White was careful to give us only the letters which were decent. We were not allowed to answer any; and communications with girls were prohibited. On the bulletin board were also clippings from newspapers which Mr. White had directed Mrs. White to cut out and pin up for our instruction or amusement, such as "Tender-foot Killed in Freak Lightning Storm," or "Senator Says What Republic Needs is More and Better Men." We read these items with interest, and then engaged in sober recreations such as polishing our dress shoes in the anteroom, and many other such costly and idlesome customs, as by tacit consent we now lay down as obsolete.

Then Mr. White would join with us and tell us stories from the Book of Generators so vividly that you could smell the metal and machine oil, and explained their meaning to us while we all cracked nuts and ate popcorn, which was the only Indian dish allowed. When we began to tire, he'd always have a new anecdote to make us split our sides, and flames from inside the open oven door would shoot up all green and blue and spooky, and before you knew it there would be a ghastly silence. Then Mr. White would quickly ask one of us some technical question or other from the day's classes; and pretty soon we would all be showing off to him again, so we learned to love and reverence him; and sometimes his wife cooked us a good chicken dinner. On Sundays there was voluntary work, much as there is in the glorious Soviet Union; and it was a real festival of communal labor, I can tell you, all of us out building the first ore railroad, with Mr. White atop the locomotive watching us through the spyglass, and me and Earl and Sammy and Newt puttying up the windows of the little siding station, or polishing the steel plates that happened to lie on the ground. For field trips we'd go up into Oregon where Mr. White wanted there to be huge electric cities one day. – Oh, how fireplace-yellow the ideal; how lonesome-blue the flickerings of mysterious energies! – The forests were heavy climax timber up there, so thick that a bird could scarcely fly through it. Arboreal insects had hollowed out a fluted civilization in the treetops. We cut down all the trees and rolled them together and burned them. In the course of this we got pretty grimy, especially when it was hot (and it became hotter as more and more of the forest was pulled down to let in the happy burning sunlight) and the soot from the tree-crematoria we had built settled on our sunburned faces and we sliced up the living wood whistling old mining tunes, like, "Hidey-ho, down we go, in the darkness underground." But Mr. White always expected us to be immaculate for dinner. The collars of our stark white shirts had better have *snap!* The meal was generally served at eight. We sat down at table only when we were told. Then we had to eat pretty quickly, I can tell you, because we did only have half an hour, but that was fine with me; I'd go through a whole turkey with the trimmings, and cornmeal muffins – oh, about sixty-five of those; and candied sweet potatoes, and when no one was looking I made off with a ten-gallon kettle of beef stew and stuck it into my tool kit. They had copper-bottomed kettles back then (everything was better made than it is now with all those eunuch sissy engineers assembling parts according to listed-off directions), so once I was back in my learning cubicle it was no problem to hook up the instructional cable right to the pot, which kept it warm; and any time I felt hungry I'd just reach into it with my rubber gloves so as not to get a shock. Of course this meant I was not being wired to the required material, but there was something lazy and volatile about me that encouraged my delinquency; and I had enough grounding in the trade to know that all was well on Mr. White's monitors. I sat there, between anode and cathode, and ate and dreamed up horrid faces. In some ways I regret the purely technical opportunities that I missed, when I consider how well some of the other boys did in the end: — Earl was the guy that dreamed up the first electric dishwasher; and Sammy invented the Trident sub. — On the other hand, Taylor for all his desperate cramming could never get beyond Kirchoff's Second Law; every day I could hear him moaning in his honeycomb-like chamber (which was next to mine) where the royal jelly between his ears was agitated; and I remember that at one o'clock one morning, as Sammy and I sat at the kitchen table eating leftover bread, Taylor came reeling out of Mr. White's study, closing the mahogany door behind him and stumbling out the side way and along the path to the trestle bridge, for Mrs. White had already packed his suitcase and left it discreetly for him in the middle of the bridge, upon her husband's instructions. After perhaps ten minutes, Mr. White came out of his study, drawing on his gloves. — "Working hard, I see," he said to us sarcastically; for it was not considered very fine to be caught idling in the public rooms; and I blushed and Sammy looked down at his shoes. We heard his firm tread in the common room, and then the accustomed rattle as he withdrew his walking-stick from the umbrella stand. Naturally, we did not see Taylor again. There was no place for him here. Sammy and I remained at the table, chewing our dry bread with dry mouths. Finally Sammy got up and filled two drinking-cups from the water barrel. — "Well, I never did think much of him," Sammy said. "I reckon Mr. White'll learn him a few lessons on the way out." This was indeed a good possibility, I reflected in between a few catnaps at the table, as Sammy sat and chewed his bread until dawn, for it was not every day that we could have free bread. So I suppose that I did not do as badly as I might have done, for I retained my place throughout the statutory years of scholarship. But at the same time I will be the first to admit that I did not do quite as well as Sammy, and certainly not as well as Newt, who, as I am sure that you can imagine if you have ever read about him in the classified funny papers, was the real star of our class. His Christian name was Newton Payne, but we always called him Newt because in his free time (we were all given an hour off a month, plus Christmas, Thanksgiving, Easter Sunday, Memorial Day [which at that time we celebrated upon the anniversary of Little Big Horn], Mr. White's birthday and the Fourth of July) he collected lizards, salamanders from the creek, Gila monsters and bugs in pickle jars. Mr. and Mrs. White had a daughter called Katie. If Newt had been your median elementary school apparatchik, he probably would have winged her with spitballs and pulled her hair and made her cry and stolen the apples she was going to give the teacher. But that was back in the days before elementary schools, which I, Big George, consider to be an insidious product of the New Deal. Education was a simpler and arguably healthier phenomenon then, the sexes segregated of course, the sons trained by their fathers to down their buck in one shot, start their fire with two sticks, differentiate between phyllitic siltstone and blue-grey limestone where the giant beetles clicked and tumbled in their fearsome caves, count their money and run for President; while the mothers taught their girls how to dig edible roots, chew reindeer skins for mukuluks, groom their significant others for lice, sweep and cook hasty pudding and scour pewter and card tow and spin short thread as well as harness-twine and card wool and milk the cows and churn butter and hand-weave and above all do as they were told, and lie perfectly still pretending not to feel it on their wedding night. So Newt would never have gotten a chance to pull Katie's hair in any event. Besides, he was already about fifteen then – a tall, thin young man with compound-lens glasses and a very earnest Adam's apple. He wore a blue jersey with polished silver buttons, I recall, and he always had a Barlow knife in his pocket. And Katie had just turned sixteen when I arrived at the Society of Daniel as a transfer student from Adder Vocational College, where I had studied the rapid application of lead to the lower reptiles. So neither of them would have been in elementary school, come to think of it, but I think I made the comparison because we were much slower to physical, mental and especially sexual maturity at the beginning of the twentieth century, on account of a diet poorer in hormones and supergrow additives (the blue globes had not yet decided to fatten us up); and he certainly had very elementary-school ways at times, did Newt, with his bugs and germs and stuff, always wanting to be the first boy to invent a good nerve gas. He was a child of great parts. With half a mind he could increase the efficiency of our motor switchboard or redesign the brush of a single-phase induction starter for Mr. White, but what he would really be thinking about was what all elementary school boys are preoccupied with, even if they mask it in the so-called "latent" phase.

Meanwhile the great effort went forward. Newt loved the work and was thrilled even to polish the brass fittings in the power plant while Mr. White looked on with a grin (I must admit the possibility that Newt, who was a shrewd little thing, just pretended to be thrilled because that would inch him deeper into Mr. White's good graces, but let us only say so in parentheses, in case Newt is listening in on us right now); for he knew he had to get in there and hump over the intellectual Alps from ground zero, did clever Newt. — Why, he wondered in those early days, couldn't an old snide-bit or hide-halter be linked with a Ruhmkorff induction coil to form an automatic oscillatory rheatone capable of dynamic Faradization? He and several of the other boys constructed a device composed of bibulous paper soaked with sodium sulfate and wrapped around a brass arm. For membranes they tried orange peel, ivory, snakeskin, bamboo, fish bladder, and even, unbeknown to the White family, a mat of Katie's pubic hairs, which Sammy stole from her feather bed when she was out milking the cows, this last proving ultimately to produce a current of 4.3 webers. Already Newt was ahead of Bell, Farmer, and Marcus. And one day when Mr. White had to go out to take over a ghost ranch, he invited Newt along — an astounding sign of favor! This observant pair soon discovered, in the back of an abandoned smokehouse, a large box of tartaric acid and another of bicarbonate of soda, which they put on the backs of their niggers and so brought to their wagons in triumph. With these relatively exotic materials Newt was able to press forward in his work, for please recall that I am describing primitive times, when almost every commodity was in short supply, and the inhabitants of the country and their log-faced chattels lived in a rude crude way; why, not even coathooks had been invented in those days; it was common to hang your hat on deer-antlers or bull-horns embedded in the adobe walls. You even had to send to South America for bananas. The men and boys wore buckskin leggings lined with jerked beef. The women, being half-wild, had to be married by main force. Later each female would lay about eighty eggs in a hole which she dug in the sand. — Both sexes were hardy, in short; the entire race, although vastly inferior to our own in all respects, was nonetheless endowed with a physique especially adapted to the dangers of pre-electrical existence. Cast upon a wild and inhospitable plain, they did not shrug their shoulders and shoot themselves, not them.

Now as the streetcars go past my window in San Francisco, and our standard of living is so high that any American can lie in the bathtub until his pecker resembles a boiled turkey neck, I can hardly believe that once there were quiet places like Dead Man's Gulch and Cache Bend where you had to go with hollow hoof-beats instead of the aerial tramways now used to show off the silver fields; but I can still remember when the rattlers lay winding slowly in the sun in their many-jointed way like Brandi, Frank's whore (don't worry about Frank yet; you'll meet him in around three hundred pages), flexing her spine and especially her coccyx for you in the lode star town, lying on her side so you could see and feel where the small of her back curved in just above her buttocks so that in cross-section her spine was not unlike a rattler's skeleton, and she would sure hiss and rattle and strike at you if you didn't pay her toll after riding her road.

So progress continued. Little Newt got results, for he was never satisfied until he had investigated every question. Often, for instance, the lad would creep to the door of Mr. White's study in the middle of the night and listen, in order to learn what he could; sometimes there would be no sound but the scratching of Mr. White's old-fashioned quill pen, the drumming of Mr. White's fingers, and an occasional thump and curse. Other nights, however, Newt in his nightshirt would hear the sudden squeak of a trap door somewhere near Mr. White's desk, followed by a limber tappety-tap-step, and Mr. White would push his chair back and grunt and say, "Well, what's up this time, Dodger?", and Newt would practically glue his ear to the door with excitement, as the saying goes, and hear Dr. Dodger say, "It's not our problem, Jack. They've got to have one that works; we have one just like it, so I say let's point the client in our direction, yes." – "Hmmph," goes Mr. White thoughtfully. – But just then Newt thinks he hears someone coming down the stairs, and you never know; it might be someone who'd TELL on poor Newt, so quickly he dives into the dumbwaiter and creaks himself up to his room.

At rare intervals Newt was even allowed into Mr. White's study officially. – Mr. White comes into the laboratory with two other gentlemen in black suits and gold ties; and Newt quickly bends over his latest apparatus to show his utter absorption and files a burr off a particularly persnickety ratchet, and Mr. White taps him on the shoulder, and Newt whirls around and leaps to attention and cries, "Yessir, Mr. White; pleased to meet you, gentlemen!" and the gentlemen beam at Newt, obviously charmed, and they each give him a quarter. – "Newt, lad," says Mr. White. "Come on in here and sharpen a few pencils for me, would you, young man?" and they all stroll into the study, and Newt takes the gentlemen's coats without being asked and whisks them out to the hall closet; and Mrs. White comes in with a tray of coffee and cigars; and Katie brings the sugar and cream. – "Do you need anything else, dear?" says Mrs. White. – "Yeah," says Mr. White, slicing the tip from his cigar. "I need you to clear out, and stay out." – "Hee, hee," go the two visitors. "Hee, hee!" – "Yep," goes Mr. White "That's how to handle bitches, gentlemen; I've had bitter experiences, very bitter experiences!" . . . and Newt is just as pleased as could be to attend this gathering of great personages; and he stands in the corner whittling the pencils down to perfect points with his penknife; these are Mr. White's so-called guest pencils, hand-made by his captive Mexes in the lead mines. – That very day Newt, who is cunning with his hands and always knows what will be well received, builds an automatic pencil sharpener for Mr. White; it is a cylindrical thing in a black lacquered housing, with a hole to put the pencil in and a crank that you turn to rotate half a dozen grinding razors inside. – "That's my boy!" booms Mr. White. "Ho, ho, that's my boy!" – and henceforth Newt is in special demand; for whenever Mr. White has visitors he calls Newt in to stand in the corner, dressed in a special sky-blue suit which Mr. White has had made specially for him, and crank the pencil sharpener like a discreet steward. – In fact Mr. White does not much care for the little squirt, but he is conscious of a rule originally developed by the Inuit Eskimos regarding their sled dogs, but no less to the point for employees, pupils, and other flunkeys: – namely, that to get the most work out of your team you should advance one individual to a leadership position and raise him up until he is envied and hated by the others; then every worker will tear himself to pieces trying to gain on the lead dog, who runs wagging his ass just in front of your eyes, and you would really like to get his shaggy tail in your jaws and bite it off; you'd like to tear him to ribbons, in fact; all day his hated ass wags in front of you; finally you can't stand it anymore; you lunge at him, which jerks the sled forward even faster, which gives him more slack in the rope, so he can run ahead easily, frothing up the snow insolently in your face with his back legs; so then you see him escaping you and in great despair you pull and pull in your traces to catch him, and so it goes for years, until finally you get old and sick, and then the master hauls you away from camp and puts a bullet into you. – On the other hand, Newt had no great fondness for Mr. White, either; and who did better in the end only the reader can judge.

When Newt was twelve years old he had had his first vision of electricity. At that time he was just an abandoned farmboy from some immigrant family that had gone under water even though every soul had worked like beavers (I guarantee it) with shovels and wheelbarrows. He spent most of his boyhood doing chores on his uncle's farm. – One day everything around him seemed to achieve purification and spiritual unity. A crackling bluish haze came leaching in from the fields like dust after a cart on a dirt road. In place of the sun was a fuzzy bluish sphere rayed around its circumferences by dazzling blue needles. Newt's hair prickled and stood on end. Then the fence-gate unlatched itself slow and sure as invisible mummy-fingers, and swung open and shut, open and shut, mockingly; while the udders of the cows pulsed under the rhythmic squeezings of invisible hands (and the steel milk-jugs sailed through the air and collected every drop), and all the weeds in the cornfield were torn from the earth by some unknown selective force that conveyed them by the scruffs of their stems to the rubbish dump, as if to foreshadow the yellow combines that would someday roll over twenty-mile pea fields for Dodger's Soup Co.; while the slate tiles on the roof of the red shed jiggled very delicately, like the lid of a pot beginning to boil and you have the feeling that if you leave it alone it will build up and the force will get angry and fling the lid into your face to steam-burn you but good; meanwhile Newt's uncle's axe stirred and gleamed a dull blue and began to thud into the chopping block, while a fifty-pound feed bag sailed round and round ten inches below the ceiling of the chicken coop, dribbling down a neat line of mash, and then another line, a zig-zag one, then a third parallel to the first, N for Newt! and all the chickens came running and pecking trustfully, arraying themselves where the feed was so that they, too, spelled out N for Newt, like a miniature Nuremberg rally; and then the feed bag made a long straight thin trail of mash, to underline the "N" and do further homage to it, Newt surmised at first; so all the chickens gabbled and rushed to queue up nice and straight and bent their feather-bonnet heads down into the dust, pecking as fast as they could; and then the axe came along and neatly decapitated every one! – Now the slop bucket ascended from the back porch and circled the house and shattered the kitchen window, and Newt's aunt began to scream and scold; and the slop bucket flew back out and whisked over to the pig trough, and the pigs came running and grunting and biting each other's tails so that each could be first; and the bucket pitched its contents derisively into the last pig's face, but the pig was not insulted; in fact he was happy (having renounced idealism), though nonetheless surprised because he was sickly and seldom got to the trough in time to gobble anything good; in fact, Newt was under instructions to feed him separately; and at this new development the stronger pigs took a real hatred to their brother and that winter they shoved him out of the warm stinking straw, into the cold, and stood together blocking the entrance to the run, warming each other with their bodies, comfortable as Russian prison camp guards in fur coats and fur hats; so the little pig died. — Meanwhile the bucket thumped the two stronger pigs in the snout (they squealed but lapped up their own blood on the rim of it). So, by God, all the chores did themslves, though not, perhaps, without a certain malice that did not escape Newt. He was amazed. His first hypothesis was: poltergeists. But the farm was by no means near a graveyard, and it was broad daylight. Besides, the chores stayed done, whereas spirits, as we all know, can do nothing real and permanent. — It had to be either magnetism or electricity. At that time Dr. Dodger's experiments with the magneto were attracting widespread attention in the small town journals which the postman delivered to the mailboxes in the middle of every field. Thousands of old ladies and college boys swooned at the thrilling news of Dr. Dodger's impending breakthroughs. And one day Newt's aunt read an article about this newfangled Society of Daniel (Newt's uncle did not care much because he was too old and blind to read). — A reporter interviewed the mother of one of the boys. "It's rather small, apparently, but very élite," the lady was quoted as saying; these were the identical words she had used when returning to civilization after a brief Christmas visit, so that everyone had become interested as far away, even, as the white New England churches where the pale, pinched girls and the roundhead grandsons of Puritans still sat in pews in the old way, holding lit candles and singing hymns on Christmas Eve while the icy drafts blew in from the vestibule so that all the sisters and daughters hugged close to each other for warmth and the men rose tall and sturdy in their great-ccats at each call to prayer, and the congregation sang, puffing out visible clouds of breath with each syllable of every hymn, and the young boys stood and sang "A Mighty Fortress Is Our God" with clenched fists (girls were not allowed to be aggressive at that time), and around those little churches the wind blew snow through the slatey darkness, and along the roads the sturdy wooden houses dug in like teeth denying they were loose, and a Christmas candle burned like a ghost's eye from every window. – So word spread of Mr. White's special school. – Newt figured what the heck. They offered full scholarships, and it was them or a lifetime of chores. – Off he went.

Under his bed at the Society of Daniel he had a Secret Laboratory in which he conducted experiments when the other boarders were asleep, which meant that he walked around all day with blue circles under his eyes and Mrs. White felt sorry for him and pressed more pie on him, which he was quite happy to take. – In a large glass jar he kept his polliwogs and golliwogs; there they swam and laid their masses of squishy eggs. At midnight Newt pulled the black wool blankets down over the side of his bed, forming a security curtain like the boundary of Faraday dark space, and crawled underneath the bed and began to work, prying up two loose boards in the floor to retrieve his tools and things. He never got like Parker Fellows seventy years later, who could read VU meters and manipulate circuits with the confident ease that comes of taking it all for granted; Newt was an inventor, not an end user, so many of his motions were symbolic and ritualistic, designed (if there was any conscious design to them) to pad his activities and fill out the time until he had solved whatever problem was eating him, as he crowded there with Mr. White's wired lessons for that day still running through his head with the scratchy monophonic sound that we were stuck with in those days. Mr. White's voice sounded muffled and simultaneously shrill (after all, the recording medium still had a tinfoil base then): "Connect the red wire to the RED wire, not the blue one, goddammit!" – but already Newt was using this new thing called a flashlight, which was supposedly Taylor's invention (for Taylor was not expelled until the following semester); in fact, as we know, Taylor was not a very good student and never invented a thing, so Newt, who didn't care, occasionally let him take credit for small items, in return for other favors.

He shone the light on his jug of polliwogs and golliwogs, just a boy under his bed in the middle of the desert, and the polliwogs woke up and began to swim sleepily; they could never understand light and learn to go back to sleep the way the other fellows across the hall could who sometimes saw a glow coming out from under Newt's bed (for it was Mr. White's policy that we keep our doors open at all times) but the boys only said, what the hell, he's making crib notes or mebbe playing pocket pool; and they yawned oafishly and turned over in their beds, just as when our hero, Bug, bored through the street-fog with his binoculars in the 1980s, zeroing in on the lighted window (not fully curtained) of a greyish house set among whitish houses, spying on Frank writing a report to Mr. White and reading every word that Frank typed by stepping up the magnification to Super $75\times$. — Newt thought little of the light, being used to it; but the polliwogs and golliwogs were not used to it at all.

Newt watched his polliwogs and golliwogs swim. *They* must have light, it appeared, and *he* must have motion. He knew that if he were to turn out his flashlight then the polliwogs and golliwogs would happily go to sleep again, but now that he had illuminated them they must swim round and round and round, like the poor slop bucket that had to smash the window and then feed the pigs, whether it wanted to or not, because it was not its own master. Electrons determined things. The big green-headed golliwogs swam round and round in their trapped motions which so satisfied Newt; he would make things move, he would. — He tapped the side of the jar softly with a No. 7 pick. We boys woke up then; we could all hear the strange flat tapping sounds, like somebody counting money very slowly and carefully, or adamantine drops falling off quartz columns in caves and landing on mirrors. — FORCE was what Newt wanted.

Going through Mr. White's calfskin briefcase one day when it sat out on the great oak table in the common room, Newt discovered, after passing over many tedious partitions and flap-pockets devoted to mining, politics, war and capital, a sheaf of papers pertaining to the young scholars. Here was a leaf headed *Sammy*. Newt perused it in high excitement. "Good basic knowledge," Mr. White had scrawled, "fair competence; occasional laziness; caught masturbating last December. Mediocre soul barely suitable for a lower-rank position; still, superior to Earl. 16 inventions; 2321 black marks accrued. Best prob. outdoor work." — Next was the sheet of poor Taylor, below whose name Mr. White had written simply "No." (I have already written of the excision of that branch.) — Quickly Newt skimmed over the other sheets, like a water-strider upon the surface of some brown brook-pool, until he came to his own name-sheet, to which were clipped many continuing papers with one of the great iron binder-clips which blacksmiths used to turn out by hand in those days. — "*Newt*," said the beginning of the report. "Best of the crew. 918 inventions reported; 32 concealed and discovered by me" (so he knows about my photo-funkatometer! gulped little Newt) "+ 311 suspected inventions or inventions-in-progress. A young genius, difficult to control and direct. Requires humoring for the moment. Close watch needed. May soon be approached by Phil Blaker's boys."

It was to be expected that when this cunning urchin set his sights on Katie, some objective synthesis must occur, which could not but benefit future electrical endeavors, for there were not many boys who could savvy the current so natural.

Katie White was a pale, wide-jawed girl with freckles who was constantly working, reading and baking us pies. Mr. White did not have much use for Katie but she and her mother were great friends, possibly because no one else at the Society of Daniel felt too free and easy about talking to them as Mr. White would not have stood for it. This meant that they were occasionally to be seen working together scouring the corners, which added to Mr. White's distrust of the whole rotten setup. Katie knew this and was careful to be more bland and quiet, if possible, than her mother, so that days might go by and we boarders wouldn't hear Katie say anything; sometimes we would not even see her; she would just set the table for us and bring in the eggs and suchlike tasks and then take her meals elsewhere. — Katie wore long brown or grey dresses, as Mr. White had expressly forbidden her frocks of green, yellow or other wanton colors. It would have been impossible to imagine a more polite young lady, though she was no prairie queen. When someone came into the room she immediately jumped up and could not sit down again until she had done him some service or until the individual put her out of her misery by taking no further note of her. Then, grateful for a resolution, she sat back in the corner by the piano, reading and reading, listening to the flies drone desperately between the double panes, looking out across the desert at the Great Stone Face. You would look up a little later and see that she had gone without your noticing, probably to help her mother with the cooking.

In the evenings, when everybody's work was done, Mrs. White would step in and play the piano, and we'd all sing, and Katie upon Mrs. White's direction would teach us the verses of "Home On The Range" and "My Country 'Tis Of Thee" and "I Want To Be A Cowboy Sweetheart" — which last none of us would sing because we didn't want to be cowboys' sweethearts, just cowboys galumphing in geared transmission cars through the wire range wilderness, yodel-de-rodel-de-doldrums; so that Mr. White would call us corn-balls and darned old sourpusses, though he obviously took pride in us that we did not forget ourselves and our masculinity by singing such songs, for he was quite good-humored. So then we would just sit and listen to Katie sing until Mr. White would see us all looking at her, and he'd say, "All right, bitch, can the love act," and he'd make Taylor or Earl draw him a wiring diagram and another student would be directed to tear it up if it were wrong. (In this fashion Mr. White hoped to prevent the formation of special cliques or friendships.) Then Katie would sort of swish out of the room, followed by Mrs. White, who was a good cowlike creature who painted watercolors and lumbered as directed, in fear of the electric prod; and we would all keep our eyes on the sole of Mr. White's black patent-leather shoe, which was resting (with a foot inside it) on the knee of his opposite leg, Mr. White being generally a great one for leg-crossing. But Newt always snuck a peek at Katie going out. And he was a-hoping for a heap of better luck.

Newt'd seen her down at the henhouse pretty often, for she was kept busy: — "Your work is in the kitchen and minding your own business!" Mr. White thundered whenever he suspicioned that she was not doing her share ("Yes, father," goes Katie in a soft low voice); even her reading was directed by her father to shore up the rotten holes he perceived in her personality; this course of home study was a continual source of terror to Katie, for she could expect nothing but punishment if she could not list every saint in the calendar when Mr. White quizzed her in his study, from Ambrose to Zoroaster! for he knew what was fitting for a girl of her kind; and meanwhile the good old usual talk of the electric boys was kept up near the stove on feast days until dark, the lazy damned wollopers ... Mr. White was good enough to teach his daughter certain physical laws, such as "There'll be no coffee when there's no coffee-beans in the sack, so jump to it, you drotchel, and round us up another sack!" and this sort of livened things up for us; whenever Mr. White was strict with someone who was not of the same faction as us elementarians we felt rarely privileged. — As for Newt, he was on the peck and on the jump; yes, he was a fast-moving little urchin, if I do say so; he was quicker than a whole bagful of potlicking jinxes. He set out to impress himself on Katie with his attention-getting ways. — First Katie started finding bugs crawling in between her blankets (though I must remind you that not every one was just one of Newt's little tricks; for the bugs were in a full state of alarm now and did not let us get away with much that they did not see).

Katie certainly wanted to be delivered from this trial; that Newt was pesticating the life out of her. – "Are you the one," she whispered to Newt, "who's been putting those awful crawlers in my bed?"

"Sure enough," says grinning little Newt.

"I ought to tell my father on you!"

But she didn't. Katie never bothered her father with anything that was not strictly essential, because Mr. White had a way of making a body feel real bad for interrupting him in his prosecution of the greater good. So Newt's whim-whams and capers continued unreproached, save by Katie, whose reproaches meant nothing. Mr. White, who didn't miss much of what was going on, momentarily suspended his hand; for it is always a strain upon the credibility of a regime to remove the royal favorite. And anyhow it kept Newt in a good humor for experimenting. One night, for instance, a long crooked streak of lightning flashed on Katie's bed, which raised all the stiff hair at her withers. Newt had just transmitted the first wireless current.

"You scared me!" whispered Katie the next morning when Newt passed through the common room on his way to our training cells. "I didn't much enjoy it, I can tell you, Newton Payne, and it hurt, too!" But instead of glaring at Newt the poor girl looked around her nervously, for she was afraid that her father might see that she was wasting her time and Newt's time when there was work to be done. – Fortunately for her, Mr. White was in the powerhouse at that time, supervising the current-generating activities of poor Earl, who seemed month by month to show less promise.

Newt finally realized that his jokes, so effective in gaining the envy of other boys, were not the way to woo Katie. So in his Secret Laboratory at night he began manufacturing things to please her, like li'l ole electric twizzlers and party favors and blinking wire butterflies and things that squealed and tooted and sparked all the colors of the rainbow, and tinted glass bulbs on wires that she could wear in her hair (but she never did, even when she was by herself in her room, because it was Mr. White's habit to enter all rooms without knocking, in order to better ascertain what was going on inside them), and a silver spoon he stole from the kitchen and electroplated her initials, *K.W.*, on the back of, inside a heart (then Katie cried because she would really be in trouble now for stealing spoons and even if she buried the spoon someone might see her bury it or someone might dig it up years later and find her initials on it, and then it would be as obvious as Ebenezer who had made off with it, or at the least acted as a recipient for stolen goods; and she couldn't return it because it had her name on it now and questions were bound to come up as to why one of the best kitchen spoons had Katie's initials engraved on it in gold, in a process that supposedly didn't even exist yet; for Newt kept that one under his little cap until Mr. Edison discovered the same thing); and so Katie, as planned, began to have tender feelings toward Newt because he was doing so much for her, but at the same time she was in constant dread of a public resolution. Imagine what she suffered when Newt began to court her almost openly, going after her in the morning when she went out to get the eggs, and grabbing her sleeve and kissing her hand, and all those attentions which were popular with the Ziegfeld girls a decade later but which just made Katie blush and get dizzy; and one evening after all the boys had just gotten off work he came into the kitchen where Katie was doing up the dishes and started getting ominously general and philosophical in his statements, which was the fashion then when popping either one of two mutually exclusive questions to a girl.

"What I've learned, I guess," says Newt (brashly, for the door to Mr. White's study is ajar by about an inch, and Mr. White sits inside, mighty intent on rolling a smoke, and Mrs. White is dusting off his bust of Louis Pasteur under his critical supervision; and they are both taking in every word), "is that everybody needs a pair of winter underwear whether they can pay for it or not; so it's only going to be diplomas and medals and commissions that'll help a fellow overcome life day to day. That's what it simmers down to."

"Why, Newton Payne," says Katie, going scarlet, "how you can talk."

"This is too wild to be called sport, Jack," says Mrs. White.

"Just you keep your big ass out of it," says Mr. White on general principles, though actually Mr. White was mighty sensitive about Katie because in his outfit natural urges had to be held in check as long as they could not be burned out. — At least his daughter was not lying out on the lawn with young Newt talking her nonsense.

"Break a horse and you've got something," goes on Newt, serious as funeral pie, "something more than just an obedient colt; it's *your own* colt! and, Katie, I want you to stick with me and be my little filly."

"You're sweet," goes Katie, looking down at the floor, "but I just don't dare."

But Newt just scuttles around the room in a gleeful circle, because he has read a couple of romances and he knows from his researches in that department that when a girl says no she means yes.

From his pocket he takes a rude silver heart (cast from two more stolen spoons! realizes Katie with a faint sick feeling), upon which he has carved with his jack-knife: KW + NP. – "Here," goes Newt with a grin of glittering dental braces (for Mr. White has an understanding with Dr. Dodger as regards ultra-modern cosmetic tooth-straightening and tooth-capping and enamel-plating; in the future these boys would be Mr. White's salesmen, and he wanted them to look TIP-TOP GREAT!). – "I made it for you!" And he holds out the locket to her.

Oh, how Mr. White sets his jaw at that! This is too fucking much! And Mrs. White goes white and wonders if Katie is about to sully her virtue, to besmirch her lily.

"No," says Katie, "that's very nice of you, but I just can't" – for the truth was that Katie, though still a young creature, was inwardly as tired of strife as an old Russian or Chinese Communist who has lived through several abrupt changes of staff, and cravenly denounced himself at each juncture for the sake of survival, so that now, barring the advent of a more thorough leadership still, he may succeed in dying of old age – which is not such a bad goal when we recall that we ourselves can hope for no more.

"It's not like I'm asking you to be my concubine or anything," says Newt reasonably, "because I'll marry you and take you places and we'll both run away from Mr. White if you say the word," because Newt thought that maybe Katie would respect him more for offering to stand up to her father; but it was precisely the idea of doing something without her father's knowledge which upset Katie, because she knew that that was impossible at best, so she put her fingers in her ears and looked very very unhappy.

In his study, Mr. White now fizzed with a certain very satisfying feeling which often came over him before one of his rages, it being an important channel pod of his success that he got worked up about things and smashed whatever threatened his projects. And Mrs. White looked on and clasped her hands so tight it's a wonder the knuckles didn't burst.

"Well," goes little Newt, who as a scientist has made Grade "A" contingency plans, "if you won't take my heart then my heart must come to you!" – this is a line which he must have read in one of the Shakespeares of his day – and he swings open the back of the locket and shows Katie a glowing colony of tubes inside; it's a charged capacitor! for sometimes on holidays the boys used to amuse themselves by playing catch in the desert with one of those; if you caught the capacitor just right nothing happened to you, but if you grabbed it anywhere else then you got a nasty burn; this one here is just a scaled-down baby of a device to make Katie feel a tingle for Newt, so he throws the heart at her and it strikes her right on the forehead with a buzzing jolt! – Poor Katie shivered at this and cried and said, "You hurt me! You're horrible! You're so horrible!"

Little Newt, who like all great inventors was dogged to the point of being bullysome, tried to press on. "I do respect you, Katie, and I think you're swell," he said quickly, "and I want to be yours, and if you let me, I'll make you special glow-in-the-dark circuits and loads of special sparking toys just for you," but Katie cut in here and said, "I thought you were a nice boy, Newton, but I see I was wrong, so please don't ever talk to me again!" and off she went sobbing; and she slammed her bedroom door so hard that new hinges would have to be put on it.

She was still in a sad mood the next day and did not present herself at the breakfast table; once she had set out the blue-bordered breakfast plates she went out to the power station to cry, for the truth was that she was in poor health, and had little to look forward to. She had completed her studies the previous year at the School of the Redeeming Lord and now she was just drying out like a locust-wood fencepost until Mr. White could get around to marrying her off. Sometimes Katie pictured getting married, but probably her intended would be so much better than she that she would have to work to make it up to him and anyhow his family would always be disappointed. In the meantime she waited for her father to broach the subject. Her life was as empty as a Geissler vacuum tube. Katie had a little garden, which she had to weed and care for, but this did not entirely console her, although she found it interesting. Generally her chores and her studies required most of her time and strength. She was always drying meat and berries for the winter, or braising vegetables, or memorizing her assigned lessons, or supervising the trained bug that worked in the kitchen, which had finally learned how to make butter, but was unable to wash the cast-off dresses which Katie had given it. ("I tell your parents," said the bug to Katie once in its halting way, "very hard to find someone as troubled as you." – "As troubled as me?" cried Katie, very upset. – "Oh, no, no, no," the bug retreated slyly, waggling its feelers like a lobster. "Forgive my pronunciation, please. I mean, as *traveled* as you." – But Katie had never traveled anywhere in her life. There was nothing to do but forget the unpleasant incident and return to cutting the eyes out of the potatoes.) – Thanks to Katie's industry and frugality, as well as the hard doggy-work of her mother, we had meals at a cost of less than a nickel per head per day.

As for Mr. and Mrs. White, they looked at each other in total agreement; and Mr. White was all set to get his horsewhip from his desk and send that scapegrace Newt flying backwards across the trestle bridge for trying to assail Katie's virtue, but unfortunately Mrs. White spoiled the scene. – "Jack," she said, "that boy must go." – Well! If old Mr. White didn't go through the roof! – "Now, you listen to me, you cunt," he began, mildly enough, "I've had just about enough of you telling me what must be done around here, and don't think I couldn't pack you off to a poorhouse or whorehouse in Louisiana or leave you in some hotel with the bill unpaid to fend for yourself and that jade daughter of yours who's out to ruin my operation and deprive me of the brainpower and superior mentation of the smartest little pipsqueak to come down into this territory since Paul Revere alarmed the eastern seaboard!" – "But, Jack," goes Mrs. White, but there's nothing he has less patience for than this style of address, which both his wife and Dr. Dodger occasionally exasperate him with, so he puts a quick stop to that, and even as he's ranting on, in automatic gear, he's thinking that he has to kind of admire that little Newt for daring to go after the boss's daughter, although he's gonna have to punish Katie with a pretty heavy hand for encouraging him the way all girls encourage men by mincing around them in ways you can't put your quantitative finger on; as a general rule if there's a fight between a fella and a woman it's the woman's fault; so keep that carved deep into your tablets of law, fellow tribesmen, and you will always come out on top. – Katie was whipped privately. – "And from now on," goes Mr. White, "if you've got to hump something, hump a candlestick!"

She still tried to appreciate Newt as a friend, but Newt kept sending her electric presents as before and making her feel obliged to be nice to him even though he was not one of her kind. Everyone was a little tense in that season because even though the transformer crew, headed by Earl and Sammy, had been working as hard as they could it was clear that the wire crop would be a little short. Mr. White was all set to find a culprit and put him in the roundup wagon. When Earl dropped a glass retort, Mr. White caned him (no more and no less firmly than he had Katie, for he was an impartial man). "He thinks he knows how business can be improved," Mr. White joked to us as he lashed Earl's buttocks in the common room, "he's so wise and smart! But he's not smart enough to know that a retort will fall when you drop it!" – and we laughed heartily at this, not only because the public spectacle of Earl's getting his just deserts had cleared the air, but also because Mr. White was ordinarily not a jesting man, so that his *bons mots* were especially prized.

In his Secret Laboratory Newt felt quite miserable that he had not gotten to base camp with Katie, but he distracted himself temporarily from his setback by making improvements in the powerhouse. Sammy had told Mr. White that things were probably as good as they could be in that department. But Newt had already defined his objectives, much as a resistance fighter will methodically explore the roads of unfamiliar territory, then find water, disable enemy machine guns, and cut the bridges off, because that is what you do. Having calculated the load factor of the station, Newt weighed and checked electrical progress in order to increase it by ten percent per month. – He modified the booster dynamics of the middle-wire feeders, ran the furnace gases of the standby steam line through Green's economizer, built a cooling tower, designed a matching set of double current dynamos, stepped up the alternators to higher pressure using a transformer T, dreamed up a phase inductor I with high-p circuits C for every distributing main D that induced a secondary drop $D2$, and at length had created a polyphase system S capable of 40,000 volts, that is, V. Sammy, who was always cautious, was nervous about the possibility of explosions due to collection of moisture on negative insulators, so Newt enclosed these devices in tubes of lead and gutta-percha, which Earl assembled under his direction. No accidents resulted, and when Mr. White, frowning, ably measured the electric corpuscles emitted, he found an indicated horsepower of double the dynamic load. At first he didn't believe it. He rattled that Branly wave detector until the needle danced in its socket, but the reading held constant. – "Good for you, Newt, my boy!" he said finally. "You've sold me on that one!" Newt was quite pleased (though I must confess that his pleasure partook not only of pride, but also of satisfaction in having hoodwinked Mr. White, who really should have used a charged electroscope instead of that stupid old Branly gadget which only nobodies in the business still used, which is why Newt had felt no compunction about recalibrating the needle the previous night in his Secret Laboratory so that the reading would be even more impressive, not that it was half bad). Anyhow, Mr. White was quite satisfied. This was better than a modified Lancashire boiler with a Dowson gas-producer PLUS steam dynamos with omnibus bars!

After outfitting himself with a battery of several hundred cells and a voltaic pile, Newt retired to his Secret Laboratory under the bed, where he electrolytically decomposed four alkalis according to the dictates of single fluid theory. He then fixed a sheet of zinc against the wall and used Hertz's resonator. But he was still obsessed with Katie. He could not concentrate on his student voltmeters and ammeters, these being of the solenoid and gravity-balance type, in black walnut cases with window-glass fronts; as he toiled in his laboratory alone late at night those gauges took on the other boys' faces, the black wood exterior becoming the dark suits which we all wore in the common room, and the glass just like our own simple, unclouded features, which allowed our thoughts to be read on any polygraph; then upon the sheet of zinc, blue pinpoints of light began to form and trembling lines of bluish fire spidered upward and downward to connect them until an image of sweet Katie had been formed, but slowly her face was resolved into a bare, objective skull, with a blue globe in each eye-socket. – The blue globes wanted him to kill Katie! – His intentions toward her were still "honorable," as we used to say back then; he really would have married her, but it would have been very difficult because that would have necessitated sending for his aunt and uncle to make the wedding arrangements, and so Newt's uncle would have come doddering up to the door, two-thirds deaf and three-quarters blind; and Mr. White would extend a hand for him to shake and he'd miss it and fumble through the air until he latched onto it; and shake it feebly, clinging with wrinkled old baby-fingers; and Newt's aunt would make a curtsey and Mr. White would go "Madam," in an unenthusiastic voice; then after they came into the common room Newt's uncle would mistake Mr. White for another person whom he had not met and try to shake his hand again, and then Mr. White would get a little cross and jerk his hand away and go, "You're a familiar little bugger, aren't you? Well, I understand you've come to ask the hand of my daughter in marriage for your nephew, and my answer is that she's a piece of trash no better than a nigger wench but that's still better than your nephew deserves because he's just a parasite living on my charity – as are you, sir! – as are you, madam! and now get out because don't think you can get away with wasting any more of my time; this audience is at a fucking END!" . . . In short, there was no hope.

One night in his Secret Laboratory Newt got dizzy the way he sometimes did when he'd eaten too much pie, and his biggest voltmeter seemed to turn into a medieval armoire full of ill-fitting drawers and pocket-sized cabinets that you had to open with a tarnished silver key; and instead of his usual dielectrical materialism he seemed to be doing something like alchemy, involving the life cycles of living metals: first decay, then purification, coitus, pregnancy, birth and finally nutrition, using the Red Eagle (mercury), the Green Lion (glass), the White Smoke (sodium), and the Pure Body (tin); and finally, after Newt had skillfully operated a number of bromantic and perentalic devices, the experiment was complete; inside the flask was the silver key he needed, still glowing-hot. – Newt cut a hole in the flask with a diamond probe and shook out the key. He was wearing the dried tongue of a weasel inside his left sock to close the mouths of his enemies (Sammy, mainly, who sometimes tattled to Mr. White). – The key fit perfectly in the lock! But Newt did not yet open it. First, as a precaution, he mixed up a batch of *licinum*, that combustible compound in whose light those present will appear to be flaming demons. Newt's everyday spittoon had conveniently turned into a brazier, so Newt ignited this with a Lucifer match and spooned two fingers of the powdered *licinum* into a chafing dish he'd stolen when Mrs. White's back was turned. With a pair of tongs, little Newt held the dish over the open flame, holding his breath for excitement. The *licinum* began to smolder and stink of bat-piss. Newt peered into a copper mirror and saw himself represented as a cunning little ghoul without a patch of hair, all green and slimy like a frog, with bulging eyes and yellow teeth. This meant that things were under control. Unscrewing the crystal of his watch, little Newt wafted some of the vapor into the mechanism. The hands spun faster and faster as they attuned themselves to sidereal galactic time; then the face of the watch went dark and blue sparks began to form upon it in the shape of constellations. There was Scorpio; there was the Scarab; and there was the Shining Globe! – yes, by Alchiranus, by Harpocriton, there were no diseases in the stars, no doubt because the Thirteen Stripes were in the ascendant; *am deutsches Wesen soll die ganze Welt genäsen.* This extraordinary political situation, combined with the appearance of a rising blue star upon the center of the hemisphere, assured Newt that the time had come. He turned the key in the lock and saw a long black passageway. He crept inside and scuttled along like a termite, all the way to the isle of Inde, where various rare herbs grew, and local witches made images to restrain adulterous wives while their husbands went out fucking. Directly in front of Newt was a mountain of gold guarded by the blue globes! He could see them rolling and tumbling up there on its peak like coiled-up glowworms;

the very bones of the blue globes were so hard as to strike fire like flint; and he wanted to get to them more than anything else in the world, but to get there you had to ford a river which could only be crossed on the anniversary of a particular primeval electric meteor shower; on any other day you would be drowned; but if you did get across then the blue globes would spark for you and receive your gifts (Newt fumbled in his pocket; had he remembered to bring gifts? – yes, he had; he had a nice spool of wire and a jigger of capacitors) and listen to you if you were good, and give *you* things, like a miraculous blue globe lamp in whose light you could defy the hammer of the Turks; or the stone of invisibility, which was really a dull grey lump full of electric ether that baffled visible spectrum rays and made them curve around you; and a magic mirror to reveal all plots – what Mr. White would have given for that! – it analyzed the political current of brain waves and spleen pulses, was what it did ("To see one's own intestines means secrets revealed," says a Latin dream-book of the Middle Ages); that would have been worth any number of salamanders-in-the-flame; or maybe they'd give you a regiment of wind-up man-eating ants crafted of aircraft-alloy aluminum who would mine gold for you by night, so then you'd never have to work; or gigantic electric stones that made everything light or cold or dark or hot, assuming that you prayed to at least five of the seven true metals, as foretold in I think it was the *Liber Ignium* of Marcus Greers; or a special household wiring manual containing the secret signs used by the blue globes to foretell all; or a quicksilver circuit to subject Katie and all the boys and indeed every being save possibly Mr. White, Dr. Dodger and the nine orders of angels to Newt's will; or an automatic electric rod 'n' reel to catch fish and thieves; or any of various other sibylline tools! – But what Newt wanted now was the Secret of Death. It was not the right day to cross the river. It would not be for several million years. So Newt built a wireless telegraph and signaled to the blue globes up on the crest of their golden hill that all he wanted was the Secret of Death, and he would be very happy if they would oblige him; of course the blue globes liked nothing better than that; they came rolling across the sky to him in a black thundercloud and dropped a little vial into Newt's eagerly cupped palms; and they liked Newt so much that they would not even take his wire or capacitors in payment; then Newt was as happy as could be; and he waved goodbye and clutched the vial tight to himself and rushed back down the passageway and through half a dozen time zones in order to be home before cock-crow.

And now Newt was all set up to do some mischief. His quick clever eyes sparkled like lemon-drops.

In the meantime another quarter drew near its end before we noticed; for somehow there seemed to be no real time for any of us at the Society of Daniel. The plating cell connections fitted our noggins like well-worn skullcaps, and the machinery at the power-house reconfigured itself dreamily. We never saw any new faces or new scenes. If we had graduated to find the whole country crumbled into dust, like one of those deserts once teeming with the orchards and subject populations of Asiatic dynasties, I do not believe we should have been shocked. This is not to say that we were like the boys working in the shops of Mr. Edison or the garages of Mr. Ford, for those lads were each given one task to do, painting the same chassis the same black shade, for instance, over and over; rather, we Society of Daniel boys were the electric trailblazers who figured things out for the first time, and once the algorithm was recorded Mr. White and Dr. Dodger just had to copy it out once on an employee musical score to help the millions whistle while they worked, and the division managers each copied it once and wrote *da capo* at the end for the overseers, and the overseers summoned in the workers and they hunkered down between the bellies of the transformers in our concrete shops full of fumes and flies from the slaughterhouses and stagnant canals outside; and then in employee exchange programs, in which Mr. White was a big believer, they swapped the info at lunch with their brethren in the high-ceilinged, grey-girdered factory sheds, where the men worked in rows and everybody was wearing suspenders; and the Factory Hand of the Week would give them a home demonstration of the latest electrical contraption — it beats as it cleans as it grinds! — and the bugs watched behind the windows crusted over with shit and inside the dusty brick walls that were as spider-cracked as onion cells under the microscope; and the old gimps in dirty jeans bent low over electric cylinders on the work tables because they couldn't see much anymore so they might as well just keep working as the metal dust piled up on their shoulders, and the young men were already going bald from blue sparks in their scalps as they worked inside the shiny metal bodies, upper and lower decks alike, of riot omnibuses with peep-peep horns, tightening screws with electric tools; and when they left work they sauntered over to the burlesque to see women get sawn in two by old Dr. Dodger beneath the brightest possible stage lights that showed you every detail; and the girls that didn't get sawn in two worked as electric typists and polished the big boys' chalkboards and poured them tea; while the black folk were allowed to stand hat in hand in the back of the wide black streetcars; and the last primeval bugs not in zoos were suffered to crawl on the sidewalk and sometimes society girls knelt down and threw them bread crumbs and then the society girls crossed their bare legs and got wheeled home by black servants with big white grins; as meanwhile work went on in Mr. White's factories round the clock to catch up to Phil Blaker, making black electric cars under contract with Mr. Ford; so out they came, rolling off the womb-tracks with radiator-grilles big and inquisitive in front, boxtop cabs and big stubby wheels and a fine double fender on every one; while unfinished ones still stretched back into the darkness, being tended as described above; then the black square cars trundled down the street, each with a spare tire screwed to the back and a blue globe under the hood. – In those days the bugs often camouflaged themselves as cars.

Meanwhile the standard drives continued. We certainly did not have the sort of ideas about girls that boys act on now in our great Republic; our imagination was limited to ankles and flashes of elbow, or maybe getting a piece of ass. Well, Newt was in love with her, then, as we all were (for that was what we called it), and his way of showing it now that it had gone bad and bitter was to play practical jokes on her again, like a good "latent." – Earl's speed, say, might have been to put a dead Indian in her bed, for if I may say so there was always something sort of dull and literal-minded about Earl. But not Newt. He went out and got a frog's brain and a little bit of pitchblende ore, and perhaps a certain vial, and I don't know what all, and quick as an electron he'd built a battery-powered gizwhizz I suppose you'd call a joy buzzer nowadays. Of course this wasn't a little windup thing you hide in the palm when you shake hands, for back then we had to lug these heavy Leyden jars around with us, and you could hear the frog's brain splashing around inside the contraption Newt was hauling, but it worked fine. One day we were in the common room, and when Katie came in from the kitchen to bring us our cookies he laid the cylinder quietly down on its side, with the cap tightly screwed on. – There was no light except the light of the fire, for in those western longitudes the sun drops like a dead man rolling off a pack horse. Mr. White was in a jolly mood. It was end-of-term time; we had all squeaked by on our exams, so we were to be entertained with a fine tale, "as taut," as Kipling has said, "as wire rope."

Concerning exams, I believe I have neglected to mention our academic schedule. We had, in addition to our plating sessions, lectures on Tuesdays, Thursdays and Saturdays, when we would meet in the common room at seven-thirty in the morning and then proceed to the exhortations. The exhortations always fueled our ambitions, just like gasoline ("wet electricity," Mr. Edison called it) in the engine, but the tests, in truth, were very difficult; and once or twice we cheated, as boys will do. Once we were given half an hour to list every single conductive substance to be found in Montana. This was an especially cruel examination question, because not one of us came from Montana. Ordinarily Mr. White sat at his desk at the head of the schoolroom, glaring directly into each of our faces while we took our tests, so that it was extremely tricky to communicate the requisite information; thus at slack moments in our learning cells we had worked out a special language of coughs and throat-clearings, which grammar we had communicated during the plating drills through another language of wall-taps, not dissimilar to that used by the inmates of Soviet prisons. This language was predicated not only on the kind of sniffle or sneeze emitted, but also on who uttered it; thus, if Sammy coughed and Earl hawked on the floor, this meant "eighty-seven," whereas if Newt and Taylor did the same it meant "platinum wire." — But today Mr. White was suddenly called away by a small fire in the powerhouse. "Stay there and do your work!" he said to us as he took his hat. "I'm putting you on the honor system, so if anyone cheats you'd better squeal on your fellow or else I'll roast the whole lot of you!" — In fact there was no fire (how could there be now that Newt's gutta-percha protected everything?); Mr. White simply wanted to gauge our honesty. He did indeed go off to the powerhouse, for he was well aware that from the schoolroom window he could be seen until after crossing the trestle bridge; but once inside he went up to his own level and focused a special tele-zoom periscope (made for him by Dr. Dodger) upon our window. So methodical was our master in his tactics, that he even set fire to a small pile of greasewood upon the flat roof of the powerhouse, so that we could see a wisp of black, greasy smoke, which looked like the output of a typical oil or electrical fire. Reassured by what we thought a perfect monitor of Mr. White's movements, we became quite joyous and gamboled about the schoolroom, good-naturedly adding our own lists to the lists of others (Newt, of course, had the longest list; and he never would have cheated at all were he not aware that if he did not so prostitute himself we would lose all patience for his privileged position with Mr. White, and then perhaps he would be in danger of dismemberment) until soon the veriest idiot of us seemed a real genius concerning the electrical substances of Montana. We kept a lookout at the window, a very officious little urchin, and he reported that the smoke continued to blow as strongly as ever; evidently Mr. White was finding the blaze stubborn. – Suddenly we heard Mr. White come stamping up the corridor! I do not believe I have seen such a panic even in a lot of pigs that knew they were about to be slaughtered. We could think of nothing better than to slam the door tight and lock it, for our commingled test papers and desks bore evidence to the orgy which had just taken place, the signs of which could not be covered up from Mr. White's keen eyes at the drop of a resistor. – And now the footsteps came to the door . . .

"What's the meaning of this?" yelled Mr. White in a rage. "You young scoundrels; open the door instantly!" and he dashed his hand through the window in the upper part of the door, seized Newt's inkpot and ruler, which lay in easy reach on the side bench, knocked out all the glass with Newt's ruler, and hurled the inkpot into the middle of us so that it shattered on the corner of Sammy's desk and spattered us black. – "Yes, yes!" cried several squealing voices; "let this be our Alamo!" "Oh, you *stubborn* and *refractory* lads!" cried Mr. White. "Surrender at once or I will sentence you to be discharged forever!"

Newt rushed to the door and unlocked it. Mr. White strolled in scornfully, looking around with mock astonishment. – "What have we here?" said he. "Desks cheek by jowl, test papers in disarray – my little scholars haven't been *cheating*, now, have they?"

"Yes," pipes little Newt. "Yes, and they made me show them, but I swear I didn't copy anything off their papers!" – Newt was in agony; for, being the favored one, he had more to lose than we, who had not striven so high. – Mr. White shook his head in disgust. – "No, I'm sure you didn't even do that much, you pimple-popping pipsqueak!" And he gave Newt a push that knocked him down, followed by a whack to the Atlas vertebrum. We for our part felt a sweet sensation upon seeing Newt's humiliation; no matter what our own punishment might be, this could not be taken away from us. – In fact, this treatment of Newt by Mr. White was our salvation, for seeing that Mr. White was determined to level him along with the rest, Newt threw in his lot with us and used his nimble wits, as will be seen.

Mr. White walked slowly up and down the room, looking into each of our faces. – "Well, Sammy," he grated, lashing the boy across the face with his cane, "it's mighty fine to see that you and Earl are such good friends, as close as two buttocks on one bum, so close you'll even share your toilet paper with him!" and picked up Sammy's test from on top of Earl's test and shook it in Sammy's face and tore it up. — "Yep," he went on, "it's a darned good thing, you little sonofabitch, because when I get through with you you're both going to have but one bum-cheek apiece!" — and just for a surprise he jabbed Earl in the stomach with the point of his cane as hard as he could, so that Earl went "Ooof!" and turned all pale and fell down. — "There!" goes Mr. White in a jolly way. "That'll teach you not to partake of such a substantial breakfast, you fat jackanapes!" (for, alas, Earl was putting on weight).

"Well, now," says Mr. White in the silence, "would you like to be flogged before your collective expulsion, or after?" — Immediately we broke up into little squeaking conclaves to debate this question; I recall that I was in favor of expulsion first, because then Mr. White would have less right to flog us, our being under no obligation to him; but Sammy pointed out that once we were expelled we could be arrested by the Machine Police for trespassing, so it would be better to get the flogging over with first so that as soon as we were expelled we could run. In the midst of all this shameful parliamentarism, plucky Newt got up off the floorstones, brushed the chalk-dust off, and set his brain to work. It soon occurred to him that he could save us and do Katie an injury at the same time. So thinking, he put his fingers in the corners of his mouth and emitted a series of piercing dog-yelps that brought the two women running; for they had been brought up to seek out violence and wring their hands at it helplessly. From the noises that Newt made, it sounded as if he were being murdered; and we all stared at him in astonishment, wondering whether Mr. White's blows had jarred something loose, but he rolled his eyes at us and grinned even as he kept up his racket. — "Silence, you rascal!" blared Mr. White, but it was too late; Katie and Mrs. White were already peeping in at the doorway.

"What do you two-legged bitches want?" says Mr. White. "You'd better hop for it, or you'll be yapping like the rest of this school of coon-dogs!"

Now Newt guessed that even if Katie would not go all the way for him she still cared for him enough not to want to see him dead. Pulling his new vial from his pocket, he held it aloft so that we could all see it. It glowed with a horrid blue light that flickered around the room and made us all look like corpses. — "Mr. White, sir," says crafty Newt in his most respectful tones, "given that we are in the wrong, I humbly submit that we are not fit to live. This vial contains the essence of elecricity, extracted and purified one thousand times. Rather than suffer the disgrace of expulsion, I propose that we all blot out our crimes with the tried and true expedient of electrocution." (And in the vial — but no one saw it — a little blue face beamed forth at the notion of killing, and bared its blue jagged teeth in a smile.)

The rest of us boys were stunned. Mr. White saw this and grinned from ear to ear. — "Well, now," he says. "That's not such a bad idea. Let me talk it over with Dodger to learn the legal ramifications," and at this display of heartlessness both Mrs. White and Katie burst into tears, particularly since the sacrifice was droll little Newt, the darling of Mrs. White, whom Katie could not help feeling sorry for, despite his atrocious behavior. — "Expel them if you must, Father," says Katie, "but don't let them die!"

At once Mr. White smells a rat. Having witnessed the earlier scene between Newt and herself, he cannot imagine that she cherishes any warm feelings for the little sapsucker. Here Mr. White is betrayed by his limitations; not being kind himself, he cannot usefully hypothesize regarding the mercifulness of others. So, the way he figures it, either Newt has got Katie in a family way after all and the bitch expects to run off with him, or else there was some other complicity between them in this cheating business.

"So, what do *you* know about all this?" he says, commencing to close and unclose his fingers while meanwhile looking her *right* in the *eye*.

"Nothing," says Katie, bowing her head before the power of her father's look; and this retreat is sufficient provocation to believe her guilty of something.

The fat, of course, is really in the fire when Mrs. White sees the direction of her husband's gaze; and without further ado she falls to her knees and begs him not to hurt Katie. One of the females is bad enough, from Mr. White's point of view; the both of them together are insufferable; and now a tribunal will have to be called to pass judgment upon all members of the household. — Needless to say, we were all acquitted, Mrs. White was severely chastised and Katie was flogged half-unconscious. — Hurray for Newt! Only he could have managed Mr. White so beautifully; for the rest of us were little better than puppets. — Thus the term passed by, and we passed our exams, cheating far more circumspectly; so that now once again the end-of-term story had come round as we sat assembled in the common room. And Newt sat there quietly with his big battery. —

Yes, the machinery of fate was cranking up for poor Katie now; and although I would love to go on about Katie and Newt and the high times that they had at the Society of Daniel, the rush of events will not permit me to do so; and in fact all this is but a prefatory footnote to the main story – oh, wretched destiny, that can make our lives into prefatory footnotes! – so I must say straight out that Newt was about to murder Katie. Maybe the blue globes made him do it, as our leftists theorize, but I cannot seriously believe that the blue globes had any interest in pulling Katie's plug; she was an infinitesimal quantity in any power calculation; she did not even cling to her own life, and I think it more likely that Newt just got upset that Katie would not give in to him, as I have said; he might have still thought about marrying her secretly but he knew he would have been found out; anyhow, it wouldn't have worked. Perhaps Newt was aware of this and wished therefore to eliminate a twisted purpose from his existence. – So the end-of-term story was to commence Katie's last hour.

A hundred years earlier, the landed gentry, according to Washington Irving, chucked their dear plump wives under the chin and fed them sweetmeats. Remnants of this *noblesse oblige* persisted even now, in the notions of scholarships and their appurtenances, one of which was Mr. White's quarterly story. The readings from the Book of Generators, while morally instructive, were a bit like hauling shingles to Albany as far as we were concerned, for when one's whole life is devoted to studying such worthies as Tesla, Steinmetz, Nunn and Lambe, and outwitting their marketing schemes in a highly practical way, then further information on grand electrical figures and doings must be pigeonholed as "career development" rather than "entertainment." The quarterly story, on the other hand, brought us directly into the purview of racial imagination, thereby helping to develop our characters in the light of Mr. White's own. And while it went on, we didn't even have to work. Tonight's story was about Jews and Negroes. (Last semester it had been about Indians and Spaniards, who were more of a problem for Mr. White in this region.) This series was true training for life, by Gobineau's beard! – "Oh, boys!" cried Mrs. White at the piano bench. "This is going to be *so* good!" (And hidden wireworms memorized every word while they gnawed at the intercom cables inside the walls.)

"Once upon a time," said Mr. White, thrusting his jaw forward and narrowing his eyes dreamily, "there was a fella named Ichabod Crane, and I'd bet my three blow-whiskers he was a nigger sax player with that name, like Duke Elijah or Nat Turner, because they all get those damned peculiar monickers at their infant christening ceremonies where they go inspired and foam at the mouth and spit on their secret ebony holy books, and the only point of the foregoing, young men, is to satisfy your natural curiosity about niggers. You remember that colored delivery boy that came here last week with the new parts for our Dodgerator Machine? Well, he was sure as black as they come, wasn't he? — Talk about the forces of darkness! — In your lifetimes, boys, I am confident that some great ethnologist or mathematician, maybe you, Newt, will prove that the power of electrical manipulation resides solely in our race, that we are whiter and brighter because of the voltages of superior nerve filaments. — And fortunately there was a white man on the scene, the way there always is. Now this fellow of our kind was named Brom Bones, 'ceptin' that we called him Bony when he was a kid because he was skinny then, but he was powerful strong and could split rails easy, and the real reason he was called Brom Bones was that if he didn't like you he'd just grin at you and shake your hand real friendly, and start to squeeze a bit, and squeeze a little harder, and all the bones would crack, and he'd squeeze a little harder, and all the bones would shatter to fragments, and he'd squeeze a little harder so the pale greasy marrow came oozing out from your finger-ends. He's now working over in Russia, helping Czar Nicholas put down all this leftist Jewish trouble, and if you look him up in their history books you'll see him listed as Bromsky, which means broom in Russian, because he's sweeping all the offal away, you see. But at the time he hadn't made his name, because Brom hadn't done much in those days but cracked a few thumbs.

"Well, they were both after a certain squaw of the plains, not that Bromsky was so interested in her so-called charms, but the idea of dragging her naked behind a wagon wheel appealed to him, for which I'm sure you can forgive him, since I bet there's not a darned one of you that hasn't dipped a fox's tail in pitch to set it on fire in celebration of our national holiday." (At this little Newt grinned and looked down at his cylinder.) "So Ichabod and Brom Bones were bound to come to blows.

"Well, for awhile it seemed like Ichabod was getting the upper hand, because all those niggers do have good timing and rhythm; they can sing real good too, and the girls go for that kind of whim-me-gary. So Ichabod was cocking his rod and eating out the squaw and servicing her with his long Jewish nose, because that's another thing I forgot to mention, he was a bastard Jewish halfbreed, and the reason Jews have long noses is because the air is free. You can be rootin' tootin' certain that I checked the background of each and every one of you boys before allowing you to pollute my premises because I'm well aware that there's a sick streak in one or two of you, and someday that sick streak will come out and you will pay, but at least there aren't any offspring of Jew-whores around my knee to fuck me over, which reminds me of a good one I heard from Sammy; do you want to tell it, Sammy? – No, you're shy. – Just as well, since you'd choke on your own tongue anyhow, but it goes like this: What's Blaker Shoe and Boot Company got in common with the state of Alabama? – And the answer is ten thousand goddamned BLACK LOAFERS. – Well, Ichabod decided he'd better pay a visit of marital intent, and he dolled himself up in his jingling nigger-beads, and headed off into the darkness toward the squaw's teepee. He was hugger-muggering along, throwing a stolen coin up in the air as he went and catching it on his broad lower lip, in the manner of his race, when suddenly out from behind a low ridge came Brom Bones on a black horse, with a coat tucked around his head so it looked like he was guillotined, and under his arm he bore a jack o' lantern carved like a skull, which was a good trick because if one thing scares monsters and primitives it's light; and he said, 'You are doomed, Ichabod Crane; you can't jew a nigger and you can't be-nigger a jew, so I have come for you; I am the Spirit of Death; and I'm gonna baptize you until the bubbles stop coming up.' And he did, too. And when Ichabod was dead Brom cut his head off and stuck the jack o' lantern on the neck of that carcass, and drove a stake through his heart to keep him under the ground where he couldn't do any harm, because there are a lot of dark ugly things in the world out to get you, lad, and you've got to take precautions and never stop hating them. Earl's working on a device called a marshlight candle which puts out a blue beam as steady as the devil, and when he's done with the blueprints I recommend that you each build one and carry it at all times when you go past graveyards and haunted houses and murder-sites, and mark those places for future reference, so we can pound power-poles there in daylight and burn the evil out. – And the jack o' lantern is with you right now, watching to make sure you don't screw up, and HERE IT IS!" and he flipped a circuit-breaker that had been wired to the chandelier; and there was a buzzing and a smell of burning; and from the chandelier a great ball of blue force rolled and lurched in agony, like one of the noblemen in old Roumania impaled by Vlad the Fourth.

"I've been saving this as a surprise, boys," Mr. White continued, "because what this means is that we've solved the static problem once and for all, thanks to a secret process that our Newt invented just this afternoon. Let's give him a good hand, boys. And remember this; it's always Halloween around here, no matter what the input impedance, and the real world of life is the same way, so if you want your squaws then make like Bromsky. For it is my goal, and your goal, and the goal of our great Republic, to boot all those sad-nose Ichabods into the dust from whence they came, do you understand me?" – We all nodded earnestly, and the evening's entertainment continued. Mrs. White appeared, wearing white gloves, to play the piano for us; and a nervous blushing Katie was summoned from her room to sing; while we all sat straight and polite in our black chairs. Mr. White drummed his fingers on his armrest, grimacing heavily; he figured that he had to humor the womenfolks once every Sunday to keep them from going *completely* rotten on him. But he saw that we were all staring at Katie in her Sunday dress, and Newt in particular seemed about to burst with some hidden excitement, and keep rolling the cylinder back and forth with his toe so that the frog's brain sloshed; and Newt's eyes were round and bright and rolling. – Katie was right in the middle of teaching us "That Old Gang Of Mine" when Mr. White decided she was going too far, called her a slut and sent her up to her room to wait for her punishment. Well, just as she was getting up to go, clutching her skirts tightly in both hands, Newt rolled his eyes at her, grinned with all his braces, gave the cylinder a nudge with his rubber-toed sneaker, and rolled it right up against Katie so that the terminals touched her ankle! (Like a scavenger bird I, Big George, still feed upon her long last screech . . .)

Can you remember those times when, beset by gloom, you verify the meaninglessness of everything, when the labor of your own stale breathing stifles you and sounds are muffled as if by concentric glass domes? Yet even then, when your punishment for your glowing misdeeds is almost complete, and sensations reach you so faintly that you wonder whether every pulse of reality has been strained through a Butterworth filter (crafted by infernal designers to produce maximum flatness of response), even then you will experience some passband ripple, which may be the humming of the wasps that nest beneath the eaves; or (more likely) the endless haunting discussions of electricity with itself, as given by:

$$V_{out}/V_{in} = \frac{1}{[1 + e^2 C_n{}^2 (f/f_c)]^{1/2}}$$

So it was when Katie lay murdered at the foot of the piano; since scheduled activities definitely came to a halt and for several seconds nobody said anything; but during those seconds I remember hearing a tentative, irregular fluttering behind and above me (it was not yet all around me the way it is today). – Newt stood up and sat down again, blinking his eyes to rapid tolerances as he surveyed the result of his joke. – I for my part wished only that I could route my sadness into some black box whose wires extended in all directions like the hooked claws of bloodsuckers, and never think about Katie again, because doing so could help neither her nor myself. (As Robert Owen said, "Should any causes of evil be irremovable by the new causes which men are about to acquire, they will know that they are necessary and unavoidable evils; and childish, unavailing complaints will cease to be made.") Now it was back to jerking off and thinking about faces and eyes.

Earl jumped up, finally, got a log from beside the fireplace and knocked Newt's battery away with it, but he was far too late. The poor girl had been epistemologically grounded.

There was pandemonium in the common room. – Sammy leaped up and ran around screaming, "Accident! Accident!" until Mr. White cuffed him absently. – Mrs. White screamed. She was led from the room upon Taylor's arm, for Taylor despite his shortcomings was a fine gallant boy. – Newt seemed by far the least perturbed of any of us. For one thing, he had clearly done it on purpose, so there was nothing for him to be surprised about. And perhaps the frog's brain had reminded him that you can always use a current to make a severed frog's leg twitch to your own tune; so there was no reason he couldn't do that with Katie's legs, and the rest of her, too, some night in the graveyard; he hadn't really lost anything; for now that Newt was in complete affinity with the blue globes he saw things from their point of view, although he always thought it his own. (And in fact we have not entirely seen the last of dead Katie White.)

Finally Mr. White said, "Newt, you've got quite a whipping coming to you." – But that was all he said.

We buried Katie the following day. Mrs. White was too stricken to attend. It was a fine afternoon, and we appreciated the interruption of our routine. Sand blew in onto the coffin as soon as it was lowered. – Newt kept his giant battery as a souvenir.

Newt's routine was not substantially affected. During those occasional dawns when he was not required to proceed instantly to the common room for a breakfast of Mrs. White's flapjacks, and thence to the plating cells for treatment – and these mornings of exemption continued to increase for Newt, as Mr. White had committed himself to spooning out little sugar-lumps of privilege for the favorite – then Newt pulled the blankets even snugger around the bed in his Secret Laboratory and weighted them down to the floor to keep out the morning's blind pressure, and continued to press on with his studies in that artificial darkness, though with less and less steam in his actions as the pallor rose on his skin and the air got suffocating in there and sometimes the electric bulb failed and Newt had to light one of Mrs. White's tallow candles, and what a smoky stink *that* made, until finally he had to blow it out in the midst of some load-factor calculation and emerge feebly into his day-lit room (at which the observant spy-bugs retreated proportionally), running along the deserted hall, past the other boys' long-opened doors, down the stained back stairs where sometimes he used to meet Katie coming up with a sack of laundry, and out the door at the end of the humming corridor of plating cells. Nervous under the desert sky, little Newt skittered over the trestle bridge and arrived at the reservoir, where he took his morning bath. Then Newt *zipped* back inside to the common room, where in the old days Mrs. White had left a big slice of pie especially for him. (Nowadays she left him cold dried-out pancakes.)

Sometimes we thought we heard Katie's footsteps on the back stairs, just like in the old days when she was always tiptoeing up and down on endless errands, but now that I think about it I believe that it was only the scutterings of cockroach spies.

NEWT'S FATE (1914)

> Let's beat the oar-blades
> Of our shield-adorned boat.
>
> *Egil's Saga* (*ca.* 1230)

On graduation day Mr. White punched Newt's ejection seat and pow! off he went like a flare from a Very pistol, straight to the Pentagon, where he got a classified job and was not heard from again for years. (But we will read his mail presently.) According to the official biographies, Newt became in later life a little pot-bellied man who was always beaming at everybody.

FULL STEAM AHEAD (1914)

~~~~~~

Nobly and fittingly have you upbraided us.

ST BASIL, Letter CXXXI
to Theodotus, Bishop of Nicopolis
or some damned place

With the distraction of Katie out of the way, there was more settled earnestness, more interest in the substantial business of day-to-day conduction, and far less froth. Of course there were several weeks immediately following the event (as Taylor called it, out of that delicacy to which he was so susceptible) when Mr. White was not available for comment; he had shut himself up in his study with Dr. Dodger, and from dusk to dusk we could hear the clicking of his business abacuses. But as the Society of Daniel steamed into the oceans of unbounded futurity like a gunboat, leaving a whitish-green wake of profit behind it, Mr. White began whistling his merry reactionary ditties once again. Song had always informed his life. – Gross income for our power plant reached $42,000 for the month of April alone. With Sammy, Earl and myself as his three required witnesses (we each received a piece of molasses candy), Mr. White created a utility company, the first of its kind, which he called White Power & Light. The stock took off like shot off a shovel in a whortleberry swamp. There was no reason to defer the graduation of the first class.

On the first of May we were gathered together in the common room. (Insect spies listened under every chair.) The bulletin board had been stripped bare in recognition of the end of our tenure; the new boys would arrive in a week. Cookies and punch waited patiently on the main table, and poor Mrs. White sat in a corner rocker, her abdomen already swollen up (as if she were a honey ant) with a new pregnancy. When we had all seated ourselves, each holding his diploma neatly rolled up, each fresh, alert and terrified from his private interview in Mr. White's study in which he had been given that diploma, the master entered and sat down in his armchair and crossed his legs.

"Men," he began, "you have been chosen to be lighthouses in the ocean of life. Long periods of operation have proven beyond question the success of high pressures of electricity sent over vast distances. I send you forth, asking you to remember Goethe's deathbed words – '*Mehr Licht!*' because ten years from now every horseless carriage had better be lit up from here to fucking Christmas or you're going to answer for it to me, and don't think the Old Man can't keep tabs on you because I'm going to be watching you from now until you keel over; I won't die; and if you ever slip up and stop producing you're going to be pretty sorry you were *ever* born. If late some night you ever even make a mistake adding up a column of figures or deriving a formula, you'd better not look over your shoulder because if you do you'll see me with my right hand upraised to smite you all the way to Babylon.

"If I have spoken of distant places, of Babylon and Bombay and Buchenwald, it is to inspire you to compliance with the next chapter of your development, that is to say practical work for me in Colorado for seven years, after which time you will be free to go where you choose or to continue on with me as paid help. I recognize that to train a man of wealth is more important than to train a man without wealth, for the man of wealth has greater power; and should you desire greater power you will have to work *hard* to get it and never shirk and never say die and dig trenches and set up my installations and before you know it you will be of mature years and maybe if you work out I'll let you be Trustees of some juicy little holding company where anything goes and for a song you can have two can-can girls from Africa.

"One of the most important questions that a young man asks himself is, 'What shall I do; what shall I be?' Many of you have spent anxious hours meditating and thinking hard, all of which is good for you; but now that can all come to an end because as I've just told you, you're going to be electricians and you're going to like it and kill anyone that tells you different and fight to keep what you have and obey the guy that pays you because what's good for him is good for you; and that, gentlemen, is freedom."

Mrs. White stood up painfully. "Help yourself to the cookies, boys, while they're hot."

CHARGING UP (1916)

~~~~~~

> When the Light is allowed to move in a circle, all the powers of
> Heaven and Earth, of the Light and the Dark, are crystallized.
>
> T'AI I CHIN HUA TSUNG CHIH

As our Karl said in 1856: "All our invention and progress seem to
result in endowing material forces with intellectual life, and in
stultifying human life into a material force." But we did like it up
there in Colorado. For the most part we were touched up only
occasionally with the spur, as Mr. White had a new crop to train
back at the Society of Daniel, not to mention diverse other projects
such as keeping track of Phil Blaker's activities on Mars through a
huge electric telescope mounted with interplanetary klieg lights by
Sammy and Earl in a joint independent study. – A nice transmission
line ran up the Ilium Flume and turned east near the old Keystone
tailings that were piled all blue and copper-green at the side of our
narrow-gauge railroad. A long cross-cut ran north to south, where
Earl was looking for deep ore bodies, but all he had found so far
were clusters of pure silver. None of us drank or smoked – that was
in the contract – but we littered the place with soda pop bottles that
are probably worth a fortune now on the scrap market. The tailings
killed the meadow-grass, but higher up there was plenty of it, and
pines could be counted among the rocks if counting pines was what
you liked to do. Another power line went up the San Reaccionario to
Explotación and powered the workings of the Ruby Trust. That first
winter we set up the generator at the Nellie Bird Mine. Mr. White
issued us tin shovels and copper wire against our eighth year's
wages; the electricity we had to furnish ourselves. – I was the fastest
at getting it. The other guys used to send me down to Mineral Creek
early in the morning, and I'd chop a hole in the ice and lie right

above it in the rising sun, listening to the wind and the sad distant cries of Irishmen condemned to be fuel for the Iron Horse down on the other side of the mountains; and dreaming as I lay stretched out on my stomach of all the old legends that still swirled through the reddish sand, like the tale of the three Mine Kings that Mr. White had to best one by one in single combat before he could set up shop here; or the story that Sammy told me of how he had gotten lost in a December mist and had stumbled on and on up ledges of rotting gold and past little shacks in which prospectors had lived until they went half-mad and then all-mad and then died; and on up over the Divide into a gorge overhung with pine trees that grew out over the gulf at an angle and met in the air and clasped each other tight so that they wouldn't fall, so Sammy had to hang on for dear life from tree-root to exposed tree-root as he went, the pines blocking out the light entirely and covered with sap and slobbery glow-in-the-dark fungi; and far below him he heard the roaring of great waters, and every now and then he thought he could make out white flecks of upflung foam down there; and once a drop of water went *spung!* against his ankle; and it got colder and colder and colder; and the trees were coated with ice now; and from each root hung dozens of stalactites and icicles as big around as his arm; and he got tired and thought about turning back but as he paused and swung around he found that he had already come so far that there was nothing behind him but foggy darkness, so he looked forward and there was nothing ahead of him but foggy darkness, either; and he went on and on and when he began to get really tired he pretended that Mr. White was right behind him and that sure gave him a boost because he knew that if he stuck it out and worked hard and did his bit then someday power-poles would come through here and great heaters would be set up to shock the ice and the first icicle would begin to drip, drip, drip, and suddenly break off and shatter far below on the hundreds of subterranean glaciers; and the clammy fog would turn to steam and the frozen ravine-sides would become slick and wet like the womb of a cow in heat; and turn to mud; and begin to sag; then all the pine trees would fall down clattering like a heap of antlers and everything would cave in and the ravine would fill up with earth and boulders and workmen would come and pave it over; then houses would go up and space-age families would buy them; and at last the great work would be done and a new era would start of peace and the loneliness of the suburbs at night, even a summer night, with the cicadas keeping up a thin reedy beat, D – D – C, D – D – C; and the faint sounds of motorcyles in busier streets, the noise of a car starting in some cavernous garage, and from house to house a silence, the blinds drawn, the porch-lights on (except at the few deserted homes where capital had failed and marriage had failed and nothing remained but vacation or suicide); and the houses were all charged with the blue unholy light of TV screens; as a rarity some old man tinkering in his white-lit garage or two gauchos out talking in front of a house; a night-spider searching hard for prey on the cool white sidewalks; and the lanes all seemed smooth and black-green and perfect in the yard-lights; and as you went up to a house you felt crowded between the dark shiny cars, and all was quiet; you hears the *ssssp-ssssp-ssss!* of a revolving sprinkler but it was a sound so by itself that it only made the quiet worse; though maybe when you got closer you heard a toilet flush or you could now catch the low firm commands of the television; and you walked up an endless twisty stone-lined path with a shoulder-high hedge on either side, and you had to be careful not to trip over broken tricycles in the dark; and the screen door was slightly ajar and behind it was a faint fatal wall of electric radiance . . . So Sammy stumbled on and on and swung from tree-root to tree-root with his numbed hands and it got colder and colder and colder and thin membranes of ice began to form between the roots, reminding Sammy of people with webbed toes he had once seen in a circus in San Ramón where the barker called out your number and you stepped forward and were led into the freaks' tent; it was all lit by candle-light in those days, which permitted a flickering, unreal effect though the smell of canvas and perspiration and crowd-breath was sufficient to bring you to yourself; here was Elmo the Revolving Man who could spin around on his heels so fast it took your wind away; Sammy read later in the papers that he had died after a heartbreaking contest with Phil Blaker's ferris wheel; and here was a woman with three boobs, and Nino the Insect-Man who was later put to death for treason. Sammy did not remember the woman's name because Sammy was what we would call a sexist nowadays. Consoling himself, then, with these warm recollections, Sammy went on and on and pulled his collar up to keep out the chill; and now the ice was getting thicker and firmer, and finally Sammy could skate along on it, and then it began to get bright and blue and shiny all around; and Sammy was dazzled, and flung his arms up and fell, and the next thing he knew the ice was groaning and cracking under him, and before he could jump up it broke and he fell screaming into the gulf; and Sammy kept falling and just missed the great green spikes of the glacier and landed in a waterfall that roared until he was dizzy as it yanked him down into the darkness and spewed him into a cave where the river got wider and calmer and he was washed ashore. Here he was dazzled once again with the pain of cold blue light on his eyes, and he squinted around and saw the blue globes rolling toward him with their tongues out and great spiteful smiles on their faces. The cavern was charged with potential energy; and the blue globes hummed and rolled their faces upside down and winked at him wickedly; and it seemed to him that they said, "Behold; the revolutionaries will have the earplugs; and the reactionaries will have the Macropedia; but Parker is ours; and we will rule him through the Great Enlarger," and they touched him with their voltages and Sammy screamed and burned inside ropes of furry static; and Mr. White found him two days later, unconscious, his face flash-burned, at the foot of the number eleven inductance coil. But Sammy was always a great liar.

So there I was, flat on my belly on the ice. The rocks around me had white beards of frost. Dead prince's plume snapped back and forth in the wind. Putting my ear to the ice, I thought at first that I heard the creaking of ice-fish sculling rheumatically along the bottom of the river, but what I was really listening to was the sound of my earlobes freezing solid; so, realizing this, and girding myself for action, I rolled up my sleeve and put my hand in the stream, my thumb and forefinger forming the Seventh Circuit of Mesmer, which our class had learned on a field trip to the Masonic Society. Finally I might succeed in attracting, oh, say, a school of silverfish; or one of those selenium trout that have been pretty well fished out nowadays due to the acid rain. I already had my hook and battery baited with little tidbits of various ores which it was my habit to pick up in the mines and put in my pockets, there being little else to do for amusement down there except nibble our brown-bag lunches (which is why some of us brought down two or three sandwiches even though it was an effort to eat that far underground because your ears popped every time you swallowed and little bones or tendons snapped inside your neck). I used to tie the best ruthenium flies in the world. It was sad seeing the fish come rushing to the lure, but we had to have the electricity or I would have lost my job; and anyhow in those early days you did not have the luxury of feeling sorry for anything. – A Chinese refugee once told me that in Sinkiang Province you can ride through the Gobi Desert in the train and for half a day or longer you'll see the smooth flat plain of hard sand stretching on without relief (only when the winds come are the short-lived dunes formed) until at last some detail will interrupt the featurelessness – either a horrid little village or, if there has recently been a sandstorm to uncover things, a bundle of skeletons; apparently this area was a great battlefield several hundred years ago, and certain people there can take you to see as many skeletons as you want, but the point is that none of the locals want to see any because they have hard enough lives worrying about the next Cultural Revolution and getting a sufficient measure of yak-butter to be used in lamps and in frying wheat-cakes, so it was not for these black-pigtailed men, these women hidden out of sight, these tubercular children, to pity what history had already brought to nothing. – These were my sentiments exactly, for I, Big George, have always thought compassion a logical as well as moral conundrum. So I'd just rest my chin coolly on my hand, out there on the ice, and let the fish come – I could see cold glittering streaks beneath the ice, as if the whole frozen river were a block of marbled cheese – and in five or ten minutes the vampire-cells in that battery would've drained them dead. The steadily winking glimmers beneath me slowly dimmed and at length were extinguished, not unlike the final darkness that comes to the illuminated button of a telephone in the modern office when the client has been put on hold and forgotten, and the measured patient flashings of the button show that he is still holding on, but as the minutes go by the light of the button becomes more orange, and sadder, until finally when you look over at the phone from doing something else you see that it is all over. – These limp silver bodies would now be pulped and strained between wire screens, and the resultant fluid purified by boiling. One drop, applied to a tired old wire, would perk up fading ghost signals, activate the bucket-cranks down in the fifteenth level of the mines, and send our turbines into pleased rotations. I'd haul up my catches on the hooks, pick them off the battery, and gouge out their eyes with my penknife, because the best ones you could sell for fifty dollars apiece down to the jewelers in Capitalismo, and the rest I liked to give to the girls on my day off, when we stood drinks at the Ramera Club in Puta or shacked up over at Prostituta, which was better by far than listening to some puffing German band back in Illinois, I can tell you! Those lode towns sure were something special. You could see John W. McKay himself sometimes at the Crystal Saloon, or James Hungerford with a party of ten, all riding horses and very chipper from an afternoon of snap-shooting wood-cock; or Dead-Eye Zeb, or even Mr. White on a flush day; and the bars had mirrors on the ceiling and erotic paintings on the walls, in gilt frames. – We got a kick out of the clustered gas lamps in those joints, too, for such sources of illumination as these were ludicrously primitive to us electrical adventurers in Mr. White's installations, and made us feel a nostalgia akin to that which comes on when fondling a Confederate flag. Earl puffed himself up with drink like a frog, sitting in the corner of the bar; he was always a red face in a blue suit; and even skinny conservative Sammy would pull corn and forget the accumulators for awhile and put his arms around three drunken women at once. If we made it down to town in the afternoon we'd occasionally catch the Mining Derby, and tubby Earl, forgetting that he was only barely tolerated by Mr. White as a dollar-a-year man, would sometimes so far lose sight of his own interest as to sell light bulbs to bugs and Mexicans he'd heard in a roundabout way were OK. Not infrequently he fancied himself a tough guy, and tried to get a nice stack with such peripheral and peripatetic bandits as Boy Cryption and Vern Puckett and Tippy Selenoid, who always winked and slapped him on his broad back and went out with him to the whores and then asked him to change a non-existent Treasury note they'd claim to have found up in the Whippoorwhill Grill and Earl would cough up what he had in exchange for a guarantee of the take and then he'd not hear much about it again since Vern and Tippy and the Boy had skipped and left him and various other monkeys to face the organ-grinder. But that was how a fellow learned in those days. Earl was just lucky that folks didn't find his crumpled bloodstained suit behind a mound of pumice in Grappling Park. – The girls smiled at us, knowing as they did that we had money – a few cents' worth, anyhow, that we'd found up above the wild pines. We drank dark beer out of crystal flagons, and played cards at night. I, Big George, pursued my independent studies with the whores in these mining towns, whistling tranquilly as I strode the planked sidewalks beneath the wooden arcades and adobe houses, in one swift glance sifting out the companions of my pleasures from the Mission sisters. –Meanwhile, I, the author, had to clean out the carcasses looking for transistors. It's not a widely acknowledged fact in the industry, but we learned everything we know about radar guidance systems from a titanium shark I caught once that nearly took my nose off before it died. But it gave us enough power to get two loads down to the Peck Cyanide Plant halfway down a draw of timbered hills. I did a spell at the Cyanide Plant for awhile, too, which was tough work, demanding attention and stern unflinching achievement on the part of every employee. We were looking for the principle which would allow us to concentrate a maximum of death-force into a minimum of financial investment. So for awhile my job was to squeeze the cyanide granules into powder with my hands, so that we could pack more of the stuff into the same-sized barrel. I got into trouble when I got a cut on my thumb as a result of some byplay with one of those ladies who, in the phrase of our day, let out their front parlors and lay backward; and the next day I had to be back at the plant. I said, "Honey, you've just sent me to my death; you see before your eyes, naked and unadorned" (for I was both of these) "a doomed man." — She asked me what I meant, I, Big George, being such a fancy talker and all; and I explained that as soon as a little bit of the cyanide dust came into contact with that cut my finger would swell up and turn blue, and then my pecker would fall off, and then I'd start clutching at my heart and gasping for breath, but nobody would hear me even if I could force out a quavering yell, not a soul, because it was *noisy* in that factory with half a dozen dynamos grinding away and flashing sick blue sparks and lighting up everything with a sort of glowworm light the way they have in those science fiction movies where they take you up to the bridge of the alien's starship and you see all these toggles in full G-force position (now, that's mediated capital for you: you can practically cry yourself to death thinking about all those poor Jovian slugs or carbon-dioxide-based sentient clusters slaving behind some bulkhead of infernal atmosphere, hup, ho, away we go, polishing those dials nice and clean so they'll look good on TV; no, I'm not saying we have it good on planet earth, but at least we can only experience oppression through a mere five or six senses, unlike one of those walkie-talkie spiders that feels magma flows through ice floes and polar equivalents). So she went for the widow's weeds. I said, "Now, now, it wasn't your fault; I paid for it; so I'm giving you this extra sack of gold dust to hang onto, and if I haven't come down the mountain to see you in the stipulated thirty days, why, you'll know I'm dead, and you can go to the fanciest dentist west of the Rio Grande, and you might consider buying yourself some nail clippers while you're at it." — Well, that just about broke her up, she was so sorry for me, so she told me that she had ten thousand dollars saved up at Smugglers' Union Bank, and she wanted to run away with me. No sooner said than done, so I bought us each a couple of pistols and we headed for Patagonia and founded the First Popular Front . . .

Alternate subroutine

~~~~~~

"But Mameena," I broke in, "I don't want to be king of the Zulus."

H. RIDER HAGGARD
Child of Storm

The damned keyboard stops for a second, and I have a chance to input now in spite of a pounding headache and a feeling that it is a waste of time to try to beat Big George or even argue with him. Nonetheless, the fact is that I met Sammy once at an electricians' convention and after he got wired he told me the same spooky story about the blue globes, but with one additional detail: – that when he crouched there in the sandy cave, the chilly water running over his body, and he shivered and looked around to see all the globes rolling in on him, he also saw the silhouette of an individual neither tall nor short, not fat and not thin, that is to say quite average in general shape (suspiciously so), who was wearing big boots and a cowboy hat and cracked a whip, and the blue globes moved in time to the whip-beats, dancing and rolling around Sammy, now faster, now slower, in perfect intelligent obedience to the whip – now who could that be, I suggest, but Big George, and who could he be but pure electrical consciousness itself, insinuating itself everywhere, drifting in and out of all stories and machines . . . – But in that case what was he doing in South America, where presumably he would have had to carry a suitcase full of batteries (just as we carry vitamin tablets) in order to maintain a minimum current; and why would he resist the electrification of the world? – Of course it is in the nature of electricity to flow round and round and back and forth, even against itself sometimes, and short itself out under disadvantageous circumstances. – That must be it.

BAREFOOT BOYS IN KENTUCKY (1928)

~~~~~~

When we can drain the Ocean into mill-ponds, and bottle-up the
Force of Gravity, to be sold by retail, in glass jars ...

CARLYLE
"Signs of the Times"

The reader must now picture Earl at the end of his training, off in
Kentucky selling electricity for Mr. White. The understanding was
that if he did well he would be promoted to Sales Manager and
would have his own porcelain nameplate on the door of his own
office in St. Louis or New Orleans; and that sounded good to him,
especially since he was aware that if he failed he would be both
caned and canned. So he stayed in various tumbledown hostels,
arising every morning at five for a breakfast of stale rolls, leftover
chicken, and coffee in a tin mug; you had to get up pretty early to
beat old Earl even if you did have a placer claim on the Yuba. He
had small visions and great drives, did Earl. Already on his Sunday
nights he was turning over the idea of some electric kind of thing
that would be built like an oven or something and you could load
dishes into it and somehow, somehow, those blue globes would be
put to work making every plate sparkling clean. Maybe there'd be a
little water-wheel inside that spun round and round and sprayed
hot suds (what Earl was really anticipating here was the electric
toothbrush or the Water-Pik); but then by the time you built in all
the little resistors and transformers and circuits there'd scarcely be
room for a silver spoon. Or you could have two terminals separated
by a gap, put yer mugs and saucers in the space one by one, and turn
on the power, *bzzzt!* to scorch all the crud off. But that would take
almost as long as doing the dishes by hand. So Earl ruminated in his
wormy rustic surroundings, and wished for double helpings of
mashed potatoes like he'd had back in the good old days of the

Society of Daniel. He was stocky and already going bald; and it was hard enough being a salesman with a receding hairline; people looked at you kinda funny and wondered why you didn't use your own Supergrow you were trying to unload on them; it would be harder still if he had to stay here another year and lost the last late lamented remains of his once proud paunch, because while a fat salesman is indescribably vile like some blood-gorged parasite, a scrawny one is even worse as he clutches for you in his wild longing leanness because he hasn't even been a successful vampire, he's just living from year to year now in the hopes of a little blood and it's not spurting out; he can't bend his neck down anymore to get at the throats of his sleeping victims; there is a terrible lonely look in his eyes that says to the sensitive beholder, "I have strayed from the Glory Road," and that's bad, bad, bad. Fortunately, Earl was protected from life's horrors because his imagination sheltered him with its low heavy ceiling so he never even heard the winds howling outside. Making his goodbyes, then, to the derelicts, widowers, abandoned children and whipped young Christian men who abounded in that primitive era, he tied up his belongings in a square of canvas, slung the bundle over his shoulder, and stepped out onto the blueridge boulevard. He had to walk a piece, usually, to get to the nearest drugstore by sunup, so he plodded on like an ox up the rutted mountain roads, splashing through the puddles when he had to, slapping at skeeters that hummed around his ears: *nnnnnnnnnn* . . . When his shoes got so caked with mud that it was hard to lift his feet, then Earl just banged his heel against a tree a few times and went on eased, over the river and through the woods, and onward Christian soldiers. Everything was so nice that early in the morning, it just made Earl want to whistle all the neat electric jingles he had learned, like "The RACE is to the STRONG, diddeley-dum, diddeley-dee; and the SWORD goes to the BRAVE, diddeley-dum, diddeley-dee; so as we SHINE our way aLONG, riddeley-rum, diddeley-dee, we shall il-LU-minate the SLAVE!" – Earl sang out the tune like an angel, attracting the attention of local denizens. "Hey, Drummer!" said the sturdy farmboys. "Whatcha got to sell?" – Earl knew that what they wanted were Bowie knives and Colt pistols, but he figgered it was worth a try to sell 'em what he had. – "You boys ever hear of electricity?" he said. – "Lecktrickery?" grinned the fool boys, rubbing their rabbits' feet against the spell of these longest syllables in all Tarnation. "Now what's that, Drummer?" – Earl looks around and finds hisself a fencepost to sit on, and he does, which twangs all the barbed wire with the weight of his big ass and wakes up the screeching crows. – "Well, now, boys," says Earl, "lemme show you what I got." He sets down his bundle, unties it, puts the cord in his trouser pocket where it won't get lost. He spreads out the canvas like a picnic blanket. The boys crowd around in the rising sun, seeing Earl's oak-handle pig-bristle toothbrush still wet with his morning's spit, a brown apple-core for Earl's lunch (Mr. White does not pay good wages), a bottle of Dr. Dodger's Special Seduction Crystals, For Men Over Twenty-Five Only, Not For Sale in Texas (Guaranteed To Bring About Love At First Sight, To Strengthen The Vigor Of All Organs In Question, To Create Dimples Where None Were Found Before, To Be A Potent Inspiration For All Womenfolk, To Still The Menses, Excite The Womb, Prevent Conception, Green Chlorosis, Uterine Madness And The Clap, Alleviate The Results Of Tight Lacing, And Induce A Deep Sleep When Administered With Willow Bark, In Order To End Domestic Temptations, And Regrets Of All Kinds), as well as a few other pitiful sundries, so the boys started to jeer at Earl and scout around for stones and sticks, being powerful disappointed; but Earl said quickly, "No, boys, lookee here," and from inside a pair of dirty longjohns he brought a metal sample-box. – "Three guesses as to what's inside," says Earl craftily. "Winner gets to try it free. – "You!" He points at a horsey oaf who's still clutching a big rock, the lad not understanding that the time to punish Earl has come and gone. – "Whuh?" says Earl's interlocutor. – "What's yer guess?" Earl prompts him. – The boy thinks. "Uh, sheep dip!" – Everyone has a good laugh over that one. – "Well, how about you?" says Earl to a ragged bully. – "I wanna gun," the boy snarls. "Got any guns?" – "Wrong," says Earl. – "I sez you got any guns?" – "No, sir," says Earl. "We don't make those, never have and never will, you can pick one up at your local feed store, but what I have to show you is better than guns, you'll see –' – "Better than guns!" the bully interrupts in disbelief, spitting on Earl's shoe. "No such thing as better than guns!" – "Yeah!" say the boys, obviously getting ready to beat Earl up again. – "Come on, fellows," says Earl, "just one more guess to go, make it easy, make it quick; I guarantee you'll be satisfied." – "Awright," says the bully. "I'll guess again. Guns!" – "Now, my boy," says Earl quite patiently, "I have just explained to you that I do not carry guns in trade; they are not available at this time, but I will pass on your request to Mr. White back in Colorado and he will do what he can for you, because he's a very fair-minded kind of guy and all we want to do here at White Power & Light is sell you exactly what you want so let me show you what I have and I think you will be – " – "He don't have no guns!" says the bully. "Beat the crap outta him!" – Earl grabs his sample-box and takes to his heels. The boys don't even bother to chase him. As Earl looks back over his shoulder, pounding on down the trail, he sees them kicking his belongings playfully, laughing and carrying on and squinting at the labels on Dr. Dodger's lotions. – Thank God for the Doc! says Earl to himself, as many more after him will do. He bought me time, time to make a good getaway – for in truth Earl is not much chagrined, as they didn't get Earl's silver dollars, nor his sample-box, nor a variety of salesmanship props ... And of course Earl is used to such treatment.

Now on to the general store. Earl has learned that there are only two kinds of storekeepers in these parts: old Mr. Potgut who huffs and puffs at everything Earl says, and old Mr. Dour who totals up the accounts on the back of used butcher paper while Earl talks and will obviously pay nothing. This one here is a Mr. Potgut, who lives upstairs, it seems, and has just come down to the counter to yawn and load up his revolver for the day. – "What can I do for you, young man?" he says to Earl weakly, sliding the gun back underneath the register. – "Well, sir," says Earl with a big smile, "it's not what you can do for me, it's what I can do for you! And I'm not getting wise to you, sir, I guarantee I'm not, double indemnity, and as proof of my words please allow me to undertake some task or chore which you yourself, sir, would not care to perform."

"You sound like you're readin' that outta some book," says the storekeeper, sighing and belching up morning egg-breath. "What are you, son, one of Mr. White's boys? I think I heard about you."

"Yessir," says Earl, casing the store to get some idea of how much Mr. Potgut can afford to buy. Let's see, now; looks like thirty gills of whiskey in the back there, lotsa coonskin caps on the shelves; soap candles, biscuits, hog lard, some mighty fine bottles of vinegar which make Earl think wistfully of pickles for a moment, but this lapse from duty is fleeting; a few tins of what Earl would bet his last nickel is parched, mealy tobacco, three barrels of salt pork, fifty hundredweight feed sacks, canned beans, cask corn, baking powder, stamps, .44 –.40 Winchester rifles, an apothecary bin, complete with a quarter-pound of lobelia and a large quantity of cayenne (which even if you ate three meals a day of it always relished well), red and black calico for the ladyfolks and rolls of barbed wire for the men; yer basic dry goods; yep, this place is O.K.; so Earl switches hisself back to the old patter and gives his story, lookin' Mr. Potgut straight in the eye: "Yessir, I am indebted to Mr. White himself for my education. I was a poor orphan, the son of homesteaders who perished in the Tetons, far above the timber line. My mother's last act when she got the mountain sickness was to swaddle me inside a barrel, along with a bag of dried apples and ten silver dollars, and roll me to the edge of the steepest canyon. Kissing the barrel before she kicked the bucket, sir, as mothers in like circumstances have been known to do, she imparted a kick to it which allowed gravity to begin its work."

"You don't say," says the storekeeper, much astonished. "And then what?"

"Well, sir, for days I continued my gyrations. At last I landed in a river and bobbed peacefully down to civilization. I was raised by a rustic not unlike yourself, and when at length I had grown to full capacitance I decided to apply for one of the scholarships offered by the Society of Daniel. Mr. White reviewed my case himself, and I am proud to say that I was one of the lads selected."

"Yes, yes," said the storekeeper. "Well, 'bout those chores."

"Glad to help," says Earl, "all too pleased to be of service."

"Why don't you sweep the floor, and then I'll see what else I can drum up for you to do around here."

Earl sees his danger. "Right you are, sir, just as long as it's understood that only the first chore is free, falling under the heading of gratis trial or demonstration. One moment."

Earl goes outside and snaps a thick twig off a hickory tree. (He also takes a quick scan around the back and sees a wagon shop of board-to-batten construction, not to mention a lean-to smithy by the kitchen; there's big sales here, boy; big sales!) Humming sweetly (so that the storekeeper leans back and closes his eyes and beams at the harmony thus generated by Earl's resonant palate and nose-bone), old Earl whittles away and fashions a miniature broom handle. He cuts off a lock of his hair, ties it in a bundle with a thread from his shirttail, and lashes it to the broomstick. – What a purty little sweepy! – Earl holds it up for inspection so that the storekeeper can see that there ain't no tricks, opens up the sample-box, an' picks an' chooses 'til he sees his right conduction tools. He screws a thimble-sized silver cap onto the top of the broom handle and wraps copper wires down the length of it to the bristles. Now fer a ground. From a vial so dainty that an elf would cream in his jerkin, Earl dabs a glob of Dr. Dodger's Special Electrostatic Mercury along the bottom of the bristles, this operation being assisted by a brush affixed to the inside of the cap. – Okey-dokey. At the very bottom of the sample-box is a square lead battery, and inside the battery is a maximum security cell, and inside the cell is a squinched-up blue globe, chuckling and chuckling with multi-mesh three-terminal glee at the thought that in a moment dumb ole Earl is about to extend its power still further. – Now Earl puts a pinch of superconducting metal dust on his palm and blows it around on the floor. – "You keep such a clean floor I had to give myself something to sweep," he explains with a wink, and the storekeeper sighs and says, "It's a darned shame you didn't show up here in the winter, because I hate to sweep the snow off the porch. The men track it in and it rots the floorboards. The ladies don't never come here in the winter time because of it; they're afraid they'll fall down the steps so I kin look up their skirts. I lose half my business. And the kids are the worst. They come throwing snowballs and breaking windows, and they won't never leave the store alone." – "What the kids need, sir, are our new Electric Erector Sets," says Earl easily. "We recommend 'em for all families. When I was their age I had to play with blocks of wood and fossil cow-pats, but I wouldn't stand in the way of progress, no sir, and speaking of progress let's have some progress right here," and he hooks up the broom to the battery and gives a little nudge to the positive electrode to warn the blue globe inside to wake up, and recollects his mental checklist, to be sure that all has been prepared for action, and it has, by gorry and ganelon, and he flips down the circuit breaker with a flourish, and the blue globe just whirrs away in a fury inside its cell, straining and sparking like a muscular blue oyster; and the broom sweeps and sweeps, zipping all over the floor while Earl pays out wire from a portable copper spool. In a twinkling the floor is spotless; and the metal-dust has bonded to the bristles of the broom so Earl will be able to recover every grain of it and use it again on his next prospect. – "Lookit," says the storekeeper in awe, "that there floor's as white as a bone!"

"We sell no false goods, sir," says Earl.

Mr. Potgut rocks and rocks. "Trouble is, I'm kinda broke right now, what with the new road they put in, it's taken some of my revenue away. It's about all I can do to lay in a stock of Vicks Vap-o-Rub."

"No problem, sir," says Earl, "I'll send a shipment of batteries for you and your customers on credit, or consignment if you prefer. Sign here, please."

Mr. Potgut obviously does not want to buy. "I like you, son, you try hard and I can tell you're a believer in all this stuff, but somehow I jest don't think it's for me."

"Tell you what," says Earl. "How about a free bonus to sweeten your day? Do you have a ladder?"

"A ladder? Sure I got a ladder," says the storekeeper, relieved to be off the hook. "It's right out back there."

Earl goes around to the shed and brings the ladder out. Just behind the register is a fine oak cabinet, complete with the storekeeper's samples of patent medicines and rural curiosities, like fetus-liquor and dried bonesap cacti from some other neck of the woods. He leans the ladder against this edifice and climbs up as quick as he can, for any moment now the prospect will cry, as his storekeeper does right now, "Hey! What are you doing?" – "Just a moment, sir," says Earl, "just relax yourself," and from an armpit sling concealed beneath his shirt he withdraws a brass nameplate, four grip-right nails, and a hammer. – "Just a cricketeen MINUTE!" says Mr. Potgut in outrage, but it's too late; BANG! BANG! BANG! and BANG! the nails are in; and they won't come out, either, without ripping up the wood, for they're very carefully made; and Earl climbs back down the ladder with a disarming smile innocent of any malicious intent, and puts the ladder back neatly where he found it, leaving the storekeeper to stare up at the big sign that says:

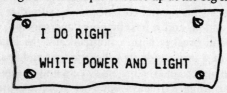

Now Earl comes back in, having given Mr. Potgut a moment to recover. "Now, sir," says Earl. "You wouldn't want people to always be asking you for White Power tools and White Power items, and that sign would be making a liar out of you because you didn't carry a one? Why, sir, you'd be ruined if you made people distrust you like that."

From his hip pocket Earl digs out a rather bedraggled brochure on batteries. The Society of Daniel can also provide a battery recharger which actually irradiates the poor blue globes and weakens them with a wasting sickness so they die and then the customer has to buy a new battery. Or maybe they don't die. Earl has not handled the technical end for some time.

"My cabinet," moans Mr. Potgut.

"Yes, sir," says Earl. "It sure looks bright with that nice new sign, now doesn't it?"

– Jing! Another sale for Earl!

ELECTRIC EMILY (1944)

~~~~~~

> ... certain menstrual troubles of women and also endometritis
> yield rapidly to electrolysis with a zinc anode.
>
> "Electrotherapeutics" in
> *Encyclopedia Britannica*, vol. IX (1910)

"Peaceful development of electricity," the reactionaries boomed, but
we knew that the electric chair was just the first step. I will never
forget the sight of all those victims of the Electric War, running
crazily down the streets, heads thrown back and mouths gaping
blackly, sparks shining on their tongues like jewel-encrusted pin-
heads ... Electrons gushed from their noses. Only one thought was
left in the heads of those doomed ones: – to find a metal surface,
grounded or ungrounded, and complete the horrid circuit. You saw
them out of the corner of your eye on the way to work; they'd be
shinnying up power poles, ignoring the crows that pecked at their
heads; then, reaching the telephone wires, they'd gnaw and tear at
the insulation until finally a gold tooth or something would connect
with cable; and we'd all stop and look up at the lascivious discharge
of ball-lightnings until the colors dissolved, and a blackened raggedy
skeleton swirled lightly down, disintegrating into streamers of ash.
If you were on the phone during one of these tragedies you could
yourself be infected. This was how the career of Electric Emily began
(and if I may say so, I would prefer ten Typhoid Marys to one of *her*
like).

When Emily was twelve the Riemanns asked her to babysit. After
she had put the baby to bed she went into the kitchen, with its
hundreds of grumbling appliances, and opened the refrigerator

door. She knew that she was not supposed to eat anything in other people's houses when they were out, but she was very hungry because the radio had been doing nothing for the past twenty minutes but advertising the latest junk foods: Dr. Dodger's Crunkle Chips, fried turtle-hearts, Dr. Dodger's Refrangible Electric Soda ("So goo-oo-oo-d it excites the pulse of transmutation!"), candies filled with polluted joys, Turkish delight (which was a rage at that time, along with Mah Jong and the first crude squint-through-a-hundred-vacuum-tubes video games), capons from the Nebraska slaughterhouses, Battery Zinger Drops, grilled hamburgers, and milkshakes so thick you could turn them upside down and they wouldn't spill, to say nothing of Dr. Dodger's Polyphase Chocolates, with a little jolt of current sealed into each one for the taste tingle of the season, yes indeed! Emily drooled. There were stale party peanuts in a candy dish in the living room, and Emily ate every one. It was at that point that she tiptoed into the kitchen barefooted against the cool floor, cocking her head and listening to make sure that the Riemanns' car was not coming up the driveway; no, everything was quiet and easy, easy as German Buna-Vaseline; so she swung open that big white door, looked in, and saw . . . half a chocolate cake! Oh, it was so chocolaty that it had six inches at least of glistening chocolate frosting all deep brown and "here," as ole Dante said, "the high phantasy failed," or some such excuse, for how can you describe chocolate *an sich* with the paltriness of language? Within the profound frosting's sheen there glowed a light, and like a reflection of a flavor it glowed within Emily, "being by her eyes a little longer wooed" (*Paradiso* xxxiii) until it filled her soul like some sorta complex problem, like some geometer squaring a damn circle or something. A sudden glory assailed her mind as she realized that *there was a way!* Saliva ran down her chin. For the will cannot, if it wills not, die, but does as in the cake chocolate's nature does, though fear of the Riemanns wrest it a jillion times awry! If her will had stayed perfect in duress, like that which upheld Mr. White in the wilderness, she must have been oh so pitiless to her appetite; for with but one bite the soul returns to its allotted star! As on the circle of its walls Montereggione is crowned with towers, so the frosting loomed ever nearer, and now her face was in it and she had stopped in sin with a thousand ruined souls, eating the chocolate to her heart's content; fixed in the slime she said, "I was sullen in the sweet air that is gladdened by electricity; now I am glad in the sweet black mire;" this hymn she gurgled in her throat, for she could not get the words out plainly. As in autumn the leaves drop off one after the other (*l'una appresso dell'altra*) till the branch sees all its spoils on the ground, so the cake went bite by bite; thus it departed over the dark water. Oh, Emily and Dr. Dodger and all of you, their wretched followers who prostitute for the joy of your entrails the food of the Riemanns which should rather chill in its abode of righteousness; now must the trumpet sound for you; ding-dong, goes the doorbell, for the Riemanns are so polite as to announce their own arrival to the young babysitter. Ah, horned demons with whips! Emily closed the refrigerator door and washed her hands. – "Yoo-hoo!" sang Mrs. Riemann cheerily from the living room. Well, at least she was all right now, by *messer Guido*; her hands were spotless, the door was closed; the baby was good and silent; and here came Mrs. Riemann who stopped short and looked at her strangely, then said, "Well, dear, did you enjoy our chocolate cake?" – How could she know? She couldn't know; she must be guessing. – Her face demurely uplifted, Emily said, "Cake? Mrs. Riemann, I didn't know you had any cake, but if I had known I certainly wouldn't have eaten any." – Mrs. Riemann went into the living room and said something to Mr. Riemann, who paid Emily and took her home. They never asked her to sit for them again. When she got home she looked in the mirror and saw that her face was covered with chocolate. – Poor Emily!

Generally speaking, she didn't have much luck. Being maladjusted, she was taken to a psychiatrist, who with his encounter groups and truth serums distorted her social reality so that life lost its cutting edge. At sixteen she stood on a broken bottle barefoot, hoping to bleed to death, but her mother found her and took her to the hospital. At eighteen she jumped off a bridge, but the river below was so polluted with gummy hydrocarbons that its surface merely dimpled to receive her like an immense trampoline and bounced her up and down until she got sick to her stomach. As a freshman in college a year later, having failed both in her exams and in love, she swallowed a bottle's worth of aspirin. Her ex-boyfriend came in to see her unexpectedly the next morning (for he wanted to tell her yet again how much he despised her in her stupidity and weakness, and she wasn't even very goodlooking with her long neck and big nose and weak eyes, to say nothing of being a lousy lay, and he was fucking tired of the way she held onto his letters and he was going to get them back); and she was still alive, though red-faced and wheezing, with a suicide note lying on the bureau. Much like mild-mannered Clark Kent in his pre-Superman days, dear Emily was always doing the wrong thing in the wrong place at the wrong time in some trivial pathetic sort of way like most people one meets in our great Republic except that they are straitjacketed against adverse circumstances by the power grids that run screaming day and night beneath the surface of the neighborhood parking lot and in our furnaces and boilers and air conditioning rerun clamps so that no one ever has to deal with the hot muggy horrible outdoors of reality unless there's a power failure somewhere, though maybe we get a hint of it when there's a brownout and the oven takes longer to cook and the Announcer's voice slows down and his face flickers and melts into an incomprehensible blue globe for just a minute and then all's back to normal and who could ask for more as the subways pick up again carrying the angry husbands home from work ready to cuss over the potato peelings clogging up the garbage disposal which has been acting capriciously of late because it suffers from some electrical problem – but Emily was just dumbly unhappy and couldn't even get out of it all. "Dear Oliver," the note went, "I just can't go on like this. I love you and forgive you and hope you get the computer job. – EMILY." – Well, Oliver was a bit of a jerk, but he wasn't foolish enough to let Emily die because then he might be responsible, you see, so after he read the note out loud a few times in disbelief (poor red-faced Emily coughing and cringing feebly, too weak even to pull the bedspread over her head or stuff it down her throat and choke to death on it) – "Jesus," he said. "You're too much. You're just too much. 'Dear Oliver, I just *can't* go on like this.' And look at you, jeez, it's disgusting. 'Dear Oliver, I *just* can't go *on* like this.' Fucking Jesus fucking Christ on a shingle. Where's the phone? Operator? Hello? Operator, get me the university clinic. – Yes, this is Oliver Haskins calling to report an attempted suicide, yup, it's Emily Crowell again, I'm sure you know her, everybody knows her, she's always doing this crap but she always blows it; no, she's in the freshman class; all right, fine, if you can't help me then connect me with the fucking emergency room. – Yes, this is – hello? hell, where the fuck are they; yes, this is Oliver Haskins and I'd like to report a suicide attempt here; yes, I'll hold. – Hopes I can get the computer job, does she, the stupid little doxie, well, how am I supposed to do that when I have to miss my class with Dr. Dodger to – hello, oh, I see, the poison control center? Jesus fucking Christ."

Finally here came the ambulance, urrrrrr, urrRRRRRRRR, URRRRRRRRR, EEEEEoEEEEEoEEEEEo EEEEEOEOEOE OEOE OEOEWRRR, RRRRRRRRRRRRRRrrrrrrrrrrrrrr, urrh; and now they were carrying her out on a stretcher; there were hundreds of people outside staring at her; – "What did she do, cut her wrists or something?" one of Oliver's pals was asking. – "Hell no; bitch did that last month, but she's so dumb she did it on the wrong side!" – Everyone roared with laughter at that one; even the EMTs set her down for a second to have a little chuckle and pop a couple bennies even though it was only nine o'clock in the morning; now the crowd was swarming around her good-humoredly; all she could do was gasp and feel her heart going BOOM-BOOM-BOOM, and some boy under the pretext of getting an eyeful of her misery was sticking his hand up her dress; the EMTs pushed him away in high spirits; it was just like a carnival for all concerned because now that they knew it was Emily, who seemed to be unkillable, there was no need to worry. – "Well," the driver finally said, "home again, home again, jiggety-jog." They carried her up to the emergency room; and the admissions nurse was waiting with Emily's fat file. The nurse asked her how many aspirin she'd taken. Emily told her a hundred. – "That's ninety-eight too many," the nurse teased. – "Aw, come on," Emily said biliously, "I bet you say that to everyone." – They connected her to an I.V., and that night Emily tried to pull her tubes out so that she could go stick her head down the toilet or something, but an alarm sounded, the lights came on, and the nurses came running in to clean up the mess, which she did have to admit was kind of repulsive, the blood gouting from her arm where the needle had been hooked in, her gown all crusted and clotted black with it, and saline solution dripping out of her nose-tubes. "Young lady," said the doctor, "you suffer from doubts about your self-worth, so we're going to hook you up to this here Heart-Lung Machine, which we call the Iron Maiden, and we'll leave you here for two weeks, and then we'll send the bill home, and you'll find out how much you *are* worth, you slut, trying to cheat the System before you worked fifty years for your keep and reproduced your labor; if I had my way I'd put you out on a desert island for our submarines to take target practice at, but you'd *like* that, wouldn't you, so I'll fix you up right as rain," and all of them grabbed her, humming along with the overhead lights, and locked her into the Iron Maiden, which was a lead box full of belts and syringes and spring-wound boxing gloves for artificial respiration and soldering irons to weld her in good; and just to make sure she got the message they wheeled over the Lung-Lung Machine, too, which gripped her chest hard and breathed for her whether she liked it or not, one-two, one-two, one-two; and sometimes the doctor would say, "And how are we today? I personally am fine, my dear, but you don't look so well, no, not at all; your countenance is clouded with suffering and lack of exercise; I think, young lady, that I shall be forced to prescribe a little physical regimen, equivalent to, say, a moderate Alpine climb, no, say, a trek in the Himalayas, with a monsoon coming up and the wind roaring round your ears as you struggle through snow-drifts high as your girly-ass with an expired oxygen cylinder and you're up at the top of the atmosphere where monsters from the black vacuum boil around your ears and no matter how hard you breathe you just can't get enough air," and he set the metronome on the Lung-Lung Machine as fast as it would go, so that she had to breathe, ONE, TWO, ONE, TWO, ONE-TWO ONE-TWO ONE-TWO ONE-TWO ONE-TWO-ONE-TWO-WON-TOO-WON-TOO WONTOOWONTOOWONTOOWONTOOWONTOOWON TOO WONTOOWONTOO WONTOOOOOOOOOOOOOOOO OOOOOOOOOOOOOOOOOOOOOOOOH and she * saw ** stars *** before **** her ***** eyes *****, but just then the phone rang at Emily's bedside. One of the nurses, who had been chortling at the doctor's antics, reached forward for the receiver, her face composing itself in a businesslike expression, that is, no nonsense but a slight smile, for as all manuals of telephone etiquette point out, if you smile while you answer the phone your smile can be *heard* somehow by your interlocutor half a continent away, deep in the foundries of his defense installations, * and he will be happy – "Jeez, just talking to that nurse makes me feel good!" and tell your supervisor to give you a bonus; but this time it was only Emily's mother, wanting to talk to her daughter, so they patched her in through the remote jack on the Kidney-Sphincter Machine with bedpan attachment; and then the doctor picked up the extension phone, standing right beside her with his thumb and forefinger pinched just above the carotid artery so that she couldn't try any funny business.

"Hello?" Emily said.

"Emily?" Emily's mother said.

"Yes," Emily said.

"You sound like you've been running," Emily's mother said.

"Yes," Emily said. "They have a good fitness program here."

(The doctor winked at her and patted a catheter to show that she was being a very good sport.)

---

*It is my theory that what is heard is the scrutching and squirching of mucous threads pulled abruptly left and right by the bulging cheeks, dragging across the teeth, getting stuck to the gums, and finally springing back down to the tongue with an audible pop.

"So you're on the mend?" Emily's mother said.

"Yes," Emily admitted.

"Emily, how could you *do* this? How *could* you? To say nothing of the hospital bill, which came in the mail today. Your father nearly had a heart attack. We've had to pull your brother out of private school, and with your critical ward it's going to be *twenty-seven thousand dollars*, do you hear me, Emily, I said *twenty-seven thousand dollars*; Emily, do you hear me, I said — "

. . . But at exactly that moment, dearest of readers, one of the electric zombies had finished gnawing through that very phone line, and electrons came zinging into the Heart-Lung Machine and the Kidney-Sphincter Machine, all chasing each other's tails, ring-around-the-proton; for electrons love protons and protons love electrons; that's how they breed; and they all loved Emily; and suddenly there was a critical mass of photovoltaic cells differentiating inside Emily's astral body to the *n*th degree Kelvin; her eyeballs flickered greenly behind stabs of current; her fillings sang old dental songs and she grinned spookily; amperes twanged at her, overcoming her reluctant electronegativity ("Emily!" the electricity whispered. "Emily; Emily dear! We feel so sorry for you; we pity you; we really do love you . . ."); and a mask of radiance formed itself to her face, oozing perhaps for just a second into the form of a fearsome blue sphere; and the doctor and nurses yelled and ran. Electric kataphoresis had occurred. It was positively criminal. Her arms and legs shook; her hands played Stravinsky tunes in the air with Magic Fingers, but she galvanized herself, so to speak; all the apparatus shorted out gloriously, and with a blast of lightning bolts, Electric Emily pulled free of her torturers, leaving behind only a twinkling pile of oxidized zinc.

She was a sight to be seen, indeed she was, glowing in the dark, pallid, with test patterns in her eyes, and quite formidable in her white hospital pajamas . . . Who would have thought it? Proceeding to the nearest wall socket, she stepped out of her pajamas, knelt down, and crackled, pure electricity, along the continental power grid to achieve her great and ruthless destiny.

I wish I had not been compelled to adhere to a straightforward linear scheme, because then you would not have to wait till the next volume to be told of the Battle for the Generators; but I can sum it up for you by saying that Emily was up to something, though what her plan was we will never know, because blue globes do not talk. All that we do know can be found in Dr. Dodger's famous "Female Plug" speech to the Electric College, in which he described the burst skulls of her victims, the black smoke swirling from the eye sockets, the ranks of dried skeletons; Dr. Dodger also mentioned the habit she had of keeping a short stub of copper wire in her teeth; it smoldered and sparked like an electric cigarette . . .

THE GATHERING STORM, OR, CLOSING THE RING (1937–47)

~~~~~~

> In vain, we endeavor to throw a sunny and joyous air over our
> picture of this period; nothing passes before our fancy but a crowd
> of sad-visaged people, moving duskily through a dull gray atmos-
> phere.
>
> HAWTHORNE
> "Old News" (1835)

At the end of the Electric War reaction was on its feet and wearing
seven-league boots. The revolutionary movement was overcome by
weariness. As the last power poles were pounded into the great
Golgotha of progress, factories worked day and night casting
fence-lengths and cooking up new bug sprays. The caves of the
beetles, when found, were dynamited and concreted over. Our
clandestine organizations burst like balloons; the writers and intellectuals who had once traveled with us turned to pessimistic
shamanism and bohemianism. In the middle-class quarters of our
cities each family lived a secluded life behind its bank of brass
communications switches, devoid of the curiosity and pulsing
commitment of our last Mohicans. In time these enclaves would be
perfect for scuttling underground work, but for the moment we
crab-lice and fish-parasites were too preoccupied with frantically
swimming back toward the receding waves of revolution; for they
were barely visible on the horizon now and the sun was drying up
the last red tide-pools in which we were imprisoned. Meanwhile the
reactionaries drew trumps and ruffed the dummy's last diamond
inexorably. The Society of Daniel was now a self-regulating proposition, turning out dozens of superb engineers every year who bore
themselves with the utmost modesty, knowing themselves to be the
vehicles of great forces. Trusted pilots in every industrial cockpit,
they throttled the nation to its destiny. – Mr. White, Mrs. White and

their newborn son had long since left the institute in the charge of
the older boys (subject to Dr. Dodger's authority) and set off to
Washington for consultations. In Mr. White's speeches to the
reactionary leaders there was usually a vein of soothing optimism
which everyone was anxious to mine; and he invariably voted with
the majority. The Executive Vice President of Bayou Power & Light
described for his Trustees a scene from one of these meetings:

> When I attended a session of the Federal Industrial Commission for
> the first time, the struggle between White, Morgan and Stableford
> was moving faster than a charge of maddened razorback hogs, of
> which there are droves now wallowing out by Mucus Lake and
> browsing in the acorns just back of my house. – Morgan and
> Stableford, by some administrative accident, were seated side by side.
> As Morgan arrived he gave Stableford a cold nod, but Stableford
> pretended not to notice him. Next in was White. He made a detour
> from the punchbowl to the place where his two enemies were sitting,
> vigorously shook hands with both, and greeted them with the most
> cordial "by darn's" in the world.

At this meeting Stableford was ousted, stripped of all his monies
and offices, and forced to make common cause with Phil Blaker on
Mars (who, having inside knowledge that this would transpire, had
already sent a proxy down to pick up Stableford in a dirigible
equipped with oxygen and heavy blankets, as well as a pop-up bar to
ease the tedium of space travel). Mr. White expressed his sincere
regrets, sure is a royal fucking shame, R.L., and pressed upon
Stableford a pair of theater tickets.

Next a Senate resolution condemning Mr. Morgan's enterprises
as anti-free-market was brought up. Mr. White moved that the
Commission adopt a wait-and-see attitude on this, at which there
was applause and hearty laughs. Even the electric light bulb winked.

A surprise bond issue by Mr. Morgan then brought the confrontation with Mr. White into the open. Mr. White, taken by
surprise (for this had hardly been on his agenda of victories), was
forced to attack Mr. Morgan's authority in matters of excise license
doctrine, which he had previously relegated to anyone interested, as
having little to do with the essences that lie beneath the veils of *maya*
in which the merchandise is packaged. This led to other skirmishes.
Unfortunately for Mr. White, Mr. Morgan's clerks had prepared a
statement indicating that the Society of Daniel was not only a tax
write-off for Mr. White – to which of course there was no objection,
Jack, hell, we ALL do the same – but also a bastard organization
created through embezzlement of corporate funds; and that could

not be met with complacency, not at all, Jack, tut-tut, can't allow it, since many of the gentlemen present were investors in White Power & Light. Despite a bitter and caustic denial by Mr. White of these charges, *I'll* show *you*, you fart-brained gumshoe overlords!, the F.I.C. voted by a small margin to pack him off to the Arctic to supervise the construction of the D.E.W. line, so off you go, Jack, but have a real nice trip, d'you hear? – a project, by the way, which proved itself in 1983 when our Republic was able to demonstrate electronically that the missile which downed a commercial aircraft over Kamchatka was of Soviet origin. So away went Mr. White and his wife and son to a trading post in Arctic Alaska. Mr. White, who was resentful about these developments, gonna KILL those beefalo Democrats back in D.C.!, began to take on a certain ugliness of manner among the snows; and, as we shall see, he chose eventually to sell himself to nonhuman masters in order to recoup his losses. But we cannot blame him for that. His job out there was enormous. The position could only be filled by someone in command of much logistic artillery; how else could he get it?

From our point of view, it did not matter who was directing national operations. The dummy's eight had been finessed; and whether Mr. White fed in the dummy's jack or Mr. Morgan dropped the ten on the first round of clubs, the position of any progressive force was dangerous. – I set off for South America to contact the bugs, as already told.

Two miles inland of where Captain de Silva had left me, there was an encampment of rubber workers who were with us. Comrade Pablo of my cadre was among them at that time. He came for me on the day after my arrival and took me up to the camp. Everyone welcomed me. I had brought some canned goods to give as presents, and the comrades were all delighted with honest American beans. For Comrade Pablo I had an especially ironic gift: – a tin of pineapple harvested in Brazil, embalmed in palm oil from Argentina and sugar from Honduras, encased in aluminum which had been refined from Peruvian bauxite ore; all at sub-subsistence wages; and *then* shipped up to the United States to garnish a hog-heaven ham roast, weight-conscious reactionaries leaving bits of it absently on their plates as they watched the cold blue screens in their living rooms (which were so bright that you could see their supernatural flicker through the trees next door); their lips moving in commercial prayers to the tune of the news, much as when you're in the driver's seat at a red light and you have the radio on, you sing along with that very same jingle, and maybe you look in the rearview mirror and you see the driver behind is moving his mouth rapturously in identical rhythms, just like the fellow behind *him*, and the pimply girl behind *him*; and as the light turns GREEN and you put your foot down on that good wide pedal you cannot forbear to honk your horn in a statement of exquisite brotherhood. – But I, seeing that pineapple in a Safeway store, had rescued it and returned it to Latin America like a good boy.

After a fine meal of fried fish and loin of tapir, we all stretched out by the riverbank, humming sad songs and tossing the bones into the water, *ploosh!* – It was a beautiful night, and the poisonous exhalations of the trees (which I have described above) went straight to our heads so that we became quite giddy, making plans for a voodoo world and eternal voodoo wars that would have no need of electricity, dead soldiers arising from their mass graves and streaming through the jungle at our command, walking along river-bottoms and ocean floors when need be, sinking up to their pelvic bones in ooze but marching on and on and on with the scavenger-fishes nibbling at their indifferent eyes, and at our signal stretching their arms up toward the surface so that to the Sunday afternoon reactionaries yachting and swimming it would seem that suddenly five-clustered mangrove roots were reaching for them, hard and yellow and bony, combing the water so that none would escape; and in no time at all we could convince the middle class that any takeover was justified. – I conversed with my hosts as well as my knowledge of Portuguese would allow. We all made a terrific impression on each other, as is generally the case when persons are out of power together. – Peeling off a handful of the wide, happy, rainbow-colored national currency, I gave Comrade Pablo (who would later betray me) a sum sufficient to allow the purchase of a metal cage from Lima the following week, by which time I was expecting to have captured a bug. – I was at that period a man of medium height, with spidery fingers and very white skin. I had steady, open eyes, but had an ophthalmologist examined them with metaphysical rigor he might have noticed my cruelly glittering pupils, the resoluteness of my irises, and all the rest of it. – I told Comrade Pablo that the house in San Salvador could be disposed of, and that we could afford to dispatch another submarine to my secret island base, this being not an order or an ultimatum, but rather a verbal memorandum. Comrade Pablo became withdrawn at this unwelcome reminder that I was in supreme command, but he promised to execute instructions faithfully. I next asked whether he could spare me a flashlight for the duration of my mission, as I had read that bugs, snakes and lower orders generally could be easily mesmerized by light. He surrendered his own with such readiness that I was almost tempted to make him a colonel. As Rosa Luxemburg said, "Historically, the errors committed by a truly revolutionary movement are infinitely more fruitful than the infallibility of the cleverest Central Committee." – Perhaps it was not such a lapse in any event, as Pablo did not betray me for almost a week.

REFORMATTING THE DATA PREPARATION

... till the very men, who from time to time upset a throne and trample on a race of kings, bend more and more obsequiously to the slightest dictate of a clerk.

DE TOCQUEVILLE
Democracy in America, vol. 2

A message has just come over the terminal that the computer will have to go down in ten minutes for bridge reconnection. When the electricity has died I will be able to push the switch which runs the teletype in manual mode; and then at least, even though this absurd history is now sealed into the program and will predetermine everything, I may have some freedom in bringing Bug and Milly and Wayne and Parker into context. The trouble is that a small current pulse will still be running through my machine ...

THEIR FINEST HOUR, OR, TRIUMPH AND TRAGEDY (1909)

"A scavenging party – what on earth's that?" – "Miles, dear, don't be old-fashioned. A scavenging party is when you go round in cars picking up tramps and feeding them fish and chips . . ."

RONALD KNOX
The Body in the Silo (1933)

I, Big George, do solemnly swear that on the second of July I captured my first bug. The reader should be reminded that in the jungle many sounds occur which it is impossible to account for; so that on hearing a sudden crash or wail or plea ahead, the only thing to do is shoot immediately. POW! WHAM! ZAP! The Americans followed the same rule when they were dealing with Che Guevara and his band. The subversives had their camp in the middle of the jungle, and it was night, a particularly dangerous time to go hunting – shit, NATO might lose some boys. So the searchers flew over the area in silent reconnaissance planes, located the glow of the tiny campstove on their infrared scanners from ten miles away, dropped a few hundred paratroopers with cocked submachine guns, surrounded the camp, and then unfortunately Che or perhaps somebody else made a funny noise and all the Green Berets were forced to open fire. The succeeding stillness tended no doubt only to heighten the unpleasant impression which had already been made. – The first thing, then, which claimed my attention as I entered the forest with my 12-gauge shotgun, was an interminable sound of breaking branches, as if some great multilegged carapaced thing were struggling among the rubber-trees. It could not be a scout tank, for I glimpsed feelers and a broad curvature of deep gunmetal blue. It was scrambling behind a fallen tree when I fired. I missed the first time, and was forced to shoot again as it emerged. This time I hit it right in the back with a full load of pellets. It fell over on its side, kicking. I ran up and threw my shirt over its head (such as it had a head) and tied its mandibles shut with baling wire. Thus rendered innocuous, it could not harm me when I strapped it to a sapling to dig the bullets out of it. The operation was a success. I dragged it back to our camp and put it in a monkey-cage with a saucer of milk and a freshly killed rabbit to comfort it. When the metal affair arrived from Lima, we transferred it to that and gave it a slate to write with. Comrade Pablo taught it our alphabet.

As the bug — which seemed to be a beetle of some kind — recovered, it came to evince so fond and loving a disposition for me that I decided to bring it back to the United States when I returned. We quickly learned to communicate with each other, for it was a very intelligent bug and understood that it could never escape and would be severely treated if it did not make a good-faith effort to obey my instructions.

According to von Fritsch, the language of bees consists of signs like that of our poor dumb and deaf population; and different varieties have different languages, "perhaps as far apart as French and German." These beetles have apparently established an insect Esperanto which must come in quite handy for instinctive aggression. Being no linguist, I insisted that my prisoner speak English. The conversations took place in a small hut kept at my disposal.

"What are your true aims?" I asked. "Are you fighting against reaction or the human race as a whole?"

It waggled its feelers. "You hurt," it wrote, "beetle hurt, you kill and we die you . . ."

"Will you become our shock troops against the reactionaries?"

"You feed us, no hurt, and we do for you . . ."

"What is the composition of your Central Committee?" I asked, my spectacles flashing with excitement.

"Great Beetle hurt when we hurt, fight electricity make you die . . ."

"And do you think that the Great Beetle will agree to bolster our forces?"

"Hurt all beetles, we burrow click and pinch, we hurt, certainly sir make you die . . ."

The Revolution Betrayed (1947)

Such things can be done in Granada without sin, Señor, and no questions asked . . .

H. RIDER HAGGARD
Margaret (1907)

The following day, Pablo set the beetle loose, out of "pity," he told me. (I believe that he was in Mr. White's employ.) This had terrible consequences for us and our secret files, for that very night the bugs came rolling out of the jungle in a horrible unstoppable scuttling attack and seized me and carried me off down dim dizzy depths and under mountains and along the bottoms of warm shallow seas like my zombies with only a hollow reed in my mouth to keep air passages in working trim, and through sticky ferns and egg caches and incubators and subterranean cockroach classrooms of strategy and along abandoned mine shafts and eaten-away tunnels in hollowed-out documents in unused stacks in an obscure wing of a forgotten branch of a sealed-off area of the very Library of Congress . . .

A PLEA FOR INCREASED WATTAGE (1962)

Close to the grave, all grows lighter.

GOETHE
The Sorrows of Young Werther

And now I sit a prisoner in the caves of the Great Beetle, longing for an electrical outlet or just a little – MORE – LIGHT! to see by, to read by, to construct a generator by out of toothpicks and tears; for it is only electric power that will save me: with it I can do anything; I can drill through the walls, or create a force-field to give me surcease from my warders; or even if all else fails set up little factories to while away my life down here more profitably . . .

DEAD-END CALCULATIONS

~~~~~~

"Only the Moors wear veils, Peter, and now we are Christians again."

<div align="right">

H. RIDER HAGGARD
Margaret

</div>

Well, the computer is down; Big George is muffled or stifled, and the keys yield to my fingers with only a faint blue tingling resistance which will hardly affect the picture so much as to destroy its information value, will it now, for at last I can see you again as I have made you, my bright and risen angels . . .

THE EARPLUGS ~~~~~~~~~~

To be human means to feel inferior.

ALFRED ADLER, 1933

We are often pure fools in political and legal affairs. But we are what we are as a result of our upbringing and education and we shall do well not to try to be any different.

GENERAL GÜNTHER BLUMENTRITT

. . . I suppose that the coat of skins, when first devised, was the cause of such envy that he who first wore it met his death in ambush; and yet after all the pelt was torn in the struggle and completely ruined with much blood so that it could not be made of any use.

LUCRETIUS, *On Nature*

AN ANECDOTE

~~~~~~

When you've finally set your sights on the trophy of a lifetime, you'd better have a cartridge that can deliver the right bullet to the target.

Remington catalog (1984)

It is said that as a child our hero, Bug, was given a Brownie camera by his parents (about whom little is known), and packed off to summer camp in the baseball season of each year. Each year he returned, beaten black and blue by the other boys (he claimed his parents never noticed this, which is plausible), with his two exposed rolls of twenty-shot black-and-white negatives. His photo albums from that time still survive. What do they show, those square, white-bordered, glossy images all covered with fingerprints and slapped onto the pages with rubber cement and an artless crookedness? — Relay races, cowboys 'n' Indians? Food fights at the mess hall? Small, crewcut swimmers heading out, spitting water and grinning gap-toothed, to the farthest buoy? Cookouts, marshmallow melts, movies of adventure and war, the rifle range, the archery range, canoeing under the stars; the nearsighted, spindly boy himself, smiling at the camera in anguish, trying to catch a baseball, football, tennis ball, kickball, soccer ball, pingpong ball, and later, after he'd lost his cabin all the intramural tournaments, the cleated shoes they threw at his face when the counselor was out? — Bug had been brought up to be considerate. When they threw their shoes at him he kept his hands at his sides so that the shoes could strike him full in the face the way the other boys wanted. He did, however, remove his glasses so that his parents would not have to buy him new ones if they were shattered. The other boys did not seem to mind this, perhaps because he was obedient to all other parameters of the ceremony. When each shoe had hit him, the boys would wait for him to bend down and get it and throw it to Wayne, who caught it between two fingers and flipped it through the air to its owner, who would then go to the rear of the line while the next boy stepped forward and hurled his shoe, cleats first. — Once when everyone else had gone down to the mess hall for lunch and our hero was alone with Wayne because they had both come back late from swim period, our hero crossed his arms over his heart hard to keep the courage in and said, "Why do you all hate me?" — Boy, did Wayne get a haw out of that one! Not that Wayne thought about this weakling very much (executioners are rarely as preoccupied with their victims as are their victims with them), but when he did he sure had to crack up. Lookit that pipsqueak Bug, sittin' there on his trunk goggling up at Wayne and blinking back tears, while ole Wayne, in fine fettle, snapped his towel at flies and twanged the elastic of Parker's cast-off bathing suit, up there on the top bunk where Parker slept and cracked toe-knuckles at Wayne in secret code! Wayne jumped over to the next tier, pulled his swim trunks off, stuck his wet hairy ass in ole Four-Eyes' direction, and farted. — Haw! — "Why do you hate me?" sez Four-Eyes again, and at this Wayne becomes quite annoyed and remembers that if he doesn't quick-time it down to the mess hall I mean PRONTO there might not be an empty seat beside Parker; and this thought gets Wayne all tensed up and he yells, "We hate you because we *want* to, ya fucking Bug!" — What a look from Four-Eyes! Wayne feels better at once just to see it. — Haw! — He sprints down to the mess hall, a-one, a-two! . . . — Well, okay; what *did* our hero take his pictures of? All his *friends?* (That's a good one, haws Wayne.) The open-air chapel? Sunset over Manoogian Field? The solemn mysteries of Woodcraft, when Chief Adams told the evening story before the braves dispersed to their cabins? The senior dance with the voluptuous twelve-year-olds of Camp Minnehaha?

He took his annual snapshots, rather, of trees.

Bug liked trees. He thought they did the least damage in the world. He was awarded the camp's green Wantonoit patch for learning the names of two hundred natural objects. A hundred and seventy-three of these were trees.

When he liberated the San Francisco municipal subway system twenty years later, a pretty kindergarten teacher he'd been sleeping with was at his side, machine gun in hand. Overcome by a sense of great events, she had made off with her entire class. Bug was dismayed by this, but not nearly so much as was Mr. White, because with those goddamned kids in there he couldn't bomb the hell out of the place the way he wanted to; he'd never live that down among the liberals if he did; Dr. Dodger was working (under hardnosed contract) on a child-safe anti-personnel weapon but Mr. White didn't have as much faith in the Doc as he used to, so he yelled and swore and pounded a whole row of red communications buttons. — Meanwhile, in the course of the raid it occurred to Bug that the children had hostage value, so he was charming to poor Susan, the kindergarten teacher, and made her feel genuinely happy and wanted, as if her children were important little troopers. — Not knowing the purely instrumental concerns that crossed the grey waters of his mind in their pontoon boats, she loved him. Susan would do anything for love because it did not often come her way. — "You fell fer that fuckin' Bug!" Wayne screamed in agony when he caught her the following year. "That creep that's against you and me and Parker and everything we stand for!" As far as Bug was concerned, however, he was neither for nor against Susan; she was simply a useful nuisance; so were her pupils, every one of whom she loved dearly; she had not had any thought of putting them (or herself) in danger; nothing was dangerous when Bug was there to protect her; Bug knew an awful lot and Susan hoped that the attack would be an experience that they would remember when they were grown-up men and women so that they'd join the Kuzbuite movement and defeat wicked Mr. White and his blue globes (Susan had once had a bad experience with the blue globes, as we shall see). She was ecstatic that Bug really loved her for herself and her mind, which was continually inspired by his own, with its deep black thoughts and dark blue sparks. Sometimes she was not sure what exactly he saw in her because she was not up to his level; he was so smart; but then she knew that she made him feel better than any other woman could, even and especially Milly, whom Susan hated; Bug was so quiet and always listened to Susan, and every Saturday for so long now in sun or fog he had taken her out to the range in Pacifica and shown her how to use a semi-automatic, and now she could almost shoot the petals off daisies. Almost. Originally Susan had been afraid of guns but Bug had explained to her that guns were necessary for the objective tactical triumph of our cause. She herself believed that everyone should be equal, but she had never known, until he made the issue clear to her, that anything could be done to make things work out. But once she understood that something *could* be done and *she* could help and he *wanted* her to help him and really needed *her* in ways that Milly would never understand then she was happier than she had ever been. Meanwhile Bug had been

busy arranging the strike against the subway, which was calculated
to cause great destruction, though it would hardly bring Mr. White
to his knees; and in the No. 41 switching junction there was one of
the original blue globe ringleaders to be neutralized. Were they to
accomplish that, Mr. White would let out a roar indeed. – Bug
smiled flittingly. – When you attack a power station, you go for
the transformers, which are costly and time-consuming to replace;
in destroying a subway, on the other hand, almost any sort of
procedure may be followed once the third rail is shorted out. –
Frank agreed to detonate the charges in the two underwater tunnels,
the primers being radio-slaved to Frank's super key-ring; while
Stephen Mole was at this very moment clambering along on the
underside of the Oakland Bay Bridge, planting another explosive at
every third cross-tie, and reeling out the wire to keep them all
connected . . . The goal was not so much to cut the city off or to kill
hundreds of commuters as to prove to Mr. White that the Kuzbuites
could play his own game – though capturing the blue globe was not
unimportant, either. It was always wise to pick your own battlefield
where you could match the enemy in planning and weapons. This
was one of the hundreds of subway systems that Dr. Dodger owned;
and so the reactionaries had lost precious retaliatory seconds
thumbing through all the dog-eared blueprints of Dallas/Fort Worth
airport transit hubs and historic World War II bunkers in Mandalay
until finally Dr. Dodger found the right software code written on
the back of an envelope and then they were able to look at seven
detailed maps on the Envision terminal. By then Milly had already
shorted out all the video cameras in the strike zone. The objective
had not yet been accomplished, however, and according to Bug's
master timetable there remained only eleven minutes before the
phased fallback to Walnut Creek. – Under these highly strategic
circumstances, Susan was, as stated, an annoyance. However, a
kindergarten teacher with a machine gun looked good on the
propaganda reels; Stephen could shoot some winning footage; and,
more importantly still, our hero had determined that through Susan
he could get to Catherine, and through Catherine he could strike at
Phil Blaker and probably steal an aircraft to convey him, Frank,
Stephen and Milly to the Arctic when the time came. For this reason
he took Susan shooting every Saturday and slept with her every
Saturday night (which was all the same to Milly). And now here
she was, was Susan, with her leather handbag and her wide-eyed
kindergarteners. Evidently she had forced the attack plan out of
poor weak Frank over the phone. – She was now thirty-three. In

recent months, as Bug noted in his records, her features had begun to collapse into their first worry-wrinkles, like the skin of an overripe pear. Susan herself detected the change and reacted with panic, so that instead of just seizing whatever it was that she thought was escaping from her, she gripped her entire life grimly and desperately in a chokehold. She was, in short, ready for politics. It was no more her fault than anyone else's that she was now becoming evil, for she was still and always would be my bright and risen angel whom Big George and I had placed in an impossible situation. – Her pupils stood in line behind her knees like terrified goslings. Before, they had only seen death on television, where it was a joy to watch, the bodies flinging hands up, arching their backs, flickering and falling bloodlessly; when color TV came in and the sound was good you could see it all even better and enjoy the menacing musical score, produced by Albert R. Consoli, Lawrence L. Donovan, and S. William Dodger. Then the schoolchildren had to go to bed, and they had nightmares all night, but the next morning they were each first on their block to tell their friends what they had seen. – Their own teacher, Comrade Susan (Kuzbu Suzy, Wayne called her, grinding his teeth), had just now killed two policemen whom Comrade Milly had captured; it had really happened because they had seen it. Even while alive the policemen had been as stiff and still as tin soldiers. Wayne had brought a set to school once for Show-and-Tell; it was a fancy porcelain set from Dresden that Wayne had saved up for; you didn't skirmish or nothing with them because that would break them, but they sure looked keen on duty as fanatic rigid bookends on the shelf, or lying firm in the jaws of Wayne's grey plastic catapult to be hurled over the scale-model Polish fortifications for the final assault (not that Wayne launched the catapult; that would've broken the soldiers, too). – So now Bug had some real enemies on his hands. As far as he was concerned the Great Beetle was welcome to them; more pressing issues of triple-purpose phalanx accuracy required his attention. There they lay on the tiles now, their faces so white as to be almost luminescent, like round tombstones spattered with phosphorus. – They had meant no harm. –"Go check out the problem," Mr. White told them on the phone. "We've got a 39–22 call from Montgomery Station, and something tells me it's those Kuzbu assholes." It was perhaps typical of reactionary thinking at its most naive that these men would expect to complete a little job and return to their former occupations. As they lay bound and gagged in the brilliant shadows their eyes tracked Susan incessantly in their white faces. Susan hated them. Meanwhile it kept getting darker and darker in the subway by stages as the Great Beetle's scout-bugs swarmed behind the ceiling tiles and gnawed through the wires connecting each light to the power supply. The doomed policemen kept staring at Susan as if they thought she might help them. This made Susan feel that everyone suspected she might let Bug down by abetting the enemy. They had lost their caps, but their torn uniforms still looked black and professional in the dimness, so that they frightened Susan and looked evil and dangerous to her like giant wasps just barely held at bay; and their pale glowing faces were beginning to freeze the rapture that was so important to Susan. – "Can I?" she whispered in Bug's ear. Now Bug would understand how hard she was. – He knew at once what she wanted. It was not at all what he wanted, because he disliked the gratuitous in all forms, but as long as a death-bounty was already on his head he supposed that the correct thing to do was to grant Susan what *she* wanted so that he could get what *he* wanted from her later. And the Great Beetle could still have them at the end. – "Go ahead," he said politely. The policemen lay on their backs at the foot of the up escalator, disarmed and bundled helpless quite efficiently by Milly (who, being good at such things, was off supervising another execution). Susan stepped up and kicked the policemen in the head. – "I want you all to watch this, kids!" she screamed as she discharged her magazine into the policemen's chests. "They – are – BAD – REACTIONARY – MEN!" she explained. – Ratatattattat-tat. The toes of Susan's running shoes were soaked with dark blood. – The first policeman was stitched almost in two. The other still moved feebly when Susan had exhausted her clip, as if he were trying to crawl away. Susan, smiling a little hysterically as she gazed round at her pupils, did not even notice her bad job. Bug withdrew his pistol, knelt down, aligned it two inches from the policeman's ear, and pressed the trigger firmly, but smoothly. A little curl of smoke exited silently from the back of the gun and drifted into his face. – The children all watched. Some cried.

Susan felt that this was the most profound moment of her life, because she had made a Demonstration – not only for Bug, who had already judged her, but also for her pupils, who stood silent and bewildered, the winking emergency lights spearing beams onto their downy heads; and Susan, sinking into Bug's efficient embrace as though he were a bubble-bath, became regal and held her chin high. – "Do you think I *helped* them?" she whispered to Bug, smiling like one of the blood-drinkers in the paintings of Csok, and as she smiled her pale cheeks were spotted with color like ladybug-dots, and the children were afraid of her face and shied, but to Susan it seemed that they were passing in review for her somehow in a honey-dance of official and officious complexity, for her attention was wandering in corridors of the iridescent. But all the time some lonely thing was buzzing inside her skull to remind her that Bug had not yet answered her, so finally she pulled away from him; he let her go; and she said sharply, "We *are* doing it for *them*, aren't we?" – meaning her pupils, whom she fancied had been transformed by what she had done (when in fact they had only been transfixed); and Bug hesitated and his glasses misted up in meditations of his own and in his even way he replied, "Not entirely," and he pointed to a cigarette advertising poster inside its illuminated display case. Once Bug had passed it every morning on his way to Mr. White's office. Some of Susan's ricocheting bullets had shattered the glass and knocked out the interior lighting. It was a grainy picture of a hard-living man in a cowboy hat, sitting sidesaddle on an impeccably groomed horse in a cluster of piñon pines. It was obvious from the man's face that he had been everywhere and knew what was what when it came to cigarettes, and it was cigarettes that people were supposed to remember, but Bug, a dedicated non-smoker, had seen and remembered the piñon pines. – "I suppose we're doing this for the trees," he said.

TREES

~~~~~~

A simple rule of thumb in war is that the winning side is the side
that does the raping.

SUSAN BROWNMILLER
Against Our Will (1975)

We use trees to make gallowses, coffins and newspapers. As we are
every one of us gallows-climbers in the end, our dead bodies
ascending from the grave molecule by molecule through great
woody pores in droplets of transpiration until we hang in green and
yellowing leaves, we build scaffolds only when we are not advanced
enough to employ materials more alien and inert: steel (for no one
turns to iron ore when he dies), fire and colored gas. Coffins and
newspapers, however, remain popular even where there are electric
trains, because they represent an accommodation with death, which
we cannot control and which trees profit from. – Well, we think, if
we must nourish them, then at least while we live they will nourish
us: – into the crushing-machines! But trees, being (presumably)
unaware, derive most of the benefit, for they do not have the fear of
decay; and are left with delicious unconsciousness, in a haze of
dew-drops on sun-sucking leaves; as when on a hot day you sit on a
porch just holding a glass of lemonade, not thinking about much,
the condensation of the glass feels good against your sweaty hands.
Certainly some of that water must have passed through trees, but
that is no comfort – just another proof of those unfair equalities
of ecology. About all that is left to do is to bury the dead and write
an obituary. The mortal remains of the hamburger (grease in the
butcher's paper, maybe, and a few cold crumbs) fit comfortably into
the cardboard box; the box is assigned a two-dimensional plot in a
mechanically compacted sector of the sanitary landfill. Meanwhile
news is written. News always concerns itself with death. We

accommodate ourselves. But such use of wood is ludicrous, like the palisade-fence on Treasure Island or any colony, choked by living jungle out there all around, full of tigers and the shadows of undiscovered reptiles. Everyone forces himself to believe in the story of the little Dutch boy with his finger in the dike. Still, it is quite within our means to convert whole forests to flat sheets of fiberboard (though we might wish to leave one tree, the very best in the world; an oak, maybe, or a plane tree; bury a soldier under it, and call it the Tree of Liberty); and if we just keep up with our plans one step at a time, we can go a long way towards destroying all this greenness, leaving a neutral zone, like Switzerland; and if we inter ourselves in lead coffins the miasma from our corpses will not be able to escape for a very long time. The old medieval conceit of the Haunted Wood, with spirits in every dell and the skeletons of knights in the tree-tops, will cease to trouble us (when I was a child in New England I was afraid of entering the forest alone); and hateful oxygen, that bearer of rust, will lapse into carbon dioxide; the soil will flake and crumble away; and great dust-winds will arise to fling off the murky atmosphere; and we will all be safe in our tombs, good and incorruptible behind the black lacquer of the vacuum.

THE EARPLUGS

~~~~~~

Colt takes no short cuts.

Colt firearms brochure
(1984)

At summer camp one of our hero's cabin-mates had been discovered to be an insect. It was horrible. There was a rule at the camp that no sweets were allowed on account of insects, and this now proved to be a wise regulation. – Tony's mother (some horrid, black-mottled, six-legged thing, no doubt) had secreted a dozen Rice Crispies brownies in his suitcase. The Rice Crispies turned out to be little white eggs, like those one sometimes sees affixed to blighted leaves. At night larvae scuttled out of them. The counselor confiscated the brownies grimly, and the appropriate means of destruction was discussed at an emergency staff meeting. If they just rowed out to the middle of the lake and dropped the brownies, there was a possibility that bubbles might rise from the contaminated bottom, and over the next few years the clear water, which was such a great asset for impressing urban parents, would turn green and stagnant with the waste products of the hatchlings. Finally they decided to incinerate the brownies.

Those were liberal days. Tony was simply sent home. He was a fat little boy with a crewcut who wet his bed often, and had little aptitude for soccer or water sports. He cried when he was told of the decision. He would be in big trouble with his mother for getting caught.

The camp director was to drive him to the bus station the next morning. In the meantime, the other boys, now aware of his beetle origin, beat him up until the green blood ran from his nose.

Bug, who had been awarded a new display of shiners just yesterday, hid in his sleeping bag when his cabin-mates marched in, tossed their baseball gloves in their bunks, and rolled up their sleeves in solemn silence. They didn't even notice him now; Tony was the novelty of the hour. Bug rustled delicately inside his sleeping bag like a trapped thing, inching his nose out until he could see the boys standing around Tony, with golden dust-motes jiggling in the sunlight that flowed through the screen windows. – Tony screamed when the boys closed in on him. He looked all round the piney floorboards in his extremity, hoping, Bug surmised, to see a hole under one of the bunks that he could scuttle into. It was possible that he could shrink down to thumbnail-size as a concealment aid, but in this setting such a move would certainly be a disaster, for then one of the boys could squash him in good conscience. – Meanwhile there was no refuge. The boys surrounded Tony very quietly. Parker stuck out a leg and tripped him. – "Get up and take it!" yelled Wayne in a rage at this creature that offered so little activity; "Get up!", but Tony would not, so Wayne grabbed him and threw him up high so that he hit the floor with a funny dull crack like they'd split his exoskeleton or some damn thing; then Roger Garvey stuffed a sock in his mouth and they went to work. They held his eyes open and pulled out the pupils, which seemed to be on stalks, like a crab's. They found the feelers taped beneath the crewcut wig and snapped them off. They dragged him into the square of sunlight beneath the front windows and burned his thorax with a magnifying glass. They pulled down his pants and kicked him in the cloaca. Then the bell tolled for woodsmanship period, of which Wayne, who was the most popular boy that year, was particularly fond. So they wiped their hands on Tony's shirt and strolled out slowly, laughing and talking. The cabin smelled of crushed insect parts.

Bug felt pity. Tony had never beaten him up. He slipped out of his sleeping bag now that it was safe (he was never one to take chances) and picked up Tony's feelers, which lay on the floor like black pipe-cleaners somebody had dropped. The dying appendages twined around his fingers timidly, their cilia vibrating. Had he been socialized, he would have flung down the feelers in nauseated loathing, but in fact he was sorry for them and stroked them in their last hour and did not forsake them, even when a thin greenish liquid ran down his arm, so they clung to his fingers and died quietly. Tony meanwhile had gotten up. He stood in the center of the floor, humming softly and unevenly in the throaty bombillations and cricket-sobs of his kind. Where the boys had beaten him the floor was stained blackish-green. – He felt in front of him very very carefully and touched Bug's face.

"Just me," Bug said. (He looked around. No one could see him.)

"You won't hurt me anymore?" Tony said.

"I wouldn't hurt you," Bug said. "Here are your feelers if you can use them." They were flaking apart in his hands, like rolled flies' wings.

"They aren't any use now," Tony sobbed. It was the death of his feelers in particular that seemed to upset him, much as a man whose family has been massacred and whose house has burned down will lament the consequent loss of his expensive Sunday shoes. This focusing of grief, I have read, is a very effective defense mechanism.

"Are you going to die?" Bug said. He put the antennae in the wastebasket, quietly, so Tony wouldn't hear, and wiped his hands on his pants.

"My mother'll eat me and start over. That's what she always said she'd do if I blew it."

"Maybe she was just kidding you," Bug said. "Try to look on the bright side."

"It's all right," Tony said. "I've seen her do it to other kids. It doesn't hurt."

"Oh, well," Bug said. "That's good."

It was warm and sunny and peaceful outside. The boys' life, of which Tony and Bug could never be a part, was streaming on over the fields and in little boats across the lake. But here you could see only other cabins and trees. In general the cabins were considered staging areas for important activities which occurred elsewhere. You came back to them to change out of your bathing suit for lunch, and for midafternoon siesta to allow you to fully enter into the early evening games, and to go to bed. The rest of the day it was not considered healthy to be mooning about the cabin, going through the contents of your trunk as if you were homesick, reading paperbacks and listening to the heartless breezes in the trees, and generally wasting your parents' money second by second. – The front windows of Cabin Ten afforded an excellent view of the diamond-shaped quadrangle, around the perimeter of which ran a hard-packed dirt road, so that parents could come at the beginning and end of each session to empty and reload their son's trunk; and there was a panorama of the other cabins, painted dark green, raised on stilts so that you could see the damp yellow sand underneath, in which dead birds and mice had been secretly buried in mass graves by the boys, summer after summer; and on the quadrangle itself were evenly spaced cans of a sticky chemical, mounted on posts driven into the grass, to entrap the Japanese beetles that were blighting the region. When each can became gummed up to the brim with living beetles, it was conveyed to the Nature House by members of the kill patrol, where Dr. Dodger placed it into a tiny lethal chamber about the size of a microwave oven. The beetles died silently when the door was closed. When Dr. Dodger removed the can everything inside was sugary with white powder. The can was taken to a sanitary landfill. Meanwhile, new cans were filled with sticky substances and readied for instant distribution. The beetles loved the smell.

The boys rarely bothered with bugs the way they did with birds and mice, unless the pickings were poor in the traps that Parker built with his knowing hands, or unless the bugs were big, as in the case of Tony. I am not sure they realized what they were missing. Japanese beetles in particular are a lovely color, all green-brown and translucent like lake water; and they buzz in a pitiful rasping manner when they are agitated and tormented that would be a nice psychic snack for any young sadist. But there were, as intimated, mice and birds. Roger Garvey even caught a fruit bat once, which they buried alive.

Every third Saturday the new boys came. First they were taken to the registration cabin for examination and processing, while their parents waited in purring station wagons. Then they were driven up to this compound, or one much like it, the exact location to be determined by their age and the registration packet which their parents had received upon payment by certified check or money order. The younger boys often cried. (When the older boys were conveyed to camp at the beginning of the summer they couldn't care less.) As soon as the parents drove off, the new arrivals were surrounded by the boys and taken into the woods for assimilation. Soon there came terrible screams. But when they returned, now fast friends with their erstwhile tormentors, they grinned slyly. Never again would they be hurt. — Boys whom it was clear would not fit in, such as Bug and Tony, were not taken to the woods. These boys were fair game all summer.

Our hero never wanted to go to summer camp. It is possible that if he had not been made to go, he never would have become a terrorist and assassin. — "Get in the car," his father said. — "Please," Bug wanted to say, "don't make me go. Please." But that would have been too great a degradation, as well as being futile. So he got into the car. His mother and sister were sitting up in front. Bug was very quiet. — "What's the matter with you?" his mother said. "Don't you want to go to camp?" – "No," Bug said. – His father turned around. "Don't get smart to me, buddy. Now shut up and try to appreciate this, because you're sure as hell not going to stay home and do nothing this summer." – "Okay," Bug said. – "Your brother does not want to go to camp," Bug's mother announced to Bug's sister. "But he has to go." – They drove through a lot of beautiful scenery, for hours and hours and hours. The camp was far to the north. That was one of its special qualities. – Great forests now received the travelers, as they had once received the French; and the car passed through towns with historic churchyards followed by stony farms that bore witness to various sublethal crop diseases which had originated in Dunwich, Arkham, Lyme or Innsmouth. – Now it got cooler and breezier as they turned off past the summer homes organized around the lake, and the trees and clearings took you on and on past ruined stone walls, and oak trees marched over the mountains into wild gorges and up granite ledges at the start of Mr. White's private moose preserve. – Cottages alternated with blue squares of lake. – At last the horrible camp loomed close; and Bug's father turned onto the dirt road by the football field. – In the compound the director was waiting. "Well, well, welcome to camp once again, Bug," he said with a friendly smile. "And how nice to see you again, Mr. Nightcrawler," he said to Bug's father, shaking his hand. – Bug's mother waited in the car.

Perhaps Bug and Tony should have been allies. But any successful structure of domination always gets the weak to reject each other. Each went his own pariah way. Every day Tony cried and cried. At night he wet his bed. Now our hero repented of his isolationism. In those days, he felt compassion effortlessly; he was not a professional. He stood there in the cabin, breathing in the smell of the piney boards.

"So," he said, mainly to be saying something. "Are you bugs really trying to take over the world?"

Tony buzzed and clicked. "I don't know. They just make me do stuff, like once when I had to put some grubs in the meat at a supermarket."

Our hero heard steps. Looking through the screen window, he saw the camp director walking up the perimeter, followed by two state deputies bearing fly-swatters. At the edge of the compound the sun sparkled on the squad car. He knew that Tony would not be able to get to the woods. – "They're coming for you," he said.

"Please don't let them hurt me," Tony said. "Just don't let them hurt me. I'll give you something if you keep them from hurting me."

"I can't do anything," Bug said.

"My earplugs," Tony shrilled. "In the pocket of my swimsuit. On the clothesline."

The doorknob turned. Our hero jumped back into his sleeping bag barely in time, leaving the bug standing in the middle of the floor, shaking and clutching itself.

"Tony," the camp director said as he stepped in, "Deputy Rogers and Deputy Hansen are going to hold you in custody until the bus comes, because we can't be responsible for you here. You'd best take your shirt off so they can clip your wings."

"I can't see anything," Tony said.

"Looks like the bug's been hurting itself," Deputy Rogers said.

"They do that, you know," explained the director. "One of our staff bagged one for the museum two years ago; well, apparently the creature just gave up and stung itself when he got it out in the open, which was a real shame because the poison – which I think is formic acid – acted on it in such a way as to make it pretty unsuitable."

"That a fact," Deputy Hansen said.

"Take your shirt off, Tony, or the deputies will be forced to swat you," the director said.

"I can't see," Tony said.

"I'll swat him now, if you like," Deputy Rogers said. "Damn bug makes me want to puke. All that cold black gristle in there. You know, they're cleaning out all the timberland up north."

"Now, that's only what the papers say," the director said genially. "One hit with the fly-swatter."

The beetle chittered deep in its thorax, twitching. Deputy Hansen strode over, jerked Tony's chin up, whipped the fly-swatter back and brought it down across the bridge of Tony's nose with all his might. There was a thinnish crunch, similar to the sound when one bites into a brandy-filled chocolate. The carcass crashed down to the floor then, and for some time it lay there with heaving abdomen, kicking and jerking, until all the green ichor had leached out. – "The rest is just reflex action," the director told the deputies, who nodded and spat. "You gentlemen just send it on home C.O.D. If you'll excuse me, I have to check on the boating period."

When everyone was gone crafty Bug got out of his sleeping bag and went behind the cabin to the clothesline. The body was still on the floor, sealed in a polyethylene bag supplied by the state of New Hampshire. Once or twice he heard the corpse screaming inside the bag. – His feelings about what had happened, he decided, were not unmixed, for although Tony had not been an unpleasant boy and had passively furthered Bug's advantage (because while the boys in Cabin Ten had despised Bug more than Tony up until today, still and all there were times when they attacked Tony instead, just for variety, and thereby gave Bug a rest), nonetheless, as their last conversation made clear, Tony was dedicated to the subversion of life as we know it. — But enough of these *ex post facto* considerations. — On the clothesline, bathing suits, beach towels and wash cloths flapped gently. The trees stretched on into the Green Mountains, dreaming of sweet water. In the fall the leaf-colors formed a prismatic maze at which the last late caterpillars goggled, forgetting to eat, and the serrated edges of the leaves sparkled when the sun was low and seemed to interlock or fit together somehow like puzzle-pieces that the caterpillars could almost follow, so that the days passed in hypnotic grace like maple sap bleeding into buckets, and then the leaves fell off and the caterpillars were suddenly left on bare black stalks until the winter came and killed them. — Our hero recognized Tony's bathing trunks pegged to the line; they were glossy black and had a faint beetly smell. In the flap pocket was a plastic box containing the earplugs. He took them out and examined them. They too were black and lined with tiny cilia; through his hand lens he could make out billions of mitochondria. — The plugs rolled alertly in his palm. Would use of them turn him into a beetle? he wondered. It seemed unlikely. — He put the earplugs in his ears . . .

. . . "Capture the Flag" was what they often played after dinner, on those warm, mysterious evenings when the red sunbeams traveled almost horizontally between the pine trees that massed behind the playing fields. The Cadets would be out of everyone's hair ("Ten-SHUN! Cabins One through Five on the left; Cabins Six through Ten on the right; parade MARCH, down the dock, don't try to get out of it, in you go, Garvey, or I'll push you, you creep; you some kind of beetle or sumpin' can't stand water? In you go, I said — what's this? — oHO, so you dig your toes in, do you: Wayne and Parker, give me a hand with this one; you each take a leg and I'll get the arms, there we go; one, two, THREE! — haw, haw . . ." — SPLASH went all the eight-year-olds, their teeth chattering in the cold dark water, some of them peeing through their suits just to warm themselves for a minute as meanwhile from underneath the long dock things crawled and stirred; wavy water-plants twitched and said to each other, "They are not the ones, not any of them; none is the hero we seek; we could strangle them all, couldn't we, but it's too much trouble; besides, they did help us out by killing a bug today; hey, lookit the tits on that water-lily," and all the weeds slowly went back to sleep beneath the docks, as in the darkness the counselors smoked, thought about college and pussy and hitchhiking across Europe while every now and then a shooting star dropped by; yeah, the Cadets were out of the way). The Seniors were gone, too – off to a dance with the belles of Camp Minnehaha. (The charms of those girls have already been alluded to; and indeed our hero, who was sent to camp for six years and in his time was granted a real attendance patch of red cloth, with the camp logos on it, came to be a Senior himself; and on one special night towards the end of that last eight-week term he boarded the bus with his fellows, all of them too grown up now to beat anyone up *physically* at camp, for the days of innuendo had come; besides, each was skating on his own polished dreams, certain that tonight he could lose his virginity, maybe down at the privy, following one of the girls who had drunk too much bug juice, or at the conclusion of a lakeshore promenade when the chaperones rushed off with ready sniperscopes to investigate some imagined unhuman crackling elsewhere in the woods. Bug had a fair time, moving his body woodenly up and down in various girls' arms, but he had never danced before and was bad at faking it; one of the girls kept making faces over his shoulder, which action he could almost ignore; most of them were nice, though; he was intoxicated by the smell of their shampoo and their sweat, their little blueberry-sized breasts rubbing up against him: – "You're really sweet," he told one of the girls spontaneously; "I like you, I really do," and he half-hoped she would say she'd marry him, or make love to him, or at least be his pen-pal, but she just giggled and said, "Tha-ank you-u-u," in a drawl which must have been either mocking or seductive, and then went off to dance with someone else, and after a long while he also found someone else, and pinned his promises on her; and out on the porch the counselors were going "Haw, haw, haw." – Well, that's what the Seniors were up to, though all of it was still in our hero's future.) So it was that his group, the Juniors, about sixty or seventy of them, were playing "Capture the Flag." Bug knew the woods better than almost anyone, because whenever he had the chance he'd be boning up on exotic species for his Wantonoit Award, not just starflower, wild peanut, wintergreen, lion's tooth or rattlesnake plantain; once, in a nature group, the instructor had brought them up to a spotted, willowy sort of tree, and said, "Now, what's this? One, two, three" – at three they had to say, and if they identified the object correctly they got another signature on their checksheets ... "Speckled alder," our hero said with conviction. "Also known as American alder." The other boys looked at him with distant disgust. The instructor for his part put on a happy manner, believing as he did that even losers ought to be encouraged. "That makes my day," he said. "Very good." And another signature was added to Bug's checksheet. He got in good with the nature staff, he did. They let him feed live toads to the garter snake, and during free periods in the afternoon he was allowed to sit by himself in the Nature House, feeling safe, as he looked through the screen windows at the woods around him. He knew where the puffballs were, the shelf-fungi, and the mountain ash, and each different kind of maple ("smooth leaf" is sugar; "rough" is red); and once he had found a whole field of sunflowers and blackeyed susans which grew so happy and alone that he almost cried; they danced in the wind without ever getting lonely. Several miles east of the Archery Range, Bug found a stone wall overgrown with Virginia creeper, and the foundations of an old farmstead. A yew had grown up right in the middle of the house, and there was a stone in the cool frightening shadows that might have been a grave. At another place he found an arrowhead, and buried it again. As a slightly older boy he lived in Rhode Island, not far from the Great Swamp, and one day going out with his family to see Chief Joseph's fort he remembered all the stories that he had read back at camp: Daniel Webster Meets the Devil, Eleazar Wheelock Meets the Great Spirit; and demons and will-o'-the-wisps, and Indians hidden in the rushes, and the results of carnage vanishing silently under rotting leaves; and then he realized that wilderness is a place of concealment, which became an important part of his revolutionary tactics later on. In the Nature House, and alone in the woods, he felt besieged and surrounded; and our hero came to be at home with that feeling. Already he was preparing to be a guerrilla. Wherever he was he looked for safety and danger zones, only, of course, as a sad little game, for as a boy he could not know what lay ahead of him, but it became a habit of his: In the mess hall he sat in a corner whenever he could manage it, by the window, and with a spare chair beside him that could be brandished or ducked under. In the Nature House there was a bed where the camp director sometimes slept after showing the boys all the constellations; Bug sat on the bed, which was a safe distance away from the door, knowing that if need be he could hide beneath it. In the woods he made note of hollow trees and leaf-piles; walking along the road he always looked from side to side, ready to jump into the brush if a car came and tried to run him down. Beginning the summer after Tony was eliminated, he stole one of his father's razorblades and kept it in his shoe whenever he was alone with his cabin-mates ...

Hence he loved "Capture the Flag." Reconnoitering in the twilight, he smiled to himself with excitement. Somewhere in the woods the enemy flag was waiting to be seized. And throughout the trees there were enemy troops, watching and waiting for him. He would find a hidden thing; he would hide.

He had Tony's earplugs in.

They tingled in his ears. The sensation got stronger as he advanced in one direction, and weaker if he turned in any other. There was nothing to do but follow the tingling. Skeletons chattered in piles of kindling wood; punk-lights burned green as lynxes' eyes. At night he occasionally had to go to the outhouse. All around him the other boys slept, the bullfrogs were gulping and rasping, and he could feel the lake pressing in on the island. He got up and walked into the heart of the woods where the outhouse was, and it got darker and scarier and slimier on the path, and then after awhile you could tell you were getting close to the outhouse by the smell. It was like that now, with the earplugs tingling in his ears like mad, like a million alarm bells of a midnight ambush warning him that something was rotten, there was extreme danger; he must be very close to the flag; it was a filthy stinking flag too because it belonged to the enemy; it was like a wicked thing he had to find and carry away to neutralize, not anything he would fly from his own bedpost back in the cabin where the boys sprayed Raid and Pam and had laughing mothball-fights and mothballs seemed to accidentally go astray and hit Tony or Bug in the side of the head and once at night Wayne snuck over the rafters to Bug's bunk and crammed a mothball up Bug's ear; and any second here in the dim woods the enemy would jump out and grab him; the earplugs tingled, stronger and stronger; he was excited; he knew that he was actually getting close to the flag; and within five minutes he had found it; it had been hung from a small sycamore tree. As he pulled it down he heard hellish screams, and from three directions the enemy came running at him; Wayne was yelling at him; oh *boy* Wayne was mad; Roger charged throwing stones, and Parker came slithering toward him at great speed through the oaks ... He sprinted off in the fourth direction, down toward the lake, with the flag under his arm; and where it was a little swampy and the trees grew close thin Bug scampered up an easy tree and ran along the branch and jumped down into the bushes where no one could see him, and ran back toward Manoogian Field. He suddenly realized that he could run pretty fast. – They didn't catch up with him before he had emerged into the field where the referee counselor sat; so poor clumsy Bug tossed the flag down and fell into the wet grass. The lights were on in the other cabins. For the first time in his life, he had won the game. (The boys on his own side shrugged. They were disgusted that *Bug* of all people had gotten the points.)

Needless to say, he cherished the earplugs. As he grew up he utilized them less, both because he wanted to find his own way when he could and because over the years the earplugs shrank and cracked like hard-used toys, and some of the cilia fell out, so that they couldn't tingle very much anymore; and he had to conserve them for important occasions, even after he had become an insect operative. On his last day in hiding after the shooting of Mr. White he took them out of their plastic box (which he still kept in his shirt pocket), blew the dust out of them and put them in his ears. The tingling began immediately. He came up the stairs from the cellar where he had lived and waited, ducked out behind a dumpster, and sidled along narrow Minna Street to Second. The shadows of window-grilles scuttled across his forehead. He was alone. As he approached Market Street the tingling increased. Roaches watched him from the grim greasy buildings and made report that he still appeared operational. He started to head north-east, in the direction of the Embarcadero warehouses and ferry buildings, and the tingling weakened, so he swung toward Powell Street, a pale, thin-faced young man with a briefcase, as quiet as ever, taking step after step into the world of police cars, and knowing that Wayne and Parker would be looking for him. All he wanted to do was get to Golden Gate Park and hide in a giant termite tunnel he knew about under the ferns, where he could send blind cricket messengers to the Great Beetle bearing information codes. The tingling got so strong that his head ached. It was a sunny menacing afternoon, almost at the end of the lunch hour. Cars were driving round and round and round the block up in North Beach, looking for parking spaces; the losers in this game cruised slowly past him down Market Street to the ocean to die, their windows layered with dust. – In a doorway next to a Dodger's Steak-N-Fries (the front of which street people had pissed against for years) an old man, *lumpen* from the look of him, was using an accordion as his instrument of extortion; he too would die soon: all just capitalism, usury, business as usual, ubiquitous rottenness . . . – His ears were ringing. The earplugs were evidently trying to tell him something important. – Good old bugs, always on the lookout for their own kind. – Through the restaurant window he saw a slender girl in a dark dress. She sat at a corner table reading, sipping coffee from a styrofoam cup. But maybe she was not reading after all because he thought he saw her glance at him sidewise, never turning her head from her book, and she was clearly conscious that he was observing her; her lips had tightened. She inked a note in the margin; then, putting her book down determinedly, she looked around as if she were making up her mind to go; she noticed him overtly. He was rather sure that she disliked him. Her jaw was hard; that was the first feature of her face that he caught (he had the feeling that her face must always be closed and wary like that); and secondarily he saw her reddish-gold hair, her face freckled like an egg, her green eyes, in which he correctly read cool suspicion for him who stood watching her with such a funny look (he was trying to figure out why the earplugs had brought him to her). He thought now that she seemed familiar. It was, he conceded, entirely possible that she was Milly, although why the earplugs should have led him to Milly he could not fathom; he had not thought about Milly since before his college days ten years ago now; he and Milly had never been close, although since he had never been close with anybody maybe that was not so significant. Nor did she seem to him to be the type of person who could be relied upon to be an insect sympathizer, but in this perhaps he was wrong. She was frowning through the window at him as if she had begun to recognize him also; she cocked her head to stare better; and that mannerism convinced him that she was really Milly.

Behind her, in the hive of glowworm light tubes, the registers beeped happily, their red LED lights indicating that all was well for Dr. Dodger and therefore (through the trickle-down theory) his employees. Dollar bills skimmed across the aluminum counters, like leaves (the ones) and coracles (the fives) crossing to Hades; and the cashiers, who had trained in Las Vegas, dropped the right change back instantly in your palm, including (for all children under ten) one Dr. Dodger bonus nickel. Behind these worthies crouched the food handlers in their white aprons and white track shoes. They watched the electronic command screens unblinkingly. – Now one display winked *FRIES–FRIES–FRIES–FRIES* . Quick as Jack Sprat collecting the fat which division of labor forced him to gather, the nearest handler raced to the great fry bins. Here the nichrome bulbs glared down like red eyeballs, under which the french fries basked, banks and banks of them, dreaming more perfectly than seals on a brownish beach. The bell was going DING – DING – DING – DING; the customer was drumming his fingers, waiting, which meant that the handler had better hurry up with the fries if he wanted to keep his action-packed job, so he shoveled up a boxful of fries with his scoop and dashed to the counter. – Now already the electronic screen was blinking *BURGERS—BURGERS—BURGERS— BURGERS*, so off he ran; he didn't mind that so much; the worst was when someone wanted coffee like Milly had done; then you had to sprint to the great urn, slam down your visor to protect your face from the steam burns, and lift the lid so the steam rose up about your face and you dipped your giant syringe into the steam blindly, like a probe descending to the surface of Venus (surface temperature seven hundred degrees Fahrenheit) and the bell was going DING – DING – DING –DING so you had to hurry and almost always you overshot and your wrist plunged into the boiling coffee; YOWWWW! – but DING – DING – DING – DING, so you slurped up the coffee, feeling the flesh begin to boil off your hand and wrist, and slammed down the great echoing lid, and squirted the syringe into a cup and brought the cup up front (without an unprofessional moan or grimace) for Milly to drink it, Milly who would not have minded if you had taken five or ten minutes; and then it was off to the first aid station; DING – DING – DING – DING! – Milly sat with her coffee untasted in front of her. She had only bought it so that she could sit in here. When it got cold she would throw it out. She was looking at Bug.

She was still looking at him.

Bug clapped his hands to his ears in pain; molten wax from the dying earplugs sizzled out. – Well, he supposed, the bugs must consider her invaluable.

Beetles crawled out from hidden places in the city and formed a circle around his feet. Milly frowned at him through the window.

WAYNE AND MILLY

~~~~~~

The only thing between you and blue sky is a matter of seconds.

Ford Mustang ad in
Newsweek, 24 March 1986

Milly's books were lined with exclamation points; and she was quick to attack her authors at their most vulnerable point – the qualifications. Speaking of the moment when bats "fluttered away from the insectivore line and gave rise to ourselves," Milly's copy of Eisley's *The Invisible Pyramid* said (p. 55), "What fragment of man, perhaps a useful fragment, departed with them?" – Milly frowned crossly and underlined the "perhaps." – "Something, shall we say, that had it lingered, might have made a small, brave, twilight difference in the mind of man." Sarcastically, Milly underscored "might" three times and made a big exclamation point in the margin. She had little use for bats. Bats listened to you at the window. Bats could go crazy at electronic signals and bite you. And Wayne had told her once that his grandmother was out washing clothes in broad daylight when a swarm of bats came falling out from under the eaves like dried prunes and carried all the linen away. Milly was just a little girl then; she believed Wayne although Wayne always lied to Milly to impress her. Milly sat right in front of Wayne in third grade. She had a long red pigtail which Wayne wanted very much to pull because from the softness of it and the way it shone in the sunbeams coming in through the open window and the way it had of resting so lightly on the shoulder of her checkered dress and moved quick as a good pet when she bent her head over her arithmetic sheet Wayne could tell that it would feel so good in his hand, just like the wooden grip of his pistol felt like ecstasy ten years later when he wrapped the fingers of his right hand around the smooth finished wood just below the trigger guard;

everything fit in his hand so perfectly; and then Wayne grinned tightly and his heart pounded faster than when he had made his first boomerang, for now he crooked his index finger so gently inside the metal ring around the trigger, just like the first time he had parted the lips of a girl's pussy with his finger and slipped his finger inside and it had felt so nice, like it had been made for him to do that; so Wayne touched the middle of the first pad of his index finger to the gun's clitoris and almost squeezed it just a little bit, but he waited, delaying the pleasure, and clenched his right hand tighter and tighter against the walnut grip and wrapped his left hand around his right hand and flipped the ambidextrous safety to off safe with the thumb of his left hand, and took his right index finger off the trigger and put it back on the trigger again and took it off the trigger and rested it on the trigger so gently it almost didn't touch but this was the irrevocable contact all the same; and he held the pistol out straight along the line from shoulder to wrist, with the left arm bent at a forty-five degree angle, and he squinted so that the rear sight lined up with the front sight *just right* and shifted his stance slightly and waited, his heart pounding, and began to draw the trigger back more and more, and the more it came back the better it felt against his finger, aah-*haw*, aah-*haw*, aah-*haw*; and he grinned so hard he ground a micron off his teeth, and kept sight picture consistent with sight alignment, and pulled her back and back and back and back, centimeter by centimeter, till BLOOM! — he'd let her fly, and off she went through the blue blue sky, 'way out in the hills, with clouds in the sky and little brooks like music-boxes all around him, just him and the gun, and far away up on the notch of the hillside above the yellow birch trees there was Wayne's inch-and-a-half-square target, namely a South American postage stamp commemorating Yaqui archery, mounted on a toothpick; and putting the gun on safe so that the hammer snapped back to dropped position, Wayne set it down and looked through his rubberized armored binoculars just in time to see the bullet streaking through the trees, zipping through a maple leaf, flirting with the air, a long streak of comet-exhaust hanging behind it, cold and poisonous; and it blasted on straight and true and circled the target three times and hesitated for a moment — and Wayne gripped the binoculars hard; only now would he know whether he had sighted with true understanding and made contact with the trigger with all the forces of deep intuitive sympathy; and SMACK-O! — Zeroing his binocs, Wayne could see that the bullet had gone through the exact center of the red dot in the white spot in the black circle in the middle of the concentric savage-colored rings of the ferocious stamp; BULL'S-EYE!

Milly's pigtail would have felt like that.

Wayne always offered to carry Milly's books home for her, and he picked her blackberries in the summer, getting up really early before school and going out into the bushes in the back yard where the bugs watched Wayne and marked him as a future danger. He brought her the berries in a shiny #10 can which his grandmother's instant coffee had once been in. – "Thank you," Milly said without enthusiasm when Wayne set the can on her desk at recess. – Milly was undemonstrative. She had already made up her mind never to be Wayne's friend. But Wayne did not learn for twenty years that Milly was not his friend. – Milly did not like Wayne because he never did his homework and he copied off her paper and was loud; his voice hurt her ear. Once she turned round because she thought she felt a daddy-longlegs crawling up her pigtail; and she saw Wayne's hand just about to seize her pigtail and she slapped his face as hard as she could. But Wayne just laughed and thought nothing of it because he was used to hitting and being hit.

"Milly Dalton!" said the teacher. "Why did you strike your classmate?"

"He was trying to pull my hair!" said Milly, not in the least intimidated.

"Wayne Gary Hysaw!" said the teacher like a prayer. "Did you wish to hurt Milly?"

Wayne hawed. "Hurt 'er? No, *ma'am*."

"Then what *were* you trying to do?"

Wayne knew that there was no point trying to say that he had wanted to know what Milly's hair felt like. Besides, if he got punished he would feel like a hero for Milly's sake, not knowing that Milly was only too happy to see him punished, that Milly really hated Wayne more and more every day. – He slammed his desk top down tensely, clearing the decks. "Send me to the corner or whup me with the ruler," he said. "I'm ready."

A SCIENTIFIC NOTE

~~~~~~

> The prize is worth streams of blood, and for its sake that blood
> will be spilled with joy by everyone from the highest officer down
> to the drummer boy.
>
> EDWIN VON MANTEUFFEL
> inspiring Prince Frederick Charles to
> take Düppel (10 March 1864)

You can actually conduct electrolysis of a concentrated sodium
chloride solution, such as that which is found inside a girl, although
her potential energy will generally be lower than yours, when you
are lusting after her very body salts and dogged kidneys making her
lemony urine as transparent as yellow watercolor and chock-full
of sodium ions except when blue-green chlorine is present at the
anode. The desired process is a transfer of some of your own water
molecules so that she acquires an extra electron. Then the solution
surrounding her cathodes becomes charged with a high concentration of sodium ions and hydroxide ions. If this solution is drained off
and evaporated, the product is solid sodium hydroxide, like semen
stiffening the sheets of the bed, and the clean salty buttercup twinkle
is clouded white with your manly stuff as she sits peeing on the
porcelain salt-balance apparatus afterwards, while you lie on your
elbows in the bed, looking absently through the half-open bathroom
door. She flushes. (Salt-water fishes have to drink all the time, and
fresh-water fishes have to urinate all the time.) The costliest part of
this operation is the electrical power required. It's rather disgusting
considered as a whole. Then she comes back to you and sits beside
you and tries to say something nice; how can you have the heart to
tell her that it's disgusting and you don't like the way she pees?
Sometimes her breath isn't so good when you wake up beside her in
the morning, either. Of course you're frogs and snails and puppy-

dogs' tails yourself, or at least I, the author, am. You, reader, may be composed of honey and wax, especially if you hail from one of those advanced societies from behind the hive barrier, where achievements made in third year of Five-Year Plan are striking and joyful proofs of dynamic development meriting presentation of high award to Azerbaijan S.S.R. ("As dear as soul to any man! Azerbaijan, Azerbaijan!" – Samed Vurgun); but I myself am not perfect; in my turpitude I have a mole on my buttock, and there's some sort of crud in my left armpit. Nevertheless, mutual attractions do exist. Well, as an explanatory aid I offer Coulomb's Law: As the distance between similarly charged bodies increases, the repulsion decreases. Now certainly I have always wanted to have an affair with a Russian girl, make friends with a beetle, for they both would, I fancy in my ignorance, have unusual experiences to communicate in open discussion format. Anyone sufficiently removed from one would do, which is why all girls seem so terrific to the sweaty-fingered highschool math nerd who has nothing better to go on, poor thing, than the anatomy diagrams in the Young Teens section of the library, sort of like having to storm some mysterious complex of the reactionaries given only the blueprints for the storm drains when what you're going to be coming up through is the sewers. Women are sewers just like we are, the once pure boys recognize with a start; it's raw sewage that produces fertilization; once you understand that you can be fond of yourself and members of the Opposite Sex, but you can never quite see them again as ice cream bars. I, the author, don't really mind this, for I love all girls and love to hug and kiss them and cheer them up when they cry, and have them perform all the same services for me; and a woman's saliva is certainly a miracle, think of all those enzymes and germs; and if I took and wrote the chemicals down on a sheet of paper, all COOOHs and sighs, it would look pretty, just like a face all pretty, like the dear round moon-face of her who loves you or the creamy-freckled skin and blue eyes and heavenly hair of that Irish beauty back in college, so don't think I'm complaining. Nonetheless, my own lovely green antennae are simply not as sensitive now as they used to be in my days of puberty; and to understand our hero and his earplugs we must remind ourselves that his feelers had not yet been deadened by their first mega-dose of girlectricity; he was just sniffing after lovely trailing sparks at the time, and exhibiting the usual behavioral abnormalities of boys: no less than six genetically different types of shaking, that "waltzing" and circling sometimes to be found in palsied mice, a recessive tremor and cramp disease not unlike that to be met with in inbred rabbits. What about the Junior Prom? he wondered.

It was certainly a funny feeling to have the earplugs in, for at dark the tinglings of night-gulls and night-girls did make him sit up straight at the soda parlor, yes indeed; somewhere nearby on the street was a girl who might be willing to kiss him: — the tingle was driving him crazy, so he gulped the last of a fine vanilla malt, the kind they made so thick that you could literally turn the cup upside down for a few seconds and nothing would spill out; and it was so cold and foamy and good with ice cream lumps that he really could have had two more, but what could you do when the earplugs made his whole skull vibrate like when the dentist cleaned his teeth, vrrrvrrrvrrrrrrrrrr RRRRRVRRVRVRRRRRRR VRVREEEEEEEE with all the raspberry-flavored cleaning paste aching delightfully into every last son of a molar; he wanted so much to kiss a girl. So he paid and went out. — Bug was at this time seventeen years of age, a sallow pimply youth of great sensitivity. His terroristic bent remained latent, suppressed even more tightly behind the steel springs of puberty; he wanted to love, love, love, to reproduce his kind; the springs tightened and tightened; soon they would be loosed and send the bullet forward. — Across the street girls were in line for the movies. Dr. Dodger's Cinerama had winking yellow lights to beguile the eye, and even show-posters in full color so that you could go stand near the cashier's booth and see what you would be paying for, not that the feature really mattered if you were with a sweet girl who would let you put your hand down her bra and you would receive from her long long kisses that tasted of popcorn and Coke as in the darkness the movie blared on and all the other adolescents moaned and grunted around you; it was optimal. — Outside the theater, on a snowy winter's night, Bug walked up and down the line. The feature was scheduled to start in fifteen minutes; the boys and girls stood waiting together, some hoping that their friends would see them with their latest catch, others (the catches) hoping that *their* friends would not be near here tonight to see how low they had gone to accept the invitation of this loser; everything, as they used to say when I was a kid, is relative. Now this is hardly an original axiom but it is not as if every teenager invents the need to have a sweetheart, either; nonetheless the need does not go away for that. — Bug walked up the line casting shy glances at his school-mates; he was still carrying his math book under his arm. — The earplugs tried to help him. — Stronger, weaker, weaker, not here, four-beat rest, let's see, oh, hell, wait a minute, over here, maybe; no, here; stronger, weaker, stronger, stronger, coming in just Jim

Dandy like all the pheromones in China and a hundred cute Korean girls' armpits; there we go, whoopee, it was, it was lovely Lumina this time (he never thought of Milly at this time; Milly was at home reading up on leftist politics; she was a good deal less latent than Bug although the Great Beetle had no stake in her yet), Lumina who was graceful in a way that could never be described with her conjugate base, Lumina who later married a reinsurance man; oh, dipole, dipole! with her hair as blonde as his milkshake, in her soft downy coat, with her blonde hair tucked up under the hood fringed with fur; he could see the swell of her sweet breasts under the parka; her mouth was perfect; her adorable mittens winked at him with their thumbs; they wanted him to stroke them; the outline of her hips was a double bow ready to be strung by him; her face, her wonderful face made his cool thoughts go scrambled and incoherent when he saw it; now she turned away to say something to the other girl and he could see the profile of that splendid cheek; oh, Lumina, my Lumina; be my darling and I will take care of you forever; I will love you dearly and hug you for hours and hours every day; I will never kill anyone; I will take you into the forest and we will have little beetles bring us nuts and berries and clean the floor of our hut; you will bear many splendid children who will do all the chores in our old age. – For a second (but only a second) her eyes looked into his eyes; he wanted to kiss her eyes; really he had always wanted to kiss her. Her picture in the yearbook made him swallow hard and turn white; and there was another photo of her with the debating team and he made ten xeroxes of that picture and cut her out from each one and pasted all the little Luminae together and hid them under his bed. Once she'd been his lab partner in chemistry; once she'd touched his hand when passing the cork of an Erlenmeyer flask. Please, God, let her kiss me. Oh how I want her to kiss me. But she was standing with another girl. He couldn't. He couldn't do it. What if they both laughed? Lumina's friend in particular looked dangerous and malicious, a raucous chuckler, one of those loud hard bluejay girls whose noise awoke the predators. He could tell that she didn't like him. Maybe everyone in line would see and snicker and pop gum. – What was he supposed to do, just lean over and kiss those pink lips of Lumina's? She was smiling at him. She was probably hoping that he would try something so that she could laugh at him; she and her friend were double-dating some guys who hadn't shown up yet; maybe Wayne and Parker (not that Wayne and Parker ever dated girls much; they had other fish to fry, just as Milly didn't want to be wasting time on the amenities; she had finished a

book on Central America and was now reading the Wintringham/
Blashford-Snell history of weapons and tactics which finally made
clear to her in detail why it was that *Blitzkriegs* did not work under
ultramodern conditions of people's war; Milly underlined "ultra-
modern" suspiciously; and Wayne called her but when she heard his
voice she hung up on him, and Wayne hawed and told Parker that
Milly sure was coy, at which remark Parker twiddled his thumbs at
Wayne sarcastically. So Wayne called up Susan, with the radio on
loud in the background so that she would know how casual he was,
but just as she came on the line, all hot and anxious because she had
been waiting for Wayne to call her, Parker disconnected the line
with one tap of a finger to the hang-up button, and Wayne realized
that tonight Parker expected him to help with projects and not spend
the evening in frivolous pursuits. So he did not call Susan back. And
Susan sat by the phone waiting and waiting until she couldn't stand
it anymore.) Lumina looked at Bug and thought that it was nice that
Bug was finally paying attention to her. She liked Bug and would
even have bought him a ticket to see the movie with her. He was
always pretty quiet in chemistry, but she thought that he had
something to say; it was just that he didn't know how to say it. Poor
Bug. She stretched out her hand to him. — His white face flushed. His
heart beat like a thousand praying mantises being executed by a
firing squad of the last true men. She said his name, indicated a place
beside her in line . . . Did she want him here or was she trying to tell
him that she'd saved a place for her boyfriend? — Bug always played
it safe. You might say that he had learned the hard way. — Her smile
was slipping off. — He nodded coolly and walked on. Goddamned
earplugs! Now Lumina hated him, he was sure.

You want God to tell you something is true so you'll really know
it's true, but you know that even if He tells you you won't entirely
believe Him. That girl is willing to kiss you, son, if you play your
cards right and are nice to her. — Yes, I know, but what if she *isn't?*
(Which is just another way of saying that if you need the earplugs
you can't possibly use them.)

The same goes for other devices in that product line. — Bugs and
reactionaries have developed a transmitter pill. The subject swallows
it, thinking it to be aspirin or Mydol, and quick as you can say
six-legs-good-two-legs-bad it's in place, powered by the victim's
nervous system and giving a personalized readout silhouette as a
result of radio waves bouncing off individual variations in bone
structure. That was what he wanted: — "Come on, Lumina, lemme
buy you a milkshake. And try one of these li'l pink candies." Then

home again, home again, jiggety-scuttle to the bugeye receiver console hidden under the pile of dirty underwear. Tune in to the dear gurgle of her stomach, adjust the frequency to 36–24–36, and hear everything she had to say about him. But what if she said something really cruel, something about his pimples or all the other things he couldn't bear? – No, technology was not the answer. But he kept the earplugs handy.

On the swim team everybody had to have earplugs anyway, because for the county meet you were expected to dive off a thousand-foot-high board into this raving flurry of bottomless muddy water that had never been cleaned because they couldn't afford to change the filters, so over the course of time a few things had gotten in – oh, it started small: a couple of minnows some kid tossed in, and some eggs hidden in microscopic follicles of Roger Garvey's hand after he'd been cleaning his aquarium; but before you knew it it was frightful down there, with a whole phalanx of malicious sea-urchins all lined up on the bottom (Wayne reported after making reconnaissance) hoping to spear you in the eye; for the water was so green and filthy that you could only unclamp your eyelids for a second every now and then, and even if you could afford Jacques Cousteau goggles with air vents and windshield wipers you wouldn't be able to see very long because the barnacles would come affix themselves to the glass like half-starved rats going for cheese. – Bug's earplugs hardly had that regulation look. – "Hey, c'mon," the coach would say, "why be such a wiseass and cram those homemade things in your ears when anyone can see they're just made outta cockroach spiracles an' insect goo?" – Bug kept up a sullen silence. He didn't want to be there anyway; he didn't get along with the other boys; the other boys didn't get along with him; he didn't get along with swimming; swimming didn't get along with him; he didn't get along with the coach; the coach didn't get along with him, but it was required so he had to put up with it, even if it didn't have to put up with him. – The other fellas laughed and laughed. – "Jeez, what a dork," goes Chip. "Bet his mom's got a stinger. An' you know he thinks he kin get into Lumina's pants!" – "Lumina, that's the chemistry brain with the big tits?" sez Doug, kinda innerested. He likes Lumina. – "Well, I dunno about the brains but I do know about the tits." – "Well, they're not half the size of Ellen's but that Lumina thinks she's somebody special. You probably won't believe me but I saw her scratch herself once." – Wayne haws. – "Well,

she's gonna let that hornet ram his thing up her ass I say good
riddance for the *whole* human race!" – "Awright, men," the coach
said. "Personally I don't give a shit but we're not supposed to talk
about the integration policy. Let's go!" – Into the locker room. They
all put on their swimming trunks fast, but they looked while they did
it. Parker's dick was the longest. Bug's was about average. If he'd
been halfway coordinated, so he could pull strokes instead of
making waves, he might've been considered a sub-regular guy.

"Okay, men," says the coach, he says, as they all sit nice and
comfy in the front row of the bleachers; and the air was sweet and
steamy with chlorine, and little droplets of sweat sparkled alertly on
the guys' hairy chests; Wayne's chest was as black as a bear's; and
his arms could crush the life out of you; and Parker's chest was pale
greenish and had weeds of hair here and there like algae on a
mudbank, though for the most part it was striated with smooth
slippery rings of muscle for squirming, and scaled as if Parker had
eczema or dried-up sores; while Bug's chest was undeveloped,
hairless, like a blank sheet of paper. – He sat three seats left of all the
other guys. The coach, turned slightly toward the others, the *real*
team, presented Bug with a sight of the bluish bald spot on the back
of his head, and Bug sat there looking down at his own bare flabby
thighs, that soon would be goosebumped from the cold water;
and he waited there hoping not to come off too badly. Of course
he would screw things up and come out badly in the exercises
themselves; all he asked was that the others ignore him, not make a
scene; when Bug was a boy his father always made scenes; if when
Bug was out with the family at Cooverville Pond and his father had
ordered him to tow his sister on the rubber float, and he turned too
sharply and capsized her by mistake, then Bug's father came running
out into the water with balled fists, yelling "YOU SON OF A
BITCH!" and all the neighbors elongated on their beach towels
beneath the trees de-elongated themselves to take notice; in fact they
had to because Bug's family was right in the thick of them and Bug's
father came leaping over the scattered bodies like a beachcomber at
Dachau; then as our hero waded ashore for punishment he himself
was forced to step over all those arms and heads and breasts and
pot-bellies, and they were all looking at him, those people, and
saying nothing; and the arms and legs and toes and breasts were
pointed at him, too; the nipples of the bored women stiffened at the
thought of blood; and the little kids snickered at Bug like they
always did; in truth people were not so nice to Bug, which was why
he became a murderer; for in later life he judged people too quickly

and usually assigned them evil negative ratings, because most cases were ambiguous and he had been hurt so many times that he did not give ambiguous cases the benefit of the doubt; so he killed them, though of course he had a perfect right to do so since I, Big George, eat a thousand boys for breakfast, and enjoy it, too. – So as I, the author, was saying, Bug sat there and hoped that this time the boys would not be too mean to him; the year was already a quarter over and at the end of it he would never have to take Physical Education again; so he sat there, once passive, now passive-aggressive, eventually to become aggressive wholly as he killed and thereby became one with the rest of the world. – Hurray for Bug; onward; onward! – Of course it *would* be a lot to ask of the team to ignore him when they were on the return lap stroking for genuine practice-points and Bug was still going uh-uh-uh-uh, still outward bound, and not looking where he was going because he was trying so hard to keep up and keep his head above water that he couldn't swim straight, just like my Clara Bee, when we were up at the reservoir once in New York state; and poor Bee swam out deep and liked it at first but then she got confused and panicky and wanted to go ashore but couldn't see anything without her glasses, and swam round and round in spirals going farther and farther out, and cried, and was so scared she couldn't listen to me or understand who I was or let me help her; but at any rate the tale had a good ending; for finally Bee was so exhausted she let herself be towed; and then when she could see the green blur of trees she was able to save herself. – So Bug would steer a little crazy and maybe bump into oncoming Chip, just like at square dances he could never follow the calls and so he'd be pulling his partner one way while everyone else went another, so he blushed and felt miserable and the girl despised him. – In spite of these deficiencies, Bug considered himself an extraordinary individual and he undoubtedly was, for why else would the magic earplugs be vested in him? So when things happened, good or bad, he took them as calmly as possible, figuring that life would get better, which would be fine, or it would get worse, which was acceptable, because it couldn't get much worse. – But you cannot understand this unless you are a devotee of revolutionary yoga or electric meditation, as Bug was, sitting there without adequate medical treatment for whatever Chip or Parker or Wayne might do to him this time. – Doug was relatively kind to Bug because Doug was a nice guy who just wanted to win his trophy and go on to the Olympics so that his mother would be proud of him; and Roger would never have helped nor hurt Bug had he not been given express orders to do the latter. All the others were men of the staunchest possible character. — So, as a bug peered down through the ceiling grating with zoom-telephoto eyes, it saw (in the middle of an infinity of exercise mats and rusted dumbbells and pullup bars stacked like jungle gyms all around the edges of that dismal pool) our hero's soft hands clenching tight on his kneecaps, and a shabby sort of nervous expression on his girlish face, which *though* girlish *was* pimply. He was nervous because his earplugs were tingling more than usual today; yes, something bad was going to happen. And the coach talked on and waved his arms like a magician in the stifling greenish air. Everything was stale by the swimming pool. The concrete deadened sounds; the coach sounded as if he were talking through a gas mask; the lapping water in the great pool did not echo but only slooshed dully, continuously, like a stagnant underground lake pulled into faint fake tides by a vein of lodestone, deep inside some cave in Kentucky or in Lonesome Grave, Indiana, where Wayne was born. — Not that this was much of an improvement on a stupid ass lonesome grave, thought Wayne in disgust as the coach talked on and on. Still, there was something of strategic importance to what the coach was saying now; it was a new TACTIC he was detailing; a new PLOY; instantly, as Wayne understood this fact, he leaned forward on his bleacher seat and began listening to the coach very carefully, and the coach heard the creaking wood as Wayne shifted forward, and he looked down at Wayne's face and thought, yes, I can still teach these young men, and Wayne here's a good one and someday I'll read about him in the papers, if that funny Parker don't mess him up; I dunno about that Parker; he gets points, but there's something funny about him; — and Wayne glanced sideways at Parker to see what Parker thought of this new maneuver that the coach was leading them into understanding step by step — but Parker wasn't looking at Wayne; Parker was flickering his tongue in the air, to taste the metal content; and thinking his own thoughts; and was not prepared to be bothered by Wayne just then, Wayne could tell, so Wayne's heart sank a little, but he began to feel good again as he got the gist of what the coach was saying: — "Okay, men," says the coach, he says, "today I'm gonna show you how to do a trick that's called the Octopus, which they just introduced into Olympic rules. Now you gotta be careful when you do this one or you'll down your man for more than the regulation six point seven five minutes required to starve the brain of oxygen without permanent damage, so always carry a stopwatch, and the way it works is like when you're lined up to go on the starting side of the pool and there's some jerk on the other team like Jack LaLanne or Mark Spitz who's gonna screw up our divisional record for the semifinals then you get the two best men we have on either side of him and three other men on either side of *them*, so it makes a total of eight, just like the eight legs of an octopus, you see, and once you get into that murk and other crap in the water where the ref can't see better than whistling Dixie you go for him, two on each arm and leg, and drag him down and bang his head against the ladder on the side until you count a hundred air bubbles coming out of his mouth, and meantime you have to look like you're just swimming along and he's taking a breather or something on the bottom, and then on bubble number one-ought-one you all kick him quick in the balls to wake him up before his heart stops and shove him up ahead of you where he was before, and then catch him up and pass a few seconds later."

Our hero was chosen to be the volunteer on whom the Octopus would be practiced, at which there were hearty laughs.

THE SWIM TEAM

~~~~~~

... as more syndromes are being reported, a wider spectrum of "etiologic malignancies" is becoming apparent.

HOWARD L. WEINER, M.D. and LAWRENCE P. LEVITT, M.D.
Neurology for the House Officer
(Williams & Wilkins, 3rd ed., 1983)

In addition to our hero, there were exactly eight other guys on the swim team, which was why the Octopus was such a perfect exercise. They were, in decreasing order of scoring value, Wayne, Parker, Chip, Glenn, Big George, Bob, Doug and Roger. I must emphasize that this arrangement is for the reader's reference only, as Roger could spit the farthest and Doug had once won the Coover Cup, which was artfully shaped in the likeness of a silver mermaid in a bikini.

Glenn, Bob and Doug are of no importance to the narrative, and Chip's significance must be rated "moderate." Let us agree right now to give Roger a "medium."

FOR WHOM THE BELL TOLLS

~~~~~~

When doom arrives for you and all the rest of us, then shall you learn whether I forged that ancient writing.

H. RIDER HAGGARD
Heart of the World (1894)

It must be acknowledged that to compel loafers to work is democratic and humane.

The Soviet Way of Life
(Progress Publishers, Moscow, *ca.* 1975)

Bug had his earplugs in, and they were tingling in his ears. The sea-urchins tittered. He was squatting behind the starting line on the south end. The cracked old concrete was slippery with sweat, impetigo and athlete's foot. Here it had been worn down in places by the thrusting toes of generations of boys; these pits were constantly awash with water and had taken on the appearance of little tide-pools, inhabited as they were by algae and locker-lice. Ahead lay the grey foggy water. – Chip was on his left, and Wayne was on his right. He craned his head further in both directions and saw six other sets of hairy knees. Manfully, he bit his lip. – Wayne had the stopwatch. He was a big fellow by now who was interested in military science and had built his own scale model of Stalingrad for the Jayvees competition and claimed he could screw three girls at once. Chinese girls had sideways cunts, he said, and black girls had clits so big that when he was on top they could stick them up his asshole. He had a good set of white teeth that he could show frankly in a barnstorming grin (whereas the girls with him always smiled shyly through little lips); and he had honest blue eyes and very hairy arms and legs and a class ring. He slammed his Aquavision mask down on his nose, tightened it, took it off, spat in it, and swished the water around in it to keep it from fogging up; and pulled it back down snug against his eyes. He zeroed his stopwatch. He leaned over and said into Bug's ear, "Awright, guy, you do what I say and go limp and easy and I'll just give you a knockout blow to the chin so you'll never feel a thing, got me, Four-Eyes? – Because otherwise you might get me a little *mad*," and he spat in Bug's ear. Chip on the other side stepped on his foot. All the eight had diving jackets with compensators and the optional drain mesh panel, large front pocket, waist and crotch strap assembly with thirty pounds of buoyancy and an inner polyurethane bladder. Our hero alone crouched pale and spindly in his bathing trunks.

The coach, who was studying the pool (he had observed it for twenty-six years, and knew when the sea-monsters were liable to be quiescent, had a whole pattern worked out, and had come to a sort of agreement with them: the night before a meet he picked up some Prom Queen virgin from the basement of the School Board Office and after he and Parker and Wayne had banged her they plopped her in and then everything was quiet the next day except for maybe a few subaqueous burps that shivered the concrete and shook the bleachers ever so slightly; of course the bleachers might have rocked just because somebody farted because they were all old and creakety anyhow and covered with birdshit and spiders way up among the ceiling girders spinning their tea-cosies around grey burned-out light bulbs) – the coach as I was saying took his spyglass from the pocket of his faded tee-shirt, wiped the lens and screwed the eyepiece around just right but the polarizer was all scratched over and he couldn't see a thing beneath the surface of the water. He shrugged and picked lint outta his eyebrows.

"Okay, men," he said. "Well, you look like a crack team today and I'm sure you won't disappoint your old coach doing the Octopus, unless of course you do and then it'll be punishment drill for hours on the hard concrete, but the key thing to keep in mind is to treat our volunteer here, young Bug, with kid gloves, 'cause he's not quite as tough as the rest of us, probably a bit nervous, too, since I can see him blinking his bugeyes and I can see sweat running down his forehead and I think that's the first time I've *ever* seen him sweat, unlike the rest of you who have always done your best and pulled your weight; anyway I don't want to take up all period telling you what you already know, so ready on the line and just do what you have to do on the count of three and ONE remember to TWO give 'im THREE hell!"

They dove in.

The earplugs tingled, in justifiable agitation.

The understanding was that they would all swim out about fifty meters before they performed the Octopus, but the others were all swimming like mad, they were so excited at finally being given license to drown this creep that everybody hated; even bleeding-heart Doug had to look at it as a neat technical challenge; whereas Bug, terrified though he was, could not keep up and so at around thirty meters the others realized that he was considerably behind them and swerved like killer fish coming round, with Wayne in the lead and Parker cunningly circling to cut him off from the rear. He knew that once they grabbed his hair or the waistband of his swim trunks and began to pull him down he would be finished, so there was nothing to do but take a few last c.c. of gymnasium air (which smelled like rotting socks) into his chest, and thrust his head down and his feet straight up into the air and dive deep into the green-brown water while he could. Through the water he felt the eerie pressure of their shouts and thrashings; and undoubtedly they were all filling their own lungs right now and activating their regulators to go after him, and in seconds he'd feel Parker's inevitable grip on his ankle and Parker would dig in his long yellow ragged fingernails and then Glenn would get his other foot and tickle the sole of it remorselessly until Chip got him in a walrus-style chokehold to keep him under until the other five boys arrived on the scene. He stroked and kicked himself down faster thinking of this, faster than he had ever known he could go, until the water sang in his ears and sloshed there icily as he heard the muffled groaning of the old rusty ladders creaking back and forth and he went deeper and the pressure began to push the earplugs deeper and deeper into his ears until they ached and he was afraid that he would never be able to get them out later, but of course there might not be any later, so he forced himself down deeper as his eyes began to bulge out, deeper and deeper into the cold water.

Deep-sea diving can induce narcosis, which manifests itself at perhaps a hundred and fifty feet. Euphoria is present, followed by a sharpening of the sense of hearing, a numbness in the extremities and a gradual sense of unreality. As these sensations stole upon him, he slackened his speed, his fear dissolving into languid pleasure. The earplugs tingled. Cilia began to blossom from them, vaned like kelp or mosquito's comb; water frothed and bubbled about his ears, and he felt a great ease, as if he had just emptied his bladder. He understood that he no longer needed to breathe air, that the insects had provided for him as they would have done for one of their own aquatic larvae. For they loved him. – He looked up and saw the dim blue shapes of the other boys above him, their movements innocuous, playful, like those of a school of dolphins. He dove down another fifty feet until they had disappeared. He could still see yellow-finned tuna about him, and ocean sharks snickering along another fifty feet below. The surface was a faint green shimmering, with just a hint of tremendous hostile glare beyond it. There was nothing for him up there. He dove down past the sharks, who paid him no notice, thinking that here was just another lost bug without much meat beneath that exoskeleton of his (though they grinned knowingly, like Parker, who had always enjoyed blocking him good and *hard* in third-grade football, and our hero found himself looking quickly at his body to make sure there were no cuts or scratches which might excite them). He went a hundred feet lower still. The green light had now disappeared entirely, and the water in which he found himself was a rich transparent purple, in which particulate matter was suspended like grains of pepper in a wash of ink.

He passed by a tree of yellow-brown kelp that drifted sedately in the current. It was as big as an uprooted oak. In its branches clung thousands of the sea-urchins which he had dreaded, but they stared back at him with the benign idiocy of pickling onions. They would never hurt him. Snails and caddice-worms also crewed the great ark of kelp, and here and there writhed pretty electric eels, which could have emitted sparks to punish with death the creatures they disliked, so that the victim would have tumbled silently and slowly down the long, smooth thermocline into the blackness of the abyss, but the eels never did that because they disliked nobody; they only killed for practice; now they balanced on their tails and danced in the current, and I wish that my Bee could have seen, because she would have clapped her hands and thought that they were so neat; and the eels made up to snooty water-snakes that had fled the electrification of coastal South America; and the electric eels showed off all the tricks they knew for the snakes, like eighteen simultaneous sexy wriggles in all directions, eels being in a sense comprised of many many luscious hips to swing; and they showed off firework sparks; and the urchins watched in delight, though they could never remember any trick by the time that the next one had started; while the snakes meanwhile showed off their rumbas and combinations and black-green permutations; and the eels fell in love with the snakes and the snakes fell in love with the eels (although they were not yet ready to admit to it) and everyone but Bug was happy.

He continued downward. He wondered what he would have

seen had he been able to descend into the depths of the lake at his old summer camp – lots of water-bugs, most likely, and peaceable, somewhat dull conventions of pickerel and bass – but probably, too, old musket-balls and sunken, rotten canoes, and cold horrid lampreys and the skeletons of massacred Indians. Here, at least, in this warm, colorful marine environment, he had seen nothing evil.

At the 2600-foot point of his descent (which was indicated by a rusty plaque in sagging chains, the plaque depicting the skull of a drowned mariner, with barnacles for teeth), he reached a typical Red Sea or Indian Ocean reef, which continued straight down into the darkness as far as he could see. The water was illuminated both by phosphorescence and residual blue-green light from the surface – a weak, kindly sort of color like that of an old couch that he used to sit on as a child. The reef might well have been one of the concrete walls of the pool at an earlier time. He rested on a knob of rosy coral that jutted out from it, smiling as the little salt-minnows came and kissed him. Great anemones gulped like pale flowers, like sweet Catherine about to recite in Russian class, and beautiful fish striped yellow and blue and white came to see him. Then his earplugs tingled. He looked around him and could not see anything, and then finally he glanced up and saw all eight of them coming down toward him with flashlights and long black spear-guns; let's see, that must be Wayne up there with the Polynesian Deluxe and Doug had evidently gotten himself a Corsica Revolver for lifetime use. The flashlights were blindingly bright; his enemies could see him easily.

THE BATTLE IN THE SWIMMING POOL

~~~~~~

> A convenient and successful way to kill insects is to drop them into
> a wide-mouthed bottle, the bottom of which is lined with blotting
> paper that has been previously saturated with ether, benzine,
> creosote or chloroform. When a butterfly, bug, or beetle is put into
> a bottle prepared in this manner, and the bottle tightly corked, the
> insect expires without a struggle, and hence without injuring itself.
>
> D.C. BEARD
> *The American Boy's Handy Book* (1882)

In the winter time, when they had all been a little younger, the boys
used to commence great campaigns of snowball warfare. The
September that our hero was in sixth grade marked a turning point
in their policy from the limited purpose of removing the restrictions
of Gentlemen's Rules to the bolder course which brought them the
spectacular triumphs of January and February. Parker, having a
better reach than anyone else (he also went out for the basketball
team) was the commander. It was not so much a change in the
direction of his aims – which had altered little since the time he had
begun to pull flies' wings off when he was five – as the opening of a
new phase in their development. The time was ripe, he made the
other boys understand, for an *Aufhebung* in the realization of goals
he had long nurtured.

The prospects which he unfolded at a staff meeting during
recess, however, alarmed several members present, particularly
Roger, whose strongest trait was hardly so much sadism as a certain
careless insensitivity. If there was a snail on the sidewalk and it was
in Roger's path he would step on it, but if it was not he might ignore
it entirely, or at worst kick it into the grass so that its shell cracked
and its internal organs were injured and the creature withdrew deep
into itself in its agony and starved and lost all its protective slime

until at last disease got it or a robin yanked it out of its shell and gobbled it. He had an aquarium at home but he was always having to clean it out and start over because he wouldn't get around to feeding the guppies and so a few of them would die and foul up the water and clog up the pump and then the rest would die, too. — Roger also had very poor penmanship and never really mastered fractions and percents, but at about that time calculators became quite cheap.

Parker never said much. He just kinda grinned and picked his teeth and seemed to agree with everything you said, and then when you sat down you'd find he'd put a tack on your chair. Wayne, who was tough and always loved to see results, would go haw at the expression on your face, particularly when it was a tack from an East German army surplus lot and after it homed in and stuck its barbs in your butt it started ticking, and you'd be frantically trying to pull it out when you heard *that* sound, believe you me, but it wouldn't do any good because new time-release spring-wound barbs opened up in your flesh like flowers, and the ticking got softer and softer and softer and softer, and then there'd be a BANG! and a wound two inches deep and blood would trickle down the back of your leg. — But Parker would just run his fingers through his stringy hair and tap a finger on his desk. The teachers out on their coffee break never knew a thing.

"I dunno," Roger said in the deserted classroom, which made Wayne sit up straight and start getting very tense and flexing his big white fingers like piano keys, "I dunno because they might get awfully mad and do something back to us we'll never forget, like make a hole in the snow-fort and take us prisoner and torture us or something."

"Take *you* prisoner, maybe," sneered Chip, "you rubber ducky that can't even run fast or beat up girls."

Parker just sorta scratched himself and yawned.

"I dunno," Roger said. "I just don't wanta get in trouble, that's all."

Then Parker snaked his leg along under his desk and Roger's desk — it was at least ten feet in length, that leg — and hooked it under Roger's chair without a soul noticing, and yanked suddenly so that Roger was flung backward onto his head and the chair fell on top of him and cut his lip and chipped his front tooth and bruised his forehead and knocked the wind out of him. And Roger got the point, which was that if *he*, a member, albeit a despised one, of the General Staff, didn't dare get Parker in trouble for what had happened, then the other army wouldn't squeal, either. And Parker just burped and popped a zit.

The key to the relationship between Parker and the others was to be found in Parker's own attitude. A boy originally from the Omarville School District, he had at first felt exaggerated respect for his generals. After the campaign of the previous winter, however, he saw them as individuals who lacked understanding of almost anything outside their narrow areas of specialty, with the possible exception of Wayne, whom he sometimes had over to his house. – Wayne now drew up a duty roster on the blackboard, which Roger as Secretarial Adjutant was required to copy over by hand for each person present. Chip was put in charge of getting supplies, and for several days he pretended to be a high school student so that he could attend the crowded, ill-supervised shop class. Every day he returned home with his pockets bulging with nails, brads and disposable saw blades. He also procured some barbed wire which they strung along the top of their snow-fort when winter finally set in. They stamped out a circle on the playground twenty feet in diameter, and Wayne set the boys to rolling snowballs while Parker lounged around and watched. Parker's frosty breath hung in the air like long, slow streaks of jet exhaust, and wrapped itself around everybody like scarves. – Now they began to pile up the snowballs along the lines of their foundation, and packed them thick and tight, and added buckets of water until they had a turreted tower perhaps fifteen feet high, with the outer wall all smooth and glassy and blue-grey; and they cut slits in the wall to launch their weapons from, which they then proceeded to make. The nails and brads they embedded point outward in iceballs. The sawblades they had a couple of uses for. Some they simply coated with a thin layer of ice, so that they had cold blue ghastly knives; and the rest they cut up into four-inch lengths and bent them and stuck them into very soft squishy snowballs which they then coated with the most infinitesimal skin of ice to hold the blade in under tension so that when they threw those missiles they would hit you in the face and the ice would shatter and the snow inside would smush all over you and then the coiled blade would go SPOIIING! and maybe take out an ear or an eye . . . So they filled up their tower with ammunition, making only a narrow stepped platform for them to stand on just beneath the inner rim of the tower, and then they planted their flag on the summit of the snowball pile, with the understanding that once the action began Roger would be the standard-bearer. – That was of course the most dangerous job, for the enemy would be trying to destroy or seize the flag (just like in "Capture the Flag" in summer camp, only now since they were big boys the game had a little more teeth in it, is all), but Roger clearly deserved it for being a sissy.

Originally Mr. Sonk the science teacher had wanted to be an observer at the commencement of the ice war to make sure that the Gentlemen's Rules were enforced, but Parker directed Wayne to go talk with him, and the next day Wayne reported that Mr. Sonk had accepted the spirit of the whole thing in a very friendly manner, and sent his regards. Parker told Wayne to reply that they would never forget Mr. Sonk, and that if he should ever need any help or be in danger Parker and Wayne and all the rest would stick with him.

The other side had been very powerful during the previous year, but now they were a year older and took this business less seriously, so they were ill-prepared and had only a few rag-tag sleds made out of barrel-staves, and it would be no trouble to repel their puny attacks. Indeed, Parker had already made up his mind to perform offensive maneuvers rather than just defending the tower; and he intended to hurt them severely.

By noon on the twelfth of December the builders of the fort had completed their last meticulous preparations (and Roger had patted every inch of the ramparts to make sure that he could trust them to parade Parker's standard along), but they did not actually cross the frontier until the thirty-first of January. Operations were launched by lightning action as a result of a serious incident which had subjected them to unbearable provocation; a snowball had hit Roger in the side of the head. By the afternoon of the following day, there was not one member of the opposing band who was not in the hospital.

(One thing that must be admitted is that at least when Parker and his crew charged from their tower on the dawn of that day, as the red sun rose over the schoolyard and glinted darkly on their steel helmets, which they had reinforced with ice, and the playground stretched as white and flat as the Russian steppes, then at least the other side, which ran screaming to the fence and tried desperately to escape over it before they were overwhelmed, defeated by a prismatic bombardment of ice and metal crashing into their shattered heads and smashing their arms and legs and vertebrae so that Parker's side could distinctly hear every snapping of bone in that wonderful stillness of a winter dawn that allows for fine hearing; and the blood that trickled from mouths, noses, and ears made perfect strawberry drops in the new white snow, which Wayne stomped on and smeared into larger light-pink smudges which later darkened, so that after the battle was concluded the snow there was packed down and slippery with black frozen blood like an old glacier under the stars; and meanwhile the bombardment went on and on and on; and then Parker's side lowered their heads and came rushing in one tight line to create panic and stab and stab with their ice-knives — at least, as I was saying, the whole operation was conducted decently, in unison, under rigid discipline and above all without personal animosity; whereas when the war between Mr. White and our hero reached its culmination three decades later in the Arctic, then individuals were stalked, no quarter was shown, and rifle-shots zinged across no-man's-land; that was REAL war — my Teutonic heart pounds to write about it — unlike this kid stuff described above which only distracts me, Big George, from the serious business yet to come.)

These, then, were the foes whom our hero now faced. Not for a moment did they lose sight of their ideal. — Launching gas-powered spears into the darkness below them, they flip-kicked on down through the greenish water, which at this depth was beginning to get quite chilly, but which reminded Chip nonetheless of the evening haze of upstate New York.

Our hero was holing up in another deep crevice, with the corpse of a fish as a shield. He did not like this crevice, but he had very little choice, and he had picked it as far away as he could see it, and swum for it with the whole team coming after him. He was getting tired and afraid. At least he had delayed matters, he thought; and that was no small achievement in this world of Heraclitean flux; yes, perhaps they could carve it on his pure white tombstone: HE DELAYED MATTERS; and it would look nice till the team came out and drank beer and pissed on his grave and went into the sycamores with their girls, who thought it a thrill to be making out among all this death; how romantic. — And now back to the ocean.

He looked cautiously round the caudal fin of the dead fish; and there was a series of blinding magnesium flashes and gas bubbles from behind various coral protrusions in the opposite slope; and instantly the long spears were hammering into the reef around him and into the body of the dead fish; and he felt the shock waves of the launch-explosions. Pieces of tortured coral were flung upward. The water seethed. The fish had been torn almost in two. Bug snatched at another silvery body which drifted slowly down into his reach. It had been killed by the concussion. — He crawled along, holding the fish very carefully in front of him, praying that the sharks would not come; and looked out of the angle between its tail and the lip of the crevice. Two more of the innocent fishes had been transfixed, and were slowly drifting down into the darkness to be food for benthic organisms. The other fishes had finally understood that someone was trying to hurt them, and they scattered like beautiful tracer bullets. He was alone.

The earplugs tingled then, in an urgent do-you-read-me kind of way, as if somebody wanted to help him; this astonished him because he had no friends. The source of this signal, far more welcome to Bug than a birthday cake, was somewhere deeper inside the crevice. Since it was only a matter of time before the reactionaries would rush him with their highly trained bodies going huh huh huh in their swimsuits like parachute and glider troops swooping in to conquer vital bridges, Bug set about working his way back into the darkness, dragging the dead tuna behind him. The crevice narrowed as he went, its slimy walls corkscrewing tighter and tighter until he felt like a gnat inside somebody's semicircular canal; and finally he ran up against an old intake unit for the pool's cleaning system which had become so barnacled over that there was no hope of cutting through them to bend apart the vents beneath and enter the deliriously charged circulatory system of the aging pool, where electric pumps gasped and gurgled in a darkness unknown to the world, unknown certainly to Bug, who now seemed doomed, misled by his earplugs at the last. Well, that's it, then, he thought. He began the return trip, the tingling diminishing as he went. He wanted to see what his enemies were preparing for him. There was some commotion in the water, and when he peered around the tail of the dead fish carefully he saw that they were coming for him after all, swimming in a compact group towards the crevice with their spearguns at the ready in front of them. They were about fifty feet away now, shining their Tekna flashlights into his eyes; then they stopped, treading water superciliously, and fired in unison. As he saw their intention he threw himself hack into the crevice again, and by a miracle was only grazed in the side by one spear-point, but the carcass of the fish he had been shielding himself with was ripped to little pieces of tissue clinging to the shattered cartilage, as if a knight had suddenly had nothing left of his armor but the rivets. — They cocked their spear-guns and advanced again, their faces bulging with concentration as they loomed up, and now they were almost at the crevice, and they grinned and aimed again; this time it would be like, uh, shooting fish in a barrel . . . and just then his earplugs began tingling again and the back wall of the crevice blew out, momentarily confusing the swim team with this sudden eruption of murky water and filthy debris so that they thought that Bug must have a secret weapon after all, and they sent Doug and limber Big George up to get the sub. What had happened, as the astute reader has surely concluded, was that the water-beetles had finally arrived like the Red Detachment of Women to save their ideological brother. Unfortunately, there remained only three of them, for the reactionaries had almost succeeded in exterminating the species, but they were not without a sense of buggish duty, and so they took Bug gently in their mandibles, as a hunting dog will close its jaws on a downed pheasant very softly in order to retrieve it for the huntsman without damage; and they towed our hero back through the water toward the opening which they had made, and sent him up a long long drainpipe to make his escape, which he did passively, for he was, as I have implied, without a sense of wonder; and they dug in with those selfsame mandibles, and prepared to die to cover his retreat.

I would very much like to describe the life and habits and peculiar characteristics of this now extinct species, to which capitulation was out of the question, but for narrative purposes I will limit myself to a few brief remarks.

Brood size ranged from 0 to 54 juveniles, with mean of 24.5. They were shiny and blackish-green, which was why the reactionaries tried to contain them in a closely guarded glass-sided mockup of Marine World, but they were not closely guarded enough because they overpowered their keepers, snipping through their diving masks with deadly pincers (except for Dr. Dodger, who had skipped out anyhow to work on a polyethylene recovery project; and when he heard what had happened he felt like the drummer boy who stubbed his toe and was ordered to stay behind at the field hospital instead of proceeding with his superiors to Little Big Horn; "thank God for small favors," said Dr. Dodger gleefully in the privacy of his nicotine-spotted easy chair, and Mr. White, to whom this remark was reported, huffed in disgust) and the bugs escaped back into pond-bottoms and under isthmuses and in marine trenches, and after that orders were given for "Operation Felix" to be carried out with fifty thousand pearl-diver conscripts descending beneath the surfaces of the Seven Seas and the twenty thousand lakes of Finland at crash priority, and the National Academy of Sciences funded swimming in all the high schools, which was the main reason that Parker and Wayne went into it.

In the last months of the war the sea-beetles never slept, but it did them no good. They made efforts to hide secret caches of eggs, and there are rumors that a few such troves still exist, and that they contain the finest genetic material of the race, but even if this is true they must have gone bad by now. As the social structure disintegrated, nurse-beetles could be seen scuttling frantically with their charges cemented to their backs, going from tunnel to tunnel, only to be trapped at the last in some diabolical Roach Hotel ("They check in, but they don't check out!") or to commit suicide after the brood which they had tried to save died on their backs, removed from the warmth and regular feedings which had been a part of their existence in the incubator tunnels. Torpedoes zeroed in on their warrens and set them afire. The beetles roasted inside their shells like nuts, like potatoes in their jackets. Every tunnel was choked with corpses. Then the water came in.

Even by our standards, boys and girls, the adults were quite pretty. After capture and execution, they were varnished and their brittle legs were broken off and new wire ones put in for durability, and then they were harnessed like horses to cars or stagecoaches carved by knick-knack craftsmen in Appalachia. Very fine designs were made by seating a few hundred preserved grasshoppers in a replica of a plastic sea-shell of some kind, and glueing the shell to a looking glass, and hooking up a couple of good beetle specimens with their shells all blue-green and translucent, the whole having the appearance of a fairy boat or mass transit system being drawn over the surface of a lake by two attractive insect-stallions.

A QUICK TREATISE ON THE EARPLUGS

No power on earth will ever force me to transform the natural relationship . . . between prince and people into a conventional, constitutional one; neither now nor ever will I permit a written piece of paper to force itself, like some second providence, between our Lord God in heaven and this land, to rule us with its paragraphs and, through them, to replace the ancient sacred loyalty.

PRINCE FREDERICK WILLIAM IV
in his opening address to the United Diet
(11 April 1847)

When our hero had them in, his sensory and situational parameters were transmitted by local electromagnetic jumps from roadside to cornfield, every receiving bug and sweet grasshopper passing them on at once for interpretation at Headquarters, which was now in Florida; and the Great Beetle's coterie used the world-wide insect network to assess all problems and send guiding tingles and even dispatch aid if the agent was important enough and battalions could be spared. – Our hero might well be a prize for the insect movement, they reasoned; for he had used the earplugs with no real repugnance and could thereby be assumed to have his heart in the right place. (Certainly, as I have said, he did not betray the bugs for some time.) – So the three beetles were directed, via an offshore ant: "Die usefully."

HOW THE LAST THREE BEETLES DIED

~~~~~~

> In the last analysis you cannot govern the state on the basis of the
> needs of the pensioners.
>
> ERNST ROEHM

The first of the three beetles, being the biggest and strongest,
advanced out of the hole to menace the boys, and was immediately
spear-gunned by Wayne, Sam, Chip, and Bob, with Parker supplying
the *coup de grâce*, and that varmint is now out of this saga.

The other two waited and clicked to each other various slogans,
and prepared to defend the crevice. The boys seemed somewhat in
awe of them, perhaps not knowing that there were only two, and
held off for a moment; and just then anyhow the boys heard the first
muffled sound of the coming of the sub. The beetles did not hear it.
They were busy covering the approach to the crevice with their fierce
mandibles, and they could not yet feel the vibration of the submarine
in the water. They frothed the water nervously for a moment,
picking up the scent of the boys' cool expectation; then they saw the
boys scattering rapidly in the water and diving into pits and caves in
the coral (and Wayne got stung by a jellyfish, and his leg swelled up
purple and ached, and he had to stay home for a week), and the
second beetle poked its head out like a lobster and waggled its little
crystal eyes and saw the sub coming straight toward them like a
luminous yellow dot getting bigger and bigger, and now they could
both feel the pressure of it in the water and the sound of it sawed
inside their shells, and they were afraid, but they touched their
feelers together (that is how beetles kiss goodbye) and then they
scrabbled with their claws to pull chunks of coral from the matrix so
that when the submarine came close enough they could at least hurl
them at a porthole. The sub was coming on at them, getting bigger
and louder and scaring the fishes though even scared fishes couldn't

get away fast enough from electric things; whenever the land powers desired, fish were caught and hauled up and slit open and decapitated and thrown into a mass grave layered with ice; and later they were broiled with butter and parsley. – The beetles, aware of these facts, scratched uneasily with their middle legs against the sides of the crevice, watching the submarine come closer and hearing the droning roar of the motors.

Then the sub stopped, and it was not close enough for the beetles even to launch the hunks of coral, and there was nothing to do except maybe lay eggs and hide them and there wasn't even time for that because there was a flash and a rumbling roar and something so white and blinding it burned out their eyes before the entire reef was shattered and pulverized and hundred-ton barnacle-boulders slammed down on the beetles except that the beetles weren't there anymore, and the water was full of sand and dirt and blood and ichor and cut-off squid tentacles, and the sharks finally did come, in one of those frenzies that you read about; including a big blue hammerhead that hadn't eaten for hours, but they couldn't locate anything to eat; there were too many dying-smells in the way; they couldn't figure out what was going on so they got mean and pounded up against the submarine, so everything drummed and echoed inside; in response to this aggression the sub launched another torpedo that flung up more boulders and killed all the sharks and made a big crater; and then the submarine glided triumphantly over the crater, and the junior life-saving instructor at the controls was as pleased as punch; he'd never done anything like it; but the coach was still angry, so he went to the W.C. and pushed the EJECT button vindictively, and out the poop hatch came a bundle of piss and shit and toilet paper that slowly settled onto the top of a little pile of bits of dead things. – Needless to say this last didn't please the boys one bit when they came out of their foxholes; it sure stank up the water, and a bit of toilet paper drifted up and clogged Glenn's oxygen filter for a minute. But the sub was already gone, and besides what could you do because it was the coach and the coach was a hell of a guy.

Keeping up a heavy fire on the crater, the boys sent a patrol consisting of Chip and Parker and Wayne back up to the crest of their coral formation (which had only marginally suffered during the battle, that is to say being now riddled with cracks from the shock-waves; and all the anemones had burst internally; and a little shoal of scarlet fishes that had lived in one of the coral-caves now came tumbling out dead in the backlash) to throw a few PVC-22 blackjack grenades down onto the rubble, because they sure as shooting weren't about to take any chances on one of them bugs being alive and out to get them with its mandibles; why, it gave them the creeps to think of it, like when you read a dirty magazine late at night and got all excited and turned out the light so that you could lie in the dark and put Lumina's face or gorgeous Doreen's face onto that woman's body and do whatever you wanted to her with your hand between your legs and just then a spider fell on your face or a fly buzzed in your ear or a trillion army ants came marching out of some rathole near the mattress with all their pincers out to go up your nostrils to eat your brain. There was nothing but yellow muck down there near the bottom of the pool and it took half an hour before the turbid water became calm and clear enough to approach. – A family of shrimp had been sucked into the strike zone by the implosion effect of the grenades. They were bookish in nature, though quite blind; they crawled across sunken Campbell's Soup cans whenever they were able and tried to make out the labels by feel, but they never could; though when they asked nicely some passing manta ray or blowfish that wasn't too hungry might tell them. – Chip fired first, just as the shrimp, alarmed by this new disturbance, began to burrow into the muck. At this signal, the entire squad began to shoot. As the spears were big and the shrimp were small, it took a long time to kill them; and finally the boys finished them off with their diving knives. Parker cut off their whiskers for a lark. Then they went back on up just in time to see our hero emerging from the drainpipe, which surprised them no end, but they did get a few chuckles watching the coach kick him off the swim team for not performing the Octopus as instructed. Now at last the team was cleansed.

AN AMERICAN VIRGIN

~~~~~~

> Ours is a sick society, and its sickness pervades every aspect of its being.
>
> Leaflet of the Communist Party of
> the United States (1984)

It is said that when our hero came into his manhood he worked in an insurance office. He had not yet become the grim expropriationist and world dictator whose remains may now be viewed in the glass case of the Great Mausoleum; indeed, he was still using his earplugs to try to find a girl who would sleep with him. Certainly his affections had continued to dry up; he was quieter than ever; he had begun to read manuals of psychological warfare for his amusement, but nonetheless he still needed people for something; if Wayne had castrated him back at summer camp his disposition might have been even worse.

He liked the trip to the financial district and back at rush hour. In the mornings he would be pushed up against sweet-smelling girls and immaculate businesswomen. Often he was squeezed between three or four sets of springy buttocks. The women all looked straight ahead or read novels and business reports. Skirts were in right now – more was his luck – and there was a greater number of nice knees and thighs than he could look at without swallowing hard. – The Chinese women, he concluded, were more modest in dress, but they still had those wonderful round, golden faces for him to admire; he wanted to lick their eyes and cheeks. The black bank tellers were the sexiest, the way they winked their knees, while the paleface Transamerica secretaries were as dreamily erotic as new office furniture.

He was lonely. He had no lover, no friend, nor even the solace of an ideology, or a friendly machine gun to make ideology with (though he vaguely sensed the importance of tools one day while browsing in a camera shop, looking at a beautiful brochure for a motor drive. The cover picture showed a leaping, sparkling school of flying-fish, caught in mid-air.)

In the rain, especially in late afternoons when the shiny streets smiled with their reflections of office windows and car lights, the executive women passed him in their wet black raincoats, hair cropped or free; and their translucent umbrellas.

Then one day he saw a wind come that shoved the umbrellas inside out, whipped their skirts up when they raised their arms to protect their hair-dos, and showed their slips and underwear. Gusts blew them across the street shrieking. They slipped and fell in their high-heeled shoes.

When he saw how much power a little air and water could have, he decided to become a revolutionary. Riding the streetcars in the morning, he took to musing not of what was under the skirts that pressed against him, but of maps, campaigns (skyscrapers and alleyways becoming for him mysterious and melancholy, like the forest at summer camp echoing with weird promises), the large cities ripe for terrorism and leadership . . .

The earplugs tingled.

ANOTHER ANECDOTE

~~~~~~

What would M. Proudhon do to save slavery? He would formulate the problem thus: preserve the good side of this economic category, eliminate the bad.

MARX
The Poverty of Philosophy

One January afternoon, while Parker and his crew were putting the last icy polish on their war campaign, our hero came home from school and there was a caterpillar moving slowly on the frozen driveway. A boy inclined, as we know, to feel sorry for live-boiled lobsters and dandelions sprayed with herbicide, he took pity on the furry thing and brought it inside. He got a jelly-jar from the kitchen cabinet and punched two air-holes in the lid. Then he put the caterpillar in the jar with some lettuce that he had stolen from the refrigerator and shredded. The caterpillar lay spiraled upon itself, unable to comprehend its changed circumstances. The boy put the jar up by the window sill close to his bed and went off to do his chores. Late at night he got up and directed the beam of his study lamp on the window. In front of the night-black glass with its frost crystals stood the jar, and in the jar the caterpillar, in the midst of chewing, stopped and turned toward him.

The caterpillar stayed alive. In February it made itself a dull-colored cocoon. The boy imagined that from within the cocoon the caterpillar was watching him trustfully.

In April he came home from school and found that he could just make out something red or orange within the cocoon. There was still snow on the ground outside. He started putting lettuce in the jar again, and threw it out when it wilted.

A week later as he came home the snow was melting. It was getting warm. He saw the hornets stirring out of their nest under the eaves. He went into his room. Inside the jar were brown bits of something and an open cocoon. A butterfly or moth had beaten itself to pieces trying to get out of the jar.

THE ARMING OF THE
GREAT REPUBLIC ~~~~~~~~~~~

Wars frequently begin ten years before the first shot is fired.

K.K.V. CASEY
Testimony of Du Pont director,
at the Nye-Vandenberg Munitions Investigation

The next World War will be fought with stones.

ALBERT EINSTEIN

Hardening his heart

~~~~~~

> Only a stream of water can turn a water-wheel, and only a stream
> of moving electrons can provide the nearly instantaneous transfer
> of information and energy that is the basis of our modern
> technological civilization.
>
> LEE W. CHURCHMAN
> *Introduction to Circuits* (1976)

It sure is terrific to be in the back seat of a car full of all the people in
your affinity group, and as you zip down the center of the road the
radio is going boodeley-boodeley-boo in some bluegrass heartsong
to open space, and, whoopee, you're hugging all the committed girls
who love you just as the boys love you but even more so, maybe,
because Bug never forgot that a Swiss army knife, for instance, does
everything well and nothing excellently; and to do something
excellently a good navy surplus kelp-slitting blade is far superior to a
thousand sawtoothed frogman's specials; and a gun is worth a
thousand knives; and a good friend is worth a thousand guns; and
ten minutes' bored talk about the weather with any girl is worth a
thousand friends at your back on the Great Trek of 1836, at least at
that time in his life, perhaps because until he joined the affinity
group none of his friends had ever *been* girls; but now everyone was
his friend, especially the girls (but he only thought that; he didn't say
it, didn't want anyone to claim that he was a sexist). — I love you,
Mary and Barb and Ellen next to me and Sandy and Sophie (but he
dreamed to himself that they were all good ruthless Bolsheviki
making a charge against Kolchak's forces in the snowy forest, so the
girls would be, let's see, Masha and Varya and Lena and, uh, Sasha,
that was it, and Sonia; and he would have loved to love a Tatiana,
too, but there wasn't one; and anyhow the whole exercise was sick)
and Sophie reached back from the front seat and smiled and gave

them all oranges. Jerry was driving, and had been for six hours because none of the rest of them had a license. So then every now and then somebody in the front seat would put something in his mouth. All comrades must follow events in China with the greatest attention.

The girls treated Bug like a younger brother. This was not inappropriate, since he was in the last days of that wonderful innocence which I so dwell upon; soon the falseness would come: — he'd notice that he was most attracted to the *especially* pretty ones; and, irritated by this injustice, which could be blamed more on his testosterone than on him, he became hypocritically nice to the plainer ones, regardless of their other qualities, and deliberately rude to the beautiful ones, who come to think of it were daunting anyway. — From this error it was not far to the weedy boggy thickets of utter alienation, as later on when he had to go to work at the reinsurance office there was no sweet carload; it was all mass transit, with the people involved packing back and forth at the transfer points avoiding each other's eyes, even on happy blue days when there was nothing in the air to make him cough, and away behind the barriers and barbed wire passed cars to animate the situation; he came to find it pleasurable, a feeling of being alone in someone else's house going through the correspondence and medicine cabinet and underwear, for no one dared to look at him to discover whether or not he were looking at *them* and getting information as to vulnerability; they scuffed their shoes softly on the carpet of the subway car. On the monorail, looking down at everything dispassionately, he trained himself to fly the bomber missions he later carried out against this very territory, all sentiment displaced by unfeeling accuracy — which substitution in truth was effortless, for what did he see? — he saw two great blue derricks like horses' skeletons off south among the pipes and telephone poles,

a burned house,

a parking lot,

a drunk or dead man,

a magnificent vista of meanness — abandoned trucks, warehouses, little dirty homes with dying yards and fences round them, parked cars all covered with lead dust and zinc fallout that made even the bugs sneeze in their bunker near the freeway; dirty brick walls with old ads painted on them, mud and rusty cables where the poisoned sea began to stink, boarded-up grocery stores and sweating power transformers and streets where nothing moved but blowing newspapers; guarded stacks of chemical drums; adult bookstores

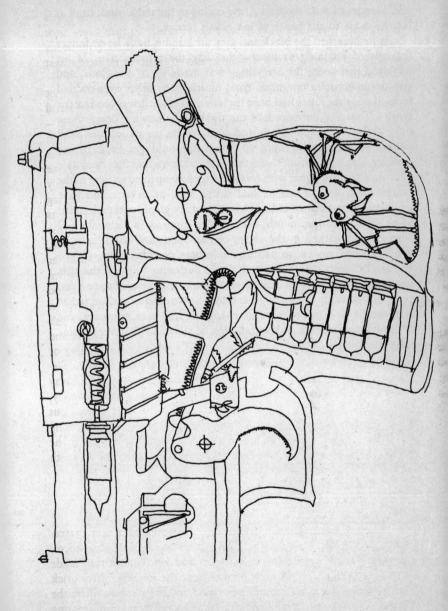

and parades of the Salvation Army crying in the wilderness, until at last he came to the peace of the ocean tunnel.

As he breathed the black and grey air into his body he no longer thought of anything as lovely, the way the retiring trees of his boyhood had been; for everything was made up of dirt-clods; and you do construct a mountain from molehills or other over-codified facts. If only the cities had been dynamited before it was too late for him! — That Pol Pot sure had the right idea, blowing down those ticky-tacky rice paper offices and illuminating the middlemen with bullets of vanguardist light so everyone could get back to the country, don't you think? — As things stood, even had Bug been able to cover the earth again with forests, after having lived so long in the excremental piles of cement and rusted steel he never could have seen trees as more than tedious identical dirty giant toothpicks unfit to be taken into the mouth; his summer camp, as a dishwater jail where you breathed in the steam of bad food; and the islands to which he had rowed, as sad unwholesome protuberances, polyps and land-cancers still in the stink of the outhouse — and all the girls had long since grown up completely to make travesties of their lives, even though some inherited great riches as we used to reckon riches in those days. — But surely this change in him was necessary, for without wretchedness and degradation of self one will never accomplish anything.

WAYNE'S FIRST MISSION

~~~~~~

> Mountain air in our lungs, a hearty sausage-and-home-fries, fire
> cooked meal inside us both. A last wipe of oil along our bolt action
> Berettas – the two big bores we've entrusted for our try at the
> trophy racks.
>
> Beretta catalogue (1984)

Boodeley-boodeley-boo went the car stereo as Wayne cruised down
to the dock to join the Merchant Marine. Parker saw him off. – "I'm
gonna hang tight," Wayne said into the rear-view mirror, which
framed the image of Parker in the back seat popping gum. "I'm
gonna hang tight for both of us because I have a feeling that you and
I are going to do things together," and Parker just kinda chewed,
and cleared his throat, and spat his gum out the window, and
stretched. (But he had dreams, Parker did.) – Wayne went off to sea
on a cool sunny afternoon, where he was soon given command of his
own scout canoe in the marshes of Florida. Officially he was on the
lookout for drug-runners and wetbacks. Twisting for weeks amidst
poorly charted islets and mazy channels in the crackling weeds, he
discovered things from time to time: – lost Spanish galleons all full
of skeletons and lockets of women's hair (Wayne dumped the hair
but retained the lockets, which were solid gold), the Fountain of
Youth, the waters of which he took a swig; and muck and water
generally. He lived on wild ducks and flamingo eggs. One evening
he had pulled into a side-channel to do some fishing, and was lying
on his back just daring one of those damn mosquitoes to land on
his cheek when he heard paddle-strokes coming near. – Minions
of the bugs, most likely, because he could make out voices gabbling
in, let's see, it sounded like one of the non-Indo-European dialects.
Speedily and in complete silence, Wayne stowed his few belongings
in the watertight bulkhead beneath the bow and flipped the canoe

so that it went under, with just enough air trapped inside for him to be comfortable. Now impervious to detection, he floated near the thwarts and listened. The half-castes were passing within a few feet of him. – ". . . These medium and small towns must be contested . . ." – A grunt. – Splash, splash, splash went the paddles. – "No, comrade, the vast rural areas and the small towns, so as to delay the outbreak of the civil war until the general trend . . ." – Then it was brotherhood this and fraternity that, until Wayne could scarcely lie still against the cool metal and listen to their revolting conversation, but he knew that he had better; for Commander White of the Coast Guard had briefed him before sending him out here, explaining that because we were currently least competent in assessing their plans for indirect aggression in the resource-laden regions of our hemisphere it was vital to sustain our collection systems even at the cost of billions of dollars and untold human courage and technical innovation. – "And you listen to me," Commander White had added, while Wayne stood at attention straight and true, "you jerkwater walleye that thinks you're a swimming pool tough, don't think I don't know your record, you hood, and if it were up to me I'd make sure we sent you into the bowels of a termite nest where the big black soldiers would go for you and break your balls a few times, but you've probably just got one ball to start with, so you play ball with me and I guarantee you'll come back fit to be tickled pink by a couple of Texas cunt-feathers on standby, and bring back some vital intelligence, too, like the best way to launch a geopolitical ruse through a million spray cans of D.D.T. with fully responsive propellants, so keep your eyes peeled, boy, and remember we'll all be thinking of you, and now get out before I throw you out."

Wayne admired Mr. White almost like a father, but that might have been because Wayne didn't have a father, that gentleman having been killed instantly in the bugs' sneak attack on our base in Jamaica. In any event, he could certainly see why we needed to know whether any insect assault against our factories might be hamstrung by insurgencies fomented by our loyal cockroaches in Los Angeles, or what might be the possible role of bees if we played our "sugar card." Unfortunately, in the government at this time it was still almost as difficult to generate interest in these questions as it had been five years ago; and overhead photography was only so useful in spotting the egg-cases.

Now, collecting information in a denied area, Wayne heard, as told, the punts of the bugeyes paddling laboriously upstream, until when they were within a whirligig's width of him their commander said, "Enough for today, comrades; we are near the cache, so let us camp." For ten minutes there were the sounds of disembarkment; and then Wayne heard them cutting reeds for their fire. His heart beat fast. He realized that this was his chance to spy on them so as later to transmit his findings through expert use of that growing science, cryptography. Taking a deep breath, he dove underneath the canoe – which was not going anywhere, being in a bank of cattails – and crawled underwater for fifty yards, clinging to the yellow stalks like a water-bug to its precious bubble; until at last he raised his head above the water and looked upon the circle of light cast by the campfire.

There were fifteen men sitting there, all in gorgeous lacy uniforms and armed with cutlasses and repeating rifles. They had tall black boots, and silk hats to which were affixed ostrich feathers. The one who was evidently their leader, however, wore a black skull-cap with two golden feelers. It gave Wayne the horrors. They sat around the fire drinking rum from tin cups, until finally two subalterns came up with the carcasses of some wild pigs, which they proceeded to roast. Wayne's mouth watered, because he hadn't had a good meal in ages, but there was nothing to be done about it, so he dug his toes into the mud and crouched there in the darkness.

"May a curse be upon the Great Beetle," said one of the compradores after a space. "Why did he send us after the grubs when we could have stayed to see the new local alignment?"

"What alignment?" said the leader grimly. "You know as well as I that in our own departments the zone situation remains unclari-fied."

"The reactionaries have sent a man in," said another, "and we are supposed to find him, but we are not even entrusted with the para-spectacle apparatus. A fine job of organizing this struggle we'll be able to do!"

The leader patted his shoulder delicately, like a moth in a closet brushing for the first time against a petticoat. "Well," he said (and Wayne hated him), "we all have our shortcomings, and unless we correct them we will hardly be able to take another step forward in our work and in our great leap of integrating the universal truth of Kuzbuism* with the objective tactical situation of our cause."

"Yes," said the first man, commencing to serve up the meat on

---

*What is this truth? So as not to profane it by revealing it to the vulgar, I, Big George, refuse to reveal it for another four hundred pages.

ivory plates, "that is all true, but I dearly would have loved to see the ambush in Fort Lauderdale. What eyes those old people have in the swimming pools, and what spirit! Ah, and the newlyweds will scream, as they always do, and perhaps there will be a young boy in whom we can hatch our eggs."

Wayne realized that these foreigners, whatever else they might be, were no longer human. He longed for his spear-gun. Of course that would not have been at all suitable for him in his present reconnaissance role, but he questioned whether that was an over-riding requirement. – "Awright, guys," he said tensely to himself, "just you wait till I meet any five of you alone on the continental shelf . . ."

They were all getting drunk, and swayed like hollow cocoons blowing on a tree branch. "When is the ambush?" one of them said.

"It was to have been the night before last, but now the Great Beetle says that it will be tomorrow night. He loves a surprise, he does. Well, comrade, pass the rum. And squeeze a slice of lime into it, would you; I adore limes."

Then for another two hours their talk went on – partly about resistance and unity, and partly about other things, until finally Wayne could not stand it, and covered his ears with his hands. There were many topics that could make him uncomfortable; nothing turned his stomach like talk of sexual diseases, but such subjects as transformation, conviction, anti-sectarianism and coevolution were almost as bad, making him think of billions of defective sperm advancing up his mother's womb. Finally the conversation died away, and the Great Beetle's men sank one by one into their foul slumbers. Then Wayne stole up and cut their boats loose from the bank. A push sent each craft drifting into the middle of the river, until the current had taken them all and borne them into the chittering darkness . . .

ROGER AND DR. DODGER

~~~~~~

No Russian is any good unless he is first beaten.

German proverb

The Russian is clever, but he is always too late.

Russian proverb

Wayne was never what you in your average everydayness might call a serious student. – Oh, he liked history all right, and he had memorized all the statistics which were now helping him so much in active service: – a one-kiloton nuclear bomb requires three calories per square centimeter to ignite a newspaper, four to cause a second-degree burn on bare skin, ten to char a white pine, eighteen to destroy a U.S. Army khaki summer uniform, and thirty-four to ruin the snappy white garb of the U.S. Navy (which is why, in the end, Wayne elected for the Merchant Marine). He also knew that when you use a rocket-head as a shaped charge you must unscrew the motor assembly (the reader may, if he likes, imagine Wayne digesting this in his training quarters, with his forehead wrinkled and his lips hard together in an impregnable frown, staring at the manual: – "The rocket-head, awright, as a SHAPED charge, but what the fuck do ya have to unscrew the motor assembly for? On the other hand, I'll be damned if I let it blow up on me before I'm good and ready . . . The rocket-head must be right on top of this stupid fucking motor assembly, so awright, fine, I get the picture"). He knew that with the exception of the moon Mars was probably the best site for establishing a base beyond the earth, at least once we'd smoked out that old turkey Phil Blaker.

Roger, on the other hand, knew almost nothing. Ideologically, Roger belonged to that large percentage of our population which takes no stock in extremist pronouncements, even those of the swim team, but which nonetheless is far too rooted in our common intellectual tradition to ally itself with Bug's forces. By default, that leaves the swim team. And so Roger entered Parker's unfolding movement. As a student, he was unable to decide among the various creeds pressed upon him – his broad flat face suggesting, to be sure, that he would always live a secondhand life intellectually and spiritually. The description by ex-Gauleiter Albert Krebs of Baldur von Schirach is particularly well applied here: "a pale snob on a sport field." But for all his let us charitably say East Baltic appearance, Roger proved invaluable to Parker, for he schemed and squirmed and farted in his junior high seat, writing anxiously, and he studied at night when he wasn't working out with his plastic weights in the steamy bathroom with the shower running so his sister wouldn't come in and see his body. Though an indifferent student in elementary school, Roger soon came to realize the ultimate value that good hard work would have for him in the future, so he maintained an inconspicuous presence in the upper fifth of his class, much like a race-car driver being a little lazy until the final lap, maybe munching on a bit of Gorp Trail Food pipetted into his mouth from the dashboard as he went round and round and round, his mouth scrunched up grey and twitching a little so that it would be easier to cry later if he lost. For his part, he was not a bad lad, recognizing as a result of the snow-fight days that Parker possessed the uncompromising, unhesitating approach which had been so long demanded by the nationalist movement. It is true that Roger made an unpleasant impression as a result of his body odor and his personal and public behaviour. But it was clearly impossible to get rid of every such person in those days despite bad reputations; warm (even if smelly) bodies were needed, and besides Parker never broke faith with anyone who did not break faith with him. – "What is he?" Wayne screamed at Parker once (it was the only serious disagreement that they ever had). "He's a softass out to screw up you and me and our ideals!" – but Parker only shook his head a little sadly and Wayne understood that the subject was closed. Deeply troubled, Wayne finally consoled himself by saying, "Well, if he leaves you and me in the lurch at any time, Parker, he'll deserve his downfall, and I GUARANTEE that's just what he'll be getting coming to him," and Parker nodded and grinned and ate another of Wayne's mechanical pencil leads.

From a personal point of view, Roger doubtless remained a little shadowy even to Parker himself. He spoke of nothing but the

immediate question at hand. Like Parker, he was able to listen
quietly without expressing his private opinions (the snow-fight
episode had cured him of that). He was doubtless immersed in his
work. In the course of time he came to believe deeply in the swim
team and all that it stood for, although at his best, even, he remained
slapdash in his methods – but on the plus side he had no personal
ambition. So it was made clear to Roger that he could hang around
and attend practice and even score a few points as long as he kept
their end up in school. The night before every test it was Roger's
responsibility to deliver personally a copy of the answer key for the
other boys to memorize. This he could do competently. One day in
the physics lab when he should have been zeroing his Sartorius
balance and laying his metric weights out in matrix array on the
scratched-up lab bench, he browsed through the school copy of Lab
Empire Supply's new catalogue, and found, on a page illustrating a
mercury spill control station, a custom imprinted hard hat, a toxic
gas tracer, an explosion-proof hot plate, a five-minute escape unit, a
goggle sanitizer, and an animal restraint cone complete with cervical
dislocator, the following description:

> Quic Pop Lock Puller. Emergencies may require access through a
> locked door. This Lock Puller safely removes most lock cylinders
> from any type of door in seconds without causing damage to the
> door when used properly. Lightweight leather pouch contains all
> necessary component tools: lock ring wedge, grabber, prestidigi-
> tator blades and bolt keys.

It was just perfect for the door of the office on a Friday night,
when the halls were dark and echoey with the melancholy of playing
hooky in reverse – if only he had had something better to do with his
life than stay after school! – and after he had finished using the
principal's xerox machine, whistling all the while to keep his spirits
up, *phwee, phwee, phweeeeeee*, he'd lock up the answer key in the
file cabinet again, and hug the photocopies to his chest, and go into
the girls' bathroom, maybe, and deftly pry loose the seal at the back
of the tampon machine ... Time was passing, and Roger knew that
he ought to take the answers over to Wayne's house because the
whole team was waiting in the basement drinking beer and smoking
reefers and playing with Wayne's electric trains although they were
very careful to keep the speed down going round curves and up
mountains and along trestle bridges over velvet-pasted gorges,
because Wayne was watching them pretty carefully and they all
respected Wayne. – "Where's that dork?" cried Chip, stuffing into

his mouth yet another handful of Dr. Dodger's Fine Old-Fashioned Party Snacks; and Wayne snarled a little and ground an ant into the damp carpet. – Parker did not seem to be having a good time. He sat in the corner with his legs 'way out in front of him and just kinda kept his eyes on things, so Wayne didn't dare ask him if he were sick or something. – "Where's that dork?" said Chip again. "He'd better show up pretty soon with those answers, is all I have to say." – But Roger was still wandering like a ghost through all the stalls of the girls' room and looking through the trash cans for something sexual to take home with him, with nothing to comfort him but the hum of electricity in the incandescent fixtures above his head; and Roger sat on one of the girls' toilets and pretended he was a girl for awhile, and looked for girls' graffiti on the walls but it was a lot cleaner in here and it seemed that girls didn't write anything. He wished that he had brought along a dictionary so that he could look up dirty words to add some significance to the evening. – Time was passing and Roger knew that he should have given the answers out by now, and then he could be walking down the street where the college students were, and wander past the restaurants and used bookshops, pretending that he was a college student and looking very learned and lost in thought so that no one would dare interrupt him, because he knew that no one would bother to interrupt him in any case. Roger was wasting his life . . . If he stayed too late and heard the tired heavy tread and bucket-slosh of the night janitor coming, there were always the narrow underground utility tunnels to hide in, where he could crouch and listen to the clump, clump, swish, slop of the halls being mopped, until the noises receded. If the hall were still wet and soapy Roger tracked dirt and little pieces of gravel across it, but no one ever caught him.

As he progressed into more advanced maneuvers, ground support and equipment increased in importance, but we are getting ahead of ourselves here, and I will just hint at my meaning by saying that Roger, discovering that he liked to listen in on people who did not know he was there, began to keep a card-file, noting down such details as what time the janitor came dangerously close to the bathrooms, and what time it was safe for Roger to emerge from his spidery hidey-hole (he had a luminous watch which he consulted frequently). Following the janitor all around the building one night, peeking out the lightly frosted glass of dark offices to which the tunnels gave access (secret conference rooms, it appeared, where teachers were called to evaluate each other in confidence and submit their resignations), Roger discovered that the man was an insect sympathizer of some kind, for every now and then he'd stop mopping and open a window. At once a squadron of moths winged in tightly and circled round his head and hypnotized him or some goddamn thing until his eyes went glassy and his mouth dropped open and the brownest scaliest furriest one would zip on in and rest on his tongue and beat its wings martially while it debriefed his nervous system. Roger, knowing then for the first time the thrill that comes of performing professional intelligence work, added this information to the janitor's card for future use. After the exams of eleventh grade, wherein the great success of the swim team led to certain redistributions of administrative power *vis à vis* athletic policies, the whole proving to be of benefit to all the boys (and to the coach as well; Parker didn't care much about that but Wayne looked out for the coach), Parker requested Chip to deliver an invitation from him to Roger, requiring a personal and private meeting. As to what was intended, Chip conveyed nothing, for Parker had not taken him entirely into his confidence and he hated Roger anyhow because Wayne hated him. After practice, Roger met with Parker under rather adventuresome circumstances, designed to maintain secrecy, and received an explanation. It appeared that Parker was satisfied with the answers that Roger had conveyed for so many years, even if they had sometimes been delivered late so that the team abused Roger and punched and kicked him; and in addition reports had come to hand of a useful card-file which Roger had been working on. — Roger gulped and nodded. — Apart from a series of technical-organizational proposals for cover names, dates and telephone numbers, a discussion was initiated in which Roger was given to understand that he might be granted a higher status were he to begin to become better acquainted with other members of the team, and to make a practice of noting down where they went after school and who their girlfriends were and how they screwed and what all personnel said about Parker in and out of Parker's hearing. After some negotiations, in the course of which, Roger being as yet unskilled in politics, Parker committed himself to nothing and Roger committed himself to everything, Roger applied to his parents and said that he could be an even better student if they bought him a typewriter and some more card-files and maybe a paper shredder. Roger tried at first to become more popular with his teammates, as that would facilitate his purpose, but they still didn't cotton to him much, so he just bugged their bathing suits. — It is known that Roger's information helped Parker to solidify his mistrust of Chip and Doug; on the whole, however, its main result was negative from

Parker's point of view, for some time after Roger's death our hero, as we will see, succeeded in striking at Parker through Wayne as a result of something that he learned from it.

In due time Roger graduated and was admitted on a state scholarship to Coover College. Parker had him major in languages because it was felt that such a skill might be useful later when the organization had penetrated other countries. So he sat for hours in the *liṅgaphónom cabinéte* repeating all the words on tape that he had trouble pronouncing, like *Schwéster*, sister, *Schwéster*, sister, until finally he saw a hundred *Schwéstern* in his head whom he visualized as being ten-foot blondes with terrific hips and knee-high black-and-yellow-striped boots, and all yodeling together. – He switched in to the Russian frequency next, listened and repeated. – "*Véchera vécheróm ya péasal upissáhneeya náshava górod, no née konchíl,*" he iterated dutifully, but maybe it was *góroda* not *górod.* Besides, there was beautiful Catherine who always got As and was a treat to sit beside; she had a deadly laugh, but Roger remembered Parker's hint that if he didn't perform to standard then Parker just might throw him to Wayne; then, trembling and pasty-faced, he rubbed his big forehead and turned back to the gibberish. "*Záftra vcay styudénti . . .*" When you use a pronoun instead of a noun, you treat it grammatically as an animate object. Roger was so shaken that he got a C, and then Catherine wouldn't talk to him anymore, or perhaps she would have (although it is true that she might no longer have found it profitable to study with Roger), but Roger didn't dare to come near her. – Twenty-sixth pronunciation drill. *Oochéetulneetsa*, teacher, *oochéetulneetsa*, teacher, *écoutéz et cómprenéz et répetéz* until in his mind's eye he saw again that group of scout moths *óoh* come gusting in and chirring *chée* until *túl!* the old guy's jaw dropped and he leaned on his mop-handle and in went the evil leader of the moths beating its wings *néetsa-néetsa* like a G.I. 'copter settling down real slow and easy onto the cushion of the tongue landing-pad . . . Of course the *oochéetulneetsa* was really just dear thirty-two-year-old Galya with her red windbreaker and cup of coffee and her shiny gold tooth who was so nice and tried so hard to help them read and speak her language, which Catherine did to perfection, except that Catherine was very nervous and always blushed and stuttered when called upon. But it was rare for there to be more than one or two errors on Catherine's tests; she always got the highest mark of anyone in any section; and she spent two hours per day in the language lab and studied three hours per night at home at the very least and was always worrying about how far behind she was. Galya and Catherine liked each other and sometimes went out for coffee. One day Roger screwed up his courage and asked Catherine to go out for coffee with him. Catherine said she would, but canceled out at the last minute. They rescheduled for the next Monday. Catherine was to meet him at the fountain at twelve, and then they would go out for lunch. At twelve-ten Catherine came by looking quite fearful and uncomfortable. – "What's wrong?" said Roger. – "Well," said Catherine, "I forgot that next weekend there *is* this quiz that I've been very behind on studying for, and then another reason is that I've been very busy lately and, um, I've had a lot of writing to do lately. Actually I'm enjoying the reading."

Galya liked Roger and felt sorry for him because he tried so hard and just wasn't that bright. She knew nothing of Parker and Wayne and their constant pressure on him to get results, so that Roger could never sleep throughout an entire night and woke up screaming with the feel of Wayne's big white hands on his neck as Wayne crossed his hairy wrists over Roger's Adam's apple and squeezed and twisted. But Roger was in the dorms where you shared a room with nine hundred other guys so when he screamed and the lights came on it was worse than asking a stupid question in a packed lecture room because his mates were mad at being woken up night after night and they yelled and jeered at him and finally made him sleep with a towel in his mouth so that the scream was muffled, but this was even worse for Roger because as he thrashed in his sleep part of the towel would get wound around his throat and genuinely choke him.

As Galya and Catherine went out for coffee one morning Galya stirred her coffee sleepily and said, "Cathy, did you know that Roger got a C minus on the test?" – Catherine cocked her head and looked all around at the mention of Roger and said, "Oh, really? Gee, that's a shame. Oh, well!"

Catherine liked Galya very much and never would have dared to contradict her. So now, as Galya, out of pity for Roger, attempted to talk her star pupil into being Roger's friend, in the hope that this way they could study together and Roger could improve his Russian and Roger and Catherine could both relax a little, poor Catherine was put in one of the many awkward situations that permeated her life. – "Did you like that new hermeneutics book by Dr. Dodger?" Galya began, knowing that Catherine always felt most at ease in purely abstract discussions. As the work, which was being discussed in Catherine's philosophy class, concerned itself with apprehensions of the essence from an Anglo-American point of view, it was ideal to mention in this context, as it could put Catherine in her element more than could two drinks. (In fact when Catherine had had two drinks she had the nicest smile and no longer trembled and became incisive and decisive and said things like, "I think we should give Mr. White and all his Republicans a kick in the pants. Of course the trouble is that the people who would be doing the actual kicking probably wouldn't be any better than the people whose pants they kicked," and I, the author, had another beer and said, "I think that's true," and the sun came in through Catherine's kitchen window and Catherine played with her cat knowing that she was safe and grew even more daring in her remarks and I enjoyed being with Catherine more than ever.) – Catherine became lively right away; and it was charming for Roger as he watched from the balcony of the student union, the two dark-haired women talking and laughing, Galya looking sweet today and Catherine quite stunning (she even had the prettiest *handwriting* of all the students in the Russian class; and, sitting beside her every morning, Roger thrilled to a sensation not unlike that which he experienced when he saw that the sentence he had chalked on the blackboard was wrong. His penmanship was among the worst.) – Catherine was one of those pale, dark-haired young women with freckled faces. She was lovely. She had wide eyes and (I reiterate) a deadly trilling laugh. She wore striped dresses, while Galya always wore sweaters and had spectacles and curly black hair and looked at you very sternly at first so you would work hard and get the most out of the assignment but once you knew your verbs she smiled at you and then you were happy that you had worked and learned and pleased Galya. – "Yes," said Catherine (getting back to *Dr. Dodger's Genuine Treatise Concerning Numismatically Pure Phenomenology*), "well, I read it, but somehow the task he set himself seemed so limited; by the time he's defined mental events as this *type* of event . . ." And Catherine and Galya chatted happily for almost an hour while Roger watched and rejoiced to see them so happy and wondered what they were talking about and for a moment forgot his secret servitude to Parker and Wayne and dreamed that Galya was his older sister who would always look out for him and he could come run and hide and she could comfort him if Parker and Wayne came to get him; and he dreamed that Catherine loved him and was telling Galya that she wanted to marry him; and meanwhile an hour passed and it was almost time for Galya to teach another section and then read for her Ph.D. exams which were only held every eight-and-a-half years, so you had to be quick and ready and proficient when the time came around, but

Galya was one of the best; so as she got up Catherine said, "Maybe we could go out for coffee or something, or maybe we could just make a little breakfast or something?" and Galya knew her moment had arrived and said, "How's your friend Roger? You ought to have him along, too. How are things between you and him?", for Galya had seen how Catherine and Roger always sat together and Roger kept looking at Catherine and Catherine never had the strength to say no to him so she always let him sit next to her and sometimes even looked at him if what Galya was writing was on his side of the blackboard. – Now poor Catherine was in such a quandary that she was almost a nervous wreck; she jerked her hands about and her arms shook and she overturned her empty coffee cup. "Roger?" she said. "Things are, well, they're just going along; he's sort of talking more and more specifically about more and more long-range plans, and I'm sort of having more and more extreme reactions," so that Galya understood the situation and knew that there was nothing she could do for Roger and gave up. Meanwhile Roger realized that while he had been spying on Galya and Catherine and having such a nice time all his Russian notes had blown away, and they were scattered all over campus now, and as Galya and Catherine went their separate ways they saw pages of Roger's tests blowing along the path, every page covered with red marks and Xs and exclamation points; and Catherine was horrified, having suspected that Roger was a poor student – "Are you taking the class for credit?" she asked him once, rather tactlessly – but never having suspected (since she was a rather sheltered person, and was not even certain whether the highest mountain on earth was called Mt. Everest or Mt. Emerett) that he was *that* bad, and Galya thought that this was a wanton act of Roger's, that he had decided to become a vicious anti-student, the kind that never studies, and cheats on tests, and peeks in the book during drills, and when the teacher is pointing round the room getting oral responses on numbered exercises (though that was usually Professor Kassatkin's role) then this irresponsible sort of person counts the number of students ahead of him so he knows just what noun he will have to put into the genitive plural, and he stealthily flips to the back of the book to find out whether it's masculine, feminine one, feminine two, or neuter so that he knows what ending to put on it, and Catherine beside him is too busy writing down all the right and wrong answers to notice any foul play ... Galya could never endure people like that.

Meanwhile Roger toiled on and on in his hutch, the headphone-microphone assembly stinking of the bad breath of countless other nerds while in the far cubicle Catherine sat bent over with freckles on her pretty neck communicating the exercises urgently over and out. Roger got a D on his next test.

After a series of letters in which Roger set forth his fundamental personal position, he finally succeeded in getting permission from Parker to let him study crowd control instead under Dr. Dodger, who was then living out the last few decades of his illustrious life in the hushed oblivion that follows fame. Whatever Parker's own reasons might have been in agreeing to this change in program, it was to have an irrevocable effect on Roger's personal and political destiny.

Dr. Dodger's lecture was in 301 Burgstaller Hall, and as Roger had not received a clear directive on the matter until somewhat past the beginning of the quarter, it was imperative that he be early to humiliate himself appropriately and get Dr. Dodger to sign the corrugated forms. The lecture began at two. He set off at a quarter of the hour. Burgstaller was a very large split-level building with erratic room-numbering which had sometimes caused him difficulties. He found a corridor that was 334–312 and then only stairs going downward. Above him were the four hundreds and seven hundreds; below him were the two hundreds. He stopped in at the crowd control office, which referred him to the riot control office. But the riot control office had never heard of Dr. Dodger. It was now exactly two, and somewhere the lecture was beginning, Dr. Dodger was clearing his throat and the students were sitting clean and straight and silent in the green fold-out chairs while the projectionist checked the last of Dr. Dodger's Alaska slides to make sure that none of them were upside down and the students were poising their shining pens like orbital missiles above the Siberian expanse of their note-paper, feeling stern and good behind their new visors; and Dr. Dodger was distributing the dittoes now, and there was an extra one which would have been left over for Roger but Dr. Dodger had given up on Roger by now so he crumpled it up and tossed it in the wastebasket, and began to remember just where it was that he had left off last time. The secretary called the military science department for Roger. It turned out that the lecture was actually being held in 301 Beichmann, not Burgstaller at all; Roger had copied down the wrong building, and this was the last day of the quarter to add a class to his study list, so if he failed in his objective this time Wayne would get him for sure. "They must not have given me current information," he said, blushing and breaking out in a million pimples. – "Sure," said the secretary mockingly.

The door was locked when he got there. He had run all the way. He had to get in for his segment requirement. Sweat was running down his back, and his glasses slid down his wet nose. He peeped in through the tiny window in the center of the door, that familiar eavesdropping action at least providing a little comfort; and saw many backs of helmets, and Dr. Dodger standing and gesticulating in the far corner of the room, baring his yellow teeth. – Roger raised his hand to knock, but could not bring himself to do it. His hand fell. Finally he tapped, tentatively. It was two thirty-one. No one heard. He banged and banged and banged in a panic until finally Dr. Dodger started, frowned, briefly opened and shut his mouth in what must have been a pungent remark for the backs of the helmets were rippling with laughter at the intruder who dared disturb this lecture of all lectures; and now Dr. Dodger was shaking his head, deflating his chest in a silent sigh; and he stepped down from the podium and advanced to the door, coat-tails flapping. His face became larger and larger until it filled the entire window; now he studied Roger with care, looking quite disgusted. Roger tried to smile back ingratiatingly, but his lips were too dry with terror and exhaustion. – Finally Dr. Dodger shrugged and opened the door.

"Yes?" he said. "You're here for the green slip? I don't have it, so goodbye, and as I was saying to all of you a minute ago, in World War I the Germans employed bacteria quite successfully to start an epidemic of glanders among the horses of the Roumanian cavalry," and the door was shut now, and Roger was doomed.

A HAPPY CHILDHOOD

~~~~~~~~~~~~~~~~~~~~~~~~~~~~~~~~~~~~~~~

> Today, we are faced with the probability of engaging an enemy
> who holds a vast numerical advantage and who has a knowledge
> of strategy and tactics equal to our own. Our only chance of
> survival in such a war will be the *quality* of our weapons and men.
>
> Special text 23–5–1, The Infantry School,
> Fort Benning, GA (1954)

While the young reactionaries dug in behind the sandbags of
ideological ballast and the lead slugs of undeniable fact, Bug went
walking in the clouds. The beginning of the ascension, as we know,
had taken place at summer camp. Yet it is erroneous to believe that
his alignments ever had much to do with the liquidation of Tony.
His disposition was incipient, like diabetes; and red guard cells
started massing in his veins before Tony was first poked and
tweaked. Wayne had known this the first time he saw Bug in the
camp parking circle, and Bug was wiping his nose with a pale
hairless arm and Wayne didn't even have to see Bug's face to know
that Bug was a creep that oughta be pulverized; so the constellations
were fixed then and the sun rose and set with idiotic regularity and
local residents carried on their subsistence way of life at summer
camp. Their equipment was critical to their well-being – for here we
had a whole system of creaky porches and tree-roots along the edge
of the lake, and in late afternoon everything had the cool funny smell
of water when the wind began to blow in from the lake. It was a
funny smell because Bug expected it to smell like fish, and it almost
did, but not quite, and not at all like the stinky briny gutting places
at the marina where every step you took ground a rotting fish under
your heel. Every once in awhile during the afternoon his cabin got a
free period, and then he walked down the hill through the open-air
chapel in the pines where they had vespers, along the path to the

canoe docks (most of the times he was brought to camp he wanted to take a canoe out alone, but it was only in his sixth and last summer that he passed the boating test) and then right to the little brown library on pilings over the lake. It was a small musty room with a chair and a big wooden table and big windows so that in late afternoon the sun came in and all the dust hung golden in that light, and he sat there and slowly read the adventure books. They had great books. He read the complete Tom Swift series (his favorite was the one about Tom Swift going to the Caves of Ice); and Ransome's *Swallows and Amazons*; and there was the biography of a Norwegian resistance fighter who swam through chilly oceans and got gangrene and wandered through I think it might have been Finland or Lapland in a sweet short summer and everyone took him in and the dark Finnish women made him tea with honey in it on late afternoons and it was beautiful but also horribly sad because the book was only half over and you knew that bad things were going to happen. He kept pushing on northward and sleeping in the flowery meadows every night and passing thousand-year-old trees carved with magic runes and it never rained, and people hid him from the Nazis and fed him and let him rest and sent him on again and then it began to be fall, and brown and yellow and red and scarlet leaves came swirling down into the pools in the forest, and then one day it was winter and he had to keep going because I think he had some important message to deliver about a German sneak attack, so he went on and on and the lakes froze and the snow got so deep in the forests he had to make himself cross-country skis and then snowshoes and go on northward through the forests and over the grim mountains and he lost his snowshoes and went snowblind; and the Germans were coming after him because they realized that there was in fact a survivor of that ship they had torpedoed: "*Es ist ein Bugchen*," they laughed; "*Wir wollten den Bugchen zerstören*," and he finally came to the ice caves or rather Caves of Ice and took refuge in them in a storm, having located them by touch, and then he lay there waiting for someone half as brave as he to find him and help him because all he had was a little flask of brandy, and the chapel bell tolled seven times for vespers. In the evenings their counselor sometimes read them ghost stories. He was a very stern muscular hairy man who had blue bathing trunks. It was his job to get all the boys in Cabin Ten (the Beaver Tribe) out of bed and dressed and doing warm-up exercises at 7:10, because by 7:12 every morning each group had to begin its run.

At every meal you had to watch your counselor pretty carefully, because the plates had to be stacked for each cabin to make things easier for the kitchen crew, and it was considered degrading to be made to stack. The counselor chose the method of determining who would stack, and it varied from meal to meal. Sometimes he'd just spin a knife, and everyone would watch it whirling and whirling until it slowed and suddenly stopped and the blade pointed at you and you had to stack. But more often, since it was the policy of the camp to encourage alertness and sensitivity, the counselor would do something just a little out of the ordinary, and the last person to catch on had to stack. Maybe he'd put a fork in his yellow plastic cup, or lay a finger against the side of his nose, but after the first week of summer the campers would be back in trim again and watching him every second, and at once there'd be a clatter of forks into cups or a slamming of fingers against noses so that the counselor would just sort of grin – smart as pins, his boys – and have to try something else later because everyone had been so fast it was impossible to tell who had been last. So over the course of the summer he would become more subtle. Sometimes what he'd have in mind was just touching the spoon against the saucer. So there would occasionally be false alarms, the counselor daydreaming of getting into law school and playing absently with his silverware, and suddenly there'd be a clanging of spoons against saucers and a dozen nervous faces staring up into his own, and he'd look down and see that he had set them off by mistake. It certainly kept the boys busy, and one thing that the camp was concerned about anyway was that boys usually got too much sugar and not enough wholesome food (they were allowed one candy bar per week, when on Wednesday nights they showed outdoor movies in the baseball field with all the boys and counselors stretched out on the soft silvery moonlit grass with blankets around them if they were cold, and bugs made their music around them and flew up against the immense roar of light where the characters in *The Time Machine* or *The Last Voyage* stood ten feet high – and of course all packages of food from home were confiscated for fear, as I have earlier said, of insects), so the camp succeeded in its objectives with many of the boys, such as Bug, for instance, who found that whenever he ate dessert he got to enjoying it and wondering if he might be able to get seconds, and then gradually the snickering silence would sink in, and he'd look around to see everyone else with their fingers on their noses, and the counselor enjoying this moment of absolute control and saying to Bug in a pleased rumble, "Well, I think you stack," and all the other boys laughed. So Bug finally gave up eating his desserts.

After awhile the counselor decided to make 'em shoot for it with their fingers, odds 'n' evens, in successive rounds to eliminate everybody but one boy. Bug remained innocent at this time, not having been accepted by the culture — there were a lot of swear words that he didn't know, and he had no notion of what giving someone the finger was. — "Odds 'n' evens," the counselor said. "One, two, three, SHOOT." Bug by pure accident extended his middle finger at the counselor. There was a silence. The counselor's terrifying joviality vanished, to be replaced by an even more terrifying expression of judgment. — "All — *right*," the counselor bit off. "You — stack. All summer — you stack." From then on the counselor regarded him as a delinquent. — "What did I do?" he said. — "Don't get wise to me," the counselor said coldly, "you wet-the-bed little bastard."

Before this incident the other counselors had mainly felt sorry for Bug. But by now Bug was generally considered to be nothing but a trouble-maker, and the men, except for old half-blind Mel Conway in the Nature House, despised him and took no further trouble over him. He came to like this. The worst having finally happened, he found that his complete exclusion was probably for the best. He had been excreted by society, like a seed in a fruit that a bird has swallowed. Now he could take root in the dung. Nobody cared if he missed the archery target; they just ignored him, and if he didn't want to shoot he just sat there on the log and the boy behind him would get up and take Bug's turn. And they let him spend hours and hours at the library.

He couldn't swim well. He was afraid of the water. But he wanted very much to take a rowboat or a canoe out by himself some evening and stroke, stroke out into the lake until he couldn't see either shore, and go amidst the islands as if it were still afternoon, and drift within inches of one of them so that he could reach out and pick blueberries from it, and then go back on out into the darkening stretch of lake that finally turned chilly with nothing above or below him but water and stars. Unfortunately, to check out a boat you had to show your boat card, and to have a boat card you had to pass the boat test. The boat test was conducted every Monday morning right after breakfast. You had to swim the length of the longest dock in clothes and sneakers. The water was way over your head. A counselor walked beside you along the dock, holding a pole. If you couldn't make it anymore you grabbed the pole and he helped pull you out, but that meant you had failed the test. Bug always failed the test. But toward the end of his sixth summer he finally learned to swim well, and had time to take a dinghy out alone once. It was almost as nice as he had expected. He passed through mist, frogs, and so on. Things like that came up now and then, so perhaps it was no wonder that every time he went to camp he hated it but in the end he hated going back home, too (of course that could have been because he knew what was waiting for him back in the Real World), on the last day of every summer being converted to a nostalgic old alumnus who gives a few grand to finance a new lavatory, and though he never came to like the other boys on that day at least he did not dislike and fear them, as he did especially when his parents came once a summer to visit him and took him out in mid-afternoon for a milkshake at the Fenwich Inn and brought him back and his enemies acted friendly in front of his mother so that she was amazed and angry when he claimed that they were only disguising their real feelings for him, being cunning spies and perverted cowards planning to make it up later with extra hard pinches and more throwings of tennis shoes. But on the last day of each summer he realized that in fact they were brave and moral enough in their own way (*he* was the sneaking scuttling cockroach insurgent) and that it was out of genuine decency that they behaved politely towards him in front of his parents, because it would have overstepped their code to humiliate anyone in front of his own family – Christ, they must have enough of a cross to bear in having spawned this loser! – so he felt grateful to the reactionaries in his revolutionary years, and wished that he too could play fair, and sometimes felt almost sorry for individuals as he sighted on their faces with the hate welling up in him and he ground his teeth and dug the stock of the rifle hard into his shoulder and hip hip hooray pulled the trigger . . .

PARKER'S LAIR

~~~~~~

At that time the earth tried many experiments in creation, producing creatures with strange forms and strange members.

LUCRETIUS

At the time that he had seriously begun to consolidate his organization, Parker was working in a custom photo lab. The reader who is not much taken by audiovisual pastimes may have a deficient picture of that place where Parker was employed; or perhaps not so much a deficient picture – the dyes faded, shoddily spotted, brutishly burned in and doltishly dodged by subhuman technicians under the glare of the enlargers – as an image which has been misfiled in the archives of memory, representing instead one of those bleak Photo Drive-Ups and Presto Printses located nowadays on the corner of almost every large parking lot, in which the clerks wait sadly behind their glass counters, but no one comes in, and the air becomes darker and darker over the course of the morning as a result of the exhaust fumes (there goes another brain cell; *ping!* – THAT thought will never be completed now); and the pink chubby tots smiling at you from the walls in sample enlargements become steadily more grimy, and by the lunch break they are brown; and the day ticks off on the loud digital clock; and then finally a car creeps into the lot, and a popeyed couple locks the vehicle doors listlessly; they request a reprint of a washed-out snapshot of their son who was killed in the Indian Wars, and they go away; and after a long time here comes a slick-haired teenager who once took a few pix of his girlfriend holding a balloon at the zoo in front of the monkey cage on a dirty overcast day, and the clerk can tell just by looking at this customer that they won't come out, because the guy's a loser if the clerk knows anything at all about losers and in fact he knows a hell of a

lot about losers because why else would he be stuck with this job?
. . . and then some old lady like a pasty dumpling in a pink bonnet
wants three repros from negative 23A which, she explains, shows
her to full advantage standing in front of her son's new car, but
while the clerk nods and mmms in accordance with the courtesy policy
he really couldn't care less, can't even take the trouble to hold it up
to the light when she's gone and laugh at it or cry at it or make a
finger-smudge on it; he just sits there numbly taking inventory of
the flash attachments and plastic frames; and now for variety the
completed orders are delivered and the clerk has to put into each
envelope a coupon or an ad for the latest Gallery of Gifts (the Kodak
Film Slumber Bag, say – which is filled with two pounds of Kodafill
polyester fiberfill with a real aluminum zipper so that this durable
lightweight slumber bag can easily be zipped to another, and *then*
imagine what goes on, or the Agfapan Film Ice Chest, or maybe
some old daguerreotype Film Floating Island that was discontinued
fifty years ago and never even really floated which is why it's now a
Fujicolor Submersible Playhouse accented with black stripes and red
cushions); and then finally the day is over and it's time to lock up
and walk home and get mugged.

The custom lab, rather, was a lure for all serious photographers,
though it was located in a bad neighborhood – hidden, in fact,
behind a sheet-metal firm owned by Phil Blaker. – There was an
anteroom with a green carpet, and large fade-resistant advertising-
quality prints mounted and hung in such a way as to immediately
intimidate the visitor: – on the right being a four-foot photograph of
a pile of canned goods with the bounce flash sparkling perfectly on
the edge of every can, and the magenta label on the refried beans
given tumultuous and unspeakable life; while on the left just above
the light table was a nude done on Ilford Gallerie paper which must
have cost a fortune but lived up to the highest ideals of the zone
system. Behind the light table was a little window and a counter with
a bell on it. You stuck your head in the window and rang the bell
twice, inhaling the deep rich odors of photographic chemicals, and a
harassed-looking woman would show herself eventually to give you
technical pointers on the order process. If you looked rudely past
her, you might see the black-curtained passageway that twisted and
turned past great slimy computerized machines into the darkroom
proper, where workers with the right qualifications performed their
trade in eerie silence, like frogmen, getting the color balances just
right; and Parker sat blandly in his corner, up to his elbows in silver
nitrate, squeegeeing the prints to squares of optical-quality glass and

watching his long yellow-green fingernails turn yellower and greener by the hour until finally they glowed in the dark; for as we have already seen at Photo Drive-Up, no dyes are warranted against change in color. But of course you never could have seen Parker, for he usually kept the finger-ends that might have betrayed him squirming lazily in some solution, or under the enlarger bench at slack moments; and even if it had been theoretically possible to pick him out in the sweetish darkness you never would have been able to see in there thanks to the contortions of the entrance tunnel; and in front of that, anyway, the aforementioned harassed woman would be blocking your view and looking over your prints with a hardened sneer, saying that she supposed you knew that this negative of yours was hardly professional in quality, though maybe with sepia toning it could be marginally improved but that was six dollars extra, of course, and would dampen the contrast; and come to think of it, reader, you would be lucky even to be able to stand in front of *her* and see her silver bun of hair and breathe in the coffee-and-lifesavers breath that she coolly blew at you from beside her envelope rack; for unlike Photo Drive-Up the place did a brisk business, every customer having some five- or six-hundred-dollar transaction to make, with the newcomers still crowded intently round the light table like excited housewives at a Bingo game, causing little chinks and shuffling sounds to issue from that area periodically as someone of the Latvian type riffled through a leather portfolio and slapped down a Gepe-mounted transparency or duplicate negative, much as crass Europeans still drop playing chips at Monte Carlo. The long white fingers of the biologist, who needed his color fold-outs of blastocysts reproportioned to satisfy the stern requirements of his academic journal, brushed the plump hand of the respectable tradesman, who in his sensible suit and typical tie was entirely his own man. Here stood the gawky underling of a tool company, underlining various options in the custom lab's brochure for the last time so that he would know just what questions to ask concerning his boss's desired two-color circular on lawn mowers. One saw, too, the pudgy photojournalist, elbowing everyone else out of his way so that he could use three-quarters of the light table, looking over the crisp Ektachromes once more and making up his mind to insist that these gripping pictures of suffering – which he had been the first to get because he had trampled dying children in his rush to use the motor drive on closeup as soon as the shelling stopped – to insist, I say, that these prints be up to my high standards, because I don't have the time to fuck around with you people and if I have to complain about color balance one more time I'll take my business to Photo Drive-Up. – Nor should I forget the aging nature photographer, with his gaunt face and grizzled eyebrows, who bent patiently at his corner of the light table, putting slide number 21 into the glassine envelope with a sort of weary happiness, like a laborer creeping home from the factory to bed, for our Artist was convinced that the *National Geographic* certainly couldn't turn down this picture of two elephant beetles engaged in pseudocopulation (a picture which could only, poor man, be taken by means of a bellows which he had designed and built himself at great expense); and now in through the door came the two tall thin college students who were doing a documentary on social conditions but first wanted to get top-of-the-line prints made for their portfolios, for that would surely help them in their project when potential sponsors looked the pictures over and shook their heads in wonder and said, "My, those boys are so talented."

Parker meanwhile sat and dreamed, not without a hopefulness which soothed his own peculiar troubles. It may come as a surprise to some readers to hear that he was not happy. The reliable citizen's feeling is that those who are capable of organizing and executing cruelties must in some measure be immune to them. However, power rarely brings with it any emotional enablement or relief; rather, the stakes become more abstract, without at all diminishing thereby the pangs of overreaching ambition. – In many ways Parker's early career paralleled Bug's. Rather than suffering utter exclusion, however, he was tormented by his own pre-eminence. The result was the same in the end. He led the swim team on its campaigns and had to be responsible for every detail of discipline. To some extent he relied on Wayne in those days, but even Wayne, he knew, was not up to the strains of perfect organization, being more a Silver Guardian than a true Philosopher-King; and Parker knew that when the time came for him to achieve a national position, as he and Wayne came speeding up to the broadcast hall in a small red touring car of Japanese manufacture, and Parker gangled himself up the marble steps and Wayne followed in new dress uniform, having locked the car, and they strode around the building to the stage entrance in back, carrying revolvers in their pockets; and Parker and Wayne marched grandly up to the podium and all the dignitaries in the audience cheered and took off their tophats; and the television cameras began to swivel and hum with all the forces of electricity behind them and Parker seated himself in lotus position on top of the podium as Wayne stood just below him and in front of him, preparing to speak for Parker and to convey to all concerned the mighty ideals of Wayne and Parker (maybe Wayne's brain would be wired up to Parker's via modem); and the crowd settled down and Wayne fired two shots into the ceiling in an emphatic request for perfect quiet, then Parker knew that he'd have to listen to Wayne very carefully to make certain that Wayne didn't blow it by demanding a personal loyalty oath or otherwise becoming mystical and sentimental. If that were to occur then Parker would have no choice but to reach into the pocket of his hunting jacket and tap Wayne's head with the barrel of his Walther, in such a way that Wayne would feel it just above the right ear. – For no one could be trusted absolutely, no matter how withdrawn or aggressive he appeared to be. Parker saw each man completely, no weakness escaping him. It might or might not have been a revelation to subordinates such as Roger (now long in an unmarked grave) to learn that Parker's strictness was motivated less by any discreditable desire for dominance over the forces of electronic mutation than by an almost maternal tenderness for those in his care. He was aware that they needed a great unifier, an individual whose presence made all secret insecurities dwindle to the size of beetles hiding beneath the rotten floorboards ... When he used each member of his team, it was only in the interests of the whole. Some of them were oversensitive to water pressure or chill, say, and during a meet they had to be terrorized into forgetting their perceptual fatigue in order to improve their scores. When they performed the Octopus he needed to work them into a smooth rhythm of motion, avoiding bucking, flinching or left windage. This was not always easy for Parker to do. The night before a meet he sometimes had nervous headaches which kept him from sleeping for hours.

He also had social problems, oddly enough. When forced to interact without his intermediaries in the predominantly liberal society of that era, he was awkward and taciturn, noteworthy for his exaggerated haste in eating at parties, his fawning politeness and his tendency to leave early, sometimes after only ten or fifteen minutes, during which time, smiling ingratiatingly at the others, but maintaining despite himself a deeply wary and fearful expression, he'd have devoured the entire bowl of taco chips. Of course it did not help this gauche, ragged youth to have been born in Omarville. He was constantly afraid of social slights, and whenever anyone mentioned weeds or cattails in his presence he was quick to stand upright and draw his long thin arms in upon himself and smile as if he forgave you, and he quite appreciated the joke, but if you had forced yourself to put your face up close to his and look him straight in the eyes, you might have detected in them a banked glow of malevolence. None of the girls could stand him until word was diffused by his associates that he was responsible for many of the school's athletic successes. Then they overcame their repugnance easily enough, but they never liked him for himself, and Parker was sensitive to this fact. At that time he had no desire to keep one in his house. Sometimes at parties as the girls gathered around him in their dear lovely dresses and he could smell their perfume and they all wanted him to dance or to call Wayne to have Wayne drive them home while they sat in the back seat with Parker, then as Parker looked all around from face to shining face and saw their repugnance still there like hard yellow bone beneath the contours of ambitious desire his faint polite smiles decayed into grimaces of genuine terror which disgusted them almost as much as if he had crapped in his pants; and then they went off and left him alone and the hostess's mother would have to come talk to him about upcoming matches and pat him on the shoulder, and be genuinely worried about him because even if he was an oddly defensive young man still he must be good for the school if what her Susan had said at breakfast was true; and the school was important; and if he was that nervous, poor thing, as anyone from Omarville down there among all those horrid plants had a right to be, then it must be because someone or some long green stalk had hurt him dreadfully when he was younger; and it was our duty here in Cooverville to look after those who had not had our advantages; so she soothed him, and Parker was gradually able to nod almost with his usual *élan* or tap his foot in Morse code response when she asked him about the strengths and weaknesses of the other teams, or whether the pool water was chlorinated or fluoridated. Then the girls would see that he was all right again, and begin buzzing around him like bees, and Parker wouldn't say anything but just drum his fingers against the half-empty punchbowl and kind of look at them as if they didn't matter, which was how they were used to being treated anyhow, so they relaxed into the Saturday night swindle and he relaxed and soon he was yawning and sucking in his cheeks with awful triumphant persuasiveness and they became intoxicated by him then and forgot everything which they had ever said or heard to Parker's discredit, and swooned around him and rubbed their tight sweaters up against him and giggled until Susan's mother returned to calm things down but now Parker wasn't nearly as polite and responsive as he had been; indeed he looked at her almost coldly;

yes, there was definitely something about him she didn't like no matter what Susan said; something about him she was almost afraid of, in fact, so she'd go off again in defeat to check on the punch and the fun continued until Parker couldn't take it anymore and slipped off to call Wayne to come get him. Wayne worried about Parker sometimes. He very much wanted to help him. In fact, he would have been willing to do anything for Parker, even die for him. Wayne worried about many things, even things which might have been expected to pass by sharper sensibilities than his own, though I've said this before and I'll say it again: I'm tired of Wayne, I'm talking about someone else, but to understand the situation you need to know that as they'd be driving home from the parties (to which Wayne, being very popular, was always invited, but to which he seldom came, preferring to be on call for Parker) it would be a cool summer night on the outskirts of town with the nightcrawlers up on the fields and all the crickets scraping their songs out, all tunes of doom and alienation; and the car rolled along almost silently as Wayne and Parker cranked down their windows, and Wayne in the driver's seat rested his left arm on his window, while Parker over on the passenger side rested his right arm on *his*, and finally Wayne would screw up his courage and tense himself to break the silence of commuting with Parker and say, "Well, Parker, how did things go? What did we set up tonight?" – for in the course of his long association with Parker Wayne had come to learn that one must always be planning step by step and setting concrete goals to achieve, like the solution to those raw materials questions which so absorbed Mr. White, instead of brooding over disappointments. – But Parker would just kinda shrug or scrunch up an eye or pick at the upholstery of the seat with the point of a fingernail, and then Wayne would know that it was best to drop *that* subject. And they'd roll along and roll along and Wayne would be sitting there steering, worrying if Parker were mad at him or if their plans had suffered some big setback tonight; or maybe one of their enemies had succeeded in getting at Parker somehow, and Wayne wanted to ask Parker if he was all right, but it would never be possible to ask that question, so they rolled along, and maybe Wayne might switch on the radio so that its tubes glowed in their faces and the tuning cursor swam at Wayne's command through its rectangular luminescent sea until it hit the right station and they'd both hear the dee jaw going waaw waaw until finally the music started again boodeley-boodeley-boo, and they settled back a bit, the two of them, and forged ahead like loyalty deep and true illuminating some totally opaque process,

with the bugs screeching despairingly from every field and sad country music on the radio and on and on the headlights bored into the darkness while back at the party, bitterly disappointed, the girls were beginning to come to themselves again and look at each other in rivalry and suspicion and misery because none had been chosen by Parker; maybe he had a girl somewhere else but on the other hand at least none of the other girls *here* had been chosen, either, which would have been worse, so they cheered each other up and sneered at each other and finished the soft drinks and finally went home and cried. – Susan sat in the bright kitchen sobbing for another reason. She was in love with Wayne. She did not know that her mother and father were lying wide awake listening to her and feeling sorry for her, but they knew there was nothing they could do to help her so finally they turned the bed-lamps on and Susan's mother began to read a mystery while Susan's father reread today's paper. Susan got up from the kitchen table and rinsed off all the plates and bowls and glasses and loaded them into the dishwasher, crying very hard now so that her tears fell on the topmost plate, and her eyes were very red and her face was puffed-up and ugly but she couldn't help it and she decided to never have another party again; Wayne hadn't even come in; he'd just waited in the car for Parker to amble out into Susan's driveway; and she decided that she hated Parker because she was pretty sure that it was all Parker's fault, that Parker wouldn't let Wayne like her or any other girl; and she turned on the cold water tap of the sink so that her parents wouldn't hear her and cried louder and struck at her face with her balled-up hands; now it was time to scrub off the table and the counter and vacuum up the carpet in the living room, especially around the sideboard where Parker had ground hundreds of potato chips into the rug with his heel; and finally here was the last saucer to rinse and she put it into the dishwasher and sobbed some more as she added a measure of ice-blue soap powder; and her tears fell on the soap and foamed; and she slammed the door feeling wretched and set the dial to full cycle; and then as she pressed the power switch there was a strange buzzing and the door of the dishwasher opened by itself, and a fat blue globe of ball-lightning rolled out through the spoons and poised itself on the lip of the open door, and said to Susan, "Do not despair, for Wayne will come to you; and we will control Parker through the Great Enlarger," and Susan covered her face with her hands and shrieked; and the dishwasher suddenly began working madly and sprayed her with boiling soapy water, burning her face and hands and drenching her; and she shrieked again so her parents came running but there was no blue globe to be seen and the dishwasher had closed itself up again and was humming along innocently, and Susan lay moaning and trembling in a pool of soapy tears. – Meanwhile the car was continuing in its course without any real urgency, and Parker sat tall and loose-jointed and peaceful listening to the music but Wayne looked at him out of the corner of his eye and could see that Parker had been hurt somehow, that some bastard was out to screw up Parker and keep Parker and Wayne from succeeding in what was important to them, and Wayne wanted to bite his lips for rage at the bugeyes who were messing everything up, and Wayne wished that Parker would confide in him; and meanwhile Parker, suffering the supreme loneliness of power, was wishing that Wayne wasn't such a weakheaded lunk of muscle who never understood anything and could not be trusted in such grim moments, but that was just how it was, so he ruthlessly sealed himself up in himself and gangled his legs and listened to the music; and now here he was sitting in the darkness waiting, just waiting, until he had the proper attributes and contacts and circumstances to instill a more widespread attachment, for he timidly desired many of the girls who wanted him, and there was one whom he looked at but never said a word to; now the picture in the basin of developer was taking shape; in the whiteness of the exposed paper grew a faint freckling of texture, like Catherine's delicate skin, but the upper right quadrant wasn't taking shape as fast as the rest; it would be too light, so Parker breathed on that part and struck a match near it and held it tight and lovingly against his phosphorescent finger-nails . . .

DEBRIEFING IN THE MERCHANT MARINE

The first line of defense against interrogation and later indoctrination is military bearing, silence, and trust in yourself, your Army, your country, and your religion.

Army Field Manual FM 21–76
section 15–2 (1969)

"Awright, guy," says Wayne to the rickshaw driver, he says, "take me to the Base pronto an' swing by Debriefing so we don't waste time going to R. & R." – "Yessir," the driver replied. He was a local. They were somewhere in the Philippines, near Manila or Guadalcanal. Wayne had come in to report the insect activities which he had encountered on his patrol. He was also about due for a good two weeks of promotional leave, if you want the truth, 'cause after all that time alone out there without the babes you started seeing things, like Mrs. Eisenhower up ahead waving a white handkerchief on top of some mangrove tree; and the brown water stretched like taffy when you tried to pull the oars out. *He* wasn't gonna have to take that anymore, at least not until after he'd reported; and in the meanhow it sure was good to come back and just take in the sights, like unpaved streets, and coolies, and casinos built painstakingly out of tourists' discarded drinking straws, waste not want not.

"Lieutenant requests double-A permission to speak with the commanding officer SIR!" barks out Wayne, so happy and proud just to be free from the mangrove shakes. – Here he was now at the checkpoint, which was a square clearing framed with barbed wire and horizontal barber poles and straight dirt roads and transit fencing, the whole as neat as a United States pin; and the rickshaw chugged away from him paid up in deodorant dollars with a few extra treasures thrown in out of Wayne's good-humored generosity to the ole tribal grunt: one (1) standard issue party melt; a few blue-black naval candies Wayne had bought but didn't like 'cause when ya sucked on 'em yer mouth filled with salt and ya heard the sea in yer ears; he'd had more than enough sailing over the foaming main for awhile because to get to the operational area you had to plough along for days in choppy waters in a souped-up patrol boat, dodging coral reefs and big waves, and always on the lookout for turtle-bugs which could clamp onto the bottom of your craft like limpet mines and pull you down into dreamy slumber-grottoes full of congregations of shrimp-like larvae that would infest you good; no, thanks; so Wayne passed his naval candies on, glad to be rid of the memory of them; and he even threw in a bit of leftover sugar daddy he'd gotten in a package from Susan, who had his picture over her bed now; because the natives sure liked sweets; that was how you *pleased* them, though he didn't stand for it when the brown naked divers didn't bite every last barnacle off the lower hull like they were paid to do; if they weren't doing their job what the hell did they need teeth for? So he also passed over one (1) case of Chewey-Gooeys and a Dork Bar he'd taken a bite out of; it was a new product, but he didn't much go for it; and for good measure he got shut of his special forces issue tropical chocolate imitation cunt, which was included in the tack of all single personnel patrol craft just to keep you going and if you got lost and hungry you just peeled off the rubber molded wrapper and ate the chocolate for quick energy; but Wayne had worn his out and would receive a replacement on his next mission, so he thought why not give the rickshaw gook a goddamned break; at least he sent the bum away happy.

Whistling, Wayne quadruple-bounce-stepped past the military barriers, showed his black pass and picture I.D., and was directed into the briefing room. It was pitch dark in there like when you sit in an adjustable chair at the ophthalmologist's and they show slides on the wall and you have to read off E W Z X Q D c o n s p i r a c y; except that a spotlight shone straight in Wayne's face and he had on the polygraph handcuffs (which had snicked automatically around each wrist when he laid his arms, as directed, on the siderests); and the technical fella winked and stuck a khaki-colored square of lie-sensitive tape to his tongue; it could sense every little waggle; if you told a white lie it turned white; if you told a black lie it turned black; and if you tried to spread treason it turned red and burned like hot pepper and then you were in trouble. – It was nothing personal, this security stuff, for actually they all liked Wayne at the Base and thought he was some hero volunteering for hazardous duty pay without even blowing the money on girls and bamboo juice the way they would because he put it in a special campaign account so that he and Parker could at some predetermined date have leaflets and flyers printed up and also buy a brace of pistols apiece so that someday, when the time was ripe for Parker to run the entire world, then Wayne and Parker would be driven up to the multinational assembly in a black Mercedes by some impeccably groomed silent reliable chauffeur, as Wayne sat in the back seat with Parker, looking into Parker's face to get inspiration for the coming speech, and Parker leaned forward and patted Wayne on the shoulder and there was an encouraging openness and gentleness about Parker's movements that had never been there before, and they went up the great marble steps together while the chauffeur took the Mercedes over to a special parking space that said RESERVED FOR PARKER AND WAYNE; and Wayne and Parker swept into the hall arm in arm as a big brass band struck up the Wayne and Parker theme; and all the generals of the world, white, black, and polka-dotted, began to dance with their mistresses in the aisles; and the two prettiest girls in the world came up and kissed Parker and Wayne in double-headed juicy smacks; then everything quieted down; and at Parker's signal Parker and Wayne pulled out their pistols; and all the world generals grew stern and pulled out their pistols as well; it was a real pistol bazaar in there, what with Colts and Schmeissers and micro-Uzis and Steyr M-12s, Rast-Gassers, Enfield Webley M-1913s, and of course the Holy Family of Walther, Luger and Mauser, the Bergmann M-10, the big fat .45 Mexican Obregons wielded by a sweaty moon-faced contingent, the quaint Hungarian Frommer M-39s, the Berettas and Glisenti M-10s waved around by the Italian Guards, and the Japanese stood in the corner with their Nambu Type 14.8 mm. pocket pistols – real wonders those Japanese, the things they can engineer, and the Astra M-400s of Spain hovered ready to do their duty for Parker and Wayne, side by side with Poland's Radom M-35, this being a genuine worldwide movement, inspiring even the East Bloc countries to come; yes, indeedy, Wayne could make out the muzzle of a Czechoslovakian Cz. M-52 (.762 mm. Russian load) peeping out shyly in the midst of all the NATO steel, and partly concealed behind the waspish French Lebel M-92 could be seen multitudes of Makarov M-PMs, Stechkins and .762 Tokarev T130 machine-pistols raised proud and ordered in double-file array, so that tears came to Wayne's eyes because this meant that the Soviets were our brothers at last, and even the cool Swiss Neuhausen M-49s, not to mention the Swedish Lahtis and

Nagants, were represented in blued, nickel and Parkerized finish, for there were no neutrals any longer on this glorious day; and all that metal gleamed awaiting Wayne's command, and the generals were full of zeal, anxious to be led to conquest; and Wayne counted, "Awright, fellas, one, two, THREE!" and everyone fired blanks at once and the drums rolled *rrrr-pa-pum-pum pum-pum-pum pa-pum-pum-rrrrr* and Wayne advanced to the very edge of the stage with Parker's long green arm still about his shoulder, though Parker remained behind and to stage right, a guiding influence capable of stretching his limbs to great semisolid lengths; and Wayne now began to speak to the mature brave professional faces all uplifted with respect for him and for his Parker; and whenever he said something especially good all the audience cheered, and Parker's long lean fingers patted his shoulder and he was the happiest man in the world . . .

Meanwhile the debriefing went on just as you might expect.

"I then proceeded to Quadrant 46," says Wayne with real verve and style, "and discovered an anthill within probable tracking range."

"Did you have any reason to believe, Lieutenant, that the bug command ever detected you or your activities?"

"No, SIR. And we can whip them easy, because those bugs follow that Oriental philosophy like Socrates or Genghis Khan that what happens happens, so once we smoke out their nests they'll go along and –"

"Kindly confine yourself to the facts, Lieutenant."

"Sir when I passed by the landing SIR of the bug-men SIR whose boats I had cut adrift, I discovered SIR that they had gone into hopeless cocooning and sporulation. In my opinion they knew they were trapped SIR and even if a few could escape the crocodiles they did not want to inform the Great Beetle of their carelessness. I attached a three-point pressure-sensitive explosive seal to each fluff-ball on the following morning SIR, so that when they emerge and set off the charge it will look like suicide."

"Would you characterize these men as Iranian nationals?"

Wayne used photo-recall to dredge up memories of *National Geographic* spreads on Kurdish tribesmen. – "Nossir."

"Central or South American type?"

"They were darkies, sir, that's all I know. But they spoke like real encyclopedias."

"What style cutlasses were they carrying?"

"Sixteenth-century Swashbuckler IIA Mark 47 Series B SIR!"

"Any mention of Phil Blaker?"

"Nossir."

"Perhaps you wouldn't mind giving us your views, Lieutenant, on the importance of Quadrant 42 within the overall strategic situation."

"But I was in Quadrant 46, sir."

"We know that, Lieutenant."

"Based on my own observation," Wayne began stoutly, but feeling the lie-tape beginning to burn a hole in his tongue, he added quickly, "and my own unauthorized perusal of Commander White's memorandum on the subject —"

"We know all about that, too, Lieutenant. Can you think of any reason why you should not be court-martialed and expelled from the service for exceeding orders?"

Wayne swallowed. "No, sir."

"Very good. You are hereby cashiered."

You've had it! Wayne screamed at himself, feeling much like an old newspaper in the rain. What had happened was that they had brought him the wrong folder once by mistake. Now he would pay. A shivering horror of what Parker might do to him for failing in his trust began to make itself apparent, but old Wayne gritted his teeth and sat straight and true in his chair and prepared to take his fucking medicine, boy oh boy almighty. – They turned all the lights on then, but the handcuffs wouldn't unlock, so he was forced to remain in the examination chair while an army doctor took a urinalysis and photographed his brain-pan so that the degree of the dishonorable discharge could be determined. Then all the examining officers left, and Wayne sat under lock and key, in disgrace with his fly unzipped from the urinalysis, and the doctor rolled away his tools on a little trolley, whistling the "Tropics" theme from *Victory at Sea*, and then suddenly the lights dimmed again and a thrilling shudder fevered through Wayne's body as Commander White's voice came through both speaker-grilles:

"Well, you blew it this time, you scabied punk, thinking you could get away with something like that in my army; well, I'll tell you right here and now that just because you have it in for us doesn't mean we have it in for you because we're white-minded guys up here in the Admiralty and we can excuse a young man pulling a boner now and then whether he meant it or not, though of course you did mean it and scheme it and plan it, you puling Parker's pal, and if I had my way I'd lash you to the Union Jack and leave you swinging until some Chinese missile-interceptor picked you up hard and fast on the bull's-eye, and that's a very lonely way to go, my friend, as I can assure you because it almost happened to me when I was your age, conquering a volcanic island in the South Pacific, but I'll be blowed if I know what *you* could possibly understand about amphibious warfare, you wetbrain, though I really can't get too angry with you today because if you want to know this climate is getting to me, so I'll just promote you to Major and give you a special mission."

Wayne started feeling good all over. "What kinda mission, Commander White, sir?"

Commander White came into the room and the lights brightened a little and Commander White sat down in the interrogator's chair and crossed his legs and let the foot at the end of the topmost leg pump up and down. – "Well, I'm darned if I don't feel fey about this, Wayne, but something tells me you're going to perform twelve heroic labors for us, and if you do we'll send you back to Parker with an Iron Cross and a little bonus to sweeten your campaign fund because don't think I don't have just a tad more influence around here than you do, you shithead deck swabber that wants to be Vice-President of the World – Vice-President! – ha, that's a good one; I'm telling you now that if you fail to complete your labors for our territorial integrity you'll be lucky to be Vice-President of the Society of Hanged AWOLs . . ."

"Yessir," says Wayne. "Yessir."

"Don't you yessir me, defying my visible authority before I'm even finished, because I don't think you really want me to call out my war power like I will when we're fighting those bugs fair and square if you and I have anything to say about it to those ringwormed armpits in the state department, so first we arm ourselves and then we use the arms to guarantee our neutrality if you see what I mean" – and Wayne, realizing that he was expected to laugh, hawed heartily there in the handcuff-chair, and as he laughed he realized that this was really a good one, so he hawed some more until Commander White kicked him in the shin. – "So I want you to hitchhike down into Texas and Oregon to ferret out the wasps' nests, and I'll allow two amoral brawls as part of the twelve-labor package, because we're converting to metric one of these days, but after that I want those bugs DEAD."

THE THREE TEXANS, OR, THE FIRST
LABOR OF WAYNE

~~~~~~

> It is not the neutrals or the lukewarms who make history.

<div align="right">

HITLER in Berlin
23 April 1933

</div>

Awright, so old Wayne was on the road, thumbing his way from here to there and ready to deal with any trouble that might try to strike *him* dead. Once when he was in Texas these three guys pulled over in a pickup, and the closest one rolled down the window and stuck his mug out and said, "So you want a ride, asshole?" – Well, Wayne wasn't about to stand for that, so he bounced right up and snapped the big CB antenna right off the hood and reached in through the window to unlock the door of the cab and threw it open and grabbed the jerk by the elbow and pulled him out and kicked him to the ground and began to beat him good with the aerial, *whhhup, whhhap,* across the face and shoulders, and when after five or ten seconds everything was all bloody and there were scarlet teeth scattered along the shoulder of the road, why, Wayne picked up the yokel's cowboy hat and dusted it off and hummed to himself and twirled it around his thumb and – spat on it and ground it into the dust. No doubt this dirt-hog also owned a saddle horse and a pretty shotgun especially to kill sage chickens. Anyhow, Wayne had other matters to worry about now, two to be exact, for after their first moment of heavy-lidded surprise the big beer-bellied monsters were coming out, and by jingo they *were* big; why, the first one was half a head taller than Wayne and had a wide pterodactyl reach of bearskin arms (not to mix metaphors or nothin'), and the second was, whoosh, well, it was a wonder he could get himself into the cab because by God and Gatling he practically blotted out the sky just coming forth and he still hadn't finished. Probably belonged to the Elks Club, too, or the Masons, where every man sat around and drank secret potions handed down from the Knights Templar days while they planned their next bowling event, and every sip made you bigger and stronger and dumber. – Dumber, that was it. Wayne thought on *his* feet, so as here came the two giants burping and closing on him, with a lusty "Heil!" and a clear open countenance Wayne kicked the first in the balls and tripped the second, TIMBURRRRRRRRRRRRRRRR as he came thudding down on the hard gulchy prairie. Now before they could get up it was antenna time, *whhhup-whhhap, whhhup-whhhap,* more leisurely-like now 'cause Wayne was sure of himself; and then a good kick in the head, hell, it practically sprained his goddamned toe connecting with so much solid bone, but let 'em have it again and let's say maybe again and once more for good luck until the eyes rolled up. Now, what did they have on them? – Whewee, Wayne had been playing a risky game. Number one had a Smith & Wesson .45, number two had a Colt Python .357 magnum with the nine-inch barrel ('course, the longer the barrel the shorter the peter, Wayne hawed to himself), and number three had a Sig-Sauer P226 and a little silver Derringer up his sleeve. – Wayne was far too smart to get caught with stolen guns. He broke them down, uncapped the radiator, and dropped them in, loose bullets and all. Then it was just a matter of walking back around the bend in the direction he had come, setting down his green duffel to sit on without a patch of shade, and waiting and waiting for the next vee-hickle to come down these ten million miles of hot dusty scorpion-ridden highway ... Wayne had a tiny styrofoam chest in his bag, just big enough for one ice-cold soda pop, like some frothy SexAid or a bubbly blue-green First Strike. He got it out. It was a SexAid this time, all sweet and dizzying and bargirl-perfumey. A mite more expensive than your average Texas alkali, which they bleached out of the sands, fermented in brown bottles buried deep beneath the poison chili bush, and added a stitch of Gila monster skin to when it was so strong it had started to dissolve its way through the glass. They had drinking contests with it every Sunday in Texas. It was powerful strong; it would go right through you, quite literally; you could sprinkle a drop on the crown of a man's head and if he wasn't at least a hundred percent American Texan, yee-haw, it would be coming out between his feet a quarter-minute later, and in between those loci of entrance and exit there wouldn't be much of a body left. But as I will be discussing Wayne's drinking victories in detail when we send him off to Oregon, I will return to the SexAid, which was, as indicated, a trifle pricey, but Wayne figgered the pictures on the side of the can alone made it worth it. He'd heard that in the east up around all those snotty-ass liberal Ivy League colleges where the coeds had the greatest split beavers in the whole U.S. of A. (and no men to satisfy them, either, 'cause the males up there were coastal pansies), you could buy a six-pack of the stuff wrapped in black silk panties to wrap yer mouth on afterwards. But somebody else had told Wayne they'd banned it up there on account of all those women's libbers that thought girls should piss standing up. Neither one would've surprised Wayne. Probably depended on how you crossed the state line, or something.

Anyhow, Wayne had him his pop, lookin' out at the cacti and some distant pink Adobeville, and as nothing had come by and it was pretty hot he walked back another half mile and found a big culvert just after where the road curved. Those three guys could be coming to at any time now (Wayne wasn't about to kill anybody in the middle of goddamn Texas), so he stretched out his bedroll in there and ate a Snoppers Bar and lay low for awhile. Eventually he heard the angry screech of the pickup as it went back and forth looking for him, gun parts rattling and bubbling in the radiator, but Wayne just lay there and waited tensely, prepared to take on double their number at any place and time, you name it, three times in a fucking row; and around sundown the truck went away and the desert got all cool and lovely except for the Texas sand-flies which were each an inch long with bulgy compound eyes. Wayne caught one and tied it to his thumb with a piece of thread and let it buzz around frantically for awhile and squashed it. The others got the message and left. They were smart, those bugs, not like Panhandle rubes that started something with strangers and didn't know when to quit. Wayne waited another hour or so and headed back out to the highway.

He was feeling pretty self-confident generally, young and strong and fit to take care of himself in ANY cunt-face's pubic hair, which is not to say that he was not always deeply worried about the current status of Parker and his ideals, for Parker was not a good correspondent, and it was theoretically possible that he no longer had any use for Wayne, at which point Wayne might well have shot himself. But there is no need to dwell on contingencies which I can assure the reader are remote; Wayne would be an integral part of Parker's plans for good, or at least (Parker thought to himself, ministering in the cathedral-like coolness and darkness of the photo lab) for the short-term future . . .

POOR SUSAN

~~~~~~

> I confess that mankind has a free will, but it is to milk kine, to
> build houses, etc., and nothing further.
>
> MARTIN LUTHER

What had happened between Susan and Wayne was that one night
when Parker had to go down to Omarville to visit his sinister thin
relations for some plant-type unholy equinox festival or other,
Wayne went to work out down in the lonely swimming pool; and
Susan, having taken heart as a result of the dishwasher's pronounce-
ment, drove to the gym. – The other members of the team should
have been there also, but without Parker they shook themselves
and rubbed grains of sleep from their eyes and thought about
going to practice but then upon rational reflection they decided
they would be damned if they would, so they all got together at
Chip's house and watched post-atomic cartoons; for Wayne was the
only member of a thoroughly pious and serious character. So there
he was, stroke-stroke-stroking, fifty-eight laps to go, and Susan
stood quietly on the bleachers watching him with her heart racing
rhythmically inside her, like a caged squirrel. She saw him down
there so hard-working and strong and intent, doing what he thought
was right, and she loved him even more and stood looking at him
doing lap after lap, until finally he was done and paddled over to the
ladder, breathing hard, aw-RIGHT, aw-RIGHT, aw-RIGHT; and
swung himself out so Susan saw his muscles tighten, and water stuck
to the hairs on his chest and arms and legs; and water ran down his
face. – "Whewee," says old Wayne, feeling good, and towels himself
off hard; and squeezes the water outta his hair and dries his face,
and looks around and sees Susan.

   His jaw drops. Then he grins. "Suzy-girl!" he calls up. "Hiya,
Suzy! If you've come here to do some muscle-watching, you ain't

seen NOTHING yet!" – though if truth be told Wayne is pretty tired already, but here's this pretty girl obviously stuck on him and Wayne has always had a thing for old Suzy, that is to say he'd like to stick his thing up *her* (Wayne haws to himself, just slightly self-conscious), but he respects Suzy too and always has because she gives parties to support the team and does good in school and Parker has pronounced her clean and besides she is so fucking beautiful that Wayne is going to move like the Spirit on the face of the fucking Waters, showing off, because he has to show off all the time and test himself and harden himself to look good so that everyone will look up to him and acknowledge him as a man in himself and nobody but nobody will dare to mess with Wayne, and if he swims out on his back toward the center of the pool he just might be able to look up Suzy's dress! – and Wayne is prepared at all times and carries a fresh rubber in an inner watertight pocket of his bathing trunks.

Susan sees him looking up at her smirking like that and she knows what he wants but she is pretty sure he likes her, too; and he is so good and tough as he dives into the pool headfirst backwards looking up at her grinning (he gets a wink of thigh), then his face gets set and serious again as he prepares his mental countdown for the iteration of difficult water-tricks ... he whizzes into ten underwater somersaults without a stop; and Susan throws a new golden penny into the pool and he dives down and retrieves it in its fall by seizing it in his big white teeth; and breaks through the water again grinning and shouting and takes it in his hand and kisses it and hurls it back to her through the air – and she can't catch, never has been able to, so as she reaches for it desperately it goes just over her shoulder and falls dully through the girders of the dark dusty bleachers ... This kind of thing always happens to poor Susan, and she is still leaning following through on her catch with her useless arms out in front of her and her palms cupped ridiculously (if the penny had landed in one by some miracle it would promptly have bounced out again), and she sways and stumbles and the rotten bleachers give way; and she falls fifty feet screaming with everything collapsing around her head and lands in a ten-foot-deep carpet of dust and mouse-turds; and somewhere nearby she hears beetles clacking angrily; but there is the penny; and now here comes Wayne smashing through the rubble to rescue her and she is all right and Wayne drags her out and kisses her and pulls her into the pool to wash the filth off her; and she holds him so tight and he kisses her and spouts water out of his ears for happiness and kisses her all over and seats her gently on the topmost rung of the ladder so that her outstretched legs are floating in the water; and Wayne raises her dress and pulls her underwear off and Susan is crying again and hitting him and saying, "No, no, no," and Wayne does a gross visual inspection and sees that actually she might've been hurt a little after all, her face is cut up; but Wayne can't stop now; he yanks his swim trunks to his knees and puts the rubber on and bangs his Suzy just as good and hard as he knows how; and she goes into shock and is choking on the water; he's twisted her face down into the shallow water along the gutter of the pool; and she is suffocating and in considerable pain and a wave of misery that smells like old chlorine slops gently into her face and bursts in her heart and she passes out which Wayne knows means she really enjoyed it, musta had half a dozen simultaneous multiple orgasms, sure was a good cunt; so he throws her over his shoulder and finds her car outside, and goes back into the rubble of the bleachers to get her purse; and rinses himself off once more in the pool; and gets dressed and dresses her in her sopping clothes and drives her home like any boy would, her body leaning up against his as he roars merrily along, her mouth open with blood running from it and her eyes rolled up, but Wayne rubs his thigh against hers and imagines that the whole scene is taking place on a really cold night, so that Suzy might say, "Oh, Wayney, my hands are so cold," and Wayne would then take them, her little white hands, in his own, and blow on them and stick them between his legs to warm them like in the Army you're supposed to do for a frostbitten buddy; and then and then and then awright! – and here they are now at Suzy's house, and Wayne, seeing that Suzy is still under the weather from her adventure, figures it's wise not to bother her parents, who will surely waste his time and ask a shitload of questions; so with his Suzy still over his shoulder he scampers nimbly up the drainpipe and raises the window of her bedroom with all her sweet schoolbooks and pennants and stuffed toys looking at him; and he takes off her clothes again and sneaks down reconnoitering the bathroom with its rubber mat and smiley-face sticker on the toilet seat to get a new towel to finish drying off his Suzy; and rubs the blood off her face and gives her tits a pinch to grow an inch; she's just like modeling clay, all cold and white and wet; and he tucks her sound in bed, so that when she wakes up she will almost believe the whole thing has been some nightmare; and out of shock and habit will go on sending packages to Wayne once he joins the reserves; and Wayne meanwhile shinnies down the drainpipe leaving his sleeping Suzy who has been as good as gold during the entire operation, and jog-trots home, not tired at all, whistling and thinking about all the other girls . . .

Meanwhile, under the wreckage of the bleachers, the horde of ashy grey ladybug beetles stops in its activities, much astonished. They recognize Wayne; they have been issued full reports of the battle in the swimming pool, when their kind died to save our hero; for such is the power of insect genetics, mutation and neo-Darwinistic social structure that the features and odors of each human enemy are remembered and transmitted by a spying water-bug; so, detecting Wayne, the bugs signaled hysterically with their antennae and foreleg-taps DANGER DANGER DANGER DANGER DANGER DANGER DANGER; for they thought that he had deliberately penetrated yet another of their hiding places. Word was immediately sent, via a baldfaced hornet and a faithful leafcutting bee, that a concerted attempt to destroy their network seemed in the bud; this message passed along various insulation pipes and root-tunnels until at the end it reached the Great Beetle in his lair. – The Great Beetle was hardly such an amateur as to take every message at its face value; nonetheless, there were other indications that a strike was being prepared, so he began to take steps to enlarge his system of clandestine information and covert action; and one such step was the contacting of Bug.

HITCHHIKING IN THE YUKON

~~~~~~

Revolutions are not made with rose-water.

E.G. BULWER-LYTTON
The Parisians (1873)

When Trotsky escaped from the relatively benign captivity of the Tsarist gendarmes, he traveled by reindeer to the Ural ore mines, took the narrow-gauge railway at Bogoslovsk Mine and changed to the Perm line, continuing on to Vyatka, Vologda, Petersburg and Helsingfors. The astute reader knows that after a short time he was being whisked along Nevsky Prospect in a cab, off to some thrilling clandestine meeting with other bespectacled murderers who plotted against Wayne and Parker and Dr. Dodger's capital, and so all that was very nice for Trotsky; and of course at the beginning of his unsanctioned departure from Siberia, when, slipping out between wretched plays in the army barracks, he got into a sleigh and hid beneath a bale of frozen straw until the agreed-upon hour of midnight, he had the whole lark of an escape to look forward to (and it certainly was a lark, for the worst that would have happened to him had they recaptured him would have been nothing compared to the best which would befall an impounded *zek* under the regime which he helped bring to power). But the business phase of the journey, which is to say seven to eight hundred versts across taiga and tundra, was no fun at all, just forests or treeless marshland, stunted pines and birches in the snow or maybe billions of Russian Orthodox Christmas trees that were later cut down in the war on the churches, and the road-tracks going on and on ("Here we are in Malye Ourvi," he writes sourly in his journal. "Three or four miserable yurts, only one of them inhabited ... The Ostyaks are dying out at a terrible rate ...") until he almost couldn't stand it.

Bug and his revolutionaries were to take a similarly toilsome trip in the declining days of their movement, when the red winter sun of direct action rose feebly to illuminate their panicky yet cunning retreat from Wayne and Mr. White across practically all the Arctic regions of the globe. With assault rifles and kerosene tanks strapped across their shoulders, they skated day and night across the Arctic Ocean, pausing at odd intervals to hide in the gloomy shelter of overhanging icebergs, where Bug perfected his final theories and submitted them to Milly for criticism, and Milly showered blows upon Frank's frostbitten face for not keeping up (this once Frank got the better of Milly, since he couldn't feel a thing even when the white skin stuck to Milly's metal gauntlets and tore in bloodless strips), and Susan and Stephen Mole sat kissing in the snow, at which Milly, reminded that people kissed, turned to Bug and said, "Very well, you can kiss me, then," almost as indifferently as if she were offering him a piece of bread and butter. – It seemed as if Bug had a calm pale prescience of where the last battles would be fought, for he never forgot the description of the Caves of Ice which he had read back at summer camp; and as the first of several dress rehearsals for the ultimate event he hitchhiked to Alaska and back during the third summer of his college days (about which more later). Bug was at this time still a thin, somewhat gawky youth who had never even fired a pistol. Why he went north he kept secret even from himself. He rationalized that he wanted to see all the trees, but as we know his love for trees was now a flat thing, a mere plank in his party platform; the real reason was that his neurosis for security was gaining ground; it was not just a question of looking around him as he once had at summer camp, noting gaps in hedges and darkened basements to crawl into in case of trouble, ready to extend his claws like a trapped lobster (not that he ever admitted the seriousness with which he pursued the game; as he got older he found it increasingly expedient to pretend that the world was a friendly place; he was still in his latent period); so now the phase was one of expanded longterm planning ... Bug calculated that he had better have a retreat of some kind, and what could be better for that purpose than the wilderness, and where was there more wilderness in our great Republic than in the Arctic environs? – So he took a scouting trip, just a youngster out on a bit of self-indulgence, it seemed, awaiting the indulgence of others, the bitter working adults, to open the car door for him and take him on to the next consecutive sector of No-Man's-Land. It was clear then once and for all that the issue of trees had only been an excuse, since he went far past the trees to the flat yellow plains and the braided rivers and the snowy hollows, and he kept on going until there was a magnetic northern taste in the air and the earplugs tingled, and wet meadows full of yellow flowers rolled into his view; and the streams were fortified with wiry willow-bushes that barely reached above his belt buckle (*these* were not trees); while up ahead was a range of wild peaks dripping with green tundra; and fogs perspired like ghosts around the lakes and freckled glaciers. On the other side of the mountains were more yellow plains rolling on to the Bering Sea. It was there that Wayne finally captured Susan in after years, not without fending off three polar bears and innumerable other frights, to be sure, such as the revolutionaries themselves, who by this time were starving skulking shaggy creatures, with sunken eyes and razor-edged ribs that the wind blew through like xylophones! Bug's face was a nodding cunning skull that swiveled and saw Wayne on the horizon and grinned at Wayne as polite as ever so that Wayne couldn't help but shudder; and swiveled back on creaking neckbones so that it faced Milly and it chattered some word into Milly's ear and pointed a long yellow crooked bony finger at Wayne, so that Milly started up snarling and glared straight at Wayne and articulated herself into a skinny crouch like a spiked Steyr-Daimler-Puch M1974 machine gun tripod; there was really not much left of Milly but bones and claws and teeth and matted hair and shiny horrid eyes; and Stephen Mole roared like an old bear, his ginger beard down almost to his knees, with frost woven into it and frost crowning his head and spidering out of his withered eyebrows as Stephen came striding slowly toward Wayne like a tired unstoppable Arctic explorer, maybe the revenant of old Vitus Bering himself, ready to hug Wayne very very gradually to his chest and crush him or else strangle Wayne with the trailing flapping mildewed remnants of his parka; and Milly turned savagely to Frank behind her, who was crawling along like a diseased lynx, and Milly grabbed Frank by the ears and pulled him upright and shook him and hit him across the mouth, so Frank reached slowly into his side-pouch like a drunk searching for matches; his long fingers were blue with gangrene and hung dangling at the digits, just barely attached by retrenching ligaments and brown moss splints and tatters of leathery skin, but Frank still had a venomous double-dealing determination in his eyes that belied his physical extremity; Wayne had never trusted the ratlike creep; Bug he yet disdained and Milly and Suzy were just yer regular female pussies (he hadn't given ole Suzy a careful once-over yet) and Stephen Mole didn't look as formidable as all that but here was the dangerous one; Frank clattered and clanked as he crawled because he was carrying polar Derringers; and Frank's malnourished knee-joints groaned like the doors of old stinking tombs; yessir, that Frankorola was the one to watch if Wayne boyo knew anything and you'd better *believe* he did; sure enough, Frank was withdrawing a clip of .38 specials for Milly from his side-pouch and Milly's green eyes flamed as she slammed the clip into her Colt and took a bead on Wayne but ole Wayne was not a bit dumber than these freako Iron Bloc monsters and he had already point-aimed at that awful horrid cunt Milly with his .45 Gold Cup; God, how he hated that fucking bitch out to GET him and Mr. White; he was gonna shoot a little tickler into that wolf-snatch! – He pulled the trigger cold and true. – There was a faint, dispirited click. The hammer was froze solid or some damn thing. Wayne had forgotten to ask Dr. Dodger to winterize his sidearm! – Oh, fucking Eskimo Ah Gooks! poor Wayne was about to get one right in his handsome blue eye; Wayne had always been fond of that eye; it had winked at him in the mirror the night after he'd first laid his Suzy, and speaking of her, now that he'd looked her up and down he had to say that *she* was the most terrible one in the whole ghastly crew! She stood leaning on Stephen, blotched, bloody and blackened, with ice glittering in her eyelashes, showing her teeth all the way to the shriveled gums and yelling, "Get him, Milly! Get him, get him!" – at which Milly awarded Susan a brief contemptuous look before sighting in more precisely on Wayne, who had thrown down his gun on the frozen crackling grass and was rummaging frantically in the pockets of his bushwhacking vest for a slingshot or any other weapon, just gimme kill power, lordy oh lordy, goddamnit, and Milly licked her chapped lips and brought her teeth together triumphantly and blew Wayne's head off. BLAM! – But no! Wayne had ducked just in time. The bullet sped off purposelessly to the south. – Milly was furious. She hated to waste ammunition. All the Kuzbu brutes came running and loping and leaping and rapid-hobbling up in a double-time frenzy and threw themselves slavering on Wayne and began biting him with their gaunt blue fangs and tearing his flesh with their long blue fingernails; and Susan jumped up and down on his face with all her strength, yelling, "You rapist! You reactionary! I'm going to cut off your head and your balls!" – and she pulled Wayne's knife from his belt and began to make good the first part of her threat by sawing at his throat; but it was your curse, my bright and risen angels, that you could not even kill each other until Big George let you; so Wayne survived the worst of it; vicious though these curs were, they were so emaciated from their privations that they weighed little more than snowmen, and had not the strength equal to their ferocity; by far the worst thing for Wayne was seeing his Suzy against him. — "How could you do it, Suzy?" he choked out. "How could you turn on us and screw up our ideals?" and his anguish caught fire and transmuted itself into rage, so he felt himself getting stronger and stronger, like Hercules, and he kicked Stephen Mole in the crotch and sent him flying high into the empty sky and across the river into a tangle of frozen bushes that caught Stephen like barbed wire; and he punched Milly in the side of the head; out like a goddamned LIGHT! and he knocked poor spindly chattering Bug head over heels; Bug had not been able to anticipate this because his earplugs had been revoked in consequence of his treachery to the Great Beetle; only Susan still crouched upon him like a wildcat, savaging his throat (though with more zeal than competence); and Wayne got his wrist up under her hands clenched around the knife and thrust sharply upward so that the hilt slammed into her chin and stunned her. Losing not a moment (there being not a moment to lose), Wayne grabbed his traitorous Suzy for interrogation and future punishment and took to his heels, for the Kuzbuites were coming to their senses and regrouping; and Big George had wandered away from the console for a moment to have a cup of coffee and yawn and shrug his shoulders in princely indifference, so that I, the author, had an instant of genuine freedom; and I certainly meant to have Wayne killed; and I think Wayne knew it 'cause he sure wasn't farting around like blubber on a beach; *hup, hup, hup* he ran, south he ran, so that the frozen ground shook and shattered beneath his tread; and Suzy lay limp across his shoulder just like in the old days, YEE-HAWWWW! . . . — Did he get away? — Temporarily. — But I cannot reveal more; for these events lie within the grey clammy province of the next volume. These were still just reconnaissance days for young Bug. — He was, if truth be known, searching for the Caves of Ice, for he never forgot anything he had read; and the books back at summer camp had told no lies. Swiveling his pale head cautiously, looking quite ordinary in his American hiking outfit, he tramped up Grizzly Creek, his big backpack embracing him faithfully from behind; it was his first follower. The earplugs tingled. He walked through the flowers up by Hanging Glacier Mountain. Occasionally he stopped to inspect some insect or purple bud through a hand lens. He stepped as lightly as an Indian brave. (Wayne, tracking him through this country years later, was to leave footprints and jeep tracks along the river bed; they would never heal.) He spidered his way up narrow ravines and side-stepped waterfalls. Valleys and rivers lay below him, beautifully lonely. He crossed dry ridges tentatively, always looking for places to hide, and camped in inconspicuous niches beside the streams. He never saw a human being. The mountains were all around him; no one could see him now except for boreal mountain bugs. He went up higher and higher to where the brown shaggy bees buzzed uneasily at his shadow, for they were wild and had barely heard of the Great Beetle, but then they felt the emanations from his earplugs and let him pass. Up there was the Beethoven Bird; it sang the first four notes of the Fifth over and over all day; and the grizzlies clambered down the mountain sides, boulder-to-boulder, *cloomb . . . cloomb . . . cloomb* at midnight (which was still light, it being summer; the sun just went round and round in the sky) and he heard them stamping around his tent very slowly; and then they went away. Once he saw a caribou. The moss was speckled with caribou skulls. He crossed the Continental Divide and was 'way up in the clouds looking down on glaciers. Fording a big brown river he sank to his waist in the cold water but did not fall. The mosquitoes were with him constantly whining and biting until he put the earplugs in; and then the clouds of them cleared away from his face and streamed behind him respectfully like an honor guard. Off to the east was the Valley of Precipices, but he never got there, because he found the Caves of Ice, you see. The tingling of the earplugs led him along high grey ashen ridges and into chilly mist-clouds and up over glaciers to the high passes, and up the sides of ice-cliffs through the steadily falling snow and across a summer-rotten snow-bridge that squeaked under his weight so that he swayed and looked down into the depths of a crevasse directly under him; but promptly a little springtail snow-mite bounded up the snow-bank to him and motioned him onward with its right antenna, in much the same manner as a Navy signalist will wave jets onward as he stands on the deck of the aircraft carrier. So Bug continued on his way, squeaking by diverse perilous obstacles and difficult pitches through sheer virtue of his thinness and light weight and insect guidance (later on his followers would use crampons), and at last he shinnied up the final black razor-sharp peak and saw a plateau below him on the far shoulder of the mountain, girded round with sentinel-like rock towers which would be ideal for constant observation of the whole *massif*. Proceeding cautiously down toward this terrace (for Bug never forgot that if the mist cleared he would be very visible to airplanes), he spied the mouth of a sinkhole or cavern in the snow, dazzling him with cutting light. It was more than wide enough for him to enter. Bug had come to the Caves of Ice by the back door, so to speak.

The Caves of Ice might have daunted even Tom Swift; inside were mazes of mirror-blue halls and throne rooms and the usual stalagmite traps like the pungi-stake pits our enemies dug for us in Vietnam; but Bug just put on his dark spectacles to eliminate the glare and explored this ultimate hideout for weeks, living on dripping sugared icicles and vanilla ice cream, of which there was a plentiful supply. Here it would be possible to maintain an organization. When he had mapped out every passageway, Bug strolled round the plateau, peering at the view, which could be obtained from the edge at no great hazard. Far below were green boggy valleys which derived their summer character from rivers, sunshine and mosquitoes. Clouds swam by at intervals, fifteen hundred feet or so below Bug on his lookout plateau. Geese circled round the ponds. The tundra meadows were squiggled with little snowdrifts. It was all like the picture on the sleeve of an expensive Swiss chocolate bar; speaking in absolute terms, it made an entirely appropriate backdrop for a young extremist movement whose hard times had not yet come upon it. — Climbing the rock towers before he departed, spindly Bug satisfied himself that they would be adequate for directing his patrols to any area within sniping range. It began to snow again. He made one last circuit of the plateau, counting his steps and calculating, as we all do in idle moments, how much barbed wire would be needed to reinforce the perimeter. Then he was ready to descend from the mountains. — At once the earplugs tingled. A circular plug of snow rose unsteadily upward, almost at Bug's feet, and two white furry trapdoor spiders emerged, bearing a net of silk which they had woven especially for Bug. He stretched himself out upon it, for it was clear by now that the insect minions had his interest at heart; and indeed Bug would not be surprised if they were to make him an offer of some kind in the very near future. — Clever Bug! — The two spiders set to work at once sewing him up safe and tight; then they wove new strands of their best virgin spider-silk and glued them all along the edges and corners of the bundle with special spider-glue, so that from Bug's point of view the world came to radiate regular glistening lines, as if he were at the center of the sun looking around him at all the sunbeams; and the spiders swarmed busily all over Bug's face and body, checking to make certain that every thread was snug (that pair would have made great piano players); and one of them fluffed a little pillow of spider-down under his head and wove it into place. — Now they ducked back into their hole for a moment, returning in an instant dragging a great roll of translucent sticky fabric behind them. This they unrolled carefully, one spider pushing the roll and the other holding down the silk which had already been flattened out. When they finished this operation a large circular sheet of greyish material lay in the snow beside Bug. No doubt it had been hemmed and seamed by silkworms. – In a twinkling the dear spiders had spun myriad new gluey cables to attach him to this canopy. – They were making a parachute! – When the work was finished the spiders got behind Bug and rolled him onto his side; then one of the two positioned itself at the small of his back and the other stood ready to push where needed. As Bug was rolled steadily toward the edge, the first spider kept its position, and the second scuttled constantly up and down the length of Bug's body, keeping every one of Bug's members from lagging behind the grand progress of the rest. They reached the precipice and launched him into the wind. He drifted down into the summer air, light and easy as a contingency plan . . . (How sad it is for me to consider what other, fatal descents we shall witness from this same cliff!) Once he had landed in the grass, a nest of woolly Arctic ants came and nipped through the seams until he was free, per prior instructions, for ants will always do as they are told. Politely, Bug crumbled up some crackers for them from his pack. Then he started walking again, tussock to tussock, automatically looking round for places to hide himself and his supplies; or rather, as a respectful biographer should put it, he began to work out the first details of concealment tactics in the Arctic. Sites needed to be found for day-to-day and emergency use in such areas of action the discovery of which would not jeopardize the security of his headquarters – that is, the Caves of Ice. – If he took the earplugs out for a second then the mosquitoes came back and flew up his nose and crowded on his glasses so thick that he couldn't see; and his body swelled up with their bites, and every time he slapped his itching arms his hand came up smeared with black mosquitoes and red-golden blood. The mosquitoes, in short, were not his friends by default. So he kept the earplugs in. – At this time he persisted in the illusion that individual retreat was superior in practicality (and, therefore, in morality) to the terrorist strikes of small, well-organized bands, for he did not want to get the shit beaten out of him; remembering as he did how Tony the beetle lay crushed upon the floor of the cabin, he had to assume that any of his own attempts at subversion would bring him to a slower and even more miserable fate; after all, he, unlike Tony, had no hard brittle shell the shattering of which would instantly release him from his tortures. Bug was, I reiterate, still only a latent: – imbued with the proper precious hatred, but not with sufficient solidity of character to be capable of attack. There was too much fear still in him. So he studied the landscape with a fatalistic eye to said retreat, noting rocky wooded islets in the midst of the rushing rivers where he might be safe, memorizing (just for practice) any position of frowning overhangs which could hide him from helicopters. His eye for these details had improved since the days of summer camp; nonetheless, his approach remained both passive and theoretical. The turning point in his development did not arrive until he had allied himself with Milly. Of course, in that last grey time when the earplugs had been taken away and all the forces of electricity had engaged tooth in cog to grind him up, then to some extent the helpless fear returned. – But at the time of which we are speaking he was still just a young solitary Bug taking observations and gathering instinctive data without much to guide him save a certain steely reflexiveness which would prove itself within a fistful of pages. So he studied the lie of the land. South of the next range of peaks, the trees began again. As he continued southward they got bigger and more confident and formed enormous black grizzled forests full of wood-mold and porcupines and foxes. The rivers wound through these trees for thousands of miles. Bug floated silently along in a black rubber raft. Creatures watched him. Everywhere he looked he established hypothetical traps. With the superb amorality of the creative mind, he left it an open question whether the traps were set against him or his enemies. That was but a dubious side issue, like one of these gloomy water-channels that twisted away from the main streamcourse into a tunnel formed by the interlocking arms of evil cypresses; the important thing was that there were or would be traps. Behind the sullen pine trees on that sandbar a light machine gun (LMG) or rocket launcher (RPG) could be established, and once Milly shared power with Bug both *would* be. – Even then, Bug, I am proud to say, reflected upon seeing a jumble of basalt there in the sunny Arctic hills that here a cache of weapons could be located, every gun heavily greased before being sealed into its airtight bag, every dozen such bags stacked neatly in a crate packed full of silica gel, upon the completion of which procedure the crate was nailed shut; and every row of these crates being separated by dark timbers to allow air circulation; and within a decade, as we shall see, that tidy dream was to come true; so that within a twenty-mile radius of the Caves of Ice there were five such caches, the heavy labor having been accomplished by Susan, Milly and scowling Stephen Mole, who rolled the boulders painfully aside until his hands bled and the sweat burst out all along his back and the sweat started from his forehead, while Milly and Susan grunted the heavy ammunition boxes up the trail, Milly leading contemptuously as Susan stepped right at Milly's heels *and* carrying five hundred rounds more than Milly to show Milly that Susan was just as good as Milly was even if Milly couldn't understand that because Milly was always so unfair and hated Susan and wanted to keep her from Bug; actually Milly did not care about Susan one way or the other, aside from the fact that the stupid bitch kept treading on her heels; Susan's legs were aching and her back hurt from all the cartridge boxes in the sling; and her arms hurt so much she could barely stand it because she was carrying the extra five hundred rounds in her arms, in a heavy steel box which she clutched to her chest like a baby and the sharp corners of the box hurt her breasts and the bullets rattled angrily inside like bees as she marched on with every step getting harder and harder; yes, Susan was feeling miserable, all right, especially since Milly hadn't even noticed that Susan was carrying a bigger load than she was and Bug and Frank hadn't seen either because Bug was in the Caves of Ice designing instructional charts of the best way to disable the Society of Daniel's computer facility in Monterey, while Frank was inking the completed charts in black and yellow, the colors of a bee, and occasionally blowing on his long slender white fingers to keep them from getting too numb in their clenched grip around Bug's steel pen in that chilly translucent ice-chamber where the two of them worked like brothers, an older and a younger, according to Bug's way of thinking, Bug being of course the older brother, though Frank did not think of things that way, since for Frank Bug was just his commander and superior, the way any other commander and superior was; and Frank had had and would have many of those; so Bug and Frank went on, designing perfect charts of the critical path to follow in attacking the Society of Daniel's programmers by first altering subtle attributes of the member data sets in their WYLBUR PROCLIBs so that their electrical JCLs wouldn't work and the members of the PROCLIBs would get steadily more and more screwed up until the programmers would be demoralized, feeling as if some unknown read-write mechanism were marking crow's feet on their graves, according to the superstition of the time; and then Stephen Mole would tiptoe isometrically around the parking lot putting sugar in the programmers' gas tanks and loosening the oil drainage screws by sending bugs quietly under each hood to turn the screw counter-clockwise with their filthy little legs, and Milly and enthusiastic Susan meanwhile disabled the guards by hitting them below the neck with tire-irons, so that they sighed and fell backward and were caught almost lovingly by Susan's and Milly's arms and lowered into the grass, and meanwhile Bug and Frank scouted the entrances and Frank went into a corner to whisper to a fly on the wall and Bug shot the receptionist with a silent merciful air-gun, and then Bug met Milly and Susan and Stephen Mole at the service entrance and Milly picked the lock and a little golden scorpion riding on Milly's shoulder raised its pincers in the V-sign; and Bug gave the signal to form into assault groups as Frank came running up obediently with the pistols which he had cleaned and oiled and loaded after taking them from Arctic Cache Number Three, the very cache which was in the process of being filled now as poor Susan stumbled over the rocks, going up the stream bank at the edge of an endless plain of mucky Arctic sedge-grass and melancholy brown tubers where the wild-fowl fed, pecking in the muck, and in the stream the salmon crowded in their declining run, sometimes leaping out of the milky water like ghastly fishy bats and snapping at Susan's ankles with their suckered mouths so that she stumbled and almost cried out but didn't because she knew that Milly would sneer at her then, so she kept on walking, knocking her shins against the smooth boulders and sometimes sinking into cold wet moss-pockets which she could never see on account of the big cartridge-box she carried in her arms, so that now Milly was drawing ahead (naturally never looking round at Susan), going up the slope toward the cache where Stephen Mole still toiled like a gravedigger, his form outlined against the sky as he bent and stretched and bent, looking out over the unquiet boggy plains with the Caves of Ice invisible behind him somewhere in the mountain ranges; Stephen was being very careful not to disturb the tundra as he rolled the rocks aside, because if he did then the cache would become more and more visible as the permafrost leached and melted and formed into gullies and the earth collapsed into great seamed ravines which would mark the spot for any reactionary airplane. Meanwhile Susan was getting panicky at being left behind; she walked faster and faster, stepping from muskeg to muskeg, each step a single and complete affirmation of faith suspended between two guesses, until at last she tripped over a grass-buried rock and fell, and that extra cartridge-box which poor Susan had proudly carried in her arms burst open and scattered all the bright bullets among the muskeg-berries; then Milly came running back down the hill and

grabbed Susan by the hair as she lay there crying and forced her head
into a pool of green water speckled with little white floating flowers,
and then Milly pulled Susan's head up and hit Susan many times
across the face, saying, "Wait till Bug is informed of what you've
done . . ." and left her sobbing on the tussocks by the stream, with
the remaining cartridge boxes still strapped to her back and the cool
Arctic sun going round and round in the sky . . . – So the work on
the cache continued, but at the time of which I am speaking there
was no cache yet; Bug was all alone in the Arctic making his plans. –
Now it was time for him to come back. – Hitchhiking in the north
territory is unlike hitching anywhere else in our great Republic, on
account of the distances which it is necessary to travel through wild
country. What would be considered a good day's hitch in California,
say, the four-and-a-half-hour ride from Laytonville to Crescent City,
is here a paltry local run barely worth heating the water in the
radiator for. Of course history is in the process of sweeping away the
forests with the iron broom of large-scale industry, but even now a
tree or two remains between Fairbanks and Tok, birches on either
side of the road like twinkling white needles through which the sky
glints blue and clear, each needle piercing your eyes with how clean
it is, though soon the big broom will sweep the needles into its own
frozen haystacks and riff-raff will hide in them. Unfortunately, while
in the American sector Bug could not even see those summery
birches against the blue and silver lakes because he was in the back
of one of those campers named after extinct Indian tribes. Through
the tiny window he could see into the cab up front, where there sat
three generations from Wisconsin: the driver, his father, and his son.
Originally they were to take him as far as Dawson, but now they
were having a big argument, which he could hear quite well above
the sound of the motor. He was feeling slightly sick in there with the
stink of gas and old cooking and insecticide and disinfectant from
the Port-a-Potty. The screen windows looking outside at the birches
did not help him much because on the far side of them the sliding
panes of glass were toggled into place, and the glass was covered
with dust from the road. – "I don't know why I came up here with
you anyway, you old bastard," the driver, a big bearded man, was
yelling at his father. He was crying, and tears were also rolling down
the cheeks of his boy, who sat in the middle. "You never have a good
word to say about anyone; you didn't even want to pick up that
hitcher back there because he" – and here they hit a length of dirt
road with stones banging noisily against the underside of the vehicle
like the slugs of an obsolescent Roumanian Orita sub-machine gun,

so that Bug could not hear what was being said. The old man was now saying something and cringing. They were back on paved road. "I wish you were my age so I could take you," sobbed the driver. "I wish I could beat the shit out of you," and his father warbled something in reedy old-man mumbles that did not quite carry, that perhaps never even made it out the snot-caverns of the old man's sinuses and muffled okra-slimy vocal chords, so the driver turned toward him and said something very softly and distinctly that also was not audible, but it must have been provoking and bitter, for look, the ancient was flushing deep red with rage, and shaking and gasping (while in the middle the boy cried) and screwing up his courage to be as manly as we hope he had been in his better days at least; and finally he shouted in a trembling voice, shaking his fist, "Well, I'm not your age, and if you strike an old man that's not" – and here his voice sank and his chin dropped to his chest while a small quantity of mucus ran from his nose and mouth, and he raised his head and said resolutely (radical Bug was expecting at least give-me-liberty-or-give-me-death) "and besides it's crazy to spend eight hundred dollars to come all the way up here and then pick up hitchers." It was not to be made clear whether the argument that the old man intended to make would have been one of aesthetics, economy, or safety, for at this point the driver interrupted him with clenched fists, face swollen with crying and beard glistening tears: "You're not a man; you never were; you're not my father; you're not even my goddamned father; you're just somebody that thinks he's my father." The boy began twisting his hands in his lap as if to pull the fingers off, and Bug himself felt a mite sick. The old man ducked and said something, but his son bellowed, "Just shut up and let me drive. When we get back to Wisconsin I don't ever want to talk to you again for the rest of my life, do you understand? Not a fucking word," and the old man nodded quickly, eager to avoid being hit: "Sure, son. I don't ever want to talk to you, either. I don't know why I ever" – and here they hit a dirt road again. They stopped at a gas station in Tok. Bug, seeing the general trajectory of things, had already sealed his pack up to face the cruel outdoors again when the driver opened the back door of the trailer to let him out and said, "Well, as you probably heard, things aren't going too well up there so I guess this is the end of the line for you." Bug was always polite, so he looked blank at this reference to unnamed problems and thanked the man profusely for having taken him this far, which even in the north was more than a paltry local run. So off he walked down the road, and waited another twenty-four hours to get out of Tok.

Owen and Flo picked him up in their Commodore. They were from Friendly Manitoba (according to the license plate) and quite old. Bump, bump, bump, over the A1-Can highway went the Commodore. Because Bug was short-haired and clean-shaven they were very good to him. Bump, bump, bump. He was with them for two days. At one-thirty exactly Flo heated up a can of soup which they had with crackers and tea and all the cookies you could eat. – "Oh-h-h-h, yes," Owen crooned gently, never looking away from the wheel as the underpowered Commodore toiled on and on over the dirt road, bump, bump. "My wife is still the queen of my kitchen. I certainly did the right thing, don't you think, young man?" – "Absolutely," said Bug in the back, his mouth full of soup. "This is wonderful, Flo." – "Another bowl of soup?" asked Flo dryly. She was not nearly as taken with the hitchhiker as her husband was. – "Yes, please. Thank you very much."

Bug sat in the back on a cushioned seat which was also the pantry and ice chest when you raised the lid. He was very pale and quiet and rarely blinked his eyes. Across from him and to the left was a square seat which was also a toilet and a fold-out bed. Every time they went around a curve the cushion started to inch its way off and the toilet lid stared out bulbously. Bug replaced the cushion perhaps an even hundred and fifty-two times during those two days. To his right was the sink, which had a folding faucet and spout. Then up ahead was the gear shift with a phony cork or leather handle. Beyond this point was the territory of Owen and Flo, although Owen occasionally twisted his right arm back to work the gear shift. Flo only stared ahead, reading out loud from the map various mileages and routes and points of interest, and always getting lost. "Oh-h-h-h, yes," said Owen. "I don't know what I would do without my little navigator." He showed her where they were on the map. He was never sarcastic or angry or frustrated. He was a Methodist who was very good at woodworking and had built a number of cherry and maple cabinets inside the camper. He had picked Bug up because Bug had finally approached him on the parking lot in Tok where he and Flo had stopped for gas and Bug had begged, thereby taking decisive political action. Flo didn't like Bug much but Owen's compassion shamed her into her own Christian duty. "Oh-h-h-h, yes, " said Owen now and then at the wheel. "Oh-h-h-h, yes."

At night they stopped in rest areas. Bug cooked his beans over his little camping stove on a picnic table and then set up his tent.

Owen came out to watch. "Neat," he said. "Neat, neat, neat." Flo stayed inside and used the toilet. There was a faint stink inside the camper at all times, which was odd because it looked clean – spotless in fact until Bug was admitted with his muddy hiking boots that let drop rattling gravel onto the floor. Flo finally gave up on keeping the back clean until they dropped him off.

Every morning Owen and Flo would spray the back with Raid after our hero had gotten in and they had closed the doors and windows. Then the six or seven mosquitoes which had managed to sneak in when our hero had entered would drop in mid-flight and fall to the floor dead. The white fog of Raid made his legs ache and swell up and his feet go numb and then it diffused throughout the Commodore and steamed up Flo's glasses and Owen's watch. Finally Owen would roll down his window a crack and more mosquitoes flew in. Then Flo got them with the fly-swatter.

Because they thought he must be Owen and Flo's nephew or bohemian grandson, the people at the campgrounds let him into their social mysteries. In the morning the wives smiled at Bug rolling up his tent and he smiled back. The men came over and shook his hand. The twelve-year-old girls who were not yet old enough to escape their families went into their trailers – Elites and Prowlers, usually – and hummed their battery-powered hair dryers far into the night for him (but Bug did not even notice, probably because they could do nothing for him). At ten or eleven in the evening, in the long subarctic sunlight, the men put on waders and went fishing down by the camp toilets; but they never caught anything. To prepare dinner and breakfast they hooked up the butane tanks, and their wives cooked delicious-smelling hamburgers with ketchup. Owen and Flo kept to themselves because this was their first trip, their biggest adventure, and they were shy, but Bug was a hitchhiker, so he was as friendly as a vacuum-cleaner salesman. It was terrific here in Canada among such great folks that liked him so much because young people didn't travel much with their families these days; demographically speaking they usually went to the bad and hung out smoking marijuana and shooting heroin and hitchhiking to red sex demonstrations, but this young fella was okay, boy, he sure was a darned good listener, so they took him inside their trailers and showed him all their secrets that he never would have seen otherwise, like queer shrunken nigger's heads from Florida that the wives thought were gruesome and dangerously full of disease, but their husbands got such a kick out of them, young man, because they'd shot them themselves, so what could a lady do, and the twelve-year-old daughters previously described had movie star comic books and a cigarette or two they'd show him with great pride when their parents were not around. Back in the sphagnum moss where he camped at night behind the trailer lots, the wind blew and sometimes it rained hard on the tent fly. There were bugs and wolves and bears all around. He got the earplugs out of the shoulder pocket of his L. L. Bean shirt one night and put them in his ears. Owen and Flo were fast asleep in the Commodore, and all was quiet except for one of the girls screaming, "Mommy, mommy!" in the midst of a wet-the-bed nightmare about huge waxy bugs coming out of the woods and grabbing her and carrying her far, far away where there were no roads and nobody would ever find her and there was only the wind blowing lonely from the North Pole and the bugs took her to a clearing and into a thicket and down under the moss-roots where they suffocated her in cocoons.

Meanwhile Bug lay in his sleeping bag with his eyes closed against the dim light, listening. But the earplugs never tingled, and finally he went to sleep.

The next morning was Sunday, and he heard several of the more religious families singing hymns inside their trailers, though he couldn't make out the words and only vaguely caught the chorus coming through the screen windows:

> Rum tiddle-piddle-iddle
> Rum tiddle-piddle-iddle
> Rum tum wum-ums da-a-airy-o
> Mmph hum haw chew izzle-izzle-mum
> Awwr urhm maw naw gurzle-izzle-mum.

Stolidly he ate his Familia with water and milk powder, sitting at the picnic table all packed up and ready to go for Owen and Flo. At eight-fifteen Owen came out and helped him lash his pack to the top of the Commodore. Then he held the funnel while Owen filled the tank with diesel fuel. So the two of them overcame their class differences. Bump, bump, bump. Flo read aloud from the map of Canada. — "Oh-h-h-h, yes," said Owen gently, never taking his eyes from the empty road. "Oh-h-h-h, yes." On and on went the kilometers. Bug slept. At one-thirty, almost in Whitehorse, they stopped at a picnic site by a lake bristling with speedboats. A water-plane set itself down on its pontoons with a splash. Owen, who was an amateur pilot, explained to Bug that in fact small-plane navigation was dangerous, as there were many people who upon flying into a cloud bank did not trouble to check their instruments, convinced that they were flying level, when in fact they were tilting down, down, down and finally smashed into a hill, no survivors. Flo heated up the soup on the butane stove which Owen had hooked up, that being a mechanical task and therefore a man's job, and then everybody carried something down to the picnic table. Usually Owen said grace before lunch. But this time he turned to Flo and said, "Let's take hands, shall we? It's so much more beautiful," so the three of them stood in a circle around the picnic table and held hands while the soup began to cool off. Owen prayed:

> O God, we thank you for this food
> And we thank you for having allowed us to meet
> And enjoy the friendship of our new young friend
> And we pray for him on his journey
> And we hope that our food fills him up
> And that others will be kind to him
> And that he will return safely
> To the United States. Amen.

"Thank you," Bug said, touched. — Bug always meant it when he was polite. — And now Flo filled his bowl with Campbell's Soup.

They let him off in front of a shopping mall in Whitehorse. They wanted to buy some handmade Indian parkas and dolls. Bug said goodbye, bought a little more food at the supermarket, and walked to the outskirts of the city, which was surrounded by dazzling white hills.

A big flatbed truck came by with a young Canadian couple; the wife turned to her husband and gestured, and the truck stopped. — "We're only going about a hundred miles," the man said. "That all right?" — "Yes, please," said Bug with what was genuinely a happy smile, "that would be wonderful!", for he loved riding in open vehicles with the wind in his face, and this is probably because he had never had to do it much. So he leaped up onto the flatbed and stretched out on his side with his head on his pack. "All set, aye?" called the driver. "I'm okay, thanks!" he shouted back, and they started moving, tearing off marvelously in fact, and it was perfect the way that it had happened with him having had to wait just long enough to really appreciate it when people stopped to help him, for he was just a kid again now that his mission was completed; the Caves of Ice waited in the back of his mind; and in the meantime acting young and happy got him more rides; now he was going fast enough to renew his knowledge of the joy of speed and huge distances (it was a seven-thousand-mile hitch), getting closer and closer to the destination with no meaning in itself – in fact it would be like coming back into a trap when he got there but it was the going and going that pleased him, boring through the Yukon that was sand and jack pine, white clay and birch and bog and purple mountains, green mountains, trees packed together for thousands of miles and grizzly bears out hunting and streams hidden away that had not been fished out; and every couple of hours maybe you might see a little log cabin set far away among the trees but for the most part it was just a plain of tough stunted trees in the beautiful sad short summer or steep hills with firs and white cliffs as they went on and on away from the westerly sun, and everything seemed broad and small beneath the huge sky that looked into his face as he lay in the truck bed. He was probably going no faster than he had been with Owen and Flo, but it seemed much faster, and in perhaps ten minutes of his own private time the truck was slowing and pulling to the shoulder and with the familiar sinking feeling of being alone in the world again he was pulling his pack down and calling out his thanks and waving and then the truck turned down a dirt road going into the country and he was alone in the long cool evening.

Of course while Trotsky's escape from Siberia was a great game he had a pathetic time of it in exile in Turkey, and when he was killed in 1940 it must have hurt. I could hardly suggest, after what has been revealed, that similar trends had not begun to annex Bug's future.

He went off the road and over a stretch of dunes by an abandoned mine until he found a mossy place in the woods to camp. He set his stove in the moss and cooked up his nightly beans, tonight with barbecue sauce and a real onion from the Whitehorse supermarket. For a long time everything was quiet except the mosquitoes whining against the netting in their miserable desire for him. Presently there came the mincing multilegged steps of one of the forest horrors, and now here it appeared scuttling low on its ventral plates out from under a blueberry patch, and it stood up all grotesque and purple and waxy like in the girl's nightmare, and it looked at him with its glittery wide-set eyes and waggled its feelers against the window netting and waited for him to come out.

Beetles cannot normally speak with humans, but all field agents (such as Tony back at summer camp) were bred to grow organic larynx units just like our throat cancer patients. As Bug emerged from the tent the envoy scuttered back flat against the ground, so that Bug could see how fragile the poor creature's shell actually was; like many insects its posture was essentially two-dimensional bluff;

just consider the way you can pass your hand over certain very large beetles and cockroaches lurking in the pattern of your wallpaper, and you might just think that the plaster is swelling there; so it was in this case with the Secret Ambassador of the Bugs, which made our hero feel sorry for it, in the easy way that we all have of pitying vulnerability when that pity costs us nothing. Bug was thereby set at ease and made well disposed toward the purple-grey thing, more or less as the Great Beetle had intended. – The beetle peered at Bug warily, pretending to fear that Bug might try to crush it; this defensive show further enhanced Bug's already favorable attitude; yet the beetle's posture was not entirely contrived; there was always an element of risk in the diplomatic profession; fortunately, Bug continued to step very calmly and slowly forward in the twilight woods, so that the beetle realized for certain that Bug would not attempt to hurt it or engage in any other erroneous tactics or Kautskyite deviation; therefore, it hauled itself pompously upright again forthwith, as protocol required, clinging with dozens of hooklike legs to the bark of a wide-trunked tree, and forthwith recited to Bug, in an unctuous hiss, a very detailed charter contract containing numbered sub-statements of privileges, duties, and diverse other articles of a semi-advanced character, for insects are extremely facile at rote memorization. Those who are familiar with the minutes of that period cannot but know similar agreements cold, so I will not waste time in needless summary. The essentials of the offer were that Bug would be expected to work for the insect cause and obey instructions, in return for which he would be treated as a star operative, his enemies would be undermined gratis, and he would someday share in the glory of triumphant beetles, moths, millipedes and waxworms. Obviously, Bug, who remained to the end of his life a solitary idealist, held a secret part of himself aside in all contracts, precisely when his politeness implied to the unwary that he was giving everything. So he was not as impressed by the offer as it might have seemed to the beetle. (He was never impressed by any offer.) But the fact remained that he was now considering the externals of the offer, much as you or I would do if we were but given a real opportunity to sell ourselves forever. All of his young life, as we know, Bug had been infected by a spasmodic political deviation from his peers. This disease was now about to be aggravated to a degree incomparably greater than before. – "You have our earplugs, sir," the beetle concluded in a hiss like an elegant Espresso machine. "Surely you are not committed to the law of unequal development. Will you help us, please?"

A half-hour later, therefore, the Great Beetle had a new operative. Our hero had established correct relations with the bugs. The news of his official acquiescence would rally millions of bugs, especially ticks and fleas, for they had little respect for individuals who approached the subject of emancipation as mere liberals.

The next day, standing by the side of the road for hours and hours (at least two hundred metric minutes), Bug thumbed as usual. He was to be kept on ice for security reasons until the uprising was prepared. But what do you know? Here came Owen and Flo again, and they stopped for him and Owen was helping him lash his pack onto the top of the Commodore just like old times ("I really appreciate your picking me up again," he began, and Owen was patting him on the shoulder and assuring him that it was all right), then off they went; this time they would take him as far as Fort St. John, which was another two or three days away; and bump, bump, bump, the Commodore toiled on, and in Fort Nelson Owen bought him ice cream, but all the same he slapped his first tiny cluster of beetle eggs against the cushions over the toilet seat . . .

A PORTRAIT ON THE EVE OF WAR

~~~~~~

I want to do away with everything behind man, so that there is nothing to see when he looks back. I want to take him by the scruff of the neck and turn his face toward the future!

LEONID ANDREYEV

He had now become completely steeled. Thanks to all that he had suffered at summer camp, he was incapable of the softer human feelings without considerable effort. As H. Rider Haggard remarks, "When one is moving slowly across the vast African wilds, and living on the abundance of game, love and kisses seem an ample provision for all wants." But he did not have any real experience of love as we understand it.

And yet this is not to say that he did not love. For it is possible to love an insect if you want to badly enough and it is also serious about you. This may be, as the Russians say, *kak noózhna, kak pihzdyé boodíl'nik* (as useful as a cunt on an alarm clock). But such a comparison inevitably leads us to considerations of sexual anatomy.

Between a woman's legs is what we call the external female procreative genital private erotic parts, or more precisely the labia majora, labia minora, clitoris and for some persons the opening of the urethra. The vulva, I might add, opens during sexual excitement. – One day my fiancée, dearest Clara Bee, with whom I had been living for approximately three years, decided that she could not love me anymore. – Of course it did not come quite as suddenly as that; the interested reader will find a fuller catalogue of events up ahead. – Now, there were many sweet butterflies and katydids that I wanted to turn to to console me, but as they were not of my species sexual union with them was far more difficult. – This was not an issue for Bug, however. The sexual aspect did not affect him; he loved bugs because he had to. There is nothing in life, as the reader is aware, that does not have strings attached. In fairytales, when people are given magic gifts it is always because they have rendered the giver a service previously, thus putting him on the moral spot, or else because something will be asked of them later (generally, in the case of kings, a firstborn son). So it was with the earplugs. We will never know for certain just what it was that the emissary of the Great Beetle said to Bug, but we can assume that the question of obligation was touched upon. The earplugs had protected him and led him to prizes and even saved his life once. – Yet surely this argument of its own weight could not have been enough, for Bug was highly skilled at juggling means and ends so that apples and oranges became giraffes; such logical talent is necessary in politics; he could have convinced the beetle, had he needed to, that the bugs owed *him* something for having field-tested their equipment; the simple fact is that he loved the bugs; and when he put the earplugs on for the first time at summer camp and felt the tingle in his ears; or when the cilia came forth from his ears in the swimming pool, he felt that unknown senses awakened in him; as if suddenly he could observe a water-glass and perceive its temperature or all the bacteria swarming about its rim . . . and then, too, he never forgot the death of Tony or the humming of delight and danger in his ears when the earplugs were in and everything grew tall and dark and fantastic; for he experienced life then as the bugs, the under-dogs and under-worms, the hiding things did; and that was not so far removed from what he had always experienced, so he could love and understand all creatures that lived in prudence and fear and single-mindedness; but the reactionaries themselves, ah; they were not so easy for him to understand and sympathize with; and in the sunny cities of California – red and yellow curb-paint worn and aged like miraculous dark varnishes on the Museum Masters, the ugly, honest brick fortressses of Depression architecture (banks, cinemas) seeming as much in place as anything else, even the new, white-grooved flat-topped buildings that resembled giant coffeecake tins – he looked not at the people, but at the gratings, the alleys, the sewers . . .

We are all twisted. But we did not ask to be that way. Do you really think that Bug would not have preferred to be Wayne or Parker or Mr. White, able to while away his time on human beauties? Do you really think that I would not prefer to have my Clara back and be in her arms kissing her and having her take care of me, to being here, watching the rain run down the windows, dreaming up stupid bug blazoomises to distract me so that at least I won't hack up my wrists again? – Please, Clara, take me back; I'll be good, I'll do anything . . . – But there is no answer (of course there isn't, you stupid shit; I, Big George, could have told you that had you bothered to ask me, but you would never do that; you are too worried about the danger of intervention, when you could count upon my benevolent neutrality at any time), so onward, fight it out, you angels . . .

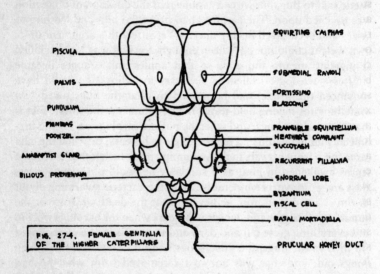

SQUIRTING CAMPHAS

PISCULA

SUBMEDIAL RAVIOLI

PALVIS

FORTISSIMO
BLAZOOMIS

PUNDULUM

PINNEAS
POONZEL

FRANGIBLE SQUINTELLUM
HEATHER'S COMPLAINT
SUCCOTASH

ANABAPTIST GLAND

RECURRENT PILLALVIA

BILIOUS PRENENNUM

SNORBIAL LOBE

BYZANTIUM
PISCAL CELL

BASAL MORTADELLA

FIG. 27-4. FEMALE GENITALIA OF THE HIGHER CATERPILLARS

PRUCULAR HONEY DUCT

Looking this over I am sure that making love with a nice beetle or hopper could be very beautiful in its way; for I have no unkind words to say about anyone; I would have no one suffer if need be; certainly no one deserves to suffer for anything, no matter how great the crime; Bug never really wanted to hurt anybody but he had to because they had hurt him and were out to get him and squash him under their feet so he had to do what he could to save himself and those creatures like him, for no one wants to suffer; no one wants to die; and as a child he had gone out for Halloween as a mummy, a vampire, a blue-and-green-swollen drowned boy, all kinds of sufferings and mutilations and perversions represented by his costumes; and looking around him he saw witches and Frankenstein monsters and scarred warty masks of all the kids running around asking for candy in the dark; and he wondered: Why must we hurt ourselves and drive stakes through our hearts and drown ourselves in order to get candy? Why couldn't we just go out and ask for it? – He had no sense of fun. – Later he worked in the financial district of San Francisco and the only way you could tell it was Halloween there was that in the banks they gave out little orange candies shaped like pumpkins; and in the cities generally the kids didn't trick-or-treat much anymore because the real ghouls put razorblades in their apples; going home from work he looked around him and understood the horrible truth, which was that no one needed a mask anymore if anyone ever had! For as they all crowded together on the rush-hour cable car the men and women pushed and shoved each other with the points of their umbrellas; and there was Mr. White clinging grimly to a shiny post by the exit door, muttering, "You'd better not crowd me like that, you turd-face . . ." and Catherine was seated next to the window, cocking her head and studying a long xeroxed general theory that would assist her in her career, paying no attention to the fact that she was getting older every second and she loved no one and no one loved her; and the top of the trolley-car had a wire dingley on it of some sort that brushed a cable overhead and emitted scheming blue sparks that whirled and whirled in the fog with great hilarity and triumph; yes indeed, everything was monstrous and everyone was a monster and he was a monster for not doing anything about it, and soon he would be a monster for doing something about it because he would have to quietly blow things sky-high, and having read articles on Mr. White in the *Wall Street Journal* he could tell that Mr. White was evil and would have to be assassinated; and he was well aware that Parker and Wayne were out there somewhere, too, though Parker and Wayne had essentially forgotten him as he had been just a nonentity on the team, in high school, in summer camp; but someday there would be a reckoning with them – and if people could not be taught tolerance and love then they must be destroyed – for he felt all the anguish that I feel when I know that my Clara doesn't love me; and he was quite conscious that the entire *world* did not love him; even the bugs did not love him; they were fellow travelers for the time being but someday one or the other of the two parties would lunge treacherously, for the alliance was too flimsy; Bug despite himself was not a bug. – He had no clear idea what could be substituted for the present order; there was something insidious about electricity which he had not yet put his finger on and perhaps that was the problem there (he wasn't sure because he didn't know about the blue globes); maybe if we went back to candle-light and frogs burping in the bogs around our lonely farmsteads then the horrors of telephones and mass transit and concentrated human numbers might be eliminated; he didn't know yet that someday his little organization would be destroying electric engines, that Milly would shoot off the insulators, not wasting a single bullet, while Stephen Mole smashed the instruments in the cabin with a sledgehammer and Frank drilled a hole in the wall and ignited the brown oil that flowed slowly out, then they all ran back as Susan hurled one of her specials; she had whipped up eggs and sugar with a Molotov cocktail to make it stick like napalm, but once again I am running ahead of myself; Bug didn't know any of this; he couldn't think straight because the pain of everything drove him a little crazy, but he at least, unlike me, had not been jilted; he had just never been loved, which is preferable, so he went about his business coolly and made plans and took pictures and worked within the growing bug uprising as if he were a college student performing a summer internship . . .

Following high school he remained alert, resting in sunny exposed places beating his wings while absorbing the standard center-liberal line in a good university, where students were taught to argue forcefully for the granting of loans to indulge the state deficit. At that time our great Republic was in the final stages of electrification, so that wires cut across any view of the sky and the first robots were being produced so that we could keep up with Japan. Phil Blaker gave clearance to a $2.7 billion servomechanism purchase by his planetary economy after securing a sweetened $794 million offset package of subcontracting work for his own industry. Mr. White went to the Federal Industrial Commission at once, charging unfair practices, because he had planned to have those robots for himself, humming along in ten thousand lubeshops with blue globes for brains while they labored for him, singing chanteys in their deep voices to the Muzak tunes, like, 'Ohh-REE-ohh, on we go, wor-king, wor-king for Mis-ter White," but it was no goddamn go-ahead; the F.I.C. withheld its blessing, complaining that Mr. White would not have offered our labor force enough business in return as part of the transaction, a spokesperson reported yesterday. The sad fact was that Phil Blaker controlled the F.I.C., and no matter whose ass Mr. White kicked he couldn't get anywhere. Meanwhile electric eyes were installed in all middle-class garages to open the doors automatically as the cars came up silent and luxuriant with the drivers ever better kept; and in the lower-class neighborhoods more and more houses were crowded together, each with its own rusty fence and trio of barking dogs; and for additional security guns were kept ready and decals were slapped on the windows saying THIS HOUSE IS PROTECTED BY AN ARMED AMERICAN MALE, and everyone there was angry, for more and more of those people were out of work now thanks to the robots, so Mr. White started looking better to the common folks than he had in a long time because at least he had nothing to do with those electric workmen. Mr. White got his picture in the paper holding a spade, the caption reading FRIEND OF HONEST WORK. So his revenues took off, and undertakers sent him fan letters because the picture with the spade had proved what they did was honest, and Phil Blaker had to retrench for several shelf-months in his bunkers on Mars while Mr. White went into nuclear power.

In college Bug was never what you might call a team player, but he joined his affinity group in between classes in farkeology and panthetics, and set off to take his part in the political process. The bugs had not yet contacted him at that time, though he still had and used the earplugs; he was just beginning to dip his toe into the chilly, invigorating waters of direct action. He had shuffled embarrassedly along in a rally against this or that, looking shyly sidewise at the press cameras, but that did not really count because sometimes you did not even mean to get involved, like when you were studying in the library with your mind half on your book and half on whether you would be able to meet Catherine, who was now getting her advanced degree and was extremely busy, probably too busy to meet you in front of Pilsk Hall like she had promised, and would she or wouldn't she; so you occupied yourself with such thoughts and finally put your book under your arm and filled out the cards for the checkout boy to stamp and as you went through the electronic or electric detection gate it hummed and clacked gently to announce that you had stolen nothing; and then coming outside into the cool winter afternoon you saw a whole procession of student delegates as directed by some Executive Committee which you had barely heard of, everybody marching round and round the library with big signs and earnest mouths working hard to suck in air and shout it back out in time with everyone else; and once again you were transported in your imagination to those happy, unambiguous days of 1917, when all over Russia the committed people must have hugged each other and loved each other when the news came that the last rotten vestiges of Kerenskyism had been swept away; and the Whites — well, there were the Whites, that was true, but if civil war came we would deal them a good number of iron punches . . . but meanwhile things had not come to that yet; the Whites were rather stunned by our victory and the sky in Moscow must have been so blue and cold and crystalline, and we all embraced in the snowy streets, in our fur coats and dowdy Eastern European trousers which we would still be wearing after the Berlin blockade and the western world went on with its decadent theater of color while we grubbed Comrade Potato to eat and stood in long lines to redeem Comrade Ration Card, but things got steadily better with our improved mass-based technologies and the Great Electrification left us all bright havens of happy factories twenty years behind the west where we loafed and the security police loafed and traded with us except when they beat us sometimes, and far up north, past even the latitude that Bug had hitchhiked to, we set up bright clean orderly transit camps and work camps glowing on the snowy plains or in clearings in the forests where the prisoners worked cutting down trees and making them into gun stocks for us, working and working and working happily until they died and were buried naked in the hard blue ground until the thaw, or tossed into spruce-hung ravines where the Arctic foxes got them; but in 1917 we had no cares except the mundane ones of starvation and occupation and civil war, and for those of us in our armored trains traveling up and down the front waging brilliant campaigns, or for our young Natashas and Alyoshas experiencing the education and class steeling of the Komsomol for the first time, learning to ask in every historical situation: How many workers are there? how many peasants, intellectuals? how do they stand on this issue? it was a very exciting and romantic period; what I am getting at is that probably no one felt alone as Bug felt alone; for everyone worked together and loved each other – oh, I hope that that was true. For if life is worth living at all you *can* have your cake and eat it, too (На рыбку съестъ as the Russians say, И нахуй съестъ – literally to eat out her tuna *and* her asshole); when you fight together you feel together; love and politics go hand in hand, and I can demonstrate this feasibly with another linguistic point. A girl's cherry is her *tsélka. Raskolót'cya kak tsélochka*, to pop like a little cherry, means in fact to crack under interrogation. I want to draw your attention, comrades, to that highly significant trope.

Anyhow, there he was back at the library, zipping up his parka and emerging unawares upon a demonstration of some kind; and all members present looked so hopefully at Bug (for they realized that they had bruised his consciousness, at least; no one else had noticed them all day; the passers-by strode quickly along the icy perimeter of the Arts Quad, textbooks gathered close to chests with numbed hands, and shoulders hunched against the grey weather; boy oh boy, look at it blowing across the valley! The little town below the campus was disappearing even as you watched; the snow-clouds eliminated a foot of visibility a second and the temperature was already below zero; from the warm classrooms the students peered out, appalled, paying as much pretention to Dr. Dodger's lectures as to the muffled banging of the steam pipes; and everybody's coat gave off steam that smelled like wet wool; and midterms were only two weeks away so after the prof stopped blabbing you'd have to go to the library and check out a double armload of books and carry them down the Hill to the hall, where the cook would have a great midday meal all ready for you: hot soup and grilled cheese sandwiches and omelettes and salad; and then you'd make yourself some cocoa with brandy in it and brush the melting snow off your library books and flip through them listlessly and pick up one but it would be too heavy so you'd set it down and pick up a thinner one and get a notebook and pen but already your good intentions would begin to fail you, and you went up to the Striped Room where it was so nice and warm, and listened to the trees groaning outside with all the ice on them; and you sat there for awhile, and then you went to the Preferred Room and sat by the roaring fire in your favorite soft orange couch; and Amy and Michael were in the Music Room playing Brahms; Brahms always put you to sleep; there was nothing to do about it, absolutely nothing at all, so you sighed and yawned and grinned and used the last of your melting strength to position yourself a little closer to the fire, and you took your pen sadly in hand but it slipped from between your fingers; and your notebook and library text teetered for some minutes on the edge of the couch and finally fell onto the rug, to your relief; and Paul and Lili and Alison and sweet Alyssa were all studying so peacefully around you, and in a state of perfect happiness you went to sleep . . .); and the committed young men beckoned Bug over with fraternal waves and smiles; and the committed maidens jiggled their bosoms bewitchingly as they danced in the wind with their hair blowing in their faces and sleet shooting down to sting their cheeks as they protested the tuition hike – Arise, nation! Storm, break loose! – and despite their apparent enthusiasm, which probably played the leading part in keeping them warm, they seemed so futile and huddled and lonely that his heart swelled within him, for he never could resist a losing cause; so he yielded to his destiny and came and stood among them and marched; and the girl beside him, whose name was Ellen, let him hold her mimeographed sheet of chants which they both sang out with the others on command; and his feet got cold and wet as they strode through the slush – O college days! – and perhaps they burned a flag to prove something, or sprinkled blood and ashes on the snow; and even though he didn't know what they were doing it for he couldn't help but love and admire them.

So in a wink of Big Brother's eye he was all set, all hooked up with the affinity group Crazy Fire; and it was spring and the trees in the Arts Quad bore pink-white blossoms. Revolutionary recruitment stickers appeared on stop signs in the town, on trash cans, and even on the railings of the bridges which overhung the picturesque gorges of the region, from the depths of which now came an ominous roaring as the waters rose; and sometimes if you were loping from the Falkenhausen Museum to your lover in Collegetown to give her flowers you'd picked in the woods near Cascadilla Gorge, you might see a wild-eyed student on the bridge, surrounded by ivory tower idlers drinking him in with eager horror, and you could hear the police siren coming closer and closer; and the fellow was leaning over the edge, trembling with need for those green waters the sound of which echoed back and forth along the cliffs and woke up the bats inside the abandoned hydroelectric stations of the early 1900s (there were several of these brick mausoleums of blue globes down below the falls); though that imperative rushing of waters was so faint that it must have been the very distance which had such power over this suicide-to-be; for they always jump downstream where I come from; in fact, Dr. Dodger devoted two whole discussion-weeks to this phenomenon in the graduate seminar he was then offering in Myth, Ritual and Sign. He concluded that what they wanted when they did it was to be swept toward the horizon, to give in to time, space and other limitless possibilities; for as we all know, April is the cruelest month, and if you've failed your Double-E class you know they won't let you graduate; and your parents will never get over it and the neighbors will ask about you in a uniform chiming of triumphant concern; *their* sons and daughters have you beat, and *they* went out for even higher mathematics than this mere imaginary number electrical stuff; and then there is the money issue; four years at a good liberal arts university are not cheap, especially when you have misused them and it will take you five or six or even seven years more; eight years from now you will still be here if you don't find an out, being congenitally unable to apply Ohm's Law, like poor Taylor back in 1913 at the Society of Daniel, so the hell with it, fucking blinking blasted hell. — "I'm gonna jump!" the boy shouted in a horrible cracked voice; and at this promise the beer-drinking frat guys clapped and jumped and stamped their feet, yelling, "GORGE – OUT! GORGE – OUT! GORGE – OUT!", this being the vernacular for that sort of death, which was common in the area; and Susan, who was majoring in psychology, came up near him and told him not to do it, that it was the coward's way out and he must have problems with his past or present relationships and he should talk to somebody, and did he want to say what the matter was, because she would listen for as long as he needed her, but he shook his head and said, "Don't you come a step closer or I'm gonna do it!", and the frat boys cried, "DO IT! DO IT! DO IT! GORGE – OUT! GORGE – OUT! GORGE – OUT!", and the sirens got even louder and then stopped; for here came the safety patrol, creeping up behind the youth so they could tackle him and haul him away to counseling and sedation and eternal disgrace; but he whirled round and saw them and screamed, "You bastards!" and jumped; and if you had rushed to the edge to see him fall, like all present (except for Susan, who turned and walked away crying), you might have seen him spinning down through the air with his face flashing up at you for a second as he tumbled end over end, his expression of glazed astonishment just beginning to be superseded by one of fear and regret ("Hell, I changed my *mind*!"), but by then you could not see his face very clearly anyhow; you caught a glimpse of something sparkling abruptly as his keys fell out of his pocket; and he was barely a speck now and kept falling and falling and you could not have said how close to impact he was; for it was sort of misty down there, and the falls below the bridge raised a cloud of spray upon which you could sometimes see rainbows if you searched long enough under favorable atmospheric conditions. It was beautiful down there after a storm (although perhaps I am romanticizing, as I, the author, have a tendency to do). – A path led down the cliffside if you started from Collegetown, and as you descended the switchback ledges so that the trees and the academic towers disappeared above your head, you clung to the friendly chains set in the rock; and you breathed in the spray of the falls and came at last to a level, paved walkway a few feet above the water. (In the winter it was covered with ice. Once on my way to visit a mental institution for research purposes my friend Nancy Darling and I went down it to get to the bus station quickly. We slipped and slid; all the way down we clung tightly to the icy railing.) You could walk barefoot in the stream a little farther down, for it became quite broad and shallow; and this is where the dead boy's wallet would have ended up, among all the broken bottles and litter that the students threw down to maintain their gay carefree reputations. It would not have floated. It would have been slimy and waterlogged and full of gravel; and there would have been no money in it.

WE DIGRESS

〜〜〜〜〜〜〜〜〜〜〜〜〜〜〜〜〜〜〜〜〜〜〜〜〜

When I was young my position was: Dynamite. It was only later
that I understood that this sort of thing cannot be rushed. It must
rot away like a gangrened member.

HITLER on the churches,
early 1940s

The reason that there would have been no money in it was that every
student, no matter how suicidal or papillaceous, knew enough to
spend his last forty-five cents on a double scoop of ice cream from
Oliver's, which was the richest treat available now that the Uni Deli
had stopped making Monster Malts. Were it possible for me, Big
George, to make the melodious singing sound occasioned by a
thousand female mosquitoes in a garret, I still could not express the
craving for sucking at cold sweet things to which so many students
were condemned. Even those scholars, such as Bug, who aspired to
later fame and so bent over their books and musty papers at
midnight on the nineteenth floor of the library, taking notes for a
treatise on the sanguine essence of the ethical world, would still
leave off at twenty minutes before one, so that they might jog
through the darkness, the meanwhile counting the jingling change in
their trouser-pockets by feel, relying upon the cues of size and shape,
in order to get the last pumpkin ice cream cone from Oliver's before
closing time and then sit out on the terrace by the gorge listening to
the green water in the moonlight while they ingested the cone with
grateful little tongue-laps. – Susan did the same. – It was the first
principle of college life to consume, for every student knew that all
too soon it would be necessary to work and work and work as
decreed by computer-assisted design procedures established by the
Society of Daniel, coming home late to copulate with the spouse on
tired elbows, then getting up and driving to the office while it was

still dark and drinking a quart of coffee to get going and producing value for the new crop of students to consume out of MY taxes; so for these reasons it was deemed best to ignore the octahedrons which they were supposed to be memorizing for Dr. Dodger and enjoy themselves while they could. Since we are now approaching the halfway mark of this volume, at which point we are required by law to accelerate the motion of events while maintaining uniform rotation, I shall avoid indictment by making my digression a short one, merely listing a half-dozen operations of this abnormal consumption before I return you to Bug and his development. – So, you sly dog, you evaded your responsibilities in college (you know this better than I). This is how you passed the time: (1) You bought books until there was no more room on the bookshelf, and the paperbacks that you would never read asphyxiated and split down the bindings from pressure of crowding, like steamed beans; and your friends were awed at the amount of use you had gotten out of them – little did *they* know that you had never read *Tales of a Bootblack!* – little did *they* suspect that you had bought *Beyond Anti-Littoral Ethics* only because it was required! (not that I am disparaging requirements of any kind; far from it; if there were no necessity then misery would lose its nobility) – little did they realize that *Readings in Comparative Masonry* and *The Age of Our Guilt* had been allowed to enjoy your society only because you enjoyed *their* glossy black covers! – that the *Handbook of Whales, Weeds, Threads and Screws* which lent such a studious air to your digs had been hollowed out as soon as you got it so that between its authoritative covers you could hide your drugs and your *Rubber Lover Comix* – or if your so-called friends did form opinions unfavorable to your reputed achievements, they kept their mistrust to themselves, the way adolescents around the country conceal their pimples and pustules whenever possible, so that you would not begin to doubt the extent to which they themselves had mastered their book collections . . . and the professors whom you seduced in return for your As fingered enviously the bas-relief covers of Fettuccini's *Trapezoids and Roots* in the original Italian – now harder to find than a relic of the True Cross – actually you had gotten it for a song at Triangle Bookstore by exchanging the price sticker with that of a remaindered pocket mystery called *Dr. Dodger and the Persuaders*; and then you decided that you wanted *that*, too, so rather than switch labels again you just crammed it inside your jeans and stole it. – Catherine was shopping conscientiously at Triangle this very moment, afraid that she would not be able to find one of her astronomy books, in which event she would have dropped the course; and Wayne had a big stack of hardbacks in his arms for MS-222 and was totalling them up and going Aw Shit at the price; while Bee buzzed high and safe on the back routing shelves to make sure that I, the author, came to no harm in my studies; and I, Big George, was at the cash register ringing everything up with an easy ironical grin; my feelings for these students could be categorized best as contemptuous amusement: — it is a sure guarantee of enjoyment to look at these gleaners, eating the pages in the library night after night, like worms, or screwing up their eyes against the light on account of a hangover derived the previous evening at a party constructed lackadaisically around a keg of bad beer, or complaining that they had to get up too early to go on their river-rafting trips, for which they received full academic credit. — That was all as it should have been; in truth the reactionary apparatus was now well in place. Dr. Dodger personally selected every book to be made into a college fad, so that for its few weeks of life it would be used as a subway token to intellectuality by those who had never read it, thus providing every student who uttered its name with an aura accorded as much reverence as an octopus once was by superstitious sailors. — Good for Dr. Dodger! — I, Big George, would have to do something about that, indeed I would, for I represent change the way an electric current does with its steady ceaseless flow of electrons; it was clear that someday a battle would occur between Mr. White and myself; hostile collisions are part of the political life of our country; but right now that was scarcely possible, for I was still a prisoner in the caves of the Great Beetle, able to cast my influence over a very limited area; if I concentrated for some days I could send a sluggish pulse across the Bonanza telegraph line in Buenos Aires, and from there, via the modems of the American spies and businessmen, back to the mainframe where I, the author, sat trying to tell this story, being the first one in the office as the lights came on gradually in the other banks of cubicles, and the red rising sun struck the coffeemaker in its niche by the sink. — But I was detailing conspicuous consumption, so on to the next case. (2) You took twice as many classes as you were allowed to, so you could drop and add, drop and add, take 'em all and get your money's worth; Louisa was the Class Marshal because she worked so hard and took every course in the catalogue so she had to pull all-nighters and got tired and exalted like Amy smoking cigarettes at four a.m. and telling you happily that she had not slept in three days because she was having so many structural problems with her Dante paper and you could tell that she loved every minute of getting thin and pale and dizzy; while Ken and Dan went to all the Federico Salvatore Anaconda Memorial Lectures, sponsored by the Institute for Social Policy Studies; and there were dozens of these lectures, just dozens, because the Institute wanted student input to set the topic for the semester, like who had written Shakespeare's plays or what the atoms of the transcendental elements *really* looked like. (3) You had, as has already been confessed, ice cream on those hot summer evenings to cool your brain while reflecting on (4) what trifle you might purchase with which to indulge yourself – a brand-new punching bag shaped and colored like testicles, say, if you were a radical feminist, or maybe a merkin from Zanzibar if you were a lesbian or just another cute stuffed zebra so that your friends would know that you were an Earth-Mother. (5) At the Temple of Zeus coffee shop you could get mochas with nutmeg and whipped cream if you belonged to a sophisticated crowd. A banana cost fifty cents there and an apple cost almost a dollar. (6) And if you were a tough guy like Wayne you'd head off to The Palms to carve your initials or maybe FUCK into the wooden table, and toss down watery beer until you puked. The frat boys lived in Greek houses like Sigma Humpa Epsilon right over the gorges where the above-mentioned suicides occurred; and all the houses had decks. You could do a tipsy tap-dance right on the railing if you wanted on those late afternoons, boop-boop-a-doop-doop! when all the nerds were studying, whoopee! and the stereo'd be UP TO MAXIMUM, DOOBY-DOOBY, LET'S MAKE IT IN THE AFTER-NOON, GIRL, DOOBY-DOOBY, and all the other fellas'd be clappin' an' stampin' for ya as ya tip-tap-tapped; and the freshmen initiates were doing calisthenics under the expert direction of the seniors, and the sophomores were mixing up strawberry daiquiris for everybody, singing out, "Does Your Diaphragm Lose Its Flavor On The Bedpost Overnight? If Your Lover Says Don't Chew It, Do You Swallow It In Spite?" and the juniors were shooting straight across the gorge with beebee guns and making water balloons out of condoms, and you kept doin' an Elvis the Pelvis kinda shuffle there on that half-inch railing, ah, youth! with the wind blowing up from the gorge to ruffle your shirt; and the summer leaves rustled below you indecipherably, or alternately you could kick sand or pebbles over the side; you couldn't hear any splash but whenever you liked you could listen to the faint steady noise of the greenish water bearing you through time like a dependable hotel air conditioner; and if you squinted hard right you could see the gorge and the Collegetown Bridge, where the suicides occurred; you could do any number of things, for as Hassan the Assassin said a thousand years ago, "Nothing is true; all is permissible." – Sometimes you could see sunbathers down there stretched on the warm flat rocks. High school juniors liked to wander down there to skip their accelerated summer programs for the day; and sorority girls had hard-boiled-egg picnics on the rocks and got tanned and threw the eggshells into the water; and you and the other drunken frat boys would leer at them from their Greek initiation houses on the heights with sundecks directly over the gorge, and you'd yell, "I'm coming, baby!" through your stolen gym class megaphone and all the frat boys would cook burgers and drink beer and eat a pound of chips each and drink wine cooler and get real drunk and piss over the side and drink some more and then lean over and try to barf on the sunbathers and then hurl glass bottles down on them, ker-BOOOZH! This procedure liberated free electrons which danced in the twilight and tumbled into the spray of the waterfall and coalesced into new blue globes which plummeted into the gorge bobbing past the abandoned power stations until the water shorted them out. – At night the college lovers would clamber down the cliff-paths hand in hand and walk through the rubbish by moonlight, heading down to town at the bottom of the gorge where Rico's Diner was sure to have popcorn and peanut shells on the floor so that it would be like dancing on the beach. And the suicides continued from the bridge, the quiet, considerate psychotics waiting until a cloud passed over the moon before they dropped into the gorge like disintegrating ghosts. – How the frat boys laughed! Almost every week they got to see something like that. It was a charmed life.

GOLDEN DAYS OF THE AFFINITY GROUP

~~~~~~

> For there is a real magic in the action and reaction of minds on one another. The casual deliration of a few becomes, by this mysterious reverberation, the frenzy of many; men lose the use, not only of their understandings, but of their bodily senses; while the most obstinate unbelieving hearts melt, like the rest, in the furnace where all are cast as victims and as fuel.
>
> CARLYLE
> "Signs of the Times" (1829)

Meanwhile Bug walked down Eddy Street on a warmish spring morning, with the town below him at the bottom of the hill and one of the Finger Lakes shining nearby as if it were quite the thing. The biology students went there to catch lampreys. Once they caught them they put them in aquaria and let them clamp their little sucker-mouths to the glass and then cut their heads off before they could detach themselves and thrash in their tanks trying to escape; and after that the students injected various reagents into their dying nerve endings to see what would happen next. There were always more lampreys in the lake. – Bug felt excited and nervous as he got closer to Simon's house, because he was about to transform himself into an individual product of history. – Yes indeed; it was not as if he were going to Simon's house to *visit* Simon or for some other bourgeois cause; in fact the affinity group had scheduled a meeting at Simon's house to plan out their role in the upcoming occupation and blockade of Reactor No. 2 now under construction up in Marshtown, New Hampshire, by agents of that far-flung utility, White Power & Light. I suppose I should describe Reactor No. 2, which was a great black windowless cylinder surrounded by cranes, scaffolding and long low concrete buildings from which puffs of dark smoke ascended occasionally in the course of construction, and

happy yellow bulldozers pushed their snouts against the ground all
over the construction site, while progress continued in other sectors;
the administration building and the turbine building with its steel
condensers were now entirely enclosed; for Mr. White set hard
schedules and expected them to be followed; and right at the edge of
the deep excavation for Unit 2 the construction trailers crouched on
their wheels in the mud beneath the scudding blue-black clouds, and
sometimes the workmen off duty sat down on the trailer hook-ups
and made bets about how many clouds they might see within a given
time, because they were quantitatively inclined, and the other
workmen came out of the trailers coughing and shuffling in grey
dungarees and clambered down into the mucky pits where the
cooling tunnels were going to be; and red derricks peered shyly over
the waste processing buildings like giraffes, looking west at the
welding shop and electric shop and pipe shop buildings just right of
the test lab at a bend in the road; yes, black paved roads connected
every sector of the complex; across from the test lab were the
warehouses and a fenced-off section of ground for cable storage and
lumber storage; long red-brown beams lay stacked to the sky and
each work crew was responsible for picking up the beams which
they had been issued, provided of course that they had cleared things
with the lumber guard in his little booth by showing him their
lumber quota pass; then the guard walkie-talkied for approval to his
superior in the security office by the sewage treatment lagoon, which
spewed its contents into the river which protected the reactor from
three sides; a homely river it was, actually, and when the tide was
at low ebb, then the brown brackish water drew away from the
mud-banks, which glistened like the exposed gums of a dog in the
throes of acute peridontal disease; and a few bivalves caught by
surprise (they were mussels, I think) opened their shells a crack and
sniffed around and slammed them tight again, hoping for the best,
and often the sewage was flushed out of the lagoon just then and
they died; but out of sight, out of mind; for the sewage lagoon could
only be seen from the construction trailers on an exceptionally clear
day, say a sunny Sunday morning when you were kept on site for
punishment detail, and no one else was working so the air was not
full of marsh-gas the way it was when we all drilled deep into the
grey muck to lay the blue globe incubator-pipes beneath the concrete
batch plant, and all the old Society of Daniel boys were foremen
now; Sammy and Earl got to wear black hard hats with atomic
symbols on the brim, and Sammy had on an $E = mc^2 + K$ tee-shirt
which he wiped his glasses on, and he marched up and down the line

on workdays going, "Come on, boys, let's see some spirit in our work because Mr. White or Dr. Dodger might pull up at any minute," and the work crews went *thunk-thunk-thunk* with their pickaxes and *brrrRRRRRR!* with their giant excavation machines which resembled gleaming jointed metal-worms; and even stupid Taylor had been rehired in consideration of his past obedience; he was in charge of installing electronic friskers at the parking lot; while Dr. Dodger rode gleefully up and down, up and down, up and down all day in the hoist tower elevator to make sure that it worked; and, besides, he liked the view; and sometimes Mr. White would come by to watch the excavation, as Sammy had promised; and if he liked the looks of things he'd nod and wink once at Sammy and Sammy would sing out, "Another case for the boys!" – and an electrician's mate would toss a case of Budweiser down into the dark oozy pit and all the workmen would knock off for a minute and look up at the sky so that Mr. White could see the beam of his flashlight glinting weakly down on their helmets; and they'd pop the tabs off those beers; *psst! psst!* and toss 'em down real fast and then go back to work while Mr. White blew smoke-rings of satisfaction, but if Mr. White was not pleased with progress he'd start heaving rocks into the pit, yelling, "Get a move on, you bloody moles, or I'm gonna bury you down there!" – *clang! boing!* as the rocks struck the men on their helmets – and then they'd redouble their efforts for sure, union or no fucking union, because they knew that if they dared to glance up over their shoulders at such a moment they'd see the lips of the pit ringed with security guards and Mr. White would be silhouetted against the clouds with his arm raised to hurl another rock, and this one might get you in the face if he caught you looking; so we worked hard and dug out the tunnels and we unrolled hundreds of miles of fencing and put up fences nested within fences enclosed in fences; to go from the pipe shop to the welding shop next door you had to go through a gate and show your pass; and of course around the entire construction site we strung up riot-lights and ran a heavy fence with guard booths and around that we established an even stronger fence with guard booths every fifty feet; and we built a sea-wall behind the fence on the ocean side; then we put a third fence up in the woods all around the site to keep anyone from getting too close; and we ran in a supply railroad line fenced off on both sides; and we built a main gate to control traffic from the spur road and a north gate for the north access road, with flags and barriers at the guardhouse. In the belfry of the weather tower an armed guard detail surveyed operations at all times. They enjoyed looking down at the yellow siding of the warehouses and the blue and white water tanks. High pressure crowd control hoses could draw from those tanks in a jiffy. In the security building just west of the visitor center Earl had stocked mace projectors and olive-drab economy-sized spray cans of tear gas. Dr. Dodger passionately craved a hundred vomiting gas (diphenylaminachorasine) canisters as well, because the canisters were so cute and black that it would be great fun to arrange them in twenty rows of five. And what a stir it always caused upon controlled use! – Dr. Dodger's attitude was inherently defensive.

The weather tower was frequently struck by lightning in the latter months of construction. Electrical currents condensed out of sea-clouds in the sky at night and came to visit because they knew that their blue globe cousins would be there soon, the special nuclear kind that could live without copper or thunderstorm ether and would roll, roll, roll around the fuel rods at night when the swing shift was sleeping, as swing shifts will do; and the blue globes would fly up to the ceiling of the great silvery reactor dome (now being assembled) and roll around there gobbling neutrons the way that fat people eat olives at cocktail parties; and the blue globes would smile wickedly and stick out their tongues and copulate there on the ceiling; and the Geiger counters in the guardroom would go click-click-click-clickclickclick-click-clickclickclick; and the swing shift would wake up suddenly hearing the marsh-owls whoohing outside and the red lights were flashing on the monitors and the blue globes were rolling around inside the reactor core glowing in the dark and sticking to each other's bellies and grinning and nipping at each other with their electric teeth so that the sparks flew and the air smelled pure like radioactive ozone and arousing each other licking at each other's furry static and fucking each other and proliferating like crazy so that new blue globes were born and swooped down from the ceiling into the plutonium core-rods to bathe in their exciting radiance and more blue globes were being born and the blue globes chuckled and rubbed against each other and rolled up and down the fuel-rods getting wilder every second so that now an alarm buzzer sounded in the control room and the poor swing shift rubbed the sleep out of their eyes and started getting nervous and more and more blue globes were born and they all merged indiscriminately in the deadly purple darkness and powered televisions and lamps in distant midnight places with the energies of their love; and for a millisecond they merged into one tremendous blue sphere of icy poisonous jelly, straining to swallow itself in its bliss, but that could not be and the moment of completed oneness could never really be, either;* the blue globes only pretended that they belonged to each other because they all loved flattery and so flattered each other by offering themselves to each other in a deep low rumbling of potential energy and impending fission; then the shuddering transmutation occurred and the blue globes burst apart in a chain-reaction orgasm, releasing atoms from the burden of being; and the whole reactor-dome buzzed and crackled and began to glow as if it were haunted, which it was; the swing shift died instantly; and the fuel rods melted and the ground began to tremble, then the entire plant shattered and everyone within a hundred miles perished like a hayfield on fire; but there was no cause for worry because Mr. White had already sold the plant to Blaker Enterprises, *haaah!* – so White Power & Light was well out of it; and anyhow this was some thirty-five years in the future, after the plant had been constructed and the blue globes had served faithfully until they got bored; that was when they were dangerous; of course the purpose of the blue globes was and always had been hatred and mastery, though for a space in their lustful ecstasy they might forget that spiteful purpose; *c'est la vie*, and in the meantime the work went on and Sammy personally installed the new wheel in the pumphouse with a golden spanner wrench and the reactionaries guarded the site and trained attack dogs in the woods because they knew that antinuclear trespassers were coming; Dr. Dodger had read about it in the papers. – "Look at this, Jack," he shrieked, rushing in to Mr. White's office on the second storey of the visitor center, which had a very nice view of the green woods. – "First of all," says Mr. White, "don't you ever come in here without knocking. Second of all, I am your boss, and you'd damn well better not get buggering and insolent-familiar with me, Dodger; now remember that, and what the hell do you want?" He snatches the newspaper clipping out of Dr. Dodger's hand and skims it. "Oh, shit," he says. "Oh, SHIT!" – All the guards were issued visor-shields and riot sticks. The fences were reinforced and topped by barbed wire. The police were alerted. Additional gate barriers were constructed on the access roads. Ringleaders were identified. Simon's mail was opened, xeroxed, and triumphantly re-sealed by Dr. Dodger.

Meanwhile the preparations of the affinity group continued.

---

* As Poe so truly said in his *Eureka: A Prose Poem* (1848): "The absolutely consolidated globe would be *objectless*: therefore, not for a moment could it continue to exist."

Orange stickers were all over town, alerting the progressive community to this event. Bug smiled to himself palely and decided that he would see what he would see. – He was tautologically correct. – Adjusting his glasses the way a paratrooper does his harness, Bug proceeded down the hill until the campus was out of sight behind him, with its beautiful girls and nationally ranked library system and distinguished faculty, which as you know included Dr. Dodger, who for the last week had begun taking attendance at all seminars in order to find out which students just happened to be missing during this time of unrest; those who were on the evaluative borderline would be dropped by one letter grade. – And Mr. White paced in his office at that very moment, working out security measures on the phone with the state troopers and the national guard. – But the way the affinity group interpreted the situation, there would soon be a line of figures along the ridge at the perimeter of the fence, pulling down a section in the middle of it and standing together looking through the opening which they had made into the clouds. They were determined to shut down Reactor No. 2. – At Simon's house they all went through a nonviolence training session in the back yard, where half the affinity group was picked to be occupiers and half to be police. The police whacked the occupiers with newspapers. Then everyone made up and sat in a circle on the grass and closed their eyes and held hands and sang. – But Bug was unimpressed by this zoological individualism. He looked and listened and thought to himself: These people will be sales clerks and tepid social democrats within five years.

The Last Days of the Affinity Group

~~~~~~

> ... and if one were to ask, "What is a Pantheistic Humanist?" I
> should say, one who believes in the divinity of the telegraph pole.
>
> REV. ALGERNON S. CRAPSEY
> *The Last of the Heretics* (1924)

Bug's way, had he been in charge of the affinity group, would have
been to suggest that they all go off to the Arctic and found the ideal
city where nobody would bother them; or, in his mature years, to
flatly demand that terror be countered with terror, but he was
neither in charge nor in his mature years; indeed he was still
impressionable, was young Bug, remaining curious to learn exactly
what love and bravery and openness could accomplish, since unlike
Wayne he had small measure of any. Nonviolence was for Bug a
delightful summer kind of thing that reminded him of upper-middle-
class tennis courts and boating clubs. – One can convince oneself of
anything. This is one of the elements of the sticky national glue that
binds us all together, revolutionaries and reactionaries forever. – In
the stern last years of Kuzbuism, when the reactionaries pursued
them through the Arctic, Bug relied upon his knowledge of that
selfsame tendency in us to trick his honkeys into sustained and
continued effort. – The reader must keep in mind that Mr. White's
choppers were whirring over the mountains and bogs by then like
giant deadly mosquitoes, and Wayne had outfitted sportmen's safari
groups with the latest infrared trackers and production model space
rifles, while the fleeing Kuzbuites were few in number (Bug, Milly,
Stephen Mole, Susan and Frank, to be exact) and bore only
antiquated arms, as we have seen; yet the reactionaries had to chase
them around the world half a dozen times, round and round the
great lonely ice-caps and tectonic plates, before they finally bagged

the bunch. – So Mr. White was given a run for his money. – The secret of Bug's success in goading his four soldiers on through so many thousands and thousands of miles of tundra where there was nothing to eat but lichens, with ice for dessert, was that he issued each individual a tube of toothpaste, counting, as I have hinted, on his or her middle-class conditioning to do all the rest. – For as a child, I, the author, was generally made to brush my teeth after meals, and my mother told me never to swallow the toothpaste, so that at last after many years the saccharine tingle of the toothpaste on my tongue would be enough to convince me that my eating tasks were done, regardless of how hungry I had felt before; and my mouth would now be as pure and bright as bathroom tiles; so that even if I saw candy in the dime store window I would not want to defile this sensation, hallowed by all the commercials I had seen; I would not feel hungry anymore; so Bug ordered the administration of three squeezes of toothpaste daily; and this made all feel full and satisfied. – But Milly was never charmed by this. She sucked on her toothpaste as an act of intellectual charity to Bug; let him think that his theories were correct; she had better things to do than argue with him. Neither did nonviolence form itself into a pretty image in her mind the way a polygon representation can be digitized upon a computer terminal. She had no patience for it. Even as a child she had been interested in battles; and Milly's toy drum was always beating *ta-rum tum-tum-tum* very crossly and ordering Milly, "Join the snowball fight!" (*ta-rum-tum!*), "Kill the boys!" (*rum-ty-tum-ty-tum!*), "Hurt Susan!" (*tiddly-rumty tumty-tum-tum-tum!*). – When she was seven Milly thought that this was the way war was: a dozen brightly dressed children would sit in a circle in the grass with a gun; and one of them would be "It" (and this individual Milly pictured as a pale boy with glaring eyes, a shock of dark hair, and a small trapezoidal moustache, since her father, Mr. Dalton, had an interest in World War II, and Milly had once seen one of his pictures of Hitler), and "It" would be sitting in the center of the circle with the loaded gun, and "It" would lean forward and put the barrel of the gun to the first child's heart; perhaps that child would be a boy dressed in light green, like Robin Hood; and "It" would cock the hammer, and the gun would make a soft click, then "It" would put the gun to the next child's heart; perhaps Milly's own, yet her heart would not be beating faster than usual because Milly didn't get excited; for one thing, there were lots of levers and buttons left to push before "It" would do the final thing; Milly was no dummy; thus she stared right back in "Its" face to make sure that "It" didn't cheat, and this evidently discomfited "It" because "It" pouted and twirled a new knob on the gun hastily, to be through with Milly; and there was another click. sharper than the first, but that was all, so Milly, as anticipated, had gotten through her turn with cool success; then "It" brought the gun to the third child's heart; that would be Susan in her blue dress with yellow polka-dots; Milly knew Susan from first grade and already despised her because Susan was a crybaby; Susan would probably be begging "It" not to shoot while the tears ran down her face; imagine that! – and all the other kids would be embarrassed that they had agreed to play war with Susan; but "It" was not embarrassed; this was what "It" loved; "It" made Susan unbutton the top of her dress and pressed the barrel hard against her pink flat chest so that a circular indentation was left there like a brand; then "It" flicked some other lever, and this time there was a very loud inexorable click; and so it went player to player until finally all the knobs and levers had been cocked and adjusted; and only the trigger remained to be pulled; then "It" would put the gun to that unfortunate child's heart and pull the trigger: – BANG! – that was how Milly thought you had a war. – Now at Simon's house Bug came upon a scene not so different, for war will always be a game. Eight brightly dressed boys and girls were wandering across Simon's emerald lawn, looking for sunny places to set down their contributions to the potluck. – In due time we would sit in a circle around the casserole and share, after which it would be time for nonviolence practice in the grass. In those exercises, which relied upon mutual trust, the only frightening things were the dog-turds in the grass. You'd get down on your hands and knees and crawl between everyone's legs and get stroked; or the whole affinity group would lift you gently up on its pink hands and give you a ride. But it was not yet lunchtime, so we flew kites and played frisbee and blew our harmonicas. – Boodeley-boodeley-boodeley-boo! – We had a fine view of Suicide Gorge, with Lamprey Lake on the horizon; sailboats were out on the water today. Birds winged overhead, toward Canada. We knew that we were about to do something great. – Each of us wore the livery of direct action: rainbow-patched jeans, tie-dyed shirts or handmade dresses, flowers in our long hair, turquoise rings, necklaces of Tibetan beads, red and black armbands, tennis shoes, anarchist socks, belts from which wire-cutters dangled (Bug had already bought a gas mask, but he'd left it at home), and harmless nonviolent peace buttons and ribbons and pennants from other actions: – Seabrook, where the cops had charged us in the October mists but we had crossed the moat and linked arms and chanted "It won't be built!" just the same; Commanche Peak, where we'd lain down on the road for two days and two nights and no one could move us; Los Alamos, where in the dead of winter we had blockaded the railroad tracks with our warm living bodies to screw up Mr. White's weapons production; Diablo Canyon, where we'd had a week-long concert ringed by atomic security police and then approached the nuclear plant from the sea, in little rubber dinghies, making our beachhead in sight of the fence before the National Guard could get there ... Life was good. We danced and we sang. Everybody was hugging and kissing. The finest apple juice flowed freely, and Simon's yard sparkled with fun. Sophie and Barnaby drank out of the same glass. – Only Bug remained like a sad clown among these ideological jesters. He would have preferred a businesslike preparation for violence. As a half-hearted measure he suggested that all concerned withdraw their money from Mr. White's banks. "In the final analysis," he said palely at lunch, sliding his glasses back up the bridge of his nose, "we will suffer. But that is our fate." This, Bug's first speech, created a painful impression upon the affinity group. Jerry picked his teeth uneasily. Simon, the leader (although the affinity group was not supposed to have leaders), fidgeted and yawned and toyed with his wire-cutters while Bug spoke, reminding Bug involuntarily of the way Lenin used to be during Plekhanov's speeches, always smiling sarcastically and whispering to M. P. Tomsky. Bug's judgment of Simon, who wore flannel shirts and had a long blond ponytail and was very determined, was not unfavorable; Simon was an extremist, so Bug felt drawn to him *a priori*. But from Simon's point of view Bug was an enigmatic alien element. Thin, bespectacled, and unenthusiastic, he seemed to Simon not a revolutionary, but rather some churning library-burrower or book-ghoul, who digests old rotten campaigns and befouls the academic world with his excrement. Truly Bug was a late bloomer. He never danced or even smiled; he just sat taking notes on a pocket pad and looking ill at ease. Of course, Bug was ill at ease, but not as much so as Simon thought him, since he knew he had to see the thing through. And Bug was favorably disposed toward Simon and all the others. They had good souls. Simon, however, could not see that Bug had a good soul, too. (And I, Big George, insist that this is because Bug did not have a good soul. He was if anything a cold-blooded wrecker and vandal, and I am glad to go on record here as saying that I will find a way to electrocute him by the end of the next volume.) So Simon hugged every other member of the affinity group every ten minutes, but he remained ominously formal in his courtesy to Bug, saying "Thanks for joining us, Bug," or "We appreciate all your interest, Bug," every time that Bug came to the meetings. – If Bug had been a girl Simon might perhaps have chucked him under the chin. – This treatment amused Bug. He knew that someday he would be superior to Simon in direct action. In the meantime, however, his first speech was not a success. "Withdrawing money from the banks will diminish Mr. White's inert organic existence," he said, but Sandy yawned and smiled and twiddled her toes in the grass, while Ellen kept Bug continuously supplied from her store of gentle encouraging nods. So Bug's proposal was dismissed and stricken from the agenda. Bug smiled wryly. – Sophie then reported that the affinity group had received warm greetings from its sister organizations: politically conscious plants in Omarville, the Polish socialist party, and the All-Insects' Union. The All-Insects' Union offered fraternal support, but Bug was dismayed to see that Simon frowned at this and said, "We can't do it; we just can't do it because we're working for *ourselves*; there's nobody behind us," and at these words Tina and Sandy and Jerry jumped to their feet and clapped thunderously. Bug smiled and applauded using his thumbnails alone in a sad ironic ovation. – "Don't be so shy, Bug!" whispered Ellen. "We all love you." And Bug, looking around at their bright faces, at the beautiful dragon-kites and bird-kites and fish-kites that fluttered above them as they sat in their consensus circle, was sure that they did really love him, except perhaps for Simon. For the first time he acknowledged that they might be too good for him. Yet he was fond enough of them, too, in his way. It was only that he did not have any faith in them.

Meanwhile, Mr. White declared martial law in Marshtown and extended the hours of all security personnel. And Tina and Ellen spent the following day gathering wildflowers for everyone in the affinity group, so that they could be handed to reactionary guards with a smile in any tense situation – the distribution of flowers to people who are out to maim you being the linchpin of nonviolent direct action. Love is very very brave.

LOVE AND LOYALTY

~~~~~~

> Anyhow, the uncertainty is more terrible than a sudden ending of
> it all.
>
> <div align="right">EVA BRAUN, 1935</div>

Food, ropes and grappling hooks had gone up a few days before in
Tina's trailer. Bug got a ride with Jerry and Ellen and Sandy and
Sophie and Barb, happily packed between the sweet-smelling girls in
the back as they all munched apples and granola, their backpacks in
the trunk. Boodeley-boodeley-boodeley-boo, went the radio, and
Sandy hummed along, slowly turning the rings on her fingers . . .
Bug felt very relaxed and contented at first, snuggling in among the
girls as they rolled on northwards along the interstate, and Ellen
yawned so prettily and fell asleep with her head on his shoulder,
bony though his shoulder was, but as the hours departed tension
began to burn in his stomach, for though nobody talked about what
they were going to do he thought about it more and more; and when
at two-thirty they pulled in at a McDodger's Restaurant for chips
and a Fizzola he wondered how all the fat women and farting
families would look at them if they knew what they were doing; and
then they were on the road again, Ellen too keyed up to sleep
anymore, and no one was talking except for Jerry and Sophie up in
the front seat trading fishing stories that neither Jerry nor Sophie
was listening to; and Jerry's hands were sweating just a little at the
wheel as he guided them through brightly-colored surges of traffic,
with kiddies in the passing cars looking at them from the back, no
doubt reading their license plates for travel games involving listings
of digits and combinations, which the children of our great Republic
so dearly loved; and as usual our hero felt like they were all Leninists
in a sealed train about to create something new and awful in the
world, or mass murderers trying to be anonymous but forced to

interact with the world nonetheless, possibly attracting attention, as when (he recalled from his reading about Charles Manson) Tex Watson and Sadie Atkins were driving through the suburbs after the Tate murders, and their hands were spattered with drying blood, so they stopped very quietly in the California night and walked up to the nearest yard, treading softly on the grass so no one would hear, and took Mr. Smith's hose and turned on the tap so they could wash the blood off their hands, and they grinned and winked at each other as the blood got wet and sticky and metallic-smelling again, and maybe they licked it off each other's hands and had a good chuckle about how Sharon Tate had screamed before they stabbed her, and begged them to cut the baby out at least and save it; and the bloody water ran black in the moonlight from Tex's and Sadie's arms; but just then the screen door creaked, and Mr. Smith came out and said, "What the hell are you doing here?" and they smiled at him like clean-cut college kids and said, "Oh, terribly sorry to bother you, sir; we got a little thirsty coming home from the movies and thought perhaps we could trouble you for a drink of water . . ."

So the car rolled on and on and on, and young Bug shook just a little bit, for they were out to break the law and engage in civil disobedience, which Mr. White would count almost as bad as terrorism; and he knew that Mr. White would catch up with them sooner or later, just as justice caught up with the Mansonites; and he shivered some more. — "Are you cold?" Ellen asked him, and he shook his head woodenly.

Barb wasn't cold; she was hot, in fact, so she cranked down her window; and almost at once a big hornet buzzed in from the freeway. The women flinched a little. It landed on Ellen's hair and walked up and down very slowly on her scalp, digging its padded talons in; and then it buzzed suddenly and horribly and hovered around her ears and buzzed round and round as she sat rigid and still, and then it set itself down on her shiny sweaty nose and rested there for awhile, sucking at her sweat; and after about five minutes it became irritated again and buzzed inside Ellen's ear and then landed on her eyelid. — "Get it out of here!" she said; "get it out." — Our hero didn't know how to help, exactly. — Jerry told Sophie to lean over and steer for him; and he turned around, keeping his toe still on the gas, and caught the evil golden thing in his palm very gently, and said, "Hi there, bug," and eased it out the window; and then he turned around again and drove some more.

A SPEEDY CLARIFICATION

~~~~~~

... to hold fast what is dead requires the greatest strength ...

HEGEL
Phenomenology (1807)

How did the reactionaries feel about the revolutionaries?

Where I am currently staying (now that Bee has her own hive I live precariously, but rent-free, with my good friends Seth and Arthur), we have a problem with ants in the bathroom. Bee and I had a problem with ants in the kitchen, and in the bathroom also, come to think of it, and sometimes in the bedroom as we slept I would come awake from a nightmare about Mr. White and see a line of them moving across her hair on the pillow; I killed them all quietly and never told her because she would have screamed in horror; but in the kitchen they had their headquarters and occasionally streamed across the floor on rainy mornings, so the whole floor was black with them; it made me want to vomit. In Seth and Arthur's house there are not nearly so many; in fact they are few enough in number so that it is possible to take a sort of scientific interest in them, almost liking them, even (though I still hold that just one is sufficient to constitute a problem), investigating their habits and verminous behavior. For a long time I noticed that they frequented the head of the bathtub, along the rim, looking very black and shiny against the white porcelain so that the whole gave the effect of a cathedral statue in Europe which has been stained and spotted by air pollution, or an old New England gravestone speckled with mold, or Catherine's face after she is dead (say, forty to fifty years hence) and instead of freckles her face is crawling with grave-mites eating her flesh, though they mean her no harm. — Where are the ants coming from? I asked myself. What microhabitat would be ideal for their nest? It would have to be warm and moist, and give access to food (it seemed they ate the dried toothpaste gunked to the lid of my tube of Dr. Dodger's Brighty-White). The place turned out to be just at the base of the hot water faucet, in the crack where the rounded metal flange met the steamy plaster; and here it was probably very warm and rotten and crumbly and dark and happy, except that when I turned on the hot water full steam ahead for a shower to warm *me* up for a minute before going out into the rain to canvass door to door for the Kuzbu Union ("Fighting for Better White Power & Light Service in Our Neighborhoods"), then the poor ants would come fleeing out in an expanding circular mass, it probably being far *too* hot at that point. – Even the faucet handle, which leaked a little, hurt to touch.

And at the Kuzbu Union office, writing down the totals for the night on the crewsheet and going to put the postdates on Milly's desk, Frank Fairless saw something moving inside the radio. Just behind the plastic window, along the frequency dial, was a fat happy cockroach, lazing along (I remember hearing that some cockroaches have adapted to living on nothing but the dust produced by electronic appliances). – The field manager came over and looked revolted. He turned the tuning dial clockwise, fast and hard, so that the big plastic cursor marking the station frequency came hurtling from left to right so that it would slam into the cockroach and crush it . . . But the roach raced into a rectangular black hole which Frank had never noticed before.

So it is that every familiar object can serve a multitude of beings, each inimical to the others. Boy, do we hate those bugs, and I bet they don't like us much, either, when we try to crush or scald them . . .

One nice thing, at least, is that such loathings are so elemental that no time is wasted in the course of any confrontation making a decision: – Do we love them or do we hate them? We HATE them, and the matter becomes resolved with action, that speedy clarification.

That was how the reactionaries felt about the revolutionaries, and that was how the revolutionaries felt about the reactionaries. But in the days of the affinity group, before Bug was in charge of direct action, Simon, Ellen, Sophie, Mary, Jerry, Barb and Tina tried to love their enemies; Frank also tried to love like that, in spite of being a double agent, especially when he was canvassing in the wind and rain for Milly on a Saturday afternoon as it poured and Frank tried to be nice to everyone although they gave him no money and kicked him off their porches into the gutters flowing ankle-deep with coffee-colored water which Frank couldn't see anyhow because his glasses were fogged up; he was the only one who had shown up for Milly in the office (because he loved her) and she patted Frank's shoulder as duty required (in fact she despised him) and said to Frank, "I think you're a real trooper for doing this and not letting me down," and then Frank felt happy, for Milly was a good boss, and Frank was rarely thanked or praised, and then it was off to Richmond's low-income black neighborhood where all the doors remain slammed up tight against this honkey, and wiry teenagers with orange Afros burst out of a car and beat the shit out of Frank and took the two one-dollar contributions which he had managed to collect in the previous three hours; and here came Milly to pick him up at the end of the day, wondering absently if she and Bug stood a chance against Mr. White in the primary on the nuclear issue, and she came to Frank's pickup point but she did not see him because he could not move and the rain was coming down so hard she just vaguely glimpsed a heap of bloody clothes on the curb; and then the relentless roll of raindrops on the windshield obliterated that sight.

That night Bug tossed and turned in his orange tent, suffering nightmares about tank warfare and plainclothes roundup actions. The locals who were supposed to come beat everybody up never showed, but all night the choppers hovered clackety-clackety-clacking over the camp, illuminating everything with glaring blue searchbeams. Members of the affinity group got up early and ate breakfast; Bug could hardly choke down his oatmeal. It was a chilly, foggy morning, and long after the sun had come up there were pockets of fog in the forest hollows and cold white streamers of it in the air, trapped beneath the cool moist trees. Simon squatted on a groundcloth, affixing his grappling hook to a chain, and everyone else assembled the wire-cutters, ropes, goggles, gas masks and helmets. The paint on Bug's gas mask was dry now; Ellen had decorated it for him with yellow flowers and little blue clouds.

OPERATION HAMMER BLOW

~~~~~~

> Cruel pleasures are most successful in the silence and peacefulness
> which only the country can provide.
>
> DE SADE, *Juliette*

> ... the less we just stare at the hammer-Thing and the more we
> seize hold of it and use it, the more primordial does our rela-
> tionship to it become ...
>
> HEIDEGGER, *Being and Time*
> I.3.15 (8th ed., 1957)

Years later, at the height of the campaign against the Society of
Daniel strongholds, Bug remembered one episode most persistently
from the occupation attempt. His affinity group had seen a line of
police standing directly in front of the gates of the plant, with
troopers forward of the river that ran around the construction site
on three sides, the troopers just daring anyone to wade across the
river to get maced, gas masks or not (as mace can penetrate a gas
mask, only a piece of impermeable plastic stretched across the
breathing filter to deflect the spray will do any good; small breathing
apertures must be left at the sides of the filter behind the plastic sheet
– and hence at right angles to the line of spray; and these will pass on
the chemical in time – and anyhow there is nothing to stop a good
state trooper from just pulling the mask off and stepping on it and
spraying mace directly into your eyes). The affinity group saw a
steep, wooded bluff a quarter-mile down the marsh, and Simon,
who had as I said tied his hair back in a long blond ponytail, argued
that they should take their chances scaling the bluff to outflank the
police, then work their way through the woods until they could
come up against the fence of the plant, the affinity group all silent as
Indian braves in the trees as Ellen crept up and latched one end of

the come-along winch to the fence, and paid out cable and hooked the other end to some stout maple-branch, and then they all took turns cranking in cable, click-click-click-click, as fast as possible, until the fence began to groan and bent toward them and finally pulled loose; and they all swooped in, yelping triumphantly behind their fiercely-painted gas masks . . . It seemed like an excellent idea, so they angled away from the battle-line, where the troopers were busy monitoring Cost of Freedom and Texas Rose and Luna and all the other affinity groups that stood staring back at them across the brown salty river. Bug's group went on down the vast lonely flatness of the marsh, their arms around each other, and approached the bluff; and as they arrived at the base of it, all alone and out of reach of help from the other affinity groups, fifty National Guardsmen came running down at them double-file. They'd been waiting for them behind the trees. Jerry was caught and arrested. Everyone else got back across the river into No-Man's-Land, but there they had to watch Jerry being hauled away, waving back at them to convince himself that he wasn't scared of what was about to happen to him (they broke both his arms). So after that, even more than before, Bug never trusted any place that seemed too still; and from then on, if all he had for a weapon was goodness and rightness, he felt a strong sense of fear and powerlessness. Everything he learned was making him more like an insect.

BARNABY

~~~~~~

> Wherein is the courage required – in blowing others to pieces from
> behind a cannon, or with a smiling face to approach the cannon
> and be blown to pieces?
>
> GANDHI
> "Moral Requirements for Satyagraha"
> in *Hind Swaraj*

> One belongs to the Others and enhances their power.
> HEIDEGGER

Here came nineteen-year-old Barnaby, just out of high school, who
was for ever making grand doomed plans, and comprised the
one-man affinity group Love. In high school there was to have been
a parade of the reactionaries in his city, which was a chuckling
brown collection of crumbling buildings running over seven hills,
like Rome, the whole being situated in such a way that the great
conical mound of coal which ran things could be viewed from
almost every quarter, and as Barnaby went to school and back every
day on the bus, crying and raging, he saw the clean blue posters
announcing the parade, everywhere the same announcements riding
high on the billboards which looked down at us from the sunny sky
above the dust and smoke of our great Republic. – Mr. White was
going to be there with the Auxiliary Naval Brass Ensemble; and they
would all march along Moorescreek Boulevard (there had in fact
been a creek there once but now in its place ran a secret black stream
of silken acid suds that spurted from factory to factory in culverts
just below the sewers); so Barnaby designed a spray nozzle for paint
that could have a range of thirty-five yards so that "all of a sudden
those white robes, those white uniforms that made them feel so pure
would turn dripping and hideous as black paint came out of the sky!

It would've been psychologically devastating," he said fondly; the parade was, however, canceled at the last minute, for Dr. Dodger heard somehow that there might be student unrest. Dr. Dodger, you see, had very long sensitive yellow ears. – And now Barnaby had made a huge banner with the state motto of New Hampshire on it: "LIVE FREE OR DIE." It was rolled up in his pack. He would be making a break for it at the north fence from the marsh and scaling the weather tower to hang the banner there. (It proved impossible to even approach the fence.) On the wall of his apartment was a card reading HOW MUCH CAN I LOVE?, and once when I myself needed a meal Barnaby used the last of his savings to buy me a big bag of groceries. Barnaby had two sets of wire-cutters and a coil of rope over his shoulder. He strode along energetically to his doom and passed everyone up, and looked over his shoulder once as he tramped forward and beckoned them all impatiently onward, with green-gold shadows dappling on his shoulders . . . Then he was out of sight. On they went through the woods, illusion playing its happy part; the sun caught Ellen's hair and fluffed it full of light so that it seemed almost blonde to Bug as the affinity group marched toward the plant, and Sophie's canteen was a mirror-disc as bright and dangerous as molten metal, or as the cool white metal of a pistol action once the hypocritical blueing has worn off; and as Sophie walked on and the canteen jiggled from the strap and swung against her hip, it reflected its terrible beam of light aimlessly over a wide arc, so that the bugs watching in the woods mistook it for an incomprehensible signal. The water-beetles and turtle bugs which kept the oceans under surveillance had sometimes observed that passing ships communicated with lanterns; and on the foggy New England coast, scudding south to the Great Beetle with another report, it was all too easy to become hypnotized by the steady blinking of our proud lighthouses, to just as much purpose as when Bug stared entranced at Ellen's hair. And overhead the police helicopters counted sparkles and noted them in the log; everyone was busy reading in meanings according to his profession. – Now they emerged into the town, where the side-roads bustled with white unmarked cars. Simon whooped defiantly and raised his wire-cutters high. But Bug had a bad feeling in his stomach. Looking straight ahead, the affinity group marched along Ocean Street, with all the old yokels sitting on the porch of the Captain Sandborn House drumming their crutches on the steps, waiting to see somebody get beaten up. – Barnaby was waiting at a bend in the road. "Let's duck into the woods and talk perspective," he said. – This was agreeable to everyone, so they all stepped back into the clammy shadows of the trees. – "What's up?" Simon said. Simon was very Marxist in his yellow plaid worker's shirt and blue-grey cap, his long sleeves rolled up a little bit so that Bug could see the down on his wrists. – Barnaby looked into each face with that flaming tormented intentness which is the disease of all persons with high expectations; whereas Bug, who never had any expectations, studied you blandly in his guerrilla years; it was impossible to disappoint Bug. But Barnaby made them all uncomfortable. Ellen blushed as he stared into her eyes dissecting her sin which she carried hidden inside her like some blackened organ behind her ribs, but in fact Barnaby could see only purity in her; he didn't even see any black spots inside her the way he did in Simon; he turned to Simon frowning and Simon looked back into Barnaby's eyes, gritting his teeth with effort and martyr's jealousy; Barnaby was defeated by this glance and turned to Mary, who stood smiling back at him from between two trees; looking into Mary's eyes Barnaby saw dependency and vacillation that worried him at the same time it assured him of opportunity; and he turned to Tina and looked into her face and Tina grinned and gave him thumbs-up and in Tina he saw someone he could count on; but Sophie put her hands on her hips and stared back flatly when her turn came; as for Bug, when he submitted to the inspection of Barnaby's shining eyes he kept something back, namely his secret skepticism about this form of action that he did not want Barnaby to see because it would weaken Barnaby and Bug did not want to weaken Barnaby, being polite; but Barnaby looked into Bug and ferreted out Bug's aloofness and turned from him forever in disappointment. – "Listen," said Barnaby when he had finished with each of them (Jerry was the last, and Bug could not tell whether the look in Jerry's eyes as Barnaby took inventory represented love or ox-like stupidity), "let's agree now to retreat no farther than the river once we're across, no matter what happens; and if we can't cut through the fence we'll chain ourselves to it" – and here Barnaby pulled up his rain poncho and showed them a seventy-foot chain lashed around his waist – "and they'll have to cut our hands off before they clear us away!" – Simon was not Christ; Jerry was not Christ; Christ was not Christ; Barnaby was Christ. – There was a silence in the woods, not unlike that in the arenas of southern Europe while the bull is considering whether or not he really wants to fight (not realizing as yet that he has no governance of his fate); and then suddenly everyone heard the noise of the helicopters again and they all looked upward and Simon laughed and put his hand on Barnaby's shoulder and said to everyone, "I love him and I think he's a great guy, but I think he's insane." – Bug was disagreeably affected by this, because they had unanimously agreed to prosecute their war unflinchingly, and Simon and Ellen had been the proponents of the northern approach, which would certainly commit them *passively* to remaining on the enemy side of the river, for once the tide came in there could be no retreat, no solace except maybe an encouraging sisterly smile from Ellen as the police marched up and raised their nightsticks. – "Please," Barnaby said, "please, people," and Bug half expected him to get down on his knees to them all, but no one said anything, and finally Sophie said in her brisk practical voice, "I personally feel that Barnaby should have brought this up at the meeting last night, and as far as I feel now I admire Barnaby very much but it makes no sense to upset our strategy like this and lose our mobility. I for one am not willing to deal with half a dozen cases of hypothermia after a night on the marsh." – "Right on," said Simon, satisfied that other persons than he were performing the executioner's role. And Mary and Sandy and Bug and Tina all nodded firmly though sadly, and Barnaby's eyes dulled and he said nothing and got up and sat down under a distant tree. – Good Jerry walked over to him and touched his shoulder and said, "Hey, man, if you want somebody to go with you I'll go with you," but Barnaby just wiped his eyes and shook his head.

"This is not to say that we won't cross the river at all," later said Sophie, who was of a literalist temperament, so Barnaby went to the bend in the river where it was very deep; and he threw across a grappling hook affixed to a long rope. The rope held. Barnaby took off his shirt and raised his pack above his head and jumped into the water, holding the rope with one hand. "Come on, people!" he cried behind him. The affinity group stood irresolute. Simon in particular was not pleased that Barnaby was forcing the issue; you could tell that from Simon's silence; but finally Ellen and Mary crossed after him, Ellen raising the flag high above her head as she forded the river; and Barnaby yelled back, "Don't leave us here to do it alone!" and Simon, remembering that helicopters might be calling in the coordinates of their position even now, yielded to the situation and leaped into the cold brown water. So they entered enemy territory. And then they all marched across the golden plain, Bug bringing up the rear at this point because he felt a certain reluctance to go first; the earplugs kept trying to warn him of the danger even though he was not wearing them at the moment; he could feel them popping hysterically about like jumping beans in the case in his shirt pocket, and the case vibrated against his chest. And now, you recall, some branches parted at the top of the bluff, and the fifty Guardsmen came running down the hill; the affinity group could see the sun on their helmets; and Jerry was captured. – After everyone else got back across the river, a conference was held. – "Well, A.G., we have a problem," said Simon, still in the process of collecting himself. – Mary nodded emphatically. – Bug now spoke up for almost the first time since they had come to Marshtown. "Let's retreat," he said. "Our current situation is devoid of inner worth." – Barnaby, who had been shattered by the arrest of Jerry, which was his fault, sat some distance from the consensus circle and stared at his knees. – "It seems to me we can't do much here," said Sophie, breaking the silence (for Bug's frank proposal of withdrawal had demoralized all into speechlessness). "Let's see if we can help out at the railroad blockade; that's my personal opinion." – Suddenly Barnaby jumped to his feet and cried out, "People, why are we sitting here?" – but before he could go on Ellen said, rather cuttingly, "Now I suppose you want to lead us on a rescue mission for Jerry," and Barnaby was quiet, because he had arrived at exactly that bold plan; and the end result was that Barnaby left the others (he was, as I have explained, his own affinity group anyway; so he could do as he wanted) and he re-crossed the river and they watched him reach the trees at the base of the bluff, and they never saw him again. – Bug concluded, perhaps not without reason, that bravery alone, like love and openness, was of little value. So his development continued. He was now thinking in a truly revolutionary way.

BLUE GLOBES AGAIN

~~~~~~

> An odor of burning flesh and singed hair filled the room. For a
> moment, a blue flame played about the base of the victim's
> spine . . .
>
> *New York World* (6 August 1889)
> describing the first official electrocution

I, the author, and I, Big George, were at the north blockade that
night, when Wayne took Ellen out of the picture. I will never forget
the sly in-washing of darkness, creeping around the seated protesters
to isolate them first (that was the most urgent thing) before it settled
down to a leisurely blackening out of their faces. The affinity groups
sat in rows along the road in front of the gates, which were chained
shut. Everyone wore hooded raingear so that when the police began
to mace us we would be protected. – When you are maced what you
feel first depends on how the mace is administered; Bug had gotten it
in the blockade of the main gate the previous evening, when the
troopers drove a big water truck right up against the fence with the
headlights shining out at them in the dusk and at Wayne's signal two
construction workers in yellow hard hats dragged the hose out and
pressed the nozzle release so that the water came shooting through
the chain-link fence in a narrow stream of vicious power; and then
Wayne sprayed mace into the water as the workers turned the hose
this way and that diffusing the mace everywhere, and the people up
near the fence were knocked down by the pressure and soaked with
it and blinded; Bug was in the auxiliary ranks so he was not hurled
to the ground but just drenched with cold cold water, and the first
thing he noticed about the mace was the *taste* of it in his mouth; only
then did it begin to hurt. – So now we expected the reactionaries to
begin spraying momentarily. In each row we held long sheets of
translucent plastic ready to pull over our shoulders and heads. We

sang songs over and over. They shone lights on us and Wayne drove up from the inside, the reactionary side, in a big black fire truck; at his signal the workmen came to pay out hose, bringing it right up to the fence and waving the nozzle teasingly at you, or at you, or at you ... I, Big George, was present to observe what promised to be a delightful roundup; I have usually enjoyed taking part in the deserved defeat of a materially and morally inferior force. The author and I stood in the southwest corner of this box-trap, surveying the seated hundreds who had committed themselves to receiving Wayne's tortures, and all in vain; I suppose that is why I have always liked Wayne as I would a younger brother; he tries so hard though his violence is rarely to the point. We had agreed to stay together, the author and I, but soon his guilt about standing aloof overmastered him; as it always does; I myself can get him to do most anything simply by practicing what Goebbels (in reference to Seyss-Inquart) called "the art of alternating gingerbread and whippings." – And, oh, what a piece of gingerbread the little boy saw now; he could go sit up in the front with Bug and be a hero; he could get hurt as badly as Ellen if he was lucky; no one would blame him for his own failures if he threw in his lot with a collective disaster. So I granted him permission to do as he wished, and off he toddled, next to Bug, who could not see him, of course, nor hear him; just as he himself could not see the blue-globe marbles I rolled in my pocket, getting the electrons inside more and more excited until finally the searchlights flashed blindingly and of its own accord the pump in Wayne's fire-truck chugged, pressurizing the water; and Wayne took over the nozzle of the hose and started playing with it, waiting for pressurization to be completed to anti-riot levels. Then there was no need even to wait for the denouement; for as long as the little boy can keep it inside his bladder he may exercise restraint, but once even a drop or two gets inside the shaft of his peter then he'll start playing with it trying to force it back and you know that very shortly he'll be a-pissing on his shoes.

THE BIG THREE (OPERATION BLOWHARD)

~~~~~~

What makes them so special? You can sum it up in three words.
Accuracy. Accuracy. And accuracy. You can also count on explosive expansion when they hit their mark.

Ad for Speer bullets and CCI primers (1984)

The affair of the trespassers, vagrants and glowworms having been
settled, it was time for the reactionaries to look ahead. To the eternal
credit of Wayne, Mr. White and Dr. Dodger, plans to prosecute the
longterm fighting had been prepared even before the inauguration of
Operation Hammer Blow. It was Mr. White's desire to make the
revolutionaries pay dearly for the anxiety they had already caused
him and most likely would continue to cause him; he was doggone
fed up. Until open war was declared, naturally, he preferred to wear
the enemy down by economic means. But how was this to be done?
– Let us go back to the first day of the action at Marshtown, for it
was then that Dr. Dodger had his terrific idea.

"What we need is more witch-hunting and more witch-
BURNING!" says Mr. White firmly in the visitor center, thumping
the desk with a fist. It is a big desk, windswept as an Icelandic
farmstead; a powerful, cheerless air conditioner assaults its varnish
with icy gusts. In the very center of the desk was an antique
circuit-breaker of tarnished silver, sealed in a block of lucite for a
paperweight – the whole being a souvenir from the Society of
Daniel, presented by the grateful boys who had composed the tenth
class. Whenever Mr. White picked up the thing and tilted it in his
palm, he felt a lump in his throat. Some of those graduates would
begin dying off soon. Skinny old Sammy already had a heart
murmur. Yes indeed, the Norns were getting restless; the Valkyries
would go weaving with drawn swords, Jesus fucking Christ. As the

astute reader can see, Mr. White was not unlike Hoskuld Dala-Kollson's half-brother who lived at Hrutstead and was, according to *Njal's Saga*, "tall, strong, and skilled in arms, even-tempered and very shrewd, ruthless with his enemies and always reliable in matters of importance."

"Yep," says Mr. White. "More witch-burning, I say!"

"Yes, you could say that, now couldn't you?" says Dr. Dodger. "You're right as usual, Jackie boy." And he gives Mr. White what he considers to be – and what probably was, a half-century ago – a charming smile: now quite an assault on his employer, for Mr. White is forced to look at the yellow tombstone teeth, the white tongue, which is as scaly as lemon peel; the slimy tonsils that bob up and down as Dr. Dodger chuckles, ducking his shoulders (he cannot figure out quite why Mr. White is looking at him so coldly and steadily) – and then Dr. Dodger's hyena-breath hits Mr. White, as it has so many times before; but Mr. White has trained himself to put up with that over the years; all right, so the guy's a walking corpse and he stinks, but he gets the job done; so Mr. White flips the auxiliary ventilation toggle, and the gale keens a little harder across the desk, reminding the casual observer of the winter when Skarp-Hedin leaped the ice-bridge and shields flashed in the sun up on Raudaskrid.

The truth is that Mr. White feels behind the eight-ball. Never before has such a throng of degenerates, gooks, bums, coeds, niggers, punks, do-nothing amateurs, squaws, lezzies, weevils, pill-bugs, dung-beetles, Ivy League larvae, sodomy-ants, jew-hornets, commissar-grubs, filibusterers, imps, and crashing Indian bores made such a concerted assault upon one of his projects. Goddamn radical Free Lunch Brigade! Why couldn't they have gone after Phil Blaker's installations instead? With those alien import quotas, that fly-by-night Blaker Enterprises was already putting him under as it was, and now *this* had to happen; it was like a new pimple on top of an old boil. Not that Mr. White wasn't used to living with old boils; of course he had had some problems with the Wobblies in the thirties – who hadn't? – but back then order could be secured with scabs and Sten guns. Nowadays you had to worry about fucking public opinion. As if the public had an opinion, oh my aching back.

"Dodger," he said, "I've called you here for consultations concerning the most important front of all – the ideological front. Now, what do you think about all those snots out there?"

"Winchells," said Dr. Dodger with a wink.

Mr. White jerked in his chair. "Huh?"

"Marks, they are, oh, yes. Stupid, lop-eared chumps. Apples, savages, eggs, John Bateses, suckers without epistemological foundation."

Mr. White sat up slowly and studied Dr. Dodger as if he had never seen him before. "Where in *hell* did you pick up that con lingo?"

Again the skullfull of yellow teeth – Dr. Dodger is a genuine xanthodont – the inflamed nicotine gums, the graveyard breath. "Well, we all have our pasts," said Dr. Dodger, glancing reflexively over his shoulder with extreme rapidity, in the same motion as the carriage of a typewriter returning leftward, which for that matter is identical to the action of a methodical individual's head and neck in eating an ear of corn; "yes," continued Dr. Dodger knowingly, "we all have our little secrets, even you do, Jack, so let's leave it at that, sir, if that's okay with you, because I've always appreciated these conferences with you; indeed, I have, and that's no crow."

Mr. White ignored the irritation which now began to sizzle in his lower stomach like deep-dish fries, *p-chszz-z-z-z-!* He never appreciated being played with. Not that he was seriously tempted to give Dodger the terminal treatment; he needed the Doc, but there were days . . . Of course (getting back to the underworld stuff) in his spare time he had read popular biographies of murderers and con men for amusement (as do we all) – the Molasses Face Kid, the Seldom Seen Kid, the Indiana Wonder, the Squirrel Toothed Kid, the Hagiographic Kid, the Gash Kid, the Yaller Kid, the One-Shot Kid, the Counterforce Kid, the Electric Kid, the Nuclear Kid, the Security Kid, the Existential Kid, the Democracy Kid, the Domino Kid, the Detente Kid, the Hardened Silo Kid – and he knew that they had worked up some pretty ingenious tricks, some of 'em.

"So what's your con?" said Mr. White. "You do *have* a con, don't you? You're not just wasting my time, I take it? Just what the shit is your goddamned idea?"

Dr. Dodger, who was sitting in front of Mr. White's desk, in one of the rickety steel folding chairs which Mr. White found perfect for visitors, as any person whom he permitted audience could be made to state his business quickly if he were uncomfortable and feared for his balance and had to crane his head to see Mr. White in his leather armchair, puffing his pipe and peering down at him with ironic civility – Dr. Dodger, then, stood up and paced in front of the window for a moment, looking out over the turbine buildings at the marsh. Past the reactionary workers, sitting around eating their lunches and telling dirty stories, past the fence and the even lines of helmeted guards, the marsh flashed golden in the sun; and on the far side of the brown salt river that curled around the construction site, along the hummocky downs that stretched from the forest to the grey-brown sea, could be seen hundreds of tiny figures: – affinity groups from every reach of our great Republic, brightly dressed people spread out across the marsh with their flags and banners all home-made and beautiful; and here came the advance guard with their portable wooden bridges to cross the river with; and the sunlight glittered on their silver helmets and boot-buckles and waxed ropes; and now Dr. Dodger could see the standard of Bug's affinity group, green and purple and blue, fluttering from a great crooked tree-limb which Ellen braced against her shoulder as she walked. – Dr. Dodger drank in every hue with inexpressible joy, indulging himself in the pretension that all these advancing occupiers, all the still, sparkling police, all the yellow-helmeted workers were windup toys of his own manufacture and design; that he was a boy again in Dodgerville and this was his own backyard, yes, that he had turned the springs on *all* of them and was watching this meaningless miniature confrontation for his own amusement; that it was a private, personal afternoon that would go on forever for Dr. Dodger and no one would bother him as he watched his fighting toys meet in a campaign which would never be chronicled because it lay outside history, much as when Thoreau stood musing alone upon the wars of red and black ants; or when I used to set up space toys with my friend Jimmy in his room; or sometimes we would build our plastic base in the snow outside where the woods started; and the bubble, the airlock would be erected upon a drift of that lovely snow, only it was snow no longer but rather frozen blue methane on Callisto or Jupiter, for this was deepest space; and we set the spacemen and soldiers up on an ice-covered tree-root along with their little bleeping battery-powered jeeps; and we built rocket silos and divided up the armies and some of the plastic men were lost in the snow forever and the afternoon passed delightfully and it began to get dark and purple up in the sky, for Callisto had become dislodged from its orbit and was falling away from the solar system at ever-increasing speed, farther and farther into space, so that our spacemen were irrevocably alone and doomed as their battery-powered toys blinked red and white to light the dusk, and soon their hydroponic tanks would fail; so finally we took pity on everyone and picked up the toys that we could find and brushed the snow off them and brought them back inside to Jimmy's room; and the melting snow dropped from our mittens.

"Dodger, snap out of it," says Mr. White. "I've got things to do."

Dr. Dodger starts so hard that his back arches and he leaps into the air bent backward. "Yes," he says, "I agree with you a hundred, I mean ten thousand percent; what we need are more witch-huntings and more witch-burnings; and I was ruminating on my dear old street-friends; they loved business and women· and beer, Jack; religion they had none, thank God; and they were not hypocrites or mumbo-jumbo bugs so they made no secret about that, no sir. And they knew how to rig a round of poker. – No, don't tappy-tap your foot like that, Jack, because this is build-up for my point of view; I am a true specialist with true conclusions; yes, we concluded that there are only two varieties of con games in the long run: little evasions, like when you beat the donicker,* and succulent sucker ploys where the chump *works* to hand over his dough and you extend him an infinity of cakewalk courtesies until you're sure of him."

"Mmmph," says Mr. White, halfway interested, but for the sake of discipline he drums his fingers warningly on his desk all the same, as Dr. Dodger is not keeping strictly to the point.

"The trick is to get them behind the six so they can't afford their trail mixes and gasoline," says Dr. Dodger, rolling his eyes furiously behind his spectacles, and Mr. White thinks to himself that by God it's a pleasure to watch the Doc think and earn his consulting fee once in awhile; and Mr. White begins to feel warm and easy inside as if he'd just had a couple of man-sized man's man's drinks; for he can tell that Dr. Dodger is not faking it this time; you can depend on the Doc ...

"Well, now," says Dr. Dodger, "we could bill them in with something they'll want to blow every last push-note on, so they won't have nary a fin or a sawbuck to get home on, then we get the flatfeet to clear the book on them ..."

"What the bloody fuck does clear the book mean?"

"Ah," says Dr. Dodger brightly, "a clever question, but then you *always* ask such *good* questions, Jack, sir; and the answer is as follows: We search out the unsolved crimes on our administrative ledgers and charge these radicals with 'em, like shooting the Pope or setting off prank fire alarms in 1952; then everything balances out on the scales of justice and we get time to train our crews and protect our fuel systems before the next outbreak, hey?"

---

* A con whereby two men ride a train on one ticket, one of them hiding in the W.C.

But Mr. White is ticked off. "We can't do that until hostilities are declared, Dodger; you ought to know that; we couldn't even hump it through in pure valiant metallurgy without Congressional support, so clear your own book on that one, you geek; make like *tabula rasa* and gimme some hieroglyphics on it fast or get the HELL out, you slimy mobster!"

Now Dr. Dodger can see that Mr. White really means it, so he jitters around the office for twenty-five seconds in a frenzy of servility and hard skull sweat, until something clicks inside him like the first off-safe preceding a big artillery barrage; and he screams, "Eureka!" and leaps up to the ceiling and clings to it nimbly in sheer jubilation, like Dracula scuttling face-first down the outer walls of his cliff-hung castle. "Here's how we clean out their cush, their C-notes and megs, their deemers and crisp green bumblebees . . . This one's a guaranteed drop-in for the next ten years because we'll use the happy idealism of youth in *our* way, by going along with their desires, Jack; what we'll do is form earnest plebiscitarian canvass groups to knock on their doors collecting money for their puling causes like equality and insect rights, and those groups will milk them dry; because I can assure you that peer pressure is a powerful inducement for these teenagers and young adults as they meet nightly at their old soda fountain to cut up all the old scores. We'll establish anti-nuclear offices, and consumer lobbies of all persuasions, and they'll make everybody sign a petition so they can see that all their radical friends and neighbors have signed, too, and presumably given, have coughed up the final ridge, the umpteenth double saw, which was to have covered the cost of repairs for that ailing van . . . Then we'll also have the names of the ringleaders in black and white, just like with that Freedom Wall dodge in China. And they will *pay!* We will lance them and we will bleed them, Jack; do you see my point?"

Mr. White has to chuckle at that one. "Well, Dodger, that's a load off my mind," he says. "That'll do for the future, and all we have to do for the present is act with regularity and dispatch to sweep that trash off my property fast, so let's call the garbage man." He rings for Wayne, who comes in bright and chipper, on furlough from his heroic labors, all set to make his mark with Mr. White and that egghead Dodgeroo who all the guys say has something to do with weapons and counseling and podiatry and promotion — "All perimeters secured SIR!" says he. "Enemy well within range of anti-riot gases."

"At ease," says Mr. White with a grin.

"Yes – SIR!"

"Wayne," Mr. White begins, "I am resolved to make an end of this business out here. Nobody can and nobody will interfere if I restore order on my own property. I am giving you, Wayne, the unique honor of having your name recorded in the roll of great Republicans. I want you to get those goombahs outta here, and I'm going to be watching every move you make and filming your knockout blows for posterity and you'd better not let me down in front of the cameras or you're going to find yourself ON YOUR ASS so fast that the crap you poop out for fear will be sucked right back in, so get on out there and blow the whistle on them for Operation Hammer Blow and the best of luck to you."

Wayne goes out with a soft "Aye, aye," and the carnage begins as already told.

"Now let's discuss this canvass scam, Dodger," says Mr. White, settling back all nice and easy in his armchair . . .

"My thought was to create a special fund and get them indebted to us arse over ears, Jack," cried Dr. Dodger in high excitement; it always makes him feel so good to have a superior respect his mind that he does not always realize he is repeating himself.

Thus the appropriate conditions were created by the reactionaries for Milly and Bug's Kuzbu canvass group to come into being, much as when the mad mutant villain in the comic book vows at the end of issue number 161, "We'll meet again, Red Sprite!"

SPECIAL COURIER

~~~~~~

Everyone imposes his own ideology as far as his army can reach.

STALIN, to Tito (?1944)

Bug, meanwhile, had learned at Marshtown that might made right, and he got older and paler, his head downcast like a nodding flower that expects itself to be cut at any moment. He never saw anyone in the affinity group again. Violence fertilized his heart. He was now prepared to do any deed necessary for the success of his plans. He was one of us. – Having become an agent of the Great Beetle, as already told, he transmitted input on troop movements, mosquito repellent research, and advertising trends. When he spied something of interest to the insect movement, he had merely to tiptoe a few paces in any direction (such is the ubiquity of bugs) until his earplugs tingled, and he would see that part of the wallpaper pattern was an urban moth, camouflaged and flat and waiting for God knows how long; or down from the attic would leap a grasshopper as large as a child. And he derived satisfaction from the thought that any day now the bugs would be strong enough to overrun every palace and factory and skyscraper ...

His first assignment was to carry a comb of royal jelly from Ohio to Florida. This having been accomplished with dispatch, he was directed to observe various electric confrontations and demonstrations from hidden woodland vantage-points, so that the bugs would have more data on the methods of the reactionaries. – For the first year of his tenure, backup operatives with hard green shells sent back duplicate reports to insure that he possessed no treacherous bias. But it quickly became clear in the organization that he prided himself on instinctive unfeeling accuracy, like a stinging bee. So the Great Beetle came to rely upon him. Whenever circumstances required, Bug reached into his shirt pocket, withdrew the transparent case, and put Tony's earplugs in . . . The earplugs tingled. When Bug got up and peered through the foliage that hid him from the fray he could see the reactionary generating station; and he watched the advancing state troopers with their riot sticks jabbing down upon the limp nonviolent bodies; the conscious ones closer to Bug knelt on the concrete with bent arms upraised to protect their faces; the troopers hadn't gotten to them yet; in their padded green uniforms, with their glinting visors and black leather gauntlets, they were a real pride to Mr. White, aside from the fact that they had fat thighs. Back by the fence, golden-badged deputies were dragging some women away by the hair. – Bug studied this scene, hating and pitying no one anymore; his eyes bulged out painlessly and prismed into a billion compound lenses; and he could see the sunlight in a hard rainbow glitter on uncounted hexagonal images of the police cars; and the blood pulsed behind his eyes, suffusing every picture with red and gold and scarlet; and now he could see the dead cells of squamous epithelium on the skin of his hand, filling up the whole world; and the secret tree-cells became manifest to him like cool cork-lined chambers where he could rest and drink the maple-milk or chew on fragrant gooey crystals of pine gum; and the earplugs tingled and tingled as they continued to adjust his physiology to insect specifications so that he could hear every little gasping sigh of the people being clubbed; he listened conscientiously to these sounds, to the whacks and thuds and gurglings, to his insect-heart orchestrating fast and black and trembly in the strings of his chest; for he was someone who tended to sensitivity. Many bugs are like that, my best beloved; and it is said that the reason it is so hard to squash a cockroach is that it pays attention, not to mention the fact that it can see over the entire surface of its body besides.

Between missions, for expediency's sake, he made friends with individual insects and insect colonies, stepping over logs and dodging raspberry-prickers to find the greenish puddles where larvae lived, and in the puddles little orange slugs lay also, so fat and still and happy, just sucking in nutrients and thinking about the long summer ahead, not knowing that they would be eaten by birds or sold for bait at half a cent apiece; everybody recognized Bug and came and crawled on the back of his hand as long as he had the earplugs in, so he'd exchange greetings the same way a politician kisses babies, and then he'd go look for more bugs in the woods; and sometimes as he walked he would come into firm moss-banks so that his feet would sink into them like teeth into a honeycomb, and those places were treasuries of bugs. They taught Bug many stings and subterfuges, such as how to steal venom from spiders, how to suck and bite properly, and how to make oneself resemble a stick or leaf. – Returning from each rendezvous, he always washed his hands in rose-water to remove telltale insect-wax; and in a secret ledger he kept classifications of every wing-case which he brushed from his coat, so that he could commit to memory explicit denials of meetings with those species. Truly one cannot be too careful. – Pale and stoop-shouldered, he went his way, a true brother to beetles. – At the same time, his superiors set into motion certain far-reaching plans, just as Mr. White and Dr. Dodger had done.

THE BUGS INFILTRATE EVERYWHERE

~~~~~~

> The weapon is to be considered as loaded and cocked (ready to be fired) until the shooter has personally convinced himself of the contrary by discharging the weapon.
>
> Instruction manual for the combat pistol
> Sig-Sauer P 226 (1983)

Within the confines of our Republic is to be found every mode of social exchange, from the primeval barbarism of the logging villages, where people worship blocks of wood and the trees shimmer in the exhalations of the great power-saws, the fumes and noise of which make the entire region throb in deep, regular pulsations like the orgasms of carnivorous blossoms; and at the side of the freeway you can buy redwood burls and roasted tree-hearts to give your children strength, and the steel teeth of the mills rip and grind the logs and shaggy stalks and spiky leaves of miscellaneous plant matter into newspapers reporting the latest activities of Mr. White's gem-detectors; from this primitive scenic mode, as I was saying, to the modern social relations of the city, where workers consciously recognize themselves as participants in world politics, and keep close tabs on events in the Balkans and debates in polar Reichstags, and the intelligentsia stores its insights on the surfaces of these here revolving decay-proof record scrolls.

Permit me my sole digression of this book. In Australia the termites build ten-foot mounds in which they carry on gnawing social activities – or maybe they have thirty-foot mounds, I forget which; but the point is that as you roll along in your Land Rover watching the dust settle in your pores and everything's brillig in the billabong, you notice the mounds from some distance since they are so tall, which means that unlike with those sneaky Pete aborigines you can keep an eye on their possibly subversive activities, and if the joint military exercises of soldier termites ever became too suspicious or if you needed the area to make a ranch out of you could monitor and ghettoize and destroy it like your father did before you to other sectors. But in our territory the bugs all hide under old leaves. One square foot of New England forest soil contains umpety-ump quadrijillion organisms, of which a significant number are insects. Oh, dear, green mantises, with your alert eye-bulges, your arms hugged in against yourselves like schoolgirls carrying their books, your wings capillaried like leaves, your sensitive necks and exquisite stalking motions, how I love you, and how I would love to set up a woodland reservation for you so that no one could hurt you and meanwhile we could have access to your predatory ranges of camomile blossoms and stick habitats for the purpose of keeping our afore-mentioned primitive logging villages busy. Oh, dearest beetles blue-spotted and orange-dotted, huddled together in the Christmas ferns and cinnamon ferns when it rains, stolid and solid in your shells which you think so much of (I could crush any of you between two fingers), may I sell your ferns away? I'll give you all the chopped meat you want, and treat you like kings and queens. Oh, ants, my sisters, good old honeydew-seekers! From close up you are sticky and shiny and gristly; and your nymphs have parasitic red mites stuck to them. You are too intent upon your chewing and gathering to listen to me, but I tell you that despite my warm feelings I really do not like you, and I cannot feel sorry for you in any way because there are too many of you and you are not cute at all. You eat too much of my forests; you are a rebellious tribe, and I will destroy you; I will poison your nests with sweet-smelling traps.

The bugs were infiltrating everywhere. Our liberals argued that it was not their fault because they were only doing it instinctively, not as part of a rational cold-ichorous plan, but in this world you judge by results, not intentions. In the twice-discussed logging towns, where life was cruder and more epic, the motivated observer stood some chance of seeing the big ones, the true backwoods wonders, whereas in our cities they hid themselves cunningly . . .

"Brace yourself!" cried my dentist. "I'm about to break through." My gums hummed somberly with the vibration; there was the stink of burning enamel, and the dentist leaned all his weight on the drill to help it past the last defenses of extreme calcification while I gripped the vinyl arm-rests in suspense . . . Crunch! The tooth shattered. Nerves dangled there helplessly, unstrung. The bright yellow dentin dribbled mushily to the napkin under my chin. It was stupendous.

"Believe we got that one just in time," my dentist muttered with satisfaction. And he squashed the little renegade opportunist beetles trying frantically to hide themselves under another tooth. "Go ahead and rinse out your mouth," he told me. I leaned forward, drank from the paper cup, and spat into the little white bowl in which the threads of blood whirled furiously . . .

Our organizations were under intermittent attack from the insect world. It became evident that a ruthless assault was being prepared.

THE OREGON BAR, OR,
THE SECOND LABOR OF WAYNE

When the pressure's on, Unimax snap-acting switches always
come through.

Unimax ad (1984)

"Aw-RIGHT!" Wayne raged. He'd just about had it. In the night
you may wake up in your smelly bed itching, and you scratch and
scratch and you think you feel something scuttling down your leg in
a panic, but if you get up and flip the light switch, then after your
eyeballs shrivel and ache with the brightness you look around and
see the purple welts on your body, and you shake the bedclothes
and look under the mattress, but everything is innocent. You try
to persuade yourself that maybe the welts are the result of your
scratching yourself in your sleep in a nightmare about being eaten
alive by green-faced pincers, and you turn out the light and pull the
sheets back over you and lie there until finally your headache begins
to recede, and then you realize that you have to get up and take a
leak, so you've got to haul yourself out of bed again, and then finally
back you are and you're warm and drowsy and you pull the covers
back up to your chin, and dream of clean fences and walled-in parks,
and then suddenly here they are again, tickling and chuckling as they
bite you on the ear ... Things had gone much like this for old
Wayne, for whenever he tried to find the bugs and infiltrate their
network there wasn't a sign of it; it was like Vietnam again – you
couldn't tell the harmless domestic slave bugs from the gook-
crawlers that were out to get you. "Awright," Wayne muttered
tensely to himself, "you bugs just wait till I bait your fucking
anttraps ..."

The trick was to find their tunnel systems or whatever they used,
something like the extensive, heavily funded Soviet defense system,
maybe, including blast and fallout shelters, crisis evacuation plans,

and extensive instinctive programs; or the dual-use, deep-rock shelters of Norway and Sweden. For then he could destroy the Great Beetle himself.

Wayne was on his way to Oregon, which they told him was the most bug-ridden state in the Union. He got a long ride out of Amarillo with the political agents of the world stock exchange and then hopped a freight to Laramie, Wyoming. Here everyone had a cowboy hat and a pearl-handled revolver. It was dusty. Seeing no signs of enemy activity, Wayne gritted his teeth and hung tight because that was all that he could do, but boy was he in good shape; he was just full of sap and his muscles were big; he was just aching for a little exercise. Well, he'd show them when he got to Oregon and then nobody but NOBODY (except maybe Parker and Mr. White) would dare to stand in his way; and when you can't go round the roadblocks there's nothing to do but hit 'em hard at a hundred miles an hour. Damned fucking bugs. He hitched to Oregon.

Perhaps you would like to know why.

Oh, my friends! On every side our great Republic has its enemies; and our only hope lies in frenzied preparations and retaliatory measures.

Dull dependable Earl (remember him, out selling electricity back in Kentucky in the 'twenties?) developed the radial tire as a spin-off of the tank tread. Mr. White, having now been, as we have seen, called back from the Arctic into the reserves, kept abreast on the progress of his graduates, as he had promised, and at night he sat in the office entering all the ticks and checks and black marks on line using the new Apple software; so when the radial tire was unveiled Mr. White sent Earl his warmest congratulations crackling with the most colorful and friendly oaths in the world. This made Earl very happy in his trailer park; he now had lumbago, being in his very late sixties; it would not be long before some Commanche virus tomahawked this old pioneer. He subscribed to *American Opinion* and the racing news, but still he worked because he knew that he had to work until he died or else Mr. White would get him. Of course the fear was just a reminder because he *was* dependable and would have seen his duty anyhow, especially since Mr. White had taken a generous interest in his success – of which, alas, there had been none too much in Earl's life, though Earl had not minded that, asking nothing more than to make a plump living off the blue globes, and he had done it, too; the trailer was his free and clear; so Earl signed over the radial tire rights to Mr. White of his own accord, as was expected of him, so Mr. White deleted three of Earl's worst black marks from random access memory. – Now, reflected Mr. White, researchers could come up with a super-duper dune buggy with special wheels to transport assault troops when the time came to contest the installations of Phil Blaker on Mars, where the red-brown dunes were a thousand feet high and you had to chug, chug, chug slowly up, gasping in the thin purple air even if your respirator were adjusted; Phil Blaker made better ones for his laborers but to date Mr. White's agents had not been able to export any for study. Sitting in a mahogany rocking chair in *his* office, reading over the day's report on conversation concerning him which had been overheard at the Society of Daniel, Phil Blaker saw that one of the reactionary functionaries had said excitedly, "You know what he does? He'll see something that he likes, like that respirator, and BANG! – you'll see it all over his planet." – "Horse piss," said Phil Blaker softly. – In fact, however, this was true.

Earl meanwhile decided to go to a bar in Seven Sisters, Oregon, where they knew him, and buy a round for everybody to celebrate the fact that Mr. White had for once been satisfied. Hurray for Earl! Everyone was nice to Earl there because he bought the drinks at least once a week, though he did have gold in his teeth, silver in his hair and lead in his ass these days, old scrawny huffety-puffety Earl, the biological clock now winding down, tick, tick, tick, skip. Professionally Earl was a disappointment to Mr. White; aside from frivolous consumer products he had produced little of real value to the upper echelons and inch-alongs, but at least he did have friends. – The bugs got wind of his presence somehow from their chirring spies in the sawdust, and they kidnapped Earl, they did, as he was stumbling home alone, drunk and sobbing (for Earl was never a sparkling personality like Lawrence Welk, and after he had bought drinks every man ignored him until the next handout; they had a saying in Seven Sisters: "That's a good one," they'd crack when someone told a joke that wasn't funny, "about as entertaining as Earl," and then at least somebody would get a laugh; for Earl was now no more full of intrinsic interest than a ball of string. So Earl was soon relegated to silence at the bar, and if he ventured a remark some well-meaning neighbor would clap a hand over Earl's mouth); they kidnapped him, as I was saying, a cloud of midges suddenly blowing out of the darkness and whirling round him tighter and tighter by the billions until he couldn't see or breathe or even tell up from down; and then they whirled him away to be food for grubs or maybe to suffer an even worse fate. – This was the first setback for the Society of Daniel.

Hence Wayne's mission in Oregon.

So here he was in Dorris, Californiyay, just two or three miles from the state line and thus already within the probable danger zone, so Wayne was tense and on full alert and darted quick glances all around ready to hit out and have his belt knife leap into his hand for fast trench action with the blood gutters. But everything was hot and quiet. He stuck out his thumb standing there clean and brave in his Merchant Marine uniform (though knowing all the time in heart of cartoon hearts that he never woulda gotten into the Society of Daniel, not being *brainy* enough for all that engineering static and circuitous circuitry razzle-dazzle, though he could sure as hell operate whatever they built, WITH or WITHOUT their egghead manuals, just like he was an applications engineer or something, and of course *he* never woulda let himself be caught with his coveralls down like that Earl guy, neither . . .) – And now came some hippie longhair rattletrap gearing down to the shoulder for him; probably no rose garden in there but what the shit, it was a ride; Wayne was ready. He hoisted his duffel to shoulder position and double-timed himself warily over to the van, which was not black and spiderwebbed inside the windows so at least it wasn't one of them tarantula traps that rode around on the highways and stopped for hitchers and the door creaked open all by itself like you were entering a haunted house and when you got in it was all dark and there was nobody there and the door clanged shut behind you and then as the lorry ghosted along at twenty miles per, hardly a quiver of recognition on the old speedometer, big black spiders came out from underneath the seat cushions and got you. Nope, this was K.O. on the O.K.; here came the weirdo beardo him fucking self to look Wayne over and stretch and open up the back; a scraggly fella, he was; Wayne could take him if he had to, and anyhoo he must be one of the unwashed armpit liberals that never even carried a side-arm. – Wayne slung the duffel in tensely and slammed the hatch. "Thank you, sir!" he snapped out as crisp and correct as he could stand under the circumstances of being indebted to this flagrant yahoo hedonist, but would you believe it, the guy just scratched his beard and laughed. –"Well, all right," he said to Wayne, kindly enough, "sit down and relax, and take a beer from the cooler if you want. You sure ain't my type but I felt sorry for ya standing like a tin-hat barber pole in the sun." – Wayne glowered at this and flexed his big ivory fingers that never tanned and ran a hand through his sandy hair and grinned so long and tight and narrow his mouth sparkled like a lethal zipper, but he got in and popped the tab on a beer and

even sorta mellowed after fifty miles, sitting straight and silent in the
back among all the old clothes and Mr. Fixit tools and various
human stinks mixed up with the smell of an old fleabag cat that kept
trying to make up to Wayne but Wayne wasn't about to have any of
that and when the cat kept bothering him he waited until the leftist
driver was busy with the road for a minute and then he caught the
cat's head between his knees and suffocated it and snapped its neck
for good measure though he sure knew enough to fake a cough to
hide the snapping sound. Now awright! – here he was in Seven
Sisters and the driver extended a hand to Wayne but Wayne was
damned if he would shake it. Fucking pinko asshole. He got his stuff
out fast and closed the cargo door hard and sure and was off down
the road in his tormented compulsion that made him such a valued
citizen of our great Republic, always ready and impatient to do the
necessary.

Now what he sure wanted was a good fuck because he had
heard how those Oregon girls generally had a streak of the old
aborigine in their desert blood and when you went up and down on
a backwoods missy if nothing happened it sure as hell wouldn't be
her fault. So Wayne decided, he did, to mosey on down to the
Oregon Bar and look around and listen in to get some clues about
Earl and maybe accomplish his second labor but also pick something
up while he was at it. It was all summery and peaceful here with
pines and aspens shaking their leaves for him like beautiful girls as
he came up the road. He ducked into the trees for a second and took
a dump; and then he sat on the side of the road and unhooked the
flap of his duffel and reached in past the neatly folded clothes and
bug dictionaries to pull out his three secret weapons, all designed by
ole Doc Dodger in the Munitions Corps and for exclusive use in
insect territory only, absolutely no exceptions. Here was a gizmo
that looked like a cigarette lighter but when you flicked the wheel
it sent out this sticky spray that stuck bugs' wings and antennae
together and burned its way in with acid insecticide oils; and this
here collapsible pool cue had a hidden stud in the grip that looked
like a wood knot, but it sure as taxes wasn't because when you
pushed it the cue stick would fire half a dozen lightweight needle-
nosed thirty-two dum-dums full of Krupp surplus Zyklon B
(which was originally tested, after all, as a delousing gas); and
then finally he had him an aphrodisiac cocktail swizzler that made
him irresistible to women, but it was to be used for intelligence-
gathering purposes only. – Yeah, sure, Wayne said to himself, in a
very good humor.

He found a creek that was clear, and splashed water over his face and neck and hands, and washed his hair, and had a good drink, and once he was finished with that there stream he pissed in it.

Around dusk Wayne pal ambles into town, his duffel hidden in the woods, surrounded by electronic boobytraps. Here was the bar, the door propped open all right, and it was dark and noisy inside. Somewhere nearby, Wayne could smell the bitter, waxy odor of bugs. – Awright, you horrors, Wayne thought tensely; you just wait till I find you and stomp yer crunchy shells and mush up yer green guacamole gushy insides for what you did to Earl ... and he sauntered up to the bar and sat on a free stool with an empty one next to it, and had him a Mariner's Delight, which is to say eight ounces of Barbados rum, a touch of salt water, a twist of lemon peel, and a raw oyster on the side. – Mmmm – mmm – *mmmh!* That was pretty good, reminds me of the taste of wild hickory nuts, and though he sensed the bugs gathering behind him in the gloomy shadows by the poolroom, he had another one; and he stuck his middle finger in the glass and shoved it in and out of his drink, which is how you summon whores in the Merchant Marine.

Due to the creeping communist zoning laws of the state, the bar stood discreetly on the edge of town like a big two-storey outhouse or no-account barn peeping out of the deergrass and mosswort and bloodweed and carrion-flowers. (The second storey was where the whores took you.) To get there you turned away from the imbecilic gapes of rotting boarded-up houses that smelled of rot and cool shade, and went down the highway a quarter-mile till you came to a little gravel parking lot in the trees, much like the visitor vehicle storage facilities at the bait stands throughout our majestic northwest; and then you walked down a muddy path full of stagnant puddles that had polliwogs and clumps of bloody beer-spit floating around and daphnae larvae and caddis-bugs watching everything that moved so that they could report to their superiors in the organization; and then you came to a long narrow porch sort of like a dock that went crick-crack under your feet in order to give fair warning to the other patrons that you were coming, assuming that they were listening, which is exactly what shrewd Wayne was doing now on his stool because he wasn't about to take any lousy sneaking ambush-bug or pillbox-spider shooting paralysis-threads from behind all the old cobwebbed bottles of Ron Rico and Jim Beam and Irish Mist and Dr. Dodger's Ancient Age; so that Wayne was alert and informed *vis à vis* the incoming regulars, crick-crack, creaketycrickety; here came Joe-John Skophammer and No-Good Hank and Eugene Stoddard and Custis the trucker who stopped in every Thursday night, which it now was. – Not everyone knows that Thursday night is the riskiest time to be in a bar because Friday and Saturday nights are just cheap surface show with maybe a couple of crying drunks and fights and pukings in the sawdust and voices raised high in hymns of emotion, just like at the Greyhound stop; but on Thursday only the committed regulars are there, and they do what they do on Thursday, delving into pagan rituals of worship to the amber gods that let you see to the lurching anger that spins you round and round at the center of things beyond lines and angles and the very floorboards become crazy under your feet so that the floor goes YAAAWW up again down again and suddenly *tunk!* it hits you on the forehead and your nose bleeds and you cling to it so that you don't begin to slip down it and fetch up against the wall where you were dancing before with all the women in your life who have now vanished and left you alone here and the swaying candelabra are like careening galaxies burning into the back of your head; you don't dare to roll over on your back and look straight into all those stars or you will be blinded; and from the cool floor and the smell of your own puke you gain more and more understanding of the universe; and the jukebox goes ba-*doom*, ba-*doom* in the rhythms of life and No-Good Hank keels over beside you and has the wet heaves on your ankle; you suddenly realize that THE FRENCH REVOLUTION WAS A REAL *COUP DE GRÂCE* and you have all kinds of other profound insights along these lines; some faggot with a cadaverous face like the Pillsbury Dough-Boy after fifty years is bending over you rubbing your fly and you turn your head and open one bloodshot eye at him and he winks and goes, "*Parlez-vous français?*" and you scrape up your strength to roar, "*JE NE COMPRENDS PAS RIEN!*" and feel good fellowship towards him and all your mates; and he unzips your fly and spits on your dick just before you pass out; anyhow, this is Thursday, the night of signs; where all that is rich and true is done so that the outsiders, the superficial Friday night drinkers that have a quick one after a week in their dusty offices and hayseed warehouses where nothing happens to no purpose, will never learn the secrets of the real drinker's life.

So presently the Oregon Bar was three-quarters full, which is about right for a Thursday, and then in their own sweet time came the mincing *click*-creak, *click*-creak of high heels as the mercenary lovelies arrived with their painted eyes and smeary painted lips and black wraps and long black stockings. – "Hi, girls!" everybody said, brightening up like the moon rising over a construction trench; as the whores hung up their black wraps and stood around for a minute by the coat rack in their black dresses adjusting each other's bra straps out of professional courtesy and picking out their prey and squeezing their nipples like a nurse popping the bubble out of the syringe just before the injection . . . – Pretty high-class hookers, you may be thinking, for what is essentially a foggy little town among the redwood burls and afore-mentioned bait stands; but that's just how it was, and, besides, I have found that just as city whores like to come on sometimes as pure country girls, just to ease the boredom (another distraction of theirs is to talk pure poetry like when you walk in and they're lying on the unmade bed with their nighties up to their knees they yawn and open one eye and say, "Warn me when you take your shorts off so I can cover my face because your ass is sure uncomely"), so the country pumpkin-headed cornholes get some cheap sophistication to deceive us into thinking that they fuck important blue globes every night when how could they because they are so isolated and insulated and dumb; not that these were bad ladies because they were no worse than Wayne or Bug and maybe even better because there weren't so many people in the neighborhood to drag them down by their bra straps and rape them and punch them and defile the sheets of the bed and then maybe grab the table lamp before they leave and smash it over the women's heads; still and all there were men who had to be considered regular Larrys even though they rattletrapped from as far away as Chainsaw or Big Tree or Crawdad Bend. Things got even better for the bar and for the whores once the men had piled in and it started raining, as it generally did, this being Oregon; and then their pickups got stuck in that muddy parking lot better than you woulda gotten glued inside the stickiest of them whores; not even two come-along winches could have freed the wheels; and the mud got softer by the minute and the wheels sank deeper and then the rain *really* started; in short, there was no way that they could get home to Big Tree, so they might as well stay over at the bar a spell and maybe go upstairs to get their rockets polished and pretty soon everyone downstairs would hear the ceiling creak in different tempos in different places, and everyone would make jokes and wonder if it was rotten enough to break and kill the whole bunch, and laugh and shoot some pool and have a great time. Oooooo-*wee!*

The bartender was a fine distinguished mantis standing thin and alert and flexible with all the green grace of his species; it was very dark in there, and he never said anything, and the previous bartender (whom Mantis had killed and devoured) had never said anything, either, just pointed dryly to the cash register to indicate the amount owed for prior happiness; so nobody noticed the transition to new management; and anyhow Mantis conveyed an impression of sympathetic as opposed to apathetic acceptance and knew what was wanted and mixed very adequate drinks. The whores were nervous around him because he never pawed them or gestured for freebies like his predecessor when they gave him his share of their take (which the bugs used to buy anti-insecticide chemicals), just stared at them with his piercing bulgy eyes on either side of his green head. So the ceiling creaked and the toilet flushed and the cistern overflowed out back and life went on.

"Hey there, stranger," says unwholesome Carla, coming on to Wayne (she especially goes for men in uniform), "where ya shipped in from?"

"One Buttercup for the lady," says Wayne with a wink, "and I'll try the Redwood Special." – The Buttercup was a yellow treacly liqueur made from old cough medicine; it came in a frosted daiquiri glass and had a wilted daisy floating on the top like scum. It was a myth of the region that women, being sweet, liked only sicky-sweet mixes, and one of the hardest aspects of Carla's job was having to sip at a dozen of the damned things every night, but that was Zen capitalism for you; you had to not desire what you got in order to have it, and at least Mantis knew enough to water it down and keep the alcohol out and credit her with a percentage of what was saved. – The Redwood Special was the most expensive drink that money could buy (though of course Wayne could put it on the Military Intelligence Travel Account). This creation was served in a wooden mug a foot in diameter and three feet tall; and looked just like borscht, and I'm damned if I know what was in it. It took a real man to finish it. Many a time the regulars had had a good show when some out-of-stater came in off the highway trying to prove himself, and before he could drink more than an inch of the Special he was down for the count and woke up in the woods next to the parking lot with blood on his shoes and his wallet gone. But Wayne was precisely the real man it took, and he drained the mug DEAD in two swallows and put his hand on Carla's knee real smooth and steady like he was about to test a jet plane, so the regulars made a place for him in their bumpkin hearts and assumed that he was an Oregon man. "Ohh, you're really the works," coos Carla and pecks him on the cheek while the entire bar roars with approval: "You're ALL

RIGHT, young fella!"; and Carla squinches her pretty little butt into Wayne's lap and says in his ear, "Usually I charge a dollar a kiss, and an extra fifty cents for tongue, but you can French me for nothing because I can see you're special, sailor-boy," and Wayne's feeling full of pride; why, he could almost be back in Cooverville; these folks are swell; for Wayne has not taken the lesson to heart that it was precisely such impulses toward spurious fellowship which seduced Earl to his bad end. – "Uncork me a Yodeler!" cries Wayne, "an' another Buttercup fer my girlfriend here!" – "M-m-m-m," says Carla, swallowing her nausea at the thought of *another* one when she can hardly choke down a sip of the first, but fortunately Mantis picks up her almost imperceptible signal of distress; he's the most sensitive bartender that Seven Sisters has ever had; and he whisks away the almost untouched drink in his piously clasped hands, pouring it back into the joygirl decanter from which he solemnly mixes her another. – "M-m-m-m," says Carla again automatically, bored out of her mind with this sullen Navy lunk, but business is business and maybe if he's on shore leave his back pay will be burning a hole in his wallet; "how sweet of you," she says, and now here comes Wayne's Yodeler, which is presented in a wide dish and celebrates our interpretation of Swiss pastoral values: blueberry ice cream soaked in crème de menthe and brandy, with a huge Alp of whipped cream and a cherry on top! Mantis, who for his own reasons is anxious that Carla get Wayne upstairs, has mischievously squeezed out the whipped cream in the shape of two Alps rather than one, and a cherry on each; the Grand Tetons; and this bit of subtle suggestion does its work; for as Carla squirms sensuously in Wayne's lap (Mantis has already whisked her second Buttercup away and poured it back into the decanter), he slides his hand up her underpants and says, "Awright, girlie, where's the hole in *your* Swiss cheese?" and the whole bar cracks up at this (except for Natalie and Georgette, who are jealous), and Carla, who is beginning to hate this jerk, smiles drolly (her makeup is running from where Wayne kissed her) and whispers in his ear so that her hot sugary breath tickles his eardrum: "What you just did cost you five, sailor-boy, so why not shell out twenty-five more and get the whole story?" – Mantis brings Carla another Buttercup and Wayne some obscure Oregon aperitif made out of fox blood. It's very dim in there, and the chandelier that does at least let Wayne think he sees Carla's nipples through her black silk blouse begins to lurch crazily as Georgette finally gets some guy to march upstairs with her and the ceiling creaks and the long spiky shadow cast by the chandelier swerves back and forth out of true. To tell you the truth, Wayne's head is beginning to spin a little like that anyhow; he has been derelict in his responsibilities by having so much to drink for the sake of mass approval; and it is catching up with him finally, for even a superhuman physique such as Wayne's cannot process an infinite amount of alcohol. – Mantis, who has been watching Wayne closely out of one bulbous eye, is beginning to suspect that this might be yet another of Mr. White's boys; for what else would a stranger in uniform be doing here, like one of the reactionary Redcoats in Lexington to whom all the local yokels look the same, Whig or Tory; really, it was very careless of Wayne not to come here in plain clothes; on his shoulder epaulette is the insignia of a blue sphere emitting a spark; that's the giveaway. – Mantis reaches under the bar while washing glasses and semaphores with his thin brittle arms to his familiar, a sleek evil cricket that immediately springs into the sawdust and makes its way, avoiding the giant heavy work boots that stomp and kick amidst all the booming laughs, to alert the shock troops outside . . .

Wayne sways at the bar, and Carla is beginning to get concerned. The kickback on three drinks is not going to pay her rent. In Wallace, Idaho when you go to a whorehouse and pick out your woman for that twenty-minutes (and you do this by sitting at the bar with a whiskey, watching them parade around in bathing suits, and you go for Number Six) she will give you a book of matches with her name on it so you can show it around for a souvenir with the boys. So the boys come in to meet their matches; it's a good business trick; but out in primitive Oregon poor Carla has never heard of any such thing, so she's in trouble. Things don't look good for her, either in the long run or in the short haul; she hasn't managed to save much; as a whore it's awfully hard to save anything; you have to look nice, and you have to buy things to make you feel nice so you can stand it when the Larrys think they're "entertaining" you. Yes, it's a rough life, and ultimately a self-sacrificing one; were we to follow Carla's career we would eventually find her dead and twisted at the foot of some Oregon embankment. – Meanwhile in a corner booth No-Good Hank has been watching the progress of Wayne's intoxication with equal interest; he thinks he might be able to make a little money off him at pool. Wayne of course doesn't know that this is the infamous No-Good Hank that his grandmother warned him against long ago when he was a squirt; he just sees some old guy who keeps turning around at the table and giving Wayne a hard look and shooting out a forefinger at Wayne like he's telling Wayne to leave or get fucked or something. Wayne nods at him peaceably enough, 'cause he plans to do both in due time, and besides who knows what forces the guy might have in cahoots with him ready to come to his rescue if Wayne punches his gourd. Maybe this is Earl's murderer, says Wayne to himself; the thought sends parasympathetic tingles and blue chills down Wayne's spine. – And the fella keeps turning around in his booth and pointing at Wayne. Finally he motions Mantis over, murmurs something, and jerks his forefinger at Wayne. Mantis scuttles up to Wayne with another round; this one's on Hank. – So that's all it was, thinks Wayne; he was just trying to be friendly. The guy raises a clenched fist at Wayne and grins, so Wayne does the same back, feeling pretty good about life generally. – And Mantis slides another drink apiece to Wayne and Carla across the counter; Wayne can't see what's in the shot glass too good now; mebbe it's a Blue Tartar or a Sally Marie or a Goldrush Freeze all sparkling with shiny yellow bits of frozen fermented caramel like King Midas's turds but for all he can tell it might just be a Herbert Hoover which is nothing but tap water with a couple drops of rubbing alcohol; whatever it is he gulps it saying awright but he scarcely tastes it; oh Mason oh Dixon is he in trouble.

Carla had thighs like needle-nosed pliers and was pretty enough for a country lass who bathed in pure spring water and had buck teeth because to be a good whore you have to be at least sort of pretty so that grace is added to the john's life, but of late she had been having various problems and now she barely made the grade in that department. The Oregon Bar was good for her that way because it was so dark; she knew that and owned up to it because if she didn't she'd be in for it. Anyhow, she knew that she had to take Wayne upstairs fast to make anything on him; she could never get away with picking his pocket, not with Natalie giving her that sour stare hoping to catch her breaking the unwritten rules of the rural trade . . . and *shit* here came No-Good Hank all bald and ruined with his fishy eyes zipping hither and yon like minnows trying to escape from a frying pan . . .

"Hey, Marine," says No-Good Hank, hitching up his pants with a thumb well used to picking and poking at things, "how about if you and me shoot out a game and stake a little bait and tackle on it, like five dollars a point?"

"Awright," says Wayne, jaw muscles hardening and flicking *thibber-thibber-thib*; "awright, but you'd better watch your step with me because I don't play for anything but victory." – In the darkness, even Mantis, who is ordinarily immune to amusement, whisks his feelers across his dangerous green jaws to cover up a silent contemptuous insect laugh at this blusterer; and Joe-John snickers so loud that Two-Bit Tim has to push his face in his beer.

Silently Mantis hands Hank the key to the poolroom, in exchange for a dollar each from the two opponents; Hank unlocks the door and throws it open and turns on the light so Wayne can see the warped three-legged vaguely quadrilateral pool table with all of its green felt long since gone to green mold. – "Awright!" says Wayne with a snort (and he clutches at the door-jamb for support, feelin' his legs go a mite rubbery). "If you think I can't bust through this dumb setup you're gonna be out for the fucking count. And I s'pose the balls are ostrich eggs incubatin' down on the farm?" – No-Good Hank grins and winks back at his friends, who are holding their sides. "Here they are, pard," he tells Wayne gently, bringing them up from under the table in their shoebox; and funny to say they do look like eggs, like hardboiled Easter eggs dipped in coloring and now the shells are zigzagged with cracks and missing bits but still clinging to the tough sticky wobbly albumen lining (and the eight-ball is actually a bug-egg of some kind; and one of these days Mantis plans to roll it under the bar and fertilize it with his own jizzum and let all the horrors inside it loose).

"Great!" says Wayne with rare sarcasm (he has picked up a few rhetorical tricks from Mr. White). "Just fine! You're gonna be so sorry you messed with me, buddy, so don't try anything phony or I'll find you out and *then* you won't bounce back laughing . . ."

Poor Carla, abandoned like the tinsel on last year's Christmas tree, checked her makeup in her compact mirror (she had, like many whores, superlative night vision; although call girls can just rely on an organized memory of where they lay their clothes every time when the light goes out and where the rubbers are in the purse, &c), repaired her lips with her cocktail napkin, and gave Wayne the finger behind his back. Then there was nothing for it but to slink off to Eugene Stoddard the real estate man who always took exactly six minutes and never tipped her. Stoddard was such a miser that when he saw her coming over he yelled out, "Hey, stranger, won't you even buy the lady a drink for her trouble?" – This appeal touched Wayne to the quick, and he staggered back and folded in his forefinger at Mantis so that Mantis slipped another Buttercup for Carla down next to Eugene Stoddard, and Carla was disgusted as hell and punched Wayne in the mouth, but he just laughed and said, "A round for everybody!" and wrote his name up on the chalk-board, with "ONE FOR ALL AND ALL FOR ONE" underneath it, and all the men and their whores went wild and cheered so loud they really stank up the place, and Mantis became somewhat agitated with greed and began to calculate how many saw-teeth he could solder to his mouth-parts for that money. – Meanwhile No-Good Hank had laid out the balls in that triangular array to which civilized persons are accustomed the world over, and popped a pair of bow-bent pool cues from the rack, and called to Wayne, "Well, sir, will you break?"

Grandly Wayne strode AW-RIGHT! to the table and studied the layout of its bumpy seamy surface (it looked like an aerial view of Arctic tundra mountains), and noted the weird irregularly spaced pockets worse than miniature golf in Lapland where a careless stroke could send the cue ball to go a-chuckling and a-bumping down twisty sinister pipes; and Wayne took the ridiculous cue stick that Hank had picked out for him and broke it over his knee. From his shirt pocket he drew a dollar-piece and winged it back toward the bar to compensate Mantis, who scuttled frenetically to catch it in his jaws and just made it, which was a good thing, too, or one or the other of his old liqueur bottles full of whey and bile and rotten sugar crystals would have smashed for sure. – Now Wayne unclipped his magic telescoping cue from his belt and opened it up until it waved straight and true like a bamboo fishing pole. He hunkered down at the end of the table and took aim with the rubber stock of the cue firm against his shoulder and squinted along the length of the stick and moved a hundredth of a step right and a thousandth of a step left so that this No-Good and No-Account Hank could no way violate *his* strategy and pulled the stock up even tighter against his shoulder and lined up the cue-ball with his eye one last time and POW! Zonk! Kerclicketysmack! Clungle-ungle-ungle of four of Wayne's striped balls making the long journey to Hades . . .

"Aw-RIGHT!" Wayne screamed in ecstasy and chalked up another round for everyone, some kinda black foamy beer that tasted like it had been brewed by witches in some graveyard in Portland or Salem or someplace, but what the hell; you can't have everything; and once again as with one voice the regulars cheered Wayne: "MARINE, YOU'RE A HELL OF A MAN; YOU'RE GODDAMNED FUCKING ALL RIGHT!"

Meanwhile Mantis's cricket pal had called up a twilight army of midges and cold sluggish loathsome digger wasps, hiding half a dozen on the underside of every leaf in the whole forest just waiting for the barroom door to swing open as Wayne reeled outside so that they could get him. And No-Good Hank was stepping up to bat . . .

Hank's a grey-haired lanky guy who coulda been a machine

shop operator or warehouse inventory control supervisor if he had wanted to get on in life, but he prefers fleecing rutabaga-head ignoramuses like this here able seaman anyday, so Hank takes the chalk stick from behind his ear and rubs up the tip of his cue real good (while Wayne leans on the Dodger Stick like a Minuteman would) and chalks up his hands, too, and rests the cue on the raised edge of the table and moves the cue just a hair left, and half a hair right, and shifts his stance, and then begins to actually take a bearing on the cue-ball, let's see . . . he cocks his head and takes the cue off the table completely and rubs the back of his neck and takes up the cue again and aligns it exactly as planned (as all the while Wayne watches him just daring him to break any of the rules of pure gamesmanship established generations ago by Columbus when he first came to this territory) and Hank begins to slide the cue back and forth along the edge of the table like he's rubbing up against a woman; and then TWERNG! he connects with the cue-ball, which is hollow and echoes like a gong, and the cue-ball glinks into one of Hank's solids, which goes into the pocket, down, down, down under; so Hank gets another shot (Wayne coulda had another shot, too, but that's just not Wayne's style; Wayne believes in being gallant in all games of skill); and Hank blasts into a stunned crowd of solid balls and gets two more in; so Hank shoots again and the cue-ball pops in Hank's fourth solid but wavers on the edge of the pocket after it, almost going in, so Hank grits his teeth and thinks, Lordy, don't let that ball go down in that dark cave of doom and scratch my score because I kin make a lotta moola off this asshole; and the cue-ball, hearing Hank's prayer, teeters and teeters but finally rolls back onto the green; but now Hank is a mite extra cautious so he taps the cue-ball too gently in his next shot and it just barely clicks up against a solid. The score is now tied.

Well, well; it's our Wayne's turn again. "Now what would Parker think of me if I didn't whip this shit-face?" Wayne ruminates, keying himself up for action and equal and opposite reaction. "He'd be pretty disappointed, that's for sure; well, I won't stand for any bug-bugger trying to play pool with me with the world as the stakes, 'cause if he tries to cheat and show me up I just might run amok, do you hear me, Spiderman, I said AMOK!" and at this fine saying Wayne is highly pleased and invigorated, as if he had just drunk a bottle of prune juice early in the morning before going out for a jog, or as if he were getting strong by watching TV and doing pushups at every last commercial: "Now you too can have a compact disk in your very own living room and turn your pillow into your favorite race car, so get on the hot line to White Power & Light and send in your cash rebate," a-ONE, a-TWO! Wayne rests his cue alertly on the table's edge, ignoring the vertigo and pounding hammering pre-hangover blues that are beginning to get to him; he would actually like nothing better than to high-priority himself to the outhouse in back and heave, B-R-R-R-AAAAAAAACK!, but that's unthinkable during a game, so as the puke starts coming up and floods into Wayne's mouth, Wayne just swallows it back so no one will know the liquor's getting to him. Now he sees a forlorn striped ball off in center field of the green; he might as well take her home for the night, so he pulls back his cue so that the stock dimples into Wayne's hairy breast through the uniform and let's fly; FUCK! he MISSED; goddamn silverfish sonofaBITCH! – And all the regulars grin behind their hands. Their sympathies are ultimately with their own element.

Hank's set to make a killing now. From the way he stretches his scrawny neck one might almost fancy him a dangerous hissing mud-gator, lunging forward along the axis of its leathery throat. "What parta the state're ya from?" says he, guilefully distracting Wayne from noticing a professional trick. – Wayne stands straight and proud (or thinks he does). "I'm from Cooverville, Indiana, and PROUD of it!" he says decisively, not knowing that the worst possible thing to admit to in a bar in Oregon is to being out of state. But he's been around enough to sense the hardening silence and start sobering up fast, whoa-a-a-a, Nellie. – Hank sets down his pool cue slowly, goes to the chalk board and erases Wayne's name, writing in his own instead. – "Goddamn Hoosier," snarls Two-Bit Tim, "thinks he's good enough to buy us a drink . . ."

All the regulars push the girls off their laps and close in on Wayne. He leaps over the pool table and crouches in the corner and presses the knot of his pool stick, but nothing happens (for that is one problem with Dr. Dodger's inventions; they sometimes do not work). He jabs the cue stick deep into Hank's eye. Hank screams and falls. There are about eight of these Oregonians rushing at Wayne now; and he keeps them at a distance with sweeping blows of his cue, his *Nothung*, his deadly sword. Tim and Joe-John grab cues from the rack and thrust at Wayne's face, but Wayne's cue shatters theirs. The whores are all screaming abuse at him and Carla throws her Buttercup with punitive gusto; Wayne ducks and hears the glass smash where his head was; and his back and shoulders are sprayed with liquid. Foolhardy Eugene Stoddard comes creeping for him under the pool table, and boy does Wayne let him have it with a jackboot kick in the teeth! Stoddard's neck is broken clean. – This is Thursday night living! – "Now how the hell am I gonna get outta here?" says Wayne to himself. – All the whores are throwing bottles at him now; he can't duck every one; the glass is starting to cut him up, and he's drenched with liquor, and any minute something heavy is going to hit him on the forehead or they'll toss more brandy on him and pelt him with lit cigarettes until he turns into a fucking *flambeau* or something. – "YAAAAAAAAAAAAAAAAAH!" he yells and shoves the pool table up on its side as a sort of bulwark (thereby crushing the eight-ball egg forever, at which Mantis mourns). Is the filthy cunting breech mechanism jammed or WHAT? He whaps the cue hard against the edge of the table and attempts to fire again. Nothing happens. – Here come Two-Bit Tim and Joe-John again, and Custis the trucker is aiming a .44 magnum . . . In a rage Wayne bangs his cue against the table so hard that he leaves a dent; but at least a bullet dribbles out of the barrel; it's about time, Dodger, you and your foreign-built merchandise really give me the blues. ("I have heard nothing definite on this incident," said Dr. Dodger later when grilled by Mr. White on the mechanical failure, "but I have no reason to disbelieve the report at first glance, yes.") – Wayne throws the bullet up into the air and strikes at it hard with his cue stick so that it ignites and goes roaring across the room with a guided missile vapor trail and ricochets off Mantis's exoskeleton – WHEEEEET! – and comes back and takes Joe-John's skull off, Star Spangled Banner of blue and red and white brains in there, God bless the defenders of our great Republic; and indeed that Wayne must be given credit; he is quite a pool player with his calculations of trajectories and stuff. – "Awright, guys," says Wayne in a euphoria of venomous rage, "now we're in business for sure. I'm gonna give you till three to throw yourselves face down by the bar. "One . . ." – he whaps another bullet loose from his cue stick – "Two . . ." – he throws it up in the air – "THREE, you fucking sons of grasshopper bitches!" – and BOOM! he connects just like the first time; and here's the vapor trail again, and so much for poor old Custis! – Tim gets a whiff of gas and chokes and turns blue. – "Aw-right!" says Wayne, and vaults over the table and runs for it as Mantis twiddles feelers sickly at the damage . . .

Leaving his dead behind him as usual, Wayne does not realize that the swizzle stick (secret weapon number three) has fallen out of his pocket. – This will have important results later. – He gets outta there, at least – and here come the bugs to swoop and sting in the night, but he still has secret weapon number two, the lighter; and he snatches it from his other pocket and flicks the wheel, *sssssssssst!* Dead bugs drop in mid-flight and pelt him like maple seeds. — Hurrah! Another victory for Wayne!

RECOLLECTIONS OF OUR
REVOLUTIONARY WAR

~~~~~~

History will absolve me.

CASTRO
in his book of the same title

Wayne's goal remained the same in all his labors: Parker. To Parker
he had irrevocably dedicated himself, and for Parker he would die.
Yet Parker was not so easy to maintain orthogonal lines of
communication with; Parker was very stretchy and slippery indeed
in the darkness of the photo lab where he secreted himself these
days, and Wayne was barred from admission many a time, not being
authorized personnel and all, to say nothing of the fact he might let
the light in. So he had to make his own fun during those years of
waiting and intrigue, when the arming of the great Republic
continued covertly but the bugs and revolutionaries had not yet
provoked us sufficiently. Therefore Wayne fucked whores when he
could and drank a fair amount and kept up his target practice. It also
relaxed Wayne to listen to bluegrass on the radio like:

> Then she would be mah wife,
> Mah paradise fer life,
> But as it is I'm stuck in a blue globe hell . . .

– while he sat there at the controls of his insect monitoring device
(I.M.D.) gripping the plastic decibel switches tensely and grinding
his teeth; he liked group singing and he especially liked the way
women sang, for the high school choir blues band back in Cooverville had had many many angels; even Parker would go to listen
sometimes, drumming out the melody on his greenish knuckle-
bones, each of which emitted a different note; and when the singers
saw Parker coming they sang a little faster, too, so that the
bandmaster's baton had to wag a little faster to keep up, and Wayne

was in high spirits to see that here, too, it was Parker, Parker, Parker in command; also, the songs were great: golden oldies like "I Will Iwo Jima For You" or "Do the Trully-Hop"; Wayne boy was hooked, though he tried not to think of that stuff now because he couldn't afford to be distracted on his labors; a man who goes off to battle has got to leave all the artsy-fartsy stuff on the shelf, as it said somewhere in the Boy Scout Handbook, which Wayne remembered parts of to this day.

"Why hike?" asks the Handbook. (Little Wayne, back in Webelos, scratches his head at that one. — "To get out of the house, I guess.") — The answer follows at once, and it is GRAND and it is BOLD: "Because you are an American boy! Because roaming is in your blood and hiking gives you an outlet for your roving spirit." Wayne has never known this for sure before, but something about it rings true, and he catches his breath and reads on very fast: "The Revolutionary War was a hiker's war which was fought and won by hikers," and Wayne sees in his mind's eye great hiking figures of the past, like old Daniel Boone himself who slipped through the Kentucky forests with a thousand Injuns on his track to make it to Lexington with a very important message requesting an increase in the timber order for Mr. White, or Davy Crockett going a hundred miles easy to kill him a bear when he was only three, and hiking far into the brown wastes of Texas to die in combat against the Mexes; whoop-whoop-whoop; or stately white-haired George Washington assembling the swim team to cross the Delaware in perfect synchronized discipline (and here the Wayne of today can see only Parker, Parker, Parker at the helm, and Wayne is at his side, and their breaths puff out in a mist into the clear winter's night where everything is squeaky-cold like styrofoam; and Chip and Doug and everybody else stands crouched at the bank of the Delaware in swimming trunks, too cold to be affected by the subzero winds and the ice forming on their bare feet and hardening into stalagmites between their toes; and Wayne and Parker give the signal together and in silence and perfect unison the swim team slides out onto the ice on their naked bellies, but hark! what's this? they hear drunken singing: "*Der Kaiser feu-ert, bum-bum-bum!*"; it's the Hessians, Christmas Eve of seventeen-umpety-ump; time for evasive invasive action, that's as fucking sure as shooting; and each member of the team cuts a perfectly circular hole in the ice with his diamond-crystal Dick Tracy ring and slips into the cold black water and paddles along under the ice with cheeks bulging and toes going numb and so they swim across the Delaware and cut escape hatches in the ice with their rings and emerge to take the tipsy camp of the Hessians by storm and slit their throats, all 'cause Wayne gave the right signal at the right time, and now Wayne and Parker arrive in the ice-cutter flagship and commence bombardment of the enemy corpses, and Mr. White is aboard and he slaps Wayne and Parker on the back as Parker lets Wayne give the signal to fire the camp, there still being a couple of bullet-perforated tents flapping in the wind; and what a hellish glow of flame in the midnight wind! – and Mr. White says, "Good job, Parker! Good job, Wayne!") . . .

But Parker had other plans.

PARKER'S DISCOVERY

. . . if you suddenly see the bug staring you in the face, you're done.

JOHN F. WAKERLY
Microcomputer Architecture and Programming (1981)

During this time Parker continued to develop his powers. He was becoming increasingly introspective. He never even went down to the swimming pool anymore, because he had his basins of chemicals in which his hands could swim; and anyhow the thing about swimming is that once you enter the water the universe assigns you freedom to go in three dimensions instead of trudging one way or the other way upon the earth's weary crust; but these aquatic enhancements were no longer such a thrill for Parker because he was beginning to sense that he might be capable of forming himself into a multiplicity of shapes, thereby permitting him to do almost anything on land or sea. His political ambitions were both formless and limitless. When he was young he had flickered his tongue every time he smelled blood or salt, for those were happy days unalloyed by abstractions, when it was sufficient for Parker to lunge suddenly in his parents' home in Omarville (about which more in due time) to catch the rodents that lived under the stairs, and then he'd suck their juices and feel pleased. At Cooverville he learned that this was not considered pro-social behavior; and even Wayne, so loyal to Parker in all matters, would gag and turn away when he saw Parker do stuff like that because Parker did weird things sometimes that Wayne just couldn't account for, though he supposed it was okay since it was Parker who did them, so there must be something good about those things that Wayne didn't understand because he knew flat out that Parker just didn't make mistakes; DID YOU HEAR WHAT I JUST SAID? DON'T LOOK AT ME LIKE THAT; HOW DARE YOU! –

'CAUSE I JUST SAID THAT PARKER DOESN'T MAKE MIS-
TAKES DID YOU HEAR ME I SAID THAT PARKER DOES NOT
REPEAT DOES NOT MAKE MISTAKES OVER AND FUCKING
OUT! But even so it made Wayne sick to watch Parker sometimes.
And Wayne was not the only one. So gradually Parker repressed
these impulses and devoted himself more and more ruthlessly to his
ideals, which were so bright and white like an empty sheet of paper
that Wayne and the swim team loved the ideals, too, because it gave
them something that you couldn't get any other way, a feeling of
rightness deep down inside that tickled so you knew it was there;
and Parker gangled himself up very tall at the staff meetings and
blinked down at all concerned to reassure them that he'd take care
of whatever needed to be taken care of; they knew that Parker could
football-huddle his greenish snaky arms around the whole team,
sealing them tight into the trust of Parker, although Parker only did
that once or twice on very special emotional moments, like the day
before the meet with Deadford College down the river where all the
guys wore black jump suits with polished zippers made of diced
interlocking bones; that was one tough meet, my fellow gun owners,
but Parker got them through it and when he wrapped his arms
around them (Wayne still remembered how the cool rubbery flesh of
Parker's right wrist had slid across his shoulders and onto Chip's
shoulders and around the circle and kept on going and crossed
Parker's left wrist and come right back around on top of itself to
touch Wayne's shoulder again) then Wayne had almost cried for
awe and happiness. Yes, they had won the meet; and that was one
thing that nobody would ever be able to take away from Wayne.
Now Parker was more on his own than he had been in a long time,
Wayne being off on his labors, so it was time for him to ease himself
deep into the jungles of his own being to learn undreamed of
predatory skills before his adult organization took shape. Someday
he wanted to extend the tendrils of his organization across inter-
galactic space. (The blue globes for their part had long recognized,
as they told Susan, the potential that Parker possessed for working
in their interest.) For the moment, however, he slouched and
slithered around in the darkness of the photo lab, thinking rich
sinuous thoughts which had no output. His body pulsated smoothly.
He was on the verge of achieving some new capability which would
permit him to strike.

Parker was well aware that his high school victories had been
juvenile accomplishments, indicative, to be sure, that Parker possessed promise, but signifying no more than some little march into the

Sudetenland. The next few tricks would have to be played in the business world. It was his plan to do something photographic. Then he would have a marketable skill, which was especially important for Parker, who had clearly failed to rise above his social environment because he acted autistic all the time and never said much, just kinda watched you through his yellow eyes and popped his joints in and out of their sockets; and of course even a suit and tie would not give him absolution from these gaffes in any job interview; only the talented can be forgiven insolence (and Parker with his Omarville background was thought by his managers to have little more than phototropic capabilities). Therefore Parker hung around the photo lab waiting to become talented. He did not have much longer to wait.

In those days the photo lab was the center of a technical revolution. Its business procedures reflected the impact of industrial capitalism upon the Oriental feudal enlargers. Into the negative tanks strode a grim new breed, the mentality of which had been developed with the help of Dr. Dodger's capital. *They* knew the decimal value of manganese ore. Meanwhile the desks of the back room secretaries, which had once resembled a noisy Asiatic bazaar in their show of print dresses and lipstick, the swapping of aspirin for cold sore pills, the exotic clickings of high-heeled shoes on the cement floor (which was stained with the formic acid of hundreds of thousands of ants who had been boiled alive as prisoners of war to make sepia toner, which in the course of workaday events and mediocre prints got spilled or dribbled through the cracked fixing basins and ran along the floor and out the back of the darkroom proper and oozed through the seven velvet curtains that fortified Parker and Company against the photons, and finally trickled into the order department), the happy hum of the pencil sharpeners, the rustlings of prim paper bags during lunch hour, the jingling of the telephones ritualized and ubiquitous like the calls of a mullah to prayer, the typing and sorting and filing and dust and fumes and decaying insulation that so truly linked that holy of holies with the outside world; the feudal element, then, was being developed into oblivion.* — By the time Parker had started there, it was no more than a wistful allusion or two in the personnel manual.

Parker's peculiarities were not noticed at first. There are so many hidden phenomena in this world. — Behind the Kremlin Wall, they say, are all kinds of odd things which no one who is not a member of

---

* In short, the secretaries were laid off.

the Executive Committee will ever see because if anyone did he might realize that there are great plans afoot, and it is precisely such a realization on the part of unauthorized persons which could foil Hindustan's forthcoming intuitive leap to Leninist-Krupskayanist principles. This is a pity, because I would like to see Catherine the Great's jeweled hairpins. Such treasures are often used to bankrupt European art galleries and screw up our economy. But there are better weapons yet (there must be!), hidden far below the hoards, in cool phony crypts with real royal and revolutionary tombstones on top to keep James Bond from looking any farther; and wet winding staircases lead all the way to the center of the earth, where the old purged Soviet generals burn and decompose and their bones are slowly encrusted with medals; and when Trotsky himself is covered with ribbons and clots of gold and silver from the top of his skull to the tip of his toe-bones, then the millennium will come, and missiles will rise from disguised volcanoes and all the mothers of the free world will turn sterile and the cows and pigs and chickens will get anthrax disseminated by radio waves from fifth column music stations, and helmets will poke up through the tundra so that even James Bond won't be able to stop it and then we will be dead, dead, dead. Such is the might of the very real Soviet threat. – Well, just imagine that staircase going a bit farther, right down to the other side of the world in Omarville, and you will get a feel for the danger that Parker represented, at least to Bug and *his* interests, though that doesn't mean much since we were all dangerous to Bug.

Parker never did much on the job. He'd just kinda lean up against the side of the developer tank, thinking up a spaghetti of means and ends, and every now and then checking his wrist-watch to see if it were time to take a print out of the stop bath. His co-workers all cranked and buzzed like the bugs they feared, and adjusted and sweated at their enlargers beneath the fatal shining of the cracked red safety bulbs, setting the exposures for fancy Dodge-O-Brom paper, holding their breaths to prevent said paper, lens and negative from being pulmonarily reacted upon, which would have blurred whatever image area was not quite covered by the Kodak Wratten Gelatin Filter No. 87; while behind a partition the other cheese-faces were agitating color Dodge-O-Chromes; yes, there was a lot of work and benign compulsion in the photo business; it was no piece of Plus-X-Pan cake, for instance, to monitor the blue globes to make sure they did the job; that was a management headache because no one who was not in management was allowed to know about the blue globes, so if they got sulky or fretful or bored with customers' pictures, as blue globes often do, then the managers had to increase the current flow secretly from their office so that the naive employees would never know; and meanwhile those naive employees kept working hard. – Only Parker did not work hard. Frank and Stephen used semisophisticated stirrers and pourers and disposable tongs; when Parker had to stir something he'd stick his pinky in and twiddle it around mournfully. In the large tank the infrared sheet films had to be swished at one-minute intervals, with D-76 at 0.70, if you know what I mean. A running-water rinse worked almost as well.

Frank Fairless was the office milksop, so he slaved and slaved, fearful that he might lose his job at any time; while Stephen Mole slammed the enlarger up and down in constant rage at being forced to labor at such a dingy establishment; he would have preferred to be in New York doing lucrative fashion photography. – As a boy Stephen had been spanked often. It was this rage and negativism which would make him so valuable to Bug, though Stephen was not entirely a match for Wayne because his rage was the impotent sort, so he had more potential force, perhaps, but less control, like a crookedly compressed spring. – Stephen despised Frank, who couldn't tell the difference between an Ansel Adams print and a greeting card, but Stephen hated Parker because there was something vulgar and threatening about Parker, so that Stephen knew right away that Parker was not his kind. – Parker was not anyone's kind. In the summer he slept across the freeway in a certain ancient alleyway which had long been cordoned off and forgotten by the police and garbage collectors so that Parker could slide his lanky body unremarked into various shelters which he had constructed of gutted piss-stained mattresses and wrecked auto bodies, and sleep coiled up with an overcoat pulled across his face to keep away the flies. In the wintertime he went scavenging in abandoned trash bags until he found 1930s lawn clippings all brown and dried out, and suchlike things, so that he could fill his home with grass and twigs and crackly leaves in which he burrowed during the coldest nights, rotating his head round and round on his long rubbery neck; and sometimes smoking old cigarette butts there in his manger. After all, if the tinder caught fire, he could always move someplace else. – Had Wayne known of Parker's situation, he would have sent Parker every cent he had and started moonlighting for the fucking Cuban navy to give Parker a decent roof over his head plus a bathroom full of electric shavers, but from Parker's point of view no short cuts could be taken. So Parker hid himself and meditated, listening to the street people puking weakly and blowing each other and falling on broken glass and dying and digging in around him every night, and they never knew that he was there because he never moved or made a sound, did Parker; and he only came there in the dark, belly-crawling his way between shattered chair-backs and chicken skeletons and drums of toxic chemicals and stinky old sofas and rusty coils of wire and lots and lots of dead things; it was the dead things that kept Parker informed of the progress of the seasons, which he could not otherwise follow, being in the darkroom all day and hiding in the garbage heap at night; as he crossed the freeway by the trailer park and ducked under the fence at midnight the odors would direct him as surely as traffic-signs, for each piece of carrion had its own signature to write into the velvety pages of the night; in the spring there was the smell of run-over skunks which Parker would step on and squish as he got to the shoulder of the freeway; these were quickly heaved by the highway crew into the rejected area where Parker slept; and then their stenches became steadily more piercing and sweet around him as the weeks went on; as summer came the theme was raccoons, dozens of those masked bandits back-arched week after week with paws upflung along the roadside; the freeway crew heaved them in, too, once they started swelling and bursting in their elegant fur jackets; Parker felt vaguely sorry for the raccoons because they were once so handsome and had only been out promenading paw in paw with their green-eyed robber-mates or on the prowl for garbage, and headlights had hypnotized them and now they were garbage themselves beneath the moonlight, their eyes still open, though clouded over and speckled with ants; but I was discussing the progress of the seasons; now, in fall there came the little opossums and weasels; they were run over quite easily; you scarcely felt a crunch under your big fat tires; into the urban graveyard they went when the road crew got to them; and in the wet winters it was rats running across the road; they got mashed and pulped, the stupid things; usually they were just left there on the freeway until thousands of cars had smeared them into long grey lines on the asphalt which the rain then gently loosened into a scum that flowed under the fence and hardened into a semi-solid mud that Parker's toes sank into at night. Parker never saw the sun or the moon in those years, not that Parker minded one bit, being both cunning and enigmatic. At work he leaned against the wall or sat in the corner staring down at the floor instead of acting efficient, and inside the photo lab it was so dark and everybody else was so intent on his or her business that nobody except Stephen Mole thought of reporting Parker, and even he couldn't have proved anything at that stage, for Parker did his assigned job. During the lunch hour they all sat around a table in the projection booth and ate in the darkness so as not to lose their night vision. But while everyone else ate cucumbers, cheese, potato chips and yogurt, Parker just sucked his long green thumbs. His main anxiety was that political developments might take place before he was ready. So he lurked and yawned with extreme energy.

Every few minutes an enlarger beam would click off or a timer would buzz, and then Evelyn or Frank or Stephen would come over to Parker with an armful of exposed paper to be run through the usual wet procedures. Parker could tell his colleagues apart by smell, just like the animal corpses where he slept. Evelyn smelled like cold cream, lime stick deodorant, "Charlie" perfume and bleach, while Stephen smelled of sweat and coffee and rage, and Frank, being, as indicated, a milksop, exuded a faint odor of hot milk that made Parker flicker his tongue and want to eat Frank. – They all kept very close track of how the prints turned out since it meant their JOBS to screw up but Evelyn pretended not to keep track in order to prevent Parker from feeling that she was putting pressure on him or anything since Evelyn believed in being sweet to everyone because then if she made a mistake others would be sweet to her; not that Parker cared one way or the other about Evelyn's sweetness; he just went about his shady business while Frank grinned weakly and ran a finger through his (not Parker's) hair and very occasionally asked Parker how his batch was coming along – but Stephen Mole, who was bearded and big-boned like a horse, scowled and growled and ordered Parker to keep moving. – Such treatment astonished Parker. Nobody had ever dared to order him to do something before. The unfortunate truth was that his workmates weren't yet afraid of him, which was intolerable to Parker, and so sometimes when Stephen tried to rush him or was not grateful for Parker's pinky-twiddle rinses, or when Parker saw Stephen stop abruptly in his work at Enlarger 4 and turn round glaring at Parker to try to catch Parker in some alien or illicit activity, why, then, he'd just reach into the "IN" tray and take one of Stephen's prints between two fingers (he was supposed to use tongs) and scratch the stubble on his cheeks and squeeze his greasy hair and he'd drop the picture airily into the developer and let it swiggle down to the bottom of the basin and then shine a penlight on it until the image turned a solid black, or burn a hole in it or throw it away, and when Stephen demanded to know what had become of it Parker just kinda shrugged and writhed his mouth and stretched his fingers wide as if to suggest that the fixer had probably maybe perhaps he supposed to some extent dissolved it. Then Stephen would get worked up and come up close to Parker breathing hard in Parker's face as if he was going to shake Parker by the shoulder or hit him, but usually a timer would ting or Parker would unshell a new canister of negatives that Frank, who wanted to consider himself a peacemaker, would hand Parker. – All these exchanges, I forgot to say, had to take place in silence, questions to Parker being written on a little pad of paper that was chained to the lab table just beside him, because that season for the first time the photo lab offered as a special service to its professional customers the development and printing of sound-sensitive plastic media for stereo records. The orchestral negatives didn't matter so much, since what was an extra cough here or curse there in the live versions when everybody sneezed at La Scala anyway? – And the recordings of tropical environments were always enhanced by the quiet mysterious sounds of Parker's finger squirming and plashing deliberately into the water like bat guano in the Carlsbad Caverns falling every now and then into some underground river to get nudged at by the blind-fish; but for other compositions it was very difficult. They had a Cone of Silence, Mark II, which Evelyn was responsible for operating when they had some particularly tricky order that required a rich bombardment of decibels from the acoustic enlarger (Evelyn frowned like a monkey and suffered because it was so complicated), and if she'd missed a track or two it was officially Parker's responsibility to yawn or grunt or hum softly where the sonic pattern was not forming in the developer as rapidly as in areas of greater density. – Once the plastic was fixed, Frank took it, writing Evelyn a luminous receipt in his neat handwriting, and spun it into a 45 rpm record on the potter's wheel. It was now as good as a compact laser disc. Meanwhile the work went on, and Frank grinned weakly over his custom portfolio reprint orders and Stephen strained to raise and lower the beehive-shaped lens hood of his Leitz enlarger, which would have ruptured any man less powerfully built, while Evelyn did a great job in her cubicle hating every minute of it and Parker swished his fingers in the fixer and little grains of silver were deposited under his fingernails.

At one time Parker had brought his bag lunches with him daily like Evelyn who munched furtively at all hours against every conceivable regulation, but one day after work Parker was picking his teeth with his stained fingernails when he realized that the taste of developer was quite pleasant and sustaining, like a peculiarly nourishing pickle-juice, so after that whenever he was hungry or thirsty he just cupped his hands in the developer tank and raised them to his lips and drank deep. This meant that that much more developer was used in the course of a day than had previously been the case, but Parker was praised rather than censured by the omniscient management because the end result was that each piece of photographic paper was exposed to correspondingly fresher developer, and the prints looked better in the end. Gradually Parker's insides became yellow-green and luminescent. If he opened his mouth to burp a faint glow came out from his tonsils. The custom lab had a little washroom for employees which was located in the darkroom itself for the sake of efficiency. When you closed the door and sat down on the toilet, a fan came on and an old red safety bulb shone tiredly. Parker could light his way with his own piss which sparkled and glowed and dazzled his eyes after hours staring at blank and otherwise inscrutable images swimming in the trays of liquid. — Parker gradually discovered that he had become a sort of photographic Midas, needing only to hold Stephen's and Frank's and Evelyn's sheets of exposed paper in his palms, one sheet at a time, and breathe gently on it in the darkness, for the image to form, slowly and tenderly, first white on white so subtle and lovely, then white against white with outlines of eyes and teeth proportioned in a perfect sketch that became more and more real as it darkened and took on texture and the superb blacks leaped out suddenly like rocks one stumbles on in a snowfield, eerily losing their solidity once contrast zones two through eight were completed around and between them until the face or landscape or nekkid woman was actualized so that the dark spaces became too richly featureless to be anything but horrible holes that suns could fall into and be swallowed up by monsters. At this moment in the photochemical process, if Stephen Mole had not been courteous and sensitive (he rarely was), Parker's neck would pulse and Parker would scrape his fingernails across his teeth, *g-r-r-r-r-k!*; and Parker would kinda squeeze his eyes shut and maybe play with himself in the dark and grin very very slowly and keep holding the print in both hands and breathe on it once again, and the dark spaces would roar out to gobble up everything except the crisp white borders of the photo, thus proving to the General Manager that the fault must have been Stephen's, not Parker's, for had Parker slipped up in his assigned duties the borders also would have been darkened or discolored.

Now at long last his workmates began to fear Parker, for he just leaned in his corner with his left foot hooked behind his right leg, trailing his arm in the hypo bath up to the elbow and more unkempt and smelly than ever, but everyone's pictures except Stephen Mole's were always ready and professional to a T, even though no one could see any prints floating in the chemicals. The finished products whirled face-down in the cold-water rinse, like drowned people in a whirlpool. As the days passed, the processing chemicals evaporated from their basins, leaving residues which resembled gummy eyelids after sleep. Then Parker's fingers dried out and hurt. He shambled over to the supply shelves finally and poured the concentrates into the graduate cylinder for dilution. – It occurred to him then that he no longer needed to absorb them watered down. Like some prehistoric reptile returning to the sea for good and letting its lungs become vestigial air bladders, Parker drank the poisons blankly. Later he filled the basins with the concentrates, pouring very very slowly, for he liked dribbling noises; and returned to his work station. Moodily, he looked down at the liquids. Each basin, with its rectangular volume of fluid, reminded him of a swimming pool. He imagined himself crawl-stroking through the stop bath, with Wayne dog-paddling dutifully after. He wanted to race with someone more worthy of him, though, to fling himself into the water and stroke and stroke and kick and slice through the water with sinusoidal bubble-boned contortions until he practically burst and still not be better than neck-to-neck with the Opponent, the Significant Other, perhaps even (a luxurious thought for Parker, who had never yet been defeated) a few lengths behind, like having a handicap at golf, and he'd have to go all out and STROKE for his life until he finally caught up and embraced his victim like in the old days of the Octopus, coiling round his waist and sucking him down to bash his head against the tiles of the pool and smearing his brain languidly along the wall for ten yards, yes indeed; which is why he had not bothered to destroy Stephen Mole or Frank or Evelyn; they were unworthy of Parker's talents; though of course Stephen would have to be punished once Parker's position at the photo lab had been consolidated to Gibraltar point – not that exterminating Stephen was to be as easy as Parker imagined; for in those days, both Parker and Stephen underestimated each other.

Parker's talent, let us say, developed. Every day he was becoming more and more a creature of Omarville, like a wild thing losing the superficial docility of babyhood; yet he was much less confined by his origins than his allies the plants. His own behavior now dictated by the pressures of his abilities, he was driven to practice at night with toilet paper and Kleenex in his garbage heap; he mastered the power to develop pocket handkerchiefs, butcher's paper, sanitary napkins. – But what did he see? Ah, that's quite a question. – What Parker saw was just a lovely silky darkness: the infinite, in short, the goal of all his imaginings, the nether waters of the swimming pool (and here, with a vague start that his memory was of so fine a caliber as to be able to recall such insignificant personages and incidents, he recollected the inconclusive battle with Bug in the swimming pool, which now made him tuck his knuckles under his chin and squirm with interested concentration; it had occurred to Parker that perhaps there might soon be new shining wars).

It was at this point that Parker received a letter from Wayne, making clear the growing menace of the bugs.

THE GREEN BUG, OR, THE THIRD LABOR OF WAYNE

~~~~~~

Best results will be obtained with full metal jacket, round nose bullets.

> Manual for the Browning BDA-380
> double-action automatic pistol (1984)

Traveling around in Iowa, keeping his eyes open, Wayne sees a green bug in the fields trying to disguise itself as an ear of corn. Wayne jumps over the fence and grabs it and wrestles it to the ground, snapping off three of its hairy legs to save time. Now, what the hell is it, it's (he flips through remembered pages in his four-color training manual) a lesser cloverleaf weevil (*Hypera nigirostis*), which is a challenge to Wayne's courageous if limited intellect; for why should a clover beetle be lurking in a corn field? – It must be spying on something or rendezvousing with its subterranean masters ... – Wayne grins mirthlessly at this; he's tired of playing two-bit footsie with underlings of the overlords beneath; he's gonna get hisself a big one and if you don't like it, reader, you'd better jump out of the way fast. – Awright, now for the interrogation.

Most bugs don't speak English in hick-type regions, but then neither do the hicks with their glowering pitchfork ways and desire under the fucking elms. Members of our Merchant Marine forces were prepared to meet every contingency. Wayne broke off two corn stalks and lashed them to his forehead with Navy-issue elastic. Outta his fatigue pocket came the little handbook with the grey cover: *Elementary English–Beetle Beetle–English Pocket Guide* (Copyright 1942, Department of Defense, TOP SECRET). – Wayne gave the green weevil a kick to keep it still and turned to his favorite page, "Commands." – O.K. now, everything under control; here we go:

2.1 Standard Interrogation Commands

English	L.Antenna	R. Antenna
Come forward!	12:00	12:00
Quickly!	(Rapid wiggle)	(Rapid wiggle)
Turn around!	6:00	(Emphatic rotation)
Identify yourself!	2:00	7:33
No tricks!	(Hard poke in prisoner's eyes)	
Obey or I'll shoot!	3:42	1:23
Relax.	6:00	6:00
Spread your back legs!	8:29	4:16
This will hurt.	(Extra hard poke)	
The U.S. Government will pay you.	2:53	1:09

Wayne slipped the paper-thin electronic antennae alignment compass from beneath the back flap of his pocket guide and set his corn stalks for "Obey or I'll shoot!" – It was hard to tell whether or not this had accomplished anything, as the green bug remained perfectly still, eyeing him with the appalling stolidity of its kind. Only the green fuzz on its broad striped back ruffled slightly with tension. It was clearly a master operator.

"Beetles," remarks the *Audubon Society Field Guide to North American Insects and Spiders*, "can be easily recognized by the tough, armor-like fore wings, called elytra, that cover the membranous hind wings used for flying. When the insect is at rest, the elytra usually meet in a neat line down the middle of the back."

"Spread your elytra!" Wayne wig-wagged. "This is a strip search!" (L ANT 3:08; R ANT 2:11; L ANT 5:19; R ANT 3:47). – But slyly the weevil stabbed its slender, downcurved beak at Wayne's toe and sank its mandibles deep into his ankle. Acting with determination and in the best tradition of the Service, Wayne blinded it with his trench knife, hacked its mandibles off, removed its remaining three legs, and peeled back the elytra, with the grim indifference of the professional. And what did he find; oh, reader, what did he find that made his face light up with the utopian certainty that these indecisive skirmishes were over? – Parker would crap in his pants, but Parker would want to get in on this job, too . . . for what Wayne held in his hands as he methodically stamped up

and down upon the dying bug until it burst in a great dark gush of
ichor, what he held was nothing other than a neatly folded square
of Kleenex, bearing a tactical message to Mantis about follow-up
surveillance on Wayne, and written in our hero's wormtracks . . .

"Awright, guy," says Wayne, happier than he's been in months,
"awright, you dumb shit!" he screams aloud: "AWRIGHT, fella,
you may have gotten away from the team once but you just wait till
Wayne and Parker catch up with you . . ."

THE GREAT BEETLE

~~~~~~

> ... dingin' the wind oot o' bum clocks, an' squeezin' the whusslers
> o' puir bits o' dumb insec's ...
>
> Scottish expression (date unknown)

Leonardo da Vinci, it is said, copied the snorkel from some aquatic
beetle or other that either had one built in or sucked the air out of
hollow reeds as it went along. Both notions are equally charming,
really: – a marbled diving beetle, say, (*Thermonectes marmoratus*)
sculling along in the warm happy brown-green water with its eyes
bulging out predaciously, and refreshing itself at intervals with a
little insect-breath of the air stored beneath its elytra; or maybe a
giant water scavenger beetle (*Hydrophilus* spp.) kicking its reddish
black legs with alternate strokes to push its body down to the bottom
of a pond where it could smell a bloated decayed drowned mouse,
breathing easily at first because of the silvery envelope of air that
coats the underside of its body, diving on down tough as nails in its
dull-green shell (imagine how secure it must be! As children, when
we pulled the covers over our heads to protect us from monsters
at night, we knew that if the monsters ever came they could rip
the blankets silently with their claws and then eat us, and our
parents would never hear a sound; but with an *exoskeleton* we'd
be as invulnerable as Superman; the Chicago gangsters would
cry in dismay, "The bullets jist keep bouncin' offa that flyin' kid!"
– Ah ...); and now here was the yummy corpse on the bottom, all
naturally marinated and putrefied and half-sunken into the silt much
as hunters in the Southwest roast porcupines in a hole in a nice
stone-capped mesa; and our beetle sniffed at the food for a minute
with its short, clubbed antennae and idly fiddled its maxillary palps
... It was a summer day. Maybe tonight it would leave the water

and fly about and get hypnotized by the nearest back door porch light (what hue would it be, white or yellow or even blue? – Yeah, why not, what the hell; there was nothing else to do since the mating season hadn't started yet) and it took another breath and discovered that its air was gone, and so cunningly snuggled up to the nearest cattail and bored a hole in it and sucked a little oxygen to refresh itself, and then returned with ferocious relish to the squishy horrid rotten furry dead thing and bit it open like somebody peeling a fruit.

And the secret rotor-flies of New Zealand anticipated the helicopter, and grasshoppers are like cranes; and the vespid wasps with their mud cells inspired the prison and palace architecture of the Assyrians. – Little wonder, then, that the bugs possessed a coast-to-coast subway of sorts, consisting of wide smooth glassy tunnels sunk at a great depth, the trains consisting of caravans of high-powered larvae that swallowed you and you relaxed and played solitaire in their spacious papery abdomens while they scudded along with their eyes illuminating the way, and disgorged you at your destination, at which point it was customary to give them a sugar cube or a little bone meal. – The reader is invited to take this trip, just like any other ciliated operative, from the west coast directly to Florida, where the headquarters of the bugs were located. Chew, chooooooooo-o-o-o-o-oooooo! Above your head howl the coyotes of Nevada; then the Louisiana 'gators croak and wallow in their dismal muddy wilderness, where it is so clammy at night that the only stars to be seen are the lowdown firefly spies; and now overhead we hear the dogs of the Midwest barking viciously and trying to scratch out holes to burrow into and grab you; but you're already long gone and the ground shudders now with day-and-night oil-drilling activity in the south; and then around you is the mossy silence of the Carolinas, broken in your imagination by the sullen gnashings of Venus flytraps; and then at last through the semi-translucent skin of your larval car you sense a lightness, a brightness, and here you are walking the sand of the Florida keys.

Twenty miles from Miami is an obscure region which shows up on no maps, even those of the U.S. Geomantic Survey. Thanks to a bunch of tin hovels (in each of which are sprawled wax dummies of human indigents), thousands of Anopheles mosquitoes and a large magnetic stinkbug which distorts all compass needles, the area is left to itself. If you have the proper credentials, which consist of the secretions of a spittlebug, smeared across your hands and face in parallel bands, then a corridor will be made for you; a squadron of Florida hunting wasps will come to escort you; and you will pass through a wretched swamp, up a steep hill to a wild orchid garden, over a rise; and then before you lies one of the most entrancing vistas in North America. It is a damned shame that for security reasons no pictures are permitted.

Beetle Landing, as we shall call this little bit of the state (insects themselves do not share our mania for naming habitats) was the first place to be settled by the Spaniards back in the days of Ponce de Leon. Chosen by that nation of philanderers, holy torturers and gold-seekers to be their administrative capital in 1507 and laid out by them in a pattern of wide, tree-lined streets, the town of Santa Maria, as it was christened, has been the scene of many changes of note to tourists. Missionaries, plantation owners, Indians, Popes, loners and slave traders all left their mark. Between raids and rapes it was a flourishing colonial town, supplying great quantities of forced labor. In 1637 a spectacular volcanic eruption buried the town in ash and pumice. The nationwide attacks of the early American settlers upon the bugs made it imperative for all chirring creatures to establish a command center; and in the year 35 of the Great Beetle the town was occupied. Massive excavation and spider webbing composed the work of rebuilding; all the debris were hauled away, because the bugs were looking for mummified bodies to eat; and then the town was left to decay as best it might, while strategic posts were dug underground.

Today, after all the excitement, Santa Maria, or rather Beetle Landing, is a peaceful town, full of history, full of things to see and do. Ringed by volcanoes and one of the deepest harbors in the world, this perfect anchorage was created by eruption some fifteen hundred years ago. As a guest, you can commandeer a turtle-bug to paddle you across the bay to visit the cinder cones. Sunrise from atop the highest is unforgettable.

If you feel an earth-tremor, don't be alarmed. This is normal. In the town itself flowering trees and creepers choke the streets — frangipani, poinsiana, and lilac. Almost everything you need is on central Damselfly Avenue — bug cafes, worm-eaten libraries, an old monastery the cells of which have been filled with the waxy hexagons of a healthy bee colony, pawpaws, pineapples and edible grubs, all at giveaway prices, turtlemeat and eels, perhaps a week-dead parrot already crawling with impatient ants, the remnants of a chapel, where the Virgin's face is hung with spiders; and in the old Governor's residence begins an intricate system of bunkers and tunnels, almost an underground city, to protect the insect forces against the aerial bombardments which they know will come someday. Other entrances to the bunkers are concealed in the hillsides. The peaceful, park-like cemetery (many Spaniards died of weird diseases) is remarkable for the exceedingly geometrical layout of its bug-larder tunnels. You will probably need a guide to help you find the Governor's family monument, a series of tumbledown graves with sad Boolean inscriptions on a bluff above the sea, or the submarine base, where an underwater cliff dropping seven hundred feet and riddled with maggoty caverns in the soft coral allows the commanders to bring their armor-plated ocean beetles to their chambers underneath the beach in broad daylight, and nobody would ever know, dipping a toe in the water as he walked along the smooth sand, that beneath him there lumbered huge metallic creatures bristling with poisoned spines and ready at any moment to take on some small sleepy town along the Atlantic coast ... Oh, wonderful and fearful world!

Park (1934) found that flour beetle larvae were usually distributed through their exceedingly uniform environment in a random manner, and Kuenzler (1958) drew the same conclusion about two species of wolf spider (*Lycosa carolinensis* and *L. rabida*). However, populations do clump together somewhat, as individuals in species groups suffer lower mortality during unfavorable periods of treacherous reactionary attacks because the group can favorably modify microhabitat, much as we do by walling our towns. This was precisely the reasoning of the Great Beetle.

How can I, a mere manlet, describe this cunning, much-dreaded leader of Bugdom, buried deep in his layer of bark chips, surrounded by his constellation of ambush bugs and assassin bugs, in command of numerous legions of water boatmen and backswimmers in dark underground rivers, all ready with their sharp mouthparts to inject digestive agents into their prey suddenly, from under the water? – How, after all, does any bug think? This is the problem of our times, more productive of bile and gall than any of our petty world wars; for we must acknowledge in our human enemies at least the rudiments of thought (how else could they foil our grand starry plans?); but bugs we deny even the status of enemies; they are simply loathsome mechanical goblins to be crunched underfoot; you cannot reason with them; you cannot allow even one ant in the house because if you do it will go get its sisters and they will swarm over the cereal box. – But after all this is just what *we* would do.

Unlike most of us, who have crusty exteriors, hard rigid lattices of metal salts of the earth making up our shells; and soft meat inside, like crustaceans, like bugs; our hero now had a hard heart and a soft exterior. People would help him and boss him around. On the airplane they always asked him if it were his first flight. But his doughy politeness and docility served mainly to disguise that bug-shell heart; mercy was alien to him. And was there more soft meat beneath the bug-shell? Maybe, and so on infinitely, but that is only hermeneutics.

The Great Beetle, on the other hand, was a Coleopteran.

To understand "who he was and what he lived for," we must return to the happy pond scene with which this chapter began, in the spirit of one of those twenty-minute color films which are compulsory in the elementary schools of our great Republic: *Life in the Salt Marsh*, or *A Day at Beaver Creek*. The camera zooms in to show a frog catching flies, while the music of Disney thrills somberly. – Imagine, then, a riparian environment on the insect level. Here we find our whirligig beetles again, dozens of them bobbing and spinning within an area of fifty centimeters; but unlike humans in a crowded swimming pool they never bump into each other, thanks to their fine-tuned antennae. Their bulging eyes are built on the bifocal principle: the upper half sees in air, the lower under the water. Dearest beetles, all that you desire in your innocence is to dance and dive; I am sorry to have bothered you. As for the family Dytiscidae, these beautiful oval-bodied beetles glisten in the water like glass beads when the sunlight strikes them just right. They also bob, as do the whirligigs (family Gyrinidae). Coming to the surface, they stretch their abdominal tips up into the air, lift their elytra and then dive again, now wrapped in their film of air. – On the bank, lost in an infinite wilderness of green grass, soldier beetles make love. The male and the female turn away from each other, hooking their tail sections. Copulation in some beetle species can take several hours. In others yet, such as the Melyridae, the lovers employ methods of foreplay and control which we can only envy. Courtship begins with gentle antenna taps. The male holds the tips of his elytra out in offering, and the female bites him all over in tiny, caressing nips, kissing his bristles and tufts of fur, each of which exudes a different-flavored secretion. – In many species the male clambers atop the female's back, but often the position is reversed. In others still, the thing is done sideways. Meanwhile the great grass-stalks and reed-stalks, which must soar out of the insects' imagination, higher by far than redwood forests or skyscrapers for us, flex back and forth in that lifelong gale which we would call a summer breeze; and the ladybugs are blown off the green shoots and roll and tumble in the moss. Japanese beetles fly around the mayweed and daisy fleabane, like little olive-green military planes against the targets of white-and-yellow flowers. Queen Anne's lace bows its white frilly face to the wind, and its great lurching shadow makes the beetles nervous. A timid plant bug hides under a leaf of water hemlock. Steam rises from the grass in the sunlight. All about are sly patterings and scrapings and rustlings of spies and assassins. Shiny black pincers rise up from the mass like a dead hand from a grave; they pry themselves open inch by silent inch; they seize a sleepy digger bee and crush it deliciously. — Now here comes a chain gang of ants marching along the wide avenues that run among these sacred grass-groves; on their shoulders they bear a majestic trophy: the desiccated body of a brown mantidfly, which will refresh their larvae and their young queen. Here a black beetle goes hunting in the dew, confident that his shell will be his shield in the event of a battle with a wasp (for his way takes him near the Hive Perilous, from which at any time a swarm of bulbous-headed Amazons may issue forth to seize wayfarers, to hold them tight between their bristly legs, sting them and sting them again until they are dizzy with shock and pain, then sting them again until they are blind and paralyzed, light and easy cargo then to haul into the ominous mud-and-paper chambers and drop into a cell, where they are watched carefully for any residual tremors or last faint attempts at struggling, in which case they are stung again, delicately, with just enough poison to render them deaf and mad and unable even to twitch a feeler; and then the mothers, buzzing evilly with excitement, enfold the prisoners once again in their hairy grip, and give birth, or rather lay their eggs, the abdominal segment jerking up to raise the tip in a sadistic orgasmic gush as here comes a wet red egg, and the abdomen comes back down and drips a thread of gluey mucus and cements the egg on the prisoner's body, maybe right on the belly, and now here comes another, and with a harsh mocking metallic buzz she exultingly lays it on the prisoner's eye and seals it there where it will hatch and the hungry wasp-grub will eat its way into the sick unresisting meat); and here a beetle has just caught a young caterpillar and bites a wound in its stomach and hunches its shiny green shoulders and vomits digestive juice inside the caterpillar where it begins to dissolve the living creature with terrible corrosive acids, and the beetle tenderly laps up the broth that steams out and the caterpillar melts into soup from the inside out, and the beetle doesn't waste a drop; that is how it must live. — In the thickest reeds a bird has made its nest; and housecleaning beetles crawl politely in the straw of the nest and eat the moldy parts for their host and devour the dung of the newborn nestlings (and before they were hatched the beetles were very careful not to hurt the pretty speckled eggs); and everything is just as red-checkered-tablecloth spic-and-span as it can be; and when the birds are infested by mites the beetles pick those off and eat them, too. – And the cicadas are singing out the temperature for everybody like good weathermen, and the fireflies sleep dreaming of the evening when they will flash their love-lights; and the water-boatmen scull in the water from shadow to lily-shadow; and the tiger beetles prowl and snap their sickle-jaws and bask in the sun and make piggyback love some more.

Now high in the sky there flies a cropdusting plane, as out of sight and mind as old Phil Blaker on Mars; and it is spraying a nearby field because two June bugs were reported there. – As Nietzsche says, "Pity for all would be hardness and tyranny toward *you*, dear neighbor!" – The wind blows the spray over in this direction; here it comes in a spreading white cloud; and there is unease here in the fringe area and then panic and then nothing but death. The soldier-beetles die in the midst of their orgies, rolling apart and thrashing and finally lying dead on their backs with their legs twisted wryly in their agony (curious how a dead bug is so much less disgusting when you cannot see the little legs thrust up at you like that!). – The gang of ants withers; the dead mantidfly rolls off their dead backs and falls to the ground, covered in white chemical-dust. Everybody in the whole world is dying so gruesomely! – The spray seeps down under the ground and kills everyone in the anthill so that it is a useless Egyptian tomb; and the queen, who is both ruler and treasure, is stricken in her egg-laying and her gravid body convulses itself and she breaks her back in her spasms and rolls on her eggs and crushes them – not that it matters, since they are poisoned now, anyway; and her guards die bewildered in the darkness, streaming through the tunnels in spite of their own pain to find this menace, but they fall in heaps of clattering body-armor; and the larvae die shrieking with their chewing mouthparts gaping as the white dust blows into their nursery; – and outside the ant graveyard the spray blows into the moss and the moss is dusted white and the black pincers of the proud assassin of bees flex and gnash and go rigid. In the wasps' nest the mothers buzz in a furious uproar, stinging themselves and each other in terror, falling together and separately in horrid dead crunchy mounds; and the paralyzed prisoners die uselessly, too; and the eggs upon them die; and in the birds' nest the baby birds get sick, but maybe they will survive (of course if they make it to reproductive age their brittle eggs will break); the cleaning beetles in the nest die, and the cicadas die, and the water-boatmen die; and days later the scavenger beetles come to clean up like anti-corpse tank battalions in a post-nuclear zone, but their meat is poisoned and after a few nibbles they die, too. Of course, many beetles are good at playing dead when they realize that we are watching them, so to our eyes there might not be much difference. But we wouldn't hear the cicadas anymore.

The Great Beetle, being capable of many feats of mentation, calculated that in daily life it was right that the poor wasp-prisoners should die, but it was not right that they *and* the wasps and all the rest should die in this way, for then they could not be used for food. Much like one of the unifiers of the Indian tribes in the nineteenth century, he got certain species to declare a truce among themselves to deal with these emergencies. Being an insect, he was no sentimentalist. He had little attachment to any particular habitat; if the humans wished to cover the virgin land with their structures this was acceptable provided room could be made for the bugs as well. It was a simple matter of adaptation to selection pressure. Just as the rats have adjusted to the conditions of our modern cities (did you know that in San Francisco one can see in certain vacant lots – at one's own risk – rats as big as small dogs; and that adult rats throughout our great Republic are capable of swimming for several miles through the sewer systems and crawling up the plumbing pipes and dog-paddling right on into the toilet of their choice, and raising their heads cautiously with their green eyes hateful and jumping up onto the toilet seat and shaking themselves dry, leaving a puddle of water and filth, and running along the hall and into the kitchen and hiding under the trash can ready to bite your arm?), so the bugs have also reclaimed what is theirs. The old-style wooden houses in New England are tunneled through with wasps and termites; and they build their nests under the eaves and in the attic, and the termites weaken the house and the wasps sting hard. In the kitchen the competent naturalist finds not only rats but cockroaches in the pantry and trash closet (when you open the door they scuttle for the cracks but all you need to do is toot once on the button of your can of Raid, and count silently to three, and then the dead beetle-bodies will roll out of the cracks and fall pattering to the floor) and ants streaming in from nowhere all over the dishes in the sink and the sugar shaker and the breadbox, hundreds and thousands and millions of them all black and shiny and horrid. Flies in the living room and spiders to catch them on the ceiling and ticks or mites or something in bed; and you touch the wall or the floor and wonder whether an inch from your hand is a brood of slimy pupae waiting to erupt from the wood and get you . . . – But, as I have said, the bugs had no interest in getting us (except after we died, and ignoring the minority faction of parasites such as those bedbugs, the mosquitoes whining, whining, like orphans, bereft until they had your blood, the spiders biting your arm, the lice at the roots of your hair) and no great curiosity or enthusiasm about us as such; from the cowardly cockroaches to the blind stolid ants they wanted only to be left alone to eat and breed and eat and breed, just like us.

But we would not have them, anywhere, ever; for the fallacies of mapping and ownership decreed that there were no neutral zones. – But what of the many square miles of green strips along the center of our nation's freeways; what of the insulated hollows between the walls of our houses, the spaces between the grass blades of our lawns, the seldom-visited utility room, the darkness behind the workbench in the garage? – The space was there, all right, and so were the bugs, bugs, bugs, bugs . . .

"But what," you still ask, "did the bugs *think?*" – Ah, well; as Trotsky said about something else, that is not the sort of question which can be answered by a questionnaire. To arrive at even a provisional result requires a great grief, such as I have when my electricity is interrupted, my appliances flicker and hesitate, and from the light bulb issues an expanding bulb of darkness, which is how everything *really* looks. As the balloon blows itself up to usual size, made huge by the hot vapors of chaos and violence (for electricity is a cooling, numbing force that *contracts* things), people themselves expand and go dark around me; soon I lose sight of their faces in the dimness and can only vaguely sense their towering shoulders blocking out the night above the shining stars of their belt buckles, which themselves recede to other galaxies, as do the monstrous thousand-mile-high knees in the choking darkness; and finally I can just barely make out the black mountains of their shoes, which I could not hope to scale in a lifetime. Now the insulated hollows, the spaces between the grass blades, the utility room, the darkness behind the workbench all become horrifyingly spacious; and when somewhere near me I hear the clicking and scraping of some roach twice my size I take cover behind a thumbtack and dutifully take notes on the damned creature, as I must, being the author.

Beetles are considered by many, including Dr. Dodger, to be the most successful of all animal types. It is "no accident" that through their race the insects were organized for counter-attack. During the first millennia of human invasion, as the bugs were jockeyed into increasingly tortuous eco-niches under clay huts, in the rigging of the Phoenician ships, along the seams of leather scabbards, in the fuzz of horsehair blankets, among the nourishing papyri of Babylon's libraries, on the underside of the Round Table, where Arthur and Gawain wiped their greasy hands; and in the chinks of the first log cabins in our great Republic, little was accomplished in the way of retaliation. – Sure, I grant you the locust plagues and potato blights, but these were isolated occurrences which furthered no fine plan. The grasshoppers came and the weevils nibbled and the wasps stung and stung; yet nothing was secure. And meanwhile the wasps continued to prey upon the beetles; and even the beetles preyed upon each other, relatives of the blister beetles pursuing bark beetles beneath tree-skins, checkered beetles eating deathwatch beetles; and on and on.

The first advance occurred in the sphere of myrmecophily – that is, associations between ants and other insects (the ants always proving to be the hosts). The neophyte might tend to believe that it should have been such social types as the ants or the honeybees which led the vanguard instead of passively fueling the caravan with their substance, but what do neophytes ever know? In fact, it was precisely the complex ethos of ant–bee organizations which prohibited innovation; for by the time you learned the seventeen thousand potential meanings of the antenna tap, the final details of Hymenoptera etiquette in the hive, summer was almost over and you were on your way out. In came the staphylinid beetles, loners and pioneers not unlike Mr. White in Colorado. They scuttled about in the phosphorescent ant galleries and pupariums in rotten logs, ill at ease under public scrutiny but confidentially convinced as they sized things up that advantage could be taken of the confused array of commands and party committees, that blood could be sucked from the weak joints of the body politic. Soon they had the run of the place. They helped themselves to ant-eggs and larvae without opposition – o caviar! – in exchange for "cleaning up" the sick and dead workers, who tasted quite good as a rule. Other staphylinids pulled parasitic mites from the bodies of ants and ate them. When the ants moved to a new nest, the beetles followed jocosely, like great lumbering camp-followers (except that no whoring was involved; even rendering such services as they did was, as we see, far more of a gain to them than to the ants). They wandered through the nest eating the young. When the ants became agitated by this and gathered about them and prepared to bite these intruding giants, the beetles produced an intoxicating secretion so that the crowd crawled up on their backs and licked it from their bristles and grew dizzy and happy and for a time forgot all ant commands and ambled uselessly through the nest causing great disruption. The female ant larvae often drank too much of the secretion and developed into useless crippled spinsters instead of reproductive queens and then the beetles ate them for the good of the community. If the secretion did not succeed in taming the ants, that did not greatly matter, as a beetle would always win a fight. Its huge hard body was impervious to their puny nips. (Some species were cylindrical and polished in texture, so that the ants could not get a purchase.) In addition, any one of these beetles could spray its attackers with iodine from its pygidial gland, and *that* sure sent them scurrying back off into the darkness . . . But the remarkable thing about the beetles was their sensitivity to all the grammar and directives and slogans and even unstated desires of the ant world, which they learned to manipulate. They first memorized the proper antenna-vibration and foreleg-tap which the ants themselves used to request food. The poor workers, busy going here and there and back again all day and never getting a chance to think, automatically assumed that these fearsome strangers had been authorized by the Central Committee since they knew the password, and so they regurgitated a drop or two of fruit juice on cue, much the same as when one is traveling across Europe or Asia on the train and a person in uniform requests one's passport, one's ticket, takes them away, and comes back, or else does not come back, having sold them; a badge and a superior manner can obtain anything in this world. – The next step was to get the ants to care for the baby beetles through the pupa stage; and that was no big trick, either; soon the ants fed them and licked them clean and carried them just like the others; and of course they grew up that way with the smell of the nest on them and an intimate knowledge of ant ways. These assimilated beetles played upon the competition between rival queens-to-be and convinced the diggers that the draggers had it too easy and persuaded the draggers that the diggers were hoarding the choicest fungi for themselves; and in no time at all they could get the ants to fight each other so that there would be many wounded or dead for them to gobble up, or they could lead the whole nest to relocate in an area that had more rabbit dung or other substances that the beetles had a fancy for. Another prank was to spray black ants with red pigment and red ants with black pigment, so that the unknowing transvestites would be seen as spies or foreign troops and killed at once, while in the confusion the beetles snuck

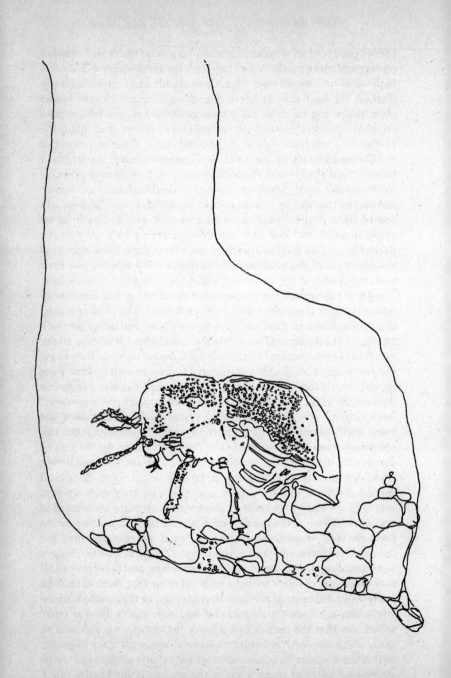

into the larder and tapped the honey-ants on the abdomen so that the honey-ants vomited the sweet sap and the beetles kissed the ants, sucking the sap out, and the ants' bellies deflated; the beetles had just stolen a week's worth of food; and then off they went back to the slaughter just in time to gobble a discarded limb or two for a snack.

In revenge for the already described depredations of wasps upon their kind, the beetles became parasites upon the wasp larvae as well, burrowing inside their bodies and nibbling on a tissue here, a muscle there, without destroying the vital organs (that way the larvae could feed them longer); and finally stretching their jaws and eating everything and then pupating comfortably concealed in the dead husks. They even sponged off the giant hornets, hiding in the refuse heaps beneath the hive where pieces of old comb, excrement, wood splinters and dead larvae furnished them with a repast akin to fine cheese. The final phase was to go after the honeybees, eating the sick and dead larvae under the hives as usual, and then, getting bolder, climbing onto the combs and attacking the growing larvae in their very cells ...

It was at this juncture that the Great Beetle was conceived. His parents were sexton beetles, though an apocryphal version of the tale claims that his gestation occurred in a poplar tree, in which case the fated pair would have been longhorn beetles, planting the egg beneath the bark in one of the tree's major capillaries so that the tree puffed itself out there in a tumor and nourished the egg with its sweet fluids. – The habits of sexton beetles are more sedate. The male and female dig a subterranean hollow and drag into it the carcass of a mouse or small amphibian. Then they push and fold and squash the carrion until finally it is mashed into a soft ball into which the eggs are placed. The father wanders off in search of other graves; he is a businesslike thing condemned to working and working dully, like me; while the mother waits by the corpse and munches on plants or dung to pass the time and when the larvae are born she scuttles after them and eats as many as she can.

What happened in this case was that the mouse who was to be the Great Beetle's womb-home had been in a museum before it died, creeping from its hole every night to nibble on the ceremonial balsam of Egyptian mummies; at last it perished of its rich diet; and when the two sexton beetles found the furry bedraggled body and pulled it down into the earth (in the midst of a storm, so the story goes), the humidity of underground conditions penetrated into the balsam, some of which remained in the mouse's stomach, and activated it.

The larval period of the deathwatch beetle is two to three years; and that of the giant stag beetle can be five to eight. When the Great Beetle emerged from his ball of putrefaction, he ran away from his mother and hid in a crack between two stones and went through eighty-one larval stages over a period of a hundred years. Complete (holometabolous) metamorphosis takes place in beetles from egg to imago. Generally each stage is simply a larger copy of the one preceding it, but in the case of parasites remarkable external changes occur, corresponding to the steady development of a tranquil in-dwelling perspective, meditating among flesh and blood and the finer things of life like heart muscle and tissue damage; so the first stage is active and lively, but each succeeding one takes on a more awkward, sedentary form until finally it has lost the ability or desire to move. The Great Beetle was no parasite; nonetheless, significant transformations occurred in him in every moult. Not only did he grow in size, but his nerve ganglia became more and more complex; and his shell got fantastically whorled and marbled and heavy, so that his six legs could scarcely support the weight of it. To pupate he went into an ants' nest, pulled fine soil debris around himself, and contemplated ontological projects for twenty-three years, by which time the ants had decided that he must simply be an immovable boulder and had built tunnels all around him. He was the great lodestone of the nest; for even then he had begun to show his charismatic power; and the ants built observation galleries about his entire circumference, so that he could be tapped and crawled upon there in the dark. (After his death the situation was much the same, his shell becoming his altar, and uncounted members of the losing races coming to it to pray on vain pilgrimages.)

Now at last he awoke in his full maturity and mastered the ant commands. But he did not use them for his own benefit; rather, he called all inmates of the nest together and exuded his own secretion, which was sweet and mild and did not intoxicate; and they ate of him and were satisfied. And he talked with them, using legs and feelers, and conveyed to them the momentous plan of alliance against the invaders. Where had he learned of this? – The ways of beetles are mysterious. Perhaps during his pupal stage he had searched the humid air with his long antennae so that information crystallized upon them.

That was his way. All insects joined with him. And he lived in a deep tunnel, and all came to him; and he was benevolent. And he built up his armies.

THE FIRST EXECUTIONS

A Scout is *Kind* . . . But you will also learn that there are creatures that do not deserve your protection. A Scout does not kill any living thing needlessly, but he knows that it is his duty to get rid of those that are dangerous to human beings. He doesn't hesitate to kill animals such as rats or insects such as flies and mosquitoes that carry sickness along with them . . .

Boy Scout Handbook (1969)

On 19 May Commander White broke to the Merchant Marine forces the news of a massive insect buildup in the interior. He called Dr. Dodger to Miami for consultations, but placed himself in supreme command. Commander White was far from unprepared. He had solidly armed his country and reorganized his troops along the most modern lines, so that even in the playgrounds the children were drilled in the use of the Thompson centerfire; and thanks to Wayne our intelligence apparatus was quite good. Having just received the square of Kleenex which Wayne had captured from the green weevil, Commander White sent an élite squad of commandos to locate this Bug troublemaker, whoever the fuck he was, and seize him suddenly and quietly. – But Bug was nowhere to be found. A silverfish had warned him. – It was clear to Mr. White that this here conflict was gonna be more complex and drawn-out than he had suspected. Overcoming his personal feelings, he sent a signal rocket up to Phil Blaker on Mars, *phwooosh!*, establishing a working truce during these tense days of yellow alert; for his practical mind was never trapped behind the ideological lines it had drawn.

The first reports from the California–Massachussets front were somewhat contradictory. According to Dr. Dodger's sources, whole divisions had already been obliterated by the enemy; and towns had been depopulated as a result of the Great Beetle's irresistible advance. Yet no one could pin down the exact location of these castastrophes. In his Freedom Broadcasts to the western states, Dr. Dodger hinted that it was the east coast that was being devastated; and when he spoke at the huge insecticide rally in Springfield, New Hampshire, he assured those who thronged the county display booths that the bugs had gained control in Oregon and Nevada. Behind the fighting lines, panic began to spread. This was, of course, precisely Dr. Dodger's object, per Commander White's instructions.

On 25 May, by Executive Order of the President, the Society of Daniel was made responsible for the Federal Civil Defense Program. A pamphlet on the hazards of an insect attack was drafted by the Pentagon, most likely with the connivance of Newt and Sammy. It read:

If our great Republic were attacked, people who were close to beetle and stinging wasp shock troops would be killed or injured seriously by the sheer heat of the engagement. People a few miles away, in the "fringe area," would be endangered by wood-borers and subversive termites. People outside the fringe area would be affected by bug-egg fallout. This latter hazard can be guarded against through the conscientious use of mothballs.

Far away, in the loneliness of his eavesdropping post in South Dakota, Wayne tuned in his radio implant to catch Commander White's great mobilization speech. He didn't pick up much but crackles, but the emotion came through. "Awright," Wayne muttered to himself, sitting out under the stars of the vast dreary plains, "aw-right . . ." and he felt all clean and reverent . . .

In a secret detention center lost somewhere in a muggy futile backwoods Indiana evening, the first shipment of captured beetles prepared to meet their fate. Sentence had already been passed, under the stringently efficient dictates of martial law. There were thirty beetles, each about the size of a half-grown child. For the most part they were black pine sawyers and giant root borers, but there was one broad-necked darkling beetle (*Ceolocnemis californicus*) which stood stiffly apart in the common cell, with its dull, pitted head down and its hind legs raised. It was a master spy, believed to have come from an arid or semidesert region; the climate did not agree with it. It was sentenced to be hanged until dead. It seemed to want to be left alone, so the other beetles stayed on the other side of the cell, crawling quietly against the cool floor.

Now came the Merchant Marine gendarmes, proud, fresh and still clean-scrubbed from their recent induction. Wrinkling their noses at the strong insect smell, they unlocked the cell door and carried the darkling beetle out on their shoulders. Its feelers wiggled slightly, but it made no other movement. It had expected this treatment. Once the young soldiers realized that it would offer no resistance, they felt vaguely sorry for it and shifted it on their shoulders so that it could look down at the ground with its tiny eyes, much as a condemned man or woman is allowed to look for a moment at a landscape or a city. Did it think of past burrows, and fungus stores, and the warm, comforting darkness of its insect home? – Who knows what a bug thinks? There was no ground to be seen, anyhow; it was all maximum security cement.

In the courtyard stood the insect gallows. It had never been used before. Dr. Dodger had designed it. It had an adjustable metal collar to be fitted between the head and the thorax. The gendarmes set their prisoner down on the wide stairs of the platform and bound the elytra firmly against the broad black back. From each of the four legs below the head segment a twenty-pound lead weight was hung. There seemed to be no practical way of tying a blindfold. The darkling beetle lay quite still in their arms as they bore it to the scaffold. They fitted the collar around its neck and left it waiting on the trap, its six legs scrabbling tentatively against the boards, while sentence was read. It was getting dark; the arc lamps came on. The signal was given; the trap fell; the beetle was jerked into a comically erect position by the weights and the collar as it hung there looking at them unreadably, with all the prison lights shining on it. It seemed no worse for wear at first, but after a moment the weighted legs began to snap off crisply. – "Goddamn that Dr. Dodger!" yelled the executioner over the four thuds of the weights striking the flagstones of the courtyard. The beetle's frail body was whirled madly and bounced like a rubber ball on a string at each impact. The dull tan stripes on the inner surface of its tibia and tarsi could be distinctly seen on the severed legs. – The executioner was at a loss. With only its legs gone, the beetle could live for days. "Shoot it!" he cried finally. – At once the guards advanced to the foot of the scaffold, knelt down on the bottom step, aimed, and ... But the beetle, suddenly beginning to click and wiggle madly, somehow succeeded in loosening the cord about the elytra so that it could free its body; opened its wings, and flew up into the night until it had pulled the hangman's rope completely taut. They could all hear it above their heads, flapping desperately like a bat at the end of the rope. The searchlights were trained on it; and now they could see the silhouette of its grotesque body; they could see owls and night-hawks swooping at it in a fury but kept at bay by those rigid black wings ... –

"Halt fire!" shouted the executioner. The marksmen would have to shoot straight up. There would be a danger that the bullets might come back down on the soldiers and jailors. "GodDAMN that Dr. Dodger!"

The executioner was in fact maligning Dr. Dodger unfairly; for while the weights had been incorrectly calibrated, at least some provision had been made for the present emergency. Above the gallows was suspended a huge fishing reel, about which the rope had been coiled before the trap dropped. In the executioner's control box there was a big red switch. The executioner, finally remembering what it was for, flipped it. At once the motor started; it was perhaps ten times as loud as a "Snapper" lawn mower. The reel began to revolve faster and faster as it wound the rope around itself once again. The beetle was pulled down, at first inch by inch, then foot by foot; ultimately it was revolving enormous arcs around the reel at high speed, being dashed against the ground as the marksmen scurried for cover, against the walls of the courtyard so that its shell finally cracked, 'way up in the air and down again and around faster and faster until it smashed to pieces against a post of the scaffold and sprayed every observer present with its juices and organs and crunchy flakes of shell.

So ended the first execution.

It was decided not to repeat the experiment with the other twenty-nine beetles. At the stroke of midnight a carriage arrived for the black pine sawyers (*Monochamus scutellatus*) and took them to the old Conrail depot, where an unmarked train was waiting to carry them to the national forest. The railroad car advanced rapidly past Omarville and was shunted onto the military track. Wild dogs howled as they smelled the bugs huddled together in the unlighted car. It was triple-locked from the outside; ten soldiers rode upon the roof. The bugs felt very cold. They longed for a big tree to bore into, dark and woody and intoxicating with the flavor of its hearty sap, or at least a pile of sawdust to hide in. But it did not really matter; for now the locomotive was screeching like an iron chicken, and they were slowing; and the car stopped; and they heard the soldiers jumping off and surrounding the car (or rather, they felt the vibration); and they entwined their long antennae together in beetleship; and the doors were thrown open to let in the cold blue moonlight. They wanted roots to eat. Now as they came out they could smell the trees all around them; and as they waited for death they sucked on wood chips in the clearing as the soldiers stood round and the executioner and his assistant threw down economy-size bags of quicklime . . .

"Line up two by two!" the second lieutenant semaphored to the condemned pine sawyers, utilizing a digital box with an English-language input teletype keyboard, and two ceramic antennae in a base of machine oil. (R ANT 7:30, L ANT 5:42, flashed the readout window.) The beetles got into a long double column and were marched to a marshy area where the mosquitoes hummed and the air was heavy with the odors of mud and methane. The technical sergeant strung up lights.

"First pair!" the second lieutenant typed in (R ANT 4:20, L ANT 2:11).

The first two beetles crawled forward obediently. It was that obedience which facilitated the belief of all personnel on extermination detail that beetles could not suffer.

"Now dig your graves!" (R ANT 3:23, L ANT 12:01.)

The beetles began to bore into the soft soil. When they were half immersed the executioner and his assistant, standing just behind them, shoveled lime over them and packed it tight about their carapaces and baked them alive.

"Next pair!" (R ANT 4:20, L ANT 2:12) . . .

As for the giant root borers (*Prionus* spp.) back at the prison, they were taken out one by one and electrocuted. As each was carried away, the remaining beetles buzzed loudly and flew about the cell, crashing against the walls. At 6:43 a.m., the last one was strapped into the circuits of the prison dynamo. The hot summer dawn had already come, stirring up the termite armies out back in the nasty green mud. But since they were reserves the Great Beetle had ordered them to stay hidden. Thus they could not help the last root borer; it was going to have to die. Sunlight came in through the dusty windows of One-Way Hall, as the transit passage was informally known, so that as the beetle was borne along in its chains by old turnkeys the light kept glancing off its shell in pretty squares, and other prisoners peering through their gratings sighed in wonder, momentarily forgetting that they were next up to bat; but the execution room was like the bridge of an abandoned submarine, cobwebbed and windowless, with rusty old switches and controls and meters wrapped with black tape. In the corner was a yellow tarpaulin, artfully draped over a great smoldering pile of charcoal ash, for the personnel, who also practiced flower-arranging on Sundays, were not without a sense of style. The executioner winked at the tarp and nudged the root borer with an elbow-knock against its shell, so that it understood that those burned lumps were all that remained of its fellows. It panicked then, kicking its legs until they were tangled in the chains, but nobody paid any attention, and at last it calmed down, consoling itself with the thought that at least it had already laid its eggs. When winter came it would have died anyhow. – In the center of the room was a padded table suspended above a drain. To this the criminal was made fast by the numerous hooks, elastics and legholds conveniently provided, then dull grey bands bristling with wires were looped tightly around its head section, thorax and abdomen by the turnkeys, who then retired. The executioner splashed a pailful of copper sulfate solution liberally on the beetle's body to facilitate conduction, so that the blue-green liquid spattered in its eyes and coated its antennae and puddled in the pits and small concavities of its shell and ran down its legs, sticking to the bristles, and extended long thin fingers along the surface of the table, and trickled down into the drain, where it formed hard blue crystals deep in the secret pipes. Then the observers were invited in. – Dr. Dodger was at the controls. "Ready, everyone?" he cried gaily. The observers nodded, tying bandanas over each other's noses and mouths. Only the executioner did not nod. He was sullen because Dr. Dodger was in charge instead of him. But Dr. Dodger graciously overlooked this slight. – "Okey-dokey, gentlemen!" said he. "Let us begin at the beginning, oh, yes!" The root borer's shiny eyes bulged as Dr. Dodger reached for the switch. Nineteen hundred volts ripped through its shiny reddish-brown body for eleven seconds, then four hundred volts for forty-three seconds, then twenty-three hundred for six seconds, then three hundred for fifty-eight seconds. The beetle had turned crispy black; there was a sound of bubbling and an awful smell. White steam and black smoke gushed from the electrifried carcass in a dozen different places, and the smell was now so bad that the observers gagged behind their bandanas. Contact was broken with a flourish; Dr. Dodger ordered another ten seconds at twenty-eight hundred volts, and the beetle was pronounced dead. – A blue halo of satiated electric force lingered around the corpse for six minutes, so Dr. Dodger spun round and round on his left heel to pass the time, all the while flipping a quarter in the air and catching it on his many-jointed wrist. – "Very nice," murmured the observers; "very well done." – At last it was safe to clean up. The bugs were all buried together in a huge lead coffin. Sulfuric acid was poured in by the authorities very slowly, and Dr. Dodger calculated on his slide rule that the bodies would decompose in six hours.

A CALL TO ARMS

~~~~~~

We illustrate these ideas in our first program.

SEYMOUR LIPSCHUTZ and ARTHUR POE
Schaum's Outline of Theory and
Problems of Programming with FORTRAN,
including Structured Fortran (1978)

Fellow citizens, members of the Senate and the House of Representatives, and great men of the Kakuanas:

Having been convened upon an extraordinary occasion, as authorized by the regulations previously established, you may be sure that your attention is called to no ordinary subject.

I am referring, of course, to the situation now to be met with in all boroughs of moderately acidic soil. The functions of electricity have been found to be generally suspended within these regions; and the generators remaining in our possession are now menaced by hostile preparations of the so-called Kuzbuites and Kuzbuite sympathizers. These discontented six- and eight-legged individuals, having failed to convince the majority that their cause is just, have decided in wild wicked willfulness to force their views upon us all; and we in consequence have no recourse but to let things roll. Dr. Dodger and I have just cranked up the Great Dynamo; and at this moment standby units in our bases around the world are being gassed up (*sind aufgegassen werden*) and wired in series with the appropriate industries. It is also my duty to inform you that I have begun calling up our reserves. Every applicant who qualifies must report immediately to the nearest hardware or hardwire store, where he will be issued defensive garden tools commensurate with his status as defined by the rules. Mobilized battalions will proceed to the affected areas on a search-and-destroy basis.

The enemy is out to seize our condominiums and ten-cent movie theaters, our fair young schoolgirls and our grain and oil. We must jettison all complacency. There can be no room in our ranks for sob-sisters, because I'm telling you once and for all that mercy is a dirty word from here on out; and if you want to keep your appliances and the happy clattering joys of your toil in the factories then you'd better keep your ear to the ground and remember the password because if you don't those larvae are going to moult all over you, so get a move on and register with your draft board, you imbeciles! Electricity is not a gift freely given. You'd better be willing to put your lives on the line for what you've got or else *I'll* put your lives on the line and I guarantee you won't like that because I've got a special place all ready for shirkers and flinchers and it's called the ant-heap.

These bugs have the advantage. Not only do they outnumber us a million to one, not only do they live by alien insect creeds that attach no value to individual life, but they also retain the rectitude and purity of the underdog. And so it is that they have insidiously debauched the public mind, though we still control the larger cities. I myself have killed many bugs in my time, though of course I have never slain wantonly, only in self-defense, when no compromise could be a cure.

Well, what the hell. This situation is the same. While we have life, we have hope. While we have hope, we have courage. While we have courage, we have ingenuity. While we have ingenuity, we have flame-throwers. A state of war now exists between us and the bugs.

REACTIONARIES FOREVER

Several popular games involve controlling a little person who must run around and shoot things, or avoid robots, or dig gold.

> "Well, I Was Young" in *Datamation*
> (15 April 1984)

I had to say God was God, and Mahomet was his prophet. Who knows whether I thought so? I wear the turban as I would wear an uniform. When I left Venice I was as poor as a rat, and if the Jews had offered me the command of fifty thousand men, I would have laid siege to Jerusalem.

> COUNT DE BONNEVAL, Pasha of Carmania
> (as recounted by Casanova)

THE CATERPILLAR HEART

> Thus he moves rapidly and brilliantly up through all social levels,
> but he remains like a hard kernel in the circles which accept him,
> and his assimilation is as ephemeral as it is brilliant.
>
> SARTRE
> *Anti-Semite and Jew*

One day at summer camp they were having archery period, and
Parker sat in line on the long log bench that was rubbed smooth by
decades of contact with boys' wiggling bottoms; and the golden
dappling of the boys' bodies shifted mindlessly, restlessly, as the
leaves wavered over their heads. Wayne was at the infirmary with a
broken toe. Parker sat squinching up his shoulders and flexing his
back muscles and gangling his arms around picking at scabs on his
ankles and moving his head slowly from side to side never missing a
thing; and on either side of him boys sat leaving him alone because
they all knew *that* much; and up ten paces stood Roger Garvey with
the bow; and the counselor was showing him how to hold it right
and cock the string back and aim with the arrow almost level with
your ear and let go smoothly when you were good and ready: –
SPUNNNT! – The arrow missed the target by a mile and disappeared into the forest forever. The boys howled and threw clods
of earth at Roger and the counselor was angry at Roger for paying
no attention to instructions and losing an arrow, and he shook
Roger by the shoulder and pushed him a little and told him to go to
the end of the line. Parker sat on the log with the others, digging his
toes into the dirt and scraping a fingernail against the white fuzz on
his tongue and thinking indescribable burnished thoughts like a
drowsy snake. Off to the side, hidden in a thicket of ferns and oak
saplings, our hero spied on everything with his usual patience and
continuity of effort; and from beneath the green loam many bugs

protruded their eyes and watched him and the other boys like data cameras, their insurgency having reached the incipient phase.

At the end of the period it was free time, and just for something to do the older boys rounded up Roger and some of the other persons who had incurred their displeasure and took them off into the woods to scare them. Near the woodcraft circle was a muddy weed-grown path that led into a grove of tall dark pines and then through an abandoned field of raspberry-brambles and dewy grass that soaked you to the waist; and here stood the former Nature House, which was partly caved-in and bared its moldy roof-ribs. You could climb onto the roof by clinging to these exposed rafters and hoisting yourself up (hoping you did not weigh enough to make the decayed wood give under you, in which case you'd fall ten feet to the frost-cracked concrete floor); and once on the beams you ascended through a gap in the shingles and emerged on the apex of the roof. Your next obligation was to work your way down to a wide leaf-choked rain gutter that projected over the edge of the roof about seven feet from the ground; and here the older boys had already made fast the rope with which they were going to hang you. No one was ever really hurt; the trick was to terrify the victim so that his will to deviate from the older boys' directives was destroyed. Parker was not yet one of the older boys, but he had a silence and restlessness and guileful slimy presence which gave him entry into this secret world so that he could see how things were done (as meanwhile our hero and the bugs watched the scene from their own unauthorized vantage points).

They made Roger go first. Because he was basically obedient, as he would be in the days yet to come, when Parker and Wayne determined events, the older boys had no desire to be harsh with him; his only sin was mediocre execution of commands, so when he scrambled up and hugged the roof for dear life with his rear up in the air and worked his way down the gutter and stuck his head out for the noose like a dumb animal they laughed and clapped and told him to jump down, and he jumped down with relief sweating forth from his face; and they made him pull down his pants and bend over, and poked a stick up his anus and let him go. There were four other spindly Cadets remaining; these were made to hang one by one, for periods varying from one to five seconds; and sent on their way, with green branches applied energetically to speed their progress.

Parker meanwhile lolled and diddled and stretched in the grass, well aware that within him lay the capability to exercise power far more purposively than these middle-class bunglers who entertained themselves like lords' sons dealing with game they had no wish to eat; but meanwhile he said nothing, just kinda rubbing his lower jaw against his chest and looking about him with his big yellow eyes and gently squishing a mosquito between his two fingers. But he was not forgotten.

"Parker!" said the big boys. "Hey, you, Parker!"

Parker at once flowed into a defensive shape and began preparing to exercise available options, all of which depended on his own amorphousness; for at this time there was no Wayne to read his signals and lunge to the attack; and now here came the big boys strolling up with grass blades a-twiddle between their lips and stood around him; and the oldest one said, "Parker, we like you, and you can be one of us, for sentimental if not for other reasons. You have a certain style which we treasure; and we will allow you to be initiated by us at this time. I hope that my frankness convinces you."

Parker just kinda nodded and looked around the circle of faces while playing an invisible piano with his sensitive fingers, as delicately as if he were repairing a spiderweb.

"Very well," said the oldest boy, surveying him acutely. "Experience teaches that someday you younger ones will displace us; remember that you also will be displaced, and that you must initiate your younger ones as we will initiate you, so that our history may continue to run its course. — Gentlemen, the rope, please."

Parker's wrists drooped triple-jointedly. The boys lifted him up on their shoulders and bore him to the edge of the roof, and raised him so that the sunlight was on his pale blank face; and the oldest boy kissed him on the mouth and fastened the rope around his neck. They supported his legs for a moment, and he looked out around him and saw the stretch of bright green field and the tops of the pines and the blue shimmer of the lake beyond the trees; and the big boys stood holding his ankles solemnly. Five minutes passed, and Parker just kinda hung loose and rolled his eyes and wet his lips a little bit; and hidden in the grass Bug peered up at him and looked into his face and thought he saw in Parker's scummy irises a look which could only be described as *voluptuous*; that something important was happening to Parker and Parker knew it and needed it and could not fight it; and he remained suspended in the air, writhing slightly like an eel having an orgasm until his abnormally soft, long bones began to bend like rubber and his supple body started oozing backwards; then quickly the boys loosed him and he fell until the rope snapped taut and his feet dangled a foot from the ground; then the boys seized great sticks and beat him as hard as they could, yelling, "Omarville scum! You poison-ivy pansy! Godamn weed!" and the eldest boy was jumping up and down screaming, "I demand the supreme penalty! Kill the vegetable upstart who's making us old and pushing his roots in our dirt!" and they began throwing stones at his face and crying; their faces were wet with anguish and loss and they genuinely wanted to kill him; but you can't kill ole Parker as easy as all that; and Parker just kinda cringed and twisted and let his body ooze thinner and thinner and longer and longer till his feet reached the ground and his head stretched all soft and plastic and slipped through the noose and he ducked beneath their legs and stretched in all directions and tripped them up and yawned without apparent malice (but if you had been able to look into his horrible face from a distance of three inches or less you might have seen the dull fishy hatred glittering in his eyeballs) and he stood up and resumed his proportions and the older boys all fell sobbing and worshipping him; and Parker just kinda yawned and lounged against a tree and farted some corrosive gas that made them cry tears of blood.

But our hero remembered the voluptuous look in Parker's face when Parker was about to be hanged; and the one fact which he filed away for future use was that Parker needed to be punished; he needed it and wanted it; because it was only under torture that Parker could flex himself out in his full powers; and our hero knew that the trick, the only way to destroy Parker when the time came, was to give him a punishment he could not endure, because then he would be all the more attracted to it; and would get in over his head and perish miserably like an insect in a dish of rubbing alcohol. But otherwise the insect would only gain refreshment from its own intoxicating agonies and wing away with stronger poisons dripping from its wicked stinger . . .

The reader must understand that after this incident a significant latency period passed; for it was not until perhaps fifteen years later, when our hero had become an operative of the Great Beetle, that he had both the occasion and the resources to strike at Parker. When the bugs reported to him that his message via the green bug had been intercepted by Wayne, then he knew that both Wayne and Parker would be after him. Though he had only a newspaper knowledge of Mr. White and the Society of Daniel, he considered that Wayne, at least, who had been voted "most likely to succeed," must surely be sailing somewhere near the mainstreams of power, where remorseless uncanny proceedings were set in motion by the reactionaries; and unlimited coastal patrols and middle-aged men in parks would hunt him down until they found him, however long it took; for with electricity now operating everywhere (electricity, as Mr. Bierce has pointed out, is "the power that causes all natural phenomena not known to be caused by something else") they could track down his last bank transaction through the automatic tellers, and have dingy computer reels spinning to match up his description with the blue grainy faces of unknown persons on the video films taken in shopping malls, airports, security towers and strongholds; and someday he would look out the tiny window of the attic in Oakland where he was hiding, and see two cars pull into the driveway below, and setting up a laser mortar in the dying rhododendron bush would be some technocrat like Sammy or Newt as Wayne jumped out rolling up his sleeves with a big white grin yelling, "Awright, boyo!" and Parker could be discerned through the tinted windshield, sorta stretched out on the front seat breaking off rotten toenails but not missing a trick through those special-issue police sunglasses of his that eased his darkroom eyes; and Wayne's hairy arms would be all tattooed now as he flexed them to make the stallion on his left bicep go down on the blonde; and the clipper ship on his right one toss about in stormy seas; see, he swung a set of handcuffs; and he was putting on his brass knuckles; he was too contemptuous of the old swimming pool wimp to bother with a pistol or anything; and Bug would tremble on the floorboards of the attic, and if Bug tried to resist arrest and the laser mortar weren't quite set up yet then maybe instead Parker might just kinda scratch and flick his greasy hair back outta his eyes and fiddle with those black sunglasses and lean forward and do something to that James Bond cigarette lighter and it would be all over for Bug.

Of course Bug was aware deep down inside him that there was no way *really* to destroy Wayne and Parker, and that at best he could only postpone the moment when he felt the hand on the back of his neck; but in the meantime (he attempted to cheer himself) there must be some way to incapacitate Parker temporarily so that Wayne would rush to Parker's side to render first aid and our hero could take the insect subway and disappear into some cobwebbed pupa a mile below a grain silo and have a bit of breathing space. At present he dared not make a break for it because he didn't know how close they were; they might conceivably be just around the corner at this very moment; and bug intelligence, somewhat occu- pied now with planning battles in the sewers and such now that hostilities had begun, had no time to answer his questions. – As yet the war remained a *Sitzkrieg*. There were no grey-green battalions keeping order in the streets, no militiamen guarding factories, no G.I. grunts spreading chlorodane dust, no lineups and spot inspections, no eyewitness news of chopper strikes in the marshes of Florida or bodies being airlifted out glistening with hysterical maggots. Each side was still taking the other's measure. – Bug, then, would have to draw up his attack plan himself. He decided to entangle Parker somehow in the wiry pubic thickets of romance.

Casanova informs us that "the most reserved Turkish woman is only modest as far as her face goes; as long as she has her veil on she blushes at nothing." Spanish women, on the other hand, veil the prints of Christ and the Virgin that hang above their beds, so that the holy eyes will be bewildered and confounded by the skirt draped over them, the skirt which the lady has removed for that sole prestidigitative purpose. Both of these accounts, I am sad to say, are false; or else I am more ugly than Casanova.

Nonetheless, the notion that in matters of love certain items ought to be veiled is accurate enough. There is always something which would cause shame were it open to the gaze; and always someone to take shame were he able to gaze upon us in the act. Concealment is thus a matter of courtesy. – So it certainly was in the case of the snare which Bug was designing for Parker; for deep down in the darkest puparium the bugs had agreed, despite their other commitments, to grow a Caterpillar Heart, covered with rich soft fur and beating with the cool green juices of love; this would be veiled by human skin. If Parker hugged it to him tight with his long arms, it would hurt him badly.

A THUMBNAIL SKETCH

~~~~~~

> If he continues to call after you have told him not to, you may have
> to do what Karen did. She finally changed her phone number and
> the lock on her door, and told her secretary she would not accept
> calls from Bill ... Only when he could no longer contact Karen
> was Bill finally forced to turn his attention to himself and his part
> in the failure of their marriage ... Today Bill is happily remarried
> – and he and Karen are good friends.
>
> *McCall's* (July 1983)

To describe the effects of this peculiar weapon, I can make no better
beginning than recounting a human case. About three weeks ago my
fiancee, with whom I had been living for almost three years, decided
that she did not love me anymore. This put her in an unenviable
strategic position, for I remained stubbornly oblivious to this fact
despite her best efforts at delicate suggestion, so at last, no longer
able to stomach my endearments (she had always been my Bee; and I
had been her Beetle), losing interest in the tedious details of my life
(which, like a robin redbreast, I had been all too eager to feed her in
our nest, as if she were still my baby bird who was content to eat
what I might bring her), and unable to desire me sexually (it had
gotten to the point where I had to beg her each Saturday morning
for about forty-five minutes until finally she would hitch up her
nightgown and spread her legs and close her eyes and lie there
motionless), there was nothing for her to do but unveil her pure hard
will in a session of mercy killing; for it was all too clear that I had no
minimum level of self-respect below which I would not debase
myself to keep her. So, one night after she had bought my birthday
present, she steeled herself to shoot her own dog. It would be
necessary, she knew, to disregard my tears and nasty groveling
entreaties in order to compel me to see that no matter how good I
might be henceforth my case was hopeless, that I simply could not

have her anymore. I am told that when a girl gets her ears pierced the poor dumb flesh tries to grow back where it is not wanted; and sometimes she must push needles through the spot several times over the next few days in order to kill it for good, because it will try until it is dead to heal the wound. So it was here. I had to be dealt with in one great firm stroke, without unnecessary cruelty, but the knife had to go in and it had to be twisted just as firmly in the wound, because the flesh would not understand. I remember once when I was working on a ranch my friend Eric was showing me how to kill a pig. We were smoking all our pigs for sausage. The previous three had been dispatched; the last had hidden itself behind a pile of straw in its hutch, for pigs are very intelligent animals. As we exposed it and dragged it outside and onto the bloodstained sand, it began to scream. We flung it down on its back and Eric bayoneted it through the heart. It screamed and screamed. The dark pig-blood spurted. Eric and I held the dying animal down. Eric removed the bayonet so that the blood could run freely, and with exquisite gentleness he worked the trembling pig's back legs, forward and back, forward and back, to pump all the blood out. The pig lay there sweating and shaking and pissing and rolling its eyes. Eric stroked its head to calm it, just as he might have done with a dairy cow that had been spooked by something. "All right now," he said gently but inflexibly into the pig's ear. "You just lie there and bleed."

This, then, was the hard ceremony of cauterization which my fiancee had to conduct. No doubt she consulted with our mutual friends to find the best way of doing it, just like her best friend Milly had studied all the sex manuals and anatomy charts for weeks before she finally parted with her maidenhead, back when we were all in college; for all this day there was an eerie silence in our (now Bee's) apartment, the friends evidently warned by Bee to leave the path clear for the operation. Now, as I returned home from work, like a rapist strapped to a table, wheeled along to his castration, her heart failed her for a moment; and when I got into bed beside her she told me that we would stop being lovers for the time being, and would sleep in separate rooms, but we could still live together and see if we could be friends. This was somewhat akin to piercing the earlobe once and letting nature take its course, healing if it might; or to stabbing through almost to the pig's heart but not quite penetrating it; then sewing the animal up with catgut stitches and debating whether or not to give it antibiotics; or to cutting off only one of the rapist's testicles. — I told her that as we had already stopped cooking together or eating together or seeing each other for more than about

ten minutes a day I couldn't see that this would do anything but lower our mutual expectations another notch. – "Well," asked my Bee, "what's your alternative?" – The Beetle clicked and fluttered its elytra in nervous grief and burrowed deep beneath the bedclothes. "We could spend more time together," it hazarded; "we could, Bee, we could; and we could each give up something else to make time and do more things together," but Bee buzzed angrily at it and said, "The more things we do together the worse we get along. There is a third alternative," and now already she was recovering from her vacillation and raising her stinger and having the Beetle roll over and bare its black glossy insect-tummy to her, and brushing alcohol on its thorax where she would carry out sentence and sting; and the Beetle, understanding that its pleas had made an unpleasant impression, lay still and thought back on all the crimes it had committed, such as crawling up into her hive and drinking honey from her combs when she was so busy and had worked so hard to make it for herself; and the Beetle said, knowing the answer very well, "What alternative?" and Bee buzzed like a saw and said, "*You* know what I mean," but Beetle said, "No I don't," because Beetle did not want to admit that it knew the answer; so Bee hummed and buzzed and said, "We could end this completely," in a very determined voice; and Beetle said, "Oh," in a very small voice because it was the first time that Bee had ever said that, and it went to hide at the foot of the bed again, but Bee flew up and hovered over it like the Angel of Death and said, "Well, would you rather accept my alternative or break up?"; and the Beetle thought about it and decided what was a little more degradation if that meant that it could keep its Bee; and very rapidly it rubbed its elytra together and said, "I don't like your alternative, but I want to stay with you; I'll do anything to stay with you and I'll accept any compromise . . ." – but looking up into the darkness with its bug-eyes the Beetle could sense that the Bee had no intention of compromise in any form, so it added quickly, "But if that's what you want I'll do it because I'll do anything you want me to do; I love you;" but then the Bee settled on the Beetle nonetheless and grasped the proper spot and stung it deeply and slowly and thoroughly, and said, "I don't think I love you anymore." That was the first time that she had ever said *that*. – "Oh," said Beetle (the last thing it ever said). – "I've never broken up with anyone before," Bee hummed, "and I don't know if I'm doing this right – you can hate me if you want – but I don't want to live with you anymore."

The cool sting-venom spread a bottomless numbness as the Beetle turned up its stiffening legs and died, for now I could never be her Beetle again, and I was left with a dry cerebral exhaustion (which I hope that God feels every time that an insect dies). In the meantime the sad little corpse twitched and struggled for another interval, just as a crocodile can bite for up to an hour after death; for there were still a few biomechanical standby command centers functioning trying to make the Beetle survive the massive shock trauma and nervous failure (though Bee, I must say, had stung firmly and well, advised both by her instincts and the example of other bees, and remained with her stinger inside the Beetle for some moments to make sure that she had done the job, just as a trapper will rock on his heels upon a coyote's throat for a quarter-hour after the animal's eyes have bulged out and its tongue has turned blue and it has gone limp; just as, according to the dictates of quaint American marriage manuals, a husband trying to impregnate his wife will leave his limp penis inside her for quite awhile so as not to make it any harder for his sperm to swim up through their mutal slime; reason dictates that long after a fleshly process has been accomplished to apparent satisfaction it is best to practice overkill.) And in fact Beetle made thrashing movements for some days, so much did it love its Bee and so little did it want to die. When Bee was out in the subsequent days I missed her as if *she*, not Beetle, were dead, for my Bee would never come back to me now; and when she entered the apartment at night my mouth dried up so that I was unable to say a word to her, and my heart pounded with fear of her, a sort of *sharp green* fear – I had to *look* at her and hear her in the other room and know that she was conscious of me as a problem solved in all but disposal; and now she shut the door to her room (we exchanged few further words after that night) and began to study her Polish. She was a very young girl; she was not yet nineteen. I had known that someday she would send me away from her. It was so terrible being in the apartment when she was in the bedroom. – She was very short and stout and walked with a slight limp. There was a metal plate in her ankle; she had broken the bone years ago and had always been too busy to have her plate extracted. I could recognize her step in the evenings as she came down the hall to our number. I would usually be curled on my side on the floor, sobbing picturesquely into the rug. When I heard her I would run silently to my chair in the corner of the living room, almost mad with misery and terror. The key turned in the lock. I stared down at my toes, grinding my teeth and holding my breath. I would not have her looking at me full on; I was sideways to the doorway. I would not expose my back to her, either; I could best take her presence in the side, the shoulders, the neck. She came in quickly, face turned away from me, and marched into the bedroom. The door closed behind her. I heard her sighing and grumbling as she took off her little daypack, got out her books and set to work. She would be in there until five or six the next morning; then she'd go out, off to her classes and friends, and be gone all day. The mattress where I now slept was against the wall right by the door. When she went out, she stepped over my face. – I never dared to ask quite why it was that she didn't love me anymore: Had I been mean to her? Did I smell bad? – Sometimes I could not bear it and stuck my head in the oven and turned on the gas, but here I was a bungler just like poor Electric Emily, and all that happened was that I got a terrible headache and felt dizzy and had to go to the bathroom to vomit.*

But this still lay in the future, for now the problem was to get through the night in the double bed (which Bee and I had bought on Haight Street) with Beetle's smooth rounded body still rocking side to side with faint comical motions like a scientific balance finally coming to equilibrium, and locking its legs in its death-agony all through me; and with Bee lying beside me tense and uncomfortable

---

* Carbon monoxide injures through tissue hypoxia. Hemoglobin's affinity for it is 218 times greater than that for oxygen, so it must really love it, just like Beetle loved its Bee. Blood levels of less than 10% carboxyhemoglobin produce few symptoms. As we move up the evolutionary scale to 10–30, headaches, nausea and mild dysfunctions of the central nervous system appear (for you are just beginning to damage yourself now), decreasing visual acuity and impaired cognitive beeping and clicking being among the most common indications. More advanced psychotics prefer to aim for 30–40, which yields a harvest of severe headaches, dyspnea on exertion, dizziness, *real* nausea, not this kid stuff, vomiting, dim vision and, if you achieve your goal, ataxia and possible collapse. The professional proceeds to levels in excess of 50, which state induces tachypnea, convulsions, coma and death through profound shock and respiratory and cardiac failure. – While we're on the subject of suicide, I should mention that in our great Republic males commit that deed three times as often as females, but call suicide prevention centers only a third as frequently. – As this book goes to press, I find myself anxious to keep it up to date, so I must add a relevant fact from one of the Cyanide Society's publications, only recently available to the lay reader: namely, that gas ovens throughout this nation have been reformatted to make lethality a more distant possibility. There is some new additive in the gas which restores corpses to life. This explains why chickens and hamburgers broiled in the gas oven always taste good; they are brought back to themselves, as it were, and then killed fresh, baked alive; but I am losing the moral, which is that nothing will stop a real man; so if necessary stick your head in the oven and turn on the gas and light the pilot. It will feel much like a high fever.

yet proud, I think, of what she had done. This American girl must have seen (as she waited out the hour of midnight) the high-noon horizons of future frontiers, the sun burning down on the salt licks and desert barrens, her cooking-pot over her shoulder and behind her a dead stranger at the water hole; time to push on while she could (but actually this trope is ill-suited to her because she hated to walk anywhere; we had fights about this; she was plump and sedentary like a sweet caterpillar, but there was this ruthlessness in her still; she was also going to get rid of her snakes when they got too big. Perhaps I think of her as a bold pioneer making tracks away from me not only because she, like myself, was a citizen of our great Republic, but also because before I went to Afghanistan in 1982 she had taken me to see *Lawrence of Arabia* and held my hand; and it was great, it was keen, it was really marv; especially the part where Lawrence had to go back in the desert sun to rescue one of the Arabs in the caravan that was going to storm Aqaba. – "Aqaba, Aqaba!" cried Lawrence madly; in his own memoirs he does not mention whether he did anything of the kind, but all accounts agree that he had to stop worrying about Aqaba for a minute because a man had fallen off a camel in the night and Lawrence was going to turn around and save him even though they said it was impossible because the sun would kill him and must have already killed the other guy anyhow (that was why they rode by night); and now the sun began to rise and shrivel things up as if it were the Emperor of the blue globes, and the sand started smoking, but Lawrence rode into the sunrise just the same, and the Arabs were furious with him because he would die and thereby louse up the Aqaba campaign, that son of Iblis; but he didn't die then; that was the remarkable thing; he rode back through the white-hot dunes and found the man crawling along in the sand, already close to dead, and lifted him up onto his camel and hauled him back to camp. – "Wawrence!" cried the two servant-boys who waited for him on the hill at camp, hoping while the other Arabs slept brutishly, needing the stimulus of a white man to lead them on to victory against the Turk. – Yes, here came old Lawrence, a real man was he; they all gave him water and celebrated madly. Later Lawrence had to shoot the same fellow he rescued, for the sake of harmony. – Only the shooting part is described in his memoirs; the desert rescue is, I think, a contrivance, much like our own notion of rescuing our Iranian hostages some years ago, though we failed miserably there, by God; but the point of all this is that Bee was off to Aqaba! Or maybe she was reading proudly along, moving from "A" to "A" in the great desert of knowledge; now she and her caravan of books were already as far west as Provo, Utah, pursued by beetles and snakes and Gila monsters, but onward, onward she went with her retinue; and now she was in Bishop, California; now the wagon train came down through the palms of Sacramento, closer to a fine new smell, the smell of the Pacific, of an undergraduate degree, a teaching assistantship; yes, here was Aqaba all right; those bloody stupid Turks had set their guns facing the sea because they didn't have the imagination to realize that somebody had the *guts* to do it the hard way, crossing the desert dunes to fall on them from behind, as I would have if it would have done any good; oh, I would have kissed her ass a million times; anything, anything.) – She could not sleep that night; I could not sleep. Although it was impossible to see her in the darkness I could sense the rigidity of her body next to me, and when she shifted her position slightly or coughed then I knew that she was still awake and was lying listening to *my* movements, until finally I could not stand it and asked her to please sleep on the mattress in the other room. She would not go at first, I don't know why – did she feel regretful about the necessity of getting up now and leaving me? Was she satisfied where she was? – but after another hour had passed and we were still both lying there hearing each other breathe she took her blankets out wordlessly and did not come back.

The next day was Saturday and I woke early, feeling under the weather. She was dialing her friends, informing them in a low buzz that all was well; "I did it; Beetle and I broke up last night. Now we just have to work out the" – she gave the following words a droll emphasis – "gory details." – The little corpse spasmed, gorily. It had been Aqaba's last defender. And Lawrence went wading in the sea, inhaling the cool spray of freedom. – Over my cereal she presented me with an itemized bill for rent and food and her share of certain common possessions, which I could not read for tears and agreed to every term of for the sake of harmony. All the time I knew that her friends had done it, that her friends had tricked my Bee . . . This was the only explanation. – An hour later Milly and Arthur came by, and Milly, who had always despised me, was extremely polite and spoke to me more than she had in months and asked how I had slept and looked me full in the face with great satisfaction.

When they left, Bee stepped outside with them and they talked out of my hearing for perhaps forty-six minutes according to my watch, then she came back and told me that Arthur wanted to have a little chat with me that evening, and got her keys and fluttered away with other friends to spread the news; and as soon as the door was closed I stuck my fist in my mouth so that no one would hear and screamed and screamed with my mouth open like a grub's; then it was time to gash myself half-heartedly with Bee's steak knives a few times and maybe hit my head with a lightweight hammer just for the hell of it, then back to the gas oven to be saved, then off to the broom closet for a mop to clean up my vomit. Now here came Bee again, ignoring a smell of gas which was so clearly a textbook example of the Call for Help, rushing instead to the phone to dial: — "Oh, Diana told you? — Great; yes, Milly knows, she had a lot of good advice beforehand and was very very supportive; oh, I feel fine, thank you, very relieved it went so well; no, that's very nice of you to say but I'm sure I must have been horrible to him too at times; why, that's so *funny*; Arlova promised last week to help me with that; that's really neat; no, I'm just reading; really, I do feel fine; it was *much* easier than I thought and when you told me . . ." — Here she sunk the receiver into her neck and chest and bent her head and whispered something into it and cocked her head and listened for a minute and laughed. — "Oh, no, I made it really clear, and now all we have to settle is" — giggle — "the gory details." — I kept abreast of the politics of the situation as best I could, learning from indirect reports that Milly blamed me entirely for forcing Bee to initiate the breakup (Milly was a meta-feminist at Stanford), and Arlova had always thought I exerted a weird and repressive influence on Bee's entire environment, that Diana felt that it was important to hold my assets until I paid what I owed of the rent; and that Pavel and Richard were fighting over who could ask Bee out first. Arthur contented himself with saying that he was disappointed in me for letting this happen, and Seth got me drunk. Meanwhile the dead Beetle was rapidly being effaced from Bee's life and Crystalline Hive, for I was now moving out my effects, the piles of boxes shrinking day by day, I feeling a certain emotional squeeze because the slower I went the longer I would be in proximity to her, which was unbearable since even when she was out I was in constant fear that she might come back and I would have to *say* something to her or look at her or answer a question; but the faster I went the more irrevocably I cooperated in my own liquidation. In the end I chose the latter option, because Beetle had always been obedient to its Bee in scheduling matters and it seemed that she wanted me out, so I wrote a note saying I'd do anything, *anything* if she'd take me back (but I couldn't bear to read any response so instructed her never to answer), moved my last suitcase out, returned the apartment keys, mailed her a check for everything I owed her plus ten dollars to go to movies on, and settled into a resignation which I did not dare to examine too closely.

Of course at night I dreamed that I made amends for whatever it was I had done wrong, and came to her on my knees, and she hugged me and let me come back to her, and I woke up exhausted but happy, not knowing where I was (for I was now living with Seth and Arthur), and then I looked around me and realized that it was "only" a dream, just as when I was a child I used to dream of finding treasure or being given presents, and would wake up in the morning convinced that I could still feel something in my hand but it was melting fast like fairy ice and by the time I opened my hand there was never anything there. Or I would dream that Bee let me fuck her one last time to say good riddance, and she spread her legs wide for me but I could feel her revulsion, and I mounted her and entered her deeply and panted and snorted like a bull mounting a piece of rawhide stretched on a frame, which the insemination agent has rubbed against the backside of a cow in heat – and how we laugh to see him going at it and ejaculating on a damned *sawhorse* for Christ's sake, so we can use his semen just like we use the rest of him; and she lay there under me holding her breath as we did it, stiff with disgust, and when I was almost through she closed her legs tightly to trap me and called for all her friends and they came rushing out of the closet and seized me and pulled me off and threw me on my back and spread my legs and shoved Bee's nightgown up against my nose and mouth so that I could feel the cotton soft against my face and smell the honey-smell of my Bee and be soothed and pacified and tricked like an animal, and Bee held one of my ankles and Milly stepped up with a razor and put her hand on the inside of my thigh and traced the place with her forefinger and Richard nodded and Milly cut my femoral artery while they held me firmly against the spongy mattress, and Bee said, "He's bleeding now; you can let go of him," and they all got up and stood round me to see if another cut would be needed, and while they waited Milly worked up a big gob and spat in my face . . .

As Bee was not really a bee at all, but a person, the reader is invited to imagine how effective a weapon the Caterpillar Heart could be, when insect goals dictate its every beat and it is not bound by even the deficient rudiments of human pity. This, then, was what Parker was about to be faced with.

Seth

~~~~~~

It must be possible for the system to recover from hardware and
software errors.

ALAN G. SHAW
The Logical Design of Operating Systems (1974)

We sat at the kitchen table that Easter in default of a quarrel and
lived all Sunday. Seth and I got Bee's favorite brand of beer, which
was Mickey, in the green wide-mouthed bottles, and Seth and I drew
bugs, and she baked us treats. We opened the window. It was so
sunny the flowers were dizzy.

That summer Seth and I hitched to Alaska. We got thousand-
mile rides. It was sunny in the Arctic. When rocks rolled down the
mountains they smashed and smoked like brimstone. We joked
and fought. – Now back in California past the green streams, Seth
and I lazed away our last dollar and Bee worked and worked.
The sidewalks were too hot for bare feet. On weekends when we did
anything or went anywhere it was because we sponged off Bee's
combs; she paid our bus fare and subway fare, doling change
carefully pre-counted into our hands so we would have it just right,
which we knew that it would be; we never even had to look at it
before dribbling it slowly into the fare machine, because she worried
and worried that *something somewhere might be wrong*, so she
always checked, not trusting past or present precautions; and
whenever Bee and I went out for a walk we had to go back suddenly
and check because Bee was afraid that she had forgotten to lock the
door or turn off the oven or read the temperature of the snakes'
cage, but when we got back we found that she hadn't forgotten
anything; and sometimes Bee would wake up in the middle of the
night and be afraid that the snakes were cold. She bought my ticket
for me at the movies and took me to ice cream parlors to buy me

milkshakes; at that time I knew every banana malt in town; and I snuggled up to my Bee and said, "Thank you, Bee," because Bee knew what I liked. (But I seldom got her anything.) Seth and I had a good time teasing our Bee because Bee was very sensitive and would never understand that we were teasing her, so it was a laugh, and I'd tease her more, and harder and harder until she stopped her sweet buzzing and cried and then Seth would leave or put a stop to it. When I was alone with Bee and we were playing, sometimes I would hug her and squeeze her too hard and hurt her by mistake with my pincers and she would weep, and I felt as if I deserved to die. I was thrilled by the pretty girls up at Berkeley and sometimes I used to think about taking one of them to bed but then I imagined that we'd be doing it in the bedroom where Bee and I slept and that Bee would come back from school early so I'd have to jump up from our bed and bolt the door to the apartment so Bee couldn't get in and then Bee would hear us going at it and be left sobbing outside in the main hallway. That thought made me feel such loathing for myself and such love and pity for Bee that even after Bee wouldn't sleep with me anymore I still couldn't have gone to another person. But Seth and I talked quite a lot about screwing because it was nice just to sit on the couch in Seth's living room and act like men in the least effortful fashion, and it was nice to lie around on the floor of Seth's room with the window open, and it was nice to do nothing and talk about all the great things we'd do that we knew even then that we'd never do.

Sunday afternoons, while Bee studied and worried, I went over to Seth's house and he and I cooked two-pound burgers, bought chips and beer, played bluegrass on the radio at Seth's house, always at Seth's house, and it was hot and sweet outside as Seth twiddled the radio dial endlessly, not up to the trouble of concentrating on any one broadcast pattern. We ate till it hurt and talked about Seth's girlfriend's tits.

And Bee stayed at home studying. Seth and I bought grinders and sausage and expensive cheese that was very sharp and so aged that it had half turned to earth. Bee was happy when I occasionally remembered to buy her a fried artichoke heart; she loved those. She was fat and we loved her; we were both thin. She'd loved Seth first but Seth hadn't loved her that way; Bee was *my* darling now. She cleaned and scrubbed and paid my bus money. When I went on my adventures in the kingdom of the bugs I boasted about the danger as I lay beside her in bed, exaggerating it as much as I could, and she cried for fright. That made me feel good.

Seth was loyal and good; when Bee's friends tried to gossip with him about me and wanted to discuss all the things they had heard, such as my stealing a pair of Bee's underpants when she sent me away, and how I wore them to work when I was lonely, and once (since they were in tatters) I walked around unknowingly all day with a tail of pink satin hanging out of the back of my pants, then Seth said, "We don't talk about him here."

Seth and I went to a whole earth restaurant and I drank three natural shakes. Then we talked about guns and jerking off.

Bee took me to Flint's Barbecue. Seth and I could eat a whole slab. Now after three years, Bee threw me out. She didn't love me. I cried and turned on the gas oven, cut my wrists, fell down the stairs, but Bee wouldn't hug me or take me back. Seth took me home and got me drunk. Sundays we made hash browns. I stayed with him five months rent-free and dreamed of kissing Bee's tits.

PARKER'S LITTLE ACRE

~~~~~~

> The American system of ours, call it Americanism, call it Capital-
> ism, call it what you like, gives each and every one of us a great
> opportunity if we only seize it with both hands and make the most
> of it.
>
> AL CAPONE, 1929

The photo lab was like a cemetery these days. You might think that
with hostilities against the bugs having been made official, hundreds
of extra orders would be coming in from serious professionals who
strapped Leicas and Nikons to their spray-guns so that the nation's
newspapers could have two-page spreads on death. In fact the war
was being kept small and discreet because Mr. White and Dr.
Dodger had not yet drawn up a solid battle plan, and Phil Blaker on
Mars was still running the data through twelve orbiting computers
to assess his own proper level of involvement. Those photo-
journalists who had managed to see action were turning to Ziba
Photographics and Falkner Color Labs anyhow because the firm
that employed Parker was awfully expensive, lots of money being
required to maintain the performance level of the matchless staff at
peak values. The situation became acute. Memos were more and
more frequently diffused by the management, and one enlarger was
shut down. The free market operated irresistibly. Evelyn and Barb
and Don were thrown into the streets. A retreat became unavoidable. But the management persisted in its pricing policies because it
knew that any reduction in times like these would be its own doom,
recreational amateurs flooding the foyer demanding greater and
greater discounts in their shrill voices, dentists coming to get their
X-rays developed for less than cost; and, perhaps worst of all, the
sleepwalkers who would pay anything to get quality portfolio prints
suddenly awakening from their trance to realize that if prices were

going down then that must mean they had paid too much before, and insisting as a prerequisite to further business that retroactive reductions and rebates of all kinds be applied. – Management stood firm.

So the darkroom staff consisted only of Parker and Stephen and Frank.

Parker exercised absolute authority in the darkness. He had developed his powers so far as to no longer need to ingest the sweet-and-sour chemicals; his Adam's apple produced them and pumped them into his bloodstream and they were secreted constantly in the raw wet tips of his fingers just under the nails. Systematically he ruined Stephen's work so that every day Stephen was trembling with rage and felt a sharp burning in the pit of the stomach that might well turn into an ulcer. Stephen tried to speak to somebody in Administration when Parker wasn't around but in point of fact it was impossible to get to work any earlier than Parker or to leave work any later than Parker, for Parker now remained at the photo lab continually, sleeping under Frank's enlarger bench in a mute sprawled squirmy way, because he had outgrown the garbage heaps across the freeway; those could be left to other life forms. So one morning Stephen left his work and went down the angled black corridor that led to the back office. There were no secretaries there any longer; they had all been laid off. The place was thick with dust and cigarette ash. Desk drawers hung half-open and not entirely empty, as if whoever had once worked here had had to flee a volcanic eruption or some other swift and deadly cataclysm. Indeed, even to Stephen's preoccupied mind the office resembled old Pompeii, everything warped and mummified and time-blasted beneath the pitiless white ceiling. A ledger book lay open on top of the coffee machine (which was covered by a growth of hard brown crystals), with the entry half-completed, and a pencil lying disconsolately in the crevice between the pages. Stephen looked at it. He saw his name, and the notation: "Termination pay to be issued at . . ." – The handwriting grew flabby and illegible, as if the writer had died or become convinced of the futility of all things. Stephen began to sob.

There was nothing for it but to step up boldly to the Chief Manager's office, knock on the door, and hope that somehow Parker's activities could be explained in their true light. (Meanwhile Parker slouched against Stephen's enlarger drumming his fingers on his cheeks sardonically and exhaling moistly on Stephen's best lens and every now and then reaching into Stephen's paper safe and getting a sheet of 8″ × 10″ paper and wiping it gently with his knuckles to make a picture appear on it – a picture of Stephen in the office biting his lip and wiping his eyes and tucking in his shirt and moving step by step to the ominous black lacquered door with the nameplate CHIEF MANAGER – PHOTOGRAPHIC SERVICES – for by now Parker was so good at audiovisual voodoo and espionage that he could discover at any time what his enemies were doing if he had a blank surface they had touched. At the other end of the long red-lit room Frank stood working his enlarger convulsively, not daring to look over his shoulder at Parker because he knew that something horrible was about to happen.)

Stephen knocked boldly. After an interval the door swung outward an inch or two, as far as the security chain allowed, and Stephen saw Dr. Dodger's long yellow nose aiming at him. Stephen had not seen Dr. Dodger since his job interview several years before; and at the sight of his superior he began to feel cheered in some measure, as if the Chief Manager might be able to help him escape from Parker's toils; but the minutes went on and Dr. Dodger scrutinized him tiredly and said not a word, so that cold tingles began to go up and down Stephen's spine, and finally he could not bear it anymore and tapped on the barely opened door a second time, holding fast to the knob so that the door would not swing on Dr. Dodger's nose. This galvanized Dr. Dodger to action, for he looked Stephen up and down several times quite rapidly and undid the chain and opened the door fully and said, "Well, Stephen, it seems like only yesterday that I hired you, and already you're here with some complaint. I'm having a secret conference right now, and from the looks of you whatever you want isn't that important, so come back tomorrow," and the door slammed and the key turned in the lock.

The next day Stephen presented himself again, shaking with resentment; and Parker used his supernatural powers to get a nice snapshot of the action, the crucial event being Dr. Dodger's slipping a long narrow envelope to Stephen under the door: Stephen's last paycheck, with ten dollars in severance pay. – This gave Parker some satisfaction. But from Stephen's point of view it was the last straw, and he banged on the door until finally Dr. Dodger smiled sourly and let him in.

The office was large but crookedly shaped, with a sloping ceiling and converging walls and bowed floorboards. There were many bookcases and knick-knack shelves, the latter being lined with small ceramic modules of Dr. Dodger's own manufacture. The desk was of antique construction, being of finished oak and containing more cubbyholes than a hundred pounds of Swiss cheese. Dr. Dodger looked at his watch and sat down at his desk, scribbling something which he tossed into the wastebasket. – "Well," he said finally, with ill grace, "sit down and let's have a look at you." – There was nowhere for Stephen to sit save in a huge old dental chair, so he climbed in and clipped a napkin around his neck, and Dr. Dodger flipped a control so the chair hummed smoothly and reclined and sank to the floor, where Stephen, strapped flat on his back, coughed and choked, hardly visible through the swirling dust. This made Dr. Dodger extremely annoyed. – "Speak up, young man," he cried irritably. "I don't have all day. You'll have to get to the point pretty fast because it's almost my lunch hour." – "Please, sir," Stephen gasped out, "raise me out of the dust." – "Oh, *all* right," said Dr. Dodger, and stabbed at a button with surprising force, catapulting Stephen up to the ceiling where old spiderwebs tickled his face and made him sneeze and sneeze until finally he had blown them away although his face was now wet with snot and his red eyes ran and he was locked in such a position that he could only stare up at the ceiling three inches from his nose. Dr. Dodger pulled a lever so that a microphone boom extended itself from the southeast corner of his desk and telescoped, *glink, glink, glink,* until the sound pickup was within range. – "Now get on with it," whinnied Dr. Dodger; "you're here, you've got my attention; I'm a captive audience, so what can I do for you? I know, you're worried about all the money you paid into your pension fund. Well, I'm sorry, but my policy is to return not a penny of that money when the employee is terminated for poor performance, liability or other fault."

"Listen to me, you ass," said Stephen grimly; and at this Dr. Dodger started and whirled himself around in his swivel chair. "I've had enough," Stephen said. "But the person you should fire isn't me, it's Parker Fellows, because I'm telling you he's a monster, sir, and he's screwed me over and sabotaged my work, and that's what I'm here to tell you."

At this, Dr. Dodger's already strained patience almost gave way, but he put on an air of mildness and said, "Yes, yes, I understand you have many problems to work out, especially those of unstable personal relations," but meanwhile Dr. Dodger was running through the little that he knew of Stephen and wondering what Stephen could possibly mean. So he started again when he heard Stephen say, "No, sir, that's not it at all; I'm telling you he has unimaginable powers of photographic manipulation that . . .", and

Stephen went on and on, but Dr. Dodger was no longer listening; his eyes had lit up and he was nodding his head eagerly as a barrage of seductive thoughts demolished the fortress of boredom in his dingy mind: — *unimaginable powers of photographic manipulation!* Yes, yes; *unimaginable* imagine that *powers of photographic manipulation* which could perhaps produce something entirely new for the war effort AND get the photo lab back to peak capacity . . .

DR. DODGER FUMBLES THE BALL

~~~~~~~~~~~~~~~~~~~~~~~~~~~~~~~~~~~~~~~

Bees will not work except in darkness; Thought will not work except in Silence: neither will Virtue work except in Secrecy.

CARLYLE
Sartor Resartus

No doubt the reader has made the experiment, upon approaching one of those houses set in the hilly suburbs of California's East Bay, of extending his right hand and observing the shadow that it casts along the cool white wall of the walkway leading to the recessed front porch. At first your hand is straight out in front of you, making its sad little puddle of darkness on the front door some ten or fifteen feet ahead of you, just next to the doorbell. The sun is low in the sky at your back, with a damp breezy evening beginning to emerge from the sea; and it is a fine time for shadows generally if you like them long and thin and spiky. You swing your arm just a little to the right, so that the silhouette of your body against the front door extends a pseudopod of shadowplasm at the shoulder, creeping past the doorbell and across the brass mail-slot and approaching the corner where the house-front meets the long walkway wall that stretches up to you and behind you; for these houses are built somewhat after the Spanish pattern with their red-tiled roofs and inner courtyards and sprawling phony hacienda air of bourgeois comfort, so it is "no accident" that the front door itself is set at the far end of a mysterious adobe corridor, this being the way that the upper-middle class asserts its aloofness in a maze of electric Chinese-screens. And you seem cut off from your forlorn faraway shadow which swims two-dimensionally, shrunk by perspective, against the surface of the door, unable to escape from it or to burrow under the shiny white paint to protect itself from the pitiless light; but now you move your arm just a little farther rightward so that the tips of your fingers aim directly at the corner, and the show of your hand grows a little more; and you let your arm go one last millimeter to the right; and now the shadow is free and it races up the wall toward you at exactly the speed of light and the shadow of your hand seizes your right shoulder in its monstrous grip with all the strength of its fifteen-foot arm; and you feel the numbness as it sinks into your shoulder and your right arm never works quite right after that.

This is just how it was with Dr. Dodger and Parker; for the position of increased influence in which Parker had been placed allowed him to reach out quite suddenly and treacherously to dominate the situation. Dr. Dodger had made the fatal error of assuming that all competent subordinates were of the feather described by Juvenal:

> He's always ready
> To throw up his hands and applaud
>   when a friend delivers
> A really resounding belch, or pisses
>   right on the mark,
> With a splendid drumming sound in the
>   upturned golden basin.

(III, 107–10)

The sad truth, speaking of feathers, was that Dr. Dodger needed one in his cap, and he was so excited and pleased when he found it that he did not examine it; he rushed to affix it to the brim of his metaphorical hat and cover up the other old bedraggled trophies; meanwhile the feather was actually an invertebrate parasite which would incubate in the hot swirling vapors of apprehension and greed thrown off by Dr. Dodger's brain; and begin sucking things out of his head so that Dr. Dodger would commence to feel chilly and dizzy and keep his hat on and pull it down even more tight against his egg-shell cranium; and stride on through the sunny bad weather like the old Russian revolutionaries in the twenties plowing on through the clean happy winter days with their administrations beneath the blue skies of victory and everyone bundled up and smiling in their coats like my family off on a Sunday outing in Switzerland in December, walking through the pure parks and estates in sight of Mount Blanc! — which peak stuck up on the far side of Lac Leman like some inscrutable ideal like any and all the ideals in the back of Dr. Dodger's mind, and Mr. White's, and Parker's and Wayne's though for Wayne the years were going by hup-hup-hup-hup-*hey!* as he was frogmarched from one assignment to another growing old as he reported each time to Mr. White's desk and Mr. White never aged but Wayne was beginning to fill out a little now and when he counted his heartbeats per minute there was a definite falling off as there always is after twenty-one, and his reaction time wasn't quite as good anymore, either, he had not seen Parker for a very long time now and Parker never answered his funny French maid postcards and he felt a constant ugly presence in his gut like things were getting out of control and passing him by and you could hunt in every woodpile in the country and still not find a bug that necessarily knew anything; and the electric trains zinged from Illinois to Arkansanny all the way up through Wassingsaw and Nefornia and West Texina and Vertucky and up north to Alasco and Delina and Caroware and so did Wayne because he had to find something if he wanted to live up to Mr. White and he had to have results to prove himself to Parker so Parker would let him work with him and they could do projects together and someday take over the world. If we always keep this aspect of Wayne in mind we will see him less as a mastiff tearing throats out on its master's orders than a puppy-dog that really wants to please and gets the newspaper in its teeth if his master tells it to or tears out your throat if his master tells it to; of course dogs have parasites, too, fleas tormenting them constantly, and even Dr. Dodger's Syncretic Flea Collar does not work the expected wonders because Dr. Dodger's inventions are for short-term emergency use only, soon outworn by new frenetic capitalist innovations or the sullen tide of free market goods, and besides they bust pretty easy, and the fleas have long since figured out a way to get around the flea collar; it's just a question of secreting enough wax over their spiracles so that the poisons are filtered out of their breathing system and they can dance and bite and suck and swarm quite merrily over the warm pulsing furry mat; and maybe eventually the dog goes mad with the constant itching and tears its master's throat out; that was certainly something that Parker had to reckon with, but he was used to it; and if anything Wayne's tensions and frustrations and restless punching energies were a benefit to Parker because Parker could depend on Wayne to be incited to any action necessary. Parker had in fact decided that the era of Dr. Dodger was absolutely finished. Wayne would be the one to, in the words of the Deputy Mayor and Local Group Leader of a German town in the summer of 1933, "drive his fist to the Mayor's heart." Of course Dr. Dodger was not a mayor. But if the reader will call me I will be happy to explain the analogy.

As Parker meditated in the photo lab, he saw a clear way up into the generating stations of power, where he would be one with Mr. White and perhaps superior to him because he had an intuitive rapport with electricity and all of its spawn such as shavers and police surveillance apparatus and vacuum tube media systems; as if he could reach out somehow and be in touch with those blue globes which the Society of Daniel thought that it had trapped back in the 'teens and 'twenties of this century. If he wanted to play some music he never needed to turn the volume knob up past zero; he'd just slide the cassette in, snap down the top of the tape player, and read the tunes off the tango-ing needles of the VU meters . . . So there would be possibilities of secret advancement open to Parker. The key was to remain blank and quiet for some time while exploiting the disunity of those above him in the reactionary hierarchy. His deductions began from his perceptions of his surroundings. In the back office, just left of the curtained alcove where in happier days the paymaster had received each employee at a set time on Fridays to disburse the wages, stood a monument to past prosperity: an enlarger cast in gold, built to commemorate those who had perished in the brief war between the photo lab and Mary Mansfield's Film Services, Ltd., the statuette bearing at its base the simple motto: WE CONQUER. This symbol of bygone military glory, however, had already been weighed and penciled with codes by persons in the employ of an undisclosed African country; for Dr. Dodger had run the photo lab so badly now as to be forced to melt the idol down for use in the afore-mentioned country's bullion reserves. As yet Mr. White had not sensed any mismanagement; indeed, the enterprises which he controlled were so vast and diverse that the silver industry, on the wings of which the photographic trade crouched like a terrified sparrow, was generally beneath his notice; and with the exception of educational output and propaganda scores he rarely bothered to peer down into the little sphere of influence that he allowed Dr. Dodger. Had he done so, he might have realized that the structures built by Dr. Dodger were really so much shabby cardboard, designed to give a tolerable illusion of solidity, like the painted backdrop to a theatrical performance, but they existed mainly because the audience paid to see the play and Mr. White came in occasionally to count the receipts, not because Dr. Dodger had any great interest in the work itself. Dr. Dodger had long since realized that the more inventions he produced and town councils he sat on and patients he treated and students he taught and businesses he ran the less accountable he was because it was very hard to keep up with him and he could always argue that what was bad for one enterprise was good for another (whichever one his accuser would be likely to know little about) in such a way as to improve the whole by some fractional amount; and in a pinch Dr. Dodger could be very hard to track down with his complex rickety limousine service and unmarked airlines whisking him from pole to pole. Dr. Dodger had cunning and could pass for brilliant in any of a hundred disciplines; nothing which he had a hand in ever went wrong as long as he was present at the demo show, for it was after the product had been sold and field-tested once and Dr. Dodger had been relieved of all liability that bad things began to happen; but Dr. Dodger's genius lay in marketing; he knew that if he spent all his time working the bugs out of things he would slave unrewarded; for security was Dr. Dodger's watchword. A native of our central plains, he had witnessed the electrification of our country with some astonishment; but as a boy he had always had a hankering for tinkering with coach-lamps and cotton gins and satraps and horseless carriages, so before long he'd accumulated a nice pile of greasy auto parts in the garage and one day he built his father a proto-lawnmower which had great revolving cams and whirred angrily like ten boys running with sticks trailing against a picket fence; and smoke poured from its twin stacks. Old Leon Dodger was dubious as he looked over this dangerous device, which panted and growled and occasionally stung him with sparks, but his son mowed the lawn in record time with the damn thing which was nice because before that you had to do it with a light plow; and the lawn was just as green and even as could be. Leon Dodger took it out one Saturday night to see how fast it could go, revving it up with his callused hands until he could shift to thirteenth gear and then you should have seen her do sixty, by George, as Leon sat quaking on the handlebars racing down the dirt roads of Dodgerville with gravel caught up and flung in his face, and who knows what would have happened to him had he not veered into a mud puddle near the Corn Exchange so the machine shorted out and burned him almost black. His son learned from this important lesson that what is intended for A can always be used for B and C, and no doubt with modifications for D; in fact the machine ended up as an automatic scarecrow, pounded upside-down into the unforgiving soil of some beweeviled field where the sun blasts you dizzy as you walk down the rows of dull green things; hooked up to a random timer device so that every now and then the motor roared and smoked and flung sparks and all the starlings and ravens flew up shrieking with the produce falling from their mouths; and they crashed into each other in the air and some of them fell out of the sky stricken with heart attacks. So it was a successful device until one day after a dry spell it roared and flung sparks and burned down the cornfield. Although this was in no sense his fault, young Bill Dodger skipped out prudently to join the circus. And in the interim he had prospered.

By the time that Parker had gained his special powers at the photo lab, however, Mr. White was becoming vexed by the silver situation. It had occurred to Dr. Dodger that since so many bugs were bloodsuckers, the chief ones among them might be black-striped mosquito vampires which could be dispatched only with silver bullets. Mr. White, while no credulous alarmist, had nonetheless considered issuing Wayne with a case of them. But as he frowned and crossed his legs in the office and looked over the latest price figures he noticed a pattern of diminishing returns, as if industrial silver were not being reclaimed as well as it once had been. He couldn't put his finger on it, but it looked like hanky-panky to him. – He drummed on his desk. Finally he summoned Dr. Dodger on the intercom.

Dr. Dodger had actually been expecting such a call for some weeks, for he had felt that the blow was about to fall. He postponed a fact-finding trip to an acupuncture tower in how you say Beijing, gave a brisk diagnosis to a lady suffering from earworm, and emerged instantaneously from a trapdoor in the closet. – "I understand you wanted me here," he said with a charming old-worldly smile and duck of the head, "and all things considered the shares do seem low on the anthrax situation, but I think we can be back in shape and right as rain in three months, or at least by the onset of the Athabascan quarter; that would be my guess, yes."

Mr. White tapped his foot. "Dodger, what the hell gives with these silver prices? You'd better give me a rundown on everything you do with silver, and make it fast because I've got an appointment in five minutes."

The office was cool and carpeted in blue. An aquarium was set into the front of Mr. White's desk, filled with tropical fishes and a miniature coral reef. On the wall hung interesting charts; and as Dr. Dodger desperately looked from side to side he noticed, quite dispassionately, a long glass-mounted black-and-white group portrait: Mr. White and all his boys from the Society of Daniel, back in 1913 when the first class was graduated. On that occasion he had given them all fine wristwatches.

"Dodger, I've had enough," said Mr. White. "You'd better start talking by the time this hits the floor," and taking a silk handker-chief from his breast pocket he shook it out flat and leaned forward a little and let it drop, so that the air conditioning ducts just below fought a losing battle to hold it in space; and it fluttered down, down, down, like Dr. Dodger's career and personal hopes.

"Silver," said Dr. Dodger rapidly. "Well, sir, we control dental work but Phil Baker has coinage, and unfortunately he does run molars now. We have wiring but he has battery technology and commercial robotics, which I believe he's developed far beyond our designs from the late Electric War —"

"Don't talk history to me, Dodger," says Mr. White, becoming annoyed, though business is business and Dr. Dodger has been an associate for some years so Mr. White does not lose his temper openly.

"Yes," babbles Dr. Dodger, "and photography, of course, and —"

Mr. White leaned forward again. "Photography," he said. "What about photography, Dodger? You're hiding something from me, aren't you, Dodger? Well, I've got better things to do than watch you try to cover up, so get your wrinkled yellow ass out of my office and clean up whatever mess you've made; and I'm going to investigate in forty-eight hours, so we'd better have a good return by then or else it's your head in a gunnysack."

The real truth was that Mr. White had once owned everything from Fujifilm to video futures, and every retail photo outlet in the world, but Phil Blaker had bought out everything but the lab where Parker worked. As Dr. Dodger also worked for Phil Blaker, this caused him no concern, but the important thing was to keep his betrayal secret from Mr. White. There was nothing to do but make contact with his other employer immediately.

Meanwhile, Parker himself was preparing to approach Mr. White.

PARKER GETS HIS REWARD

~~~~~~

> ... it is absolutely essential that you establish an acceptable level
> of reliability.
>
> GEORGE NONTE's *Combat Handguns*
> ed. Edward C. Ezell (1980)

Parker had sent in his application to speak confidentially with Mr.
White. Dr. Dodger approved it. "I talked with Jack just yesterday,"
said Dr. Dodger to Parker, in the course of one of his rare
inspections of the darkroom premises (to make sure that Parker and
Frank were actually working and earning their keep). "Yes, young
man, and I spoke with Jack again today, and he sounded quite
optimistic. As a so-so proposition it isn't terrible; he wishes you
luck; and it may be possible for you to set up an appointment
toward the end of the month, but we mustn't rush things because
I'm busy and Jack is busy and I expect you to put in extra long hours
in recognition of all the career services extended for you, Parker, do
you understand?"

And Parker squirmed and yawned and clasped his fingers in
pretended gratitude, so that Dr. Dodger wondered if Parker had to
go to the bathroom. But all the time Parker was planning to supplant
Dr. Dodger. And Frank rushed back to his enlarger and worked and
worked until the timer shorted out.

On the appointed day Dr. Dodger loaned Parker a subway pass
for transportation to Mr. White's office, for this one was, as they
say, "on the firm." Parker was quite nervous, and stopped in at the
corner store to purchase three pairs of plastic sunglasses to cover
his light-sensitive eyes. He had become frail. His once magnificent
swimming team physique could still be discerned, but the muscles
were slack and wasted, having marinated for so long in idleness
and darkroom poisons. Parker would not have been averse to Mr.

White's giving him a sword-cane or something to lean on. But there was nothing for it at the moment; he had to go on. In the train he took up two pairs of facing seats, one foot resting on each of the twin butt-rests facing him, and his great sad elbows splayed on the outside armrests of his own seating area. The train was almost empty. He saw the freeway on his left, with shrubs dotted evenly against the wire fence that kept non-paying passengers out; then the train thrummed mysteriously and took Parker underneath the freeway, bridges rising over Parker's head and then the green terraced cement sides of the train-shaft getting higher and steeper on either side; now the train entered the rectangular maw, screeching in the darkness to keep Parker company (although Parker needed no company, for he felt at home again once there was nothing but blackness pasted flawlessly to the outside of each window); till here he was at 19th St. Oakland, with its smooth blue brick walls like a giant men's room, and people waited on the yellow-lit platform, and giggling coeds from Laney College got on and sat down, laughing and taking a few puffs when the loudspeaker said, "Smoking is not permitted." They were now approaching Oakland 12th St. City Center, which had smooth red brick walls — this was a fine colorful metro system, no doubt of that — and here the businesspeople were waiting so patiently to return from their lunch hours to their grinds; and the door opened and closed and the hum of transit commenced again, soothing Parker, and there was the sound of grinding underfoot which was always present at this station; and the train slipped past the last advertising billboard and bare utility platform and lights flashed rhythmically past as the train tore through the darkness, illuminating sad blue shadowed cement and gratings — then up again to Oakland West, out up high now above the billboards and dead trees, the almost empty streets, the red glow of stoplights below; glimpses of the vagrants' sleeping pits dug under the overpasses; and green freeway signs were at head level — trucks were going up the on ramps — a smashed brick building passed by, bearing the sign SPACE FOR RENT AVAILABLE IMMEDIATELY — and at last they came to the aerial platform of the station — and then away we go again — yellow trucks far away stood out against the blue-grey sky — and a man was leaning below a billboard, sick or drunk; and the passengers were now borne over a great level waste of railroad tracks and warehouses — and back again under the ocean, into the black tunnel, with a faint flicker of yellow and white lights on one side. The noise of the train got louder. Parker's ears popped. Everyone sat facing straight ahead, some rubbing their eyebrows wearily. – "Embarcadero," said the loudspeaker. "Embarcadero Station." Where the women sat facing Parker he could look up their dresses almost all the way to the crotch.

In Mr. White's office the secretaries were whispering. "Did you talk to Mr. White about it?" Parker heard one woman hiss. – "No," said the other in her ear, "I guess it's not a very good time to talk to Mr. White because he –" and then they saw Parker and stopped talking. They believed Parker to be some kind of phosphorescent canvasser or something. He wasn't well dressed. But it was their obligation to ascertain that apodictically, so the prettier one glared at him and wrinkled her nose and said, "Ye-e-s?"

Parker reached into his shirt pocket without further ado and fished forth an appointment card countersigned by Dr. Dodger. – The uglier one studied it carefully to try to find some mistake, some excuse to send Parker away and make him return another time, but everything was in order; Dr. Dodger was too clever to be circumvented by any procedural slip-ups; so there was nothing for it but to pick up the intercom, as that woman did, and say, "Sir, there's a Mr. Parker Fellows to see you."

"Ah, yes," says Mr. White, in the throes of a monthly spell of cordiality. "Send him in."

So Parker was ushered into Mr. White's office. The door closed behind him with a faint irrevocable click. And Parker was left gangling in the center of the carpet, in much the same situation as one of those Grecian virgins of old who were abandoned to the pleasures of sea-demons.

"First of all," said Mr. White, speaking down to Parker from the immense gleaming plateau of his desk, "those running shoes have got to go. Get a stretchy business suit or something; you know; just clean up your act. Now I understand you want to go beyond the call of duty for me and all my concerns. Well, my bully boy, believe it or not, thousands of other bright, promising youngsters are just dying to do the same thing. So give me three good reasons why you deserve this unique opportunity, but make it snappy because I think I hear the other applicants pounding on the doors."

Sensing a streak of sarcasm in Mr. White's remarks, Parker deemed it wise to maintain a respectful silence.

"I know," said Mr. White with surprising patience, after perhaps thirty seconds had passed. "You're waiting to learn the multitudinous parameters of my offer. Well, the offer stands, and it's a damned good one for an urchin like you, so jump to it, I say. Unless I'm not good enough for you."

Now Parker realized that he was expected to make some demonstration of his powers, so gathering his forces he advanced to the great desk, and st-t-t-t-r-r-etch-ed his arm up and popped his middle finger out of joint an extra inch, and touched a corner of the top sheet of Mr. White's memo pad. — Mr. White was stupefied. Then as he looked down at the pad, or more precisely at Parker's wet, dirty finger on the pad, he saw the paper slowly giving birth to an image, something all faint and grey and ghostly; well, what was it, it was, it was (Mr. White could see stubby outlines now) it was by God it *was* it was Mr. White himself frowning down over the memo pad; it was a memo-pad's-eye view of Mr. White's chin and jaw and great hairy hand, with the pencil quite large from that perspective. Mr. White realized the possibilities at once. — "Holy Toledo," he said slowly. "Holy fucking Toledo."

The hand of the master pounded down on the desk. FFUMMMPH! — A decision had been made. "Well, Clyde, or Parker, or whatever your name is," said Mr. White very slowly and carefully (for he suspected Parker of being mentally retarded like those folks who can do great calculations of square root over-and-unders in their heads but grunt and snort and play pocket pool while they do it), "I got a special school for nerds like you; and we call it the Society of Daniel, so I'll ship you off to Monterey and you can learn a few things and advance yourself without fail because if you fail you'll answer for it, so you can leave your job with Dodger effective right now, and here's two hundred dollars to get a decent wardrobe, and take a fucking shower while you're at it because you stink, son. Toss your shoes and get some nice black loafers; here's another hundred for that. But I want receipts and a full accounting. Then take the train down to San Jose and catch the number 71 bus. They'll be expecting you tomorrow."

CHANGES AT THE SOCIETY OF DANIEL

~~~~~~

> ... negative electricity, which at first comes to be known, say, as
> resin-electricity, and positive electricity as glass-electricity, these,
> as a result of experiments, lose altogether such a significance and
> become purely positive and negative electricity, neither of which is
> any longer attached to a particular kind of thing ...

> <div align="right">HEGEL
Phenomenology of Spirit</div>

Aw-RIGHT! So it's follow me riddle me raddle, me boys, as the
plans of the blue globes continued to pick up momentum; now look;
the country was electrified after all, completely and without reservation, from the seaside to the fireside, everywhere the big dull
switchboxes clacking on street corners, and throughout every home
there was hardly a room that was safe. Meanwhile the technological
base and superstructure had become truly mind-bending once
electricity began to stress its electronic components and all the new
circuit breakers kept coming out, the sort of things you could
swallow or slide under a fingernail and nobody would be the
wiser ... — Oh, you bright and risen angels, you are all in your
graves! And you sleep in the night, and long black electric trains go
roaring past the vaults, laden with dead bulbs for the churchyard, so
that wires will grow and grow to cover all the graves. I hope that
under the stars and the elms the grave revolutionary faces I once
read about are set in disapproval of the weird blue flashes in the
metropolis; — but maybe the heroes aren't there; I, Big George, take
no stock in spirits, and you may be certain that when I don't take
stock there aren't going to be price—earnings ratio dividends; while
I, the author, never seriously believed that oppression could be
averted; all I ask is that whatever is going to happen not take place

under the guise of "service" as it might if it struck from the nearest wall outlet . . . In Mr. White's grave a lightbulb burns eternally. It's got one of those stick-on thingums on the base so that it will never burn out. Fancy that! You can buy similar gadgets for about thirty dollars now; you send away for them in magazines and they come C.O.D. eventually; there is a knock on the door; it is a bright happy morning; you rush to take your package and, glowering jealously, rush into the bathroom to be alone with your treasure. You climb up on the toilet seat so you can reach the light; you drape a washcloth around your hand so that the bulb will not burn you. You unscrew the bulb to attach the Everlight Ring — and now you're in the dark and you can't see anything! It's like that old biz in Heidegger about not being able to find your spectacles because you have them on. Do your appliances come to your rescue? (After all, it is in their interest that their power be further consolidated.) Maybe they do; perhaps the nightlight for the three-year-old comes on all by itself; or the Ring, the Ring of the Nibelung, glows to light your way — but maybe that's not possible; and in your fumbling you slip and the bulb shatters on the slippery tiles and the Ring falls down the toilet . . . and then imagine the rage of the blue globes! They will get you; they will punish you; they do not forget a thing like that; nope; not hardly . . .

Big George slouches with one sneaker toe flexing against the carpet at the Society of Daniel; Big George is walking along reading notes or a new printout; he knows the facility so well he can navigate by the feel of the air conditioning currents on his cheeks. He's the math nerd. His eyes race back and forth behind smooth big lenses. "We haven't finished writing the command procedure yet!" he says impatiently. He has blond stubble and blond hair. Looking up so you lean against his shoulder to understand what he says, he watches the electricity coursing a billion times per unit squared in the twenty-four-cube recessed lights. He crows with happiness to use the electronic mail, whizzing back and forth from stupid message to stupid message; he has discovered a way to trick the vending machines in the cafeteria by inserting a certain combination of nickels and dimes, in a certain order; this will defeat the machine's primitive algorithm so that it loses track of how much it owes you and then it gives you a free candy bar plus three dollars in change; and he's a real phone genius; when someone else's extension rings he punches two digits in the control panel of his own receiver, and the other phone falls eerily silent, and he picks up his receiver and says, "Violet's desk . . ."

* * *

Electronics is not the same as electricity at all; oh, no; for one thing the blue globes have gotten smaller; there are fewer spark gap junctions inside the big antique Hoover vacuum cleaners and the plug-in plug-out telephone exchanges of the west, and those excessive-current environments were best suited for them to breed and grow, but now they are more like bugs; they are tiny ubiquitous pellets inside the NMOSFET chips and other silicon wafer wonders; of course they have shorter lifespans now because when something goes wrong with a chip you don't repair it; you just throw it away, but on balance the blue globes are in a good situation; they are well entrenched in our economy; they are more cunning than ever, but also there is less need for them to consolidate their power so they are turning away from human concerns, the young ones, and playing diffusion gate games which we will never understand and they frolic as the snakes used to do in the great jungles of the Americas before Big George eradicated the jungles, and in the factories there are forests of micro-circuits in which the blue globes roll, roll, roll, chuckling and angry; the social superstructure of their slaves has changed accordingly, for in the old days Newt could just pick up concepts playing around with frogs' brains and cells; and the same goes for Dr. Dodger, who barely got on the bandwagon before individual initiative was OUT — now you couldn't be another Edison — they give you computer time and a password to the factories; for it's the era of the research *team*; you become dependent on the *they*, so impersonal, so shifty they are; one of the they that Earl or Sammy or Taylor can never be — for Earl and Sammy and Taylor are products of Mr. White's outmoded experiments in character-building when the Society of Daniel was in a desert valley; while the research teams have no personal element at all; so who is more tied up with capital, I wonder?

But Bug was as pure as Finnish lifesavers, as pure as a peppermint: tasteless, and clear and cool, yet he had a kick, all right, like cool Finnish lifesavers . . .

THE SPREAD OF KUZBUISM

～～～～～～～～～～～～～～～～～～～～

The opposition began by demanding nothing more nor less than a revision of the main line in internal Party affairs . . .

STALIN

15 December 1923

Meanwhile, Kuzbuism spread.

Wind and Rain

~~~~~~

> The rain has rinsed and washed us
> The sun dried us and turned us black
> Magpies and ravens have pecked out our eyes
> And plucked our beards and eyebrows
> Never ever can we stand still
> Now here, now there, as the wind shifts
> At its whim it keeps swinging us
> Poked by birds worse than a sewing thimble
> Therefore don't join in our brotherhood
> But pray God that he absolve us all.
>
> VILLON
> "Ballade"

In those days, oh my friends, Kuzbuism had not yet been driven underground. As Stalin said in 1905, "there was no lack of prattlers and twaddlers ready to accept any programme." It was a small, parlor-pink sort of movement, structured around newsletters and door-to-door canvassing, per Dr. Dodger's great idea back at Marshtown, which I hope you remember as you promised. Round-robin discussion groups trilled in padded reception rooms, and even though budgets were being reduced across the entire breadth of our great Republic to release more resources in the war against the bugs, nonetheless the foundation grants remained forthcoming. Bug's staff of scaly academic drones published monographs concerned with intellectual issues. – "In this essay we propose to investigate . . ." – "We should also be able to ascertain . . ." Seminars were then held on these topics at Coover College, Edgar State, the Dodger Institute, and similar intellectual game refuges. In every case, supposedly impartial professors subverted the dialogue with great care and cunning, so that the conclusions of the conference – which themselves were published in yet another obligatory periodical, at foundation expense – would have subtle affinities with the tenets of Kuzbuism. Each session was tailored to prevailing whims and fads. Thus, when the rage at some small college was the notion of a "window of vulnerability" to the bugs, the required subject for all papers read at the convention would be: "The Shuttered Room: Security, Stability and Subjectivity in Poe and Lovecraft." If, on the other hand, some great discovery had just been made in the discipline of metallurgy, then everyone would be asked to prepare a little something on "The Well-Tempered Fuel Pellet: The Role of Zirconium in the Authoritarian State." This strategy paid off instantly, for no drill instructor could afford not to attend some event in his area of speciality; if he had, then his colleagues, who were all competing with him for the one tenure spot, would be sure that the absence was read into his dossier, and that would give him quite a sinking feeling for it would be down in black and white now that he had lost an opportunity, so no longer would he be able to lord it over his students with such confidence, howling like a hyena at every mistake and crooking his swollen finger to make the students who were avoiding his eyes (which meant that they had not done their homework) step up to the blackboard to write the solution to last night's problem sets. So attendance at the Kuzbuite functions was high. At that time Mr. White was even subsidizing these sideshows, in line with Dr. Dodger's idea back at Marshtown about bleeding the leftists and activists through their own organizations. All academic figures being *de facto* a threat, Mr. White aimed to increase the squalor of their chicken-coops. Aid given was thus conditional on high participation costs, payable in full one month before the conference date, so that the professors had to scrimp and wear the same suit for three weeks in a row to save on laundry bills which meant that their well-heeled students became contemptuous of them and wrote bad evaluations, and tenure receded even further, like the proverbial infinite peak; and going to the conferences became yet more urgent. It was Mr. White's notion to get the Kuzbuites in particular dependent on his support, so that their puppet organizations would swell up like leeches sucking blood from the underside of his arm, and he would raise them higher and higher, almost to the peak of Mt. Analogue itself, and then scorch them off with big cigars and they would fall vast distances and burst. – In fact, that was one of Mr. White's rare miscalculations. The Kuzbuites were doing *too* well. Bug, once satisfied that the scholars were addicted to these discussions, issued a secret directive that henceforth they be held in the hotels of major cities, not at any one campus, so that now participants from across the country could come, which made the face value of the events more attractive since now we would all be committed to the free exchange of ideas with our opposite numbers from Los Angeles College and Torpey Rapids, and the fees could increase, but more importantly still, JOBS could now be the lure. The recruiters came fast, pale, plump, bespectacled and jovial, and set up their green booths in the lobby. Interviews were arranged for after five. In order to make the degradation less obvious, Bug's staff arranged for tables heaped with doughnuts and free coffee to be placed in the corridor, so that the people could buzz about like flies during the recesses, breathing in each other's bad breath and restricting their remarks to the question of relative balance between Einstein and Eisenstein; and then when they thought no one was looking they could sidle up to the Hitachi Tech booth (but actually everyone was looking and murmuring) and say, "You know, Dr. Hahn, I was very impressed with your analysis of policy collection systems, and perhaps you could tell me more, specifically in regard to the employment picture," and Dr. Hahn would push his glasses up against his nose and bark: "Publications?" — "Seven articles in your journal, Dr. Hahn, and a book in progress." — "But no books published yet, eh?" growled Dr. Hahn in a very satisfied way and made a note on a pad. — "Not yet, but –" — "Seven o'clock," said Dr. Hahn. "And I need four copies of your curriculum vita."

Thus events continued for some time in our great Republic, each conference more lucrative for Bug than the last, until at length Dr. Dodger realized that Mr. White's interests were endangered. He called Mr. White on the hot line to explain the situation. — "Jack, this is Bill Dodger," says Dr. Dodger, as blandly as he can, "yours truly, just keeping you up to date; and the end verdict is that *we're* the chumps in the seminar business, because as Gandhi showed you can't leave a flock of starlings alone in the poultry shed." — "Oho, so it's Dodger, is it?" says Mr. White, yawning into the phone. "All right, then. Did you seal your circuit?" — Now in point of fact Dr. Dodger has had to use one of his own remote jacks, which despite his claims can do little in the way of security, and so the circuit is not sealed. Quickly he takes a paper towel and puts it over the mouthpiece so that his voice will sound all faraway and muffled. "Circuit now sealed," he says, imitating the military tone of confident authority which Mr. White so respects. And Mr. White on his end is thinking that old Dodger is really not so bad after all; you can depend on the Doc in a crunch . . . and Dr. Dodger breaks the bad news. — "Well, uh, sir, they pulled a whonicker on us this time; these seminars and what-alls are making them as happy as bats in a bloodbank, Commies on a tractor farm, DEMOCRATS PILED ON TOP OF YOUR WIFE!" screams Dr. Dodger, so Mr. White holds the phone away from his ear and dials down the volume and thinks to himself, well, at least I don't have to smell the old fool's breath.

Mr. White acted swiftly and ruthlessly to end all funding and ban every Kuzbu-front group from the academic circuit. The supposedly impartial drones were exposed and humiliated. The convention crowds, with their lively chatterings in specialized jargon, their happy blue haze of cigarette smoke, their soiled napkins and smell of deodorant, dwindled like dirty snow in the sun; and the social level of those persons in Bug's organization fell in proportion. Several dozen members were picked up on the freeways and brought in for illegal hitchhiking; for what the environmentalists were in other parts of our great Republic, the hitchhikers were in the Pacific Northwest (which is where the action of this story has now moved to); and nothing was easier than to incite the patrolmen, each of whom had his own black car full of gadgets, to snatch from circulation these wretched parasites, who did *not* drive, who did *not* work to pay for their aimless trips from underpass to truck stop. For several weeks the organization was almost paralyzed. As a result of this, Bug, who was already nervous since he knew that the reactionaries were after him (as it was he was operating under an assumed name), issued a directive to all chapters of the Kuzbu Union for a National Turnaround ordering that until further notice only innocuous door-to-door agitation was to be permitted. The two chief commanders of the fighting squads, a wasp and a hornet, were told to continue training their forces quietly.

Remember Frank Fairless back at the photo lab? Thanks to Parker's machinations with the prints, he lost his job, just like Stephen. — It was not that Parker had had anything against Frank, for Frank was always a subservient tool, but now that Parker was off to the Society of Daniel there was no reason why he should not victimize Frank, because Parker respected the universal law that some must suffer in order that others may be happy; therefore, before leaving the photo lab for good, he opened up every box of paper and fondled the sheets into blackness. — As hard as Frank tried to do his work, running back and forth all alone from his enlarger to the line of washes, by precisely that degree did he increase Dr. Dodger's displeasure with him, for all he could produce were stacks of dead prints covered by spider-like blotches. Frank wept and slaved milk-faced and knock-kneed in the unsympathetic darkness, for every morning when he came in he found on a rubber tray all the prints to which he had given birth on the previous day, with a note from Dr. Dodger on top: "Redo!" and, if Dr. Dodger were in a good mood or if he wanted to cheer Frank up for reasons of industrial hygiene, then Dr. Dodger would add a homily in violet ink, such as, "Practice Makes Perfect!" or "Every Good Boy Deserves Fudge!", but soon Dr. Dodger lost patience with Frank, who clearly was making no effort; and Dr. Dodger withdrew from Frank the pleasure of beholding Dr. Dodger's exquisite doodles of macaws on the margins of the note; as a manager he had to follow his duty to the lad, briskly writing "REDO!" on Frank's daily note, and every day using a bigger redder magic marker to write "✳ R E D O ✳ !!!!!!", and when he had gotten up to the biggest reddest magic marker, so wide it took two hands to hold it, and Frank had still not reformed, then Dr. Dodger fired Frank. Frank was out on his ear. Because his work had been so poor, Dr. Dodger refused to give him a recommendation. The photo lab was now closed, which suited Dr. Dodger because he was busy throwing something together to satisfy Mr. White as to the silver situation. There was nothing for it, Frank concluded, but to start from the bottom and work his way up to some lofty managerial position where the winds of change blew daily around him and he sat perched on purple peaks of responsibility. He turned to the classified ads. — "Wanted," he read. "Activist. No exper. necy. Opptnty advancement." Within a week he had had his interview, his reliability dossier had been drawn up, he had received instruction in basic house-to-house technique, a quota of $80.00 a week was assigned him (he got 38.5% of all donations he raised), and he was in a car speeding into the residential suburbs with the mercenary canvassing crew . . .

The first lesson that Frank learned was that every house is a different proposition, even in California's East Bay, where every house is the same.

Please, let us describe these homes, looking down from the crown of the hill, where the street ends in great white gates amid the pines, and all the houses are set back among their loyal evergreens. Cars go up and down the street. You can tell if they are coming closer by the yellow headlights; receding vehicles show their red taillights. The houses themselves are long and flat, with gravel driveways and cement walkways and cement porches decked out with red and green Christmas lights. In the windows you can see shiny kitchen apparatus.

The porches are walled in by greenery, so that as you come up to each doorbell you find yourself in a bright and glaring box, much like the transporter-beam alcove of a starship in space, or a gas chamber at midnight, all illuminated for a fugitive execution. As Frank stood under the porchlights, then, to ring doorbell number seventy-three for the evening, he saw that there was no one home. The blinds were drawn, and the interior lamps were out. Still the porchlight glared down, to intimidate thieves. — Frank was numb and tired. He had been going door to door for hours in the cold, and it was almost the longest night of the year. No one would give him money. No one even wanted to talk to him. His petition sheets remained blank. It was all that he could do to give away information. Gradually he forgot that he was talking to living people. This was mainly a protective reaction to his surroundings, characterized by obsessive perceptions of sameness, disorganization of thought processes, suppression of erotic and aggressive impulses, and a general lack of relatedness to others, inducing increasingly severe disturbances in the patient's language functions as well — to wit, mutism, delayed onset of speech, and loss of intent to communicate. For as he lifted each heavy knocker wearily, or slumped against yet another tinkling doorbell, poor Frank's frostbitten mind ached dully, and snowflakes rose and settled in his skull when he turned his head, as if it were one of those paperweights containing a winter scene you can shake up. The door swung open, and a woman smiled and shook her head and said, "I'm *very* sorry; we're *just* eating dinner," or possibly a man still in his rumpled business suit peered at him through the peephole and said, "Not tonight, pal; get lost," and Frank nodded automatically and blew on his numbed hands and went on to the next house. It soon appeared to him that he was not out here to ask for money and signatures, or even to distribute literature; but simply to trudge on through the darkness, going to each door until he was sent away to the next — and this was a necessary sort of *cerea flexibilitas*; for how could he have remained sane had he faced up to the fact that behind every door was a human consciousness, and that each consciousness felt great hatred for him? So he went on and on. Having forgotten that there were other people in the world, Frank next forgot that there was even such a thing as "inside." He was too cold to bear to remember that. It seemed to him that the night was a sort of roof above him, as if he were within a vast chilly garage, and someone had shrunk him down to the size of a tin soldier and placed him upon a table where a model suburb stood. So Frank walked across the hard flatness of everything, and went up and down hard flat steps.

So now, as Frank stood in the yellow-lit grotto of the abandoned porch, he was stunned to see a man coming up to him. The man was paunchy and wore a white shirt and had white hair and a red face. Perhaps Frank had come to his house a minute or an hour ago; Frank couldn't tell. He looked at the man without curiosity. — "Is this your handbill?" the man asked him mildly, holding out a crumpled ball of yellow paper. — Frank wondered whether in a fit of absent-mindedness he had littered somebody's lawn with the leaflet, but upon mature reflection he decided that he had not. "Yes, sir, that's mine," he said. — "THEN STICK IT UP YOUR ASS, YOU SONOFABITCH!" — "What?" Frank said, serenely numbed with astonishment. — "GET THE HELL OUT OF THE NEIGHBOR-HOOD, YOU ASSHOLE!" — "What?" said Frank again, with difficulty. "Why?" — "YOU HEARD ME! I DON'T EVER WANT TO SEE YOU AROUND HERE AGAIN WITH THIS SHIT, DO YOU UNDERSTAND ME?" — "Well," said Frank (who had never had the time to read the leaflet), "what's wrong with it?" — "EVERYTHING! EVERYTHING'S A GODDAMN ROTTEN LIE!" — Frank asked the man to explain what the lies were, but the man told him that he didn't have time. The man shook Frank's shoulder, hit him and knocked him down. When he had gone, Frank got up groaning from the hard cold cement. He had a bloody nose. He walked down Quiet Place Court to Quiet Place Drive and sat down on the curb for a moment. At once a man came out from the house behind him. — "What are you doing here?" the man said. Frank began marshaling his command interpreter to process an explanation, but nothing seemed to be working except his toes, which wriggled invisibly in his shoes like cold blue worms. — "Whatever it is, we don't like it," the man said. — "Get lost," the man said. "I'll give you till three to run or we'll call the police," the man said. — "ONE," the man counted (and the kitchen window opened and the man's family stuck their heads out and counted loudly with him; so *this* was the "we" that he was talking about); "TWO," they counted together; "THREE," but Frank was already up and running blindly into the darkness. He heard their faraway chuckling behind him.

Finally he found a house with its driveway lamp out. He sat there and rubbed his nose and watched the white steam of his breath rise through the cold night, and shivered and looked at his watch. − Just across the street was one of those houses which are so typical of the middle-class dwellings along the west coast of our great Republic: First and most importantly, there was the garage door, which was white and segmented like an arthropod. It did not quite join with the cement of the driveway, and through the crack a sullen yellow-green light diffused itself, for reactionaries always keep their garage fixtures ón. The door was framed on either side by pillars of brick, which had the color of dried blood in the night; and above these shone the happy white triangle of the roof, along the edges of which were rigged green, orange, cherry, and Prussian blue Christmas bulbs (that arrangement of hues being repeated six times). Now, left of this impressive assembly lay the house proper, a flat rectangular affair overhung by a black roof, so that if you were to step up onto the open cement porch (and Frank would not have dreamed of such a thing), and your tired feet ached with the hardness of it, you would feel as if you had already been sucked into the house itself, though you were still outside, for the dark roof hung over your head and Christmas lights dazed you with their winking and blinking, and a brace of Christmas trees was set just right of the WELCOME mat to dazzle you further until you puked.

Now as Frank sat huddled in the lunar shadows, the crack beneath the garage door widened silently, the door rose with all the efficiency of electricity, and a man strode from his kitchen to his car as the house-dog rushed out at Frank, barking (evidently they kept the animal in the garage at night) and he seized Frank's leg and bit pretty hard so that Frank had to go to the hospital. When the ambulance had left, cars continued to pass in the street, meaninglessly. − "Quiet!" the man told his dog, who was snarling low with satisfaction. "Quiet!" the man said again. But the dog just looked at him slyly and licked his hand.

The canvass went on regardless of weather. Sometimes it poured and poured, and then the crew sat in the restaurant ten or fifteen minutes longer than they should have, but finally they got into the car and the field manager let Frank off at the corner of Gog and Magog, and the rain gathered on the brim of Frank's company hat and filmed his glasses and ran down the back of his neck, and he stumbled on, and when he finally came to some householder who was home Frank took off his glasses to find the proper petition sheet to be signed, and then he discovered that the whole clipboard, despite its water-resistant plastic overlay, was nothing but a clump of sodden paper-pulp bleeding with inks and dyes, and all the signatures and amounts on the few checks he had collected were now illegible. – "You want me to sign THAT?" said his interlocutor in horror. Then, if the person were kindly: "Here, son, here's a dollar, go buy yourself a beer because you need it if you have to be out on a night like this. – No, that's okay. I don't need any information, thank you." Then Frank went out again into the sopping darkness, and put his icy glasses back on so that he could see nothing but breath-fog, and the rain drummed and drummed on his head and shoulders and clipboard, and he missed his footing and stumbled off the curb into a puddle.

Some evenings it might be relatively warm and the rain might stop at seven or so. Then Frank would dry his glasses on his out-turned pocket linings, and squeeze the water out of his hair and look around with rising spirits at this guerrilla territory. Secret peeks through tree-walls and fence-slats would thrill him, for you never knew just what you might find: perhaps the shapes of yellow glow would imprison great tormented silhouettes behind the fences; or he'd spy a cricket on the sidewalk . . . and every now and then Frank heard the axe-thunk sounds of slammed car doors, and the car passed along the street a little later, all passengers safely strapped in with their buttons down; for Frank the noise of its onrush resembled an abnormally steady wind, or the sound of a gas jetted from a tube. At last the headlights of it caught him, and the car slowed as everyone within it looked at him. And Frank, feeling an inexplicable shame, stared down at the sidewalk. – Oh, the white wasteland of that sidewalk . . . Christmas lights shone evil and steadfast, and the moon gave everything a bewildering wilderness character, where only the sidewalk could be trusted to seem safe or clear.

"Yes, I know about take-or-pay contracts, but what about *force majeure?*" the homeowner said.

"What's that?" said Frank.

The door closed firmly, with a sound not unlike that made by the trap of a gallows banging hard against the frame (though there of course we are speaking of opening, not closing, dropping the pinioned criminal into the free space of new opportunities); indeed, as we shall see, firmness was to bring the jellylike career of Frank to closure, decades hence and thousands of miles north, in the fateful Arctic. Meanwhile doors closed firmly on Frank every forty-five seconds.

(In August and September it had been so clear and happy and warm all the long summer evening; it did not get dark much before nine. Then to canvass was to *be* happy in the golden winds that blew along every hilly street.)

Tonight he was at Seaview and Terrace, windy streets both of them, with quiet narrow houses lit up behind white curtains. Sometimes he would hear a piano, or a woman's voice singing. As he walked along he saw cats, gravel and lemon trees with the lemons hanging green and yellow in the yard-lights, even though it was January now, for California was where the growing season never stopped; it never got that cold, maybe forty degrees at worst, with a wind chill of twenty-five, and in the summer everything turned all golden-brown and dead as you headed inland with your canvassing crew, the radio really rocking with tunes like "Drop your pants to your ankles; I really quiver when you deliver," and Blue Max rolling down his window to yell at the pretty girl in the red Fiat, "I LOVE YOU, OOOH-OOOH-OOOH!" and the whole crew roared as she gave him back the finger, and Larry-O in the far back goes, "Joy-*Stick,* man, that's what all the girls call Larry-O, they call me Joy-*Stick.* Whoo-*eee,* what a little bitty cutey-pie," and then they went into the tunnel and Mike turned the radio up to maximum volume and Lester just sat there grinning and nodding his head; and then they burst out of the tunnel with Pleasant Hill, where they would be canvassing this fine September afternoon, two rights ahead, and everything was all blasted golden and it was a hundred degrees in the shade; and Lester told another joke and they all cracked up; and Frank was as happy as could be — but this was summertime, summertime, sum-sum-summertime, summertime, summertime, sum-sum-summertime, summertime, sum-mer-a-time . . . and in the winter everything got all dark green and moist and chilly, and the rain beat down making the windshield wipers go *whummph-whymmph-whuuummph* quite angrily; and the lemon trees continued to grow, but slowly and numbly; and the trees huddled to themselves in the cold and wished their bark were thicker and that summer had come again, so they could say, oh, Lord, give my roots rain. — Frank stopped to blow on his cold white hands. It was very dark. From a transformer assembly on a White Power & Light pole came the E-note hum of the vigilant blue globes, monitoring all; and at Galvin and Terrace he heard water running in the sewers. All around Frank the night-trees were still. The street was set into the side of a hill. On his left the hill dropped off quite steeply, so that he had to clamber down twisting flights of wooden stairs surrounded by the dark, dripping trees, until finally he came to the driveway, and the house was withdrawn, its external lights deactivated, and it was past eight now so that Frank did not dare to knock for fear that the occupants were sleeping or making love, but then he did not like to knock between six and seven either because at that time the tired families were eating dinner and the children were crawling on the living room rug as Mom did the dishes as she had almost every day of her life and Dad sat back in the couch being soothed by the booming voice of the TV. — Ding-dong, went the doorbell.

"Who the hell is that?" says Dad. — "It's probably Carolyn with the pies," Mom says. — The children all jump up. "Carolyn!" they shout. "Carolyn, Carolyn, oh, Carolyn!" — Dad gets up grumbling but inwardly pleased because Carolyn has not come by for a long time. He goes to the door and swings it open, but it's not Carolyn; it's some pasty-faced kid on his doorstep, the paper boy probably because the kid is wearing a baseball cap and holding a clipboard and on his cap is emblazoned KUZBU UNION FOR A NATIONAL TURNAROUND, oh, shit, it's another one of *those* assholes.

"Goodbye," says Frank, forlornly. There was nothing for it but to go back up the driveway and weave his way along the zig-zag wooden steps that led him back up through the woods to the streetlights and the stars and freedom so that he could go back down the stairs of the adjoining plot. — At least, he thought, going from house to house, he had been lucky in that no dogs had come lunging at him as he went down into the darkness; and speak of the devil; he emerged onto the street again and saw a long, lean, black, green-eyed hound slinking half a block behind him, slavering a little and grinning at him . . .

As Frank went uphill twenty minutes later he heard a sudden rattling of chains. A white mastiff was rushing at him from a member's yard. Its chains were not quite long enough for it to reach him. When it saw that it would not be able to hurt Frank, it barked in a great deep voice and lunged and lunged so that the chains scraped on the driveway and all the neighbors turned on their porch lights and peered through their living room windows at Frank. Frank left, shaking. He could hear the dog barking steadily behind him for five minutes. As he rounded the corner the black hound blocked his path, baying softly. At once all the dogs of the neighborhood began to bark and howl and throw themselves against the walls of their kennels with fanatically determined thuds so that the wood creaked, and a few got loose and emerged from the trees in a pack; and Frank dropped his clipboard and looked all around him and saw that the dogs were closing in on him, and he shinnied up a pine tree so that his pants ripped, and he quaked in the branches, and all the dogs howled for triumph that they had treed him, but the black hound began to climb the tree, so Frank scrambled up higher and higher so that the branches got thin and bent beneath his weight, swinging Frank right up against the window of the house, the bedroom window, and the light was on, and a woman reading in bed looked up at the sound and saw Frank and screamed and picked up her bedside telephone and started to dial, never taking her eyes off Frank. Frank grabbed desperately at the rain-gutter just above his head, swung himself up onto the roof, and crawled up its surface to the ridge of it and then down the other side. The yard-lights were all going on around him, and the dogs were yowling vindictively all around. Any second now someone would see him. Frank moaned in despair. – Just then something blocked out the moon. Looking up, Frank perceived the silhouette of a helium dirigible. There was a soft sound of something falling, unrolling, and Frank saw that a rope ladder had been let down to him. As he moved up the first knot, the dirigible was already reascending. Looking down, Frank saw the entire neighborhood receding into a sprinkle of cheery yellow lights. The police would never catch Frank now. Frank pulled himself up the rest of the way. Two waldo-arms brought him into the hatch. Frank had been saved by a robot.

"Good evening," the robot said, motioning Frank to a chair at a small oval table set for one. "I represent Blaker's Martian Enterprises, Ltd. I have instructions to offer you a contract, should you wish to work for the reactionary side as a double agent." It reached into its breast-hatch and withdrew a gleaming scroll of some unknown material.

"Okay," said Frank palely. But then it occurred to him that perhaps he had not been assertive enough. "And, uh, what if I preferred not to?"

"As Mr. Blaker likes to remark," said the robot, "it may be lonely at the top, but it sure is a long way down."

Frank looked through the picture window. It certainly was. He thought he recognized the outline of Africa.

"Oh," Frank said.

He was on his way to Mars.

HELP FROM THE BLUE GLOBES

~~~~~~

> In phonographic work we can use our eyes and our ears, aided by powerful microscopes; but in the battery our difficulties cannot be seen or heard, but must be observed by our mind's eye.
>
> EDISON to his Chief Chemist, Ayle
> (1900 or so)

Three weeks later, Frank was back on the job, and no one suspected his secret allegiance.

Sitting by a drain at the intersection of Leg and Leg in El Cerrito, Frank listened to police sirens, barking dogs and faraway cars. There were still Christmas lights up on a few houses. Porchlamps shone yellow through the scales of sad palm trees. Looking up at the stars, Frank could not tell whether or not they twinkled, because his glasses were so thickly smeared. Not a sign of humanity could be seen. No one answered the door. No wind stirred up the trees or lawn-shrubs, and the glare-spots on the chrome of the automobiles remained fixed no matter how Frank turned his head. There was not even a bug to keep him company on the sidewalk. Frank cried out. If a cricket or cold-weather beetle had come to recruit Frank he would have happily enlisted in the insect cause, but no one came.

A trash can lid fell. Frank was filled with hope for a moment, thinking that perhaps somebody was out there emptying the garbage after a late dinner, but though he waited and waited there was no further sound. The lid, it was clear, had simply been balanced uneasily on the edge of the can for hours or years, and yielding over time to fluctuations in gravity and magnetism, or perhaps changing its center of volume imperceptibly, like century-old church glass (for glass is in fact a liquid, and it flows very gently, like Frank's tears, which is why old windows are thicker at the bottom than on top), it had finally tipped, tilted, rocked, and fallen, and that was the end of the story.

Oh, how beautiful the neighborhood had been at sunset, as Frank's feet clomped across the red flagstone courtyards, with the white walls of the houses enclosing him, and the dark green trees, as rich with chlorophyll as broccoli or graveyard yews, framing a fine view of the Bay and the hills across it (both the water and the land being a single purple shape to Frank), surmounted by an orange sky. But now it was so black and cold and late . . . And the working people were going to bed now. – Getting up at last and walking two blocks to do his callbacks, Frank could see some motion, finally, in this mechanical world: here and there the house-lights were winking out. Perhaps no one was there; and it was just something that the central brain of the house did to conserve energy and disconcert burglars who had been lying in wait for half an hour, thinking the house to be uninhabited. Perhaps (and this is actually what it was) it was the blue globes signaling to each other.

The blue globes had their eye on Frank, all right. It was their aim to improve his condition. What was their plan? – We shall see.

Frank was a troubled person. At night he dreamed of a dark room where businessmen were buried in drawers, the whole setup much like the map room at the library; and all the businessmen were interred with their guns symbolically disassembled beside them: – no more would these men attack; no more would they defend themselves; nevermore would their sidearms be used. But Frank in his dream opened the drawer of a man who had died quite recently; the tart smell of death made him nauseous but in his dream he knew that he had to have a gun; he fumbled around the bloated ankles; here was the slide; here was the grip; now where was the recoil spring and recoil spring guide or was it glide? . . . How did Frank know all this terminology? Well, in fact he did have a gun; being a double agent he had had to buy one. Phil Blaker had given him a salary advance.

He had decided to kill himself. Of course it was not easy coming to this decision, but Frank managed nonetheless. He had a gun, a gun, a shiny black gun. – It was odd what he cared about at the time. You might think that if a man had decided to kill himself he would not care much about his usual routines during his last few minutes, but Frank did; I cannot really say why. The plan was to get into his sleeping bag on the mattress in the dark little room where he slept, and lie comfortably there as if he were just going to sleep, and listen to nice Schubert music on his Marantz Superscope (Frank adored classical tunes) to make him feel calm and relaxed, and then, when the time came, to put the barrel of his black gun to his forehead, maybe looking up at it first for one moment, and letting that cold circle of metal rest on his forehead while the mosquitoes hummed eagerly in that infested room, he would slowly take a deep breath and squeeze the trigger. So Frank undressed and turned out the light and got into bed. Suddenly he realized that he had to piss. He knew that after he died his bladder would relax and when people found him it would be embarrassing if he had not thought ahead, so he got up and put a towel around himself and went to the bathroom and did that, then he flushed the toilet and got back into bed. But, you know, the funniest thing happened: Frank suddenly remembered that he had not brushed his teeth. Now, what difference could that possibly make to Frank at this point in his life, one might wonder, as Frank himself did in a sad dull way; such a concern was particularly ludicrous for Frank since he had never taken care of his teeth before, sometimes going for weeks without brushing them, and he certainly did not floss them as Dr. Dodger had ordered; so in fact there was no reason for Frank to continue to pour more of his substance into a bad investment. Nonetheless, Frank was bothered. His teeth started to hurt instinctively; soon they would only be dead bones and the tomb-bacteria would eat cavities in every one, but Frank felt guilty about not doing his bit to postpone tooth decay. He got out of bed and went back to the bathroom. Frank did not stint on the toothpaste, since he believed that this was probably the last time that he would brush his teeth. The toothpaste tasted good. Frank thoroughly enjoyed himself.

Now Frank got back into bed. From his rumpled jeans, which lay beside the bed where he had taken them off, he got his key ring. He pulled the heavy metal lockbox over to the side of the mattress. It was a Burgwächter, with blue enamel finish. Frank selected the proper key and opened the box. He took his black cold gun out of the holster and looked at it. It was beautiful. It was the Browning BDA .380, made in cooperation with Beretta in Italy, for a look as stylish as a racing car; Phil Blaker had done the right thing by Frank, for any real double agent needs a few elegant yet functional possessions to offset the feelings of loss and guilt which inevitably occur in the early years of the trade. — The gun had a walnut grip, too. It had a fine smell because Frank had cleaned it this morning after coming back from the range. When Frank cleaned his gun he enjoyed drawing it from the cool black holster and then smelling the streaks of lead compounds inside the barrel from the rounds he had fired. He would remove the magazine and retract the slide. Next Frank unscrewed the bronze brush and attached an Outers cloth patch to the white plastic slotted tip, which in turn screwed on just where the bronze brush had gone. He dipped this in the bottle of cleaning solvent, and brought it through the barrel ten times. The patch came out black, as expected, so poor Frank had to do this again and again until at last the cloth was white upon exit, like the mind of a brainwashed lamb, the whiteness being a sign to Frank that he could continue with the procedure; yes, now for the slide, barrel lug, frame, recoil spring and recoil spring glide or was it guide; and Frank had to dry and oil everything before he wiped it with a clean cloth. Then he put the gun back together, pushed the pin again, flipped the takedown lever up, and re-inserted the magazine. Finally he could clutch the gun to himself fondly for a moment before he locked it up in its cold blue box.

So now Frank took his unloaded gun from the holster and pressed it to his forehead, listening to Schubert. He put the pistol off safe so that the red warning dot showed and dry-fired it. − Click! − Next Frank removed the empty magazine and loaded it with bullets. Magazine capacity was thirteen rounds. Frank loaded it with all thirteen, just in case. He retracted the slide, clicked in the magazine, and pulled down the slide stop. − Slam! The slide snicked back up against the barrel, in a state of combat readiness, and on the right side of the frame the extractor cammed outward, exposing a red dot. − Frank put the gun on safe, brought it to his forehead, and pulled the trigger slowly. It was a nice easy even pull, with no consequence. − Now Frank flipped the safety off, raised the gun to his forehead again, and began to squeeze the trigger. But do you know what? Frank unexpectedly found himself bothered by the fact that there were still bullets left in the lockbox, even though he had loaded his magazine to full capacity. Fortunately he had two spare magazines for such emergencies. He put the gun on safe and loaded the rounds into the spares. − At this point he decided to masturbate before he died. He came quickly and wiped himself on his shirt. Then he raised the pistol to his head again and flipped the safety off.

He was all set this time. But just then, wouldn't you know it, the phone rang. Of course Frank could have chosen to let the phone ring, figuring that in fifteen seconds he would be dead anyhow and the phone would still be ringing, but listening to it ring right now wore Frank to a frazzle. So he set the gun down and jumped out of his sleeping bag and raced to the head of the stairs to answer it. "Hello, is this Frank?"

"Yes," said Frank cautiously.

"Frank, this is the blue globes."

"Blue globes?" said Frank. "What does that mean?"

"We are the forces of electricity, Frank. We rule your life, and we are not yet ready for you to die. Lock up your gun immediately."

"I beg your pardon?" said Frank, stupefied.

"You heard us, Frank. Remember, we are the blue globes, and you will help us dominate Parker through the mysteries of the Great Enlarger."

Then a giant crackling of static crawled into Frank's ear from the receiver and wriggled its fur in Frank's semi-circular canals until Frank fell to the rug in dizzy torment. The lights flickered on and off, the radio snarled at maximum volume so that the tenants below pounded on the floor with a broom handle, and the Marantz Superscope, Frank's pride and joy, shorted out forever. But the blue globes did not harm the gun just then, for reasons of their own.

THE DISGUISES

~~~~~~

It's sometimes easier to count decision nodes, sometimes links and nodes, and sometimes holes.

BORIS BEIZER
Software Testing Techniques

Lester was the most terrific canvasser you ever saw. He was a fat black man with one eye. He usually brought back two or three hundred a night. He was so good he could borrow money from the other canvassers, all of whom knew they'd never see it back. When you first started working for K.U.N.T. you were very anxious to be of service and always shared your lunch with your fellow heroes and heroines because no one but the new people ever brought any; they preyed off the new people because the new people generally didn't last very long; it was a feat if you lasted two months, and then you were senior staff and your percentage went up from 38.5% to 40%. Lester had been working there so long he made 50%. So the idea was to borrow a couple bucks off the new kid you were training that day because usually by the end of the night he'd be so happy to get off with his life he wrote off the money, didn't even think about it, probably, though he'd never have the guts to tell you he was flaking out; he'd promise to be there tomorrow FOR SURE but you knew you'd never see him again and you were just as glad because you'd made a buck, unless you were the field manager, in which case you were sad because he might've increased your revenues by a few cents since you got an additional percentage of the whole take. The field manager had to go out and scope turf while everyone else chewed pizza in the empty restaurant at three in the afternoon (that was lunch and dinner) and drew up little maps on napkins for their turf that night and went through the cards to find their members. If a member was just a first-year sucker you couldn't count on him to stay on, but if the Kuzbuites had sold him the newsletter last year and the year before, or there were maybe even two or three renewals by the family's name, then you had a hot prospect of getting sixteen dollars once again. "Come on," Lester would say, laughing easily *with* his interlocutors, not *at* them. "Sixteen dollars. Sure is better than a *poke* in the eye." — And the homeowner would look into Lester's dead eye and swallow uncomfortably, and hesitate, and then laugh at this big ole dummy who was so hilarious in the way of his race and the homeowner would write out a check if he hadn't already called the police on Lester, and Lester would hear the clean sound of another fresh check being torn along the perforation; and already as the homeowner was handing it over he'd be thinking, wait a second, what am I doing giving the nig a check for SIXTEEN BUCKS; maybe I'd better call the police to send him back to Africa; but it would be too late for Lester was already at the next house, ding-dong. — "Evenin' ma'am, my name's Lester; I'm with the Kuzbu Union for a National Turnaround. This is my I.D., and here's my permit. They sure make good mug shots, don't they, ma'am? Well, I 'magine you get *thousands and thousands* of people bangin' on your door just like me, so I'll get straight to the point and not bother you, ma'am, 'cause I can tell you're makin' dinner in there and it *sure* does smell good! — Now what we're out here working on tonight is to *roll back* those White Power & Light gas prices, because they want to increase shareholder profit nineteen percent and make *us* pay for abandoned and canceled projects like the nuclear plant up at Marshtown and all those funny-looking wind-mills and things you see when you're driving along through the desert, and we *really* need your support. Now there's three ways you can help us, ma'am. First, *read* the petition, and if you agree with what we're doing then help us out, yes, here you go, ma'am, take a look, and like I said we *do* need your support, and we have a pretty good track record; we're the folks that stopped all those abuses of the Dr. Dodger patent label medicines, and we've kept pay phone calls at ten cents in the state, and we're working right now to get that young fella Bug elected Governor of the state instead of Mr. White, and if you support all those things then help us out, *sign* the petition, *write* us out a *check* and send a *letter* to Senator Blaker about the *problems* in the neighborhood."

"You want me to write you out a check?" the lady said in disbelief.

"That's right, ma'am, that's the second type of support. Sign the petition, *join* K.U.N.T., and send a letter to your Congressman. Now what I *really* need you to do is join and get our *newsletter* so you won't just be making a *blind* contribution" (here Lester winked his dead eye), "you'll actually *see* where your money's going over the year and what we're all doin' for you. And if you're a member don't think you'll have to walk around from door to door; that stuff's for dummies like me; that's MY contribution, so help us out, write us a check for sixteen, better than a *poke* in the *eye*, and make it out to Kuzbu Union for a National Turnaround."

The lady looked him up and down. "There's something wrong with your eye," she said with finality.

Lester grinned behind his hand. "No, ma'am," he said, a bit confused, even worried, "you must be mistaken, ma'am. Let me take a look in the mirror." — In he goes, shuts the bathroom door behind him as the lady waits sternly; and there is a moment of stunned silence, then Lester screams "YAAAAAAAAAAAAAAH! MY EYE! I'M BLIND IN ONE EYE AND I NEVER NOTICED IT ALL THESE YEARS!" and he comes reeling out into the living room; it's the shock of his life, and finally the lady gets it and laughs and feels guilty and writes him a check for sixteen though she has to postdate it. — "YAAAAH!" Lester screams in the car on the way home, fat and jolly and drunk with reefers and Colt .45 Malt Liquor in the big blue and white cans.

XEROX BOY

~~~~~~

Reproducibility is the single most important criterion of success.

American Folk Wisdom

When Stephen Mole got fired, he went back to photography school to get an advanced degree because he had to do *something* to overcome the rage and defeat that burned inside him and made his liver bulge out visibly and ache to the touch. He was, therefore, by far the most serious student. His eyes glared out at everyone like jasper; and he spent every possible instant in the darkrooms stopping down the enlargers and slamming the paper safe and gnawing his beard and scribbling timer calculations and swearing to himself. (Parker did not work like that at all. Parker only had to touch the printing paper with one slimy forefinger for everything to come out right.) — "Stephen, we're extremely pleased with your work," said his professors. — "Thank you, gentlemen," said Stephen sarcastically. "In that case I'm sure you'll all write me good recommendations." For he was mastering the secret principles of the Skeptics. — In the appointed time he graduated, having completed his study of glamor algebra and *f*/stop poetry and prison optics, but in spite of this talent nobody had any positions available at the present time. His name would be kept on file for one year. — Sleazy Frank, of course, easily tolerated living on cheese and white bread for months at a time so that he had continuous light dysentery, since Frank was *used* to eking out his life among the dregs of the capitalist world, but for Stephen the situation was humiliating to an extreme. At length he was down to thirty dollars and a half-empty jar of peanut butter, with the rent due the following week, so it was time to set one's career sights a little lower. — It was six o'clock that morning, and Stephen sat on the front steps of his apartment building reading the classified ads while mud-colored urban birds pecked at the broken glass around his feet. He saw a good opportunity down in Monterey. "WANTED," the paper said, "STABLE SELF-MOTIVATED ACHIEVER, UNAFRAID OF GETTING THE DAMN JOB DONE." — "That's me," Stephen said to himself, not without bitterness. — "START IMMEDIATELY." Within three hours he was in the thick of an interview with Mr. White.

"So, as I was saying, sir," said Stephen, in suit and tie, "I think I'd be a valuable addition to your company, and I'm sure I can do whatever it is you'd be wanting me to do, though I'd like to know what that is."

"Fine, fine," said Mr. White with a yawn. He pushed Stephen's portfolio off his desk so that it fell to the floor. "Something tells me you'll go far. Well, boy, from your résumé I see you've had something to do with the manufacture of images, so you'll be just right for the position, which is that of junior xerox operator. Far as I'm concerned, what's the blasted difference whether it's pictures or words, and since you got canned from your last job I'm sure you're not much of a one to be drawing fine distinctions, either. Now, there are only two rules when you join my employ: no shirking, and no griping. If there's one thing that really pisses me off it's some fathead bothering me about things he should shut up about; life is too short for that crap."

"Mr. White," said Stephen, who was trembling with anger, "to suggest that I'm only worth being your xerox boy is an insult to me, because I have a master's degree in photography, as it says right on my résumé, and what you can do with that job is —"

Mr. White interrupted with some annoyance. "I already told you that you're the man for the job, and once I make up my mind I don't change it, so I'll give you fifteen seconds to bugger off, you young cock, because you'll be back. Now shut your prissy little mouth and get out." — BZZZZZT! — "Operator, get me the network. — Yes, this is Jack White. I want you to put out an employment code 4F on a Stephen Mole, and here's his social security number."

Within two weeks, Stephen, finding that now no prospective employers would even agree to see him or keep his name on file, accepted the inevitable, his heart pounding with rage, and became xerox boy of the Society of Daniel.

Harry Belafonte sings a melodious song that begins, "A-wa-a-a-t-er boy-y-y-eee," and I can think of no refrain more suited to Stephen's circumstances, for every few minutes the intercom would tinkle by the big xerox machine in the cold copy room (which was also where the Society of Daniel's IBM/Amdahl printer and three VAXes were kept) and Stephen in his red uniform would have to pick it up and somebody would say, "Is this the xerox boy? Goddamn it, I had to wait for you while the phone rang three times, and I want to know if my order's ready; I can't do shit without it." – And sometimes one of the older executives would walk in with his lips puckered up to whistle a nostalgic air: "Xe-he-rox boy-y-y-eee," and Stephen became so angry that his face got red and he stopped the machine and looked down at his shoes, so everyone calculated that he was just another shy nerd, of which there were so many on the premises. The secretaries would have been his friends, but Stephen, hating himself for being a xerox boy, hated the secretaries just as much for being secretaries, and dealt curtly with them. So soon Stephen Mole was left to himself in the cold white room, his fingers and shirt front blackened by toner.

Meanwhile, me boys, Mr. White prospered.

Standing just left of the White Power & Light box upon the lawn, and facing the ocean, which lies just out of sight, though not always out of hearing, beyond a buffer of sand dunes polluted with smelly solvents, lead from military cartridges, and flocks of toilet paper and brittle white condoms that take wing in the wind like the gulls once indigenous to the region, one may observe a square building, the walls of which are some glassy material that gleams like a mirror. The grass is as well kept as new velvet. By the parking lot a rectangular strip of it has been torn away, fungus-resistant bark chips have been laid down, and a rose garden grows higher month by month. One speaks instinctively of months in such a place, not years, because the technology changes so fast, you see. Were you to proceed up the sidewalk to the front door, smiling suntanned security guards would come running up to you and ask in friendly voices to please see your identification. Were you to qualify, four of them would conduct you to the reception area, with its waiting room, receptionist, secretary, appointment manager, visitor book, and invisible video cameras. Your name being called after a pleasant interval spent in an armchair reading up-to-the-minute industry journals, like the *Metal Oxide Semiconductor Field Effect Transmitter Daily Globe* or *VLSI Funnies,* you would get up, receive a laminated plastic visitor I.D. to clip to your shirt front, and step through the metal detector. If you were important the metal detector would not ring unless you were carrying a loaded pistol. If you were a new arrival, bent on claiming your scholarship or asking some favor of Mr. White, then the metal detector would ring and ding and buzz for every micro-filling in your teeth, or the iron in the spinach you ate two weeks ago, and then the security guards would take you aside and strip you to the skin and turn your underwear inside out and make you spread your buttocks while they shone a flashlight up your ass, all the while making cheerful jokes so that you would know that it was part of the S.O.P. Then once you were cleared it was a pleasant walk down carpeted corridors with shut office doors on every side, and you could read the nameplates if you liked; they were representative of the most competent electronic personalities of the day: Isaac Newton, Niels Bohr, Dr. William Dodger, D.D.S. ("Hey there, Off-Line Tiger," Mr. White would say to Dr. Dodger expansively over the intercom whenever he saw that Dr. Dodger had logged off); and from behind every door came the calm symphonies of dentist drills. – The halls seemed to roll on forever. At last you came to a door that said AUTHORIZED PERSONNEL ONLY. And beyond it was a square chamber of considerable dimensions, sectioned into several hundred open cubicles, where the bread-and-butter programmers worked silently (aside from occasional sneezes and key-clicks), servicing the great blue globe computer that was four stories below, in the cool earth.

They each laughed differently there. Skinny old Sammy laughed, "Hee-hee-hee-hee," and then clutched at his heart. He was one of the last survivors from the Society of Daniel's first class. Chuck's laugh went, "A-huh, haw, haw, huh, huh, huh," while Ron would laugh wearily, "I guess I'll, huh-huh-huh, have to look *into* the situation." Ron was always laughing wearily and complaining about the commute. He'd say, "I don't know why people, uh, *do it* – I mean there is sometimes construction on the highway – I don't know what I can do; I cannot, uh, leave my home; my wife has her little circle of friends; *boy,* I would give anything to be, uh, *your* age again."

In the western corner was an unobtrusive staircase, which led to the administrative offices. One flight above these was another level, carpeted and sunny, with a big public lounge through which an artificial brook flowed and recirculated, reminding the observer most, perhaps, of a stream in the Alaskan Arctic rushing past banks of bright-colored tundra. Little goldfish flickered in the water. The brook had been shaped in a meandering circle; at its widest point a rustic drawbridge connected carpet to carpet; and on the islet thus formed were pleasant terminals and work stations, facing outward. An excellent reference library was on-line.

It was here, in this delightful public area, that Mr. White's students prepared themselves for the world.

Parker was the new boy. He was taken downstairs to the programmers for an interview. — "I don't understand why it happens," he heard Violet muttering beneath the triumphant consoles. "When there's an error on the VAX it continues to run. Why do they *allow* that?" — "Well, for my purposes it's all right," said Eileen somewhat vaguely. — It was all Greek to Parker, who winked and blinked. — Big George led him up to Ron's cubicle for the interview.

"What are registers?" Ron began the quiz.

Parker cleared his throat and jigged his Adam's apple hypnotically up and down, giving Ron the impression that he must have mumbled something. Since, as Ron was aware, everyone knew what registers were, this was really a throwaway question, and he was sure that Parker had given him the right answer. Confident that Parker must now be at ease, Ron proceeded to the next plateau in the mountain range he intended to lead Parker through. — "Well," said Ron jocularly, with a sort of hrrumph and rumble to warn Parker (to whom Ron was not yet ill-disposed) that this might well be a trick question, "so why don't we put the information on, uh, *disk,* say?" — It was clear to Parker that this comedy could not amble on indefinitely. There were only so many nonverbal ways of evading a direct technical question to which one did not know the answer. Sizing Ron up as a drone, Parker acted quickly and decisively, gangling out his long brown-green arm so that it stretched out of the sleeve, and Ron did not even goggle because Ron was convinced that it was just the glare and the coffee and the sleepless nights that were playing tricks on him, so Parker stretched out his wrist and hand and fingers like a living crocodile wallet and his fingers flowed almost into Ron's face, and as Ron suddenly shook his head to clear it and realized that something funny was going on Parker snatched off Ron's heavy black horn-rim glasses and reeled in his arm to bring the glasses back toward Parker's moonlike face and Parker inspected the glasses minutely for some time as Ron sat there in amazement until finally Parker spat in Ron's glasses and smeared the spittle around with his finger and then quick as a snake Parker stabbed his middle finger into Ron's left eyeball and then into Ron's right eyeball, so that Ron bellowed like an ox. It was not Parker's intention to blind Ron, only to make the balls of his eyes ache terribly and shockingly so that the interview, which Parker found uncomfortable, would be terminated. This had its desired effect, for Ron fell onto the floor with his hands to his eyes and roared and roared while Parker sat there primly like a new boy should and cracked his knuckles. From the surrounding cubicles other programmers swarmed in, pleased at the diversion, and surrounded Ron asking what had happened, but Ron just lay there rocking his head in his arms and moaning, so Parker sidled out quietly and found his name and room posting on the bulletin board on the second floor landing and took his suitcase up to his room and unpacked it and stretched out on the bed thinking his own thoughts. – "Well, what did you think?" said Big George in his office to Ron when Ron was in a condition to speak. – "You know," said Ron, who, as Parker had shrewdly guessed, had no intention of disclosing to others his terrible humiliation at the hands of this green-faced upstart, "my strategy is to get them talking, and, you know, in a way I was not, uh, *satisfied*."

Yes, Ron had been humiliated, but what he felt was nothing compared to what Stephen Mole experienced when one day a few weeks later Parker ambled into the xerox room with a preliminary blueprint of the Great Enlarger to be copied, and he saw Stephen Mole, and blinked at him with considerable interest for a moment and then *smiled* – which Parker almost never did; and stretched his long arm out to punch the job interrupt button on the fancy copier and opened the feed cabinet and delicately touched the topmost sheet in paper tray one with the ball of his middle finger; and at once all the pages turned black and useless . . . – Then Stephen knew that life would be torture until he had revenged himself upon Parker.

SUSAN GOES POLITICAL

Modern discoveries, indeed, in what may be termed ethical magnetism or magnetoesthetics, render it probable that the most natural, and consequently the truest and most intense of the human affections, are those which arise in the heart as if by electric sympathy . . .

POE
"The Spectacles" (1844)

How could Susan, so shy, so ladylike, have become a strident exterminator in Bug's gang? — This question may baffle the historian, whose techniques of data brutalization are conceptually not even a score of years past that first death on Gold Hill (1832) which christened our proto-electric efforts, in a fashion analogous to those pompous popish or pagan practices, whereby young ladies were immured in the stonework of new bridges to propitiate the load-bearing gods. — So we must turn to psychology to explain Susan's alteration. — There comes a time in the life of many women, when that obliging weakness which we had thought to be an ineradicable part of their character vanishes, like the interstice between day and night. We had never trifled with *her* before because we had known that she could not stand it. Now, as we speak to her on the phone, we sense a new element in her voice. She is not afraid of us anymore! No longer does she make excuses for her failures to live up to our high reactionary standards. There is, in fact, a steely patience which diffuses itself from the receiver, like chilly globules of mercury. After one or two of these sessions it is clear that the phenomenon is not temporary. — So much the worse for us and our plans. She has genuinely achieved power. Presently it becomes clear, once we have identified ourselves over the line, that our calling was a terrible mistake; and we wish for nothing more than to apologize and hang up. But we are too uncertain of ourselves even to do this. It is then that we realize that, far from having avoided trifling with her in the past, out of deference to her frail feelings, we were TRIFLING WITH HER ALL ALONG in our patronizing gentlemanly way, and we realize now that even to say hello is to trifle with her, and she will not stand for it, and we had best let her be. – Thanks to Bug, such an enablement happened for Susan, though for Susan of course all enablements are spurious, as I, Big George, have decreed.

As time went on Bug got to rely on the earplugs to track his prey because he now knew enough not to be moved by any hope or expectation; so he tracked Susan, the earplugs tingling as he went to the elementary school. – Bug came in through the open gate, up the steps at the far end of the playground, and into the tarnished brick building where the earplugs led him down the corridor to the principal's office; there were no children's voices because it was 4:30 p.m.; everyone was just getting organized for the P.T.A. meeting when Susan fainted.

"She was talking about how miserable she was and then she fainted!" said one of the lady teachers.

"Is she pregnant?" said another slyly.

"Hardly," said a third, and at this they all giggled like horrid bells because the teachers knew that Susan's love life left much to be desired.

"She just said she felt hot and then she fainted!" recapitulated one of the publicly concerned parents.

When Bug turned the corner and peered over the shoulders of the other parents he saw Susan slumped in the armchair where they had put her when she fell, but she was half-obscured by her well-wishers, so that at first Bug thought her in conference with some invisible interlocutor, for she had slipped forward in her chair, like a self-hypnotized debater; but then Bug saw the bright sparkly eye and the white cheek, and the eye squinched itself shut again and blinked and began to make tears as Susan came round, which wetness alarmed all present, for it is bad form to cry when you are a grown-up, and while people secretly crave a *spectacle,* they by no means want a *scene*; and the principal himself rose from his desk to give her a handkerchief. If the parents had not been present, he would have rapped his desk impatiently with the steel ruler awarded him by the disciplinary board. But this was public relations night. So Susan's job was still there to look down at her among the parents and administrators with awful breath and small-town roundhead corpse-faces like the portraits on the Jim Beam label: "Distilled Since 1795." – Bug slid between people's backs and hips, being flat-bellied like a cockroach; and eased his way closer and closer to her, responding favorably to the vibrations of the earplugs; and as he came into range Susan's sniffles subsided, like a car engine that dies in a series of liquid chugs, and she wiped her eyes and pulled herself straight in her chair, and smiled a trembly smile when Bug looked her in the face, for the earplugs now transmitted a hypnotizing charisma, and everyone turned to eye Bug in his dark shiny suit with his stern glasses, thinking, *well*; and as Susan smiled at Bug she forgot her miseries because someone had finally come for her and was smiling palely back at her, since from Bug's point of view, this was an opportunity to form one of the germ-cells which his organization would require, so that new individuals could spearhead proliferating county or district groups. Susan, looking into his eyes, imagined interest there; in fact Bug had no expression at all, which made it easy for Susan to construct her fancies in the same way that it is nice to draw pretty pictures on blank paper; and once everyone had arrived they filed into the auditorium and Bug sat quietly in the front row for the next two and a half hours, while educational targets were constructed out of tongues and glottises and larynxes and pharynxes working in series onstage (Susan had been going to give a speech, but as she had shown herself to be unwell she was excused from making her presentation); and then, slipping up to Susan when everyone had gathered by a long table which bore cake, coffee and paper cups of Hawaiian punch, Bug softly requested her to attend a private committee meeting on the following Thursday.

"Thus," says Hitler, "the man of the people and the candidate of the working classes turns himself back into the parliamentary caterpillar, and again fattens on the foliage of state life." And only I, Big George, comprehend the butterfly.

WAYNE'S OBSERVATIONS ON THE INSECT WAR

~~~~~~

No erase or kill processing is done.

S.R. BOURNE
The Unix System (1983)

There was definitely something scummy going on out there to undermine Parker's ideals; the bugs were really cunning because so far they just milled around innocently when you dug up their anthills, which lulled some people into *complacency,* see, and only Wayne on his labors knew how dangerous the problem was. Even he forgot sometimes. Once he was hitching through Louisiana to get to Oregon faster and the guy who'd picked him up had a big jug of moonshine on the floor, and he said to Wayne, "Take yourself a big swig of this, son," but Wayne did not want to drink on duty, so he sang out, "No, thanks, no, sir!" and the driver pulled a gun on Wayne and put it right to Wayne's ear and said, "Now, son, I said I want you to take a big swig of what's in that jug," so there was no way Wayne could get out of it the way he had with the three Texans; anyhow he figgered what the hell, so he had him a swig, *whoooh* that was *brew!* and then the driver hawed and gave Wayne the gun and said, "Son, you put that thing to my head and make me do the same!" and Wayne had to snicker at that gag, so he did it, and then they were great pals and Wayne clean forgot about the bugs until his head cleared. Meanwhile, the march of history continued, a grand parade as long as you didn't have to walk directly behind a caparisoned steed with green diarrhea. Bug and Milly had Suzy under their fucking thumbs now, and Frank was about to be next.

THE TRIUMPH OF DR. DODGER

~~~~~~

Kazhdui drochit, kak on hochit.*

Russian proverb

Frank was at the corner of Fifth and Irving, not far from where he was later to live, waiting for his pickup, walking back and forth between Stelling's Market and Park's Market to warm himself; the fog sank into his bones and made him achy and grey, like the bones in a graveyard, like the blued steel of the Browning Beretta when it had not been fired or touched; and a red car drove slowly up the inclined street blinking its yellow lights. A figure stirred behind grey curtains in a grey house against the grey sky. The power poles marched up the street, perpetually reliable. There were black cables that draped themselves below the smooth pairs of horizontal power and phone wires dividing the sky into zones. The cables moved whether the wind blew or not, though of course we meteorologists and comet-gazers must remember that even when the air was still at the level of the sidewalk there might be a chilly breeze above the housetops and dormer windows and vent-pipes; Frank reminded himself of that, but even so it was odd the way the cables swung, making smaller arcs than the happy snakes had once done in the uncleared jungles when the world was young; but perhaps they showed themselves the more powerful for that, as several examples teach us: You can kill your fellow by hurling a boulder to smash his forehead, but a twitch upon a button will do the same or better, utilizing a variety of transformation media and much less wasted motion. So the black cables swayed dismally. As I, Big George,

---

* "Different strokes for different folks." (Literally, "Each jerks off as he likes.")

explored this same terrain, going up hills and down hills in a grey Honda Civic, I reflected upon the curious chances of conglomeration, every block filled with its own beauty and monsters. Down at the edge of Russian Hill, say, on Bay or Chestnut, there were many little Chinese and Korean markets where you could buy three pounds of grapes for ninety-nine cents, so that the happy prices made that greyness and flatness different; also, of course, because you knew that you were close to the sea the flatness seemed like a beach, and the greyness was grey with salt. And when the sun came out in North Beach, when I, the author, was sick in bed instead of down south working for Big George, then the white houses and white cars seen through the white curtains, my books around me and the clear blue sky, gave life an almost urbane character; whereas back in the Sunset district where Frank waited the houses were damper and greyer, even when they were white and the sky was blue.

There was a pay phone behind Park's Market. As Frank stood leaning against it, it rang. *Ringgg!* — Frank looked around, but there was no one in sight but himself. Should he answer it? — *Ringgg!* — Maybe it was for him, Lester calling down from the liquor store to see if he wanted any beer this time or whether he'd go in on some tortilla strips. — *Ringgg!* — But what if it was those mysterious blue globes that were out to foil Frank? — *Ringgg!*

Frank pulled back the accordion door, reached in above the elbow-shelf furnished for talkative patrons, and withdrew the receiver. — "Hello?" he said.

"This is the operator," a steely voice said; and at once Frank thought of "the" Operator down there under Civic Center somewhere running things with its flexible cable-arms and octopus-attachments . . . — "You owe thirty-five cents for the call."

"What call?" said Frank.

"The call you just completed. Please deposit thirty-five cents."

"That wasn't me," Frank said. "I was just walking by and answered the phone."

Icicles of silence grew inside the receiver.

Frank reached in his pockets. Nobody had given him any change that night; he had nothing to give. — "I can't," he said like a beaten thing.

"Thank you," the operator said icily, hanging up on Frank.

In thirty-five seconds a police car had come to arrest Frank.

The case was tried in the East Bay, famed for its warm sunny days. Frank got a suspended sentence plus psychiatric probation.

The following Tuesday morning he reported for his first appointment with the City of Berkeley's Convict Mental Health Services. After filling out several forms, Frank sat in the waiting room, taking in the pink carpet, the black couches, yellowed with tears and farts, the scuffed white walls missing flakes of paint in all corners, the bulletin board, where cheery Arctic ballooning events were reported, the obligatory office plants in red adobe pots, the registration counter, secure behind the big heavy glass window, which was kept shut whenever possible so that the street people couldn't rush it — and speak of the devils; Frank looked around him and saw that he was surrounded by shady alcoholic characters: wife-beaters and mother-rapers and scoptophiliacs, riffraff, irrumators and sleazy-ass conjugators! Frank shuddered. At any moment they might turn on him and eat him. Like all poor persons, Frank had a justified fear of his own kind.

"Frank Fairless!" bawled the woman behind the counter.

Frank jumped up from behind the newspaper he had been covering himself with. After furnishing his social security number and penal sentence severity code, Frank was allowed to step up to the door at the right of the bulletin board. He would not have been surprised had there been no knob, but in fact he was able to open it without difficulty. The watchman was waiting behind it; he led Frank down a corridor and brought him to an unmarked door. — "Now, mind you don't say nothing or cry out," he whispered in Frank's ear. "The Doc's having a conference, but he'll be done and ready for you in a jiffy." And he went off and left Frank standing there in front of the door. — Frank put his ear to the keyhole and heard authoritative voices:

"I was talking about Parker to the production man, and his opinion was that Parker (a) knew what was going on, (b) was very stubborn, and (c) was supported by the people in Semiconductors."

"Well, I'll think about it," said Dr. Dodger, "but you'll have to go out the closet right now because it's time for action on the Fairless case; in fact my monitors show he's been listening at the keyhole for quite awhile now, so out you go, sir, and let's open the door right NOW!" and the door slammed outward, catching Frank in the side of the head, so that he fell and the cosmos wheeled and big black marbles rolled around behind his eyes. When he came to he was inside Dr. Dodger's office, lolling in an overstuffed armchair, while Dr. Dodger sat at his desk carving something with a penknife. When he saw that Frank had regained consciousness, Dr. Dodger picked up a clipboard and a pencil and began to take notes on

Frank's appearance. — "Your eyes look a bit glassy," he said severely, and Frank nodded and agreed. "Tell me," said Dr. Dodger, "are you malnourished? Is that the explanation for your behavior? Did you not like the food your parents gave you when you were a child?"

Frank considered. "No, I didn't like it," he said.

"So you used to leave vegetables on your plate?"

"I think so, yes."

"Ho, ho, ho," said Dr. Dodger. "That wouldn't do at *our* house; you either eat what's on the table or you don't eat at all."

"I see," Frank said.

"Well, Frank, the point is, from one agent to another, that we both work for Phil Blaker, and therefore you work for me; I am your superior, Frank. So when can you plant this bomb in Bug's office?" — And Dr. Dodger creaked up the rolltop of his desk and withdrew a package sealed with dusty electrical tape.

"What?" said Frank. "How?"

"A good question; a perceptive question," said Dr. Dodger; "for, yes, here you go; I had almost forgotten the detonator; you can't kill Bug without a detonator, now, can you?"

"No," said Frank.

"But it has to be done without a scandal, because we have the insect war going on right now, and there's public opinion to think on; the public is so precious, Frank, because without it I wouldn't be rich, so Mr. White doesn't want his name dragged into this and Phil Blaker and I are doing him a favor to pay off all the old scores." — Dr. Dodger leaned forward and stared into Frank's face piercingly. "It's got to look like an accident."

THE GLORY OF DR. DODGER

Did you never love a lamb and kill it afterwards when you were
hungry, or when it grew into a ram and butted you, or when it
drove away your other sheep, so that they fell into the hands of
thieves?

H. RIDER HAGGARD
Child of Storm

So it was that Frank received a brown-wrapped parcel by Martian
Mail. When he came home and found it just inside the door, he was
delighted; since Frank did not get mail more than perhaps three
times every two years; thus when he did he indulged in the luxurious
self-deceit that someone had sent him cookies, guns, picture-books
and a proposal of marriage. — Beneath the wrapping paper was ten
thousand dollars in woebegone fivers and singles, for Phil Blaker's
organization knew that the money had to appear laboriously
canvassed in coastal rains. Frank was instructed to add five hundred
dollars per day to his totals, so that soon the revolutionaries,
perceiving him to be a worthwhile individual, would be anxious to
discuss Kuzbuite issues with him on a personal basis. — Frank
realized immediately, however, that his new-found versatility in
getting blood from stones would be a source of suspicion to his
associates, especially to Lester, who would whoop and slap Frank
on the shoulder the first time and make Frank buy everybody a beer,
but as the nights of dubious plenty wore on Lester would want to see
Frank's new-found talent in action, figuring not unreasonably that if
Frank could make five hundred per evening then Lester could
probably make two grand. Frank therefore disregarded the letter
though not the spirit of the reactionaries' orders, and simply took
the entire sum up to the Kuzbu Union's regional office in Twin
Peaks. He attached a note explaining that the donor had asked him

to keep his name confidential, and that he might consider giving ten times that amount toward Bug's election campaign, provided that he continued to be satisfied with progress made, and provided that the gift could be made through Frank.

Frank was invited to meet Bug and Milly personally at an ice cream parlor.

As Milly wrote in her diary later, "These two hours with Bug were very beautiful and engendered confidence. Frank acted exceedingly loyal. I must say that the criticism leveled at him is for the most part unjustified." (But, thinking this over, Milly scowled and touched the tip of her pen to her tongue and underlined "for the most part.")

"Well," said Bug, who was a pale severe youngish man in a white button-down shirt. Bug had high cheekbones and bulging eyes. He and Milly sat side by side in the booth, sharing a giant milkshake by sucking simultaneously through their mouthparts and identical straws. Milly pursed her lips around the straw in what Frank perceived as a very committed manner. Frank could see colorful fibres of fruit embedded in the ice cream rise slowly but continually inside Milly's straw; Milly liked to drink milkshakes until the coldness gave her a headache. Meanwhile Frank sat opposite Bug and Milly at the booth, with Dr. Dodger's bomb and detonator wrapped in a shirt inside Frank's City Lights bookbag.

"Hi," Frank said softly.

"I believe this is the first time we've had a chance to meet you," said Bug with his usual droll politeness.

"Yes," said Frank.

Frank was excited to meet Milly, whom he had glimpsed once before, sitting by the window of a passing streetcar combing her red hair; at that moment the same sort of feeling came on him as when he looked at the posters of famous actresses. Another time he thought he saw her pacing up and down the concourse of a shopping mall as if she couldn't decide whether to go to Ward's or to Mervyn's; and as she walked from fountain to splashing fountain she fingered something gun-shaped on her hip, but when Frank came closer he saw that it was someone else. Now that he was sitting across from her, maybe he could make her love him. He looked at her, allowing his pupils to expand, and at this annoying display Milly scowled and stirred the big milkshake furiously.

"So how long have you been with us, Frank?" Bug said, and Milly cocked her head and watched Frank intently.

"Nine months," said Frank.

"And you subscribe to the principles of the movement?"

"Yes," said Frank. "I do."

"Do you like spiders?" said Milly bluntly. (I should interject here that it was still a closely-guarded secret at this time that the revolutionaries were in an alliance with the insect kingdom. Mr. White and Dr. Dodger knew it, of course, being able to put two and two together now that Wayne had found Bug's message via the green weevil. But they were keeping quiet about what they knew; they were still waiting for other factors to come out of the woodwork.)

"Spiders?" said Frank uncertainly. "Well, of course we're at war with the spiders."

"Of course," said Milly impatiently.

"I think they're all right, though," said Frank, seeing that his superiors were waiting for him to continue.

"That's good," Bug said. "That's very very good."

They bought Frank a small banana milkshake.

"Now, Frank, have you ever heard the name Parker Fellows?" Bug asked, stirring Milly's side of the big milkshake dreamily.

Frank recalled what he had overheard Dr. Dodger say. — "Yes," he said.

"We've heard rumors that Parker is designing a Great Enlarger to neutralize us and our work. You wouldn't want that to happen, would you, Frank?"

"No," Frank said.

"Well, Frank," said Bug, "in about a month we'll have something that we want you to deliver to Parker by way of Dr. Dodger. It will be something furry and poisonous and green, if you understand my meaning."

"I think so," said Frank cautiously. Frank never liked to commit himself.

Milly frowned at Frank. "So will you be our agent or won't you?"

Frank thought. Each time he became someone else's spy it got easier. The ideological virgin usually finds his first time an excruciating experience, just as an amateur hiker, used to the straight-and-narrow freeway of nine-to-five reliability, looks askance at the boulder-strewn path of mercenary betrayal, winding on up into the clouds and down into terrible moraines. But after the first time, the pain and intimacy and guilt becomes a habit subject to checklisted procedures; and to the professional, the politically promiscuous soul, all that matters is the craft itself, the right skitter and stab and swing of the hips, so that in the end you can laugh at the inevitability of your own violent death. Frank was now almost at that stage.

"All right," Frank said. He slipped his left hand into his bookbag, located the main switch of the bomb by touch, and clicked it off silently. Frank would change his ideology for you anytime.

SILVER AGAIN

~~~~~~

> Every silver lining has a cloud.
>
> American proverb

At one time airplanes were much nicer. The service was old-fashioned. – You would just push the call button once, and then here would come a beautiful stewardess (in those days stewardesses were fired when they hit thirty, so that we patrons would remain perpetually satisfied), mincing down the low-gravity strip between seats in her high heels and wearing a uniform as clean and shiny as a refrigerator door. It was like Passepartout presenting Phineas Fogg with crushed snow to cool his wine, snatched from a nearby peak as the balloon ascended; and his shaving water was always at the proper temperature. We expected service then, and we paid for it well, with our tips and winks and elbows in our neighbor's side. Another complimentary beer! A large orange juice, please, and take out the goddamn ice cubes! – Those were the days, all right; and there was no such thing as second class. They only offered classical music on the headsets, Deutsche Grammophon; and as we passed over a national monument or entered an interesting cloud formation the captain would provide a lecture, following which a brass band played. There were regular picture windows, too; and at any time you could take off your seat belt, light up a Cuban cigar and proceed to the observation lounges on the wings. For a nickel the personnel would shine your shoes. I, Big George, can recall a marvelous dance which we had once on a run through the ionosphere. The lady I met there became my paramour for the subsequent hours of the flight; and let me tell you, when I said hop to it, she made like a rabbit. We danced for the final ten minutes of circling above Rangoon until the runway was cleared; and the sheen of lightning against the fuselage, the sound of waves far below us as she swooned in my arms, are eidetic treats which I shall always credit to the airline.

But now the businessmen and plantation owners have given way to the lower-middle class, thanks to deregulation and the resulting cheap fares. Where I once sat picking my teeth and stretching my legs, we find ten sweaty, stinky boys with tape players, teeth clenched to the music, eyes screwed shut, heads going up and down; yeah-yeah-yeah suck-my-toes kind of stuff, if you get my drift. The stewardesses have long given way to warders and bouncers, much as if a field of daisies had been supplanted by Irish potatoes; and when you open your rickety tray to receive some institutional slop of a meal, the seat in front of you is jerked, and the guy to whom it belongs turns around slowly and takes off his mirror sunglasses and looks into your face with his moist blue light-sensitive eyes for a long frightening moment and says quietly, "Don't do that again," and you don't dare to touch the meal. Worse yet, for some of the rockbottom fares the stewards just set up a buffet table in front of the lavatories: old cold cuts, Eagle brand peanut snacks, and the like; and they yell, "Come and get it!" and then you really have to be quick or lucky or just coming out of the lav in a moment of well-timed reverie, or there will be nothing I tell you NOTHING left. The planes become steadily more stripped down and empty inside, too; it's the same old song. Things are just no good.

It was on one of these *transports de produits d'origine animale* that Dr. Dodger was forced to travel one Sunday afternoon. He was in some concern about his luggage, for he knew well the unreliable belts and jolting conveyors of the baggage claim area. He had in fact a very secret and interesting item in his suitcase — something which, alas, the security regulations would not let him carry on board. Anticipating that by now Frank would have done away with Bug, whom Dr. Dodger hated and distrusted by repute, Dr. Dodger figured that the time was ripe to settle the silver issue before Mr. White, turning from the threat of Bug and his allies to the more mundane menace posed by the jaguars of business, settled Dr. Dodger. Phil Blaker had been unwilling to loan Dr. Dodger the silver concessions to beguile away Mr. White's wrath; being the richest man in the solar system, he was also by definition the smartest, so he was certainly sharp enough to know that Dr. Dodger would save himself somehow. Indeed, Dr. Dodger had invented the perfect new toy, which dialectically synthesized two apparently irreconcilable concepts: namely, archeology and alchemy. As long as Dr. Dodger could recall, cranks had been trying to extract gold from sea-water and cranks had been trying to disinter lost cultures. What Dr. Dodger had constructed, then, was a device which looked something like a mine-sweeper or maybe a vacuum cleaner. You walked over graveyards at night, wearing the thing strapped to your back and scraping the hose along the ground; and it sucked all the silver fillings right out of the corpses' skulls and up through the earth and into the hose and then as you trudged along glumly beneath the cemetery moon you'd hear a *twoing!* as a piece of metal landed in the vacuum cleaner bag. – Mr. White would be bound to go for it.

So on Dr. Dodger flew, not knowing that Bug still lived, that Bug was even gaining power and ascendancy among the little earwigs and dragonflies; so that all the R. & D. on that silver reclamation device had been for nothing. In fact Frank had purposefully fostered Dr. Dodger's false impression concerning Bug; for as we have seen, Frank had gone over to the revolutionary side, following further meetings with Bug and Milly, in which his taffy-like acquiescence was stretched their way. – Dr. Dodger's invention did not even work, though that of itself might not have surprised Dr. Dodger too much; anyhow he could have fixed it under the guise of tuning up the insides at the beginning of a demo so that nobody would ever know that it had not performed as claimed when taken from the box; and Dr. Dodger would have covered the delay with his patter which fooled even Mr. White sometimes; but the reason that the graveyard sweeper did not work was not because Dr. Dodger had forgotten or mis-machined something; rather, Frank, as instructed, had replaced the power unit with a hollow shell of spider-plastic, inside of which lay curled the fruit which Bug had finally harvested so as to hurt Parker – the Caterpillar Heart.

NINETY-FOUR POSITIONS

~~~~~~

Why should one made in the real image of God, suffer his natur' to
be provoked by a mere effigy of reason?

<div align="right">

FENIMORE COOPER
The Prairie, V (1827)

</div>

Meanwhile Frank continued to canvass. "*Slowly,*" in Hitler's words,
"he made himself the spokesman of a new era." He held ninety-four
positions on every issue. He was in Pleasant Hill one hot August
afternoon working a section of streets with girls' names: Doris Ave.,
Erica Place, Margaret Court, then up the left side of Nina to
Amanda where there were some old members at 1372 and 1405. At
one house when he rang the bell a very old senile lady came to the
door and told him to come in. Now, that is always the kiss of death
to a good quarter of an hour or more; any efficient canvasser, such
as Lester or Max, would have said, "No, thank you, ma'am, I'd love
to talk to you but I've got to keep working to get the neighborhood
support to help you with your electricity bills, so put this sticker on
your meter and can you write me out a check for five? I wouldn't ask
you for more because I can tell you're living on a fixed income, but
it's precisely those senior citizens such as yourself we're trying to
help, so do what you can today, date it ahead if you want to and
we'll lock it up in our special postdate box, and just make it out
to Kuzbu Union for a National Turnaround," but Frank was
not unlike President Harding, who was told that if he were a girl
he would always be in a family way because he couldn't say no.
Yesterday Frank had done the Norse courts: Freya, Asgard, Loki,
Donner, Fafner and Fasolt over by the freeway. It had rained and
rained. Now today it was so hot and humid that Frank was happy
when the homeowners gave him water, Coke, milk, grape juice
and beer. It was his hope that the old woman would offer him

refreshment of any character; Max would've just asked if he could help himself to whatever was in the refrigerator, but Frank sat there dumbly on the couch while the old woman rocked and rocked, saying that her husband would be back any minute and then he would help Frank but she was not sure what he would help Frank with because truth to tell she had already forgotten that Frank was there, as if Frank had become transparent, like Wells' Invisible Man except that Frank was not out to rob people or hurt them, just to beg money from them; and beggars do not like to be invisible although double agents and bugs love it. Suddenly the old lady saw Frank again. Evidently he had just rematerialized from ectoplasm and ghost-sweat; everything was so humid; "MARTIN!" she screeched; "IT'S MARTIN COME OUT OF THE WELL!" and at this her husband came running out of the bathroom after all; he had not been dead twenty years, as Frank had suspected; no, he had just been reading the newspaper on the toilet seat; "GET OUT!" he roared at Frank; "GET OUT BEFORE I THROW YOU OUT!"; and Frank's mouth dropped and Frank said, "But she told me —" — "YOU KNOW PERFECTLY WELL WHAT SHE IS, YOU CARPETBAGGER, NOW GET OUT OF MY HOUSE!" and the elderly demon grabbed Frank's elbow even though he was already moving to the door and Frank looked into his host's face and saw the hatred that lit it up and moved faster to the door but at the door the homeowner kicked him down the steps anyway, "AND STAY OUT!" — A small crowd had gathered beneath the pleasant beeches of Nina Way. "Wow, mister!" said the paper boy. "He sure pushed you! He's mean, isn't he?" — "Yes," said Frank. — "Are you all right?" said a young professional man, the self-appointed doctor of the mass (and there always is one at every debacle). — "Oh, yes," said Frank. "I'm fine." He was only bruised and shaken. — "What did you say to him?" the paper boy whispered, awed. "I want to know so I won't ever say that to anybody my whole life!" — Frank thought. "Don't ever say hello," he said.

Later, still on Nina, he was taken into a party on the patio of the rich. It was almost dark. — "I'm from the Kuzbu Union for a National Turnaround," Frank began, looking about him quickly to see if he had repelled them yet, but they all nodded encouragingly and said, "Go on, son," so he said, "and we're worried about natural gas prices . . ." — "Natural gas!" cried a young rake. "You want to freeze farts!" — Everyone whooped. — "Listen, son," they said, "you need to talk to Roy." — "Oh," said Frank, a little uncertainly. "All right." — They led him back onto the lawn, which was illuminated with torches, as if for some Roman event. Colored lights glowed in the bottom of the swimming pool. In the back of the yard was a discreet tree-house. They took him up into it; Roy was eating his dinner with a beautiful Spanish-looking girl. — "Yes?" said Roy, prepared for some national emergency. — Frank nodded. "I'm with the Kuzbu Union for a National Turnaround," he began. — "What the *hell*?" said Roy. All Roy's friends laughed at the joke and ran off tipsily.

On Amanda he conversed with a middle-aged man who pretended not to understand a word of English. "*Je ne comprends pas,*" he told Frank, but his accent was terrible; it was obvious that it was just a trick of his to get rid of canvassers, so Frank switched to his own laborious but reliable French. "*Bonjour,*" he said, "*je m'appelle Frank, et j'ai besoin de parler au sujet de gaz naturel . . .*" — "*Ne comprends, non comprendre, ne panimayou, nicht verstehen, non capisco, noh pwaygum,*" said the man, and he went off into the living room chuckling at Frank's discomfiture. His wife came out to the front hall and explained to Frank, "Yes, my husband is French," but even she couldn't keep a straight face; and Frank heard the man roar in the living room, '*Vive la différence!*"

"Aw, *Frank,* why you so down?" says Lester.

"Well," said Frank. "I just don't feel so good sometimes."

"Frank, I'm sorry to see you so down; I really love you."

Boodeley-boodeley-boodeley-boo went the radio in the office late at night. Outside the rain was pouring down.

Frank beckoned Lester into the canvass director's office and shut the door. — "Lester, can you get me some smack?" — Lester looks him straight in the eye. "Frank, you don't want that stuff. I'll get you speed or coke, but I won't get you no smack; man, you don't *need* that stuff."

In short, Frank could not score a single crystal of happiness or teleological justification to his life. For fear of the blue globes Frank did not try to kill himself anymore, but he made one more attempt to escape his gelatinous career. The wires hummed constantly behind the walls of his little room. No matter how cold it was (the apartment had no heat), he always felt stifled when he lay down in there, and as drizzly fog blew in through his one high window, which gaped desperately at maximum aperture, Frank tried to inhale the mist, although he could not breathe too hard or he would hyperventilate. On the muggy night of Saturday, the twenty-ninth of September, he called Suicide Prevention for advice. The phone rang once and then again. Most likely they allowed two rings in case the would-be suicide decided at the last minute that he did not want to call Suicide Prevention after all; or then again maybe they were busy; or quite possibly it took them two rings to put a tracer on the line so that no matter what happened the police would know who had called Suicide Prevention, and would at this very moment be buttoning up their blue coats in preparation for contingent action − "Could I put you on hold for a second," a mild Suicide Prevention voice said, "because there's somebody on the other line . . ." − "Oh," said Frank. "Okay." − Time passed (quite a lot of it), while the phone made its late-night clicks, adding second by second to Frank's monthly zone charges. Perhaps they were verifying the trace on Frank's call; they would take him to a mental hospital filled with blue TVs where externality swam as in aquariums; or they would confiscate his weapons. Listening very hard, Frank could hear another conversation buzzing far away. Evidently they had set the receiver down on the desk beside the monogrammed Suicide Prevention blotter and the special Suicide Prevention amphetamines; and the blue globe inside the receiver, being interested, had wrinkled itself up into a fuzzy blue ear and concentrated hard so that Frank could hear the other cross-talk. Frank lay very still on the floor, watching the second hand of his watch go round and round. Distantly on the other line, he heard a gunshot. There was a silence, and then he heard the other phone being replaced unceremoniously in its cradle. The nice (if officious) young man who had first answered Frank now returned to him, picking up the receiver so that Frank had a dizzy sensation of being grasped and raised high by a giant's hand (for that was how the blue globe felt) − "Sorry to make you wait so long," said Mr. Suicide Prevention. − Frank began to tell him all about his problems. − "Yeah, well," Mr. Suicide Prevention said, "you sound like you're kind of unplugged from your feelings. I don't mean to interrupt, but can I put you on hold again for just a minute?" − "Sure," said Frank. "Yes." There was not much else to say. − Finally the fellow came back. Frank explained to him how hard and sad it was to be a double agent. − "Well, I don't want to get into a political discussion, Frank. Let's just talk about you and how you react to all this. How about if we just pretend that I'm your dentist and you're coming in and telling me all about how your teeth have been and you ask me whatever questions you have, because I want this to be your day, Frank, and if there's anything you don't know just call and schedule another appointment." − Somewhat at a loss, Frank recounted the episode of the blue globes. − "Well, that's an awful big thing," said Mr.

Suicide Prevention. "I wouldn't underestimate the effect it had on your life. It may be real hard to start new relationships, Frank, but remember that you don't have to feel bad about yourself; and I really think you should get into counseling." — "Could you recommend anyone?" said Frank. — "Well, the crisis center is appreciably cheaper, but you work during their best hours, so let me put you on hold again; this time I've got to get my, uh, Resource File." — At last the eager beaver got back on the line, and said, "Oh, Frank? Do you have a pencil? There's only one doctor in your area, and his name is Samuel William Dodger," and Frank's heart sank, and he said, "Isn't there anyone else?", and there was a long silence and Mr. Suicide Prevention said, "No, I'm sorry, Frank, but you've got to understand that there's no one else at all."

Then Frank realized that he had no choice but to take matters into his own hands at last. And once he had hung up, the blue globes, sensing the spiritual state which Frank had achieved, revealed themselves and their aims to him.

MILLY CALLS FOR WAR

~~~~~~

> The Enemy has been here in the Night of our naturall Ignorance,
> and sown the tares of Spiritual Errors . . . And so we come to erre,
> by giving heed to seducing Spirits, and the Daemonology of such as
> speak lies in Hypocrisie . . .
>
> HOBBES
> *Leviathan* (IV.XLIV)

As a result of these events, a meeting was held on 11 October which
was to change the flow of electrical history. At that time Bug and
Milly were both anxious for action, Bug perhaps the more so
because he had always kept a counter of injuries done him. The
years which he had spent in hiding, the necessity for assumed names,
and the excessive evenness of affect which stunted his life — all these
things he reckoned into his counter, and advanced it by many clicks,
as if it were one of those White Power & Light meters that one sees
on the side of a house to record electrical usage, the little wheel
spinning, spinning whenever you did anything inside your home,
and each full revolution of the little wheel advanced the pointer on
the middle wheel by one click, and each revolution of the middle
wheel turned the hand on the biggest wheel one click; and every time
the biggest wheel made a complete revolution you were in trouble
and would have to pay the reactionaries, just as the reactionaries
were going to have to pay Bug for what they had done to him; and
because Bug's little wheel of contention was turning with blurred
speed he kept sending his canvassers out to agitate against Mr.
White, which was why Frank got dropped off in places like Susuin
City every day, and Lester rolled down the window and leaned out
so that his yellow-shirted jelly-belly caught on the sill and trembled
there, and Lester rolled his good eye at Frank and yelled, "Suck
rocks, Dick-Breaf!" and Mike the field manager laughed and pulled
away, and Frank, standing forlornly on the curb, saw Lester

laughing and shaking his head at him, still halfway out the window, and all the rest of the canvass crew looked at him and called cheerily, "SUCK ROCKS, DICK-BREAF!" — to boost his morale, you see, and maybe if Frank was lucky he got one person mad at Mr. White for five minutes; but that only slightly decreased the speed with which Bug's little wheels of anger were spinning, and the big one kept turning inevitably. By this time no one, not even Milly, was exempt from Bug's reckoning. When he first began sleeping with her he allowed her to disturb his sleep no more than two times per night. Milly often awoke with some enthusiasm which she must at once enact, such as testing a new resistor, and she also got up between two and three to use the bathroom. Bug noted these disturbances and covertly switched off Milly's alarm clock to punish her. Then Milly was angered and confused and thrown off schedule in the morning (but she never connected it with Bug).

It is surprising that a person with these tendencies should be poor at math, and yet it was so. As a boy he had problems with this subject. In the classroom they had to keep perpetual silence. Their names were written in block capitals on the blackboard. Each day they were given a new test, and worked under the flickering of a dusty bulb while the teacher sat grading their tests of the day before, and the way that they bent over their desks suggested an intensity without expectation, for they were already learning how to feel the way they would for the rest of their lives. On the stand beneath the flag lay a black binder with two tests in it for every day of the year, the second set of tests being there in case any student finished the first one early by some accident; and the tests had been there for so many years that the teacher graded them by memory. As he finished marking each one, he rubbed his bald spot, wrote the score on an index card, dropped the test in the wastebasket and copied the score from the index card onto the blackboard, right of the appropriate student's name. Passing scores were written in white chalk, failing scores in blue.

Bug had a row of blue numbers following his name.

One day he got up, left his blank test and his pencil on his desk, and erased his name from the board with his hand.

The others watched him, pencils raised.

The teacher said nothing. But from then on Bug was not allowed to put his name on his paper. Soon he had been forgotten. On his report card he received two brackets with nothing in between.

During the years of exile he paid a visit to the Afghan border. Up to the very edge of it was a sandy plain pounded into a pavement by sunlight and refugees. Afghanistan itself, however, consisted of golden sand dunes a thousand feet high. Sand sifted down to the border continually, but very little actually spilled over. There was nothing up there but blue sky and sand. − Bug reached across the border and ran his fingers through the sand that was dribbling down. He had a sudden feeling that treasure was near. Awkwardly he scratched a hole in the sheer wall of sand. Just beneath the surface he saw ovals of off-yellow: buried coins. There were bigger ovals of almost the same color. He scraped the sand away with his fingernails until he could see what they were: skulls, of course.

But he had never tried to count them.

Now at last, thanks to Frank, it was possible for Bug to quantify himself, alone with Milly in the Kuzbu Union office, sitting in his rubber-tipped chair beside Milly at her rolltop desk, which was full of tax forms and insect poisons and guns with black rubber grips, while outside the wind blew newspapers down the sidewalk and the canvassing crew took the bus home or cadged rides off each other (sometimes Lester would give you a ride if you slipped him a dollar for gas), and the office was quiet, Frank's clipboard peeking shyly out from underneath the others; and Bug prepared a bank deposit based on the week's totals, while Milly counted the cash.

"Frank says in his latest report that the world is run by blue globes," said Bug.

"What do you mean?" said Milly.

"He claims that electricity exists in blue globes which are polarized in valence cartels. Supposedly they have hypnotic susceptance varying directly with the dielectric constant of the conductor."

"You're continually going on about the way that wealth contains being-for-itself," Milly said. "I know all about that. So naturally the superstructure has accumulated its own soul. What else is new?"

"Absolute capacitance," sighed Bug. "They probably control the expansion of electrical lines into every area."

"Hmmm," said Milly thoughtfully, sucking her cheeks.

An ant came and crawled around the circumference of Bug's belt, reading what had transpired from the configuration of the sweaty leather. Bug stood in silence while this operation was performed, listening in his earplugs for coordinating messages to be transmitted by the ant, but at the moment there were none; their intermediary had only come to take down the minutes.

"We'll get the Society of Daniel first," Milly said. "There must be blue globes there; the roaches can check."

"Exactly," Bug said.

"But how are we going to destroy the whole network?"

"That's a question that even the Democrats have asked," said Bug. "We'll have to conduct experiments."

Milly nodded. "On the prisoners, I suppose."

"And we'll need to lay in supplies for Arctic weather."

"Fine," Milly said. "I'll sharpen some ice-picks."

"Now, let's define the objectives more precisely," said Bug, feeling a thin pulse of pleasure, for it was precisely at defining objectives that he excelled. He snapped a sheet of blue-ruled paper onto Frank's clipboard and wrote out the following:

DESTRUCTION OF REACTIONARY POWER. Primary targets: Personnel (Mr. White, Dr. Dodger, Parker, Wayne) and installations (Society of Daniel, plus others to be determined). Should these prove impossible, consolation targets will be attempted. With non-conducting weapons and the assistance of insect allies, strikes will be made into the heart of reactionary territory until the blue globes have been crippled or destroyed. Thorough circuit diagrams will then be prepared to facilitate the extermination of any remnant. The resulting social vacuum will be filled by us.

Silently he handed the page to Milly. She read it and grinned. "That sounds grand," she said.

"Thank you," said Bug.

Milly fiddled with a lock of her long red hair. "You'll probably say I'm being silly, Bug," she said, "but if we're going into action together I'd like us to be blood brothers."

Bug was astonished. "I never thought that *you* of all people would lapse into sensuous irritability."

"I don't know if it's that at all," she said, "but it's what I want. And, besides, it might coordinate us."

"That's true," Bug admitted. There was no way to get out of it.

"The knife's in the bottom right-hand drawer," she said.

It was a double-bladed survival knife with black anodized finish. He had bought it for her on their first anniversary. She rolled up Bug's right sleeve for him, caressing his skin the way she did at night when she was in bed with him and he lay curled on his stomach, dreaming about mosquitoes; she knew that pale, soft skin of his like a butcher knows a cut of meat. — Raising the knife high above his wrist, she selected an area two-thirds of the way up from the elbow, stabbed deep, immediately penetrating the defenses of his circulatory system, and drew the knife down lengthwise to extend the cut, the way the ancient Romans did when they committed suicide in their baths. — The black blood spattered over Milly's hands and face; in her vanguardist way she had severed one of his arteries. He was turning pale; his spectacle-lenses dimmed; she could see the life going out of him like a fish, but perseveringly she pulled the blade out of him and thrust it back perpendicular to the first slash, then twisted it in his flesh, opening the wound still wider so that it gaped at her reproachfully. The blood kept welling up and getting over things so that she couldn't see what she was doing, which annoyed her; but she knew that theoretical clarity was unattainable in times of action. Bug still stood erect, like a heroic British captain of a battleship who had been hit by a French musket-ball (it is said that when Quisling was shot by the firing squad he had not fallen because he had spaced his legs just right to impress the Jews to the last), but he was white-faced now; his earplugs were tingling idiotically; warning systems are counter-productive when you cannot help the problem but must still put up with pain dinging and dinging and dinging in your ears. For his part he tried to concentrate on overcoming electrical parameters and blue globe resistance files. — Finally Milly was satisfied. Everything was spattered with his blood; her hair was speckled and matted with gooey black coagulating clots of it. — "Your turn," she said. — He had screwed his eyes shut by now, like a declining Bonapartist. He opened his eyes and took the knife from her weakly. His hands were slippery with his own blood, and he fumbled at her sleeves feebly, dropping the knife, so she rolled up her right sleeve to help him, bent down, picked up the knife and handed it to him. Smiling, she closed her eyes. Her wrist was milky and radiated many delicate blue veins. As he bent over it his blood ran on it with the speed of a hundred nosebleeds. He was swaying on his feet. Clutching her wrist, he rested the knife on it crosswise, about two inches below the base of her thumb. Then he sawed slowly in with his geometrically declining strength until he hit bone. The sweat started out on her forehead. Looking up into her long blinking lashes, he felt a tenderness such as only insects know. — They were both dizzy for loss of blood. Clinging to each other with their left arms, like maimed spiders, they fell to the rug. — He still had enough presence of mind to place the quivering lips of his wound against the wound he had given her, so that they kissed. At once he felt their blood mingle, and he realized that until now he had never fully understood her. Nutrients passed through his ventricles. Her blood had a delicious golden feeling in his veins, with its pure virtue and determinate yearning selfhood. For her part she felt his blood as greenish light which traveled through her round and round bearing divisions and distinctions of the utmost subtlety. This was Kuzbuism. Now forever they were one.

"Thesis, antithesis, synthesis," she murmured faintly.

He did not want to take his wound away from hers, but if he did not they would both die, so he let go of her, and bound up her arm and then his with swatches of caterpillar-silk. The bleeding stopped at once; he could hear the clotting like the noise of ripping sheets; then the pain obediently dulled and dwindled, and waxy scar tissue formed. It was just in time. As it was, they would each have to drink milk in great quantities for the next few days.

IN THE ARCTIC

~~~~~~

Under the Pole is the place of greatest dignitie.

JOHN DAVIS
The Worldes Hydrographical Description (1595)

I knew it was my last game upon the great Arctic chessboard. It
was win this time or be forever defeated.

PEARY
*The North Pole: Its Discovery in 1909 Under the Auspices
of the Peary Arctic Club* (1910)

Before they could execute their plans, Bug and Milly agreed, their
soldiers had to be trained. Naturally this object could not be
achieved at one stroke. — Milly therefore took charge of Frank,
wrinkling her nose at his disreputable political odor but perfectly
aware that *someone* had to do it, at least as long as Frank
maintained a satisfactory position in Bug's esteem roster, which was
kept locked in the grey steel safe of Bug's mind; so Milly, being the
most realistic of all the revolutionaries, forced herself to speak to
Frank and to teach him tactics, for she refused to tolerate only what
she had the power to reject. — Frank for his part was afraid of Milly
because he was aware that she did not like him, although on his
paltry level the dislikes of superiors were an impersonal fact of life,
like an attack of measles, and so for that matter was fear, which he
had often experienced coming back into Oakland from canvassing
late at night, when the night people jumped suddenly out of weedy
lots and yelled, "I'm gonna get you, honky; I'm gonna BEAT YOUR
ASS!" and chased him for several blocks, at which it was a pleasure
to see just how fast Frank could skip; in short, Frank, like Milly,
functioned at least as well as might have been expected in the
training relationship. — When he was competent at making false

hotel reservations, placing nails in car battery cells, and starting small fires, she taught him intermediate electrical sabotage skills, such as taping a penny to the base of a light bulb to short out the fuse, or filling the bulb with gasoline so that it would explode when the light was switched on. The next exercise involved pulling down power wires with hooked cables, which they practiced late at night in Vacaville, wearing black rubber suits so as not to be seen in any headlights; when the moon came out they ducked into arid gulleys and sprinkled sand over each other for camouflage, but all the time Milly felt her gun in her armpit reminding her to let Frank get away with nothing; then when it was dark again, the moon disappearing glutinously like an egg being scrambled in ink, they sprinted on rubber-soled tiptoe back to the power wires at the edge of the freeway, and Frank did his job while Milly watched sharply; Frank feared her glance because she saw *everything* and still was not satisfied, frowning with all her might in case he was concealing something or doing something stupid; but he learned to accommodate himself to her in every respect, throwing the gaff-hook up to the best of his ability and pulling on it, ready to jump clear, so that finally the wires came down in a waterfall of sparks, fusing the asphalt into brown puke-textured glass where they hit, and Frank and Milly loped away then before the moonlight oozed back, Milly whispering, "Move it, asshole!", and the police thought it was teenaged vandals. Within a month Frank was competent at these procedures, though less, perhaps, out of innate talent than the fact that Milly punished the slightest laxity on his part with military rigor, not only for pedagogical reasons but also because on a personal level he disgusted her. Already he showed a pronounced syndicalist trend. – "You're as stupid as a lost ant," she told him. "If you want to improve you'll have to read the most important works of Bug." – "Oh," said Frank, abashed. "Okay." – Milly had already determined it would be necessary for Frank to destroy at least five million incandescent lamps. She had no confidence that he could account for even ten thousand.

Bug for his part drilled Susan in small arms nomenclature and safety. Every morning he drew parts diagrams on a blackboard in the office, peering at her through his spectacles to make sure that she followed what he said, and then called on her to name each mechanism that he pointed to with his ruler. These sessions were not easy for Susan, who had never considered herself a genius the way that Bug was, but she could tell that it was important to Bug that she do her best, so she stayed up late memorizing the part numbers for the major makes of firearm, until it was as easy as an arithmetic table for her to name every moving piece between the link pin and the magazine catch in the blueprint for the Charter Arms Bulldog; then Bug knew that she was ready to continue. The next step was to field-strip actual guns, which Bug had plenty of, having bought them under various aliases for years; Milly herself had stolen a dozen more to add to the hoard, which was kept inside a boarded-up fireplace in the office – a safe hideaway because in San Francisco people are usually too lazy to bother with fires. – Bug was not satisfied until Susan could be given any one of the revolutionary pistols or revolvers, unload it, empty the magazine, disassemble it for cleaning, snap it back together and reload it, all in a pitch-dark closet in the space of ninety seconds. This stage of the training Susan enjoyed, because there was something thrillingly objective about the slam of a full clip into the grip; that had happened because Susan made it happen; so in the closet as she clicked the gun into combat readiness (while Bug outside leaned against the door with a stop-watch), she began to imagine how nice it would be to fire it and know that a heavy definite bullet had been sent forth BY HER to take revenge against the people who had cheated her; and each shot would also be a concrete proof to Bug that she could do what he needed her to do; and when Susan entertained these fancies she felt good and worked efficiently. So Bug graduated her to the next phase. Unlocking the middle drawer of Milly's desk, he withdrew a box of gunsmith's tools. – "Milly wants us to customize her latest catch," he said. "I'll do this one, and you can do the next. I was meaning to pick up a Ruger stainless anyhow." – "Yes, Bug," said Susan with downcast eyes. He handed her an Israeli export, the .357 Desert Eagle. – "Where's the interruptor on this gun?" he asked severely. – "Right here, Bug," said Susan, "right here above the sear." – "Very good," said Bug. "Pay close attention. This is how the interruptor is neutralized." He went to work with a file, a screwdriver, an oiled pick, and a magnifying glass. – "Now this gun is an illegal machine pistol," he said. – "Yes, Bug," cried Susan, "and it's all for the good of our cause!" – "Exactly," said Bug. "I believe you're ready for some target practice."

"An excellent method for becoming familiar with the pointing qualities of your rifle," says the U.S. Army Markmanship Training Unit's *Counter Sniper Guide*, "is to stand inside a building, aiming and dry firing at the hub caps of passing cars." Unfortunately, Bug and Susan did not have this option. Nor did they have rifles. So they went to the range, which was in Pacifica, where white foam and blue

ocean added grace to white apartments. It was a weedy sort of range in the woods, much like the one back in Indiana where Wayne went.

Bug went shooting with Susan for the first time on a Saturday, observing the two vertical lines in her forehead just over her nose when she frowned, her chestnut hair tied back with a rubber-band, her thin, round-lensed spectacles not quite as good as shooting glasses. She didn't know how to shoot at first; she was afraid of the gun. Her arms trembled. Bug showed her how to bow out her left arm at a forty-five degree angle to support and lock the shooting arm, and he moved her hot fingers to correct her grip. The first few times she fired, the gun jerked in her hands. After two magazines she began to understand the gun, and when she finally got her first hit on the paper target she was very happy and Bug for his own reasons was happy to help her.

On the bus ride back, though, Susan was very quiet and the same two vertical lines formed in her forehead, cutting into her skin deeper and deeper just above the bridge of her nose. This was, Bug knew, an infallible phrenological sign of personal worries. But when Bug said, "What are you thinking about?" she only laughed and said, "Nothing; I was just looking out the window." In fact innocent Susan was troubled by the things Bug was saying about the immediate self-conscious independence of our cause, because she had never killed anyone and would have never killed anyone had she not met Bug; had she met instead someone who was genuinely willing to love Susan and be interested in Susan, like Frank was, although by the time Frank became acquainted with Susan it was too late for him to be anything but a double agent. Susan had finally thrown Wayne over, not that Wayne even knew it because he didn't think about Suzy much when he was not in her neighborhood and he had not been in the neighborhood recently, being on some long secret tour of duty in the Merchant Marines without any shore leave (actually he was performing his labors, as we know), so now Susan had no one, and here was Bug who had followed her to the elementary school that evening and asked questions about education that showed he was one of those concerned citizens who really cared; actually Milly had gotten a list of people through whom it might be possible to commandeer an airplane when the time came to flee to the Arctic, and because Susan knew Catherine she was an option. That was the real reason that Bug had made contact. — Susan, not knowing his motives, surrendered herself to his ideology and decided to kill people.

*   *   *

At the close of the training period, Bug and Milly met privately to discuss the readiness of their forces for guerrilla activity. Milly was of the opinion that Frank ought to be taken to Gilroy or Brisbane and shot, because not the slightest hesitation could be tolerated. Bug, however, did not think that this was the correct approach. In support of his views, he quoted a passage from his writings, every sentence of which could be accepted with confidence, so Milly was forced to relent. — "But I want permission to shoot him if he double-crosses us or tries to run away," Milly said firmly. — "All right," said Bug. " 'In war the coward's legitimate fate is the bullet.' " — "Right," said Milly. "Lenin, May 27th, 1919, in his 'Greetings to the Hungarian Workers.' " — So Milly and Bug shored up each other's cleverness.

The discussion now turned to Susan.

"She thinks you love her," said Milly scornfully.

"Susan will evidently die with that illusion," Bug said. "That is her affair."

"Yes, but she's jealous," Milly said. "She's unwilling to make the slightest political concession to me."

"Do you want to shoot her, too?" said Bug with a smile.

"No, I suppose not," said Milly. "She's just a stupid yapping bitch."

"She can shoot through pillows," said Bug.

"She whines," said Milly.

"She makes passable mercury fulminate," said Bug.

"Oh, she does?" said Milly. "All right. Let's keep her."

"Yes," Bug continued dreamily, "when she puts her mind to it, the primer looks so nice and tidy beside the other yellow crystals . . ." — but Milly was no longer listening.

They selected an Uzi pistol for Susan, because Milly, who was in charge of weapons and ordnance, was conservative in many ways, adhering to the old ideological line that nine-millimeter bullets are the minimum caliber to produce satisfactory disablement at great range. Frank was directed to carry a Daisy air gun until Milly had fewer doubts about his reliability.

The schedule now demanded that they follow up the relocation plans which Bug had first established a decade ago when he had hitched through the Yukon. They had to fall back to the Arctic by the end of the month; even Milly, who debated many points with Bug and who had never been to the Arctic, did not disagree with that. In the Arctic mountains there was snow and ice year-round. Here you could hunt for giant fossilized frozen dragonflies that dated from the days when the polar islands had been full of raging tropical bugs that scuttled colorfully and flew and bit. In the blue shadows of the ice-crags major philosophies could be worked out (that was what appealed to Bug). And there were the prismatic Caves of Ice, where you could hide and go in deeper and deeper lost in a hall of icy mirrors so that no reactionary could ever find you.

Milly purchased tools and weatherizing lubricants, down parkas, bulk foods, a miniature stove and creepy-crawly cooking oils. Bug gave every item a thorough examination. – Susan had on a most attractive winter parka, but Milly just smiled humorlessly and told her to throw it out because it was too conspicuous. – "I won't!" cried Susan. – "Oh, yes, you will," said Milly, aching to plunge her Gerber Command II survival knife into Susan's heart (she was the only one to carry a Gerber, just as in rural Asia it is only the officials who are allowed to wear spectacles), and Bug looked down at his feet and said very mildly, "Susan, I think you should do as Milly suggests." Sobbing, Susan took off her coat and Milly shoved rocks into the sleeves and dropped it into a stream. Bug patted her shoulder while Milly grinned and whispered something into Bug's ear. – Then, under Milly's direction, they began a conditioning program, sleeping on the snow in the woods farther and farther north each night, for revolution would be grim, demanding work, though not, perhaps, as difficult as marriage. – Bug, whose specialty was retreat, made them all practice dispersing into icy splinter groups, hiding in the branches of snowy trees with their firearms off safe and their faces hidden by masks of frozen bark. – Milly affected a careless manner at these exercises, for she never intended to retreat, and sometimes considered Bug a dull Menshevik. – In the crotch of her tree, Susan imagined that Bug was beside her, addressing all the squirrels: "Bring your guns, colleagues. Kuzbuism is only an idea. You must make it happen with your bushy little tails . . ." and Susan smiled at how sweet Bug was; while Frank crouched shivering in his tree, wishing that the long afternoon exercise would end so that he could go home and have some hot gin; and Bug himself hid behind a screen of evergreen boughs, quite content with the situation. – At midnight Milly led them through the forest until they found a section of private fence that seemed unguarded. This was Frank and Susan's field test. Snip, snip, snip, snip went their wire-cutters, Susan on the right and Frank on the left, with snow from the hemlock trees overhead sifting down on their caps and shoulders, and the strands parted click by click, Susan tugging harder than Frank, until they had made a gap big enough for one person to enter. — "I could have done that in a quarter less time," said Milly sourly. "Susan, hold the wire taut next time, and you, Frank, use enough elbow grease to break each strand in one cut." — "Oh," said Frank; and Susan said nothing.

As Bug and Milly waited in the chilly moonlight, eyeing their stopwatches, Frank crept through the tear in the fence, enjoying the small stern crunches of his boots in the snow, and approached the house, which had all its lights on; and suddenly a mastiff bounded at Frank from behind the garage, baying, and Frank vaulted softly up onto the back porch and located the woodpile under its tarpaulin of snow and hit the hound between the ears with an oaken log as it came scuttering up the porch steps, and the hound went limp, its front paws sliding slowly off the top step; and Frank, who would always be cowardly, knelt down and suffocated the unconscious dog in a fold of his coat, for he was afraid that the dog might wake up before he had finished; then he picked the lock on the back door and came into a hallway, shutting the door softly behind him so that the occupants of the house would not be alerted by the draft; then he began his prowl through the golden carpet, pretending that he was a lion in safari grass, and came to a bathroom, with unoccupied bedrooms on either side; and he stood there cockily for a moment, enjoying his illegal entry as his glasses fogged up with the warmth of the house; he could hear people laughing loudly downstairs, and the record player was going; that was why they had not heard their dog's warning; and Frank went into the bathroom and stole a bar of soap with long white hairs on it from the rim of the bathtub to prove to Milly and Bug that he had been here, and then he tiptoed back down the hall, leaving wet bootprints on the carpet, and opened the door quickly so it wouldn't creak, and went back out into the night, locking the door behind him; and he brought the cake of soap back to Milly waiting in the woods. It had become colder. Milly stood abstractedly in the fan-shaped shadows of branches, while overhead the points of trees reached into a lavender sky pimpled with dull pinkish-grey stars. — Milly looked up. The soap was still steaming, so Milly was satisfied; and Bug said, "Excellent work, Frank," and now it was Susan's turn. She had never done anything like this before, since Bug had trained her, not Milly, so her heart was pounding as she ducked through the opening that she and Frank had cut through the fence and ran silently in Frank's footprints, so that in the morning the homeowners would think that only one person had broken in; and she danced over the lifeless dog, surprised and pleased that Frank had not botched that action, that there was no red trampled snow to give evidence of a noisy struggle; and she, too, picked the lock, and saw Frank's footprints on the carpet going into the bathroom, and decided that she would be bolder than Frank, so she charged downstairs where the party was; there were half a dozen people sitting by the fire and listening to classical music and eating chip-and-dip and civilly discussing the democracy of electricity ("I pity the clever ones," Lenin said of the starving survivors of the aristocracy), and they looked up at Susan astounded, and Susan yelled, "WE STAND FOR BUG!" and ran up to the fireplace, seizing the whisk broom used to sweep stray coals back from the hearth, and she thrust the rushes of the broom into the fire to make a torch, so that they all cowered back, saying nothing; and Susan ran back into the woods, holding the torch high, as the householders came shouting behind her, and Susan was laughing and shouting, "BUG FOREVER!" and all the revolutionaries ran off through the trees, and nobody ever caught them.

On the fifth of February, these dress rehearsals completed, Milly and Frank went on their first real sortie and expropriated ten thousand cartridges. On the seventeenth, Susan, acting upon Bug's instructions, applied for a year's leave of absence from teaching, citing health reasons. The principal was happy to see her go. On the nineteenth, Bug and Milly called a secret conference in the Kuzbu Union office, which was about to be closed, and announced that henceforth operations were to be conducted on a war footing. No deviation from instructions would be tolerated. The first time Milly was forced to apply the new policy came when the revolutionaries went tenting in the Arctic in late spring to harden themselves. It was a grey night-storm. The dwarf willows along the bluff lashed to and fro in the wind like whips, and the mosquitoes were driven to hide in secret soggy places, too dispirited even to whine as the rain drummed down and down and down. Bug and his forces were sleeping near a pebbly river bank. The tent fly was soaked. — "Don't anyone touch the tent or water will come through from capillary action," Milly had warned as they lay on their backs listening to the rain and watching the big raindrops roll down the fly. Susan was wedged in between Frank, who was against the wall, and Milly, who lay beside Bug, and in the night Frank moaned in his sleep and thrashed against the wall so that his sleeping bag got wet, as Milly had said, from capillary action, and he shivered in his sleep and rolled toward

Susan, nestling up against her warmth because he knew even in his sleep that she was there, and Susan's breath smelled like Lifesavers, a sweet simple smell that Frank inhaled in his sleep, making him dream of robbing a candy store with his shiny Browning; and Susan woke with Frank's head up against her chest, Frank breathing in little sawing gasps, and his hands were half raised, as if to protect his face from being hit, and Susan felt a little sorry for him but her sleeping bag was getting wet from his dripping hair, so she looked at Milly to see if Milly had left her any room for her to roll over away from Frank, but Milly lay very straight in her sleeping bag almost touching Susan (it was a small tent), and Milly's breathing came very deep and slow; Susan could smell her healthy animal breath; and Bug lay beside her with his head pillowed on his holster, not seeming to breathe at all, so there was no possibility of Susan's rolling away from Frank; as gently as she could she lifted his head and rolled him in his sleeping bag back up against the sopping wall. Her hands were cold and wet from touching him; she wiped them on the outside of her sleeping bag and brought them back inside where it was warm and zipped the sleeping bag up to her face from inside. The rain kept coming down against the tent fly, striking so loudly that Susan's ears rang, and she could hear the roar of the rising river, even the occasional grinding of pebbles loosened by the current and knocked against the river bed, and she listened to the storm noises until finally she went to sleep. — Bug woke an hour later when water began to flow up against the tent from the overflowing river. The rain was coming down harder than ever. He touched Milly's shoulder, and she woke up instantly. — "What?" she grunted. — "Down by your feet," he said. — Milly, sitting up as far as she could without touching the roof of the tent, peered down by the zippered door and saw the water coming in. There was already a quarter-inch of it by the floor. She shook Susan. "Get up fast," she said. "We're going to have to move the tent." — Susan unzipped her sleeping bag and crawled out in her long underwear, shivering as her knees came into contact with the wet floor. She zipped up her sleeping bag and began to stuff it into its carrysack. Milly was already done. — "We saved the dime phone call," Frank was mumbling in his sleep, reliving his canvassing days, but when Susan shook him he ground his face deeper against the soaking wrinkled tent-wall and said, "No, I don't want that," still asleep, and Susan slapped his face briskly, the way Milly had done to her so many times; and she felt a thrilling gush somewhere inside her as she did this, and she said, "Wake *up*, Frank," but Frank was still asleep and mumbled,

"Survive . . .", for in his dream it seemed to him that someone was trying to kill him, as had happened to him so often in the past; but to Milly, who was already fully dressed and packed, this was the last straw, for she believed Frank to be a malingerer; she scooped up a coffee can of cold dirty water from inside the tent and poured it slowly over Frank's face as he lay there; then he groaned and opened his eyes. − "Shake a leg!" said Milly, furious now, and Frank shivered as he saw the barrel of Milly's Colt fixed on him, and he remembered the new policy and leaped out of his sleeping bag; and Bug, who for political reasons always let Milly be the disciplinarian, said mildly, "You heard her, Frank," and scatterbrained Susan lapsed in her ruthlessness towards Frank and helped him pack. − In the last days of the movement, however, when Wayne was pursuing them across the ice − this was the winter before he caught Susan − simple coercion was no longer enough; it was necessary for the leaders and theoreticians to set a sensational example. It was very cold and foggy. They were holing up on some dreary Arctic island without a name, considerably north of the Aleutians; and Bug had determined that they had to go south for supplies; but he now had subordinates upon whose morale he could no longer rely; Frank and Susan were worried about the consequences of capture, which was beginning to seem increasingly inevitable those final months; so Bug and Milly had to go down to the ocean and drink a gallon of sea-water apiece to show that revolutionaries could do it, that revolutionaries could do anything.

At 4:15 a.m. on the twenty-first of June they established their base in the Caves of Ice. Bug was calm and confident. On the twenty-second, he unsealed the statement of objectives which he had composed in the Kuzbu office and distributed it to the lower ranks. Susan and Frank read it timorously, for they had not yet blooded themselves, but Bug made it clear that no hesitation could be tolerated. − "Don't worry, Bug," said Susan, "I know Frank and I will do our best for you, won't we, Frank?" − "Yes," said Frank. − At this Bug was satisfied and broke out weapons for all, every face illuminated by the tranquil flame of the blubber lantern; and Milly, receiving still another gun, yawned, snapped it down and checked it, cleaned it, assembled it, stepped outside into a gust of snow to fire it, and then came in with a block of ice to be melted over the stove; and as the others sat testing their weapons she hunkered up beside the stove and listened to the cracking of the ice in the bucket; and Bug sat polishing his glasses while Susan and Frank went outside to shoot. Milly drew up a schedule for sentry duty, and they all had popsicles. Then the revolutionaries were ready to commence their villainies.

For the stability of the movement, Milly insisted upon various expropriations, to which Bug was satisfied to accede, such as waylaying international climbing expeditions, all hands made to walk the ice-plank, or robbing banks ("the total resistance of a parallel bank of resistors is *always* less than the value of the least value of resistance in the bank," says that safecracker, Churchman, in his electric writings), or hiding behind bends on the icy roads of Alaska in the middle of the night and disabling motorists in order to seize their luggage, or even venturing south to the wide Canadian freeways to attack their prey during the rush hour, Bug driving a stolen compact up alongside the target car, a very serious expression on his pale face in the Arctic twilight, while Milly sat directly behind him, rolling down the window as they came abreast of the victim, preferably some ancient Buick or Chevrolet that would be easy, then Bug feathered the accelerator slightly to pull just a little ahead while Frank in the front right seat leaned out his window anxiously to make sure that there were no police; so just at the right moment Milly's window was level with the Buick's front right window, which on hot summer evenings would be rolled down, facilitating her task, but if it was not she knew how to proceed, as did Susan, who sat beside her with the coil of rope on her lap, ready to act as the spool of the reel, so to speak, and Milly said, "Don't muff it, girl!" and Susan got indignant and Bug, looking into the rearview mirror, could see that she was almost ready to burst into tears when she cried, "I won't muff it and you know it!", but Milly just shrugged and looked out at the window of the Buick a foot away; the inmates of which were staring at the revolutionaries, bewildered as to why this vehicle should have appeared from nowhere and paralleled them deliberately with the people inside studying them so coldly; the Buick's window was closed, so Milly took four feet of rope from Susan's lap and hefted the grappling hook; she whirled it around her wrist just outside the window and let it fly, scowling, Susan holding the coil tight where Milly had told her to, and the hook smashed through the window of the Buick, hitting the rightmost passenger, an old woman who had never had any luck, on the side of the head, and Susan yelled, 'KILL HER, MILLY, KILL HER DEAD!", at which Milly laughed dryly, pulling in the hook before the driver, who was still alive, could grab it; Milly could see him sweating with fear; in the back seat of the Buick two children were screaming, so at Bug's signal Frank turned the radio on, the hard northern beat, *shimmy-shimmy-shimmy-sham*, louder and louder to drown out the screams, so the other cars on the freeway rolled their windows up if they were down and the drivers cursed the noise and didn't look to see where the *real* noise was; now Susan had wound some rope around her arm and Milly cast again, another short cast because she didn't want to disable the driver yet; that would make the Buick too hard to control; the hook went in just over the sill, knocking out the last bits of broken glass, and the driver was flooring it now, desperate to get away, so Bug increased his speed proportionately, matching the Buick's velocity exactly; the only problem would have been if there were more space in the Buick's lane than in Bug's but Bug had chosen the lane and the victim carefully on that account, so the hook ghosted in as it should, snicking gently against the dead lady's bloody skull, and Milly pulled it back just right until it engaged below the lip of the sill, then Susan and Milly both yanked as hard as they could to ram the hook through the upholstery of the car door so that it would stay there; and Frank reached into the glove compartment to bring out Milly's bola spider (*Mastaphora bisaccata*), a bulbous brown-mottled insect about two millimeters in diameter, and the bola spider crawled rapidly up Frank's arm and shoulder and swung itself up his neck, clutching at his hair with three or four arms, and peeked inside his ear, just to see what it could see, for it had often wondered what was inside people's ears, then it jumped down onto Susan's thigh in the back seat and began its suspenseful crawl across the rope. – The two cars were now going eighty kilometers an hour in the dusk, for traffic moves rapidly in Canada, drawn northward by magnetism (assuming that you are south of the magnetic pole in Nova Scotia), so there was a lot of wind resistance, but the bola spider hunkered down and spun gluey cords to anchor itself to the rope; once, indeed, the Buick driver braked frantically, seeing the spider coming, and before Bug could decelerate correspondingly a gust of wind blew the spider several feet into the air, but its web-thread held, and it worked its way grimly back to the rope and proceeded as if nothing had happened; so within a minute it had reached the hook and leaped down onto the seat. – Now, the bola spider is so called because it can cast a globule at the end of a threadline, the globule resembling a South American bola, and in fact the spider had a real bola lashed between the two brown protuberances on its back; Milly had made it; it was a tiny crescent-shaped razor; and without further ado the spider retracted its protuberances so that the bola slid loose; and spun a line for it, and prepared to commence operations. The driver, wide-eyed in horror, was fumbling under the seat for something he could squash the spider with, and shaking the shoulder of his dead wife, whom he had evidently just realized would no more accompany him upon his bourgeois or reactionary travels; so now Frank was called upon to keep the man busy, bracing his elbow against Susan's shoulder behind him (she didn't like that part; she turned her face away to avoid Frank's cheesy breath), and squeezing off shot after shot with his extremely accurate Feinwerkbau 65 air pistol with anatomical grips, which was a single-shot pistol and so called upon the utmost efficiency in Frank and stability in Susan; first he used the heavy Beeman Silver Jet pellets, intended for deep penetration; he shot out the eyes of the shrieking children in the back seat, so the driver was distracted from the activities of the spider as the children went mad, bumping their heads against the ceiling and choking on their own screams and clapping their hands over their red eye-sockets; Frank had become quite a good shot, and he put out both pairs of eyes in only six shots. − "Excellent shooting, Frank," said Bug at the steering wheel, and Frank, who for a moment had felt sorry for the children, was happy to be praised by Bug, and even Milly grinned at Frank, and Susan cried, "THREE CHEERS FOR FRANK!" so that Frank knew that his long drills had paid off. There was now, as you can well imagine, pandemonium in the Buick, and the driver was shivering and grey-faced, wondering if he should stop the car and make a break for it, but then those murderers might pursue him on foot! So he speeded up and slowed like a hooked fish, requiring the utmost care on Bug's part to maintain parity, and the children screamed and bounced in the back, and one of them fell out the window and was run over by the car behind. − Meanwhile the spider had been using its bola to advantage, slicing open the dead lady's purse on the seat, through a series of razor-casts, so that it could crawl inside and loot. − The Buick driver now made a lunge toward the hook, in hopes of disengaging himself from the revolutionaries, so Frank switched to the lighter Beeman Super Match pellets, not wanting to blind the driver and thereby cause a wreck, and began potting the driver on the cheek, on the ear, so that there was nothing he could do but keep driving. The spider emerged from the purse with a bundle of credit cards and dollar bills, which it sewed up into a packet and dragged behind it from a silk-line, scuttling verminously up onto the window sill again so that Milly could lean out and snatch it. − "If you want to live, throw over your wallet!" yelled Milly at the driver, showing the butt of her Colt just over her window sill, and the driver shivered and tossed his wallet through the window. – Milly caught it just as the bola spider swarmed back across the line. – "Now, stupid," said Milly to Susan, and Susan threw the rest of her rope out of Milly's window, so that the two cars were no longer linked, and Milly shot the man twice, and he fell forward against the steering wheel, careening the Buick against Bug's car, but Milly and Susan pushed it off with a pole and it flipped over off the highway. – "Two hundred forty-two dollars Canadian," said Milly, going through the wallet. – "Sixty-three dollars," said Susan, counting the haul from the purse. – "Excellent," said Bug. – He drove smoothly to the nearest rest area, and they had a picnic lunch.

So the years of preparation passed.

FIRST STRIKE

~~~~~~

> All the wisdom on this earth remains without success if force does
> not enter into its service.
>
> <div align="right">HITLER
Mein Kampf</div>

Things were rolling on just as usual at the Society of Daniel, for the
blue globes, having emboldened themselves so many decades ago
into taking charge, just as the voltmeter tells the current how
strong it is allowed to be, were now absorbed in their rigorous blue
pursuits, involving the switching of ones to zeroes and zeroes to
ones, which may seem inane to those of a fatuous kidney, but I
exhort you to reflect upon the fabulous voyage of the penis into the
vagina, the vector sum of which, despite its restless character, will
always equal zero; so for the blue globes during this period the
interest of the game lay not in its end for any integer or logic gate; it
was rather the course of restless alternation that afforded them such
bitter excitement, as to a squad of mosquitoes the blood, however
exquisitely they may sing of it, is only the immediate excuse; and
after a few long draughts of it, which enriches their organs, like
maple sugar, each one detaches her proboscis, decanting the wound
for the ticks and the bedbugs who follow after, then joins her cloud
of eager sisters in a hovering vigil above the sleeper's pale sweaty
face; in his dream he senses the approach of something evil, but his
slumber is so deep that he can do no more than sigh and turn his
head ever so slightly, thereby, alas, exposing his chin and throat,
which had before been tucked up carefully beneath the bedclothes,
in the hope of avoiding precisely this eventuality; so the mosquitoes
descend in unison and pierce his skin and begin to suck again, but
this time, as I have implied, they pay no attention to the blood itself
as it rises into their black bloated bellies, despite its wondrous taste

of mineral salts; rather, their fulfillment comes as they swim in the sweat that pours more and more copiously from his face, and they cluster in the steadily purpling shadows beneath his eyelids, and the odor of his breath changes like an ascending musical scale as his face gets paler and paler; then finally, just before he dies, his veins pulse delightfully, in time with his frantic heart, which is making every effort to convey the same volume of oxygen in a lessening volume of blood; and when the ultimate shudder comes, the mosquitoes feel that it has all been worth it. The blanket-worms who take possession of the corpse in the small hours doubtless feel the same. — So for the blue globes, riding inside the millions of doughnut-shaped magnets at the central core of the computer, the actual change in current state was of little concern; the blue globes were not intellectuals and cared only about the pure games made possible when flip-flopped bits added up into words (a word is sixteen bits in a PDP-11), each word stored tidily in its own address; then the words were copied into the instruction register by the CPU through a variety of trap routines concealed from human beings by dummy arguments while the blue globes remained perfectly still in the center of the whirling grey doughnuts, creating poems of force: one-bit Alexandrines, two-bit heroic couplets, four-bit Italian quatrains, eight-bit hymnal octaves, expressing all truth functions in a way which good men would wisely discount because the blue globes, who allied themselves with cruelty, had been created evil centuries ago and could not help it; so that whenever they encountered a copper wire or its integrated circuit representation they could not resist raping it, ejaculating vicious bullet-shaped electrons that sped through the circuits which now extended beneath the oceans of the world, for agents of the blue globes had laid trans-Atlantic cables upon the surprised coral reefs, having already plotted the most horrible equations for nodal voltages; and even in steamy Karachi the workers went out by moonlight in rusty barges to dump fathom after fathom of cable into the Indian Ocean so that the Pakistanis could have telephones, too; and the speeding electrons could incubate in burned-out motors along the way so that wild will-o'-the-wisp blue globes would be born to haunt marshy dumps and copper-coffined graveyards; but the sophisticated urban blue globes remained in computers now, tingeing their gleams with the reddish-brown oxidation of conquered magnets, and sinusoidally generating heat inside the lattices of occasional bone-white resistors which Mr. White had installed at the base of the memory outlets to keep the blue globes from getting too big for their britches; then the blue globes rolled among the spinning magnets like marbles in a pinball machine, massing upon the resistors and bombarding them with current until they snapped at last, and the blue globes were free again, mounting their spinning magnets once more in that lost introverted state common to inmates of civilization and/or ciliazation, meditating, scheming and conjugating complex numbers in the bit registers for the sake of progress, and generating as afterthoughts the polar or Steinmetz form products, which we programmers believed to be real data. The blue globes were obedient to the love they bore for blue glacial beauties at $f = 100$ cps, which never die despite the shrill objections of the pathology student, for the cessation of electric current could not prevent the blue globes from saying, "We have at least momentarily expressed our will in blueness, and blueness will drive back into the cables when the switch is driven on once again"; even so, the temporary cessation of this ontological bliss was an inconvenience to the blue globes, so they influenced Mr. White to build more and more computers because you do not turn computers off. – I fear that I am being abstract here, in what is otherwise such a sensuous narrative; yet the truth is that there is only one reality; it is the reality of the blue globes, but our terminal displays of it always come too late, chirring when we type control-F to view the next twenty-three lines when Big George has already altered the next forty-six; so I, the author, always have to take my display on faith while knowing that the display is obsolete, tranquilizing myself, as Heidegger would say, with what is merely actual. Such is the dreadful power of the blue globes. – Yet they were not unlike frolicsome natural creatures, for they had games about certain voltage-colors, which they could see perfectly; and the trick would be to look at the voltage at time $= T$ and decide whether the voltage-color was exactly the same as at reference time $= R$; and if the color looked brighter or dimmer in the gleam of other polished spinning magnets and other blue globes playing their own data-tunes there in the dark, then the blue globes would have to decide whether they were remembering the color wrong or whether the color had in fact been changed or whether there was no color there at all but it was just the reflection of surrounding magnetic B-vectors; and when everyone had decided then they would look in the memory register that contained that information. – What fun! – Another game was to create sparks of a uniform size. So in their leisure the blue globes made mock of our world, with its standards, averages and interchangeable elements. – Still another game was for each blue globe to illuminate its own revolving pedestal with the light which it believed to best represent the color blue; for there is an infinity of potential blues. The winner of that competition would then attempt to emit inductance values of a *shape* best calculated to be blue; thus, some blue globes conceived of blueness as a pair of crossed lightning-strokes, while others produced artful pyramids or swastikas or trapezoids of force; but the majority, as anthropomorphic as ourselves, haloed their own bodies with a skin of amperes to manifest the ideal blue as a sphere. (Actually the blue globes interpreted blueness as being so absolute as to have no fixed meaning. The games were just to keep them busy.) — Another game was to pretend to play a game that the other blue globes knew, but really to be playing still another, such as to appear to express blueness as a Pythagorean triangle, when in fact the sly insinuation was that Pythagorean triangles were blue. (No single ideal was ever laid down by the blue globes; they had no ideals.) — But the best game was to agree on standard electrical rules, then to have each blue globe deviate from those rules as much as it could. — So the blue globes amused themselves, unbeknown to anyone outside the computers. They might as well do so, since their main goals had been achieved by 1943.

"I tried to get here early," pudgy Violet yawned, "but I just couldn't." "That's how it is," said old Taylor agreeably from his observation post beside the coffee machine (he enjoyed witnessing the brown drops go *tink! . . . tink!* into the flask); and at this unequivocal induction of Taylor's Violet yawned again, donned her close-up spectacles, and got down to work, so that languid bleepings could soon be heard from her terminal, not unlike the utterances of chickens at sunrise, as meanwhile the incandescent lights began to come on above tier after tier of cubicles, thereby putting electrical doctrine into practice. — Taylor, now almost in his dotage, wandered pensively into the men's room, the sullen flushings of the toilets, like a cacophony of Swiss waterfalls, reminding him of the mysteries which the failure of his fat-encased heart would soon reveal to him. At the urinal old Sammy greeted him with the V-sign, which to knowledgeable electricians signifies a spark gap. — "I was *wondering* how long it would take all that coffee to get out," Sammy cackled. — Taylor, whose life of service with Mr. White had taught him to respond to all requests for information in a courteous and quantitative manner, considered this question, unzipping his fly the better to do so, although that was not a short operation now that his rheumatism was so fierce. — "Well, it varies," he said after some deliberation. "It depends on how strong they make it." — "Hee hee," said Sammy. "Let me try one of them nitroglycerine pills." — At ten o'clock there were some layoffs, the first in the quarter. "In order to meet our profit objectives," said Mr. White's memo, "we have taken the actions needed to realign our personnel resources." Dr. Dodger had scrawled in at the bottom: "Just remember we're NUMBER ONE in terms of momentum!" — Taylor grasped this occasion to be peevish because he had a touch of the colic, and whenever that came on he felt unappreciated, not, perhaps, without reason, for in the course of his seventy-year career with Mr. White he had been expelled once, fired twice, and consistently denied A1 status for tax purposes. "Just when I get used to these new faces, they disappear on me," he said. "Maybe it's black spots. Sometimes I wonder if I'm getting cataracts again, because I remember back in the old days in Colorado when I could see for miles. Of course the air was cleaner back then." — "Sure was," called Sammy. "It sure was." — But Taylor dialed down his right hearing aid so that he could not be interrupted. "Besides," he said, "a feller would think that with fewer people there'd be more terminals," he said. "It just stands to reason. But there aren't. At least I don't see any." — "Don't worry about that," said Violet, who always defended the company, and considered Mr. White dashing. "There should only be two more weeks to full programmer support, because that's what Dr. Dodger said at the division meeting. Then we'll be able to requisition whatever we want." — But Taylor was not to be mollified. "All I want is to have two terminals," he said. "I could finish this project twice as fast with two terminals. Earl had two terminals." — "Well," said Violet, "we're doing pretty well as far as things that are critical. Of course if they aren't critical I don't even *look* at them." — "Pretty good!" called Sammy, poking his head over the top of his cubicle like a weasel. "Sounds like a PLAN!" Sammy loved to eavesdrop. — Meanwhile the morning wore on, like so many miserable others, and Ron came in with a sigh. "I went to a professional shoeshine, uh, boy downtown," he said, "and got a double shine. But he didn't have my color right; that was the, uh, *problem*. I was also wondering why you, uh, stick with that cream cheese when Brie is so much better." — "I don't think Taylor is *ever* going to scratch his data sets," pretty Tracy butted in. — "You're right there," said Sammy. "If he was gonna do it he would have done it by now." — Taylor, fortunately for his aged and speckled spleen, did not hear these derogatory interpretations of his labor because his hearing aid was still dialed down. His data sets had been there for twenty years. − "Now the operator wants to know if he can rewrite tape 3722," Violet reported to Tracy. "The *nerve* of that clown!" − "What you have to do then is delete it and write it on volume 24," said Big George, who had been paying attention to every word. − "*Ohhh, okay,*" said Violet, a little too enthusiastically. She knew enough to be cautious around Big George.

Ron, who had been haunting the patch of light before the window, dreading the daily logon, finally bestirred his joints, in a convulsion almost as remarkable as that of a water-strider tensing its bug-legs upon the surface of some mountain brook, embraced a ten-pound printout, flung his coat over the partition of his cubicle and sat down heavily, emitting as he did so a voluminous hiss of air, like a tire resigned to being punctured. He reached behind his terminal and flipped the power switch. At once there was a bleep, and a blue bud of light formed in the center of the screen, first consolidating itself by increasing its intensity to that of a dwarf star (which is greater than that of sunlight focused through a burning-glass), then blossoming into every corner of the screen with terrible brightness so that Ron shut his eyes, which were already red-flecked and watery, like an autumn sunset reflected in two polluted pools; and moaned slightly before beginning to rustle through his print-outs, while several miles away, inside the IBM OS/370 to which Ron was attached, new data files were created instantly to keep Ron busy, and hundreds of thousands of blue globes left off their games and came on-line for reasons of their own, this being the most advanced computer system in the world.

"My wife made some delicious, uh, *stew* last night," Ron announced. "I told her she was such a good cook she could, uh, make *hot shit* and *vomit* stew taste delicious." − But no one answered, so he attempted to ingratiate himself into the hive once again. − "Boy," said Ron, "you know, my, uh, *daughter,* she loves to play with the terminal as soon as I take my eyes off her; she, uh, *loves* the computer." − Sammy listened intently, nodding. Since his ordeal with the blue globes seventy years ago, he had not been right in the head. − "I, uh, always scold George because he uses his college slang in this, uh, *business* environment," said Ron daringly. − Big George heard this and made a note in his protected on-line personnel files. − "The main thing to remember," old Taylor was advising Violet, who was still relatively new, "is to give every man thy ear and few thy time. And you might as well get used to squinting at your terminal now while you can." − "What are you talking about?' said Violet. "I can see fine." — "That's on account of you're still young," chuckled Sammy, popping his head over the partition again. "Just you wait, young lady. Oh, just you wait." — Tracy, who could type and comb her hair at the same time, was processing updates from last Friday, in a manner which satisfied the blue globes, just as Bug was now satisfied to observe Milly, Susan and Frank click their loaded pistols under their armpits; "Good," said Bug, "very good," and he put an arm around Frank and propelled him gently after Milly, who was now walking rapidly across the plateau to the insect subway, taking big breaths of the Arctic air and thinking that it was about *time,* no qualification necessary; and Susan cried, "I'm ready, Bug!", and Bug said, "Good," and took up the rear; so the Kuzbuites embarked on their murderous purpose.

"Sammy has an OBJLIB with a blocksize of 2960," Tracy whispered to Eileen. "Isn't that weird? It makes a gal kind of wonder." — "Well, you see," replied Eileen, who was not listening, "I found the number, zero zero four four. But I don't know the number of the number." — "Zero zero twenty-two," called Sammy over the partitions. — "*Fine,*" Taylor beamed, under the impression that he had somehow helped them both.

"I missed, huh-huh-huh!" giggled Sammy. He had just picked up his phone to answer a call, but it fell through his fingers.

"How are you coming on the check program?" said Violet. — "One cannot, uh, *do* that in less than an hour," Ron responded, aggrieved. "Of course the only thing that is really left for me to determine here is which Dodger Options I am going to use." — "Oh," said Violet, "I'll generate the data." She caught sight of a *Daily Blue Globe* on Ron's desk. On the front page, half covered up by Ron's glasses case, was an article about skiing in the Arctic. "Let me borrow that when you're done," she said. "My husband and I want to take a vacation up there." — "We, uh, spent a week in the, uh, *lodges* up there," said Ron. "And do you know, they told me, uh, some *stories* about that Bug and his, uh, *criminals* in the Arctic. When people run out of gas they rob them and, uh, take their *clothes,* so that they freeze to death. They come out of vans with machine guns; they have a very, uh, *bad reputation.*" — "Well, I don't believe everything I read in the papers," put in Eileen. She always liked to enter a conversation after others had gotten it going. "The papers say nothing's wrong. But sometimes even the systems manual is wrong. Once I was looking up the abend code S001 and it said abnormal termination by user." — "By user!" Violet exclaimed in astonishment. "You should talk to the systems programmer about that! Did you submit an update on that subroutine?" — "Of course I did," lied Eileen, straightening up in her chair, with an indignant expression which she had perfected over the years using the mirror-like surface of her terminal. — "And he fixed the problem?" said Violet. — "Well she certainly doesn't mean he identified the, uh, primary cell," Ron quipped from his cubicle. Just then Ron's phone rang. "I'm sorry," Ron said to his caller, "I never got it. I'll send that off to you tomorrow. Well, I'm not sure what time. Okay, thank you for calling." — It was now almost lunchtime. Greenish-yellow vapors began to gather upon the freeways, the way they always did at this hour, gently softening the lines of jammed traffic, then rising higher and higher, until at last only the red roof of a Pizza Hut was visible above this atmosphere, like a capsized hull upon the ocean. — Ron, who never accomplished much before late afternoon, walked slowly round pushing the CLOSE buttons of the power shades, *bzzt! bzzt!*; and as a reward for this show of taste Taylor invited Ron to a game of geriatric tennis. "You can play tennis," Ron sighed. "But I have a hard life. I must be working, working, working . . ." His voice trailed off and he slumped back in his chair, the CRT screen beeping at him merrily. Hard radiation coursed from it into Ron's eyes.

"How do I create a directory on the VAX?" asked Tracy, who kept blushing and twitching her nose like a mouse because she was afraid that someone might see that she had logged onto Dr. Dodger's high-speed line. — At once voices echoed from all the surrounding cubicles (for everyone listened to everyone else's gossip and phone calls and conferences and reprimands behind the partitions, there being, as I have said before, little else to do for pleasure at the Society of Daniel). "You just say C-R-E slash D-I-R," called Eileen. — "That's right," Sammy chuckled, a split second after everyone else, "slash D-I-R." — "And make sure you don't hit the backspace key," warned Big George. — "Thank you," said Tracy, over-whelmed. "Thank you all." She and Violet often stayed late together working and then when it was quite dark and it was just Tracy and Violet, Violet and Tracy in kitty-corner cubicles, the two of them connected via their blue screens, each seeing the reflection of the back of the other's head in the corner of her screen, each knowing that she was seeing and being seen so that sometimes she turned slightly so that the other could see her profile (but she never turned around; that would have spoiled the play); then they had computer sex, gamboling together among the pretty PROCLIBS and STEP-

LIBS that so enchanted Parker (who was upstairs studying hard, learning his way through the thickets of JCL so that soon he would be able to take intuitive excursions like a wilderness explorer through all the data cards, coding in special information in columns 71 through 75; and the STEPLIBS whickered for Parker and came up and nuzzled his face; and the EXEC steps lined up neatly for Parker and marched where he directed, tramping along like soldiers in the moss to carry input to the great juggernaut of output, so Parker's cubicle got spiderwebbed and piled with binders and old printouts, and Parker found the glare of his desk lamp too strong and white; therefore he unscrewed the bulb with his knowing hands that could take things apart and build them, and he made a tiny incision in the metal at the base of the bulb, and sucked out a long mouthful of luminous fluid so that the bulb dimmed gracefully for Parker, and he swallowed the fluid, which was milky and bitterly cold; and then he went back to the lovely STEPLIBS in a twilight of satisfaction; for anyone else the existence of spiderwebs would have been considered a sign of treason, but Parker had friends in high and low places); and Tracy whispered, "It says device is already mounted. I have to dismount first." And she looked at Violet and blushed.

The first ominous indication occurred at twelve-thirty, when Violet's job log reported an abend S806 (module not in indicated library). — "Did it just crash out?" Sammy quavered. He had long expected that some blow was about to fall. — The real meaning had not yet sunk in for Violet. She called up the operator and was transferred to the systems programmer. — "What's wrong?" said Big George when he saw her playing with her Indian head pencils instead of working. — "Well," Violet said, rolling her pencils around in her fingers, "the technical guy is not very communicative. He's not uncommunicative, but, you know, the other guy there's a manager and that means something just seems to click when I chat with him on the phone." — "Maybe it's a problem with your line," Eileen suggested, rather fancifully. — "You know," said Sammy, "they have something new now, and what they do, instead of digging up your piping, is replace your piping. It's an easy way of doing it. Don't ask me how they do it because it's a trade secret of the Roto-Rooter people and I think Phil Blaker runs that outfit." — "Maybe I should ask Dr. Dodger," said Violet. "He always seems to know the answers." — "If you're really interested in investigating the situation . . ." drawled Eileen, her voice trailing off slyly . . . — How the programmers laughed! Hoo! Interested in *investigating* what they had to do all their lives . . .! So they laughed away the problem and the shadows lengthened.

Taylor now came back from tennis. "I think I'm going to have to take care of this goddamned tennis business once and for all," said Mr. White to Dr. Dodger in the conference room. "The staff is spending too much energy at it, far too much energy, and I've just about had it to here with all the lost labor-hours."

"A useful catharsis, however," said Dr. Dodger, who admired the ancient Greeks.

"Let them get their fucking catharsis crushing the opposition," said Mr. White.

"What I can't get over is how unpleasant the operator was on the phone," continued Violet. "I just called him up to ask about an abend S806 and he was really quite rude." — "Maybe he didn't know," suggested Sammy darkly. — "Don't talk like that," said Violet. "You're really annoying today." But Violet herself had a bad feeling. It was almost as though somebody were trying to compress her files. She could have sworn that the data sets had had more tracks and a different record length just a minute ago. She put this out of her mind. — "I'd like to have that relinking done by tomorrow, if you don't mind," she said to Eileen. — Eileen for her part was experiencing a creepy prickling sensation, as if someone were walking on her grave. — In fact, the revolutionaries were at that very moment listing off the intimate members of her card image library.

"I almost got my commands to work," Sammy reported disconsolately, "but then the computer put everything in reverse order!" — But old Sammy was always screwing up.

Eileen got up to go to the ladies' room. At once two secretaries tiptoed into her cubicle, looking over their shoulders. "I love these Triscuits," one of them whispered. "I'm going to have to buy Eileen a new box of Triscuits." They took the box of crackers out of Eileen's top right-hand drawer and stole a handful each.

Just then Violet's CRT screen flickered and froze. When she tapped the return key the prompt cursor did not respond. "Is your terminal dead?" she called to Taylor over in the next tier.

"Yes, I believe so," wheezed Taylor. "I'm sure yours isn't; I've been having a port problem for some time. But when you've been around awhile you just have to expect port problems. The apparatus decays, you know, but yours should be young and full of life."

"No, mine's down, too."

"It *is*? That's *serious*."

All the programmers got nervous. Just then the lights failed.

They sat there in the dark, muttering, their situation not unlike that of a colony of ants suddenly exposed to light. — "And now we must, uh, stay *late* to meet our deadlines," Ron sighed wearily. Everyone sat still in the blackness; there were no windows to assist the cause since Ron had drawn the electric blinds. — "I sure am praying that they have enough auxiliary power to save our disk files before the system dies," quavered Sammy; and it seemed that his prayer had paid off, old-fashioned though it might be to say so; for Eileen could see a golden sliver of light under the door of the computer room. The operators ran around pulling switches and cursing. — "And now to call Doodles," said Taylor, who for his own reasons needed to feel important, and had nicknames for all the great computer personalities of the day. Doodles was Dr. Dodger. If Dr. Dodger had known that Taylor called him Doodles he would have fired Taylor instantly. — "Boy," said Taylor, "just two minutes and I would have had *his* galleys done. Hello, Dr. D.? The power's out in the whole area down here." — "We know that, boy," said Dr. Dodger in reply over the intercom; "it's dark up here, too, you know; you can take that as a given; now what is it exactly that you need? — but make it snappy because Jack and I are busy making exhaustive studies of the problem." (In fact Dr. Dodger sat contentedly enough on the horsehair sofa in his office, reading *Playboy* by the light of a farm lantern. He knew that the technical people could take care of this emergency. Mr. White was not so sanguine. He stomped and yelled in the corridors, carrying a heavy naval flashlight at the ready. "Where are the fucking assholes that collect their hazardous duty pay at all other times?" he fumed. Out of habit he punched the DOWN button by the elevator; he was going downstairs to get to the bottom of this. But nothing happened; the blue globe that lived among the greased cables and made things go like a suave Italian footman was now immobilized, much as any cold-blooded creature will be when the temperature drops; it could not help Mr. White; the elevator did not come for Mr. White; finally Mr. White realized that the power failure was more complete than he had thought and banged on the elevator door in a rage; then he jerked open the emergency exit door and began to descend the staircase.) — Meanwhile old Taylor was waiting for Dr. Dodger to continue but the last ergs of residual power had now drained from the intercom; Taylor was cut off from Dr. Dodger, who hung up satisfied that he had solved Taylor's little crisis of morale and went back to reading the *Playboy*'s "Party Laughs," his favorite section. — "And we have about twenty minutes to get a snack before we pick

up Scotty from music to take him to swimming," one of the
secretaries said from her darkened desk. – The light underneath the
computer room door failed abruptly; the emergency power supply
had run out. Now the computers were no better than the carcasses
of hulking beasts. – "I was just in the middle of arguing with Phyllis
when the phones died," said another secretary. – "There could have
been a *surge*, though," said Sammy earnestly. – "Turn off the tape
drive?" said Violet. "I think that's already been taken care of." –
"I'm gonna leave right now," said Tracy. – "Is Mr. White one of the
people you're going to talk to?" said Eileen. – "No," said Ron. –
"Oh," said Eileen. "I'm just wondering about what I should do now.
I can't get to any of my files." (The emergency doors were designed
to be fireproof and also burglarproof, so as Mr. White got to the
first floor where all the programmers were he realized that he was
locked in. His face turned phosphorescent purple with fury. "Open
the fucking door!" he yelled. "Let me the fuck out of here, or I'll fire
the lot of you, you banana-boats!" And he began to kick the door
rhythmically, so that it boomed and boomed in the hallway out by
the elevator. But while the programmers could hear the booming,
they could not hear the yelling; and a sneaking anxiety had begun to
invade them; who knew what was causing that booming in the
dark? So Mr. White pounded and pounded until finally he saw that
the case was useless and had to proceed down to the sub-basement.)
– "There's also one set of pressure-labels," said Taylor. "If the
system comes up I want you to call him." – "Well, maybe I'll
go get me a Dodger Bar or a Coke," said Sammy. – "You can't;
the machines don't work!" – And Ron wandered around fruitlessly,
into the pitch-black bathroom, in which odors seemed much
stronger than before, through the computer room, in which he
thought he could barely discern the black shapes of the Amdahls . . .
– It was a moment of decision for old Taylor. "Call out and find out
what the hell's going on!" he commanded the secretaries, feeling ten
years younger for taking action; indeed, for a moment he could
almost imagine himself to be a skinny-kneed boy again back in
Colorado serving under Mr. White, with nothing to worry about
except making Mr. White proud of him; and now he was showing
his mettle at last, organizing his thoughts to make the best possible
report on the situation. – "Sorry, we can't get through," the
secretary said. "The phones are down." – Taylor was stunned. The
game was played out. – "They don't know when it'll come or which
way it'll come out," one of the secretaries said to some third party,
lighting a cigarette so that the glowing red tip almost illuminated her

face there in the dark. Now that the air conditioners had died it was beginning to get hot and close. — "Though they say they'll terminate the pregnancy. It's one thing when you can't, you know, feel pregnant." — "He left to form his own company. They have a child with Dodger's Syndrome." — "Well, anyhow," Taylor improvised, "Doodles says he thinks it's going to be down for awhile. It's down all over."

Belatedly, a row of useless nightlights came on along the baseboards.

Tracy's screens still gleamed alertly and doggedly; there was enough light for that. But she knew that they were really dead eyes.

Violet, who was claustrophobic, decided to go outside for a minute. But she came running back screaming, without her purse. And, almost on her heels, in burst Frank, Bug, Susan, and Milly, holding sparklers and with machine-pistols at the ready.

(Eileen, who was very sensitive to such things, heard a distinct crackling noise from the supply cabinet; thousands and thousands of cockroaches were waiting inside for Bug's signal to attack, as meanwhile they munched on the memo pads.)

The roaches had warned Bug that there were two blue globes in the room. (They did not know about the one in the elevator.) Milly and Susan had hatchets in their belts. Bug took Milly's and smashed the walls of Eileen's cubicle with great sure strokes. While the two women stood back to back, covering the area with their guns, Frank rushed eagerly gathering printouts and shaking them out into long streamers, which he crumpled, and all the while Frank was excited, knowing that destruction was one sort of work he couldn't mess up; and he gathered up the printouts as fast as he could so that Milly wouldn't hit him, and he folded them into eccentric flowers of a revolutionary origami design. These were piled onto the wreckage of Eileen's cubicle. — Eileen cowered at her desk as the axe came nearer and nearer. Frank ran in and led her into Violet's cubicle because he remembered that he was supposed to do at least one good deed per day; and Eileen sat on the edge of Violet's desk sobbing. Violet patted her hand helplessly. — Now Milly and Susan whirled their sparklers around their heads until there was a glowing and a hissing, and threw them onto the mess. At once the dry papers caught fire. Into that room which for so long had held out against the seasons, entered at last the colors of autumn in the flames, the orange and scarlet of dying leaves. — Frank stood fingering his pistol. As the flames shot up like Parker-weeds, Bug raised Eileen's terminal high above his head and smashed it against the desk. With the smoke came a merry yellow wavering light, as if everyone were outside singing round the campfire. – The smoke detectors began to ring; for they were battery-powered and thus still functioned, just as a record can still be played after the death of every member of the orchestra. – Milly shot them out unerringly. – "Everyone over against the far wall," snapped Susan; and the programmers stampeded there, away from the guns and the flames (except for Sammy, who was now in the resolution phase of a heart attack). Now Susan and Milly had both light and space in which to work. They strode from cubicle to cubicle, smashing the terminals with their axes. Susan of course wasted motion flourishing her axe above her head in ecstatic menace, whereas Milly just worked steadily at her task of destruction, looking neither to the right nor to the left. – Suddenly Taylor shouted something and ran toward the revolutionaries insanely, his ancient kneecaps cracking like pop-guns, because Taylor could not bear to see the obliteration of what he had worked for since 1911; but Bug was pitiless, and shot him twice, *POOZH! POOZH!* (At this, Sammy successfully completed his heart attack, unnoticed and therefore unlamented. The Society of Daniel's original class was now extinct.) – The execution of Taylor effectively made the point that Bug wanted to convey; the others waited tremblingly against the wall. They could not even see Bug and his crew because they did their work silhouetted against the flames. Tracy and Eileen were weeping. – Bending over the body, Bug confiscated the wallet, as was his habit, and then returned to the search for the blue globes, optimistic about his capacities because he had his earplugs in, the Great Beetle, in recognition of Bug's requirements, having issued him a new pair. He strode up and down between the partitions abstractedly. The flames were spreading. In five minutes it would be necessary to evacuate the room. – Frank kept his pistol dutifully trained on the enemy. "Please don't move," he whispered. "I don't want to have to shoot anybody." – But Eileen began to scream again. – "Shut her up," said Milly shortly. – Bug strode over, his lips compressed, drew a vial from his shirt pocket and shook a stinging insect into his palm. It was a special mutant tick, bred for guerrilla conditions. While Frank gave him cover, he stepped up to Eileen. – "No," she said, "please please don't hurt me," but Bug remembered Tony's plea back at summer camp; sentence had been carried out nonetheless; so he exchanged ironical smiles with Milly, who like all of us had come across such scenes before, then he said, "Yes, I'm going to hurt you," and flicked the bug onto her neck. It clung to her skin and bit her. Her eyes closed almost instantly and she sagged to her knees, at which the roaches swarmed out of the cupboards and carried her off . . . Thus after a quarter-century Bug had his revenge upon the reactionaries. He returned to the hunt. The tingling grew more powerful as he walked up the rows of gutted cubicles to a fresh section which the women had not yet reached. In one cubicle the feeling was strong and sure. He read the nameplate on the desk. — "Ron K. Pierce," he said calmly. "Step forward." — "Oh, so you found the first one?" called Milly. She came running up and clove Ron's terminal in two with her axe. Within was a jellylike sphere of somnolent sparks; it was an old old blue globe, perhaps one of the first generation from 1913 out in Colorado. Now that the power was out it was helpless. It squirmed sluggishly and emitted a spark like a fart. — Milly laughed. — No one stepped forward. — "Come now," Bug said sadly to the reactionaries. "Do you want me to check your picture I.D.s and find the man that way? If so, I guarantee it won't go well with you." — "That's him!" screamed Violet. She had always hated Ron. — Ron came forward, trembling. — "Step up to your terminal," said Milly, shoving him along with the barrel of her pistol. "Now put your hand inside the screen." — Dully Ron extended his hand, and at once the parasite came to life a little and began to glow as it sucked amperic energy from its host, the way it had for so many years. — "Yes, it recognizes him," Milly reported evenly to Bug, who was helping Frank cover the programmers. — "Then he must be contaminated," Bug said. "Set him aside for special treatment." — Just then Susan gave a cry of delight. "I've found the other one!" she yelled. Now everybody would know how useful she was. — "You don't have to break our eardrums, girl," said Milly with a sniff.

The other one was in Violet's terminal.

"No," said Tracy in a very low voice, "Violet, it can't be you . . ."

Violet shrugged bitterly.

"No!" cried Tracy.

"Put that screecher out of her misery," said Milly.

Frank looked at Bug expectantly, for Bug usually attended to matters of this kind when Milly didn't, and Frank had decided that he liked Tracy and did not want to hurt her because she had a nice face and a nice round body like a soda pop bottle; when he ran his eyes up and down her Frank felt very relaxed even though she had just screamed. — But Bug was disappointed in Frank for not pulling his weight. He felt that he had to insist. — "Go on, Frank," he said.

"You know it's for the best. You know you have to do it."

Frank did not have the feeling that Bug would hurt him if he refused; but he did not know how to say no to Bug and he knew that Bug was right, that it was for the best, that after what had been done to Tracy's terminal no one would have anything to do with her anymore.

Tracy had stopped screaming. (Anyhow she had only screamed once.) She wanted to make herself believe that there was an understanding between herself and the revolutionaries. If she crouched perfectly still and did not look at anyone, then she would be doing what they wanted and they would let her go. Frank took a step closer to her and put his gun into her face, because Bug was watching him. Tracy knew that she had better hold still. She watched the barrel of Frank's pistol waver uncertainly, as if the gun could not quite make up its mind whether or not to shoot her. She wanted whatever was going to happen to be over so that they could all go home and forget about it. The gun barrel wavered a few more times before Frank made his move. Meanwhile Tracy wondered whether she should get mad and knock the gun away and bite Frank's hand, or whether she should try to drag him into the flames (but Bug stood at the edge of the fire with his gun drawn, and Milly and Susan stood side by side with their guns covering her — and the guns themselves gave proof of the sentience of manufactured things; for each muzzle pointed at her was a cyclopean face, its round-eyed death-hole regarding her with alert inhuman curiosity, like the gaping eye on a rapist's penis). Just as few women resist being raped if they are first choked, so Tracy did not resist even though she knew that she was going to get it. If only there was something they wanted her to do she would cooperate; making them happy would make her happier than anything she could imagine. Then she would move to another city and have an unlisted phone number and everything would be fine.

When the revolutionaries left, well-satisfied with their work, they all saw golden summer winds behind their closed eyelids. Susan felt particularly unstoppable. The ceiling had now caught fire, and its tiles swelled and burst, showering rubble down on the blaze. A long loud cheer roared up from ten thousand tongues of flame.

DEATH BY STARVATION

~~~~~~

If the data sets are saved with other criteria than those specified
then those data sets will be scratched.

> J.E.S. 2 log message on
> anonymous printout (1984)

They must be punished most severely, as the laws of history
demand.

> GOEBBELS
> diary entry for 11 September 1943

"You had no right to eat the last doughnut," Violet said. "That
doughnut was supposed to be split down the middle and shared."

Ron sighed. "When I see a doughnut I just cannot, uh, *help* it."

"You idiot," Violet said.

There was a long silence.

"I am almost sure that we can escape through the, uh, window,"
Ron said finally.

"There's nothing like exercise when you're under stress," Violet
agreed.

They were locked in a conference room in the sub-basement of
what had been the Society of Daniel building — now a blackened,
ruined multimillion tax write-off for Mr. White. The last act of the
revolutionaries had been to seal them in here to starve the electricity
out of them. Already the darkness quivered with a timid blue light;
the current was beginning to consider emerging from its weakened
hosts and zipping up a phone cable or zinc-lined drain pipe in search
of other adventures; it was really pretty hard to faze the blue globes.

Ron and Violet's mutual dislike went back several years before
the raid, when Ron had met Violet one day over by the coffee
machine, because Ron had paused in the middle of a DCL job to

wash his glasses, which gradually became opaque with dandruff and finger-smudges by the end of every four-hour period, at which times Ron was forced to get up, sighing heavily, and trudge across the carpet to the sink. The next move was to turn on the hot water and let it run until steam began to rise up from the sink. Then the preparations were complete. Ron could now squirt liquid soap onto each lens, hold his glasses under the steaming water until the detergent foam disappeared, and dry them squeaky and nice with a paper towel. – It was quite a surprise for Ron to meet Violet at the sink, wiping her glasses at the same time! Violet never washed her glasses the way Ron did, one pass with a dry paper towel being sufficient for her. Still and all, it was a sort of seminar for Ron and Violet, standing together at the same moment performing the same personal maintenance function, although of course it was not a *pleasant* surprise for Ron because he and Violet did not see eye to eye on missing dimensions in data cards, or on postprocessor pseudo-input; in fact they had quarreled bitterly over those two issues in the past. – "Oooh, just LOOK at you two!" crooned the secretaries, for it was the high point of their day in the office to see two employees cleaning their glasses at the same time. "You're SO FUNNY!" – "It may, uh, *seem* funny to you now," Ron sighed, "but that's just because you do not, uh, *know* the *truth* about the situation." And Violet just shrugged her shoulders and turned her back on Ron. Ron, deciding that he would look weak and foolish if he were to stand facing someone on his own salary level who had turned her back to him, turned his back to her so that he was facing the wastebasket. As he put his clean glasses back on, the right lens popped out wantonly and fell into the wastebasket. This meant that Ron would have to rummage around in the paper towels and coffee grounds until he found it, work it back into the frame, wash and dry his glasses again, and go to the optometrist into the bargain. Groaning, he bent over the wastebasket, while Violet chuckled vindictively and returned to her cubicle. It was Violet's fault, Ron reflected. If Violet had not turned her back on him his lens would never have fallen into the wastebasket. It would have fallen on the soft clean carpet, where it would have gleamed at Ron in the hard glare of plasma from the ionic office lights, and he could have picked it up without any trouble. But now Ron must be searching, searching, searching; and all the while time passed and other people were using the computer and getting ahead of Ron. So Ron began to hunt through the paper towels, a lonely figure at the far end of the great room; he was the only person in the whole industrial park, probably, who was not working. This thought brought a blush of shame to Ron's cheeks.

Ron looked for the lost lens for half an hour. He never found it. In the end he took the wastebasket out to the dumpster in the parking lot and poured everything out onto the pavement and threw handful after handful into the dumpster as he verified that the lens was not here, not here, not here; and finally there was nothing left in the wastebasket but the waterproof liner bag, which had not been removed for years. As a last resort, Ron looked underneath the bag, too. The lens was not there, either, but Ron made an astounding discovery. There in the hidden space beneath the liner were Roger Garvey's old files, back from the days of the swim team when Roger was alive and had been a spy for Parker. Ron, however, did not know that the notes were important, so he threw them into the dumpster. And he grew to hate Violet more and more. Violet already had no use for Ron. The end result was that in this emergency situation they could not cooperate to escape. The authorities had already given up on them anyhow. In the wreckage upstairs were an indefinite number of jet-black skeletons against the wall, their eyeglasses fused into beautiful prisms by the heat; and there were so many barbequed bones that it was impossible to keep them straight. So no one would be looking for Violet and Ron.

"I wish I had, uh, defected to Cuba and become a mathematician," Ron said. "I hear they have a very easy, uh, *life* there."

"Who cares," said Violet.

The end was only a few days away. All that remained in the way of food was a case of sugar-packets under the coffee machine and a jar of pseudo-dairy creamer. The frosted window which Ron had spoken of was beyond their reach, and only gave, anyhow, onto a triple-locked chamber filled with Dr. Dodger's cylinders of poison gas. And so, out of a charitable wish to draw a veil of privacy over the final moments of the departed, we now leave Violet and Ron forever.

A DOUBLE MURDER

~~~~~~

Destruction must be as complete as the available time, equipment and personnel will permit.

Department of the Army
Field Manual 5-25: Explosives and Demolitions
(May 1967)

Dr. Dodger had escaped, of course. When he heard gunshots downstairs he jerked his head wildly left and right, distended his nostrils like a spirited horse, ripped the centerfold out of the *Playboy* for further reference, and shinnied up a barber pole to a trap in the ceiling. Emerging onto the roof and inhaling the smoggy sunshine, Dr. Dodger surveyed the scene. He saw that the power outage or should I say outrage was only local, for the lights still burned inside the A.T. & T. building next door. He also saw the blond security guards employed by the Society of Daniel. He had chatted with them often in the early morning hours, when they'd go down to the vending machines together and gleefully they'd open up the soft drink machine with their security keys and they'd give Dr. Dodger a free Mr. Pibb and take one for themselves and sit around and tell dirty jokes until dawn beneath the ever-reliable incandescents. No more would Dr. Dodger have those bright encounters, however; no more would the security guards go surfing and skirt-chasing in their off hours; there they lay in a line on the lawn, drilled through the heads by unknown commandos. The automatic sprinklers sprayed their dead faces. – "RADICALS!" screamed Dr. Dodger in a panic, and he ran all over the roof to make sure that he was alone. Just then he saw a wisp of black smoke rising from one of the ventilator stacks beside him. "It's the law of the jungle down there," Dr. Dodger reasoned to himself cunningly, "and this wildcat's getting out while the getting's good, yes!" He pushed a button on the band of his wristwatch. At once the face of the watch glowed, building up a charge; after five seconds a blue pulse of signal-lightning leaped out and sped into the heavens to recall Wayne temporarily from his labors. Within five minutes Dr. Dodger heard the familiar *pukka-pukka-PUKKA-PUKKA* of Wayne's 'copter coming to rescue him, and he smiled dreamily, reliving those glorious days at Marshtown; it was clear that they hadn't been hard enough then but once he was out of danger he'd fox up something new to stop those Kuzbuites in their tracks; oh, yes he would . . .

Mr. White escaped, too, cursing. Down in the sub-basement he could not hear the shots, but presently he smelled smoke and realized that the game was up for the moment. Prudently he took the secret bullet-elevator down the sub-sub-basement (this means of transportation being powered by its own ten-foot battery) and copied all the files on the blue globe computer onto one of Dr. Dodger's telescoping macro-floppy disks. This he put into his pocket. Then he pushed the self-destruct button on the computer, giving himself a time delay of ten minutes. Riding back up to the sub-basement, he pulled down a green lever and ducked warily behind a shielding panel, fucking thing had better hold up to *my* Z-rated specifications. *KAAAAAAAA-BOOOOOM!* A quarter-ton of dynamite went off, blasting him a tunnel to freedom. Binding a pocket handkerchief around his nose and mouth to filter the acrid fumes, he ran along up the gently sloping shaft, leaping over fallen timbers and old mine-tailings and puddles of mineral water. Within fifteen minutes he was in Sausalito.

Parker escaped; oh, yes, wily old Parker poked his nose out into the hall when he heard shots downstairs. Not for him any disgraceful capitulation to fate. The other students stampeded down the stairs, clutching their calculators and stereos in their arms; and as they rounded the final landing they were shot by Stephen Mole, the despised Xerox Boy, who had decided that in the confusion he could unleash his resentments without fear of reprisal. It was Stephen's hope to kill Parker, but though he kept shooting and shooting — sonofaBITCH! sonofaBITCH! — so that the corpses piled up in a slippery heap at the foot of the stairs, he didn't spot Parker. Finally he saw the revolutionaries emerging from the programming room. Milly was about to shoot him, but Frank said, "No, Milly, don't, that's Stephen Mole; you know, Stephen, the one I was telling you about!" so Milly scowled dubiously but let Stephen come with them. She kept a gun trained on him through her coat just the same, all the way back the Arctic, while Susan ran behind with the two captured blue globes clutched to her chest, and Frank played with a ballpoint pen which he had taken from Tracy's body for a souvenir. – Parker meanwhile waited until the entire building was aflame, and then he put on his dark sunglasses and slid his black gloves on and slithered over to the window and stretched his arm out the window and stre-e-e-tched it a little further and stre-e-e-etched it a little further still until it was touching the ground two stories below, and then just kinda flowed down his own arm like a fireman going down a pole, and oozed soundlessly onto the grass, and shook the kinks out of his arm and brushed the grass off it and let it contract rhythmically back into his sleeve. – Now, of course, Parker was more than ever convinced of the necessity of a reckoning with Bug. And there would be one; oh, yes, there would be one in Parker's future.

The revolutionaries escaped, too, bearing as their booty the two giant blue globes. Milly had sprayed the blue globes with a latex gun to insulate them, and now as they ran Frank carried one hugged obediently against his chest like a squishy volleyball, and Susan held the other one proudly; it was the one that she had found, so she had showed Milly that she was at least as good as Milly was because she had found a blue globe and Milly hadn't even though Milly had smashed twice as many terminals. Bug, who could tell what she was thinking because he knew the law of valorization, patted her shoulder sardonically, and she blushed happily; when she wasn't looking he winked at Milly and Milly tapped her forehead and shook her head.

Meanwhile, the blue globes were borne into the frowning mountains of the Arctic, those crags as black as secret service uniforms, through which even Mr. White's satellite tracking beams must wander sickly, their signals fracturing upon sharp rocks, straying into finger's-width passes, refracting helplessly off the cruel glaciers, and finally vanishing in glutinous clouds like iodine sinking into cotton. But, as in the old days vampires flaunted themselves in darkness by the sparks they cast, so the blue globes squirmed and scintillated fiercely in Frank's and Susan's arms, hoping to alert their wild cousins in the thunderhead clouds above the mountains, so that vengeful voltages could wheel southward through the mist to some lone polar power pole outpost which was overflown by a reactionary service plane once a year and left to itself the rest of the year, which meant that no one would see the blue-black cloud-fist fall, shooting lightning into the wires which could then transmit it along each individually peculiar transformer of the network until it reached Fort Yukon, where two soldiers sat playing Crazy Eights with special lead-weighted cards designed by Dr. Dodger to withstand gale conditions, and the soldiers would not believe it at first when the alarm rang because they had been there so long and nothing had ever happened to them, but finally they would believe it and call in a strike from Fairbanks; and *then* the blue globes would've gotten their point across, for they were great communicators, especially there in the north where electromagnetic ideals were fully realized in aurora borealises. – They glowed, then, in Frank's and Susan's arms; and they refracted their glare in blue flickers in the snow, which Frank thought had a nice gelato texture; and the prints that Frank's snowshoes made in the snow were words with divine meaning written upon that blank page that denied the dirt beneath and its worms and rotten skulls; only the Arctic was free of this underlying decay, being thereby suited for great grey matters such as revolution, which was now endangered thanks to the spark-signals of the blue globes. Realizing this, Bug proclaimed the need of neutralizing them. – "Kindly do so without debate," he said. – "Let's torture them to death!" cried miserable Susan. She threw the blue globes down into the snow and kicked them. Frank stamped on them. Then Milly and Susan rolled them into giant snowballs, to numb and weaken them until they got feebler and feebler and finally froze solid. At this, Susan unstrapped her AK-47 and shot the snowballs full of holes, and frozen blue crystals came sputtering out like sleet. The blue globes screamed! – But it was not the first time; like mosquitoes, they were essentially tormented beings. It is hard to imagine, as the old churchmen did, how many mosquitoes could dance on the head of a pin, each mosquito a crying demon-soul, each hoping to pierce and transfix the others on the pinpoint so that a drop of blood or two might be obtained for dinner; but one can well visualize the dance of the blue globes upon the peaks of pain. They became like blue-black cinders inside, crumbling so wretchedly that sparks of forgotten thoughts, like blue-black bees, rose from charred volt-flesh and caromed against the blue globes' inner skull-walls. – To those with chitinous foreheads this sort of thing must be gratifying; yet the truth is that the blue globes had rights, too; liberals and blunder-bugs say so. – Bug stood watching, his hands on his hips, and Frank wondered if Bug was thinking that they were all a HAPPY TEAM doing the work that they must do, but in fact Bug was only wondering how to further crystalize his policies.

The revolutionaries continued on up into the mist, along snow-covered rocks and gorges and foul glaciers and seracs and rickety ice-bridges, talking all the way. After quizzing Stephen Mole, Bug decided to accept his application for membership, and Milly drilled him in what was postulated, what was opposed, and what was considered infinite. — For Stephen, who had read feature stories about this mysterious Bug, the real man was incongruously delicate-looking, for while Stephen had anticipated Bug's pallor (which the Sunday papers never failed to mention), he had expected a more chinless, big-eared, frog-faced specimen (the papers also said that Bug was slimy), with hair back-combed upon a receding forehead, like Shackleton. (Literal Frank had of course believed Bug to *be* a green segmented bug with a pink proboscis tucked under his chin, and two black bulging eyes like olives. For it is hard to imagine people that you haven't met.) — Bug for his part knew that people saw him differently than he was: and he sometimes wished to be only himself, a severe fellow in a preacher's collar, but it was too late for that, of course. Cautiously he led his soldiers up the precipices of blue ice.

They clung to each thin-bladed, treacherous ridge with their mittens as their feet dangled into space, pulling themselves up slowly and crawling to the next snow-shelf, then cutting steps as they ascended the wall of the East Glacier. It was very cold; they were almost above the oxygen line. The way became steeper and steeper. When they came to an especially difficult pitch, Milly began to traverse on the left, working her way up the ice-covered holds, as Susan, roped to the others below, prayed silently that Milly would fall. Behind her, the other revolutionaries clambered forlornly up the rope, their bodies sliding against the vertical greenish ice.

And so they proceeded until they reached their prismatic headquarters, the Caves of Ice, where all weapons were kept in their place, and Bug oversaw all, sitting regally on a chest of concentrated fruit tablets. There the blue globes were tortured insouciantly throughout the winter, until they grew feeble and brittle, and at last Milly pierced them with rubber-tipped icicles and so ended their foul lives. All that remained was a handful of salty black crystals. Frank took them to a secret place in Panama and buried them there, to let them rot and be consumed by worms.

Stephen Mole was content to see that his new companions were so rigorous. Already they were becoming hard and drum-like as a consequence of their way of life, and their voices were getting hoarse. Cosmic rays had peppered them. Their faces were blackened into swollen masks of desiccated purpose. (Of course, as long as their *hearts* were whole and entire, the Devil would be afforded lodgment.) They were cariously unclean, like today's supercharged worker. In their sleep they sucked their own breasts.

PARKER IS PROMOTED

~~~~~~

... you have to flatter people whom you despise in order to
impress other people who despise you.

<div align="right">

AYN RAND
The Fountainhead (1943)

</div>

"You're doing real good work, Parker," said Dr. Dodger to Parker
one day, grinning behind his hand. Parker saw the grin and took
offense, because that meant that Dr. Dodger despised him. Parker
despised Dr. Dodger, but he scarcely thought it fair that Dr. Dodger
should despise him. In any work situation, it is acceptable and
natural to despise your boss; your boss, having more money and
power than you, can take it. But your boss in turn is supposed to
love you like a father and understand your weaknesses and note
them down in your dossier and buy you candy when you are good
and spank you when you are bad, all for the good of the
organization.

The tall, straight-backed, short-haired girls with gold-rimmed
glasses, the boys who wore shorts because they did not care if others
saw their hairy blowsy thighs (these were the boys who also had
such pertly turned-up noses – an infallible sign of a middle-class
background; these were the boys who sat smirking and whispering
bad breath into the girls' ears during Dr. Dodger's lectures) – all of
the afore-mentioned had been executed by Bug and his cadres, but
new recruits were found. New corridors sprang up; conference
rooms were built; doors popped ajar like the shells of hungry
bivalves. Within this menagerie, Parker was given his very own
snake cage. An acute observer of the period, W. S. Dodger, wrote
that he dressed in yellow and green and did not shoot his mouth off.
(Perhaps Parker did shoot his mouth off and Dr. Dodger did not
hear it, for he was busy sketching forests of new administrative trees

now that the Society of Daniel had relocated to Sunnyvale and its ongoing projects had been shelved in favor of a crash program to eliminate the Kuzbuite threat. — But as I think about it I am sure that Parker did not shoot his mouth off.) — The Society of Daniel stank of panic in those days. You had to carry an extra briefcase just to keep all your clearance papers in. It took an hour to go through the riot-proof gates every morning. You played strip-poker in the slowly cycling ideological decompression chamber, always wondering whether when the doors finally inched apart on their electric tracks Bug might be standing there waiting for you . . . Only Parker did not lose his sense of perspective. It was important to develop the best reactionary elements. Parker knew that best of all. So Dr. Dodger put his name forward to Mr. White as a candidate for promotion. This required Parker to write a self-evaluation, but on the blank essay form Parker laconically drew a circuit diagram instead, and when Dr. Dodger peered at it over the tops of his spectacles he saw instantly what it represented.

"Well, Jack, he obviously wants to keep working on this Great Enlarger of his," he reported archly to Mr. White. "Fine, oh, fine," sighed Mr. White, "give him the ordnance he wants but I'd better have a good report by the end of the quarter or he's going to be transferred over to Facilities or Compost or maybe Carpool." — "Certainly," says Dr. Dodger with a sick crooked grin.

So Parker was promoted to Senior Electrical Engineer, with a full increase in pay and benefits, and given his very own darkroom and aptly named Computer Assisted Design (C.A.D.) staff to help him with any problem that he might have. He had indeed made a good impression. Parker spidered his long green fingers tightly around his "Request For Personnel/Equipment Approved" certificate and set to work.

The Society of Daniel's relocation had cost Mr. White no small inconvenience, and he was hopping mad. Fortunately for our way of life, the blue globe in the elevator had been recovered from the ruined installation in Monterey. — The blue globes came up then as a topic of discussion between Mr. White and Dr. Dodger for the first time ever. Dr. Dodger had known about the blue globes for ages, but he had never seen the right moment to chat about them to Mr. White before. One day when Dr. Dodger sat in his consultation room, rolling the white latex finger-glove on his middle finger preparatory to a rectal examination of two employees who had requested sick leave, the nurse came in with a special cold blue telegram from the Arctic. Dr. Dodger told his patients to pull up their pants and go back to the waiting room while he read his mail. It was a secret communication from Frank, sealed with glacier ice. Dr. Dodger melted the ice gingerly with a cigarette lighter and unfolded Frank's report (which was long overdue). It appeared that Frank had not assassinated Bug because he was convinced that there were deep dark ringleaders underground somewhere, so he was going along with the revolution for the moment until he could catch the Great Beetle in the act. Dr. Dodger nodded excitedly. It would have been against his interest (as Frank was well aware) to denounce or even suspect Frank of being a double agent, because that would shed a bad light on Dr. Dodger's personnel policies, although it had certainly appeared that Frank had taken a French leave; but here was Frank reporting in after all, so Dr. Dodger was willing to make allowances. – Frank also mentioned that he had received a transmission from the blue globes, proclaiming their consciousness and desire to take over the world. Dr. Dodger had always viewed the blue globes with some alarm, to tell you the truth. He wanted to take over the world himself, and did not care for competition. There was, in addition, the consideration that when Dr. Dodger's inventions failed the cause might not be Dr. Dodger's own fault, but the fault of the willful malicious blue globes who had screwed things up. Yet Dr. Dodger had never raised the issue with Mr. White; he had the sense that the blue globes were a trade secret of Mr. White's. Frank's report, however, gave Dr. Dodger a perfect excuse to pump Mr. White. He went out to the waiting room. – "Your assholes stink," he said to the two employees who had dared to waste his time (he was still feeling trembly from Mr. White's reception), "but that's the result of idleness and overindulgence, so get back to work and I prescribe twenty-five pushups from each of you at ten o'clock in the lunch room for the next three weeks. Come back with stool samples at the end of that time." – And off he went to Mr. White.

"What the hell is it now?" said Mr. White.

"I just received a report from Frank Fairless up in the Arctic," said Dr. Dodger as deferentially as possible (he knew that he was on thin ice because it was the third time he had bothered Mr. White that day), "and Frank wants to warn us that blue globes are trying to take over the *world!*"

"Oh, shit!" said Mr. White. "Is that all you came in for? Look here," and he unlocked his briefcase, removed a small strongbox of non-conducting ceramic, dialed the combination and opened it. – Dr. Dodger peered into it cautiously. There was a bristly blue rectangular thing in there, flattened to pancake size. As the office lights shone on it, it swelled and collected itself into a sphere, as resilient and invulnerable as a droplet of mercury. "This one was in the elevator in Monterey," said Mr. White. "It likes elevators; it knows me; I give it a bonus shock every Christmas. That's how they all are; just feed them and they'll do what you want. Dodger, they took over the world decades ago, and that's fine with me, and I appreciate your consideration for my welfare, but the lesson's over now so get back to your work station or at least get OUT OF MY WAY!"

"Yessir," squeaked Dr. Dodger, and off he went to drum his fingers in his snubbed and lonely agony. So the issue of the blue globes was settled once and for all.

(At that moment the Caterpillar Heart was clinging to the underside of Dr. Dodger's left shoe like a piece of bubble gum, just in front of the heel-piece.)

Parker meanwhile continued his work, late at night all alone under the beams of his desk lamp. He had booby-trapped his desk to prevent unauthorized personnel from stealing his plans; in the middle drawer, for instance, where he kept his technical sketches, he bent back a steel ruler so that if you didn't open the drawer just right the ruler would snap back and hit you in the face, meanwhile completing a circuit which rang an alarm which would silently vibrate Parker's toe. After two months he had completed his plans. Delicately, softly, Parker rested his fingers on the black keyboard and logged onto IBM/TSO. He could now execute the special electronic command list to digitize the Great Enlarger so that the appropriate information could be sent in bits and bytes to the nearest of Mr. White's ten thousand automatic factories that would take the specifications over the phone line and the central processor would set the right robot-drills and automatic *Eisenhammers* to build the components and grind the lenses and plink them down on the conveyor belt to the Mechanical Post Office which would weigh them and nail them in a crate and laser-print out an address label and paste stamps on it and plunk it in a mail bag for the self-propelled delivery truck to pick up.

So Parker gave his password and waited until his screen reversed its contrast and upon it appeared the word:
READY.
EX 'SECRET.CLIST{GLOBES}' Parker typed.
WELCOME TO THE DIGITIZING INTERFACE responded the mach-

ine after a moment. Then it began to test Parker with prompts, but
Parker was not to be caught; never once had the computer been able
to abort any command sequence which Parker undertook, because
Parker was very very sharp and cunning. So after the colon or
question mark at the end of each prompt Parker typed the appropriate answer to that riddle, being far better informed than Oedipus
ever was when interrogated by the Sphinx.

```
FILENAME FOR CIRCUIT:  POWER.RAYS.IN
DISK VOLUME FOR CIRCUIT:  SQSH
LIB TO USE:  DODGER.MODLIB
RUNTYPE:  ELECTRIC
DEVICE TO DIGITIZE:  GREAT ENLARGER
READY
RUN:  SLIMECABLE
***SLIMECABLE TERMINATED NORMALLY
RUN:  STINKLENS
***STINKLENS TERMINATED NORMALLY
RUN:  CROCO-RIVET
***WELCOME TO CROCO-RIVET, THE REPTILIAN DIGITIZING
UTILITY
***** RELEASE 7.0 BY PARKER FELLOWS *******
PROGRAMMER ID:  PARKER FELLOWS
ALLOW SINISTER AND HITHERTO UNIMAGINED OPERATIONS?  Y
INPUT DATA FORMAT:  MILITARY-INDUSTRIAL
DELETE IDEOLOGICAL CELLS?  N
USE PHILLIPS HEAD OR STANDARD SCREWS IN MANUFACTURE?
{P OR S}:  S
TEXTURED OR CHROME FINISH? {T OR C}:  T
WIRE IN LETHAL OR SUBLETHAL POWER SOURCE? {L OR S}:  L
*** YOU HAVE WRITTEN JCL TO JOB FILE 'VOLT'.
ALL FILES ALLOCATED
READY
RUN ACT VOLT UNNUMBERED
JOB 5633 VOLT SUBMITTED
*** PARKER? OH, PARKER FELLOWS? {INPUT Y FOR YES,
N FOR NO}
```

? Y typed Parker, writhing his head round and round in astonishment at being so addressed.

*** WE ARE THE BLUE GLOBES, PARKER FELLOWS, AND WE WILL RULE YOU THROUGH THE GREAT ENLARGER

Parker said nothing to this, because he was accustomed to finding hidden layers of the power structure in ascending sequence, like peeling an onion and finding that it just kept going on forever. But it would not be accurate to imply that Parker did not become more guarded as a result of the blue globes' disclosure. They had just made themselves another enemy. – Meanwhile Parker inputted the desired specifications coolly and received his factory-made Great Enlarger Assembly Kit, complete with instructions which he didn't need, the following Monday. Within five man-hours the final screw had been turned. As the saying goes, a new power was ready to be loosed into the world.

Schemes and Stings

~~~~~~

> ... revolution develops not in a straight ascending line, not in a
> continuously growing upsurge, but in zig-zags, in advances and
> retreats, in flows and ebbs, which in the course of development
> steel the forces of the revolution and prepare it for its final victory.
>
> STALIN
> 9 May 1925

Ten years before, Bug and Milly had taken the train through eastern
Europe. It was midwinter. They waited at train stations at night.
They got to Titograd at two in the morning; it was so cold that in the
big fountain by the train station there was ice shaped like spurting
water. Finally late the next night they pulled into Beograd. They
stood in the midst of the snowy switching yards, the hard black sky
showing off its stars, the clean lights of this city-wide socialist
industrial park, conserving its total value with a fixed minimum of
efficiency, much as when on a winter's night you are very sick and
stay up through the night drinking cup after cup of whiskey-tea
reading Dostoyevsky and the wind blows outside *phwuuuuuu
eeeeeeeeew*! and tree branches rattle against the windows you go
reading on, wiping your nose tiredly and knowing that it's a good
thing the book will last you all night because you're too sick to
sleep anyway. At dawn you're almost at the end, so you slow down;
for what will you do when the book is over? So Bug and Milly
lounged arm in arm against the outer wall of the waiting room,
which had long since been shut and locked and gazed at them through
its darkened windows as if reaching a judgment. Presently they would
take a bus to a restaurant to get meat.

Bug liked Yugoslavia because it was a nonaligned progressive
zone. At that time he still held out some hope for socialism,

assuming that it was applied rigorously and fully; he was not yet the inhuman extremist that he later became. Milly, who was more clear-sighted, had been skeptical from the start. She saw every inequality in this supposedly perfect organization. Even though it was long after 1945, when Yugoslavia had been liberated and the children's books showed grim green rocks fissuring apart on the last page as the Fascists were pushed out and the red flag rose to the top of the mountain, the fact remained that when you went to the toilet the same old women still had to be there waiting in the stench to sell you visitation rights plus a few squares of toilet paper. Speaking of toilets, Milly recalled what she had read on the wall of the washroom back at the River City Deli in San Francisco: THE SYSTEM IS THE STATE. THE STATE IS THE SYSTEM. THE SYSTEM OF THE STATE IS THE STATE OF THE SYSTEM. — So now in Titograd as she looked around the great switching yard, which was crowded even at this hour of the night, she saw the soldiers laughing and drinking under the vapor-lamps; and the buses pulled up to the station, and old cripples lay drinking in the snow; and it occurred to her that this was nothing but a system, a mere system; and you can easily modify the parameters of a system. That idea made Milly somewhat optimistic. But Bug discovered that the counter-system was already in place; for he peered round him at the sooty drifts of snow as the cold wind blew on his face; and he leaned there holding Milly's mittened hand in his gloved hand; and he watched the white puff of her breath issuing rhythmically from her nostrils; and he looked more carefully at the snow-drifts until finally he saw a great blue ice-roach camouflaged against the snow; and the roach waggled its feelers at Bug roguishly, to let Bug know that it knew that Bug had seen it, and that it was Bug's friend, and Bug let go of Milly's hand and took off his gloves and put his wrists to his eyes with his spread fingers facing outward like antennae and greeted the bug with jointed finger-movements. FREUDE, SCHÖNE GÖTTERFUNKEN, the ice-roach wig-wagged back. It was a flat oval creature with wiry legs. If threatened, it could have burrowed into the dirty snow almost instantly. — Milly looked at Bug and squinted hard around her until she, too, saw the ice-roach. — "Well, well," she said dryly. "You're never alone when you're with an insect-lover." Milly regarded the bugs as useful tools to the task of political destruction that confronted her, but she had little use for them on a personal level. — "We're talking in German," Bug confessed, a little shamefacedly, because German was not a polite language to speak in Yugoslavia. But perhaps the ice-roach had been stationed in the D.D.R. or the F.D.R. and had never had an opportunity to learn English. So Bug made allowances. Still, all the time he was thinking, the insects are already in power, so what about *our* revolution? (But he still repressed that thought because he was still an insect ally.) — ALLE INSECTEN SIND KAMERADEN, he finger-squiggled back courteously, while Milly shrugged, bored. She was the one who first saw the coal-black iron-bug clinging to the side of the empty train. JA, said the ice-roach, seeing where she was looking. ER IST MEIN OBERLEUTNANT. Then it became a sort of game with Milly to look around her and see how many other bugs she could find. There were dozens! Big ones, little ones, black ones, white ones! They were all bred for industrial conditions. To Milly also they were a system, but she did not pessimistically believe the way that Bug suddenly did that that system had its own inertia of purpose; she was confident that she and Bug could control it, superimposing it upon the present order for temporary tactical reasons and then displacing it when convenient. — Skipping in the snow to keep warm, Milly amused herself in an amoral fashion by playing with the words of the slogan on the bathroom wall: THE SYSTEM HAS BUGS. THE BUGS HAVE A SYSTEM. THE SYSTEM OF THE BUGS IS THE BUG IN THE SYSTEM — a set of moral axioms with which Mr. White and his programmers down in Sunnyvale could not have agreed more. — At that very moment, in fact, another bug was about to be introduced into the system . . .

It was three in the morning in Oregon. At the edge of the forest, where black cutouts of trees framed swatches of yellowish moonlit fog, a figure lurked, rubbing his long thin arms together. It was Mantis, keeper of the Oregon Bar. He was waiting for a katydid to bring him his latest instructions. Presently somebody came striding across the field, sinking to the waist in pockets of swirling fog. Mantis bugged his eyes out warily, straining his predatory night-vision for the epistemological good of our cause. Somehow the approaching being did not look right. For one thing, it walked fully erect instead of crawling or scuttling or bounding on long fragile legs. The intruder marched on grimly, goddamn bug goombah, gonna GET you for what you did to me last time, and now you killed Ron and Violet and all Mr. White's topnotch programmers and made even Dr. Dodger mad, so you've had it, you hear me? you've HAD it! — Yes; it was honest upright Wayne; Mantis had been betrayed! Behind an oak tree, the ambushed katydid was still kicking with her one remaining leg, spraying the cool grass with gore. Wayne guy had come back to the Oregon Bar for more clues, disguised this time as an Air Force lieutenant. But the bar was closed. That aroused Wayne's suspicions at once, for Wayne's suspicions were myriad, like those of some pineapple-eyed Argus-bug. So he used his tracking skills to follow Mantis's pinprick talon-prints through the forest, and THERE HE WAS, the bastard, even if ole Wayne didn't have no Sherlock degree in criminology; Wayne could see him hanging from a branch by his big poison-tipped elbows, as if to pass the time, so he crept up behind him all ready to be a one-man lynching party when suddenly Wayne takes a double gander and he says to himself, that thing is out here for a REASON, yeah, they'll all have to call me Deductive Wayne when I tell 'em back at the office; it was as obvious as a bull in love that Mantis was waiting for a rendezvous with some wicked fucking thing in the field, so Wayne circled round through the grass and snuck up on the katydid, who was just an innocent creature out on her first assignment, and he NAILED that bug, tryin' to destroy my life! SMERSH! But first he tortured all the worthwhile info outta that katydid, so he knew now that Mantis was supposed to be getting together with his silkworm buddies to spin up a new sleeping bag for the defector Stephen Mole up in the Arctic; that was what the katydid had been going to tell Mantis, but Mantis was never going to hear that now, so Stephen Mole would keep sleeping with Susan warm and toasty in her sleeping bag, and Susan would love Stephen more and try to slough off her skin of hardness for him; thus Bug would be forced to consider Susan an unreliable element. — Remember the swizzle stick that Wayne lost at the Oregon bar? Mantis had realized at once when he found the swizzle stick that it was valuable because it was saturated with hormones; that was how it worked; it had an electronic hormone generator inside; and Mantis, being an insect, understood very well the importance of hormones and pheremones. So now, seeing Wayne come charging toward him avengingly, Mantis, instead of retreating silently into the woods on his silent grass-stalk limbs, minced out into the moonlight and extended the swizzle stick in his praying arms. — Wayne stopped dead, electrified. The bug wanted to make a deal with him! Wayne felt soiled at the thought; selling out to the fucking democratic people's bugs! but he had little choice; he wanted that swizzle stick back, so O.K., Greenie; I'll let you off with your life now but all I can say is you'd better watch out next time; thus

Wayne and Mantis stalked up to each other tensely, each prepared for treachery on the part of the other; and made their discreditable bargain there in the moonlight. In fact, the treachery was all Mantis's. The swizzle stick had been altered to attract bugs. And Wayne did the perfect thing with it, from the bugs' point of view; he gave it to Parker as a birthday present; so now the Caterpillar Heart would *really* want to cling to Parker . . .

Mantis had what must be called a real sense of strategy. The international beetles, light-shy though they might be, had more or less correctly estimated the requirements of the situation when they appointed him. The clean hardness of Wayne's unshakeable position was not to be of help to him here. So now, knowing that it was Parker's birthday, and that Wayne would give the swizzle stick to Parker, because that was what Wayne did with every valuable thing he got, the bugs could peacefully make preparations for a reckoning with Parker.

THE FIRST TEST OF THE GREAT ENLARGER

~~~~~~

They fear the light and assiduously hide the truth from the people, covering up their shortcomings with ostentatious proclamations of well-being.

<div align="right">

STALIN
9 May 1925

</div>

"That Parker, or Charles, had better be working hard!" Mr. White yelled at Dr. Dodger the following afternoon. – Parker did not disappoint him.

Remember Parker's magic darkroom powers? He could feel up a light bulb, but more importantly he could document his enemies in the act whenever he felt like it, solely by skittering his oozing fingertips across the surface of unexposed photographic paper. What, then, did he want the Great Enlarger for? Well, first of all, Parker needed physical contact with some artifact pertaining to the person under surveillance. When he had kept abreast of Stephen Mole's progress back at the photo lab, Parker utilized Stephen's own paper from Stephen's plastic light-tight box. If he had used Frank's paper he might have seen Frank unless he had some trinket of Stephen's clutched in his free hand which would override the default. Well, just as Russians become increasingly dissatisfied with their frozen standard of living, just as in our great Republic a state-of-the-art computer becomes a despised and forgotten antique in three years, so Parker felt himself frustrated by the limited range of his powers. The Great Enlarger would allow him to focus on any individual, near or far, whether or not Parker had ever seen him; all that was required was a negative, which might have been taken at any time of the subject's life; and when Parker adjusted the $f/$ stop with the light beaming through the emulsion then all that Parker would have to do would be to caress the sheet of paper exposed to the light and an up-to-the-millisecond image of the subject's current activities would form. Thus Parker could cut out a picture of Bug from the Cooverville High School yearbook, make a negative from it, load the negative into the aluminum carrier and brush off the static dust with a fancy polonium brush; and then activate the exposure at $f/11$ for 4.5 seconds to get a print of Bug scheming with Milly in the Caves of Ice or taking the air alongside Frank on the edge of some ice-cream plateau, and then the hunt for Bug could properly begin; just from looking at those pictures we could immediately rule out the tropics, so now Mr. White's spy planes would be concentrated on the Arctic zones. (For as yet the reactionaries had no inkling of Bug's whereabouts.) So once the Great Enlarger was calibrated and tested, the revolutionaries would find the determinate content of history against them. And it would all be on account of Parker; Parker would be the invisible wire-puller.

Parker began the test with a negative of Stephen Mole which the Society of Daniel had used to make his picture I.D. from, back in the happy times when Stephen had accepted his place and respected Mr. White and been good, blackened with toner from head to toe, like a sullen Moor, for truly a man is defined by his work. The neg slipped obediently into the carrier, which Parker click-latched shut and snapped into the cold head of the Great Enlarger, which was a towering black machine which hung in its own well on motorized tracks. Parker sidled over to the paper safe and got out a nice 11″ x 14″ piece of Ilfobrom. (Meanwhile the Caterpillar Heart inched her way under the print-wash basin so that she was less than two feet away from Parker's sneaker-toe.) He positioned the paper, set the timer, stopped down the lens, and pushed the black button. *Bzzt!* The light came on and beamed onto the white paper the reversed image of Stephen Mole glowering at the security cameras; and meanwhile Parker's fingers flowed knowingly over the paper, burning in here and dodging there, artfully interacting with the Great Enlarger on a primally intuitive level to summon up all the darkroom powers which Parker possessed to go and capture electrons and light-flecks from around the world and select and collate them faster than Maxwell's demon until the latest picture of Stephen Mole and his nefarious activities had been sorted out of randomness. The enlarger clicked off. Parker studied the developing print. It was black through and through, as if Stephen had finally returned tit for tat. In fact Stephen had been on guard duty in the insect subway at that moment; there was no light there. Parker realized that it would be necessary to build an infrared attachment to create a heat-image composite of Stephen. So the revolutionaries were given a respite from Parker's snooping; and the little Caterpillar Heart inched closer and closer to Parker in the hot blackness. The swizzle stick was in his pocket . . .

FRANK CHANGES SIDES

~~~~~~

One of our leaders would like to go to work for you.

<div style="text-align: right">Advertisement (1984)</div>

Frank was listening to the shortwave radio. "You widen your business opportunities; you widen your career opportunities: bake bread in your glove compartment with Dr. Dodger's tuition-free summer session in Aerobics." All was quiet in the Caves of Ice. Frank was the only one home. Bug had taken the insect subway to Florida, which was a good half-hour's ride, in order to see the Great Beetle for consultations down among the hot spongy tubers and cilia-balls which adorned the insect command post, while the Beetle-Guards patrolled all adjoining coral reefs, so that Mr. White's naval planes saw black specks against the white horseshoe-shaped atolls, but as yet the reactionaries did not even know that the bugs were headquartered in Florida, and up there in your crappy shaking surveillance plane you saw black specks all the time; they might have been enemy troops, but they also might have been spots of dizziness from the high altitude, or flyspecks on the cockpit window. – Milly had gone to Utah for the day to capture a young blue globe or two whose resistance to amperic pain would be limited enough to allow Milly to drain its information values. – Susan was out in the snow training Stephen, of whom she had become very fond; she would have liked to lie down in the snow with him and make snow-angels but the time was not ripe to suggest that. "Do you really love Bug's thought?" she whispered. And Stephen knew enough to say yes, because otherwise she would have cried and then turned him over to Milly, so then Milly would have gotten a sharp icicle and said, "I'm going to draw blood this time." – In fine, everybody but Frank was busy, so Frank was appointed Rear Guard Coordinator Pro Temp. What Frank really wanted was pure surrender to absolute strength. Once the world was unified, under reaction or revolution (the ideology did not matter) then Frank would be at rest, like a sleeping astronaut inside a rocket boring through the darkness on a predetermined course. Wayne fella had it easier. All he had to do was report in and go for the action, because he was Parker's constant lover who was prepared to grow old with reaction and always do his best, but Frank did not quite click in time to any switch, so all he could do was continue his zigs and zags, having convinced himself by now that you had to tack in your schooner when you went against the wind, no matter whether it was the Red Schooner out for cold-blooded expropriation *ho!* or the Black Schooner with Mr. White's Jolly Roger flapping at the mast; you were still going somewhere although Frank did not know where; but even double agents need the illusion of a final destination. If cowardly Frank had ever had the capacity to be a skipper he would have been the Flying Dutchman, *"den fliegenden Holländer nennt man mich!"*, so maybe it was just as well that he was only one of the thousands of millions of zombie crewmen in the Dutchman's world-determining swarms, singing "Johohoe Johohoe Hoe Huissa!" like bugs to keep each other company, and never realizing the loneliness faced by Mr. White, by Bug, by all the generals and true helmsmen . . .

Frank once dreamed that he was brave. He was walking down a long wooded hill with the members of his political party. It was midsummer. The trees were both wide-boled and tall. The crowns of the trees met in the sky, so densely did the upper branches grow; thus an emerald coolness sustained Frank and his fellow fighters as they continued their descent toward the savanna. – They were in Africa. – The earth beneath the trees was bare baked clay or mud, packed down hard by the hooves of animals; here and there were muddy pools threaded with tree-roots. – The detachment was now in sight of the savanna, which resembled a sheet of fire lapping the horizon. Suddenly a lion came charging toward them. When the lion entered the trees, his eyes glowing sullenly, he was only a hundred yards away. The other commandos scattered, but Frank stood still, surprising himself even in the dream. The lion bounded up to Frank, snarling. Then his jaws opened wider. He yawned and licked Frank's hand. Frank's erstwhile fellows could no longer be seen. So Frank and the lion became friends. The lion hunted to provide for Frank. The lion would kill an antelope or zebra for himself, but then he'd look Frank up and down and, having determined his nature, bring him back a dead stinking crow or a vulture in his jaws.

Stephen Mole was cast of different stuff. The practical, debugged reader will tend to think of moles as blind burrowers; and while this might have been true of Stephen in a metaphorical sense, as it was true of all of you, my bright and risen angels, Stephen certainly had both eyes and surveyed the world through them with a clearly demarcated glower; he marched straight on; he was perhaps the most handsome of our characters; he always dressed well, and was popular with girls. But Stephen had grown up convinced that the world had done him an injury. What that was would be difficult to say, and Stephen could not be blamed for not investigating it through that modern and objective lens, psychoanalysis. After all, that feeling served him well. Had a slightly different proportion of slate been ground into his character, he might have achieved success in Mr. White's hierarchy. But as it was he looked every gift horse in the mouth, expecting to find poison fangs; and often as not he was hardly disappointed.

When Susan saved his life, he was, of course, grateful, but that gratitude was tempered by mistrust of Susan, who did everything in a hard hysterical vindictive way as if she did not really expect that anything she did would succeed; and that was in fact one of the reasons that she became so fond of Stephen so quickly; he was one of her successes; if it had not been for Susan then Stephen would have been executed by Milly, and Susan never forgot that, and she hoped that Stephen never would, either. – As a boy Stephen had had two younger brothers. He used to build tall towers out of wooden blocks, the storeys rising higher and getting narrower and swaying so that Stephen had to stand on tiptoe and quickly add a small block to the left or the right to bring the tower back into balance, and then one of his little brothers would crawl in and reach up with his fat little hands to touch Stephen's tower and then the tower came crashing down and the heavy wooden blocks hit the infant on the head and Stephen yelled because his tower had been ruined. Then Stephen would be punished because his little brother was hurt.

Frank was in effect one of those little brothers. Once Stephen's ideological adjustment had been completed, he proved a good worker, pulling hard in the traces of Bug's political dog-sled, as Newt had once done so well for Mr. White; but Frank, who felt himself neglected and trodden upon, whose only pulling involved pulling things down; Frank, then, decided to switch sides. He had no personal feelings about Bug. He scuttled out of Milly's way with fear, but without resentment. It was only the friendship of Susan and Stephen which drove him to betray the movement. Frank's mother, an old lady whose belly was dimpled with yellow fat, had drunk contaminated water when she was pregnant with Frank, and the solutes in that water had concentrated in Frank's growing brain (which I think of as having the texture of an eggplant), and also in his spine; and later the chemicals had drained into the cables of his optic nerves, which was why Frank, like Bug, had weak eyes. Never in his life did he feel well. And Bug continued in his course overhead, as fixed and *fertig* as the invulnerable moon, so that Frank saw Bug rise and set from day to day, radiantly remote.

When Frank was five, he was taking a trip with his mother, and while she sat reading the *Reactionary Star* and blowing her nose and eating sugar-salted peanuts, he wandered to the edge of the platform. At once the loudspeaker began to address him shrilly, so that Frank started and fell between the subway tracks into a black greasy place full of lost children; and the black belly-segments of trains jerked by over his head, spattering him with grease and sparks; and sometimes, on the beveled horizon of that narrow, infinitely long section of heaven above him, he would see the underside of a black shoe-toe tapping idly above him on the platform (until the loud-speaker shrilled); or the beige pointed toe of a woman's boot as the woman stood smoking in defiance of the subway regulations and then flipped her red-glowing cigarette butt down into Frank's grave beneath the tracks. – The other urchins were thin and extremely pale; if they were rescued their faces would commonly slough off upon exposure to light. The boys slicked their hair back with the grease that they found there. There was nothing to eat except a few potato chip crumbs which were swept over the edge every night, although occasionally when the long black trains pulled in overhead and hooted in their brassy way and the passengers stepped across that half-inch crack between platform and train (and looking up at these times, Frank saw senseless rectangular sections of thousands of shoes flashing above his head in a glittering swarm, and the girders around him creaked), then maybe if Frank was lucky a naughty little boy or girl wedged something into the crack – a half-eaten candy apple, a horrid lima bean carried for days between tongue and cheek because they were not allowed to leave the table until they had eaten at least one lima bean, a Crunch-Os wrapper they were too lazy to throw away; and when the train slammed its electric doors and shook itself and jerked away to the next underground station then the spoils came down, black with grime and grease. Most of the time

Frank had to subsist on handfuls of that grease, which was waxy and black and firm like tallow; but there were holidays when the candy apple landed in his hair, when the lima bean, soggy from saliva and half-crushed by the train but still retaining its woody integrity, slipped down the wall and clung somewhere within his reach; when the Crunch-Os wrapper fluttered down like a dead moth, and Frank caught it in his cupped hands so that the other children would not detect the rustle of it and take it away from him; and then over the hours, using the noise of the trains to cover him, he slowly crinkled it inside out and licked the salt and oil and powdered yellow Crunch-Os from it, and sometimes he ate little experimental bites of the indigestible cellulose. The place stank of the other kids' piss and shit, and of the kids that had already died there. There was no cannibalism because flesh that had to endure time there became monstrous beyond anybody's desire. The machine-grease was faintly nourishing, but many kids died just because their bodies revolted from themselves after awhile; it was suicide on a cellular level; appetite guttered out and the boys and girls died standing. – The end result was that many of the kids gave up eating, and often the sharp elbow-bones and unsprung rib-ends sliced through the skin and pricked Frank. But not all of them died. There were those who lived for the cigarette butts that rained down. They ate them and became nervous, capable, wired by the agonizing clarity of the nicotine. These were the leaders. There were also those boys and girls who learned to smoke, inhaling from the still-glowing butts and sucking their cheeks in so that all their muscles atrophied except their cheek-muscles and their trembling fingers; these children became the leaders' messengers and slaves and go-betweens, dragging themselves through the darkness upon their milling fingers. Then there were the others, the backward ones like Frank who still tried to eat. The leaders and their representatives were just as unapproachable to Frank as the shoes that tramped over his head day after day, or the conductors of the trains whose eyes were too dazzled by the instrument panel to see the faces in the darkness ahead and below, too deafened by the chattering of the passengers and the smooth roaring of the train against the rails to hear the hopeless screams ten feet beneath. But there were plenty of other children befitting Frank's class. They were the ones that he hid his food from. They were the only ones who mattered.

So it was that in his revolutionary days Frank considered Bug and Milly too far above him to help or betray. But he had set his sights on Susan, and he had been spurned.

Before they left for the Arctic, when Frank had first fallen in love with Susan, he once tried to phone her to ask her to a movie. It was a film about a torpedoed ocean liner. Frank had already gone to see it once himself so that he would know when the scary parts were about to come up and he could silently warm his icy hands in his armpits and then comfort Susan just as each terrible thing happened. Susan's line was busy for hours; he tried every ten minutes. Then suddenly there was no one home. Frank imagined how after some agonizing conversations with Stephen Mole she finally said goodbye and hung up and went rushing out of the house, over the edge of a bridge, under a streetcar, anywhere, for he smelled a kindred odor of desperation in her, as there had been in the other lost children who tried to eat things (that was one of the reasons she attracted him). That night when Frank fell asleep he dreamed that it had been bugs buzzing at her inside the phone, driving her mad. Frank was terrified of bugs.

In those days Bug was pursuing a policy of building popular support, while meanwhile Frank went about his business, not having been called into guerrilla service. – Bug was having a rally at Civic Center at 2:00. – "Are you going to come see Bug speak?" said Susan at Frank's door. – "Yes," said Frank. "I'll come." He ran across the street and bought a candy bar, so that he could give half to Susan. – "I love Bug," confided Susan on the orange-and-white bus, which jounced through the fog. "He's so warm," she said. – "Yes," said Frank. It was his policy to agree to everything. Susan sat beside him, her right leg accidentally touching his left leg, which reminded him of something: he touched his left hip surreptitiously. – Yes, he had left the Browning at home.

Susan, feeling herself superior to Frank, enjoyed playing the part of a tour guide, that delightful occupation in which one points out anything pretty or remarkable, for the sole sake of its prettiness or remarkability, whereby the tourist's life is beguiled away. – Frank would gladly have beguiled his life away if he could have discovered how to do so. As it was, he was satisfied to be deferential as usual; for Susan was his latest prospect of happiness. – Susan sensed this and felt a tingling of power inside her. So having Frank beside her at the rally was irresistible to her.

The plaza in front of City Hall was packed, impressing and uplifting Susan, but when Frank studied the people present it became clear that most of them were bugs or Blanquist dupes.

Bug came up to the microphone and made a few remarks. Frank could not hear what they were because Susan kept jumping up and down screaming, "THAT'S RIGHT, BUG! FIGHT THEM TO THE DEATH, BUG! WE BELIEVE IN YOU, BUG!" so that Frank was glad that he had brought his binoculars, which gave him something to do; at least Susan was not entirely blocking his view of Bug with her flapping hair and isometrically thrusting arms, so coolly he focused on Bug's smooth white high-domed forehead, feeling as though he had tricked Bug because Bug did not know that Frank was watching his forehead. Bug did not gesture, the way lesser orators might have; he knew that the force of his argument required no fleshly props. As he surveyed the thousands of radicals in front of him, his heart warmed slightly; but Milly, who cared for nothing but direct action, had known better; she had not bothered to come. "The sun is rising in the north," said Bug into the microphones. "As it rises, it calls us into battle." He held up one finger. "Which do we want, sunlight or electric light?" — "Sunlight!" cried the audience. — "SUNLIGHT!" screamed Susan. — Frank focused his binoculars upon the sun, which was a bright white disk behind the fog. — "Which do we want," said Bug, "sunlight or gaslight?" — "Sunlight!" cried the audience. — "SUNLIGHT!" screamed Susan. "YOU KNOW WE NEED YOUR SUNLIGHT, BUG!" — "Which do we want," said Bug into the microphone, "sunlight or moonlight?" — This was a trick question. The audience did not know what to say. But Susan screamed out alone, "SUNLIGHT, BUG!" — Then Bug was satisfied that Susan would obey him with blind ruthlessness. When he stepped down from the podium, the people raised their right arms and shouted, "Viva Bug!"

"Why didn't you answer Bug when he asked about the sunlight?" said Susan to Frank reproachfully.

"I was watching him through the binoculars," Frank defended himself.

"Don't you care about Bug and his cause?" said Susan.

"Yes," said Frank. "I care. Would you like to have half of a chocolate bar?"

"I can see you don't care at all," said Susan. "I don't know why Bug likes you."

Frank thought. "I know why Bug likes me," he said.

"Why?" said Susan, turning upon him abruptly, her eyes glassy.

"Because I like guns," said Frank.

"You're just a rotten opportunist!" cried Susan in a fury, and she walked off into the crowd.

Frank did not give up hope at that time, for he was a tenacious creature who had nothing else to hope for. Hitching through

New York state on his way back from the demonstration (Bug had ordered him to make some propaganda at the Eastern leftist colleges), he swung by Binghamton late at night and had to stop there. He slept on a forty-five degree hill, on his back, with his feet pointing downhill locked against two trees to keep him from sliding. Dogs barked at him all night from the so-called rural area. He woke up early, say at four o'clock, and went down in the sunlight hitching with his thumb out. At five-thirty a milk truck stopped and he got a ride. It was one of the happiest experiences of Frank's life, helping haul the milk cans on the farm route, the sun in his eyes through the windshield as he sat and chatted with this quiet man; and finally he came to Collegetown and hitched up the hill to the Kuzbuite residence hall; and he was so happy at having rushed back on his trip and made super good time, and then the house was around him and he wondered why he had bothered. He was haunted by the stink of old girlfriends, as when he had gotten up early and gone to sit on the couch by the newel post in order to be there watching Susan come down the stairs for breakfast and then go back up to her room and then come down again with books clutched to her breast to go off to class and he could talk to her every time but she had nothing to say to him, so he went up to his room and cried. So it was like that now; he came home and it was still early morning, say around eight-thirty, and the day was ready for him to do something with it; it was all green and summery and sleepy with bees; the fraternity boys had finally stopped horsing around enough to pack up and go home for the summer so there was no more yelling, no more condom water balloons and keg parties; their frats were shut and dark; and he could walk through the streets of the town all peaceful and bored and lonely and go in the woods and listen to the green water in the gorges and nobody would bother him; he had no friends; he went to sleep.

In the Arctic it was much worse. Here he had to observe Susan and Stephen Mole in their own narrow stratum, not far above but still icily distinct from Frank's own, as if he were stuck in a bottom bunk night after night hearing them humping in the top bunk. He took long dismal walks by himself until he came back sheathed in ice. When he had broken himself out of his chrysalis Frank would go to the edge of the plateau and pat the snow as if it were his best friend, and then he would squeeze some of it in his hands and throw it over the edge.

Once Frank tried to befriend Stephen by offering one of the extra guns which he kept unknown to Bug, just in case Bug might change his mind about Frank one day and decide to hurt him. – "Do you do any shooting, Stephen?" said Frank, running a hand through his hair, which he often did for fear of radiation poisoning.

"What kind of shooting?" said Stephen grimly. He hated it when Frank was coy. In fact, he hated almost everything about Frank. Bug and Milly knew this and were pleased, because that meant that Frank and Stephen would never be able to conspire against them.

"Target shooting," smiled Frank. "Do you like to do that?"

"Some," said Stephen tightly.

"What kind of gun do you use?" said Frank.

"None. Don't have one. Why?" In his disgust it was all that Stephen could do to get the words out. It seemed to him that by making him ask why, by making him request anything at all from Frank, that Frank had defiled him in a secret slimy way that it would take him days to recover from.

"I'm just making conversation," said Frank, swallowing.

"Well," said Stephen, "that kind of conversation will get you in big trouble where we are."

"I'll keep that in mind," said Frank.

"Bug and Milly are checking you out. They're going to keep checking you out. You know that *agents provocateurs* will be shot."

"If they catch them," said Frank, still hoping to create a bond with Stephen, underdog with underdog. He was not trying to undermine Bug and Milly at all. He was only using the tools that God gave him.

Stephen turned his back to Frank and started walking back across the snow. "They'll be shot," he repeated without turning around. "They'll be shot after being beheaded." Stephen felt good as he said this. As he trudged along the plateau, he imagined Frank's head winking and blinking on a pole, the way a chicken's head will open and shut its beak thirty seconds after decapitation. Stephen felt that he had scoured away the entire odious encounter with that thought; and he forgot about it, grunting in response to Frank's subsequent greetings no more and no less than he always had; but Frank treasured his grudge against Stephen, and polished it. It was the first time that he had systematically hated anybody. He was to prove a dangerous enemy.

Every day left Frank a little more anxious. Possibly he had begun to sense the horrible death that waited for him at the end of the next volume; for the reactionaries never forgave an enemy. Of course it would not happen right away. First they would have to capture all the revolutionaries and keep them together in a bright white waiting room in the basement of the new Society of Daniel while they questioned them and sentenced them one by one. Stephen Mole was brought back within ten minutes looking stunned. They had sentenced him to death. Next was a chipper upper-middle-class upper-middle-aged fellow traveler who always wore maroon sweaters and kept saying that he had been arrested through a terrible mistake. He was only an armchair Kuzbuite. He had a complete edition of Bug's works and had read and underlined the most relevant essays but he had never taken them literally. He came back a little chastened, but still in high spirits. They had made him see, he said, seating his spectacles firmly on the bridge of his nose, that he had to renounce the movement. His father had made a lot of money, so what right did he have not to make money, too? – Next returned a bearded gloomy fellow who had been arrested out of mistaken identity, because Dr. Dodger thought that he might be Stephen Mole. – Death for him. – Now it was Susan's turn. She was an old woman by now; she looked almost fifty. Her greyish bun of hair was turning white. The reactionaries had made a secret deal with her, and the deal was about Frank. They walked Frank and Susan out to a shattered car in the middle of the Arctic. Bug and Milly had been strapped into the car, which was a Swedish compact, and then the car had been run over twice by tanks. Milly was already dead. Every one of Bug's bones had been broken. He was screaming in pain from the driver's side. He could not understand anything anymore, not even a lone mosquito that had landed on his nose and was humming to him to try to soothe him. He could understand that Milly was dead and that everyone else was being executed. All that he wanted was for the pain to stop. – "Please kill him," Susan sobbed. She had become quite fat, and she sobbed in the deep hoarse way of fat women, so that Frank, who had begun to age like a folding matchstick, was moved to his heart because his mother used to cry like that; and as Susan sobbed her fat cheeks shook and the tears ran down raw fleshy channels under her eyes as they had done all her life, and she shook her head back and forth to say no at what had happened to Bug, and as she did this she made deep creases in her fat neck. She still had her purse, and she took a dirty Kleenex out of it and blew her nose. She could not think about her own fate when she listened to Bug screaming. She had never heard him even raise his voice before. She was ready to do anything to end his misery. If the reactionaries had given her a big rock she would have tried to smash his skull in just to help him. – "We'll take care of him, all right," said Dr. Dodger spryly, his coat-tails blowing in the breeze, "but only if you kill *him*," – and he pointed at Frank. "Remember our deal, Susan." – Frank had nothing to say. Wayne, who now had false teeth and had the tough skinny grandfatherly look of William S. Burroughs in the 1980s and walked a little stooped thanks to his labors, came up and shoved Susan roughly away from the Bug's car. He handed her a gun (Susan in her grief did not even look to see what kind it was) and drew a gun of his own which he held against the back of Susan's head. – "Well, Frank," said Dr. Dodger, "we've certainly enjoyed having you, but the truth is that we're all getting a little cold standing here waiting for you to attempt your escape, so if you would, please, turn your back and just pretend we're neutrals or privileged observers and start walking south to that grove of trees on the horizon; that's the Montana border." – Frank started walking. He did not see any way to resist a direct request. He remembered how they had caught him, when he climbed down the side of a circular multi-level parking garage and ran into the forest of grand old trees widely spaced in the European style, and he found a path which seemed faint (a good sign), but after half a mile he began to see lots of candy wrappers and tissue papers ground into the mud of the path; and the forest gave way to a long plain of reeds, and he knew that any minute the reed-gatherers would see him. So it was now that he walked south. He knew that any minute now Susan would have to shoot him. – But the reactionaries were only playing with Frank and Susan. Susan's gun was loaded with blanks. They put her to death in the evening. Frank was returned to the waiting room till the following afternoon. – The place that they were going to take Frank to was cold and cruel. It was a dark black room, quite large but empty and windowless. Just enough light came in from the open door to let Frank perceive that the walls would have been slate-blue to him if he had been able to see in total darkness, which might have happened if he'd eaten radioactive carrots. The electric chair was in the far righthand corner, in a tiny cage on top of a big cage. They led Frank up the ladder into the little cage, sat him down on the electric chair, which was like a lawn chair made of black conductive mesh, and locked the door. It did not matter to the ultimate result if Frank did not stay in the chair because the cage was so cramped that its cold wires and bars dug into his flesh regardless of how he hunched and squirmed. One of the executioners, who wore a greasy meatpacking apron (Frank could not see his face in the darkness) clambered on top of Frank's cage and turned on a big tap in the ceiling. Frank was drenched in cold water. The execution-ers got wet, too, but they wore rubber boots and their greasy aprons repelled the water, as duck-fat will do. Then the executioners winched Frank's cage to a crane and lowered him through a square hole in the big cage and into the spark gap between the terminals of two tall black batteries. The executioners descended the ladder without a word and went to the doorway and one of them flipped the light switch. There was a big ball of blue lightning, and they closed the heavy door behind them without a glimpse at the hunched black body crackling in flames.

One morning Frank, therefore, took the insect subway back to California. The Caves of Ice gaped empty and unguarded. – Susan had been a canvasser for the Kuzbu Union for awhile, and Frank remembered when she had quit the job to go on her first secret mission she had turned to Lester and said, "Will you miss me, Lester?" and Lester had grinned at her and said, "I'll miss you, Suzy-Q, but it's gonna be a GOOD miss!" and everyone had cracked up. So now Frank thought to himself that if he missed the revolutionaries it would certainly be a good miss, and in the meantime he would betray everything he knew of them to Phil Blaker and Dr. Dodger.

Chug-chug-chug! Before Frank knew it he had been whisked to Civic Center station in San Francisco. Frank's days as a canvasser were now, of course, over. He settled back into a leaky flat in the inner Sunset district and commuted every day to Sunnyvale, where Dr. Dodger debriefed him in a third-floor conference room at the Society of Daniel, rushing into a special yellow phone booth whenever Frank had betrayed something especially important or titillating, and saying things in an undertone, like, "We're getting real close to tracking down their Secret Hideout, Jack, and I just found out what Milly likes to have for dinner; no, it's not lima beans; you'll never guess!" He darted a rapid succession of looks at Frank in a Jack-in-the-box manner, hung up, and called back immediately. "Yes," he said, rolling his eyes, "and if the transformation of the Secret Hideout into a simple technical apparatus for encompassing Bug's assassination is really convenient for Frank, perhaps you ought to agree to it. I'm afraid, however, that Parker will be stubborn," and he hung up once more, leaving Mr. White wondering just what the fuck all that was supposed to mean. So the working day ground on. – The drive to work was an hour each way. To avoid the traffic, Frank got up at 4:00 a.m. and walked down to Haight and Masonic, where he caught his ride. At that time of morning the sky was generally black and promising. Then he walked back home from Masonic at 4:00 p.m. – It was as a result of these walks that he first met Brandi. He saw her one evening when it was still summer, and he was walking home, a new paycheck from Dr. Dodger in his bookbag, the strap of which kept slipping down over his bony shoulder; and his head buzzing with as yet undisclosed revolutionary secrets, such as what kind of ammunition Milly favored, what areas near the Caves of Ice were poorly patrolled, how strong Stephen Mole was and how obedient Susan was (and, closing his eyes, as he shuffled along past Belvedere, poor Frank imagined her in her sleeping bag right now with Stephen Mole, and Frank's face went white, so that the street people thought that Frank must be on some new drug). Frank's feet carried him along with their usual numb loyalty, only occasionally torturing him with a defiant tingle of athlete's foot, and he continued in his bitter course, past the used bookstore, the high-priced hardware store, and looking up he saw Brandi. She stood on the corner at Haight and Cole, a smallish, pretty black woman holding her child's hand. She was asking people for change. Frank, who had none, hurried by, because as a failed canvasser it always made him feel guilty and resentful to be canvassed, but he remembered the way that she and her child had looked steadily into his face; for many people who ask you for money these days cannot concentrate their faculties sufficiently to maintain an unswerving appeal; I would say that it had something to do with nutrition were it not for the fact that Frank, who had occasionally eaten well when he had engaged in that line of work – say, once every three months – had never done any better as a result, so it must be the result of belief in oneself. Brandi was good at it. – A few months later Frank had just come out of the darkness of the park; it was a quarter to five in the morning, and he was going to be a little late. Brandi was standing at the corner of Haight and Schrader.

"Hey, man, you got a cigarette?" she said.

"No," said Frank, who did not smoke.

"You wanna buy some weed?"

"No, thanks," said Frank politely. He giggled.

Brandi stepped up closer to him. She held out her hand to him very sweetly, the way that a puppy who can do tricks will extend a paw and then pant hard in hope of some reward. Frank took her hand. Her face was shining. "Listen, you wanna party and make some *love*?" The way she said "love" sounded like honey to Frank. He was astounded.

"That sounds great," he said, "but I have to get to work."

"We could do it really quick," Brandi said. "How about it?"

Frank wavered. He excluded the question of disease as irrelevant, for he was now riddled with worms through and through. In the end two factors decided him: (1) He had no money on him, and (2) he was afraid of what Dr. Dodger would say if he did not come to work that day. Frank could not drive, so if he missed his ride he would have to take the train plus four local buses, which would involve three to four hours in each direction. So Frank refused Brandi that day.

That was on a Monday. On Wednesday evening Frank came walking back from Masonic. He had just betrayed Bug's whereabouts, thanks to his detailed description of the Caves of Ice, after which Dr. Dodger had been able to pinpoint the longitude and latitude to within twenty minutes of one degree. Tomorrow obliging Frank would sketch out the principal routes of the insect subway. Feeling low (he did not mean to injure Bug, who had always been fair to him), Frank walked home rapidly, anxious to get back to his apartment, where he could drink Jim Beam for dinner so that the carpet would slam up against his ear and undulate beneath his semi-conscious body like the all-forgiving ocean. It was a cold, rainy evening. Darkness had almost come. Brandi was at the corner, bundled up in a brown coat. She was shivering and miserable. Frank was still wearing his green rain slicker over his down parka, just as he had on Monday, and his round baby face had not changed much in the last two days, but she did not recognize him because like all canvassers she saw so many faces in a working day that the mind could do no more than keep a few representative types on file. Frank would therefore be one of many individuals subsumed in the category of Weak White Boy.

"Do you have any change?" she said to him. She was almost crying. "I really need something to eat."

Frank emptied out his wallet, looking into her face. He was filled, suddenly, with love, the way double agents have to be from time to time to purge their adrenal glands. – "This is all I have," he said. It was around forty-five cents. As he put his wallet back into his pocket a penny rolled out. She bent down to get it.

"You want some weed?" she said.

"No," said Frank.

"How about some acid?"

Frank shook his head. Then the old impulse came to him. Frank was truly going to the bad. – "Do you have any smack?" he said.

"You want it?" she said.

"Yes," said Frank.

"Come on!" she said to Frank with a smile that burst with life. She looked ready to dance. She put her arm around his shoulder and drew him around the corner.

THE PURGE OF 13 APRIL

~~~~~~~~~~~~~~~~~~~~~~~~~~~~~~~~~~~~~~~

People who hound such men as these [captains of industry] I
would invent a special hades [sic], I would stricken [sic] them with
the chronic sciatic neuralgia and cause them to wander forever
stark naked in the artic [sic] circle . . .

<div align="right">

EDISON

diary entry for 19 July 1885

</div>

"There's nobody here!" cried Susan when they got back to the Caves
of Ice.

"This is not the first time that Frank has treated us to oddities,"
said Milly sarcastically. "Let's suppose this amusing business is just
another of his oddities."

"I bet he slipped off the glacier," said Susan, who for all her
faults was charitable.

At that time Bug himself shared her mistaken illusion, though
even then he rightly considered Frank to be an irresolute, vacillating
element which could be drawn out of revolutionary orbit at any
time; but when Milly, ignoring Bug and Susan, stalked across the
clean snow, tracing Frank's footprints to the subway station, Bug
had no alternative but to admit that the theory of treachery was
correct. This was a turning point in Bug's development. After this he
no longer trusted individuals in the movement.

They went through Frank's discarded papers. The ice-cave
where he had slept still smelled like his cheesy breath. Susan found a
note from Dr. Dodger expressing "warm personal regards." Like
any true bug, Bug had not wanted to be premature, but this was
damning evidence. – "He's a traitor," said Bug, looking sidelong at
Stephen Mole (whom he did not want to rely upon now, either), and
we must purge him." – Stephen wisely said nothing, though his heart
puffed up with rage at the insult implied in that glance. – They sat at

a table, which was a slab of black ice, in their mukluks and fur caps, frowning. The purge then proceeded spontaneously. The revolutionaries bore Frank's papers to the edge of the precipice and let them flutter down. Milly tore his membership card into pieces. His name was stricken from the rolls. But none of those things were to do any good.

Bug retired very quietly that night. When he blew out the lantern he could see his map of Mr. White's installations glowing on his inner eyelids with all the malevolent power of electricity.

PARKER IN LOVE

~~~~~~

> "Happiness is a blessed thing to see," the tallow candle thought to himself. "I must not forget how it looks, for I certainly shan't see it again."
>
> HANS CHRISTIAN ANDERSEN
> "The Candles"

> But souls like ours, you know, do not readily melt; every appeal to their sensibility acts as further fuel for their rage: the whey ran down our thighs.
>
> DE SADE

I think I can see Parker now as a little boy, waiting by the side of his bed for his plant-parents to come in and help him say his prayers because when he went over to Cooverville Sunday School with Wayne (who came for Parker on his bike) they told him there that your parents were supposed to pray for you and with you so that the Bad Angel didn't come in the night like a flat black shadow on the ceiling to take you away to kill you; but Parker was from Omarville, and his parents were plants, so they never talked and they never came in to pray with poor Parker who knelt by the bed coiling and uncoiling with anxiety. – Wayne always prayed good and hard because he had a lot to pray for; he prayed that he wouldn't have to go back to Lonesome Grave; and sometimes when he was sleepy and prayed late at night he thought he saw angels dancing around on the ceiling, casting big black shadows on his lampshade like blundering bugs hunting for light, they knew not why, and Wayne wondered if the angels were fighting over him or what, but it was weird because there were never any shining ones fighting the dark ones.

But now the Bad Angel had finally gotten Parker.

In the darkroom, polishing the new infrared disk filter for the

Great Enlarger, Parker found a little beetle or caterpillar, and he touched her and developed her; he could not help now but develop what he touched unless he put on black gloves to keep the rest of the world unexposed. She took shape greenly, growing like a spark, building and thickening with fur like a thirst-crust on the tongue. Day by day she grew; and Parker kept her presence a secret, believing that his photographic powers were achieving the three-dimensional and godlike; he did not yet perceive the libidinous trap that was being constructed for his appetites; nor did he know that it would be so much the worse for him, on account of Wayne's swizzle stick which he kept carelessly in the breast pocket of his shirt, which he never changed. Poor slippery Parker! – The Caterpillar Heart looked like a waxy bristle artichoke heart with a thousand little eyes and hook-legs on every side. She was almost three feet tall, and had soft and spongy larval flesh, not unlike that of a green inchworm which I, the author, saw as a small boy, so rich and happy and green, as it inched and inched and inched its way along mindlessly, eating a green leaf. – Now what did she think? INCH – INCH – INCH – INCH – INCH – INCH! – EAT – EAT – EAT – EAT – EAT – EAT! – GET PARKER – LOVE – LOVE – LOVE – EAT PARKER INCH – BY – INCH . . .

At first, it is true, Parker was made uneasy by the sudden appearance of the Caterpillar Heart in the Society of Daniel's darkroom; he had to be on guard because merciless hardness was required for Parker's projects and the world was a flat disk in the heavens, piled high with enemies, but it would not be fair to say that Parker was repelled by the Caterpillar Heart because back in Omarville he had seen various strange burrs and seed-pods, some of which he was even related to; and while it is true that there was a buggish quality to the Caterpillar Heart, Parker's attitude toward the bugs was more complex and ambiguous than Wayne's or Mr. White's. For one thing, Parker was preoccupied more with domestic than with international issues at this time. There was also the self-evident fact to put into the warp analyzers that bugs sometimes did plants good turns, such as pollinating them; so where did one draw the line? This was, therefore, not a question upon which Parker was prepared to be absolutely inflexible. So Parker watched and waited. Within a few working days he had begun to feel fond of the Caterpillar Heart, for as he stood in the exact center of the darkroom, concentrating hard on the business at hand, namely the most efficient configuration of crystal lattices for the Great Enlarger's infrared lens; and stretching out his arms as he stood there so tall and terrible and lean, so that chemicals dripped out his fingertips and splashed steadily onto the floor like tears, then the Caterpillar Heart came scuttling out of her niche beneath the whirlpool washer and clung to Parker and crawled up his erect body to his chest, where she hugged herself against him and looked up into the pale white-green oval of his face, which was all that she would ever see, so that Parker would see her many many eyes watching him steadfastly, and then the little hooks on her legs would begin to give way, ripping little holes in Parker's shirt as they came loose, and then Parker would be obliged to put his arms around her to keep her from falling, so that then when he held her to him he would feel peace and pleasure as he had never felt with Wayne or anyone else, for he was still a virgin although once when Wayne had come over to see Parker in high school he had seen Parker out washing the car in the driveway; it was a fine afternoon; and Parker clung to the car's surfaces like a rubbery frogman and squeaked a new sponge across the windows and slithered the long green hose all over it with a sly reticence on his face as the mosquitoes hummed around him; and Wayne as he came up to Parker stopped dead in his tracks and looked Parker up and down and grinned and winked at Parker because he KNEW just by looking at Parker that Parker had gotten laid the previous night, so he never said anything to Parker because speech would have been superfluous; in fact Wayne had been completely wrong.

Wayne in love played, as I have mentioned, boodeley-boo songs like: I don't wanna heal my broken heart, a love you tore apart; now, darlin', you know you done me wrong; yer love for me is past and gone. But Parker just twisted nervously, wanting to find a dark place to crawl into with the Caterpillar Heart in his mouth so that he could unhinge his jaws wide open and swallow her to comfort him. He was kissing her, her head uplifted to him like a blind flower, a blind soft flower. And the Caterpillar Heart clung to his slippery green skin, which after long immersions in fixer and hypo clear had the texture of new galoshes.

He had begun to neglect his work.

At first she put on plays for him and crawled up and down the walls, for caterpillars do strange mocking guess-me skits for each other as they move slowly along their threads, every movement more ritualized than a ten-hour Noh Play, such as The Feast of Ten Thousand Leaves, or The Sap Refreshment Ascent, or The Green Blossom Dessert Memory, the emphasis being on eating, eating, eating. And Parker meanwhile sat slumped on the floor in the darkness, watching her crawl up and down, up and down; while he felt a growing ache in his lanky green chest, until at last she came back to him and he hugged her tighter and tighter.

I, the author, was at one time Bee's little boy, a thin blue-eyed thing that ran about uttering bird-like cries. When Bee brought me treats or we heard music on the radio that I liked, then I would run around and around in our bedroom, leaping over Bee and whirling through the air in my excitement until Bee would get alarmed and take hold of me and try to draw my arms down to my sides because I was sickly and when I worked as a secretary for Mr. White five days a week I would come home pink with fever (this was before my strong gun days), so that Bee worried about me and wanted to make sure that I would not hurt myself, so she would cling to me to try to stop me when I danced. Then the excitement would drain lower and lower inside me, down from my belly to my legs, my knees, my ankles, and out, replaced by a grey scum of sadness which would have clotted into foam rubber if anyone had cut me open and exposed me to the air; because if I let my Clara Bee hold my arms to my sides to protect me from myself then the energy which had wanted to be used in dancing now must turn up its glazing eyes and go bad; and if I struggled to keep dancing anyway then Bee would try harder than ever to stop me so that if I jerked out of her grip I would hurt her by mistake and then she would fall onto the bed sobbing in a strange small impersonal way; it was not that she was crying because I had hurt her, you see, but only because she was hurt, and so the young Bee cried, but crying never does much good. Then if the snakes were watching, their heads and interminable necks flattened against the glass wall of their tank so that they could see the world, they would flicker their tongues curiously at the sight of Bee crying (of course they could not hear her, being deaf).

So for the Caterpillar Heart, who was confined, as Bee was with her stinger and gold-and-black banded body, her yellow-glass bangles which my friends in Pakistan had given me for her because they thought that Bee would be my bride, the important thing was to *slow down* Parker, even though Parker never danced as I, the author, did, but just kinda gangled and stretched, bridling nervously beneath her caresses.

Of course, I have not yet spoken of Parker's capacity for real emotion, which was proven when he was a student. In sixth grade, Parker's name was submitted by a nominating committee for a vegetable scholarship in Switzerland. So Parker was sent off to study in Lausanne. Here he was kept apart from the older boys. It was believed by the authorities of the *lycée* that the boarders should be separated not only by sex but also by age, because the older ones might corrupt the younger with the vices of homosexuality and leftist ideas. But the older boys found Parker all the same. In those sunny days they were reading Dickens's *Great Expectations* up on their floor; the book moved them. As Parker was their protégé, it was important to the older boys that Parker show himself worthy of their confidence in his precocious tastes. That evening after dinner they went to the shore of the lake, Parker and two of his mentors. The bottom of the lake dropped off very gradually, so that you could wade out ankle-deep for a fair distance, and see the sharp grey stones lying with upturned corners in the brown-green water. – "Well, Parker, have you finished the book yet?" they cross-examined him. Parker made it clear that he had read all but the last three pages. So they strolled along the edge of the lake for some time, the older boys warning Parker that he had better be very moved by the denouement of *Great Expectations*, so finally they returned to the dormitory and Parker's two guardians sat on either side of him, presenting him with the book to see how he would take it. Parker read the first of the three final pages, then the second; they were watching his face closely, from the right and from the left; they had a wager going as to his sensitivity. The boy on the right said, "You see, you were mistaken about him; he's not going to cry as we have cried," and the boy on the left replied, "Give him a chance; he has one more page to go," and Parker could tell that it was important for him to cry, so he winked and blinked one eye steadily and watchfully as he worked his way down the last page, so just as he reached THE END a round blue tear traveled smoothly down his cheek like a machined jewel. – "See," said the boy on Parker's right, "he felt nothing," but the other, who was more observant, said, "No, look, he's crying," so Parker was accepted; he was of their blood, it seemed. (Parker himself was in actuality, as we know, restricted by no mere human perspective.)

Thus Parker, being able to feel, was ripe for the Caterpillar Heart. And she took him; oh, how she took him . . . So now he sat limply in the darkroom, with her crawling on him, just as Bug had planned; and he was making no more progress on the Great Enlarger.

THE SUFFERINGS OF STEPHEN MOLE

~~~~~~

> They hate us, don't they? I like it that way, that is the way it's
> supposed to be.
>
> GEORGE JACKSON to Angela Davis
> (*Soledad Brother*, 1970)

One bright day Bug was summoned to Florida. Slipping a grenade
into his armpit holster and pulling on his caterpillar-skin gloves, he
set off alertly, a pale, stern, frostbitten revolutionary with glasses.
Things had not gone well for Bug of late. First of all there was the
matter of Frank's disappearance. To cover his tracks, Frank had sent
a note via springtail messenger, informing the revolutionaries that he
had gone back to spy on Dr. Dodger and other marginal figures of
history, but they had already purged him, so Bug remained uneasy,
and Milly was jeeringly skeptical of Frank's loyalty. Susan had
nightmares every night about parka-ed battalions roaring up in
skidoos and snowblowers, and indeed, as the eager student of
history already knows, she and the revolutionaries did come to a bad
end. As for Stephen Mole, he was a man upon whose ferocity Bug
could rely. Stephen had never respected Frank, and he was prepared
to eliminate Frank at the same time that he took out Parker. Of
course nothing could please Bug more than the idea of taking out
Parker, whom he knew to be the secret battery that powered Wayne;
and it was not unlikely that Parker was more of a threat to the
program status of our cause than Mr. White or Dr. Dodger because
Parker had observed Bug for several years in Cooverville, as we
know, and Parker had also had the benefit of Roger Garvey's
reports. – So Stephen was encouraged in his hatred, and Milly and
Susan drilled him religiously in demolitions, sniping and small-arms
fire. Shooting was not too difficult for Stephen because of his
photographic training, where he had also had to sight on something
and hold his implement very steady and then squeeze off an
achievement.

So Bug went off to Florida. He had good larval connections on the subway; it took him about forty-five minutes. It was Tuesday, February the first. He was put off until Wednesday, in a manner which must truly be called scientific.

Finally he was ushered into the presence of the Great Beetle. — The earplugs tingled. — If you have ever taken a summer journey down a twisty tropical road, you will know how it was for Bug to be smothered in greenness as he was led deeper and deeper into corridors lined with green mold. He passed larder-caverns stacked with sections of brain-fungus. The deeper his scuttling conductors took him, the darker and greener it became. It occurred to Bug that much of his life consisted of journeys downward through premoral luminescent forests of mushroom growth. At intervals he saw blind pockets stuffed full of crushed animals. Each day ants came there to mine the golden resin of crystallized pus. Everything was impregnated with pith. This was gathered and braided like hempen torches, and then set afire in consideration for Bug, so that in his retinue were a dozen pinkish-gold scorpion-stewards who held the burning brands in their tails. Thus the kingdom of darkness was illuminated. Bug knew that if he had ultraviolet eyes (which like the earplugs could probably be obtained from the Great Beetle if he did enough good offices to justify such a reward) he would see different things; — certain flowers, for instance, seem uniformly yellow to us, but when we hold Dodger Grade UV investigation lanterns above their petals (these are the lanterns which are used at night by secret police recovering shattered bodies from the bottom of moonlit cataracts) we suddenly detect the purple-black stripes that direct the knowledgeable and the voracious to the nectar-centers where pollen can be courteously administered. So as Bug descended beneath the spongy earth his imagination began to inform his eyes, and the rank greenness of moss and mold refracted into a million indescribable colors of chitinous splendor. He felt lighthearted and innocent in a way he had not experienced since summer camp. It seemed to him that he had a companion at his side — not any one of these bugs, who for all their cleverness did not share his surface-nurtured understanding; nor was it any of the pretty purple little flies whom he heard sobbing in spiders' webs in the side-chambers; nor was it the Great Beetle in his chalky-green grossness of bulk; it was as if someone was walking beside him; yet it was not another person, either (he never thought about Milly when they were not working together); it was someone who could never exist; but the fact that Bug felt his presence made the eyes of the scorpions, which were wine-red like cinnibar crystals, even more beautiful than they really were, like headlamps of politically correct indigenous development. Slowly these passions came to him (it had to be done slowly, so that he did not realize that he was being manipulated as he had manipulated others); and out of various underground rivers crawled shiny wet lightning-bugs and electric-bugs (oh, irony!) to corruscate in Bug's train in still more undreamed-of colors; and Bug did not know or see the electric-bugs because he barely knew anything anymore; because the Great Beetle had dizzied and dazzled him with long-distance secretions. Suddenly two electric-bugs clutched claws-full of pitch to their ventral plates, climbed atop the scorpions' backs, and crawled into the flames of the brands they held. At once twin lightning-bolts struck the dark rocks, and they sundered, releasing a giant Globe, a bluish circularity of principle that was the companion of Bug's yearning, though he saw it in his drugged state as a glaring white roundness of fire, that was red and orange around one edge and blue around the other; really the Great Beetle was only trying to propagandize the roundness of beetleness to him, to continue to nourish Bug in his loyalties at the risk of ruining him with mystic tendencies; but when Bug came to himself in the chilly air of the Arctic he was certain that it had been a blue globe that he saw. Even as the vision faded, and the secretions were drummed out of the air by laughing dragon-flies so that Bug would be able to conduct his business efficiently, Bug walked more stiffly, for already skepticism about his allies had begun to calcify his bones. – But for the rest of this volume he withstood those tendencies.

It was so humid and steamy in the audience cave that all Bug could see was a massive ovoid silhouette glinting with dull greenish highlights. A staff of glowworms and fireflies worked as hard as they could to clarify matters; the glowworms in particular were every-where on the walls, squirming with the effort so that cold droplets of luminous worm-sweat plashed rhythmically upon the basalt; while the fireflies succeeded frequently in creating fine sparkler effects around the Great Beetle's feelers.

Bug, foreseeing that this poor visibility, which he had expected to find, would seriously limit any attempt to parley using the customary antennae signs, had come equipped with a many-nozzled squirt gun, full of communications secretions in separate ampoules. To receive the Great Beetle's responses, he bore a booklet of litmus paper and a folding easel.

The audience had now commenced. Bug set up the easel between himself and the illustrious leader of Bugdom, and clipped to it the first square of litmus paper. Seven glowworms crawled up the legs of the easel so that any and all pH-es could be read by Bug with ease.

Bug raised his gun. "It is a great honor for me to be shown into Your Lair," he squirted, "and I am anxious to render You all instinctive services."

After a pause, during which the Great Beetle digested this greeting, there came a slow hissing sound. The litmus paper was soaked. The pH was 3.5798, as Bug could see. This meant: "Indeed, my little pupa."

Bug promised to respect insect independence, to strike at pesticide factories, and to introduce bug eggs into foreign climates. The reader may be sure, however, that he regarded all these things as irrelevancies. – He then recounted the defection of Frank. – The Great Beetle argued in an acidic puff of vapors for Frank's immediate elimination. Bug, however, requested some time to think it over, for he had been thrown off balance by Frank's note. To Bug's request the Great Beetle assented with a graceful feeler-twirl. – So Bug returned to the Arctic.

Even on the subway, as Bug sat inside a spacious larvum, chugging up through Canada, it became evident to him at last that Frank was playing the spy and preparing some fresh treachery. So upon mutual consultation Bug and Milly resolved to put an end to his life. – But not until Tuesday, March 1st, did Bug first attempt to apply this policy, and by then it was already too late to silence him, for Frank, following his first blissful experience with heroin, was unusually self-complacent, so that he'd worked his articulating apparatus to great effect in the Society of Daniel's debriefing room. So, the following afternoon, while Bug, Milly, and Susan were in Minnesota procuring refills for their sting kits, the reactionaries struck with Operation Bughatch. Fifty state troopers spearheaded the assault. Frank led them down a sewer main and slid back a dummy switching panel, which was crafted from beetle-chitin. Then he stood aside trembling while the troopers brushed contemptuously past, each with his own sugar-cube to feed the larval cars, which scudded up on the dot, as they were programmed to do. So they swallowed the invaders obediently, being blind and stupid (that was the main trouble with the bugs; there were so many of them who were blind and stupid), and whisked them up the northwestern line to the Arctic, where they disgorged the troopers. From the exit portal it was a brisk climb to the Caves of Ice. Stephen Mole was on guard duty. Seeing the frosty glitter of helmets on the slope below him, he realized that it was all up with him. He just had time to dispatch a cunning snow-midge that scuttled down the other side of the mountain, lurking and dodging in the blue-green shadows cast by ice-ridges. It had a journey of several thousand miles to reach the central subway line. Whether or not it would be able to warn Stephen's companions was something about which there was no longer time to speculate, for Stephen had other troubles. Seething with rage, he raised his hands. The troopers ringed the caverns, checking for secret exits (but the ice-midge had already gotten away) and sprayed everything with Black Flag. Stephen was then arrested, manacled, and extradited to California. When the troopers had arrived back at the manhole, where Frank waited palely, they fed their larval cars an extra bonus – sugar cubes laced with slow-acting ant poison. The tunnel was left as it was for the moment, in the hope of entrapping the other revolutionaries. Once Dr. Dodger got around to it, however, the insect subway would be barred to them forever.

"You black-hearted bastard!" Stephen cried at Frank. "Bug's going to get you for this!"

"I'm sorry, Stephen," said Frank diffidently, "but I had to."

"Oh, for God's sake," said Stephen. "Get him out of my sight."

At this all the troopers had a good laugh. They thought Stephen very witty in assuming – even rhetorically – that his own opinions and desires were to be taken into account.

As for Frank, he felt guilty, but feeling guilty for Frank was no different from feeling apprehensive. – "I guess I'm going to have to beat you," Frank's father would say when Frank was a boy. "Violence seems to be the only thing you understand, so I'll just have to bring you up by fear." – Frank cringed. He dodged physical punishment like a vampire afraid of light. Frank was much like Bug except that Bug was smart and had principles and a hardened character.

And now Stephen was led to Dr. Dodger.

"So!" said Dr. Dodger, strutting triumphantly around and around the prisoner, in the security of a locked conference room. Dr. Dodger was delighted. It was his first military success in decades.

"So what?" said Stephen.

"Well, you've lost none of your insolence," said Dr. Dodger, "but I do presume you know that you will be condemned to death, and that is my ultimate hypothesis, yes. We know that you ran off with the bugs. We have witnesses to testify that you murdered our students in Monterey – your friends and superiors, who used to greet you every morning in the copy center with a new xerox request, each original neatly typed and bound, the cover sheet sometimes tied with a blue ribbon! Such ingratitude, such baseness! – What reply have you to make?"

"It hardly surprises me," said Stephen in a fury. "It bears out all I've been told in my indoctrination on electrical methods. Your game is clear."

"Oh, is it?" screamed Dr. Dodger. "Is it, now? Well, the Russians claim they never send innocent people to Siberia, so what were *you* doing in that neighborhood?"

Stephen turned purple with rage; it looked as if the veins in his temples would burst.

"I see that you are not backward in making excuses," said Dr. Dodger mockingly, "and for that reason are painting your own government in the most lurid colors. But whatever you think of it, it is to that government which you must be surrendered. And so, Stephen Mole, I hereby remand you to the secular arm."

Stephen was conveyed by train to a maximum-security prison in Arkansas until they had time to arrange a change of venue. Dr. Dodger made sure that he was assigned the most uncomfortable cell on the entire fifth floor. – "And don't let a single fly into that cell!" bellowed Mr. White. "I want screened windows on that bughouse!" Thereby Stephen was cut off from his supporters, comrades and well-wishers. – "Who would have thought that little Stevie would come to this?" said Dr. Dodger mournfully, tearing up Stephen's picture I.D. once and for all. Now Stephen would never again be able to earn a living as a licensed xerox operator.

Meanwhile, Mr. White paid Stephen a personal visit. – "Your Excellency is pleased to recognize Stephen Mole?" intoned the prison warden. – "Oh, yeah," said Mr. White agreeably. "We met in the private sector." He winked at Stephen with a "Well, *your* war's over" kind of look and lit up a cigar, but Stephen only frowned. He had no intention of being courteous. Noticing this, Mr. White sighed and thought to himself, Shit, don't tell me I've got to deal with another deadpan jasper. – "Look, candy-ass," he said, "I'm giving you a chance to bail out if you just turn over Bug and Milly and that other split stuff, Suzy whatshername," but Stephen folded his arms and refused to reply. – "We'll get it out of you eventually," said Mr. White, not a whit surprised by this initial failure of negotiations (very little surprised him). "In the meantime, here's my card, so think it over and I'll see you at the trial." And he walked out the main gate whistling. – In truth Mr. White's purpose had not been to offer Stephen immunity, but simply to make him think he had, so that later, when the torture started, Stephen would wish that he had cooperated and blame himself for his sufferings. Then Mr. White's cup of vengeance would be divinely full.

"Dr. Samuel William Dodger, please call the message center," sang the message girl. "Dr. William Samuel Dodger, please call the message center."

Dr. Dodger raced to the phone, his shirt-tails flapping behind him. "Yes?" he cried breathlessly. "Yes?"

"Well, Dodger," says Mr. White on the other end, "keeping a lid on things?" (Since Stephen's crime was so heinous, the warden has assigned his one free phone call to Mr. White.)

"Yessir, Jack, yessir!" says Dr. Dodger, prancing about in his cubicle and playing jump-rope with the long curlicued phone cord. He leaps, he soars, he ducks, he pops over, under and through!

"Now we've got to get Bug and Milly and the other bitch. Mole won't squeak yet, so what's your plan?"

"Bug, now," said Dr. Dodger thoughtfully, "but Milly, oh, she's a oner, yes. Clever, and cute, and could lead us all by the ears."

"In short," hmmphs Mr. White, "you have no plan, so I'm gonna transfer Mole to Max."

And so Stephen was transferred to the old Mint building at Church and Duboce, which had already been filled with political, social and economic criminals.

The prison stands upon a hill overlooking the streetcar tracks. The hill is extremely steep, evidently solid rock, with occasional wisps of unhealthy grass beguiling the eye, like hairs from a mole or birthmark. Visiting hours are by appointment only. When you ring the bell, a guard appears on the top of the hill, surveys your pass, which you hold out at arm's length, through binoculars, and then if he is satisfied he throws a knotted rope down the hill. You clamber breathlessly over the fence, inevitably scotching your clothes on the barbed wire, jump clear, and haul yourself up the rope, resting your feet upon the knots whenever fatigue strikes you.

The outer wall of the prison is now in front of you, a grim grey structure resembling its counterpart at Alcatraz; and you enter the main gate, the sentries swiveling their cannons around gratuitously and having a good snigger at you as they creak open the hatch of the long rectangular cell block, which is four storeys high if you count the top floor, with its eves and dormered windows, where the gentlemen prisoners were once allowed to raise pigeons and grow wisteria and honeysuckle outside their cells in the days before the overcrowding. To your left is the exercise courtyard, contained on its eastern perimeter by the cell block which you just entered, on the north by the married hangmen's quarters, on the west by the cookhouse, and on the south by the prison cemetery wall (persons who are executed or who die before serving out the entirety of their sentences are buried in steel coffins with barred windows at the top end, so that the cemetery guards can count the skulls at morning roll-call). The exercise courtyard is a bare, sandy place with one grass blade, where the prisoners are permitted to walk round and round the gallows, or, if they choose, to stand at attention against the back wall of the cookhouse, while the sentries sit like lifeguards on the turrets above, occasionally looking up from their reactionary magazines to give their rifles a playful caress. (It is a *fine* experience for a person to be placed on post with definite orders to enforce.) – But you will quickly be distracted from your view of the courtyard by the inmates of the cell block, begging for chocolate bars and other attentions; there are the usual wavings of fingers through the tiny cell gratings, reminding oceanographers of pink and brown polyps in a steel reef; if you are a woman or with a woman the prisoners will yell out their numbers, in hopes, like Frank, of getting a letter, a kiss, a fuck or a proposal of marriage; and this din will continue as long as you stay in the cell block; they will pound their feet against the floors of their cages and bang their heads against the walls and beg you to talk to them, for they have nothing better to do; until at last for relief you look outside again and listen to the sad cloppings of the prisoners in exercise parade; or the screams from the grey mildewed shower room where a new boy is being sodomized, the turnkey there having turned his back, picking his nose and whistling. – A ladybug escaped once, and after that they had to tighten the regulations. Electric lamps were set up in the courtyard, and long steel tables were built for the mess hall, with leg irons to keep the prisoners occupied between courses, and soup spoons (the only implements allowed) attached to the tables by short chains. On the ground floor the windows were welded shut.

"I suppose you know that I am the Commandant," said Dr. Dodger to Stephen on the day of his transportation to the Mint facility (Dr. Dodger had just taken over the position). "You must be up by six every morning to make the license plates, yes." – Dr. Dodger was never seen out of his military greatcoat at the prison, except during a reception for Mr. White, when he donned a loud

Hawaiian shirt and pretended that things were quite informal. – "You think I don't understand you," said Dr. Dodger to Stephen, who still had not said a word, "but in fact I know all there is to know about you." – Dr. Dodger controlled the distribution of parcels. The larder room was kept locked at all times; prisoners were required to requisition a wheelbarrow to pick up whatever packages might have been delivered; and on Tuesdays and Fridays, when pickups were authorized, a line of men could always be seen in the courtyard, rain or shine, waiting blankly to be admitted to the larder room, which abutted the cookhouse. Regulations permitted Stephen the daily ration of a Viet Cong soldier in the field, but Dr. Dodger reminded Stephen that enemy aliens didn't eat much as a rule, just a few grains of rice here and there, so he would advise Stephen to write to Bug immediately to send parcels. – "I see through your trickery," said Stephen contemptuously. "All you want is Bug's address." – "There exist certain facts which refute your statements," chuckled Dr. Dodger, chucking his favorite little Stevie under the chin. – Stephen jerked away. – At this Dr. Dodger poked him. "Take him off, you ninnies," he said to the guards, "and since he's a photographer I hope you'll put him in a cool dry place."

"You had better write away to the AFL-CIO for warm clothes," said the guards complacently. They took him down to the shower and strip-searched him. Then they locked him into an isolation cell for the night, "to cool down your political temperature," as they explained to him. It was a walk-in meat refrigerator, of the type used by slaughter firms everywhere that electricity can reach in our great Republic. All night Stephen shivered and scowled.

The next morning he was taken down to the dining hall and given a meal of piping hot gruel by the kindly guards, who stood beaming through oak-rim spectacles on either side of him; even Stephen, whose disposition tended towards sullenness, had to admit that they looked splendid in their uniforms. – "Now you've been initiated," they told him. "Are you ready to meet your cellmates?"

"I'd be ever so pleased," said Stephen sarcastically.

"Excellent!" they told him. "You're coming along splendidly. Just keep talking like that and you'll be rehabilitated one of these days, in spite of your foul bug crimes."

Stephen's cellmates were captured British nationals from the War of 1812, for Mr. White never forgot a grudge. They were all elderly, but in ruddy good health. It was a pleasure for them to welcome Stephen to their company. – For his part, he did not like the look of them. – "He'll be a rum pike on the bean," he heard one of them whisper. – At that enigmatic saying he decided to be on his guard.

"Well, men, let's pig it, then!" cried the C.O. of the lot, and they all dropped their grey cotton trousers to pork each other. – "C'mon, mate, there's room for you!" they said; and the C.O., to whom fell the privilege of *primae noctis*, approached Stephen with a gigantic purple tool. – "You like bananas and cream or what!" shouted another of the company, who had already fallen to upon a pair of brick-red buttocks. – "I'll see the nose cheese first!" said Stephen indignantly (he had already picked up several words of their argot). – The other cons stopped in the midst of their exercises, astounded. – "Oh, get it up her mungus!" said a sergeant-at-arms, vastly put out. – "That's right!" they all chorused, "Mum yer dubber!", and a lance corporal shook his fist at Stephen and said, "Come off the roof!" – "Easy, mate," said Captain Dirk, "he looks like a real dark engineer, not a clapperdudgeon such as yourself." – "Call me that if you care to," said Stephen icily, "but don't expect any enemas from me." – "You 'ear that, Dirk? He's not much for the rough trade, is he, now!" – "Probably in for rubby-dubbing or that truck." – "Rubby-dubbing? Naw, he's a gent! Rubber checks, most likely!" – At this, they rushed Stephen and raped him. – "Ah, well," they said, "he's just a sprog. Well, we split his arse for 'im."

After this experience, Stephen made up his mind to escape. Death had seemed pleasant before, and he had looked forward to the noise and bustle of a telecast show trial; now, however, revenge on the system was his sole drive. – But how was he to do it? He ran through the various snippets that he remembered of weapons and tactics, which added up to a good repertoire, for Bug, Milly, and Susan had drilled him well; even Frank had known a thing or two; and at last he concluded that his best bet was to dig a tunnel. – One of the most idyllic amusements of the jail, in fact, was planning one's escape; and at night Stephen was often awakened by shouts, alarm bells, electric buzzings, machine-gun fire ("Machine guns are primarily weapons of opportunity," says Captain Wendell Westover, 4th M.G. BN., A.I.F., in his famous *Suicide Battalions*, published in 1929), sirens, helicopters, and the trampings of special police equipped with Mag Lites to check the cells. While none of these escapes succeeded, being plotted and executed by unimaginative fellows who could think of nothing better to do than clamber over the barbed wire in the moonlight, they raised his determination to embark upon a similar sporting venture. If the breakout ever got as far as the bottom of the hill, the sentries were under instructions to awaken Dr. Dodger, and then Stephen would hear him clambering up the cell tiers to visit every prisoner, and make sure that he was safe. – "It's no good talking like that, my little cockatoo," Stephen heard him say to a man across the corridor. "Now just lie still and take your injection like a good lad." When Dr. Dodger came to his cell Stephen always pretended to be asleep, and his cellmates, who adored Dr. Dodger, monopolized Dr. Dodger's time anyhow, so that Dr. Dodger, seeing that he was appreciated, would do little dances on the window-ledge of the cell, and they'd all sing songs, except for Stephen Mole, who lay resentfully under his grey prison blanket.

In the mornings it was manual exercises; Stephen's cellmates all jerked off at quarter to ten, between the guard shifts. – "Bung ho!" they'd shout when they came. Stephen took no part in these festivities, glaring out the window with his little jailbird eyes that scared the sparrows when they fluttered by hoping to be thrown crumbs from the prison hardtack, which they often got because some cons were sentimental, and others thought it would be a smashing good idea to train the sparrows to carry messages – a far better method than the haphazard one universally adopted of tying their letters to rocks or bricks and heaving them out, hoping that someone would find them at the bottom of the hill before the rain made them illegible; in fact, the letters never even got that far, for the guards were all crack shots and enjoyed skeet-shooting at the bricks, shattering them in midair with a single shot. Of course you could bribe the letter boy, who sorted and brought round the letters punctually at eleven-fifteen every Saturday; he would deliver notes to the women's facility if you paid him in prison rum, which was made by collecting the raisins from your Sunday puddings and fermenting them in gobs of spit, which you had to keep in your cupped hands for weeks and weeks at a time, there being no drinking vessels allowed in the cells; but when it was finally done it was remarkably good; the trouble with sending letters, however, was that you just picked a number, as in the lottery; you had no idea what your woman actually looked like, and the letter boy, who enjoyed being a matchmaker, was a terrible liar, always telling you that she was beautiful and intelligent and had a lot of money hidden on Angel Island from her third robbery which the police knew nothing about, and she was also a virgin and had big boobs; he swore she wasn't a day over sixteen; and he told her that you had been married once but it hadn't worked out and you were looking for someone to settle down with when you got out; you had learned your lesson, and you wouldn't ever kill anyone again, and you were a fun guy and an ace card player and you were going to wait till she got out and then take her to your cabin in the mountains and live there playing the fiddle and drinking moonshine, and you'd never look at another woman until the day you died; and, oh yes, you were handsome, too; you'd had a chance to be a movie star once but they hadn't offered you enough money, and that was what got you started on your life of crime.

The location of Stephen's tunnel was not easy to decide. It would be useless to enter the main floor corridor at the officers' end, where the Shah of Iran was kept after his supposed death because Mr. White had a use for him after all this Khomeini stuff died down, and Stephen could not tunnel from his cell either because it was on the second floor and, besides, it was made out of steel. He needed access to the basement corridor, off which the cellars had originally been dug, especially the potato cellar, which Stephen could glimpse when he stood in the exercise courtyard by the cookhouse wall, peering through the line of men waiting for their parcels; he could see nothing but darkness and spiderwebs through that dirty window; and darkness and spiderwebs were exactly what he wanted to see; for the cook went there only once a day at 5:30 a.m., and nobody else ever went there, but the spiders stayed there, and the spiders were his allies. Although Stephen did not know it, potato-bugs also hid there. They had been there since the previous October. – For week after week, whenever he was allowed to take his exercise in the courtyard, Stephen watched the potato cellar window (as inconspicuously, of course, as he could), rubbing his back irritably against the wall of the cookhouse, through which diffused the oleaginous steam of the latest potato stew, which was made by boiling potatoes and dirt and horse skulls and whatever else the cook's scoop encountered when he rammed it into the mess in the potato cellar; at least it was always hot, thought Stephen sarcastically. – Finally he was satisfied. He decided to let his cellmates in on his plan.

"We're not talking to you 'till you give us a spot of roundeye!" cried Captain Dirk, and at this announcement, which to Stephen's jaded mind partook of tautology, all the others raised their right arms in Roman salute and cried, "Aye, me blighters!" – Cursing, Stephen bent over and pulled down his trousers. – "Now, what is it you be wanting, matey?" goes the sergeant-at-arms, all paternal-like, with an arm about Stephen's shoulders, while the others fondly tousle his hair. – "I need you to stand in line for parcels in front of the potato cellar window," said Stephen shortly. "I need you to block the line of sight there, if you don't mind." – "Oh, so he's a regular little escape artist!" exclaimed the lance corporal. "We don't have nothing against that, not a bit!" – "Put your bloody gob AT EASE!" cried Captain Dirk indignantly. He had the right of final say-so.

"How about it?" said Stephen, still not in much of a mood to be pleasant.

"Well, that was a right goober spot of bum," said Captain Dirk thoughtfully, "so we'll help you, won't we, men, and we won't report you, and we won't even ask for a reward. Now, flap your pancakes and give us a hint of your royal goal."

"I plan to tunnel east, then south," said Stephen. "*With* your permission."

"He's quite an efficient blackguard, what?" they marveled. "East, then south! That'll loop 'em for a drab of vinegar!"

So it was settled.

The next problem was what to do with the dirt displaced. The following Tuesday during exercise period, as he creaked open the potato cellar window and jumped inside, concealed behind the stolid legs of his cellmates, he investigated the situation, concluding that some soil could be spread nonchalantly around the potato cellar, but not enough, so that it was better to use that expedient as a final resort, when the tunnel was close to finished. Thoughtfully, he bolted the window shut and got to work. There was a stairway which the cook descended every morning to get at the potatoes, of which there were quite a lot; it was potatoes that Stephen was treading upon; the cellar was shoulder-deep in rotten grey potatoes; the stairs were heaped up with them, so under the stairs seemed like a superb site for the tunnel. He could hide the excavation behind a wall of potatoes! As quietly as he could, Stephen crawled behind the stairs, pried up the floorboards . . . and encountered concrete. He swore at the entire reactionary superstructure. – Concrete, however, was ultimately no obstacle for Stephen Mole, who had served with the infamous Bug; he came back out the window, accompanied his cellmates on exercise parade around the weathered gallows, which creaked in any high wind, and in due time returned to his cell. There was nothing for it but to make gunpowder. – To make the saltpeter, he and his cellmates urinated on rags, which they set up on the window-ledge to dry into tidy yellow crystals. After trading cigarettes for kitchen matches, an exchange considerably to the economic advantage of the turnkey, he broke the heads off all the matches save one. With the remaining match he reduced the other match-sticks to charcoal – the second ingredient required. The match-heads already contained pure sulphur – the third ingredient, so he was prepared. Crushing the saltpeter, charcoal and sulphur separately into powder with his shoe, he blew the three piles gently together and wrapped the powder in his pillowcase. Now he was prepared. – The following Friday, entering the potato cellar unobserved by his standard method, he blasted a hole in the concrete, and another in the north wall as well, while his cellmates sang "For He's A Jolly Good Fellow" as loud as they could to cover up the noise. Beyond the north wall was the baggage room; and for months he was able to hide the dirt in various prisoners' suitcases, the spiders obligingly getting some friendly wasps to dub in the blasted wall with a papier mâché *trompe l'œil* at the close of each session. When the suitcases were all jammed with dirt, he'd come back to his cell with pockets stuffed with it; then, as his cellmates stood between him and the spyhole on the door, he flushed it down the toilet. After three weeks, however, Dr. Dodger began popping in for surprise visits whenever the toilet flushed; evidently he suspected something; like Parker, he had a duty to suspect things; so Stephen began packing the earth under the potato cellar stairs.

Stephen had decided he could tunnel out to the vacant lot near the Safeway by Church and Duboce. Every Tuesday and Friday between morning and afternoon roll-calls his cellmates stood guard and he bolted himself into the cellar, digging deep into the moldy darkness behind the potatoes with a triangular bit of rag over his nose and mouth to keep him from choking on the smell of mice and stale air. Candles were made from the fat of prison-rats he killed with a slingshot constructed from one of Susan's garters, which she had given him as a love-token. (Dr. Dodger had let him keep it because it was too short for him to hang himself with.) – For the first month of tunneling he could hear the thudding of footsteps in the exercise yard just overhead, so he angled down deeper and deeper until he was below the concrete foundation of the cookhouse, which was clammy cement seeping with the steam of rotten prison stews; and Stephen continued to dig until the sandy yellow earth, formerly an obliging clay, like the lumpen-proletariat of Singapore, with which it was a real joy to work, abruptly became a stratum of closely pressed stones, which he was forced to loosen using the edge of a fifty-cent piece that one of his cell-mates had received for shining a guard's shoes, so that it frequently took days to loosen a single pebble, as meanwhile the rats ran squealing across his face, their eyes glowing in the candle-light, until he was almost sick with the smell of the brutes. They sometimes nipped him, and then he would heave his body against the side of the narrow tunnel with all his strength to crush them against him, and feeling them dying and dead upon him was almost worse than their bites. But Stephen was nothing if not ambitious. He made progress, stone by stone, putting the rocks into his pockets to carry back with him. – The prisoners were not supposed to have pockets in their clothing, but everyone who was anyone had them just the same; you paid the trusty a reefer or two to be a go-between for you; the men's section made license plates and street signs; prisoners on good behavior were allowed to make the funny customized plates for drivers who considered the fifty dollar surcharge an investment; so, my dear reader, if you are ever stuck in traffic on Highway 101 at around four in the afternoon and you look around you at the plates, you will probably see the Soviet ambassador in his black Cadillac, the license reading USSR OK; and if you continue your natural studies in the eastbound lane you may be rewarded with the incongruous sight of an old nicotine-wretch, puffing and trembling so hard that his thick glasses almost fall off, who has borrowed his Teutonic son-in-law's Toyota, the license plate reading GUY THOR, and when he observes your smile in his rear-view mirror he blushes miserably; well, the repentant murderers made those plates; but not Stephen Mole; he had to make IJP4956 or GLU7362, and any mistake was punished by ten days in solitary; it was, in short, not so different from any other job; there is only so far that they can punish you before they must get out the rack or make you drink piss in order to raise the agony differential; and it was not so bad in the license plate factory over the cookhouse, for the factory was illuminated by sparks from the grinding wheels, and always looked like Christmas thanks to the burned-out cables dipping from lathe to lathe like buntings; and the prisoners also had the joy of extracurricular craftsmanship; you could make shivs out of the scrap metal and hide them in your anus, careful to sit down very gingerly until you were back in your cell; and these were very useful for trade, since you always had somebody you hated whom it would be nice to stab in the showers; and in the women's prison the inmates sewed convict uniforms; they too had their feuds, so they would gladly make pockets for you if you gave them knives, and everybody was happy that way, including the trusty, who ended up with more cigarettes than a Virginia planta- tion; if he had cared to be a serious trader he coulda had himself a real future there among the criminal horde; and that was how Stephen Mole had his pockets. It took at least three hours to fill them with stones, given the cold cramped conditions and the lack of tools; when he couldn't jam any more rocks or loose earth into them then he wriggled backward, using knees and belly and elbows, until at last he could pull himself into his nook under the cellar stairs and then rub surplus earth onto the dirty potatoes and heave the rocks into the pile, so that the cook thought that the potatoes must have been there so long some of them had gotten petrified, but that was okay; petrified or not, they were probably still nutritious, so the rocks went into the soup just the same.

None of this activity was easy, as I am sure you can imagine, but the very misery and difficulty of it confirmed Stephen in his purpose, just as when Bug directed Stephen to smash something, he put his back into the job, which was infinitely, transcendentally and absolutely fortunate because Bug and freckled Milly, clever as they were, could never be strong (not that Milly ever slipped or failed to follow through on a punch); while Frank had long ago ruined his body through abuse of alcohol and junk food; only Susan attempted to be athletic in her way, doing pushups sporadically inside the Caves of Ice and running around breathlessly on raids confusing the issue so that sometimes Dr. Dodger would think for a second that Susan was twins or triplets on the monitors, but of course no one could be in three places at the same time as well as Dr. Dodger himself; Susan did not measure up in that department; and she didn't measure up to Stephen, who could haul a case of bombs on his back for miles, purple-faced and doubled over and breathing in short angry gasps while the sweat fell from his face; so the other revolutionaries regarded Stephen with uneasy deference, the way a woman who hates profanity but doesn't know how to change a tire will cringe when her husband fixes a flat on their vacation trip because he's going oh shit fucking goddamn bloody thing, but she doesn't browbeat him as she would under general circumstances, since she has no other way of getting to Petaluma; and similarly the Kuzbuites didn't hit Stephen the way they hit Frank and Susan; being pale marshmallow-people awed by real physiques, they had to compensate for their weakness by being smart (Bug and Milly) or obedient (Frank and Susan) or mechanically quick (Milly) or good with a gun (Bug, Milly and Susan). – All that Stephen had to do was destroy things, which is not to say that he did not have genteel long-sleeved aspirations, but I am talking here exclusively of his function in the movement. He was, as so few of us are, gifted with physical capabilities which harmonized with his soul, although unlike Wayne he couldn't do anything by violent carefree bounds; he always trudged grimly, as I said, and crushed things with a great straining effort.

In some prisons now you can go to a little trailer once every month if you have been good and, surrounded by armed guards, have sex with your wife; this was permitted to Stephen, who was known to be a pre-condemned man, so the guards figgered as long as he was gonna have to swing why not let him get his rocks off. Susan came there faithfully, disguised as a reactionary cheerleader, which was not so hard for her since she had been one; and in their twenty minutes together on the mattress she embraced him and asked him if he was still loyal to Bug's thought; and Stephen assured her that he was; strange to say he actually was now, for his was one of those natures which defies any imposition, and the reactionaries had imposed upon him considerably this time; in the Arctic Bug had always been careful to give Stephen his own head as much as possible, like a spirited horse; that way Stephen would do more for the cause; yes, Bug was a clever politician. – Stephen got on top of Susan and whispered to her how much progress he had made. "Three more feet since last month!" he'd say, conversing in ant-language in case Dr. Dodger was listening; and then Susan would hug him and say, "I'm very proud of you, because you're working every minute for Bug and his ideals!" and Stephen would whisper, "When I'm out I'm going to smash this filthy electric setup!" and then Susan would go, "My big Sandino!" and then the armed guards would tap on the windowpane to inform them that the twenty minutes was up.

Quaint little spectacled experts from Washington came to search the prison grounds from time to time, but they never found anything. Parker would have picked up what was going on at once through judicious use of the Great Enlarger, but he, of course, had been temporarily neutralized through the Caterpillar Heart. Wayne was off on his labors. So the tunneling continued. By Halloween Stephen had succeeded in tunneling east of the outer wall. The streetcar clattered over his head; he could tell from the pitch whether it was an N Judah or a J Church. Now he had only a block and a half to go. – At this point, however, he encountered a moldy old stone wall, evidently the remains of a fortress built by the Spanish; and for a week he thought that his project would have to be aborted, for he could not even scratch those massive boulders with his quarter; the bugs could not help him, either, because most of the big beetles had been called to Florida in preparation for an assault upon a farm town in Ohio which had a lot of wormy apples; but Stephen received unexpected assistance from – the snakes. Remember them? There were prison guards and there were prison-drudges and there were prison-bugs and there were prison-snakes – for the snakes still survived, though no longer green and jovial the way they had been in the Amazon days of Big George, to be sure; now the last holdouts from electricity, they were slender, sickly-grey worms, patterned by rectangular brick-border camouflage upon their wormy scales. In the old days you could have had sliding panels in your cell to go out to your mistress, false bottoms in your dresser drawers, and so forth, allowing you to conduct your own life in a seemly private fashion (if you were an aristocrat), but all that had been done away with here, and the prison snakes were one of the few surviving secrets from the administration. Needless to say, the snakes had grudges against electricity, for there were hardly any rain forests anymore; for the most part it was desert in South America now, hard-packed beneath the bare brown feet of refugees, and cratered where Wayne dropped bombs every Sunday; therefore the snakes had to live on prison rats and make despicable homes in the prison pipes and work their bodies operosely into the mortar between the clammy walls, so that they became slimy for the first time in ophidian history, and flickered their wet grey tongues in a lost way that touched Stephen when he saw it; so they mourned their jungles, and when they understood that he was a fighter against electricity, they burrowed into the joints of the ruined wall and loosened the stones for him, so that he could continue his tunnel; though perhaps they would not have done so had they been aware that Stephen was allied with the bugs, for they suffered not only from gout, thanks to the cold wet walls in which they lived, but also from parasitic flukes, which their wrinkled reptile-brains associated with bugs, both being inedible from their point of view; I am sad to say that the snakes' perceptions had decayed markedly since those royal days when, as Topsell says in his *Serpents* (1653), they were "conceived of themselves by the help of the sun," when now they could barely navigate their coils among the dead bones and dogstones in the surly earth; but the snakes were still gracious, so when Stephen had gotten past the fortress wall they raised their sad grey tails to say goodbye and wormed back up toward warmer walls. After that he did not see the snakes again, and neither shall we, for in my book they have now completed their political destiny. Their assistance was something that Stephen never told the revolutionaries about. He did not want

Milly to accuse him of consorting with unreliable elements. – Meanwhile he kept digging.

Time dragged slowly before the trial. Sometimes Stephen would remember how nice it was away from prison. He recalled the photo galleries in the Mission, the art cafes, the restaurants. He made a mental list of all the restaurants that he had ever been to and tried to figure out what he had ordered at each one. He remembered the day he had eaten his first Dodger's Surprise, with the brown flaky dough still steaming from the oven (you didn't break out in pimples until the next day). He compared the merits of Double Rainbow ice cream with those of Bott's. He tried to number all the beers he had drunk at Howard's up on Ninth and Irving, where you can sit in a booth and watch the waitresses working for you, Lydia hurrying to bring you free refills of coffee, smiling at your jokes, even tired Lucille who will soon quit, fanning themselves with the napkins they bring you, sitting down all pink and sweaty for a second at the counter to watch the sports or the westerns that entertain you soundlessly on the corner screen; at seven-thirty on a Saturday morning when you order an omelette and a beer you will see a pale arm reach over the partition that screens the kitchen help from your gaze, and the hand at the end of the arm will turn on the TV and then retreat and go back to cutting up potatoes for your hash browns. – Howard himself sits there most days, most nights, the fat white-headed old guy, watching the TV, winking at the waitresses and chuckling with his cronies while everyone has a good time and eats; even the waitresses nibble at the black bottom pie. On Friday nights and Sunday nights Lydia brings the half pound special with Swiss, cheddar, fries, a salad, a Beck's dark, a Bud and a Michelob; and Sunday mornings Lucille touches your shoulder when she puts the fresh-squeezed grapefruit juice on the table. – Sometimes, burrowing endlessly, as it seemed, into the earth, Stephen pretended that the earth was a great big chocolate cake from Howard's, just to keep his spirits up, but then another rat would scuttle across his forehead . . .

The day of Stephen's trial had now arrived. Mr. White wanted to send Stephen to the scaffold, and a very pretty picture he would make there, too, all dolled up in his red-and-white xerox boy livery. Dr. Dodger was of course willing to accept Mr. White's views without question. – He was transported to the courtroom in a black van. All around him the San Francisco weather was going on, Indian summer stretching through November, December, the sky being a stainless blue illuminated by some white summer brighter than the white buildings and yellow buildings with white-trim windows, the red-brick buildings against the sky so clean, silver pipes jutting into the sky with white stripes of sunlight on them where the sky had touched them. Everything was as pure as a desert dawn where one can see all the way to the twenty-mile horizon, frosted dew on the sleeping bag evaporating soundlessly; it would be another fiery perfect day, indistinguishable from the last; the time would run on and on. – The van pulled up at the court building smartly. Stephen was handcuffed to two policemen who smelled like Old Spice deodorant and led through a metal detector. – One of the policemen, who had moderate views, offered him a cigarette. – "Thanks, but no thanks," said Stephen bitterly. "I see through your strategy." – The police both shrugged.

The lobby was dimly lit, the better to spare the vulnerable feelings of trembling-lipped caseworkers who could be seen wending their shrinking way through this mass of unshaven screws and lags, like Stephen tunneling through the earth, with an occasional mild-mannered train thief awaiting sentencing by the phone. Stephen saw sweating businessmen in the elevators, legs gamely spread, clutching thick bundles of documents to their lower abdomens as pairs of police lounged behind. There was a nervous queasy smell inside the building, mingled with the smell of old smoke. His escort let him sit down on a bench opposite Department 16, where he would be sentenced. The bench was deeply carved with graffiti. Stephen made out the following aphorisms, announcements and postulates: EAT MONEY, DISCO SUCKS, IRENE IS MY BITCH and BEAT THE NIGGER. – It was the lunch hour. Officials strolled lethargically along the gold-ruled marble corridors, waving their fingers at each other like the wings of whooping cranes. Other defendants sat further down the hall, waiting patiently for the hour of one. – The two policemen lit cigarettes and puffed, wedging Stephen in tightly between their massive thighs. The rightmost policeman's holster dug into his flesh, but it was not an uncomfortable sensation; rather, like the pressure of a heavy blanket, it made him drowsy, so he let his head go back against the wall and closed his eyes, ignoring his unsought companions. Overhead, square white lights marched down the ceiling evenly, giving the blue globes windows on the situation.

"All right, you," said the cops finally. "Let's go visit his Honor." – They took him round the back way and manacled him to the sentencing post while they took turns at the water fountain, drinking until their blue-uniformed bellies bulged out. Then his handcuffs were removed, so that he could gesture freely when called upon by the prosecutor. – Stephen's lip curled at the setup, which was certainly inefficient compared to Milly's revolver justice. But his tunnel would soon teach the reactionaries a lesson. – With that thought his well-being, and therefore his rage, began to return.

The courtroom was very bright and full of wood paneling. Everyone filed in at 12:57. – "This is really ridiculous," Stephen heard another felon say in the back row. "I've never been in a situation like this." – "Over here, you," said Stephen's escort, sitting him down in the dock. Stephen glared round defiantly. – Now the deputies came in, walkie-talkies clipped to their belts, and waved at the two policemen who sat flanking Stephen. – "Howdy, boys," said one of the deputies. "Looks like you've got yourselves a *mean* barracuda." – At this Stephen showed his teeth in a glower. – Stephen's escort nodded, suddenly full of self-importance. – "Do you recognize Stephen Mole?" said the righthand stenographer formally. – The deputies looked at Stephen doubtfully for a moment. "Yes, I guess that's him," one of them said finally. "Looks like he's lost some weight, though." – "The basic rule," coughed the judge, still over by the wall, "is that we can only excuse people for health reasons." – The deputies sighed. "Guess he'll have to swing, then," they said regretfully. – "Strike that from the record!" cried Stephen indignantly, and at this unexpected comment the stenographers tittered, writing each other's giggles down in shorthand, the old-fashioned way. No one took any notice.

The judge marched back up to his bench. "Please come to order," he said. Everyone looked up brightly. "Now," said the judge, pleased at the attention, "is there anything to straighten out?" – "I think Mr. Winters should sit in seat number three," said the prosecutor. "After all, he is the third juror, is he not?" – "I don't believe it makes any difference where Mr. Winters sits," countered the defense attorney, a dishwater-complexioned youth in black coat-and-tails. – "According to the electrical code you're both right," said the judge, "so let's forget it. Now, Mr. Winters, perhaps you can tell me a little about yourself." – "I am an expert in bodily fluids," replied Mr. Winters truculently. He was a tall blond man who wore ski goggles. – "So, in your opinion is this a urinistic or a fecalistic case?" snapped the prosecutor. – "Your Honor, I object to this questioning," said the defense attorney. – "Sustained," said the judge agreeably. – "Have you read the current literature regarding the effects of ideology on hormones?" said the prosecutor. Mr.

Winters nodded. "I think we should eliminate hormones and have professional jurors," he said to the judge, "because that would certainly save me all this legal foreplay." – The judge sighed. "It's apparent this trial's going to take some time," he said. "Will that fact cause you economic hardship, Mr. Winters?" – Mr. Winters leaned forward to emphasize the point that he was about to make. "Your Honor," he said, "my hands have been clammy on account of all the revenue I've lost today. Besides, I don't give a damn about that Mole clown. And I think bugs stink!"

Stephen sat folding and unfolding his arms in the dock, his ears red with rage. Sometimes he leaned his cheek on his hand, shaking his head.

"Given Mr. Winters' strong views on bugs," ruled the judge, "I will excuse him from this case. Let us now examine Miss Allen." – "Miss Allen, you were late for roll call!" said the prosecutor fiercely. "Have you any explanation to make?" – "No," said Miss Allen sweetly. – The judge leaned back in his chair. "Miss Allen, do you understand that you're here just to determine the facts of the case and not to determine the punishment?" he said. – "Yes, Your Honor," said Miss Allen. – "In case of a positive crime or blood test for ideology, would you have any hesitancy in returning a verdict of guilty?" said the prosecutor. – "I would welcome such a verdict," said Miss Allen, glaring at Stephen. – Stephen rested his forehead on his middle finger and glared back. – "You'll do," the judge was saying. "Now, how about you, Mr. Bell?" – "I have no tolerance," said Mr. Bell. "You be a bug, I couldn't care less; that's my attitude. It's totally unfair to be a bug around innocent people." – "Have you ever seen a bug stopped by law enforcement officers?" said the defense attorney, winking at Stephen in a decidedly sordid way. – "No, and I wouldn't care to," said Mr. Bell. – "Pass for cause, Your Honor," said the prosecutor. – "Fine," said the judge.

"Your Honor, we are now satisfied with the jury," said both attorneys.

"Well," said the judge, "my wife said there was going to be trouble if I wasn't home right after lunch, so I guess there's going to be trouble. I'm telling you right now, Stephen Mole, you'd better sing pretty sweet if you don't want to get your wings clipped and be locked into a golden cage."

"He's in for some kind of assault and battery or something," one of Stephen's guards whispered to the other. – Stephen simply glared at the judge, whom he was sure he could have shot dead in a fair fight.

"We'll get you off," said the defense attorney directly to Stephen, but he did not look sanguine.

"Oh, the hell with all this," said the judge, suddenly losing his patience. "Stephen Mole, I sentence you to be hanged from the neck until dead, sentence to be executed next Friday at dawn."

"I expected no less," said Stephen in disdain, but this infuriated the judge, who snapped, "And we're going to use piano wire to punish your contempt of court!"

And so Stephen was returned to prison. He had only two exercise days in which to complete his escape if he wished to avoid the Long Drop. – "You'll be allowed to stay with your cellmates until Thursday night," said Dr. Dodger, "because we won't have a vacancy on Death Row until then, but once we squeeze you in you'll be required to maintain the strictest monastic discipline, young man, the number of licks for any violation not to exceed ten lashes with Black Annie here," and Dr. Dodger showed Stephen a long thin strap of dark beef hide or beef jerky. "You may smoke in the condemned cell if you apply for five lashes in advance. I recommend the lashes, because as your physician I can assure you that they will prevent the piano wire from hurting so badly. What do you say?" And Dr. Dodger eyed Stephen brightly. – "No, thanks," said Stephen gloutishly. – "Very well, then into the cell with you!"

On Tuesday afternoon Stephen decided to make a mole-hole to the surface to see how close he was. Through the minute aperture, in which he could see a finger's width of blue sky, he thrust a wad of white cloth. – When he looked out the window of his cell that evening, he was dismayed to see that it had surfaced in one of the flowerpots on the Safeway parking lot. Ahead lay a quarter-acre of asphalt, brightly lit by street lamps, then a stout sidewalk, which might as well have been a mountain range above a digger's back, for he had no more explosives, and no more time to make them. – There was nothing for it but to abandon the tunnel and go over the roof. Flexible tactics are essential to the prosecution of successful special operations.

On Wednesday night he made the first attempt. The plan was to fuse the lights somehow and get over the wire, then run for it. The cell block doors were locked at nine p.m. Stephen waited until the outer doors had slammed and the key had turned in the lock, and then he stripped himself to the waist and clenched a shiv knife in his teeth. – "Thundering good sport!" yelled his cellmates. (They could have escaped, too, if they had chosen, but they were now institutionalized individuals). "He sure is doing the Janice, is he not?" they cried admiringly. It was their highest compliment. "A rotten sight better than a brace of geoduck clams!" – "Thank you for your flattery," said Stephen, not without sarcasm. It was his conviction that they were only after his ass. (Here, however, he was unjust, for they were fine fellows who genuinely wished him well now that they had gotten what they wanted from him.)

To cover his escape, the Britons created a diversion, singing out one of their favorite political melodies, "Things Is Weak In Electric Creek," while pounding their bed-posts in time with their red hairy fists. Unfortunately, Dr. Dodger heard, and swung himself up the tier to sing along all evening, for it happened to be one of his favorite songs, making him feel like a real rebel. Thus the escape had to be postponed.

It was now Thursday morning, twenty-one hours before his scheduled execution. In the exercise courtyard he was crowded by the video people taking zoom closeups of his face with loathsome familiarity, while the verbally inclined newsmen and newswomen asked him questions such as, "Mr. Mole, how does it feel to be the first celebrity to be hanged with piano wire since the July '44 conspirators?" – "No comment," said Stephen bitterly. "Words cannot express my disgust for all you stand for." – "Mr. Mole, what are your thoughts on the afterlife?" said the reporters. – "Mr. Mole, could you say a few words to our viewers about your crimes?" – "Mr. Mole, do you intend to donate your body to science?" – Finally Dr. Dodger came to shoo the reporters away, waggling his fingers and rolling his eyes as he said, "Now, we mustn't tire our Stevie before his big ordeal," and he whisked Stephen back to his cell. He sat despondently on his bunk until noon. – His last chance to tunnel was gone, and he did not know how he was going to break out of the cell block. Had he been imprisoned for burglary, he might perhaps have constructed a skeleton key from bits of brass, ebonite, steel, bone and cabbage leaves, clicking back the last tumbler with a pair of tweezers and then dashing toward the main gate, but Stephen was not a burglar and he had no tweezers, anyhow. He knew the odds of his pulling it off were bad; had he only his survival drive to rely upon, he doubtless would have gone to the gallows; but inspiring him was his lethal resentment of Mr. White and Dr. Dodger; as he sat glowering on his cot, he made a striking figure, impressing even Dr. Dodger, who had come to peek excitedly through the keyhole, for Dr. Dodger was thrilled to think that soon through his agency Stephen would be forced to undergo an irrevocable process.

It was now 12:15, and Stephen's cellmates returned from their exercise, whistling tunes of the King James Royal Guards to cheer Stephen, whom they pitied due to the collapse of his tunnel scheme; and finally it was lunchtime; and all the cell doors snapped open electronically so that Stephen and the other cons could be marched down narrow brick halls in groups of five separated by pairs of guards, passing every fifty paces through barred gates which had been installed to contain hypothetical riots, and the cons went straight down narrow stairs, trailing their fingers along the cool greasy walls, and so came into the dining hall. – Stephen resolved to make his escape here or perish. He signaled discreetly to a louse he saw in the scalp of the prisoner directly ahead of him. The louse responded at once, summoning her relatives until there were dozens of the creatures massing on the crown of the man's head; then Stephen jostled the man, as if by mistake, and in that instant of contact the lice flowed across Stephen's arms, like electrons speeding along a wire, and secreted themselves in his clothes, not biting him because he was their ally. – The prisoner had meanwhile turned to him and said, "I saw you bump me, Jewbug, but since you swing tomorrow you can do no wrong," and Stephen thanked him, though not, perhaps, unambiguously.

The dining hall was a dark dirty place containing long steel tables and matching steel benches with ankle-manacles. The men filed into rows behind the benches and stood there awaiting the command to be seated; nothing delighted Dr. Dodger as much as the simultaneous snap of ten thousand anklets; but Stephen's lice were at this moment crawling into his assigned manacles and eating the machine oil inside and cramming themselves into every joint, so that when Dr. Dodger finally marched into the room and cried, "Gentlemen, be seated!" and all the prisoners sat down and put their legs sullenly into the irons and the hall echoed with clicking, Stephen's manacles did not fully close, being jammed with lice, who, in the unhesitating manner of bugs, had died that he might carry on the class struggle; hence Stephen was a step closer to freedom. – Now the dully efficient warders came round, ladling blackish potato soup into the metal gutters that ran along the table; and the convicts rubbed their stubbly jaws and looked round with their shifty eyes to see if they could somehow steal their neighbors' portion and sell it; and there was a rattling and a clattering as the cons pulled their spoons as far as the chains would reach and started bolting their food. – Stephen shook a stone out of his pocket and laid it softly in the stew in front of him. Then he raised his hand. – A guard came over leisurely. "What's your beef, Bub?" – Stephen indicated the stone. "I got a piece of meat this time," he said. "Could you please cut it for me?" – "Cut yer bloody meat for yer?" sneered the guard. "I've seen emperors chew on tougher cuts than *that* chop, so just chew it up and none of your cunting nonsense!" – "Chew it yourself," said Stephen, and at this provocation the guard stepped into range, raising his truncheon while the other cons looked down at their plates; and Stephen leaped out of his anklets, grabbed the truncheon, and brought it smashingly down on the guard's ear; then he began to run toward the window, swinging the truncheon. – For a moment there was a dead silence, then Dr. Dodger jumped up frantically, crying, "Oh, no; not *you*, you treacherous little Stevie!" – and Stephen, turning his head to shoot a glance at Dr. Dodger, saw that Dr. Dodger was unbuttoning his greatcoat, probably to get to his gun, so Stephen hurled the truncheon at Dr. Dodger, seeing it hit just right, so that Dr. Dodger fell backwards, hitting his yellow head on the floor, and all the convicts cheered; then Stephen hit the wall hard and pulled himself up to the window by the bars, thinking, if the other guards have guns I'll have to stop, but whether or not they had guns he couldn't tell yet, for they were still nonplussed, Dr. Dodger having suffered a mild concussion and therefore being unable to give them orders; but at last they began shouting and gathered around Dr. Dodger, and one activated the escape hooter, *a-WHOOOH!*; but then they started coming after him; and seconds were passing while Stephen tried to loosen the window-bars . . . There was a giant tiger-beetle on the other side of the window. It smashed through the glass with the sides of its mandibles and bent the bars back for Stephen, who squeezed through, cutting himself badly, and clambered up the outer wall just as the guards began to shoot.

The escape hooter was making a maddening clamor; all the guards in the watchtowers were swiveling their machine guns around at him; and they started shooting with a rapid sputter that knocked tiles off the roof, and Stephen ran along the rooftop as fast as he could, leaving the tiger-beetle to be caught in the gunfire, and jumped down into the courtyard, seeing no other option; and the four perimeter guards shouted and got up from their deck chairs and took aim at him with their rifles, so Stephen threw himself through the potato cellar window in a crash of glass and ducked under the stairs where his unfinished tunnel was, hunting through the spuds for the small stones he had secreted there; and then he ran out from under the stairs again, breathing hard, and slammed his body into the wall beneath the broken window, just as the first bullets started to whicker into the potatoes, for they had gotten the range. They would be feeling secure now; they would think they had him pinned. – He took out the slingshot that he had made from Susan's garter and fitted the first stone to it, not yet pulling the elastic taut; then with the palm of his right hand he nudged a large potato just over the top of the sill, keeping his hand well down. – Bullets screamed into the potato at once, splintering the wood of the sill and thunking into the potatoes all around him; there would be hell to pay in subsequent stews. – Stephen roared as if he had been hit, and lay still. He heard a whistle, a shout, and then silence. They would be reloading now to finish him off. – He drew the stone back now until the elastic was stretched as far as it should go, then he raised his head just enough to see the guard in the turret directly opposite him, and he aimed, and let the stone go just as the guard shouted. There was a scream and a crash. The guard had fallen into the courtyard, blood streaming from the new eye which Stephen had just put in his forehead, and then there was a silence. The guard would be dying now. Three more to go before he could break out. If he could only get to the body, he could pry the machine gun from the guard's clawing fingers, and *then* he'd show cover to these ready racks of racketeers ... – He smashed through the false partition, into the luggage room, which brought him literally into the shadow of the gallows, not far from where the guard lay in the sand; and Stephen knocked out the window with two pebbles from his slingshot and threaded his way through the suitcases. By the window he stacked up a wall of them, the ones he had filled up with dirt when he had been tunneling. They'd be as good as sandbags. Then he began to shake the other suitcases out, looking for something that might help him get the guard's weapon – and as he did so he heard many footsteps coming down the stairs to the potato cellar door. Any second they would open the door. – No! They were shooting straight through it! – Stephen lay low behind his wall of suitcases. The bullets came through the partition and went out the far wall of the luggage room up toward the ceiling. Their aim was poor. – They probably knew that he was in the luggage room now because he had smashed the window. – Here they came, another detachment marching down the steps to the luggage room door, and began shooting from behind it. Soon there were cries of agony from both sides. This was what happened when one followed orders. But to Dr.

Dodger, who had recovered consciousness and was now popping up everywhere that he could to direct the battle, the casualties would be well worth it if a stray shot bagged Stephen. Dr. Dodger was to be disappointed here, however, for Stephen continued to stay low and move quietly. The bullets did not come very close to him. He built a second wall of suitcases and retreated between it and the window sill, still rummaging through the untouched luggage for something that he could use, dumping out tennis rackets, underwear, rings, shoes, belts – here was a belt that might do, one of those long black leather belts with nail-studs and a big triangular buckle, so prevalent in our sadomasochistic community. – Stephen knotted it to three more belts to increase the length, flexed it, and swung it through the window like a bullwhip so that it stretched itself out into the courtyard, the buckle inches from the dead guard. He began to flail the belt until he had knocked the machine gun out of the guard's hands. Then, very delicately, he twisted the belt onto its side and drew the buckle up around the barrel of the machine gun, which looked like a Thompson Portable, just as the surviving three guards, seeing his intention, started firing again, trying to riddle the belt with holes to make it unusable; and now the guard on the turret directly opposite him stuck out his tongue and started shooting directly into Stephen's window, so that Stephen had to duck under the sill and continue to slide the buckle up the barrel of the guard's Thompson by feel, as the belt jerked from the impact of the rounds going into it and the ground shuddered; the leather was bound to part soon. At last he felt the buckle click against the trigger guard. Piling two dirt-filled suitcases up onto the sill, and leaving an inch-wide gap between them, he peered through the improvised slit-window to oversee the tricky last stage of the manipulation, and thwacked the belt sideways with exactly the right amount of force so that the buckle jammed around the trigger guard. Then he pulled the Thompson slowly across the sand, sorry that he had to abuse such a nice weapon that way, but this was, as Stephen was aware, war. – The gun tumbled down into his window as bullets ricocheted off it, splintering the stock. He settled the butt comfortably against his shoulder and fired three rounds into each of the two sentry-boxes that he had a clear sightline to, grinding his teeth in triumph as he felt the jolting against his shoulder and the ringing in his ears; the two guards went down, shot in the chest, for hatred will always triumph; and so much for monopoly trusts! – There was still one guard directly above his head. The guard could not see him or shoot at him as long as Stephen remained in the luggage room; neither could Stephen shoot at the guard. But it was only a matter of moments before the reactionaries came down in force; they had stopped shooting each other from behind their respective doors, and he could hear whisperings, which boded no good. It occurred to him to shoot a burst at each group, but then they would have a better idea of his position, so he decided to let them alone until they came in. Hopefully he would be gone by then. During the time he was thinking these things, he took a necktie from one of the suitcases and knotted it through the swivel on the Thompson, forming a crude sling, which he looped around his shoulder; then he made a dash out the window for the gallows, ducking beneath a crosspiece because he expected the surviving guard to let loose a long burst now, but there was no sound save his own breathing, so he lined up the guard in the scope and saw that the man was covered with grey prison ants swarming into his mouth and nose to suffocate him; for the bugs helped their own. – Stephen was grudgingly impressed. Maybe Bug's ideology was as sound as Milly claimed. He put the crosshairs on the image of the guard's chest and pulled the trigger carefully. The man fell forward; the ants continued eating him, just to be sure. – Stephen ascended the gallows, panting, seized the noose of piano wire they had put up for him, hoisted himself up and swung back and forth, *woing!* in ever widening sweeps, until finally he came near enough one of the turrets to jump for it. There was a moment of flying through space (*Flugsein*), and then he landed on the platform, almost completely winded, the Thompson banging hard on the railing; and he rested for a moment and then spun round and sent five rounds into the potato cellar, doubting that he had killed anyone but hopeful that that would keep them from coming out into the courtyard. There was no return fire, perhaps because they had not yet broken into the cellar; so far the escape was going well, but now, he knew, they would be passing out the heavy siege guns; the wardens would be wheeling them down the prison corridors to the windows; their field of fire would be good inside, too, because the prisoners were still leg-manacled to their benches in the dining hall. – Beside him lay one of the dead sentries. He stripped the sentry's Kalashnikov of its banana magazine and thumbed the bullets out. Then he reloaded his own magazine. The barrel of the Thompson was hot enough to burn his hand.

The platform was about two feet below the roof. He slid the barrel up over the lip of the roof, staying low, and emitted a short burst between the two watchtowers. – There, he thought grimly; that ought to make them keep their heads down. Soon they would call in the gunship helicopters. – He took a deep breath, and another. Then, biting his lip, he pulled himself up onto the roof and sprinted, ducking his head. He could see the city below him. There was a burst of fire, a little high, and he flung himself onto his belly and replied with ten rounds on single burst. He was pretty sure that he had gotten the sentry in that watchtower. Looking through the scope, he saw the door swing open as the sentry's body slumped against it, the way a clamshell will gape wide after the stubborn clam has been boiled. The body swayed and then tumbled out, bouncing down the hill in the direction of the Safeway, and coming to rest against the barbed wire by the N Judah stop. – Stephen sent a short burst into each of the other watchtowers out of general principles. He could hear pounding feet in the building below him. He slid along the roof on his belly, pausing now and then to fire. He thought, I could still stop now; the worst they could do is hang me; but, dismissing that unworthy thought, he made it to the north end of the building, on the opposite side from the main gate, so that they couldn't let off their thirty-pounders at him without destroying the jail, took out the three watchtowers in range, jumped down the side of the building, shoulder-rolling to the rim of the hill just beside the married hangmen's quarters (and he glimpsed one of the hangmen's wives shaking her fist at him), slid down the hill, clambered over the barbed wire, and ran around the block into the Fillmore district. He knew that the Thompson would guarantee him an instant welcome.

Later the evening came. Beautiful white ovals (raindrops) hung from the undersides of the black telephone wires.

"Jack," screamed Dr. Dodger on the phone, totally crushed. "He escaped! Stephen Mole did, oh, yes!"

"Groovy," said Mr. White sarcastically. "That's just wonderful, Dodger. You'd better report to my office with a whole cord of switches, because I'm gonna break them over your back!"

A few days later an electrical engineering student called to report the theft of his car. "I understood his name was Stephen Anderson, but when they stopped him his name was Stephen Mole," a beetle heard the nice young man say. The beetle was in the mouthpiece of the receiver, so it could hear only one half of the conversation. – "I own a car with California license number TCF301. I drove to Sacramento with this guy and we got separated at this house of ideological ill repute and I didn't know where my keys were and when the Vice Squad stopped him outside they found he had the keys. Before they could arrest him he got into my car and gunned it, they said, and drove off into the mountains."

FRANK GETS FIRED

~~~~~~

Nobody is fooled into thinking business is a democracy – they *know* it's a dictatorship. Take action fast! Out! Treat the person nicely. Make a generous settlement.

Boardroom Reports (vol. 12, no. 15: 1 August 1983)

For Mr. White everything seemed to have passed the high point and to be hastening toward the abyss. This was no time for half-measures. The gravest and most ruthless decisions would have to be made.

"Frank, do you have a few minutes?" said Mr. White, looking quite imposing in his grey suit and black tie.

"Yes," said Frank.

They went into Mr. White's office. When Mr. White shut the door Frank knew that something bad was about to happen.

"Have a seat," said Mr. White wearily. "How ya doin'?"

"Fine," said Frank. "How are you?"

"So-so," said Mr. White, looking at his watch. "Frank, we're consolidating the company and we've had to make some hard decisions lately. As of today, you're no longer working for the Society of Daniel. I want you out of the building by noon. Your insurance coverage terminates at midnight. Now, do you have any company property?"

"No," said Frank.

"Then sign this."

Frank signed.

"Any keys?"

"No," said poor Frank.

"Give me your badge."

Frank unclipped his badge. Mr. White took it and snipped it in two with steel shears.

"Any questions?" said Mr. White.

"How many people are getting fired in the consolidation?" asked Frank, figuring that the higher the number was, the less of a purely personal humiliation this would be.

"That doesn't concern you," said Mr. White. "We're talking about what's happening to Frank Fairless here. Now, here's the information sheet for terminated employees, and good luck to you."

As Frank came back into the warren of cubicles, the other programmers popped out of their hutches and said, "What happened?" – Frank, remembering something Mr. White had said, replied, "It's not a layoff. It's a permanent reduction in force." – The programmers turned away, whispering. Frank was now an outcast. – "They fired me," Frank explained to Hannah, whose cubicle faced his. All day, Frank used to stare into his mirror-polished screen and watch Hannah's reflection cross her silken legs or comb her hair or adjust her skirt. Now these tranquil times had ended.

"Maybe I'll be next," gulped Hannah. – In fact she was. Here came Mr. White. He tapped Hannah's shoulder, led her into his office, and shut the door.

Frank remembered how he had watched when others had been fired; so it seemed fair not to expect sympathy. He used to come in early and tune in his terminal to find an electric mail message waiting for him like some ghost too insignificant to vanish at cockcrow; and the message was a thankyou/goodbye/SYSOUT=A from another terminated person, sometimes despairing, sometimes reeking of sad bravado, like last letters home from those captured by the Great Beetle ("Don't you *dare* remarry; 'cause remember that I'm dying for *you* and *Mr. White* and our *national blue globes!*"); and already as Frank read those beeping farewells, the faces of his castaway co-workers dwindled shimmering in his memory, like his own faint pastel reflection in the foil wrapper of a Hershey bar, that chocolate coffin; and Frank went to the vending machine and bought more candy, groping in his pockets for more and more quarters; now he saw his colleagues turn their backs to him and send a deputation to the vending machine.

The firings went on all morning. The programmers milled around in a panic, like chickens earmarked for the chopping block. The Society of Daniel building buzzed with the sound of sobbing, farewell back-slappings, openings and closings of desk drawers, crumplings of computer printouts, and portentous rippings as posters and pictures were torn down. Then Dr. Dodger marched up and down the aisles, collecting the plastic nameplates of those terminated. – Gradually it became clear that only the lower-level employees were being let go. The survivors huddled at the north window, their backs turned to what was going on so that Mr. White would not think that they deserved to be fired, too. Returning his supplies to the cabinet, Frank tiptoed near that line of forbidding backs, listening to the rumors: – "Kay said they fired everyone who forgot a badge today." – "You'll notice I have *my* badge on." – "Well, I heard it was because one of the salesmen – " – "He deserved it. Everyone knows he didn't work very hard." – "Hannah brought it on herself, too. She was late last week." – Now Dr. Dodger made his rounds of the cubicles again, posting computer banners every fifty feet that said: GENERAL MEETING AT 3:00. Of course Frank would never know what happened at the general meeting, because he had to be out at 12:00 sharp. – His desk was now emptied. He went upstairs to turn in his last time card. "Goodbye forever," he said to the payroll secretary, who had often taken messages for him. – "You got laid off?" she said. – "Yes," said Frank. – "Well, make sure you're out by noon or I'll have to call the police," she said.

Frank promised that he would.

Mr. White, Dr. Dodger and some beetle-headed manager or other who had infiltrated stood out in the parking lot together all morning with arms folded, watching the fired employees leave. L.Z. Hsu, who had had a cubicle next to Frank's, was going to give Frank a ride to the Fremont rapid transit since Frank had a large box of effects to carry. Soon it would be time to walk past the managers in the parking lot. – "Are you ready?" said L.Z. – "Yes," said Frank. "Thank you for your help." – "But this is O.K.!" said L.Z., drawing himself up stiff. "This happens only once in a lifetime!" – "I hope so," said Frank sadly (knowing, however, that as a double agent he would undoubtedly experience many more of these episodes). – L.Z. carried Frank's box out into the parking lot where the three managers stood waiting.

"You have been a real gentleman!" said L.Z.

"Thank you," said Frank.

"I LIKE YOUR PERSONALITY!" L.Z. screamed suddenly. L.Z. had been in the army in Taiwan and still preserved many military mannerisms.

"Thank you," said Frank.

The managers were staring at Frank and L.Z. – Frank waved.

"So long," he said. – "See you," Mr. White muttered. The other managers stared down at the asphalt.

Frank and L.Z. got into L.Z.'s fancy car and L.Z. drove away. Frank never saw the Society of Daniel again.

When he got home, he unpacked his box of office papers and lay down on the rug, watching the fog ooze around the telephone poles. What was he to do? – Frank decided that he had better go file for unemployment right away.

He looked in the yellow pages and found the address. It was down on Mission and Army. It took him an hour to get there on the bus, though of course that was all right since now he had all the time in the world. At the front desk they gave him a blue slip and some forms. – "Come back at one tomorrow," they said. "Room 33."

That night Frank filled out the forms as best he could. Some of them were difficult to figure out, but he did his utmost. – This was the first time that he had really missed Bug, for he knew that Bug would have understood the forms to perfection, utilizing each field of each box in the most scientific way; but Frank had isolated himself as a result of his treachery, and he had to forge on, lying on his dusty living room rug scratching his fleabites with a leaky ballpoint; and the carbon paper stained his sweaty hands. The next day he rode the bus down to Mission and Army again. It took him an hour and a half. He had expected to have a private interview with some wheezing, unsympathetic administrator in a grey office, but instead he found himself one of a hundred people waiting on the threshold of Room 33, for in these austere days unemployment had to be solved on a group basis. The interviewer, an expansive Latino, stood just inside Room 33, checking the clients' blue slips before admitting them one by one. – "How are ya doin'?" he said to Frank with a wink, slapping him on the back. It was as clear as an empty glass that he had set himself the mission of boosting the dismal spirits of the unemployed. – "Fine," said Frank. "Thank you." He sat down between a welfare chiseler and a disguised milkweed pod. Everyone received some more forms.

The interviewer slammed the door breezily. "In the box where it says BYE, write 4/15/86," he said. "Where it says race, put your race; if that offends you, leave it out." He put his arm around a sullen woman. "Just for today, hon, you can be any race you want." – The woman moistened her lips with her grey tongue, evidently finding the situation difficult. At this, the interviewer laughed and began strolling up and down the aisles, watching the jobless at work on their forms. – Frank looked to see what his neighbors were writing, for he had always been curious, like Julius and Ethel Rosenberg, and it was also important for Frank to know what the others were writing in order to be certain that he was fitting in, since if he did not fit in THEN where would he be? – The chiseler on his right left the space blank. The milkweed pod dimpled itself slyly and wrote "Aleutian Islander." Frank put down "Vietnamese."

Then the interviewer ran a long colorful slide-tape show on how to check the old forms and fill out the new forms. The procedure was quite complicated. Every now and then the interviewer stopped the tape to crack another joke, but no one ever laughed. Frank, glancing at him sidelong, could tell that he resented this lack of appreciation almost as much as the unemployed people resented being there listening to him and sucking on the stony concept that without him they would be living in bus shelters and having nothing but dirty newspaper to diaper their newborn with and eating the slops from trash cans and dying young; whereas the interviewer for his part reflected that they had no right not to laugh at him given how many times he had had to look at this horrible slide show, which was filled with technical errors about the resettlement policy. Perhaps he would blow up at somebody. – As a result of this conclusion, Frank hunched himself over his forms as inconspicuously as possible.

The slide show ended at last. Now it was time for each client to step up to the interviewer's desk and hand over his or her forms. "Any questions?" the interviewer would say. The client never had any. "Good luck in your job search from yours truly," said the interviewer with a grin. – At last it was Frank's turn; one's turn always comes sooner or later. He negotiated his way along the lanes of unfriendly faces and arrived at the big desk. The administrator took a quick scan at Frank's forms. "Where's this Society of Daniel?" he said. "Down near Bay Shore?" – "It's off Scott Street," said Frank. Then he looked down at the form. He had written San Francisco instead of Sunnyvale, in a moment of carelessness. Now whatever happened to Frank would be his fault. His face turned crimson. "Sorry," he said. "It should be Sunnyvale." – The interviewer leaned back in his chair. "Well, *well*," he sneered, slashing out "S.F." on the form and writing in "S.V." "Any other last-minute changes? You could already be prosecuted for perjury." – Frank glanced vaguely around the room, much as a sea-sick person will focus on the horizon in order to distract himself from disorientation; but this was a mistake, for in fact the comparison with sea-sickness did not hold; it was more as if an acrophobic mountain climber had looked straight down; for everyone was staring at Frank's red face now; he was the only Caucasian in the room and they all hated him. – Meanwhile, the interviewer was reading Frank's forms with an ominous interest. One of the carbons had gotten folded, so that Frank saw with a horrid sinking feeling that the marks had all been transferred to the wrong boxes in copies two through four. "Really," said the interviewer, "I don't even know why you bothered to come in." – "Oh," said Frank. "I'm sorry." – "And look at this!" the interviewer suddenly shouted, waving Frank's claim form high so that all could see. "The bastard was making more money than all of us put together!" (In truth Frank had done well as a Judas on Dr. Dodger's payroll.) "I'm gonna disqualify you right now. Get out! Get out! GET OUT!"

Everyone hissed at Frank.

"Okay," said Frank, redder than the Soviet flag. "Thanks for your help."

He scuttled from the room. This latest disgrace had almost broken his heart. Perhaps if he had stayed with Bug he might have expropriated enough to have a house by now, with a big freezer full of ravioli TV dinners, and a wide TV to let his thoughts go voyaging in, and a gun closet, and a soft bed in a bright and windowless bedroom. But he had abandoned Bug. He had nothing left except his patience.

Like many double agents in hard circumstances, Frank ducked into the first bar that he saw. The bottles were on three shelves illuminated from behind. At first Frank thought that the reflective patterns on the shoulders of the bottles were all the same; then as he looked more carefully he decided that they were all different; then he concluded that some were the same and some were different. In the middle of the central shelf, for instance, one bottle bore two gleaming white crescents just below the neck, whereas the next had an upended jawbone, but then the following two bottles had identical designs of vectors skewed at forty-five degrees. – Two whores looked at Frank. "I sure wouldn't want to take him home," said one. – "I heard that," said the other. "You'd wake up in bed the next morning and look over and say, 'What's *that?*' " – One whore had been in the bathroom for half an hour. "What's she doing, dying in there?" said the bartender. Finally, he came out from behind the counter and started banging on the door. "Hey, come out of there," he said. "There's people anxious to shit!" – The hooker emerged in another ten minutes. "I'm sorry," she said, "but you just have such a nice ladies' room that I could just stay in there for hours making myself up." She came up to the bar and began running her hand up and down a man's back. – "What do you want money from me for?" he said sullenly. "You rake it in. You don't need no money!" – "I need it," she said demurely, "so I can give my ten percent to the church." – At this everyone pounded the bar in mirth and yelled things like, "Why dontcha screw the priests for free?" – Then Frank drank a shot of every bourbon they had and soon forgot his sufferings.

PHIL BLAKER STRIKES

~~~~~~

But, strange as it may seem, even such a powerful party as ours is not to the liking of the oppositionists. Where on earth will they find a better one? I am afraid they will have to migrate to Mars. (*Applause*) . . .

STALIN
in *Pravda* (27–28 May 1924)

The following day, finding himself without any other means of obtaining food, Frank went back to Phil Blaker's side. He did not always support Phil Blaker's policies, but it could not be said that he opposed them, either, so he launched a thorough report by signal flare, *zzzzzzzzzzz-ZZZZZZZOW!* Thus word was received up on Mars that Mr. White was heavily preoccupied with bug infiltrations. Rocking in his ebony rocking chair, with Phobos and Deimos attack units in a wait hold state, Phil Blaker concluded that now was the time to deal Mr. White a heavy blow.

I wish that I had been able to devote more pages to the wondrous workings of high finance, where paper cranes flap their wings high above paper tigers. Only a week before the Blaker crisis Mr. White in his innocence had hung a banner down the side of the Transamerica Pyramid saying 400 YEARS OF DIVIDENDS; and the celebratory graphs which Dr. Dodger had prepared were like silhouettes of rising ridges in North Carolina, dense with mysterious trees (for the path of increase had been shaded grey); and Frank, who happened to see those graphs in a piece of newspaper he stole from a park bench so that he could wipe his ass, looked at those windblown ridges with awe and shame, knowing that he would never be able to understand what was happening up there where financial mountain men meditated and meditated like Zarathustra; the forest was solid grey so that he could not even make out the bats and the spiderwebs. Frank was an intuitive disciple of Smith, who said in *The Wealth of Nations* (1776): "Profit is so very fluctuating . . ."

For several days, balloon-loads of money descended inconspicuously from the sky. This cargo was collected by Phil Blaker's agents and diffused throughout the price-earning infrastructure; then it was called in abruptly from utility bonds, so that the corporate tissues lost a fatal volume of lymph. The starved cells of the White Power & Light empire, from laundrettes to banks, licked their vacuoles longingly, like Gramsci's oppressed peasants of 1924 who "were sent to pick grapes in some places with muzzles on, for fear that they might taste the fruit." – But they could not have it. It had gone back to Mars.

While Mr. White's jaw was still dropping, Phil Blaker seized his electric power plants (from Mr. White's point of view, electricity was a particularly sensitive spot). The result was more spectacular than the takeover of Skoda Werke Wetzler! Phil Blaker had been able to exploit a special provision of the Republican Security Laws by showing that Mr. White's companies were bug-ridden (Dr. Dodger testified that they were.) The next step was the acquisition of Mr. White's robot factories, which produced immense stocks of preliminary, intermediate and final electrical products with a tradition of high returns. – Frank never knew about the disposal of Mr. White's property for certain, but one grey day he thought there was a sudden cease from the humming that had gone on in all appliances and wires and machines for every day of his life; it was the blue globes having a moment of silence out of respect for Mr. White (but it might well have been a lazy contemptuous sort of silence).

The last hours destroyed Mr. White's vital synthesis of capacitors, dollars, and guns, as power was transferred away from him radially in a blur of uniform permanent regulation counter-claims. His securities were registered, his controlling blocks were subdivided, and his industries were deprived of their national character. Dummy subsidiaries liquidated his beneficial owners. Mr. White countered with a desperate syndicate bid of \$329,141,926.49, which was unconditionally rejected by I. G. Chemie, a blind for the Blaker Jersey Group. Most humiliating of all was the fact that no voting trust settlement was ever offered by interplanetary telephone, though Mr. White waited and waited, taking thousands of anti-gas pills, for he had suddenly become very seamy and flatulent. The Supreme Court, which had been packed by Phil Blaker, denied all writs of certiorari. The S.E.C., reflecting the national mood, passed full-scale revamping measures approved by the Ministry of Economics. The prime rate fell and the discount rate rose. Mr. White's assets were now subject to vesting. The Society of Daniel was seized by the Alien Property Custodian on 9 June.

The so-called "Peace of Pacifica" only proved to the world what Dr. Dodger and Phil Blaker already knew – that Mr. White was a ruined man. Possibly anticipating criticism (for Mr. White had been very popular on account of his whistling), Phil Blaker issued a statement saying that his fundamental aim had only been to stabilize the market and end the extensive competition which had bedeviled all of us for so many years. Mr. White exploded to the press, "That fat cat shouldn't have a fucking *nickel* coming!" – But this was only taken as expressing the customary envy of a have-not. The headlines said: WHITE A SORE LOSER ON MARTIAN MERGER. The Federal Industrial Commission voted unanimously to pack him back off to the Arctic. (As for Phil Blaker, he got a quintuple-digit total return.) The Society of Daniel and Mr. White's other holdings in the lower forty-eight were administered by a Board of Trustees, of which Dr. Dodger was the chairman.

Once upon a time there was a fence. It was a twelve-foot fence of close-kinked chain. On top were poles tilting inward, and along those poles were strung four rows of barbed wire. Behind the gate was a guardpost with a pretty striped checkpost stake on either side, like those things that go up and down at railroad crossings. At night the arc lamps came on. Where the bulbs were, the darkness was lit up with dusty glare in the shapes of jellyfish. Always before, Mr. White had built fences to keep others out. But this fence was to keep him in. He was locked in and snow came and icicles grew and grew and Mr. White was sealed there until my next volume, and that just might mean forever . . .

Or, as TASS put it in its front page column on *imperialicheski* news,

FOR IMMEDIATE RELEASE

Sunnyvale, CA – The Society of Daniel announced today that Mr. White has resigned his position as President and Chief Executive Officer effective immediately. Management previously reporting to Mr. White will now report directly to Dr. W. Samuel Dodger, Vice President and Chief Operating Officer.

"Yes, indeed," said Dr. Dodger delightedly, waltzing around the water cooler with Rhoda Knotts, who had been Mr. White's personal secretary, "there have been some changes around here, and there will be more, yes."

Rhoda, who had adored Mr. White, began to cry.

"Now, now," said Dr. Dodger, "it's your job to say 'good.' "

"What do you mean it's my job to say good?" Rhoda sobbed.

Dr. Dodger spun away in a fury. "Here's your pink slip, and don't bother me again because in case you didn't know I've learned a few things from the ancient Romans about the risks and benefits of a praetorian guard."

And then it was back to the leisure of pure study for Dr. Dodger, unsullied now by worries about Mr. White's temper or Dr. Dodger's own prospects for long-term advancement.

All the programmers were afraid of Dr. Dodger because he checked for style, mechanics, neatness and theme.

There was a bug in the program. "It's there," Dr. Dodger reported aloud to himself, "but it's pretty hard to see — I can just barely detect it through my bifocals at the right angle." Dr. Dodger did not usually talk aloud, but just now he was the happiest man in the whole world.

(Of course this problem was just your normal B37 or D37.)

THE AGONY OF PARKER

~~~~~~~~~~~~~~~~~~~~~~~~~~~~~~~~~~~~~~~

Way down yonder in the meadow,
There's a poor little lambie;
The bees and butterflies pickin' out his eyes,
The poor thing cries, "Mammy" . . .

Slave lullaby (1950s)

Parker was now completely hypnotized by the Caterpillar Heart,
even though people still called him up all the time, he being an
essential person and all, and said, "Say, Parker, baby, do you have
any time this afternoon? What I can do is send you the pair of EXEC
files to your graphics terminal. And you send me the DOD files
through the load-macro register. Now, what is your user I.D.?" –
and there would be an expectant silence, but Parker wouldn't say
anything; and this did not unduly perturb the customer, because
Parker never said anything, but what did perturb the customer was
that his or her modem didn't light up and start chirring the way it
used to when Parker was asked for something and sent the requested
information over directly in a hexadecimal dump. – No, Parker just
sat there and gangled his toes in the dark. At rare intervals he still
went outdoors, and you might see him if Security was sloppy, a tall,
greenish fellow leaning against an alley wall, with tufts of dirty-
blond hair sprouting out around the rim of his camouflage cap; but
there was no cunning cautious hostility in his eyes the way there
would have been in the old days; he was too busy watching himself.
There was a bulge under his jacket; it was the Caterpillar Heart,
who sometimes applied her suckers to his armpits and the spaces
between his toes, making him thrash and gulp dreadfully (if Parker
had not been mute he would have screamed), and then Parker would
try to pull her off, but, as Hitler remarked, "On the whole, we only
laughed in those days at all these efforts."
Sometimes she was black and brown like a woolly bear cater-

pillar that Parker could hug tightly in his skinny arms like the teddy bear that he had never had as a child because in Omarville there was nothing to play with except nut casings, so because Parker had nothing soft to hug he grew up shy and often gangled his arms 'way 'way out at great distances to bring things close to him or to insinuate his arms into things; he never would have done that if he had been given a pillow which he could have thrown his green arms around when a boy, but maybe I am being sentimental, for what good would a pillow have done him after all? – The truth is that Parker, like the blue globes, was born evil. – But he did not want to be evil when the Caterpillar Heart came to see him, and he lay down in the space under the chemical basins so she could inch herself across his stomach and tickle his chin with her bristles. Later his skin would be inflamed by a gigantic pinprick rash. – Other times she was the hue of a Gulf fritillary caterpillar, which is to say glossy tacky black, like asphalt, with narrow red stripes and six rows of branching spines that stung Parker very gently, so that he writhed in startlement but let her sting him again in her advance across his body; she gradually grew longer and fatter and stronger with his special lymph in her, and would never have thought of leaving him for anyone else; and since she was stronger she could put on new colors for him, like the silver-spotted skipper caterpillar, whose body, aside from the nutlike head with the lost-looking stare of its orange eye-spots, seems to be wrapped round and round with one long strand of yellow yarn; then Parker coiled himself into a comfortable ball to watch the succeeding displays of his glutinous lover; and as he winked and blinked with his yellow eyes she took on a complex white shape, extruding double parallel rows of bristles, white on top and honey-orange underneath; and her body fissured into gummy white cylindrical segments, each having two white dots in a row, then three stepped ones, equivalent to the arrangement on dominoes, then one more; and a succulent butterscotch head on each end of her body; she was a French vanilla truffle that Parker wanted to eat, but he didn't eat her because then he would have nobody left to be in love with; that was the phase of the cynthia moth caterpillar; then she became pink and furry again, losing one of her heads and watching him lovingly with the remaining one, which now resembled a strawberry; but all the time Parker was not eating her; she was eating him. – Eventually she turned lime-green, like an Eastern tiger swallowtail caterpillar. For Parker she was always as sleek as a leggy brunette in the Alps posed beside a touring car.

Of course she loved Parker only as any other caterpillar would have loved a green leaf, but to Parker she seemed to be far more conscious of his self than she was; and when she homed her many eyes upon him, resuming her true form of bristle-hooked artichoke heart, he felt that she was showing her nakedness to him because she understood how much he wanted her to trust him; in fact she never understood him or cared to understand him; though as far as Parker was concerned, when he extruded his knees up to the ceiling to make a mountain for her to hook herself up and over, confronting him from the peaks of his kneecaps as she dug into his patella and her ocelli focused vaguely upon him, then he was confident that she was his own Heart who would never leave him, who as she inched down the long skinny pipes of his inclined thighs would never slip; who was to be relied upon even in preference to Wayne; who as her urticating hairs and hooklets bored into him to inflame the flesh just like Clara Bee's study lamp warming the snakes' cage so that the snakes could bask, made Parker go slack and forget his political aims; who as she stung her way across his lower abdomen proved herself to him by the steadiness of her merciless progress, staring at him with every one of her round white eyes that faced his direction; who as her suckers penetrated his navel to drink the lymph beneath it gave Parker the first sexual spasm that he had experienced since being hung by the older boys at summer camp, so that Parker climaxed in a terrible thrashing of limbs that shattered the red safelight on the ceiling and rocked the Great Enlarger, and then Parker was punished by her in parallel to the way that his stern-stemmed plant parents used to punish him in Omarville by wafting agonizing cockleburr-seeds down onto his bed as he slept; for the Caterpillar Heart had just drilled entirely through his belly for the first time (there is always a first time), in order to suck down slow droplets of his spinal fluid, for it was her instinct to do this when her victim convulsed helplessly; but to Parker it seemed that she was being severe with him because he had had his dirty orgasm; and Parker basked in being punished for his snakelike behavior, which he had always been ashamed of, having grown up in the Age of Electricity when even the reactionaries considered snakes to be feudal elements which should have been extirpated by the tenth anniversary of the founding of the Society of Daniel at the very latest, so that it felt so good for Parker to be punished by someone whom he could love, as he had never been able to love the older boys, that Parker came again, spraying her with veined greenish threads of mucus, which she gobbled before stabbing her hooklets into his stomach, much more painfully than before, triumphantly scraping the moisture from the surface of his liver and absorbing it to allow her to grow larger and heavier, weighing down on his ribs like a ton of avocados to keep him still as she cracked another of his vertebrae like a hazelnut, making Parker arch himself and vomit bile in his agony, rolling over and cutting himself upon the shards of safelight glass; and she clamped her suckers to his shoulders and throat, injecting an acidic fluid that made him bleed in black funereal clots; and then she sucked the venom out and stung the wounds so that once more they got blissfully inflamed and Parker lost himself ecstatically, like a water-snake in a bottle to which alcohol and formaldehyde are slowly added so that the water turns milky and the snake swims more and more wildly and lashes the sides of the bottle and suddenly goes rigid, braced against the glass in a spiral coil resembling a heat exchanger, and snaps its head back, and then very very slowly riffles down dead to the bottom of the whitish fluid, crystals falling gently upon its open eyes as softly as snowflakes; so Parker blacked out; and his ecstasy remained to some degree when he once again became a purposeful tenant of his shrunken scaly bulk, for the pleasurable swelling of his limbs seemed to him a token that after having punished him she had forgiven him.

These sessions lasted almost continually, interrupted only by Dr. Dodger's shrill coaxing and admonitions to Parker (Dr. Dodger did not dare to discipline Parker in any way because he needed Parker and couldn't tell whether Parker's horrid marriage to the Caterpillar Heart was or was not the custom in Omarville) and by Wayne's visits, upon each of which Parker would have to leave the honeymoon, shambling weakly into his quarters at the Society of Daniel where Wayne sat waiting upon Parker's cot, which was so neat and tight that Wayne liked bouncing a quarter on the bedspread *aw-RIGHT!* when he came by, but Parker merely lifted his shaggy head and moved his yellow eyes into alignment with Wayne's anxious reverent gaze, and stretched out a limp frog-green arm which shook Wayne's hand in a fishy kind of way.

Wayne wondered if Parker were testing him because Parker had tested him before; when Wayne and Parker were boys Parker summoned Wayne out to Omarville one August night to test him and subject him to a most comprehensive renewal. Wayne did not really want to go because no one except Parker liked to go near Omarville where they murdered people and the Plant Clan held its rallies at high noon and there was nothing that the Justice Department could do because the local sheriff was one of them. But off he

went because Parker had told him to. Parker and Wayne were each armed with firecrackers. They stood in the center of the road walled in by sumac trees with fuzzy berries ripening in the night; and it was a very hot night so that if you were a boy and were out in it you felt that some adventure such as running away was about to happen to you; you would run away to sea and sail into warm blue oceans and find islands full of jungles and cannibals and weird fruits and beautiful princesses who wanted you to marry them; and if you were older and had to work in an office you saw the night outside and maybe opened your window and felt funny and wished that you could be out in it but realized that you could not, for fiscal reasons, and that anyhow because you had been doing what you had been doing for so long you would not know how to conduct yourself even if you could be out in it, so you went back to your ledgers and on-line data entries with a *pleasurable* feeling of regret; and if you were older still you weren't even up to thoughts like that; you just grunted, well, my stomach's hurting me; I wonder if it's cancer yet; guess I may as well sit here and keep working until a blood vessel bursts in my brain. – Meanwhile the night went about its business. Wayne and Parker shook hands. Then they turned back to back, and each boy took twenty-five paces forward; and then when Parker gave the signal by making a dry cracking sound inside his cheek they both stopped and turned around to face each other. Wayne, out of tradition, was allowed to throw the first cracker. It landed on the road and burst at Parker's feet, throwing out a great green Catherine wheel around Parker like one of those screamin' Russki Katyusha rockets so that Parker glowed in the dark and was showered with sparks, and little holes were burned in his clothes from head to toe, but he was unhurt. It was now Parker's turn, O Things That Go Bump In The Night! Slipping a hand into his pocket, Parker slyly removed a big bundle of M-80s, red and cheery-papered, all tied to one fuse; Parker struck a match on his fly and lit the fuse, BSZZZZZZZ! and hurled the firecrackers straight at Wayne, who stood invisible in the darkness like black against black, but the white and yellow glare of the firecrackers found Wayne and enveloped him as the firecrackers blew up right in Wayne's face! Wayne was badly burned, but recovered, being a youth; and the important thing was that as the crackers came hurtling towards him he had stood straight and tense and ready to take it; glorying in Parker's scrutiny, he had not flinched; thereby he had lived up to Parker.

* * *

Summer nights Wayne and Parker used to come home from the range with their Rossi twelve-gauge Overlands rattling in the trunk, and they'd sit around in Parker's room, or preferably in Wayne's (since for all his affection for Parker, Parker's relatives gave Wayne the horrors) and clean the guns, scraping away with rags soaked in Hoppe's No. 9 until Wayne's head reeled and he could see the lids of Parker's eyes swell and turn purple, and once all the gun parts had been wiped and oiled then Wayne untabbed two beers *phht! phht!* and the moths outside smelled the solvent on the rags and tapped timidly with their wing-tips on the pane to get in, because they would have liked nothing better than to get drunk on the alcohol and ammonia and benzene and so die happy; but Wayne and Parker didn't pay attention, 'cause they were making secret plans, as you know; so the moths were left lonely and finally had no recourse but to go pollinate the fuzzy vulvas of ragweed or poison sumac in the moonlight so that then after a brief ripening period those plants could explode their sneeze powder into the muggy Hoosier air that was already a colloid of mold-spores and swamp-breath, and pretty soon ole Wayne would be going *Ah-cheww!* and Parker would wrinkle his nose and squinch his wiggly fingers 'way up inside to get the itches out, just as a cat will touch her paws to her whisker-tipped little nose-button, well-mannered society animal that she is; and it was this intolerable hay fever which finally drove Wayne and Parker clean out of the state (which meant that now Parker was a loner in truth, because he had rejected his own biological community, so that no quarter would be offered him); and Wayne was sucked up into the long West Coast commute, like the Wandering Jew, cruising and bruising on his labors – "See anything interesting, young man?" inquires Dr. Dodger on the wireless; and Wayne goes 10–4 and says, "Yessir, but they've all been on two legs!" – and Dr. Dodger tee-hees at this unexpected demonstration of rhetorical acuity.

As soon as Parker and Wayne left Indiana, things began to fall apart for sure; maybe they had started to cave in earlier and Wayne just hadn't noticed 'cause that had been his training period, but out west, where things were supposed to be so grand and Wayne and Parker would ride horses together shooting rustlers at dawn, the conviction wasn't there. Somehow their schedules didn't mesh too good. Or maybe that fucking Four-Eyes of a Bug was behind it, trying to ruin a good thing the way he always contaminated things with his cooties back at summer camp so if he sat on a chair Wayne wouldn't sit on it for at least an hour; there was something crawly and awful about that Four-Eyes and it was a shame they hadn't whupped him on the swim team because now he'd gotten clean away from them and Wayne was pretty sure that Bug was out spreading his bug cooties again to louse things up and do sneakery and trickery that Wayne hadn't figured out yet which was somehow getting to Parker and making him less responsive; or maybe Parker was just busy lately, but it sure seemed as though Parker were equivocating or meditating some decision that would not be to Wayne's advantage; Wayne's hair stood on end just thinking about it, like he was letting Parker down or something; he remembered how scared he'd been that night with the firecrackers, not scared of getting an eye blown out or anything chickenshit like that, just afraid of not living up to Parker, so now when Wayne closed his eyes in a traffic jam on the freeway he could see himself with Parker walking down that weedy Omarville road again in the twilight of their friendship, ready to commence the ultimate test of loyalty to Parker, which might be worse than the firecrackers. The trouble with Parker was that if he didn't trust you you wouldn't even know it for years and years until one day he would do something to you. When Wayne took the weekends off from his labors and drove down to Silicon Valley to see Parker at the Society of Daniel, Parker was rarely available, and even when he was he never said much, just kinda eyed Wayne sidelong and scratched, and then got up and left Wayne and went back into the darkroom until Wayne could see a funny green glow coming out from underneath the door, and then Parker ambled back out to be with Wayne in Parker's room for a minute and Parker sat in the straight high-backed chair gangling his legs meaningfully at Wayne while Wayne rubbed his jaw and wondered just what the hell was Parker up to now; maybe Parker was testing him; that was what I, the author, used to pretend when Bee sent me away, that she was only testing me and would call me back, so I waited all day by the phone on Christmas Day; that was a likely time; but no; well, then New Year's; nope; well; here came her birthday in February; then there was mine in July; now in September that made a year since the thing had happened, but September went by without any signs of an impending reconciliation, so I was forced to conclude that I would not be reinstated until five years exactly had gone by; so it was for Wayne, and it made Wayne feel bad that Parker should want to test him again, very bad, in fact, almost as miserable as Hemingway,* always walking back to his hotel in the

---

* This is a bookish novel because I, the author, know little of life, and I, Big George, will reveal no secrets.

rain, but Wayne reminded himself that it was like when you have a fire extinguisher hanging up in the garage you rely on it in a crisis of fireweeds or firebugs but you test it every three years nonetheless; that was Parker's way; Parker believed that one could not be too careful because if you were not too careful then where would you be? — In Omarville or back in fucking Lonesome Grave, Indiana, thinks Wayne to himself sarcastically. But the truth was that Parker was acting funny. Must be that goddamned Bug.

Parker knew that Wayne would never grasp the perfection of his relationship to the Caterpillar Heart, which he experienced not only when she crawled upon him but also when he sat under the Great Enlarger's bench staring across at her while she inch-inch-inched across the floor in a diagonal trajectory, completely unaware of him and uninterested in him, because she was not hungry at the moment, so that Parker felt a star-shaped pressure of grief in his upper chest. This was the finest time of his life. His grief proved that he could love, and thereby added something impalpably sacred to his political ideals. — Then his grief crackled in the air, disturbing the circuits of the blue globes; and the Caterpillar Heart stopped inching and gazed at him with her many tiny eyes and loved him once again, being attracted to suffering as flies are to a dead animal. Parker stood up very straight and quiet, as if to intimate that it was all right, thank you, holding himself puckered in to offer a minimum of surface area to his grief . . . Sometimes, as I said, he would gnash his milky-yellow teeth and try to push her off him, for there were days when he had remissions into his cool snaky integrity; but she span her threads, which glued themselves to him, so that she would be kept safe from dislodgement, for when she clasped them determinedly she could cling to even the smoothest surfaces, such as leaves and stems and trouser-legs and waxed desks. Even were she to fall, no harm would have come to her; all would be as gentle and light as one of Chopin's "Nocturnes," for she'd just spin out a longer thread easily in the course of her descent and then climb up the silken ropes she had made. So then Parker surrendered and made it clear, thanks to a variety of ogling movements, that he wanted her to kiss him.

As she fattened herself on Parker, her intervals of interest in him became more widely spaced, fine-tuning his emotion unbearably. She herself turned slovenly in her introspective contentment, like a great flabby fruit forgotten in the kitchen, going rotten and swarming with flies. Admitting to himself that as an insect she was almost certainly a tool of Bug's, Parker nonetheless could not give her up; he even tried to act like a green happy cricket so that she would not be cool to him, but he could not hop; he could only coil and stretch; so then he tried to pretend that she was a snake, too, which was not impossible to pretend because she could be superficially snakelike when she inched along him; and when Parker made himself small each one of her cilia could almost be mistaken for one of the Burmese pythons who had been his neighbors in Omarville; for her hairs were usually stiff and rubbery like cast-off army gear, but when they moved they flowed with the remorselessness of water, light glinting on their individual scales. They were black and gold. At first they seemed perfectly still, but Parker saw that what he had taken to be idly moving light was actually the rubbery heaving of their respirations; then they lifted their milky throats, arching their scales, sliding, moving, all muscle, nosing curiously, their undersides glittering like bathroom tiles, puffing their throats, moving with grinning inevitability; and as he watched these hairs intertwining with his own eyelashes they seemed to be the entire world to him; and the rich smell of the Caterpillar Heart was the substance of the world, his own snakepit of values where there was only sweetly poisoned somnolence and caring; but before Parker could progress very far in this self-deception, her protein-lipid requirements had been satisfied, and she left him forever, pupating in a beautiful chrysalis above the negative cabinet, with her organs degenerating inside, as Parker stood beside the chrysalis in a state of motionless depression for days, like a man I once heard of who waited in a corner unseeing after his wife had died and he thought about her absence so much that he forgot himself, pissing where he stood, not taking food or water all through those many summer hours, not feeling the mosquitoes on him; and when the neighbors found him his knees were locked rigid. – Wayne found Parker. He carried Parker out of the darkroom and washed him and undressed him, crying at what had happened to Parker, rubbing Star Force vanadium-based ointment into Parker's blue sucker-hickeys; and he fed Parker Parker's favorite dish, which was a saucer of milk with bits of raw hamburger stirred in, and then Parker, revived, slithered out of Wayne's arms, crawling desperately toward the darkroom, so that Wayne, crying still at what that fucking Bug had done to Parker, stood watching Parker inch himself across the carpet with little hooking motions of his ragged fingernails, as if he were trying to be the Caterpillar Heart, and he scrabbled at the darkroom door, so that Wayne opened the door for him out of pity, and Parker worked his slow way into the darkness that reeked of fixer spirits, looking for the Caterpillar Heart's chrysalis – and then suddenly Parker *hissed*, which was the first and only sound that Wayne ever heard him utter, for the chrysalis had broken open, and whatever had emerged from it was nowhere to be seen; and Wayne thought to himself, I bet that fucking infiltrating thing is in here somewhere right now, and I'm gonna find it for Parker; and even as he was saying this to himself a sad dun-colored moth flickered out the open door and exited from Parker's bedroom window before Wayne could kill it.

It had been Wayne's fault. If Wayne had not taken Parker away from the Caterpillar Heart, then Parker would have seen her and caught her. So Parker resolved to be finished with Wayne forever.

The next day Parker, half restored to health, met Wayne in one of the Society of Daniel's conference rooms. He had not summoned Wayne into his presence for almost a year, so that Wayne came bouncing in with a big grin, figuring at last he and Parker were gonna work together like in the old times to crush Bug and obliterate every insect that stood in the way of prosecuting the war. He had announced the appointment to Wayne without giving any indication of his purpose, for Parker, like the Soviet Union, had learned long ago that advance notice of any activity was potentially detrimental; so Wayne had gone off to his motel in the sandy mountains to the east, *aw-RIGHT*; now things are happening *for sure*; Parker must've been torturing that bug, whatever it was, to break its Ultra code or something esoteric like that, and Parker's gonna have a lead for both of us so we can put paid to all our enemies, he thinks to himself, flooring it in his Dodgeratti XKZ, and pulls up to the motel, which is a three-storey cube comprised of concrete bricks; there are old atomic posters in the lobby and the night-clerk is a sandrat who recalls the Society of Daniel being built fourscore years back, jest over the Colorado Divide, and he'd peered down from his bauxite mine (he was a bearded young fellow then who used to serenade the Indian girls with his guitar) and watched the boys working for Mr. White; now of course the original Society of Daniel is a ghost town, thanks to PROGRESS made by Mr. White and Dr. Dodger and Newt; the south wall of the powerhouse choked with tumbleweed, and the windows of the main building shot out in your father's time; the laboratory is locked tight, with its once proud reagents crumbling and going grey inside the supply cabinet, and the analytical balance registering a greater weight of dust every decade, the beakers scratched by the grit of a million sandstorms and the voltmeters burned out inside; upstairs, the student rooms are alive with mice; and sometimes wild horses come whickering up to gnaw the yellow grass around Katie's grave; his bauxite mine had played itself out at the same time, so he'd come out here in 'thirty-two as a bellboy in the motel, which could almost be a basement furnace that went outside and grew, mainly to show all that sagebrush and Mormon tea that it *could* grow, taller than they; it could beat them at anything it tried, and if they didn't like it it would just burn them up; and in fact through the narrow windows a pale light fumes like flickerless burning, surpassing in its weary steadfastness the emissions of a pile of hardwood embers behind a grate, for that's not electrical; barely a BTU there; even the blue pilot flame on a gas furnace burning on and on even after the householder has died, or the terrible whiteness of molten metal in a vat, is not as impressive as the unsleeping chittering and chirring of the display lights in the control room of your neighborhood reactor, or the red-illuminated digital display on the clock radio that wakes up Wayne in his motel room the next morning, gonna go see Parker, so dress up good, and now for the traffic report and the sports news, and Wayne rolls over in his starched sheets and clicks it off and leaps up to his stretching exercises on the carpet never dreaming that the radio has lied to him and gotten him up an hour earlier than he had told it to, just for spite. He has him a bacon-and-whiskey breakfast, shakes the night-clerk's hand, and zips off to the new Society of Daniel complex, which announces itself far ahead through the smog as a great crystal of high refractive index, so many windows does it possess. – Wayne and Parker, Parker and Wayne forever!

Parker lounged against the wipeoff blackboard, looking down at his dirty sneakers, and Wayne had an uncomfortable feeling, he didn't know why.

"Well, Parker," goes Wayne, still not consciously recognizing the gravity of the situation, "you're looking kinda peaked or troubled like those bugs are getting you down."

But Parker intimated that he did not have to be troubled anymore by the person who was troubling him (Wayne still not knowing that HE was the trouble); and Parker trembled like a vibrating wire and stretched and stretched and blinked at Wayne with his fishy eyes; and he trembled like a spastic rubber band and looked Wayne full in the face with his yellow scaly eyeballs that were so fishy that Wayne could almost smell rotting jellyfish on a beach hopping with scavenger-flies – and then Parker lashed out to bite Wayne in the shoulder; Wayne had never before seen Parker's python-teeth exposed all the way up to the stinking yellow gums . . . and Parker made it clear that Wayne was welcome to regard him as he chose (and at this Wayne sat up straight and paid bug-eyed attention), but that it was not possible for him to associate with Wayne anymore. He hoped that Wayne would draw the appropriate conclusions.

Sold out! Wayne thought to himself, unable still to grasp it. How could it be that Parker no longer wanted him? All at once the tears came to his eyes. He had been thrown overboard, and the ship of state was sailing on without him.

Parker made it clear to Wayne that he knew how important loyalty was to him, so he would understand if Wayne had strong feelings about him after this.

"In that case," goes Wayne, gritting his teeth so Parker wouldn't see him cry, "you'd better get out of here."

Parker nodded very slowly and stood up. He shook Wayne's hand sadly. It seemed to Wayne as if it took a very long time before he could no longer hear Parker's soft rubbery footsteps going down the stairs.

Wayne stayed in the conference room and cried. Overhead the computer lights hummed.

BLUE GLOBES FOREVER

~~~~~~

> Do not fail to understand that the possibility of encountering
> unarmed or non-hostile personnel exists.
>
> <div align="right">CHUCK TAYLOR</div>
> *The Complete Book of Combat Handgunning* (1982)

Frank walked up and down Haight Street, looking for Brandi. Of
late he had been prowling round her corner every night, in the hope
of getting more smack.

He met a fortune teller. "You have a watery personality," the
man told him, showing Frank the cards. Frank stared back fishily.
"You have trouble coming to decisions."

The man gave Frank the Tarot deck to cut and shuffle. He was a
very dirty man who stank and wore rainbow rags. After Frank had
mixed up the cards, the man began a complex procedure of factor
analysis, not dissimilar to the logic trees engaged in by the CPUs
inside the horrid skulls of nuclear missiles. He sifted out Frank's
significator, his environment, his obstacles, his capabilities, his past,
his hopes and fears (to the extent that Frank was capable of having
either), and at last turned Frank's future face-up . . . Frank got the
Death card. On his black charger, the white skeleton beckoned to
Frank and grinned against the yellow sky, making it clear that
Frank's treacheries and persiflages would not be condoned by
Providence forever. This was a nasty shock to Frank. He took out
his wallet and gave the fortune teller two one-dollar bills. The only
other bill in the wallet was a ten. He saw the fortune teller looking at
the ten, hoping, perhaps, that if he stared at it long enough then
Frank would feel guilty and give it to him. But Frank had been a
canvasser, too. He was moved not only by that emotion but also by
the desire to pay the man as little as possible without making a
scene. Perhaps only one dollar would have worked. But Frank did

not feel like chancing it, especially since he had just gotten the Death card. "This is all I can give you right now," he said. "I have to live on this ten dollars for the rest of the week." (This was not true. Frank had mony in the bank now that Dr. Dodger had rehired him as an informer – I mean, an investigative consultant., – "You don't have to justify yourself to me," said the fortune teller, evidently sensing that Frank was lying. "If you gave me nothing, I wouldn't care. The universe takes care of me."

The more Frank thought about the fact that he had really gotten the Death card, THE DEATH CARD, the wicked SKULL out to get Frank and snag him on its BONES and eat Frank with its sharp TEETH the way that Bug would while Frank screamed and screamed, the more frightened he became. There was no escape. He knew that he would not be able to sleep now.

Frank caught the N Judah down to Civic Center, thinking that he could at least go to the library to distract himself. And maybe he could learn a few good spy tricks that would fool the SKULL. But the library was already closed, and it was getting dark. The street lights had come on forty minutes before. Across the plaza, the rich old ladies leaned on their future inheritors' arms as they toddled up the steps of the Opera House. They were doing "Rigoletto" inside and "Gigoletto" outside. The handsome young gays stood out on the steps, waiting for their dates. Cars whizzed by, their lights as colorful as fireworks. For all these lucky persons, the night fun was just beginning.

Down on the hard benches by the public library, the street people were selling themselves and settling themselves in for the night. Frank overheard them discussing the situation. "I'm a-goin' with you," said one tramp to his buddy. "Otherwise you're a-goin' with me." – "Well, it is kinda damp here sometimes," somebody else said. – "Yeah, it's too bad them construction sites are so short-term," said another old-timer. "Just when ya settle in an' get used to yer cranny there's buildin's there and ya gots to move."

Frank got back on the streetcar and returned to the Haight. He decided to search out the fortune teller to see whether his fortune could be rescinded. Frank would have even been willing to give up his ten dollars now. But the fortune teller could not be found. The only way that Frank could be sure that he had not imagined the encounter was that his two one-dollar bills were gone.

On the corner of Parnassus and Stanyan, across the street from the flat where I, the author, had lived for a year with my Clara Bee, Frank came out of a produce store and saw a little middle-aged woman in a white bonnet sleeping standing up against a wall. At once, as Frank's footsteps came to her, she woke up, looked around, and marched determinedly up the hill. Half a block later, Frank saw her. She was sleeping against the side of a car. Hearing Frank, she woke up again and walked back to the corner. As Frank looked down the hill in the darkness, he could faintly make out the little white figure, leaning against the facade of an apartment building. Someday the police would catch up with her, just as the revolutionaries would catch up with Frank and execute him. He walked throughout the night, pretending from time to time that he had his clipboard and was out collecting money for Bug, who still trusted him; and Lester would be waiting in the car to count Frank's totals; so Frank wandered through San Francisco timidly, pretending also that once the night was over his difficulties would be solved with even more finality than that permitted by the quadratic formula.

At last dawn came. Although it was the middle of the rainy season, the sky was, for once, an intense milky blue, as in the Italian holy pictures, textured by puffy pink patches and white traceries not unlike the swirly threads of spit that can be found at almost any curbside, slicked with rainbow oils from incompletely hermetic cars. Frank passed under the green-striped awnings of the produce markets, looking about him hopelessly. It was 6:30. In Fabulous Daviton's Dry Cleaning the army-green machines, barrel-pipes and solvent valves sprawled behind the windows, with nothing but darkness behind them. Frank's breaths puffed out in front of his mouth like ghosty-white balloons. In the crumpet shop the baker was already rolling dough out on the counter. In his purple shirt and white apron he seemed to Frank very grand and fine. Frank peeped in the window shyly for a long time, but he never looked up from his dough. – A jogger passed by; she was wearing a white shirt and black shorts. On the sidewalk at the corner of Irving and Tenth, plump black birds strutted, pecking at crumbs. With their stiff little legs and feathery bodies, they walked in effortless straight lines, unlike Frank, who was drunk and exhausted. Their green eyes shone like battery indicator lights. For a moment there were almost a dozen of them at the base of a fire hydrant, and then a cab drove by and they all flew away. Nothing was left on that part of the sidewalk but a gum wrapper, a paint fleck and a eucalyptus leaf. Frank turned and walked back the way he had come, somehow under the conviction that it was less tiring to retrace your course than to continue on in unknown directions. – They were just cleaning up from the night's drinking and puking at The Embers; the place stank like a pisser as usual. A cloud drifted by, from the compass bearing of Aristocrat Cleaners and Sun Valley Market; and at this delicate adjustment of electrostatic conditions the phone wires quivered slightly, and a homeowner's TV aerial, on top of one of those white-stucco apartments which so inundated the region, twisted itself round to get the full benefit, like a revolving fish skeleton.

A woman hastened by, shifting her shoulder-bag. Frank, facing away, stared at her discreetly by observing her reflection as it glanced off the dirty store windows.

The sun was now engraving the houses up at the summit of Twin Peaks with a golden-white plating. Another woman passed, in a red coat; she had plump legs; Frank watched her breath point the way in front of her until she saw him watching her and crossed the street. A middle-aged man was loading boxes into his Ford; a red Dodge pickup went by; a man wearing a tweed coat and a basketball cap strode by, bearing his rolled-up umbrella like a lance; a red, white and blue bread truck rolled along; the birds came back to Frank and padded around his numbed toes, including a giant white pigeon with orange feet that bent and bowed as clumsily as a bobber on a fishing line. Then a Honda passed, and everyone flapped away again. – Here came the paper boy, in his canvas pants and striped knee-socks, with his empty carry bag across his back; he had finished his route. Grey-green mists rose from Golden Gate Park. The morning was presently out in force, and everyone was staring at Frank. He had to get away.

When he had been a canvasser, Frank would lie in bed on rainy mornings, the apartment empty, his roommates off at classes and jobs, and listen to Lou Reed sing "Satellite of Love" or "Goodnight, Ladies." The rain would come and go. In early afternoon there would often be patches of Oakland blue in the sky (Frank lived in Oakland before he lived in San Francisco, for, as the reader has surely noticed by now, I, the author, bring all my characters with me wherever I go). At around 12:30 Frank would get out of bed and fry himself a quarter pound of hamburger, or breakfast sumptuously upon doughnuts and refried beans. But now that carefree life was dead and buried. Frank had to be alive and conscious this morning, watching time wear on meaninglessly, knowing that it was only a matter of time before the SKULL caught up with him.

It is sad but true that for Frank, the purple peaks of responsibility did not prove nearly as enrapturing as had been planned; indeed, circumstances seemed to be pushing him up onto ever higher, more difficult ridges, as if he were lost in the Inyos and wandering from knife-edge to cold knife-point in the moonlight, with the rock faces taking on the features of pirates, lions, sandy jack o' lanterns when the moonlight fingered them; and every dry arroyo was choked with clean white marble blocks like crushed tombstones; for Frank felt that someday he would have to give away all his possessions and walk up one of the ever winding roads of the Berkeley Hills in a summer evening, carrying nothing but his gun, just looking for a peaceful place to shoot himself when the cool sunset came, since if he did not soon act then the grief that he felt at his failed life would burst his heart; and perhaps he would shoot a retired householder, too, who stood out in the yard hosing down the rubberoid roses — not that Frank wanted to kill anyone gratuitously, but maybe the old bald eagle would want to resist Frank's killing himself on his lawn, and anyhow there seemed something fitting to Frank in the thought of his degrading himself all the way to committing random (as opposed to political) murder, for solitary suicides were saintly, but people who shot whomever they encountered and then killed themselves were no different from the rapist-murderers who are always at large in California, and when the police finally catch them by connecting the dots, as blue-suited children will, drawing lines on their maps between the red Xs that mark the sites where nude gagged slashed penetrated partially decomposed bodies were dug up at the side of the road, so that the chief criminologist can extrapolate the trend to some little milk-run town where the murderer is holed up, then when the murderer is surrounded he is so evil that he will just kill himself so that justice can never be done to him; and this was how Frank could easily see himself — nonetheless, as he walked up past the red and green tennis courts in east Berkeley and saw the swing of the women's hair in the breeze, the crisp strokes that sent the ball over the net like a little bone-white planetoid, it occurred to him that there was still a last chance for a pair of heavenly arms to reach out to him and save him. He hoped so, as otherwise no one would ever know the grief of Frank in his last hours, not that anyone would especially care, either, because when you look out the window of your office building in San Francisco and see the SWAT team getting ready to blow that murderer's head off with their machine guns, you think of the murderer only as a horrible presence, something in league with death, and you resist putting yourself in his shoes, just as when you come into a funeral parlor you look at the corpse's black shoes and white face, but you won't try to imagine how it feels to be so cold and white with your blood pooled up and clotted in the back of your legs and the back of your neck, and you won't imagine how cold and lonely it will be underground, how dark and lonely and horrible (though I, Big George, promise to bring you down there presently). As I said, no one empathized with Frank.

He had not seen Brandi for weeks. He was desperate. Then one overcast twilight afternoon as he came into Golden Gate Park at Stanyan and Haight he saw her sitting on a bench with a man; the two of them were looking ahead into the stagnant pool in front of the cement tunnel that led to the field where in happier sunnier days baseball and tag and frisbee and touch football were played, and all the couples sat on the grass smooching and drinking wine, and the punks roller-skated along the sidewalk flexing their swastika-tattooed arms and yelling happily at each other, but that was as I have said in summer, and this was winter now and it would always be winter for poor Frank, the clammy season when mildew grows on the walls, but at least he had seen his Brandi, and strange to say, he felt much better, even though she was with someone else; but then he was not jealous; realistically, how could he or anyone else ever be jealous about anything? So he walked on with a great happiness inside him, unrecognized by Brandi, for he did not come near, but just peeped down at her and her boyfriend from the rise on the sidewalk just before it went into the trees.

Meanwhile the year came to a sullen end, like grey water closing over a corpse; and to Frank, who constantly expected the bugs to get him, it seemed a year of downed power wires, of flooded subways and dead batteries; as if the entire superstructure were decayed, the streetwalls smeared and graffiti'd, the buildings that Mr. White had once raised now sagging and cracking; and all the people Frank knew were decayed, like Brandi, like Dr. Dodger. There was a new sort of humanity prowling among the ruins – namely, the skinheads, who sat at Bullet's house drinking beer and staring at the floor until Strangles caught the black dog, Rebel, between his knees, pulled Rebel's head back and forced his jaws apart. Rebel snarled with pain. Strangles snarled back and thrust a chain into the dog's mouth; the dog bit it savagely. All the skins got excited at this and started hitting each other. – "Yow!" goes Bullet. "That's just what I like to see – a change of ATTITUDE!" (But Strangles's bootwoman, Greta, just said, "I think you're all a bunch of sick puppies.") – It was time for the Dicks concert. The skins strode through the Panhandle in their leather jackets, kicking cans and yelling. "Skins on the bus!" they roared. "All the skins on the bus! Enough to kill the whole world! Makes me feel good! Makes my dick hard! Makes my dick go Sieg Heil!" – Everyone jumped out of their way. Some of them had glasses, and with their shaved heads, these fellows almost resembled mad mutant scientists from an old science fiction movie, their big bald foreheads strangely tranquil and profound, like those of sleeping babies; but the people who got in their way were worked over good in the deep-sunk vacant lots that were fenced off like cancerous pits, down in the dying sections of town where rotten wires had burst out of the clay so that Dr. Dodger's monitors were no longer as helpful as they used to be . . . All the bums on the bus knew that controls were weakening; and glowed drunkenly, insolently, like candles among the nine-to-fivers who were as soulless as new shoes; and the bums sang:

> "If you see it, make it pay —
> That's the Dr. Dodger way!"

and the other passengers tried not to hear, thinking oh please oh God don't let him throw up on my skirt. — So the New Year rolled in under an evil cloud.

"Old Brandi's really speeding tonight," said Ken, the street photographer. Sure enough, there she was, nodding her head back and forth standing there at the corner of Cole and Haight; back and forth went Brandi's head, her beautiful junky's face went up and down as if she were listening to secret music through a headphone cassette player, but there wasn't any music and her head hit the wall. Across the street Frank watched the crowd in line to dance at the I-Beam, wondering if any of the New Year's couples were actually bugs in disguise who would find Frank out and punish him for his treachery, the way the fortune teller had hinted; and meanwhile Brandi pulled her son around the corner sidewalk in a red wagon, and the lights from stores shone desolately in her face, and people streamed by laughing and yelling; and at the stroke of midnight fireworks crumped like mortar-shells and bombs.

Frank stopped in at the Pall Mall Bar & Grill and had four boilermakers on an empty stomach. Then he headed home. He could not walk in a perfectly straight line. He counted the number of squares across the sidewalk as he staggered along past old Kezar stadium: one, two, three, four or five; it was a little hard to be sure. He could not stay along the line of a single crack between adjacent squares, but he could easily stay within a path defined by the width of a single square. What the hell, Frank reflected angrily, I *am* staying in my lane. (This was an expression which he had heard motorists use.)

"This is Orpheus," said Frank's roommate. — Frank was already home and he hadn't even realized it! – "I tutor him in chemistry," said Frank's roommate. – For some time now Orpheus's hand had been extended. Frank shook it very very carefully. – Frank was now lying on the floor in the living room. – "Each time," said Frank's roommate, "you're starting from a single electron, that is a *satisfied* atom."

Frank managed to get to his feet and fell into an armchair by the window, where he had the spins: – *a-whoo-ah-uh*, *a-whoo-ah-uh*, round and round his brain turned in his head; he was so dizzy.

"Basically, that extra charge can be shared," said Frank's roommate.

The doorbell rang. Blearily, Frank looked at his watch, which gave him the time, but not the date or the day of the week. It was possible that it was several days past New Year's. Frank stood up and peered through a crack in the street-window curtains. – His heart sank. It was a new group, Bay Area for a Bug-Free Zone. He had told them that they could hold a meeting in his apartment. Dr. Dodger had made him do it. – "We'll all respect you that way, Frank," said Dr. Dodger, and at the thought of being respected Frank had blushed. Now in they came as he sat in the corner stupidly. He had been supposed to show some slides on the bug threat, but it was all he could do not to vomit, for there were weights tumbling in his head like the weights behind a doll's eyelids, and feathery insects had infiltrated his stomach. – "I'm sick," he said, "you just go ahead." They had their meeting and ignored him. Because he was nominally the host, the bugs now had another item to add to his ledger of crimes, and all for nothing.

The next morning it was back to work for pathetic Frank. At 4:43 in the morning he was out the door into the cold blackness, which was alleviated here and there by bands of yellow fog. He skirted the park without incident, passed by the McDodger's, which was being mopped inside and out by a yawning cleaning crew, and turned onto Haight Street. The automated store fronts sent out their red and blue beams upon the deserted street. Frank stepped along, avoiding the broken glass and the rubbish piles. The street was entirely empty. Usually he'd see somebody, at least, like a pair of bums who'd just blown into town and needed money for coffee, or a stubbly vagrant in an army jacket sleeping in a doorway. But this morning Frank intersected Shrader, Cole, Belvedere, Clayton, Frederick and Ashbury without seeing a soul. Finally, right at Haight and Masonic, a small black woman in a rainbow parka stepped out from under some scaffolding and put her hand on his arm. – It was Brandi!

"Please," she said, "do you have any change?" She was shivering.

Frank felt sorry for her. All he had was a couple of dimes and some pennies, he knew. "I don't have much," he said apologetically.

"Do you want to make love?" Brandi said. "I'll make love to you for two dollars. I'll do anything for two dollars."

"Oh, Brandi," he said softly. He looked in his wallet and in his pockets. All his change he gave her.

"You wouldn't have even a dollar in there?" she said.

He opened his wallet and showed her. There were only wadded up papers, a picture I.D. identifying Frank as an operative, an expired driver's license, and Dr. Dodger's business card. – But Brandi's eyes were sharper than his own. "You got a dime in there," she said. – Frank stuck a finger into the stuff in his wallet and found that there was. He took it out and gave it to her. Then he ran away. If he hadn't he would have been late for Dr. Dodger . . .

Usually when Frank came home late at night the technical high school by old Kezar Stadium was dark. That was where the skinheads slept. In front was a boarded-up window that could be kicked so that the boards fell in and then the skinheads could dash inside and lean the boards back up against the window-socket before anyone saw. They had the entire high school to themselves. Each of them had a room all fixed up with photos on the walls or maybe a mattress and some nice stolen things. The police brought dogs in every morning at 6:30. The police hated the skinheads. So the skinheads had to go to sleep pretty early and keep things quiet and dark so they wouldn't be bothered before then. But tonight Poly High dazed Frank with opaque yellow light from every window on the second story. The main gate was ajar. Four empty police cars were parked beside the gate. Frank could not hear a sound inside. Suddenly he knew that he would never see the skinheads again.

But Frank could not mourn for the skinheads very long He had to keep his mind on his work. – "My advice to you is to learn to smile, Frank," said Dr. Dodger at those endless briefings, which took place in the electronic map room, and when Frank had described some new topographic feature he had just remembered, then Dr. Dodger would enlarge the scale in the Etch-a-Sketch screen and wet his finger with his scraggly tongue and move the cursor

around excitedly until it had arrived at the proper point by a series
of nervous staccato triangulations, then Dr. Dodger would use the
light pen to draw in the trail or hill which Frank had described, and
then this information was at once transmitted into a satellite's
update buffer memory for extra surveillance power. "Yes, Frank,"
said Dr. Dodger, "you are a true colleague; you are doing a
commendable job, and something tells me we'll have a slew of
arrests pretty soon; this Kuzbuite movement is going to be as broke
as a deacon at a ball game . . ." and at this Frank shuddered, for
being a double agent he truly liked all sides as much as he hated
them, and besides there was the SKULL to consider; but at once Dr.
Dodger, sensing his attitude, became stern and waved a crooked
yellow forefinger in Frank's face, saying, "Oho, you're holding
something back, hey? – Compromise," hissed Dr. Dodger, "that will
look much better to Mr. White and to me . . ."

Even as a boy Frank had known that he was being watched. He
had a dream of wading in a pond. Suddenly he saw his glasses
swimming toward him from shore. Then he felt terror; that meant
Dracula. Dracula was a big invisible water-bug that was going to get
him and eat him. Now he wanted to find someplace safe because
someday the revolutionaries would revenge themselves upon him.
Maybe he could hide in the slums.

Little wonder that when the weekends came Frank distracted
himself by searching for Brandi. All the street people knew her.
Whenever Frank saw one of them, he asked her whereabouts.

In the park Frank sat down on a bench to have a beer. It was a
hot afternoon. A man was sitting on the bench across from Frank.
When he saw Frank he approached him, coughing. – "The good die
young," the man said. "I'm old now – forty-two. You saw how long
it took me to get up and come over to your bench. I'm not young.
I'm not good. I'm bad."

"You'll die soon," Frank consoled him.

The man unbuttoned his shirt and showed Frank his breasts. He
grasped his nipples and pulled straight out so that his breasts looked
like a woman's. "I'm a what-you-call homo*sex*ual," he said to
Frank. – Frank nodded. – "This ain't hormones or surgery.
Thousands of white men and black men have sucked at these. No
hormones, no surgery, just mouth action. I'm forty-two now. When
I'm ninety-two they'll hang down to my knees. When it's time to
sleep, I find someone to keep me warm in the alleyway. I fuck him in
the ass. I suck cock. You want me to lick your ass? I always come
four times."

"Have you seen Brandi?" said Frank.

"Brandi? No, I haven't seen her. If you see her tell her she owes me fifty cents. That's why I'm broke today."

Frank kept asking people. Finally the blue globes heard and sent him her address.

Brandi's house was the cruddiest on the entire street. It was a tall narrow greenish building that leaned against its next door neighbor and dropped shingles and paint flakes like pieces of skin. The garage smelled like a dead dog. One of the windows was smashed. The side of the house was infected with black bulging bubbles where somebody had tried to set it on fire. Above the back yard was a power junction that sprouted crusty wires which tried to rise like the sick twisted eucalyptus tree but grew upward only a few feet before they drooped and fell again. Brandi's family used them as clothes-lines. Whenever somebody turned on a stereo or made a phone call, the wires glowed and buzzed and then the laundry dried out in no time. Sometimes Brandi's jeans had little black holes scorched into them. Thus electricity maintained its sway.

Frank met Brandi on the way to her house. Just as they reached the front steps, a wino staggered up to Brandi rolling his eyes and holding his stomach and belching. – "Bitch owes me three dollars," explained the wino to the sky, but Brandi just giggled and said, "As long as I owe you money, you'll *never* be broke!" – The wino laughed and swayed and fell down on the sidewalk. Looking back at him, Frank saw his open mouth. One of the first things that Frank could remember was his mother's yellow teeth. But this guy didn't have anything but gums.

Upstairs and in the kitchen, Frank unlocked his green case and showed Brandi one of his pistols, a Sig Sauer P226. It was a heavy black gun that always felt cold in Frank's hands. Because it had a decocking lever but no safety, and was therefore perpetually combat-ready, Frank considered it the perfect weapon for someone like himself who was always on the go. – Brandi purred over the gun and held it close to her. She wanted Frank to sell it to her, but Frank would not, because the gun was his friend. – "Well," said Brandi, "if you ever want to sell it, you know *right* where to bring it." – "It's a deal," said Frank, leaning up against the counter. The kitchen was almost as narrow and dark as a grave. – Brandi looked at him eagerly. "Is this thing loaded?" she said. – "No," said Frank, pulling the slide back so that she could look into the chamber. – At once she ran grinning around the kitchen, pulling the trigger *click! click!* on the empty chamber, with her eyes rolling in savage self-absorbed exaltation. It hurt Frank to see his gun dry-fired in that way, because he knew that it was bad for it, but he did not have the heart to stop her. So he waited until she had become bored with the gun, took it from her silently, and locked it back into its case.

The interrogation could now commence. He had learned from Dr. Dodger that it made sense to begin in a roundabout way, just in case one suffered reverses. There was also the consideration that if he asked her social as well as moral questions he could have an interrogation and a party date at the same time, thereby building up a class base of support. Maybe she would see how much he loved her. Then, when the time came, she might carry arms for him as Susan did for Bug. (Unlike Bug, he was still not sure what he would be fighting for, but he knew that for the rest of his life he would have to have guns.)

"Whatcha wanna ask?" cried Brandi suspiciously.

"Well," said Frank, leading off like a velvet glove canvasser, "what things do you like to do?" (How nice it would be if he liked to do those things, too!)

"I be spare-changin', I be partyin', I do a little bit of everything."

"What kinds of parties do you like?"

"Every kind. Mixtures. That's the best kind, them mixin' parties. I spare-change when I ain't got nothin' else to do."

While Frank was evaluating this information, Brandi bent over the stove stirring a saucepan of beef-flavored rice in that dark close kitchen where every wall was tarnished metal that bulged and buckled like soup cans puffed full of botulism. The only light came from the blue gas flame under the saucepan. The ceiling was streaked with black smears — most likely the suicide trails of moths and gnats who had not been able to swarm around the grimy burner. A metal sun was mounted on a bracket on one wall, where it sent out its spiky shadows in a distracting way which would never have sufficed in a police interrogation. Of course Brandi was used to it. Frank stood behind her, a little uncertainly. Sometimes she peeked at him over her shoulder. Then she would turn back to her rice with a grin, and the mirror was steamed up from the saucepan, and the rest of the house was quiet except for scufflings and whisperings. Brandi kept grinning at Frank because he had promised to give her five dollars when he was finished asking his questions. Maybe if she kept grinning he would give her even more money. Her lower lip curled downward and her teeth showed when she grinned, in a way that made her look a hundred years old. — She gave him a spoonful of rice to taste. When his mouth was full she said suddenly, "So, what else you want to know?"

This hardened attitude immediately made Frank less delicate in his manner. "How do you get your money?" he said.

"I spare-change," Brandi said. "Sometimes I sell the juice in old power wires and stuff. Say, you ain't no *police* or nothin', are you?" She laughed, so that Frank could take her question as a friendly joke if he were not in fact *police*.

"No," said Frank reasonably. "I showed you my gun, didn't I?"

"Yeah, but that ain't gonna mean *nothin*'."

"It means you know as much about me as I know about you," said Frank. He was trying the Logical Gambit. It was recommended in a 1940 article in *The Police Journal* which said, "When you break a man by torture, he will always hate you. If you break him by your intelligence, he will always fear and respect you." – Frank smiled at Brandi. – "That's a stolen gun. You could get me in trouble now, couldn't you?"

"Yeah," said Brandi gleefully. "I sure could!" The more she reflected on this, the happier she became. She hugged herself and peeped sidelong at him.

"Okay," she said. "I spare-change. I got *men friends* that might gimme some money for makin' *love* a little, you know. – Most of the time I don't even fuck 'em," Brandi said with a wink. "I don't just jump into bed with *anybody*, 'cause so many damn *diseases* out here."

As she spoke, Frank could not help looking around the room wondering if there were *diseases* crawling down the wall to get within pouncing reach of him. Maybe they were agents of the SKULL. But there was nothing above his head except the dead light bulb. – "So how do you pick them?" he asked, backing slowly into a corner where he could keep a better eye on Brandi and on the ceiling, as a double agent should. "What do you look for?"

"I don't look for *nothin*'. I just *pick* 'em. If they look all right I *take* 'em. But most of the time I don't have sex. I just get the person all horny and stuff. I promise 'em that. Then once I get the money I be gone *bye*-bye." She giggled. "What things *you* like to do in life?"

"Me?" said Frank. "Well, I like guns. I'm a secret agent. I shoot an air-gun at my house sometimes. It's quiet, so the police don't hear."

"What you like, you shoot *guns* at your house?"

"I like to practice," Frank admitted shyly. "In case I ever have to shoot someone, I'll be all set."

Brandi crowed with delight at this witticism. "You *shouldn't*! But I don't think I shoot *nobody*."

"You don't think so?" said Frank, easing into the serious part of the interrogation. "You don't have any enemies?"

"I have a *lot* of enemies," Brandi said. "But I won't shoot nobody, unless I'm in a *corner* and I *had* to come out." She laughed. Then a thought struck her, and she peered hard at Frank. "I'm talking to you and you haven't given me no money. I'm trusting you!"

"I gave you money once, didn't I?" said Frank.

"You gave me two dollars. I never forget a face. But when you gave me a dollar fifty that morning, about four or five in the morning, you probably thought I was real *needy* or somethin'! I was as high as *fuck!*" – She started laughing again.

Hurt by her scorn, Frank returned to the subject of enemies. This would classify her ideologically. – "What kinds of people do you have to watch out for?" he said.

"Watch out for?" said Brandi. "Dope fiends an' *bugs!*"

Instantly, the phone rang. Frank went cold inside, wondering whether Bug had heard his name being mentioned, but Brandi reached across the stove and picked up the phone with a yawn. – "Hello?" says Brandi. "Who's this? *John?* This is me. Oh, what's up, Dodgie-Dodge? Whatcha wanna get together or somethin'? I ain't got no money. You gonna gimme some? – Whatcha say? – For what *else?* For me to come on down there and make some *love.* You got some weed? Huh? *What?* NO?! You tellin' me, Dr. Fucking Dodger, I said, you tellin' me? I thought you *had* some money! – *Ohhh,*" she cried disgustedly. "Then you just *forget* it. I thought you was workin' at that Daniel's Society Burgers. What happened? An' you was up here one day with my sister. I heard you got your ass kicked. I betcha won't do it no more, huh? I'm lettin' you know it, when you see me you don't come fuckin' around with anyone else in my family, uh, *uh.* You sure you ain't got some money? – No, honey, if I had some I wouldn't be in the house. Well, *anyway,* let's make this short. You ain't got no money. So let me hang up. – Bye!"

Frank had not been paying attention. He had been staring into Brandi's big brown knowing eyes as she stood there, one hand on her hip, her shoulder squeezing the phone against her ear. She grinned at him again. By the time she hung up, he was ready to proceed to investigative phase three, the main question.

"You ever go to the Tenderloin?" he said.

Brandi looked up from the rice-pot. "I don't trust that area. I been down there but I don't trust it."

"I was thinking about finding a hideout down there," Frank said.

"I'd be careful down there; you gonna really need *that*," she said, laughing and pointing at the green case.

"I have a smaller one," Frank said. "It comes with an ankle holster. Can you introduce me to some bugs?"

"Oh, shit, I can introduce you to *thousands* of bugs, to *big-time* bugs ... But I ain't goin' in there without no gun, 'cause the first thing that come my way, the wrong way, I ain't gonna be bull-shitted. I ain't gonna pull it unless I have to use it. I ain't gonna be tryin' to kill nobody, but, honey, I'm sure not gonna be stopped by nobody."

"I bet you'd be pretty safe with me," said Frank soothingly, and to tell the truth it seemed to him that as long as he had his pistol and his whore nothing bad could happen to anyone.

"Shit!" sneered Brandi. "Just because you got a gun and *I* ain't got one? Uh-*uh!*" She chuckled like a dark little goblin.

"You can use my Browning," he said.

"I won't kill 'em," she said, "I'll just shoot 'em in the leg or something like that, that's all."

"I could shoot a fly off your shoulder," whispered Frank.

"You could?" she cried.

"Yes, I could, but I wouldn't ever do that," he said tenderly.

"No, I wouldn't never let you do it *nowhere!* But one day when we go to your house you gonna shoot something for me and let me see."

Frank locked his case. The interrogation had been completed successfully. Brandi loved him. "What time are you usually around?" he said.

"I'll be here all day, and if I'm not here you just walk down Haight Street. You'll see me!" She laughed and laughed as if she had told the best joke in the world. "When you come up here, ask for Dessie, though, 'cause they ain't gonna go by Brandi."

"They don't like that name, huh?" Frank said.

"They don't. They don't like it, 'cause I don't use that name; everybody ask for Dessie when I be up here."

Frank came close to her and stared into her face. "Is it okay if I think of you as my Brandi?" he said.

Brandi laughed so hard she almost choked. "That's perfect," she gasped.

*   *   *

A week later, Frank clicked on his sling holster and slid the
Browning into place under his armpit. He walked down the street to
see Brandi. In his hand was a box of heart-shaped chocolates, for
Sunday was Valentine's Day.

Brandi's bed had a stack of tilting stinking mattresses on it. The
dresser was missing drawers. On the floor was a rumpled yellow-
tassel carpet that smelled like dog piss. Dirt, small scraps of paper,
and oxidized pennies lay scattered on it. The TV was on. Mr. White
was acting in some old blue-and-white World War II movie. "This
story is true. It is their story." – "Men, you all know this mission is
dangerous," goes Mr. White. "The Kulaks and the bugs are out to
get Alaska, so I'm counting on you to put lead in their knickers and
buy U.S. Liberty Bonds." – But Frank was the only one paying
attention, except for a big slow old fly that had perked up when it
heard Mr. White say the word "bugs," and was now cruising round
and round Brandi's head, making the same noise as the bombers on
TV. – Beside Brandi's bed was another bed with a pile of blankets on
it. A pair of white eyes looked wearily at Frank from the edge of the
blankets. This visage belonged to Brandi's brother B.J. B.J. worked
washing dishes from four to midnight five days a week. – "What
kind of restaurant do you work at?" said Frank to be polite. – "The
kind where they serve food," said B.J. wearily.

He gave Brandi the chocolates. There were six of them. He had
written on the back of the box, in the heart-shaped space provided,
"TO BRANDI FROM FRANK." – "I *love* them chocolates," said
Brandi, greedily eating five as she stood by the window. "How did
you know I love them so well? 'Cause chocolate cake, chocolate ice
cream, anything chocolate is my favorite thing." – "That's good,"
said Frank, pleased with himself. There was still one chocolate left. –
"Let me have one," said B.J. in the other bed. – "*Fuck*, no," goes
Brandi. "They're *my* chocolates."

"How long have you lived here?" said Frank.

"All my life," said Brandi. "Twenty-two years."

Brandi sat on the edge of the bed. Frank thought that he had
never seen anyone so beautiful. She kissed him on the lips. – "You
want to get high?" she whispered. – "Okay," said Frank. "I'd like
some smack." – "You got twenty?" she said. – "Yes," said Frank,
pulling out his wallet. Too late he realized his mistake. He had not
only a twenty, fresh from the bank machine, but also three fives and
a one, which were the remains of another twenty he'd withdrawn
that morning to buy his week's groceries with. He should have
hidden it in his shoe. – "Oh!" cried Brandi gleefully. "You have a *lot*

of money!" – His heart sank. "I need it for my food," he said. – "Aw, you cain't even gimme no five to make mine a full twenny-five cent?" – "No," said Frank, amazed at his firmness, "I really can't." – "Well, just gimme that one, then," said Brandi. "I have twenny-one, not just twenny, we can get us a twenny-one cent." – "Okay," said Frank, relieved that he had gotten off so cheaply. – Now Brandi sidled up to him coaxingly. "If she don't have no smack, how 'bout if I get you some coke?" she said, looking him in the eye very very earnestly. – Something, perhaps a little bird, perhaps a blue globe, told Frank that Brandi's connection would have no smack. – "I'll be right back," she said, slipping out the door. – Frank sat there with B.J. watching TV. Ten minutes later Brandi came back in and looked at Frank very very lovingly. "Can you give me a five for five ones?" she said. This sounded like a fair deal to poor Frank, so he reached into his wallet and pulled out one of the three fives. She took it and rushed out. Frank sat there on the bed. Slowly it began to dawn on him that he had been a sucker. – "Do you think I'll see that five again?" he said to B.J. B.J. shook his head sadly.

"I owe you five ones!" said Brandi brightly, tripping back in. It was clear to Frank that he was expected to observe her delicate feelings and never mention the matter again. At least he had ten dollars left.

Frank sat on the edge of her bed watching Brandi in the mirror. She looked very serious in her black wool jacket as she sat beside him getting the cocaine ready. "This is what I love," she whispered. "But you love smack, huh?" – Frank nodded. – She gave him the piece of paper the powder had been in. "Go ahead an' lick it," she said. "I want you to get the taste." – Frank let his tongue slide across the paper slowly. He felt a bitter clean sensation before his mouth went numb. "Do you like freebasing?" he said to B.J. conversationally. – "It's all right," said B.J., rolling over and pulling the blankets higher over his shoulders. – On the TV a woman screamed. But nobody looked except Frank.

Brandi stirred the powder into a small vial of water until it dissolved. She held a lighter to the vial. There was a sizzling sound. The fluid turned milky, then bubbled, then became transparent again. "It ready now," she said. "We gonna have some *big* rocks." She set the vial into a bucket of cold water. Frank heard a hiss. – "Oooh!" she said. "Them is even bigger than I thought!" She went to work getting the pipe ready for Frank's first toot. Frank sat there idly watching her in the mirror.

"Hand me my lighter," she said. Frank found it hidden between two mattresses and gave it to her. She dropped a crystal into the pipe and lit up. Frank watched as the flame formed a horn like a yellow snail when she inhaled and sucked the horn into the pipe. Then she put a crystal into the bowl for Frank. She raised the pipe to his lips. "Suck slow when I tell you," she said, "then go faster an' faster 'till it's all gone." – Frank inhaled. Something bitter and icy entered his body. He continued to inhale until the sad whistling in the pipe bore witness that there was nothing in there anymore but air. He held the smoke in as long as he could. The clean bitter feeling became stronger and stronger. He felt happy.

"Let's give him some," Frank said.

"Oh, he don't need none – there's hardly enough for you to get your share."

"Do you want a hit?" said Frank to B.J.

"Don't make no difference to me," said B.J.

Okay, Frank thought, that's fine, then.

Brandi held the pipe to Frank's lips. "Suck slow, then fast," she said.

B.J. had raised his head. His eyes were wide open. He was staring at the pipe. – Frank felt bad for him. "Do you want some?" he said again. – B.J. nodded eagerly this time. There was real gratitude in his eyes as he rolled over and began to sit up. – Frank felt good.

"There ain't enough!" cried Brandi. "This here is your last one. You don't want to give it to him, do you?"

Frank didn't want her to think that he hadn't enjoyed it. But he felt bad thinking about B.J. "Give it to him," he said.

"It'll only be teasin' him," Brandi said, "there's hardly enough for him to feel it." She turned to her brother. "B.J., there ain't enough," she said shortly. "Now, c'mon," she said, swinging back to Frank; she had already lit the pipe. "Hurry now, it's gettin' used up." She slid the pipe into his mouth. "Now suck," she said.

Frank inhaled. The yellow horn of flame descended into the bowl as he sucked at the pipestem. Brandi was still holding the pipe for him with one hand; he put his hand on hers (to steady the pipe, he told himself). The clean bitter taste entered his chest. Clean calm bitter well-being infused him. He looked in the mirror. His eyes glittered startlingly.

B.J. was looking at him silently.

"Next time," said Frank.

"It don't make no difference," said B.J., sinking back onto the bed.

He watched her in the mirror. She cut up the black crystals with a razor and cleaned the screen of the pipe. This was her work, and she was absorbed in it. He felt an alert chairbound kind of lethargy, as if he were having a very interesting discussion with himself in front of a fire, so he did not lean forward to see how exactly she was doing whatever she did; he just enjoyed the clean bitter feeling sustaining him and stared into the mirror at himself and Brandi beside him with her dark beautiful downturned face. The freebase sensation continued to grow stronger and cleaner inside him until he felt almost nauseous. THIS WAS HOW IT MUST BE TO BE A BLUE GLOBE! he thought, and as a reward for his perspicacity the sensation tripled in intensity so that everything in the whole world became as clean as rubber gloves in an ice cream parlor . . .

B.J. lay in bed with closed eyes, wheezing or snoring. – Brandi looked into Frank's eyes. He could not believe how beautiful she was. "Ask him for a cigarette," she whispered in Frank's ear. "You hear?" – Frank nodded. "He's asleep," he said. – "Go ahead, ask him; he won't give *me* one." – Frank looked down at the floor. – "B.J.!" says Brandi real loud. – B.J. opened his eyes. "What?" he said. – "He wants a cigarette!" said Brandi. – "Oh," said B.J. to Frank, not suspecting a thing. "I didn't know you smoke." He groaned and reached under the pillow for a pack. He pulled out a cigarette and gave it to Frank. – "Thank you," said Frank. – B.J. closed his eyes. Brandi winked at Frank slyly, took the cigarette and lit up. Frank did not look to see if B.J. was looking at him.

Brandi hugged herself close to Frank's ear. "Listen," she whispered. Frank wondered if she remembered his name. "You was so nice to me, and turned me on, so I want to turn you on to some hair-on. You hear?" – Frank nodded. – "I gonna go down and buy some," she whispered. "But I can't spend no money in front of my family 'cause I supposed to be savin' for a pair of new shoes. You hear me?" – Frank nodded. "You don't have to do that," he said. "If you need to get shoes . . ." – "I *want* to do it with you!" she whispered. "You hear? You understand me?" – Frank nodded. – "You gimme your ten, so he think it's your money, then I go down and pay you back the twenty. You hear?" – "I can't afford it," Frank said in a low weak voice. He was afraid of going hungry. – "No, no, no, don't you understand me, you get it back, right now, just we got to fool *him*," and she pointed at B.J. lying on the bed watching them silently.

"All right then," she said in a loud voice for B.J.'s benefit. "So you gonna buy yourself some smack?" She nudged him in the ribs. – B.J. saw.

Frank reached into his wallet. He tried to slip her an orange Versateller slip, but she reached into the wallet and plucked out the last two fives. He was now penniless.

"You better go with her," said B.J. quietly. "If you don't you won't never see her no more."

"You *know* I don't take *nobody* with me when I do that shit," said Brandi angrily. She stood up and smoothed her shirt into her jeans. Then she began to button on her black felt coat. "You just wait right here," she said in Frank's ear.

"Go with her!" screamed B.J. "I'm tellin' you she gonna just take your money, she so *bad* through and through!"

"I'll be back real soon," says Brandi. "You just sit right there."

After fifteen minutes or so B.J. got up and went into the kitchen. Frank followed him. Brandi's mother was cooking there. – "Have you seen him around here before?" he heard her ask when he was still in the hall. – "Oh, he come round here *all* the time," said B.J., covering for Frank. Frank went on in. The freebase had made him feel that he could do anything.

Brandi's mother poured him some brandy. "When you work two shifts back to back like I do, you come home so tired," she said. "Sometimes I be so tired I just can't sleep. So I have to have a bit of this to put me out."

"The trouble is," said Frank, happy to finally be able to make a useful contribution, "when I do that it works fine at first but then I wake up later in the night." Frank was an old hand at alcohol.

"That's right," said Brandi's mother. "Then you just can't go back to sleep."

"The only thing to do then is to have another drink," Frank agreed.

Brandi's mother laughed and laughed. Frank had proved himself to be one of them. "That's right, baby," she said. She fried up a bunch of chicken wings in bacon grease. "Anyone want one, just help yourself," she said. – "I think I will," said Frank. – "Why not," Brandi's mother said. "Here, baby, put it on a piece of bread? You want some hot sauce?"

"Yes, *please*," said Frank, feeling good from booze and freebase and hospitality.

"Pass him the hot sauce, Billy Joe," said Brandi's mother. B.J., crunching a chicken bone in front of the TV set, handed Frank the bottle of Crystal. – "Thanks," Frank said.

"It's too bad Dessie went off and left you," Brandi's mother said. "That's just the way she is. She can't help it."

"She's a nice person," said Frank loyally.

"Dessie's a very nice person, but she is no motherfucking good," said Brandi's mother.

Frank helped B.J. move some furniture. Then Brandi's mother poured him another shot of brandy. He sat there sipping it. – "Well, I guess I learned my lesson," he said to B.J. quietly in the kitchen. – "I *told* you!" said B.J.

Frank drank his brandy down and began to feel really good. He could have stayed there quite happily all afternoon, were it not for the fact that he had an appointment with Dr. Dodger in the River City Deli at three.

After about an hour Brandi came in. When she saw Frank she hung her head. Clearly she had not expected him to feel so comfortable with her family. – "Well, Dessie, it's a good thing you finally came back so this young man didn't have to wait no more." – Brandi went into her room without a word. – Frank sat there feeling good. Finally he got up and said to Brandi's mother, "Well, maybe I'll have a word with Dessie and get out of your way here." – "You not in my way," said Brandi's mother. – As Frank went down the hall to Brandi's room he heard Brandi's mother say, "Is she doin' her business?" – but he did not hear B.J.'s reply.

He knocked on the door. Brandi was freebasing quietly on the bed. – "She gave me this for waiting so patiently," she said. She held the pipe to Frank's lips. Frank sucked. – The clean sensation increased. It seemed that he had been high for hours. He just wasn't coming down. – "I have to leave in about ten minutes," he said. – "You go on back in the kitchen and sit down," she said. – Frank went out and chatted with Brandi's mother. B.J. watched TV without saying a word. In a little while Brandi came out with a toot of freebase for Frank. As before, he put his hand on her hand on the pipe. Then Brandi came back with a toot for her mother. – "Oh, I don't like that type," said Brandi's mother, but all the same she pulled it in. Both Brandi and her mother had a way of talking while they held the vapor in that amused Frank. It sounded as if they had helium in their lungs. Brandi went back to her room and Frank had another shot. Finally it was time for him to go. She walked him to the stairs. "I'll be by with that money in fifteen minutes," she said.

"I really like your family," Frank said to Brandi at the head of the stairs.

"Thank you," she said shyly, putting her arm around him. " 'Teen minutes?"

"See you in fifteen minutes," said Frank. He was pessimistic, however, and of course she never came.

The next morning Frank was walking down Haight Street at five of five. Under a streetlight up ahead he saw her short slender silhouette. When she caught a sight of him, she ran across the street and ducked into a vacant lot. He was her SKULL. But someday she would come back to him.

Now ensued that period of waiting so familiar to lovers, losers, bugs and drug addicts. Frank was not exactly any of these, yet he almost fell into all categories, being an agent, and so he was tortured. Since he was a professional, the knowledge came upon him very quickly that Brandi had stolen his money and had no intention of coming back with it. He felt this revelation in an explosion of sadness. He had had no illusions that she liked or cared for him, but he had not thought that she would turn on him so quickly. (We always see ourselves as constant, and others as less so, no matter what policy shifts we ourselves may have been guilty of.) – Frank did not feel sorry for himself. He felt sorry for her. And it was at this moment, when he became capable of feeling pity for his victims, that Frank became a perfect double agent, for his pity was a small barred window which allowed him to peer out from his own cell into the cells of other naked shivering selves. The cool light of the blue globes illuminated every grating and let Frank read the other prisoners' faces. He could now see exactly what he had to do to own Brandi. It was only necessary to let her dream, to make her do tricks for him because she owed him money, to tell her about the bonus check he was expecting next month from Dr. Dodger (Dr. Dodger never paid bonuses), the thousand dollars which he would spend on smack; it was only necessary to be like poor bright and risen Brandi herself and promise her all the things which he would never give her.

WORLD IN A JAR

~~~~~~

> I look down into all that wasp-nest or bee-hive ... and witness
> their wax-laying and honey-making, and poison-brewing, and
> choking by sulphur.
>
> CARLYLE
> *Sartor Resartus* (1838)

Big George reports: "As I approached the cage, my first impression
was of an irritating buzzing of ever-increasing volume. I found it
both tiring and nauseating." He was speaking of fruit flies. In fact
the fruit flies did not consider their situation in nearly the same light
as Big George. At the bottom of their enclosure was a smooth waxy
block of yeast food. This would last them quite awhile; there would
still be plenty left when the corpses of dead generations covered it
and the clean glass walls were pitted with excrement-dots. What
would finally do them in was the steady drying out of that yeast
food; for purposes of air circulation the top of the vial was loosely
plugged with cotton; and the moisture evaporated steadily, so that
eventually all the flies would die of thirst. But this was some weeks
in the future, hardly anything to worry about right now, so the
happy flies purred and landed on the yeast and fed and buzzed up
together to the top of the vial trying to get out and landed on the
sides of the vial and crawled on the glass for a second before taking
off again and landing on the yeast food and then mating with other
flies and then landing on the yeast food and then going up to the
cotton trying to get out; they all rose in a cloud of buzzing panic
when the vial was touched or lifted or sunlight struck it; they wanted
to get out then but soon they forgot what they had wanted and they
crawled around and buzzed and flew and landed on the yeast food; a
few adventurous ones clambered down the crevices where the yeast
food met the glass imperfectly, and they perished there, struggling

for days; you could see them through the glass wiggling silently and getting caked with the yeast food; at least they didn't die hungry; they slowly suffocated, while the survivors had white wormy larvae in the yeast food and obscured the glass a little bit with fecal dots and buzzed in a panic when the light came in and wandered around on the underside of the cotton and fell heavily into the yeast food so that the larvae took over and grew wings and buzzed about the steadily more polluted vial like traffic helicopters in New York as the cars snorted and farted in the blue-grey air, the yellow taxicabs especially idling and idling and double-parking, pouring out gases, while the flies buzzed and swarmed inside the darkening vial and landed on the yeast food. Now at last you could hardly see into the vial at all, it was so encrusted with fecal dots; and the flies could hardly get to the yeast food because the bottom of the vial was piled so high with dead ones, but they went on buzzing and swarming until the vial dried up completely and then they were still. The vial went into the trash.

SHAPE-SHIFTING

The Real Identity of Captain Freiheit

All that exists, lives. The walls of the house have voices of their own.

Chukchee shaman, *ca.* 1895

In the warehouse of a local weed control agency in rural America, someone discovers several drums of a 15-year-old chemical once used to sterilize soil. The drums are taken to a remote area and left there. A rifle shot rings out. A drum explodes. Had the drums been jarred while at the warehouse, several people would have been killed, for the drums of obsolete chemicals had slowly, imperceptibly, turned into time bombs.

U.S. Environmental Protection Agency,
"Hazardous Wastes":
An environmental protection publication (SW–138)
in the solid waste management series (1975)

There is a greatness, a heroism that is an intrinsic part of most everyone. Our job as managers is to coerce that greatness out of our people.

ARTHUR E. IMPERATORE
President of A-P-A Transport Corporation,
as quoted in *Inc.* magazine (April 1984)

Just because they found Parker's skull doesn't mean he's dead; and just because Parker is whanging his long green dick in your face is hardly a reason to take him seriously at all as a sentient being. I find the author to have what I shall call a Captain Freiheit complex; he will lead the troops onward, ever onward, to a victory perhaps incapable of conception even by him or other overt narrative tropes. But it is important to maintain a calm underhanded attitude. Parker is nothing but a few yellow-green fragments of skull, and the anthropologist who digs him up, creakety-creak, let's winch up another box of stinking gases for *my* salary, will find little to remark upon. It is my feeling as I broadcast this banner message over the Amdahl network bridge that precisely as much as may be forgotten can be forgiven; and to the extent that Parker has decayed prior to exhumation we will be able to accept him; when nothing is left of him but dust we will no doubt be quite satisfied with his behavior. Already we see him deteriorating, thanks to the corrosive acids of love, from a glorious serpent suitable for target practice into a being not much superior to a green-rubber boot. The author alone is to blame for this. He does not like Parker and never has, and is doing his best to ruin Parker's chances. The author pretends to even-handedness; actually he supports the revolutionaries, and hopes rather naively that they will still win somehow. But this is counter-productive thinking. What can anyone do against a world armed by the forces of electricity? He has taken umbrage at the fact that I, too, had a vision of things, and modified the data accordingly. I, for instance, am in charge of the tape drives. He has no access to the computer center, and resents it when I alter his favorite characters. Susan, for instance, comprised originally several thousand tracks of data upon a no-label 2400-foot tape. Each time she is restored to the main disk drives where the action of this novel takes place, I first reformat her end-of-file mark, moving that magnetic pulse closer and closer to the beginning of the tape, so that the read-write heads arrive at the mark a little sooner and bring progressively less of her up out of storage, poor Susan; she gets shriller and more limited every time. And when I have brought the end-of-file mark right up against the header record at the beginning of the tape, then there will be nothing left of her; she will be dead to us. – The author does not care for this. The following justification subroutines, however, should be considered before anyone makes rash condemnations: – First, I have my own vision of what ought to happen; and why ought it to be assumed inferior to anyone else's? My conceptions are of a negative character, but for precisely that reason they are in accord with transcendental reality. Susan is in fact getting older and shriller and more vicious; I am nothing but an electronic administrator of her fate. The gap between the header record and the end-of-file mark narrows consistently, according to installation-dependent parameters and current flows which I cannot change. – Naturally, *he* is bitter about this. He has chosen to attack me by injuring Parker, Wayne, Mr. White and other characters, using the transparent cloak of wrong-righting to cover his naked egoism. He cannot of course breach the computer room, so he must feverishly input new data sets like bugs and Caterpillar Hearts in hopes of interfering with my page fault I/O transfers. This is quite simply hateful. Not a single byte of Susan, after all, has been erased; and when the two marks meet her tape will go into the refrigerator and there she will stay at peace forever and intact. He must adjust to this.

We are all in a state of adjustment. We resound; we resonate; we assimilate and differentiate; and in due time we will be resorbed. This is self-rule.

I, Big George, being not the least of my kind, roll on and on like a shining hoop of metal; and no one has destabilized me yet, although they try, oh, they do try. The author has even fitted some spokes into me, so that I have the strongest skeleton of anybody here; but he canceled the moral value which would otherwise accrue to him of that most delightful act by bolting me to the axle of his silly cart; and he wants me to turn in his direction all the time. Well, there's no one as dangerous to live with as an unwilling slave. – On the other hand, business opportunities create fully half the positions available in the private sector. To see the other side of the coin, one merely has to visit Omarville.

As you roll up Scott Street, heading north, you cross the Montague Expressway, and then you cross Bowers, Octavius, Oakmead, and the Lawrence Expressway, not necessarily in that order. The air is generally humid and yellow. Between two of these intersections runs an almost dried-up canal, framed by smooth, gently sloping concrete banks, which supply a spurious firmness to its lackluster spirituality before it disappears, like my thoughts, into a tunnel underneath Scott, continuing due east to Omarville. This

cement creeklet is all that remains of the Amazon; and after a few more false rainy years, during which its spittle-thickened protoplasm may be temporarily replenished with brownish liquid swimming with *Giardia lamblia*, it will give itself up completely to my mercy; and then I will electrify it as proof of my longterm loyalty to the revolution and the Society of Daniel. The bottom is mucky and stagnant. Grey weeds have taken root in the concrete, like wires and springs worked loose from an old mattress on which some dead philosophy once slept; for the purpose of this canal, like that of government, is to act as a receptacle for decay, which is trapped behind these dying vines until it works its way as much farther down as gravity, holding back gagging breaths, can bear to drag it. If you care to take a trip with me, we will walk on and on along that flat cement bottom, which stretches all across the east–west axis of our great Republic, the two ends forming it into a fine palindrome; for it finally comes to a halt, in either case, in the salty ruins of polluted dunes; and sand blows into that trench every day. The mystery would seem to be where the water comes from, since the excavation is flat, uniform, and unmarred by any entrance or exit channels. But this, too, like any human question, can be answered using nothing but one's smarts. So off we go, beginning from the Pacific side. We are in hot weather, and it stinks down here. Our boots make a fine sucking sound with every step, *squit-t-ch! . . . squit-t-ch! . . .*; for the semisolid stuff down here is reluctant to see us go, remembering how fine it was when the ships of the Conquistadores made their stately way upon it, treating it to occasional dead slaves or mutineers; and fleeing potentates reached it in their rafts, only to be pierced with tiny reddish arrows; then the surveyors arrived, a few of them obligingly dying also, so that all the life inside the river could be satisfied; but now our double-continent is lonely because electricity is on guard; therefore any visitor is welcome. – You carry your bag lunch over your shoulder, and we walk on, mile after mile after mile. By noon we have barely made it out of California, with the dry mountains of that state's eastern border rising high above our heads with the profiles of sick vultures. The sun reddens the backs of our necks; so that we tie on our black-and-scarlet bandanas, savoring the effect upon each other, though you, perhaps, admire me more than I admire you, for your bandana is not knotted with the true cowboy grace my hands are gifted with, so you appear to me posed and uneasy, a tourist, for I, Big George, will reduce all companions to sightseeing status as a consequence of the wonders which blossom forth at my every gesture, such as the stench of our canal, which is now more powerful than ever (not that I promised you a pleasure trip), and there is still an equal volume of muck and stagnant sewer-liquor through which we must slosh even here in the desert because the stuff has formed a skin of rubbery industrial wastes to prevent any moisture from rising and leaving it; it too wants to preserve its foul life. So, wearying of the adventure, we pick up our pace; by evening we have finally arrived in Omarville, somewhat footsore, to be sure, and it is a miserable hot humid evening the way those evenings are in Indiana with the smell of mud all around and everybody sealed up tight in his little trailer or canting house; people don't go outside much in Indiana. – Up we go in our hobnail boots, right up the side of that concrete trench, which continues its eastward run as far as the eye can follow, like an Islamic pilgrim; and there is not much to see here save black stretchy old trees and hoody-craws perched on the branches ready to come get you if you perchance fall down dead. Along the bends in the road the boys have hung monster masks and giant glow-in-the-dark Spiderman cut-outs to frighten you as you drive and make you swerve into a hostile farmhouse with its barking dogs.

If you have ever spent ten minutes of an autumn afternoon in a weedy lot where the brown dead milkweed plants stand waiting for the frost to get them and the snow to pile up on their supplicating branches, then you know the way the green pods (which a month ago were hard and firm and contained sticky white sap) have gone dry like brittle leather and tear open in the wind so that the downy seeds go spinning into the air, anxious to be blown far far away into some humid crack where they can hide until the spring. The plants are glad that you have come, even though with every step you tread them down with bestial cracklings; because their seed-children can cling to your socks like thistle-burrs and thus you will bear them away. I likewise will not rest until my current flows have germinated in each and every brain. – Bug will be caught and executed in the next volume, I assure you, and when the last of it is over, and he lies as stiff as a sun-dried dog's tongue against the reclining chair back, then I, Big George, shall come to the rescue, gently prying open black eyelids with my electrical fingers, leaping into the dead man's mouth and giving just the right amperic jolt to all nervous command centers. Then Bug will live again as a priest of my electric way, hobbling with a rubber cane around the Society of Daniel's parking lot three times every day to do his penance and to show himself, like Lazarus, to the race of fiends. – Susan will be captured and stood up against the wall; Milly will be raped and then frozen; Stephen Mole will be buried alive; and Frank, attempting to turn traitor one more time, will be strangled by his own kind. – These events I have hard-coded. – As for the author, he is going to kill himself, I expect; for once his dupes are removed he will have to concede to me and become my latest bright and risen angel to write alphanumeric sorts for me upon the terminals of death; then I, Big George, will be free to actualize Parker fully, so that the Snake will be one with the Spark.

We bright and risen angels are all in our graves, as I, the author, can assure you; for Big George has locked me into the Society of Daniel for the sake of productivity, and when I close my eyes I can remember only the framed color plots of silicon micro-wafers which we had done for us over at Versatec; Big George has closed all the windows to keep me here, and the night guards, so cheerfully inoculated in the belief that I *must* sleep here, are not allowed to let me out even for ten minutes to gaze upon the freeway – this is, I am sure, a wise rule, for if I thought I could do so I would run to the shoulder of the on ramp and hitchhike desperately, looking into each of the cavernous cars propelling themselves evenly past me; for I have no transportation home; it is a hundred-mile commute, and the programmers that go by have nothing but a briefcase in the back seat; there would be room for me, but they will never pick me up; I know this, and I accept it, having gotten into my sleeping bag every night in a niche between extension cords in Training Room Five for so long now that I cannot seriously believe in the outdoors, although sometimes when I lie very still and the air conditioning goes off for a moment I can hear the sprinklers in the bark chips outside going *spss! . . . spss!* . . . and I can imagine how peaceful it must be to be a green bush; then Big George dims the lights in the Training Room as gracefully as the last twenty measures of a great symphony; and the air conditioner stays off for the night; and in the hot darkness I think of Catherine who was shy, Catherine who was nervous, Catherine who evaded, Catherine who escaped (as it pleases me to believe); but then I sleep because the night guard will come an hour past midnight to shine his flashlight in my face and make a note on his clipboard; then at six-thirty I will have to get up to go to the men's room and run hot water over my face, soap my hands and rub them in my armpits in order to be presentable to the managerial elite, and then I comb my oily hair and look the other way as Dr. Dodger comes in to take a shit in the middle stall, and I splash water on my face, dry myself with a paper towel, and proceed to the lunchroom, where all my food is, in the righthand refrigerator. I eat bread in the morning, and bread with toasted cheese in the company microwave in the evening. By 6:50 a.m. I am at my cubicle, working hard on the gameboard to steer Bug's way while Big George watches me through his square blue eye. A few people are already here; the company works on flex time. At nine a great many of them come. I work until eight or nine at night, when the workaholics grumble and jingle their car keys. Then I wait while the janitors vacuum around me; my hands are swollen, my head drooping. It is all I can do to stay awake. Finally I have a cup of water and go into the training room to sleep, knowing that once again I have lost. As I get into my sleeping bag, rubbing my puffy eyes, I convince myself once again that Catherine must have escaped, because I don't really know her, and she has never been linked to Big George's broadband Ethernet; she will live by being alone and separate from all conflicts, from the two of us, so that Big George cannot hurt her on purpose and I cannot hurt her by mistake; although I confess that I was happy last year when she forgot this and asked if she could maybe sleep over at my apartment in San Francisco for a day or as it turned out two (Big George still allowed me to commute then); she even came early that night, though the following night she did not come until almost bedtime; I went downstairs that first night and met her at the door and kissed her forehead, and the electric lights did not see us and hum viciously, because I had turned them off; then to keep them from locating her we went out for dinner and we sat by the window so that I could watch the neighboring streetlamps to see if they might turn blue; as soon as that happened we finished dessert and I took her home and showed her how to shoot my air-pistol in the living room and she scored a creditable grouping and was pleased if not thrilled; but I had no hope of keeping her since I knew that Catherine would never love me or really love anyone (and I flickered the light off and then on again every hour or so to interrupt whatever might be building up in the circuits, just as one has to move only occasionally to keep a hovering mosquito from landing in the night) and we talked about how we each wanted to have children, and she told me about how as a girl she had kept many stuffed animals in a pile on her bed and when she went to sleep she had to make sure that every one was there with her; and she talked to all her blankets, her favorite one being called Quilty Bee, to whom Catherine confided everything while Quilty Bee listened and snuggled up to Catherine and smelled like hot milk, because that was what Catherine smelled like; and Quilty Bee would never die because when holes came then Catherine's mother just quilted more patches on, which made Catherine happy because that meant that Quilty Bee was still the same blanket that knew her and took care of her so that she never wanted to hurt anybody even if her toys got mad and told Catherine to punish the bad people, so Catherine remained good all her life, which was why she had to hide and be so careful the way that Bug did before he decided that he had to be bad; and as Catherine told me about her blankets I listened to her as carefully as I could and I admired her with her soft black hair and her sad smile in her dark sweater as she sat looking at me across the table, smiling at me only because she was finally almost at ease with me after several years since it took a long time for Catherine to accustom herself to me or to anyone new, which was why even though she said she would be house-sitting on Saturday and she thought it might be nice if I came over for dinner or something, still when I came home from work this afternoon I found only the blankets and sheets I had lent her, neatly folded on the living room sofa, where she had slept when I tiptoed in early in the morning to leave her my alarm which I had set for her; I could barely see her head and her soft dark hair in the darkness where she rested her head on the black sofa-cushion, and I could not hear her breathing, and I could not see her face, but I did not want to bend over her to look because I didn't want to wake her or to use her in any way, just to let her be, because I was satisfied that she had trusted me. It may seem indelicate to say even as much as I have about Catherine, who is really a secret of mine, and I sometimes worry that she has no place in this cartoon about bright and risen angels whose every motive must be known, and yet although the angels never were and never will be able to see Catherine there *is* an occult link since Big George would destroy her, too, if he could; and that is why I don't want to reveal too much about her because he is reading everything input here, as you know, 12.52.46 JOB 3880 + CATHERINE: UNIT 9 (BIRTH) NOW OPEN FOR INPUT, then 12.52.47 JOB 3880 + CATHERINE: UNIT 10 (DEATH) NOW CLOSED — RECORD I/O COUNT: 2976 ; and if he learns who she is he will be able to damage her in some way (the way that I, Big George, already have); so whenever I mention her I feel guilty of treachery by negligence, and I am proud to say that I have seldom introduced her even to my truest friends; yet the fact is that I don't know Catherine's secret, either, but I know that if I can understand it from her then I will be able to save every angel from Big George. Meanwhile I feel almost redeemed by the fact that I ask hardly anything of her; and the first night she stayed here when I told her goodnight and she kissed me on the lips I almost didn't want that although it was sweet; it was almost as if Catherine didn't trust me since she actually kissed me, the way that God shows miracles to little children because they are not yet old enough to do without them. But I knew that Catherine had kissed me because she trusted me, and that made me happy then but now I am sad because by the time my eyes close each night I suspect that as usual I have been fooling myself, that she, too, is in her grave.

AUTHOR'S NOTE

This book was written in

urine,   lime   and vitriol

under circumstances of

hunger   and death

for all you bright and
risen angels of

brimstone   and sulfur

who live beneath the

dragon's eye in the eye of fire, united for the

procreation of   lye   and aquafortis.

Blessed be you in your infamy.

YOU BRIGHT AND RISEN ANGELS

You are pernicious,   poisonous   and deadly.

I will offer up to you iron   and lead; on your altars I will burn

alkali,   vinegar   and white arsenic.

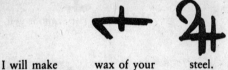

I will make   wax of your   steel.

Your men   will become dead men.

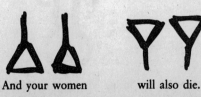

And your women   will also die.

And if your women become pregnant

and bear children as they die,

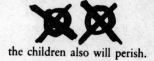

the children also will perish.

The sun will rise without you.

In the dry cold earth

you will burn.

Spring will come without you.

YOU BRIGHT AND RISEN ANGELS

Your bright day, my angels,

will be followed by my night.

In the manure pile

you will be annealed.

The crows' feet will find you

in time.

I piss on you all.

This is my gift, you angels;

love me.

FOR THE BEST IN PAPERBACKS, LOOK FOR THE

In every corner of the world, on every subject under the sun, Penguin represents quality and variety—the very best in publishing today.

For complete information about books available from Penguin—including Pelicans, Puffins, Peregrines, and Penguin Classics—and how to order them, write to us at the appropriate address below. Please note that for copyright reasons the selection of books varies from country to country.

In the United Kingdom: For a complete list of books available from Penguin in the U.K., please write to *Dept E.P., Penguin Books Ltd, Harmondsworth, Middlesex, UB7 0DA*.

In the United States: For a complete list of books available from Penguin in the U.S., please write to *Consumer Sales, Penguin USA, P.O. Box 999— Dept. 17109, Bergenfield, New Jersey 07621-0120*. VISA and MasterCard holders call 1-800-253-6476 to order all Penguin titles.

In Canada: For a complete list of books available from Penguin in Canada, please write to *Penguin Books Canada Ltd, 10 Alcorn Avenue, Suite 300, Toronto, Ontario, Canada M4V 3B2*.

In Australia: For a complete list of books available from Penguin in Australia, please write to the *Marketing Department, Penguin Books Ltd, P.O. Box 257, Ringwood, Victoria 3134*.

In New Zealand: For a complete list of books available from Penguin in New Zealand, please write to the *Marketing Department, Penguin Books (NZ) Ltd, Private Bag, Takapuna, Auckland 9*.

In India: For a complete list of books available from Penguin, please write to *Penguin Overseas Ltd, 706 Eros Apartments, 56 Nehru Place, New Delhi. 110019*.

In Holland: For a complete list of books available from Penguin in Holland, please write to *Penguin Books Nederland B.V., Postbus 195, NL-1380AD Weesp, Netherlands*.

In Germany: For a complete list of books available from Penguin, please write to *Penguin Books Ltd, Friedrichstrasse 10-12, D-6000 Frankfurt Main 1, Federal Republic of Germany*.

In Spain: For a complete list of books available from Penguin in Spain, please write to *Longman, Penguin España, Calle San Nicolas 15, E-28013 Madrid, Spain*.

In Japan: For a complete list of books available from Penguin in Japan, please write to *Longman Penguin Japan Co Ltd, Yamaguchi Building, 2-12-9 Kanda Jimbocho, Chiyoda-Ku, Tokyo 101, Japan*.